LAW FOR
TOMBSTONE

**Center Point
Large Print**

**This Large Print Book carries the
Seal of Approval of N.A.V.H.**

LAW FOR TOMBSTONE

CHARLES M. MARTIN

CENTER POINT PUBLISHING
THORNDIKE, MAINE

This Center Point Large Print edition
is published in the year 2004 by arrangement with
Golden West Literary Agency.

The text of this Large Print edition is unabridged. In other
aspects, this book may vary from the original edition. Printed in
Thailand. Set in 16-point Times New Roman type.

ISBN 1-58547-431-2

Library of Congress Cataloging-in-Publication Data

Martin, Chuck.
    Law for Tombstone / Charles M. Martin.--Center Point large print ed.
        p. cm.
    ISBN 1-58547-431-2 (lib. bdg. : alk. paper)
    1. Tombstone (Ariz.)--Fiction. 2. Large type books. I. Title.

PS3563.A723274L38 2004
813'.54--dc22

                                                    2003027802

THIS BOOK IS RESPECTFULLY DEDICATED
TO MY GOOD FRIEND
CAPTAIN JEFF D. MILTON
WHO NOW LIVES AT TOMBSTONE.
CAPTAIN MILTON IN REAL LIFE
IS THE WELLS FARGO MESSENGER WHO SHOT
AND FATALLY WOUNDED THE NOTORIOUS OUTLAW,
THREE-FINGER JACK, AT FAIRBANKS, ARIZONA.
A BRAVER AND KINDLIER MAN NEVER LIVED;
LOVED AND RESPECTED
BY THE THOUSANDS OF FRIENDS WHO KNOW HIM.
MAY HIS SHADOW NEVER GROW LESS.
TO YOU, JEFF, I AM . . . LIKE ALWAYS,
"CHUCK."

CHAPTER I

Pop Whipple swung his lash and coaxed his four-horse team deep into the collars for the long pull up the Pedro grade. The old driver swore profanely while his little gray eyes watched the catclaw thickets bordering the stage road. Then he sighed softly and elevated both gnarled hands while his scarred boot found the brake and stopped the old Concord on the very crest of the hill.

"Keep 'em up, Pop, and keep healthy," a sneering voice advised brusquely. "She's pay-day at the mines!"

Pop Whipple was five-feet-four, and he had lived sixty-four years because of his ability to take orders. His tobacco-stained lips curled back to show toothless gums when the speaker rode out of the brush on a tall bay gelding, and his bent elbows dropped slowly and cradled against his ribs to support the long leather ribbons looped around his calloused palms.

"Yo're goin' to jack up the Company one time too many, feller," he warned shrilly. "They'll bring in some Law for Tombstone, and you can tell Three-fingered Jack I said so!"

The masked bandit laughed softly. "They've tried it before," he sneered. "Now you kick down the box like usual. Reason you've lived so long is because you stuck to yore job of driving. Three-finger will make all the law Tombstone needs!"

Pop Whipple spat disgustedly and tipped the iron box with the toe of his boot. It thudded to the sandy ground and bounced to the edge of the road with a rattle of metal, and the tall bandit's horse side-stepped daintily with little ears pricked forward. The hold-up stiffened and faced about slowly while his slitted eyes followed the pointing ears.

"Drop the hardware, brother," a drawling voice intoned slowly. "Like old Pop Whipple done told you, the Law has come to Tombstone!"

The bandit was caught at a disadvantage. The drawling voice came from just behind him and a little to one side. His own right hand held a cocked forty-five, but he could see the sheen of metal backing up the authority in the stranger's careless voice. Pop Whipple cackled shrilly and lowered his skinny arms, and the bandit threw caution to the winds.

The spur on his off boot raked slyly while he twisted in the saddle like a tree cat. The heavy gun swiveled in his hand and roared into flame when the bay under him did a pinwheel to face the stranger. A fast-moving target is hard to hit, but the bandit jerked backward over the cantle when an old Peacemaker echoed the roar of his own gun.

The tall stranger sat his big red horse easily and caught the bucking gun to ear back the hammer on the recoil. The bandit's horse made three jumps and stopped when the split reins coiled down to anchor him with a ground-hitch. Old Pop Whipple stared at the twisting bandit and raised his eyes to squint at the rider on the big red horse.

"You said the Law had come to Tombstone, stranger," he almost whispered. "What for kind of law if I ain't talkin' out of turn?"

"Well, Pop," the stranger drawled softly. "There's several kinds of Law you might say, and I'm all of them. Arizona is a long ways from my home range, but me and my Snapper hoss has traveled them all. I brings you greetings from El Paso, and looks like you will have a passenger to take into Tombstone."

Pop Whipple swallowed hastily and began to cough. Tears ran down his weathered cheeks while the Adam's apple bobbed in his scrawny neck. The tall stranger watched the struggle with interest until the old driver gulped noisily and reached for a huge plug in his hip pocket.

"Ugh," Pop Whipple wheezed. "I swallowed my cud when you got the drop on me that away. Yo're Alamo Bowie, or I'm a gentle Annie!"

"The same, at yore service," and the tall Texan smiled with the corners of his hard mouth. "Tom Scudder sent me up here to set on the bench, you might say."

"Tom Scudder," the old driver murmured, and bit deeply on his plug. "He's General Manager of Wells Fargo!"

Alamo Bowie nodded and shrugged. "This jigger," he said, and pointed to the bandit near the trail-side brush. "Light down and strip that bandanna from his face so's we can mebbe call him by name."

Pop Whipple slid from the high seat with the agility of a boy. His fingers tore the handkerchief away

9

eagerly while an old Hawks-bill Bisley .41 covered the stirring bandit. Cloudy blue eyes stared sullenly up at him when he stepped back with a muttered curse.

"It's Lantern-jaw Peters," the old driver explained. "One of Three-finger Jack's men!"

The tall Texan nodded calmly. "Caught with the goods this away, he should ought to get ten-fifteen years over at Yuma," he remarked quietly. "Reckon mebbe you better take this piggin' string and rope his hands behind him. He ain't hurt anyways bad, seeing that I throwed off my shot and took him high in the shoulder."

The old driver holstered his Bisley and frowned. "You should have drilled him center," he complained. "They ain't a heap of what you might call law in Tombstone."

Alamo Bowie was a tall man even in the saddle. He frowned thoughtfully and punched the spent shell from his right-hand gun while his gray eyes studied the wounded man. Then he shrugged and thumbed a fresh cartridge through the loading gate and holstered the weapon in the moulded scabbard on his long right leg.

"We'll have to give it a try," he answered at last. "Wrap him up and dump him in the stage for the trip to town. I'll tail along on Snapper and make the complaint."

Pop Whipple rolled the bandit over and made his ties while he grumbled under his breath. Lantern-jaw Peters was sick from bullet shock, and he climbed inside the old coach without argument. The little driver shouldered the strong box and raised it to the brake-step where the Texan helped him place it under the seat.

"Yo're wasting time," he muttered, and mounted the box to unwrap the ribbons from the brake. "The only kind of law these jiggers recognizes here abouts is sixgun law, and they carry most of it themselves!"

Alamo Bowie smiled contentedly and rubbed the worn grips of his twin guns. His worn range clothing was white with alkali, but the long-barreled forty-fives were spotless and bright. He sat the tall red horse like a cowhand, and he was still smiling when the old stage rattled down the grade past Boot Hill and swung into Allen street.

Miners and trail-drivers stopped to stare when the stage careened around the corner of Fourth and turned into the O K Corral on Fremont. Pop Whipple was cracking his lash to herald his approach, and the big red horse racked alongside with an easy dog-trot. His rider scanned the crowd quickly and swung to the ground with both hands easing his guns of riding crimp while his jaw jutted craggily when he reached for the handle of the stage door.

"Unload, Peters," and his deep voice was brittle. "You and me is taking a *pasear* down to the jugadazo!"

A wide-shouldered man with a star on his vest stepped forward with hand on his gun. "I'm Ed White, stranger," he introduced himself civilly. "Town Marshal of Tombstone."

"Howdy, Marshal," the Texan drawled. "I'm Alamo

11

Bowie; special agent for the Wells Fargo Company. Caught Peters here holding up the stage on the Pedro grade."

"I'll take him," the marshal grunted, and allowed his eyes to swing over the crowd. "Time we was getting some help here in Tombstone, and this jigger will get the limit!"

A tall man pushed through the crowd and stopped to face the Texan. Black Stetson pushed back on his greasy black hair to show a high forehead and small glittering black eyes. Cowhorn mustaches framed his thin bloodless lips, and long-fingered hands rested lightly on the grips of his balanced Colts. Gray pants tucked down into polished fifty-dollar boots with the crossed gunbelts of the two-gun man riding low on lean hips.

"I'll pay the limit now," and his voice was deep with a note of arrogance. "She's twenty-five dollars and costs for killing a Pilgrim, so fifty ought to cover the damage!"

Alamo Bowie glanced at the newcomer and shook his head slowly. "What for kind of law is that?" he asked softly. "I caught this *banditto* robbing the Benson stage. Throwed off my shot so's he could stand trial and do his turn over Yuma way."

"Yo're new here abouts, stranger," the tall man answered softly. "My name is Three-finger Jack just so's you don't make any more mistakes."

The Texan's gray eyes lighted up suddenly. "Heard of you," he admitted. "Been wanting to meet you for a spell of time."

A half-smile rode his hard tanned face while he stared at the tall outlaw. Three-finger Jack was the brains of the gang that had terrorized Tombstone and vicinity since the silver camp had started to boom. Twenty-five men rode in the gang and took orders only from their chief, and the tall Texan dropped his eyes to study the twin guns thonged low with the tie-backs tight.

"So yo're Alamo Bowie," the outlaw murmured, and his black eyes were suddenly respectful. "Fastest gun-hand in Texas if reports are true."

Alamo Bowie shrugged. "Texas ain't such a big place," he drawled. "Me and Snapper goes from here to there, among other places. This time we're bringing the law to Tombstone!"

"That's right, it ain't," the outlaw agreed thoughtfully. "You took the law to the Big Four up in Deming. Now some of them fellers was fairly rapid, but they didn't carry enough to chouse over this away. You see the light, Mister?"

Alamo Bowie smiled one of his rare smiles. His gray eyes lighted up with a smoky brilliance that gave him the look of a hunting hawk. Battle-scarred and tough from the long trails to make him look older than his thirty years. Six-feet even with gray sprinkling the temples under his droopy Stetson.

"She begins to glimmer, Three-finger," he murmured softly. "Yo're meaning to break it to me gently that One-Shot Brady was plumb slow on the draw," and again he shrugged lightly and turned his back. "I'm talkin' to you after me and the marshal beds

13

down this maverick we caught robbing the stage!"

His right hand swiveled while he whirled on one high heel. Glinting metal flashed in the early sun and stopped the tall outlaw in the middle of his draw. The special agent smiled and jerked his head at Peters, and he held the crowd while Ed White herded the prisoner down the street and into the adobe jail.

"I usually finish what I start, Three-finger," Bowie murmured. "You better send a Croaker down to patch up that hole in Peters' shoulder. The trial will come off just before second drink time!"

The tall outlaw glared and set his teeth. Then he shrugged and turned toward the Crystal Palace. "I'll be at the trial," he answered evenly, and made his way back to Allen street.

The Texan nodded and holstered his gun. His boot lifted toward the stirrup and paused when a stocky man shouldered through the crowd and called sharply. Alamo Bowie dropped his foot and turned slowly to face the speaker, and his gray eyes flickered to the badge on the worn vest.

"The name is Joe Blaine, stranger. Sheriff of Cochise county. I'm handling the law here in Tombstone!"

"Howdy, Blaine," and Alamo Bowie rubbed his chin to hide the smile on his face. "I just now brought in a prisoner."

"You made the arrest outside the city," the sheriff answered gruffly. "Which don't sit well with me account of Ed White shooting over my head. Where's yore authority to make arrests here in my bailiwick?"

Alamo Bowie flicked his vest back with his left hand. Thumbed a worn star into view while his gray eyes bored into the beefy face of the sheriff.

"Deputy U. S. Marshal," he explained softly, and dropped his hand. "What you might call a roving commission."

"Yo're a known gun-fighter, Bowie," the sheriff answered sharply. "Special agent for Wells Fargo with a dozen notches on the handles of yore cutters. That won't go down here in Cochise County!"

"How come it won't?" the Texan drawled. "Looks to me like you'd be glad for some help."

"When I need help, I know where to get it," the sheriff barked. "There's the troops at Fort Huachucua, besides my deputy!"

"They don't seem to do much," Bowie murmured. "The stage was robbed three times last month. Tom Scudder didn't like it none to speak of."

"Tom Scudder is in Texas," the sheriff answered sharply. "This here is the Territory of Arizona, and my advice to you is to back-track while you got yore health!"

"My health is something that I'm right careful about," and the tall Texan nodded his head slowly while his eyes studied the truculent peace officer. "You got any suggestions to make as to how I could improve same here in Tombstone and way-points?"

Sheriff Blaine relaxed and laughed pleasantly. "That sounds like sense, Bowie," he chuckled. "Tombstone has her man for breakfast every morning, and she's partial to Texans. I was you, I'd hit the trail

15

east and find business else where. Like up in New Mex, for instance!"

Alamo Bowie straightened slowly and stared at the officer. "You ain't me, Blaine," and his voice was gruff. "I ain't never back-tracked a trail once I set my Snapper hoss to riding down sign. Robbing Wells Fargo has got to stop, and if you can't cut 'er, yo're due to get some help regardless!"

"We don't want no more killings here," Blaine answered sulkily. "We got enough as it is."

Again the tall Texan shook his head. "Not near enough," he contradicted bluntly. "And what you have is on the wrong side. Three-finger Jack is roddin' an outlaw spread of twenty-five men, and they spend their loot right here in town!"

His deep voice crackled while he made the accusation. Sheriff Blaine scowled and bit the end from a big black cigar. Not so tall as the Texan but wider of shoulders to carry more weight by twenty pounds. When he answered, his voice was ugly with threat.

"You better take my advice and high-tail. We're satisfied with the law in these parts, and if it wasn't Three-finger, it would be some other salty gang. I'll round them up without no help when the time is right!"

"There's some things that just won't wait," Bowie remarked judicially. "The Wells Fargo Company would be broke before that time got here, and just this morning I saved them four thousand dollars."

"It's their business to carry a shotgun guard on the box," and the sheriff fired his cigar and puffed vigor-

16

ously. "I offered to furnish guards, but Tom Scudder turned down my offer."

"Let's see," Bowie answered musingly. "Last month we lost three shotgun guards, including the shipments. All three of them fellers was knowed to be honest, and all three of them was buried up on Boot Hill. Them hold-ups never give 'em a chance!"

"That was an outside gang," Blaine barked. "I followed the sign my ownself, and it led down toward Nogales on the border!"

"Where Three-finger Jack has a hide-out," Bowie answered softly. "Looks like you'd be interested in seeing that gang cleaned out."

"I've lived three years here in Tombstone," Blaine answered with a smile. "Three other sheriffs before me lasted four months all together!"

Alamo Bowie stared hard. "Meaning that you value yore life more than law enforcement," he answered, and made no attempt to conceal the contempt in his deep voice.

"That's enough from you, Mister," Blaine snapped angrily. "I'm the law here in Tombstone, and I'm telling you to drag yore rope!"

"Old Tom Scudder was afraid of that," the Texan sighed. "So he had me made a U. S. deputy Marshal, the same not being subject to any orders from yore office. I reckon I'm all talked out, *sheriff* Blaine!"

The sheriff smiled with his lips. "I reckon you won't be needing that big sorrel much longer," he remarked carelessly. "I'll bet a thousand against him that you don't last forty-eight hours."

"Took!"

Alamo Bowie accepted the bet promptly and looked over the crowd. His gray eyes lighted on a tall thin man with the gray of disease in his wasted cheeks. Gunman and gambler was written plainly all over the slender figure of the stranger, and he stepped slowly forward when Bowie asked a question with his eyes.

"Yo're Doc Holliday," he said quietly. "You mind holding the sheriff's *dinero?*"

"Put up or shut up, Blaine," the gambler said softly. "I'll see that you get the hoss if Bowie cashes in before forty-eight hours."

"I warned you one time, Holliday," the sheriff snapped. "I told you not to buy chips in any game where I was holding a hand!"

The slender gambler smiled. "You warned me, and I'm buying chips," he answered flatly. "So what, Lawman?"

Joe Blaine glared and dropped his eyes. Doc Holliday smiled gently and held out his hand. His left hand. The right stayed close to the ivory-handled gun under the tails of his black coat. The sheriff shrugged and dipped into his hip pocket for his wallet.

"She's only a bet," he excused himself, and thumbed several bills from a thick sheaf. "At least you always pay off!"

"Might be well for you to remember that, sheriff," the gambler agreed, and pocketed the money. "I met Bowie once before down in the Panhandle, and I'm backing any play he makes!"

"Three-finger will be glad to hear that," Blaine snarled.

"I'm betting a cool hundred he hears about it inside an hour," Holliday answered pointedly. "I saw him riding out toward Skeleton Canyon ten minutes ago!"

The sheriff flushed and bit on his cigar. "What Jack does is his own business," he muttered.

Doc Holliday smiled grimly. "Looks like," he agreed. "Peters belonged to Jack's gang, and Peters was caught holding up the Benson stage. What you aim to do about it?"

The sheriff threw his cigar away and grinned. "The trial will be in an hour," he answered lightly. "Suppose you drop down to Tough Nut street and find out for yoreself!"

"I'll be there," Holliday promised, and watched the sheriff walk away. Then he reached out a thin white hand and shook gravely with the Texan. "Glad to see you, Alamo," he said quietly.

Alamo Bowie gripped hard. "Better take care of yoreself, Doc," he drawled. "You ain't looking so peart."

The thin gambler smiled frostily. "Ten to one it gets me before a bullet does," he whispered, and smothered a hacking cough behind his hand. "I'm living on part of one lung right now."

"This high desert air will cure you," the Texan answered softly, and his gray eyes showed the pity he felt. "Better let me play it lone-handed, Doc."

"Did you let me play it that way down in Texas?" and the gambler glared with his greenish-gray eyes.

"The time those five owl-hooters went on the prod because I won all the loot?"

Alamo Bowie sighed and nodded his head. "I know it's no use talking," he agreed. "Let's drop over to the Oriental and wet our whistles. The trail-dust is ankle-deep in my throat."

Doc Holliday shook his head. "Make it the Crystal Palace," he suggested. "I'm running the games in the Oriental, and that's one place where I watch my back."

"Keno," the Texan agreed. "Just one with a chaser of the same, because that trial comes off in an hour!"

CHAPTER II

Alamo Bowie knew that word of his coming had preceded him to the Crystal Palace Bar. Sullen-faced loungers dropped their eyes when he came through the swinging batwings with Doc Holliday, and the two found an open place at the head of the long bar.

"Name it," the gambler chuckled, and waited for the tall Texan to give his order.

"Whiskey straight with a chaser of the same," and Alamo Bowie rumbled the order deep in his throat. "What's the word, Doc?"

The gambler shrugged lightly. "Same old sixes and sevens," he answered softly, so as not to set off his cough. "Marty Williams is local agent for Wells Fargo, and you met Ed White, the town Marshal. Joe

20

Blaine is sheriff, and Fred Rutledge is his deputy."

"Plenty law for a town this size," the tall Texan murmured, and reached for the two glasses on the bar. He downed the first one neat; whipped up his left hand and sighed gustily when the chaser hit bottom. "Looks to me like them outlaws ought to be some scarce."

"This Three-finger Jack is fast," the gambler warned seriously. "I doubt if even you could shade him enough to come out alive. He's got the Indian sign on the law, and Blaine wants to be re-elected."

"Politics, eh?" Bowie remarked quietly.

The gambler nodded. "They run their law according to politics, and they don't want any outside help to spoil things. You'll find Ed White a square shooter."

"We better get down to the Court house," and the Texan hitched up his belts. "Lantern-jaw Peters is due to sweat a few years away over at Yuma."

Doc Holliday shrugged and led the way to the street. Men stared at the pair as they climbed the Court house steps, but the Texan high-heeled along and gave no sign that he noticed. Sheriff Blaine stopped them just inside the door and held out his hand.

"Check yore hardware here, gents," he requested pleasantly. "New town law just put in effect."

Alamo Bowie stopped and eyed him coldly. "That law don't apply to me," he said thinly. "I'm representing the government of these here United States."

"You get 'em back after the trial," Blaine answered. "Or you don't go in!"

Alamo Bowie continued to stare until a slight sneer curled the corners of the sheriff's mouth. The Texan's right hand blurred smoothly. Joe Blaine backed up with a gasp of surprise when the muzzle of a forty-five bored a hole in his belly.

"Do I go in?" the Texan asked quietly.

A soft voice spoke just behind him. "Pass him in, Joe. He gets salty, I might win that bet for you."

Alamo Bowie turned slowly to meet the mocking black eyes of Three-finger Jack. The outlaw was surrounded by a dozen hard-faced riders, and all had hands on their guns. The sheriff shrugged and jerked his head toward the front of the big room.

"Get along," he muttered. "You and me will settle later . . . if you last that long!"

The Texan ignored him and stared at the outlaw. "I heard you," he said softly, and his voice was the same slow drawl. "You can have it now if you feel lucky."

The outlaw shrugged. "Not now," he refused carelessly. "I want you to see the trial first."

Doc Holliday was watching with a feverish glitter in his peculiar eyes. His left hand was under the right side of his coat, and the men behind Three-finger Jack hastily raised their hands. The gambler spoke low to the outlaw.

"You make a pass in here, and I aim to scatter you and yores all over the place. I reckon you know whether I mean what I say!"

"No trouble, Doc," the outlaw murmured. "I didn't know he was a pard of yores."

"I'm sidin' him all the way," and the gambler dropped the sawed-off shotgun back under his coat. "Let's sit in the back, Bowie."

The Texan nodded without changing expression. Doc Holliday had been a Dentist until the dreaded disease forced him to abandon his profession. Always fond of gambling, he was known as a square shooter and a fearless gunman over the entire southwest. They took seats where they could watch the crowd, and the Texan nodded to Marshal Ed White who was sitting with the prisoner up front.

The Judge came in and seated himself behind the oak desk. He was a fat little man with a belly, and his importance made up for what he lacked in stature. He cleared his throat loudly and hammered on the bench with an old gavel.

"Court will come to order," he barked. "The prisoner will take the stand!"

Lantern-jaw Peters stood up and took the oath. His right arm was in a sling, and he looked around the room until he found Three-finger Jack. The color returned to his face when he saw the crowd of outlaws, and he straightened slowly when the judge rapped again for order.

"You are charged with attempted hold-up of the stage. Guilty or not guilty?"

"I never took a dollar, yore Honor," the prisoner answered promptly. "I was just going to ask old Pop Whipple the time of day!"

"Sit down," the judge ordered sharply. "Alamo Bowie will take the stand!"

Silence in the big room while the Texan made his way forward. He took the oath mechanically; seated himself in the witness chair and waited.

"You shot this man?" the judge barked.

Bowie nodded. "I shot him," he admitted. "Caught him robbing the Benson stage, and he forced the driver to kick the strong box off the seat."

The judge stared. "Never saw you before, stranger," he grunted. "How come you to take the law in your hands?"

The Texan frowned. "I am a deputy United States Marshal," he answered gruffly. "And a special agent for Wells Fargo," he added.

"You say this prisoner held up Pop Whipple?"

"That's what I said."

"Pop Whipple will take the stand!"

Marshal White interrupted. "Whipple is out on his run, yore Honor. He won't be back until tomorrow."

"Humph," the judge muttered. "Did the prisoner do any killing?"

"He didn't," Bowie answered. "All he did was threaten to kill the stage driver."

"I understand that you are a law officer," the judge said sternly. "As such, you doubtless know that it is necessary to have witnesses to prosecute a prisoner. Case is dismissed for lack of evidence!"

Alamo Bowie stared at the little judge and twiddled the fingers of his right hand. Lantern-jaw Peters grinned and let out a whoop of triumph, and the outlaws in the back of the room applauded loudly. Sheriff Blaine came forward and grinned at the Texan.

"How do you like our law?" he asked pleasantly.

"Law hell," Bowie blurted. "You gents knew he was guilty, but me, I learn quick!"

"Meaning what?" the judge demanded.

"Is court adjourned?" Bowie asked innocently.

The judge banged the gavel. "This court stands adjourned," he roared.

"Then I can talk man to man," Bowie drawled. "Along side of you and the sheriff, a jack rabbit is a roaring lion. Guess I'll be getting about my getting!"

"You shoot off a gun in town, and I'll bring you in myself," the sheriff blustered.

"You won't," the Texan corrected. "Three sheriffs were killed and nothing was done about it. You cut my sign, and a fourth one won't be missed much!"

"You heard him, Judge," Blaine muttered. "He threatened to kill me!"

"I'll fine you fifty dollars for contempt of court," the judge barked nastily.

Alamo Bowie smiled. "You dismissed court," he reminded the jurist. "And I understand the penalty for murder here in Tombstone is twenty-five dollars and costs!"

His gray eyes swept across the room and rested upon the little knot of outlaws in the doorway. Brushing sheriff Blaine aside, he stomped purposely down the aisle with Ed White and Doc Holliday on either side. Three-finger Jack smiled sneeringly and kept a hand on his gun.

"Get him, Ed," the Texan whispered. "That new law Blaine was talking about."

Marshal White faced the outlaw and drew his gun. "Yo're under arrest, Jack," he said quietly. "For packing firearms in the court room!"

The tall outlaw smiled and folded his arms. "The sheriff let us in," he answered. "Talk to him about it."

His hand moved like a flash when the marshal turned to glance at Blaine. Alamo Bowie leaped forward and slapped down viciously with his gun barrel. He stepped back when Three-finger Jack went to his knees, and Doc Holliday swiveled the sawed-off from under his coat to cover the other outlaws.

"Up!" he snapped. "Hands up or I'll cut you down!"

A dozen pair of hands went shoulder high when their owners glanced at the merciless face of the gambler. Marshal Ed White leaned down and clicked a pair of heavy cuffs on the wrists of the stunned leader. Sheriff Blaine came racing down the aisle tugging at his gun, but the Texan stopped him cold.

"Shoot if you draw," he warned coldly. "You quoted the law your ownself!"

"You can't do this to me," Blaine shouted. "I am the sheriff of Cochise County!"

"I don't care if yo're the Governor," the Texan retorted. "You helped to make that law, and these jiggers was in the court room with their hardware on while a trial was taking place. Looks like we might as well have another one!"

Judge Hart waddled up importantly and cleared his throat. The Texan cut him short by waving the gun in his right hand. The judge spluttered and retreated to the bench with Bowie following him closely. Doc Holliday swiveled his murderous weapon and started his drive. Marshal White herded Three-finger after the

26

crowd and forced him in the prisoner's dock.

"Open court," Bowie grunted, and stared over the barrel of his old Peacemaker Colt.

"I declare this Court open," the judge quavered weakly. "The prisoner will stand."

"Prisoners," Bowie corrected gravely. "Thirteen men were sitting here in court with sixguns strapped on their legs. Violation of the new law put into force this week!"

Three-finger Jack stood up when his name was called. "Guilty or not guilty?" and Judge Hart refused to meet the glittering black eyes.

"Not guilty as charged," the outlaw muttered. "The sheriff gave us permission."

"Are you a peace officer?" Marshal White asked.

"The court will ask the questions," Judge Hart barked.

Alamo Bowie smiled and tapped with his gun. "Ask him," he suggested.

"Are you a peace officer?" the judge squeaked.

"You know I ain't," Three-finger Jack growled angrily. "You trying to hooraw me?"

"The penalty is twenty-five dollars and costs, and three days in jail," Marshal White said grimly. "And this time I have two witnesses. I refer to Doc Holliday and Alamo Bowie!"

The judge glanced at the sheriff and shivered when he saw Three-finger Jack watching him. He swallowed noisily and cleared his throat.

"This court has no alternative," he almost whispered. "I fine you, and each of you twenty-five dollars and costs, and sentence you and each of you to three days in the county jail. Court is dismissed!"

"Listen, Pot-gut," Three-finger roared. "You won't keep yore health long if you try to make that stick!"

Marshal Ed White prodded the outlaw to his feet with his sixgun. "Some more of that and you'll get a stretch in Yuma for threatening the bench," he warned coldly. "Now you gents march unless you prefer to be carried to jail!"

The outlaw turned to sheriff Blaine. "You going to stand for this after what I done for you?" he asked softly.

The sheriff dropped his eyes and twisted uneasily. "What can I do?" he muttered. "They made that law legal just last week."

"The judge can suspend the jail sentence," the outlaw shouted. "And he better do it!"

Judge Hart brightened up, but Alamo Bowie smiled grimly. "The judge has already dismissed court," he reminded them. "The sentence stands as ordered. Take 'em, Marshal!"

Through the empty court room and down the broad steps; men stared when the little procession wound around to the jail in back, and Doc Holliday stared them down while he swiveled the deadly sawed-off in his thin white hands. They knew the gambler and his reputation for cold courage. They also knew that the shotgun ran nine buckshot to the barrel, and after all it was not their quarrel.

In the jail office, the marshal emptied pockets and collected the fines. Alamo Bowie stood by until the last prisoner was locked up. Marshal White took a key from his pocket and spoke softly to the outlaw leader.

"Turn around, Jack."

He unlocked the cuffs and stepped back with his gun in hand. Three-finger Jack glared at him for a long moment and walked to the empty cell.

"You win for now," he muttered. "But three days ain't such an awful long time!"

"That's just a starter," the Texan cut in gruffly. "I told you that I was bringing Law for Tombstone, but you figgered you was bigger than the law. The United States government speaking, and after this I aim to do my talking with sixguns!"

"I'll tally for you one day soon, Texan," the outlaw promised quietly. "The man don't live who can buffalo me with his cutter and live to brag about it!"

Alamo Bowie shrugged and holstered his gun. "Any time after three days," he answered in his quiet drawl, and followed Doc Holliday to the jail office.

Marshal White sat on the edge of his scarred desk with a frown on his tanned face. "I might as well order my coffin," he muttered. "There were four town marshals killed in two weeks, and all four were shot in the back."

Doc Holliday grunted softly and eased the sawed-off under his coat where it hung by a strap. "I'll take the job if you want a vacation," he offered quietly, but there was a deadly glitter in his greenish eyes. "That way I could work legal with Alamo."

Ed White shrugged angrily. "I ain't running," he protested. "I took me an oath, and I'll live up to it. But

29

I got a feeling just the same!"

"Spoke like a man, feller," the Texan applauded softly. "Tom Scudder told me you didn't booger worth a hoot. Three days gives us considerable time to work, and if Tombstone has to have her man for breakfast, it might as well be an outlaw!"

The marshal frowned again. "It ain't that sheriff Blaine is crooked," he explained. "Only he's a danged politician, and he is afraid of Three-finger Jack. Good reason, too," he added.

"He could get a conviction if he went about it like a man," the gambler said bluntly. "The trouble is that Three-finger helped elect Blaine, and not only that, but he helped him collect taxes back there in the Dragoons where Blaine didn't dare go alone."

"And this is the County jail," Bowie said thoughtfully. "It might save a lot of trouble if some of those outlaws were killed while trying to escape."

"We can't do that, Bowie," the marshal protested, and glared at the Texan.

"Reckon yo're right, Ed," Bowie admitted. "But it's dollars to dimes that Blaine turns the lot of them loose when you go off duty. That's what I meant about them escaping."

The marshal sighed. "He's the sheriff, and my superior," he muttered. "If he turns them loose . . . ?"

"Impeach him," the gambler suggested. "For malfeasance of office."

Ed White shrugged irritably. "That's politics, and I don't play politics," he objected. "Not only that, but the fellers that worked to put him in office would do night work to keep him there, if you know what I'm getting at."

Alamo Bowie scratched a scar on his chin, a habit he had when deep in thought. "About Pop Whipple," he said suddenly. "We can call him in as witness if we have any more trouble with Peters. He's the only one of the crowd that kept out of jail, because he didn't have a gun on him."

"Old Pop will come too," White agreed. "But I'd hate to call him, Bowie. It would be too easy for one of the gang to pick him off the seat when he's making his run."

He led the way outside with a worried frown on his tanned face, and almost collided with a tall square-shouldered man. The newcomer reached out a powerful hand and steadied the marshal, and Ed White wiped the frown from his face.

"Howdy, Fred," he greeted. "Want to make you acquainted with Alamo Bowie. He had a little run-in with Three-finger Jack and his gang."

"Howdy," and Fred Rutledge studied the tall Texan without offering to shake hands.

Alamo Bowie flicked his gray eyes over the deputy sheriff and offered his right hand. "Glad to know you, Rutledge," he said quietly. "Reckon you and me will get along."

The deputy shook hands without changing expression. "Joe Blaine is my boss," he answered soberly. "I give him the best I got, Bowie."

The Texan nodded his approval. "You would," he drawled. "But I heard a little of yore history from a gent over in New Mex. He said you played yore cards across the top of the board, and that's good enough for me."

"This gent," and Rutledge narrowed his eyes. "You mind giving him a handle?"

"Name of Joe Grant," Bowie answered. "Sheriff of Luna County."

A new light came into the steady gray eyes of the deputy. "One of my best pards," he muttered. "And he likewise told me about you. I'll do what I can, Bowie."

"We were talking about these prisoners," the Texan explained. "According to the new town law, they do three days in jail. You reckon they will?"

Fred Rutledge was on the young side of thirty, but like Bowie he looked ten years older. His eyes narrowed thoughtfully for a moment while he pulled on his upper lip. Then he set his mouth and held out his hand.

"I can't say they will," he admitted honestly. "But I will see that you know about it if someone else turns them loose. Might save a bush-whacking that away, and you'd do the same for me."

A whistle blew hoarsely across the gulch where the silver mines were located. The deputy straightened his shoulders and waved his hand.

"Got to check some Posters," he muttered, and stomped into the office. "See you fellers later."

Ed White glanced down the street and nudged Bowie. "Joe Blaine coming," he whispered. "Fred didn't want to be seen chinning with us."

Doc Holliday stared at the thick-shouldered sheriff with the trace of a sneer on his thin lips. "I'm getting along," he muttered. "I never did like him, and I'm in no mood to take any more of his lip."

"Let's go up to Nellie Gray's for dinner," Ed White suggested. "Bowie will have to meet her sooner or later."

"Not interested in women," the Texan answered quickly. "Unless they can cook as good as I've heard about Miss Gray."

CHAPTER III

Alamo Bowie glanced curiously at the houses set well back on Tough Nut street. Most of them had red lights over the porches with shades drawn down even at mid-day. Tombstone was noted for her night life, but none of the habitués were visible. Here and there a curtain moved slightly to show that the ladies were interested in the marshal and his tall companion. Doc Holliday needed no introduction.

Ed White stopped at the corner of Fifth street and pointed to a sign over the broad porch of a rambling frame building. Alamo Bowie read the sign: RUSS HOUSE. Then he followed the marshal and Doc Holliday up the steps and took off his battered Stetson when the gambler bowed to the stately woman.

"Howdy, Nellie," Holliday greeted, and his usually brusque voice was soft and gentle. "Want you to meet

Alamo Bowie. Bowie; Miss Nellie Gray!"

"Pleased to know you, Ma'am," the Texan muttered, and twisted the hat in his strong fingers. "Been hearing all along the trail about the meals you set up here."

Nellie Gray smiled with her large brown eyes. Black hair combed straight back and parted in the middle. Fearless eyes set in the kindest face the Texan had ever seen. He guessed her age at twenty-six or seven, and she held out her hand and gripped him like a man.

"Glad to have you with us, Mister Bowie," and her voice was throaty and low. "Of course I have heard about you."

She released her hand and led the way to the dining room. The Texan followed her with his eyes until Ed White nudged him.

"Yo're not interested in women," he reminded. "But wait until you get on the outside of some of her grub. Folks here abouts calls Nellie the Angel of Tombstone."

Alamo Bowie jerked erect and flushed under his tan. "Imagine her in a place like this," he muttered.

Doc Holliday smiled. "They ain't a man in Tombstone but what would kill for Nellie," he said softly. "The preachers do a lot of talking with their mouths, but Nellie she gets out and nurses the sick, and feeds the hungry. Let's eat!"

"Right down here on Tough Nut street," and the Texan shook his head.

"People is just folks to Nellie," the gambler

explained. "She would just as soon go over and nurse one of the girls in a bawdy house, as take care of the sky-pilot's wife. Quit staring at her that away!"

Alamo Bowie sighed deeply and tore his eyes from the tall woman at the other end of the room. All during the meal he watched Nellie Gray attending to the wants of her guests. She greeted rough miners and cowboys with the same sincerity that she gave to the merchants, and the Texan marveled at the respect they gave in return.

They were finishing up on apple pie and strong coffee when Fred Rutledge came into the big room and ran his eyes over the crowd. Then the deputy spotted them and high-heeled between the tables. His face was grave when he touched Alamo Bowie on the arm.

"I said I'd let you know," he muttered. "Three-finger Jack and his crowd are loose."

"Joe Blaine?" and the Texan flexed the fingers of his right hand.

Rutledge nodded. "He's the sheriff of Cochise county. Nothing I could do about it, but I thought you and Ed ought to know. Red Dodge and Bisbee Thompson were in that crowd, and they aim to get you when you come into the Crystal Palace!"

"Thanks, pard," Bowie murmured, and pushed his chair back.

"More bad news," Rutledge said slowly. "The Benson stage was held up again. Old Pop Whipple was shot through the heart!"

Alamo Bowie turned and locked glances with Ed

White. The marshal frowned and rubbed the grip of his gun. Doc Holliday nodded his head slowly and leaned closer.

"They were afraid you would call Pop as a witness," he whispered huskily, and smothered a cough. "It's only a block to the Crystal Palace."

"That's right," and Bowie stretched to his feet and made his way to the door where Nellie Gray was waiting. "That shore was a swell feed, Ma'am," he said earnestly. "I'd take it kindly if I could eat here regular and often."

"I'm glad," the woman answered with a pleased smile. "Must you kill them?" and her brown eyes were suddenly grave.

Alamo Bowie knew what she meant. "They are waiting to kill me," he answered. "And I am bringing the law to Tombstone!"

She held out her hand impulsively. "Good luck, Alamo. I'd ask you not to if it were anyone else, but no one can stop that gang of outlaws. Don't forget that we will have corn fritters for supper."

She squeezed his hand and turned away to hide a tear. The Texan swallowed noisily and stomped to the porch. Doc Holliday was waiting with an expectant smile curling the corners of his thin mouth. The Texan turned to Ed White.

"You better not go, Ed," he said quietly. "It's me they want."

"I'm town Marshal," White said gruffly. "And old Pop Whipple was a friend of mine."

"He was killed outside of town," the Texan pointed

out. "This is a job for the U. S. Marshal!"

"We'll all go," White answered, and started up the street.

Crowds of red-shirted miners lined the streets when the three shouldered up the walks under the board awnings. Cowboys in buckskin and leather chaps leaning indolently against the tie rails with veiled glances of anticipation in their lowered eyes. Around the corner to Allen street and across the dusty road where the swinging doors of the Crystal Palace Bar beckoned a welcome.

"After me, yo're first," Bowie said to Ed White. "Like Rutledge said, it's me they want!"

He twitched the handles of his guns and shouldered through the batwings with his Stetson cuffed low over his gray eyes. The scar on his cheek stood out whitely against the deep tan, and the Texan walked to the center of the room with long arms hanging loosely at his sides.

Doc Holliday stepped through the doors and placed his thin shoulders against the front wall. His greenish eyes were glowing with a strange light while he reached under his long coat and found the stock of the sawed-off. Ed White leaned against the side wall and waited with a grim look on his face.

Three-finger Jack was not in sight, but the crowd had drawn away from two men drinking at the far end of the bar. One was a lanky desperado with a stubble of red beard on his vicious face. The other was a stocky man of forty with wide powerful shoulders and long black mustaches. Both were watching the Texan in the center of the room, and Red Dodge began to talk loudly to his companion.

"Now you take Texans, Bisbee," he sneered. "Up here we use them kind up quick. All I want is a chance to set my two eyes on that long-jinted gun-slinger what throwed us in the jug!"

"Never saw one yet that packed any sand when he was on his own," Bisbee Thompson answered. "This here is a free country, and he told the boss he was bringing Law for Tombstone. To hell with the law!"

Alamo Bowie spread his long legs and stared at the two outlaws without speaking. Red Dodge glanced up and nudged his companion. Both acted like they had just seen Bowie as they pushed away from the bar and separated.

"There he is now," Bisbee Thompson announced loudly. "Speak of the devil and yo're bound to hear his chains rattling!"

"Yore boss heard them this morning," the Texan answered clearly. "When we put the bracelets on him and dragged him to jail!"

Red Dodge swore under his breath and went into a crouch. "That was the first and last time," he growled. "You likewise threw me in jail and I'm taking it personal!"

"I heard you was," Bowie answered softly. "You doing something about it?"

"We got a spot picked out for you on Boot Hill," the outlaw sneered softly. "Along side the rest of those star toters that thought they could bring us some law!"

Alamo Bowie smiled with his lips and hunched his

shoulders. Red Dodge had both hands hooked in his gunbelts while Bisbee Thompson gripped the handle of his gun six feet to the side. Both were leaning forward watching the Texan who faced them with empty hands.

"You talked out?" Bowie asked softly.

Red Dodge slapped down suddenly with both hands. Bisbee Thompson lurched forward while his right arm began to jerk up. Doc Holliday watched with a little smile twitching the corners of his mouth while the killer light glowed deep in his eyes. And still the tall Texan watched and waited.

Suddenly his powerful shoulders twitched to hurl his hands down to meet the grips of his guns. None saw the Twins leap through the smoky air until red gunlight gouted from his brown hands like heat lightning on stampeding longhorns.

Bisbee Thompson jerked back and sat down with the gun spilling from his grimy hand. Red Dodge whipped into a half-turn and triggered a pair of slugs into the bar when his guns cleared leather with the shock of the bullet that shattered his right shoulder. He stomped his left boot down hard and whirled with thumb dogging back the filed hammer of his left-hand gun while a roar of rage blasted from his throat.

Alamo Bowie caught the bucking gun in his right hand and dropped hammer just as Red Dodge finished his right-about. The gun flew from the outlaw's hand when a crimson splotch leaped to his left breast and rocked him back on his rounded heels. He teetered a time or two with his jaws agape before he buckled his knees and crumpled to the dirty sawdust.

Three seconds of slashing flame and thudding lead while the crowd held their breathing against aching chests. Silence while boot heels rattled on the planking, with a gunman's halo of black-powder smoke making a widening ring above the head of Alamo Bowie. The scar on his chin was normal when he holstered the Twins and turned to face the crowd.

"Them two was outlaws," and his voice was harsh. "They been robbing the stages, and it's my job to make 'em safe. Do I hear any objections?"

His gray eyes flicked over each face while he waited for an answer. When none came he dropped his hands and made the same careless rapid draw of a moment before. Jacked the spent shells from his guns and thumbed fresh cartridges through the loading gates, and once more the Twins disappeared when he waved his hands. He stiffened when a hoarse voice shouted from the front door.

"Hands up, Bowie. I'm taking you for murder!"

The Texan turned slowly to face sheriff Joe Blaine. "You ain't," he contradicted softly. "Both those gents passed notice on me!"

"I turned them loose," Blaine growled angrily. "And the judge heard you threaten to do yore talking with sixguns!"

"Which same I done," the Texan admitted calmly. "All these gents saw the deceased draw first."

"You can do yore talking in jail," the sheriff shouted. "Make a move and I'll drop you in yore tracks!"

"Now I wouldn't do that if I was you," a soft voice interrupted. "I got both barrels notched back, and the muzzle not more than a foot from yore spine!"

Sheriff Blaine straightened up from his crouch with the color draining from his beefy face. He knew that thin soft voice just behind him. The same voice that called the cases night after night in the Oriental. Beads of fine sweat broke out on his forehead, and then the heavy gun sagged low in his trembling hand.

"You can turn around, Blaine," Doc Holliday said softly. "I wanted to keep you honest!"

The sheriff whirled and cursed angrily. The dapper gambler was facing him empty-handed, and he whipped up his gun to regain the drop.

"Hold it, Blaine!"

The flustered sheriff whirled back to face the Texan. Alamo Bowie flicked his hands and came out with a full house. The Twins cuddled against his palms with the hammers eared back while he spoke softly to Joe Blaine without raising his drawling voice.

"I told you once before, sheriff, not to draw yore cutter unless you aimed to smoke. What was you saying when you come in?"

"I might have knowed that gambler was bluffing," the sheriff growled. "You caught me on a sneak!"

"Holster your gun," and the Texan's voice was brassy.

Joe Blaine fumbled and holstered his Colt. Alamo Bowie flicked his hands again and the Twins disappeared. Then the tall Texan started from scratch.

"She's yore play, sheriff," he said softly. "These

41

killers sent me warning, and I'm only a deputy U. S. Marshal. I killed them both and I'm saving some of the same for their pards."

"It's a frame-up," the sheriff growled, and stared at Ed White. "I'll have yore star for letting this happen!"

"Take it up with the Town committee," the marshal answered quietly. "I was going to take them two, but I couldn't match them with a hand gun!"

"You hear about Pop Whipple, sheriff?" the Texan asked carelessly.

"What about him?"

"The stage was held up again," Bowie answered. "Pop Whipple was killed so he couldn't be a witness against Lantern-jaw Peters!"

"Mebbe Three-finger did it," the sheriff sneered. "And him in jail!"

"Mebbe some of his gang did it," the Texan retorted sharply. "It's my business to find out, and I aim to do it!"

"You can ride in my posse," and the sheriff changed his tone. "I'm riding out to cut for sign right now."

"Just you keep right on riding," Bowie answered with the trace of a sneer in his voice. "I usually work alone."

"Them two," and Blaine pointed at the bodies on the floor.

The Texan shrugged. "Boot Hill," he said harshly. "The government will stand the expense and save money on trials!"

"Reckon yo're right," and the sheriff showed one of his rapid changes. "Better ride with me, Bowie."

"Better not," Doc Holliday interrupted coldly. "Like as not there will be several of them outlaws riding with the posse. It wouldn't be the first time!"

"Meaning what?" and sheriff Blaine turned slowly to face the gambler.

"Meaning that Three-finger Jack rode with you to collect taxes," Doc Holliday snapped, and held his breath while he reached for a handkerchief to smother a sudden burst of coughing.

The sheriff watched his struggles with no sign of pity on his hard face. Doc Holliday held to the door for support until the paroxysm had passed. Then he wiped a pink froth from his lips and smiled wanly.

"You heard me," he added softly.

The sheriff raised his hand to his mouth and coughed mockingly. The gambler narrowed his eyes until iris and pupil melded. Little red flecks danced to the high cheek-bones against the dead white of the gambler's skin. His right hand moved like the flick of a snake's tongue, and the sheriff gasped when a long-barreled forty-five bored a dent in his paunch.

"Cough one more time," Doc Holliday pleaded earnestly. "Cough once more so's I can drop hammer and scatter yore innards all over the floor!"

"Guess I taken a cold," the sheriff whispered. "I didn't mean nothing, Doc!"

The gambler holstered his Colt with a sneer. "You ain't got the guts of a horny toad," he said softly, but the tones bit deep. "Now you better get about rounding up yore owl-hoot posse before I remember again what you did!"

Alamo Bowie watched the little scene with pity in his heart for the sick man. Doc Holliday's days were numbered, but he would be a fighting man until either the white plague or gunman's lead cut him down. The sheriff backed through the swinging doors, and the Texan waved his hand toward the bar.

"Belly up," he invited. "I'm buying for the house!"

The crowd began to chatter as they rushed for the bar. Alamo Bowie stood at the end with a glass of whiskey in one hand, and a chaser of the same in the other. Two swift passes, and then he wiped his lips with the back of his hand.

"You handing in yore star?" he asked Ed White.

The Town Marshal shook his head slowly. "That's up to the committee," he muttered. "I wish I could ride with you this afternoon."

The Texan shrugged. "I like to ride alone, and I've been missing my Snapper hoss. I'll see you tonight while yo're making your rounds."

He left the saloon with a nod for Doc Holliday, and made his way to the O K Corral. A gaunt raw-boned man came out on the platform of the stage depot and called softly. Held out a hand when Bowie came close.

"Howdy, Bowie. I'm Marty Williams, Agent for the Company here in Tombstone."

"Knew it," and the Texan shook hands. "You might let Tom Scudder know about Red Dodge and Bisbee Thompson. There was Posters on both them jiggers for a job over Deming way."

"They dead?"

Bowie nodded carelessly. "Tell Tom the sheriff is

getting a warrant out for me for murder. You hear about Pop Whipple?"

The big agent nodded slowly. "Pop was the best driver on the division," he said sadly. "They got six thousand in gold."

"Damn the gold," Bowie muttered profanely. "With Pop as witness, we could have got a conviction against Peters!"

Marty Williams shrugged his big shoulders. "You got other law," he suggested quietly. "And don't forget the Company is behind you all the way!"

"Where was this last hold-up?" the Texan asked abruptly.

"Just the other side of Contention," Williams answered. "The shotgun guard came in on one of the horses. He said they had just passed the Drew ranch going up the grade."

"Be seeing you," and Bowie walked across the corral to the barn. The big red horse whinnied a welcome and muzzled his master until the Texan brought out a cube of sugar in his palm.

"Been a missing you, Snapper hoss," he crooned softly, and stroked the satiny neck.

"Alamo?"

The Texan turned slowly when the soft voice called his name. Nellie Gray was dressed in a riding habit, and she sat a side-saddle on a deep-chested bay. Her brown eyes were shining with happiness, and she reached down a white hand and patted the Texan on the shoulder.

"I'm so glad you were not hurt," and her voice

made a tremor race up his spine. "Promise me that you will be careful."

"Who? Me, Ma'am?" and the Texan stared his unbelief.

"You are an honest man, though a hard one," she answered softly. "We need you here in Tombstone."

"Huh?"

"There are two classes here, Alamo," she continued. "The decent element can't stay unless the law comes in. Oh, I know we have law," she said with a frown. "But we need the kind that gives everyone an equal chance!"

"Yes'm," he agreed soberly. "We got that kind too," and he tapped the worn scabbards on his long legs. "Holster law," he added gruffly.

"Killing," and the woman shuddered. "I've dreamed of the day when things would be different. There is wealth here for everyone, but only the outlaws get it. They spend their loot over the bars and down on Tough Nut street, and nothing is done about it!"

"I'm a gun-fighter, Miss Nellie," the Texan said gravely. "But all my life I've sold my guns on the side of the law. It won't be no different now!"

"Poor Pop," she murmured. "You are going to ride out there where he was killed?"

The Texan nodded. "And I always ride alone," he muttered. "Begging yore pardon, Ma'am."

He twisted uneasily when he saw the quick look of hurt in her brown eyes. "I thought you might want me," she whispered. "I get lonesome here at times, Alamo."

"Reckon you do, Miss Nellie," he muttered. "Well, I'll be seeing you come supper time!"

His fingers tightened the cinchas, and then he was in the saddle. A touch of his heel and the big red horse was across the corral and through the gate. Nellie Gray watched wistfully and tossed her head. Then she sent the bay roaring in pursuit.

CHAPTER IV

Alamo Bowie heard the clatter of pursuit as he raced up the long gradual hill where the windswept cemetery guarded the crest. His nostrils distended like a stallion going into a fight when he saw three Mexican laborers digging a pair of graves in the rocky soil. The big red horse whinnied softly and pricked up his ears, and the special agent sighed softly and waited for Nellie Gray.

"Alamo," she chided reprovingly, and came close to rub stirrups. "You ran away from me."

The Texan pointed to the new graves, and his voice was harsh. "That's why," he explained. "And there will be more of the same before I finish my work. It is always the same where men want gold that does not belong to them!"

"This work of yours," and her voice was still gentle. "Must you always mete out the extreme penalty?"

The Texan refused to meet her brown eyes while his head nodded vigorously. "Nearly always," he grunted. "Like last year when the Company made me a lawyer as well as their special agent. I had to catch the stage robbers in the act, and then I held trial and sat on the bench in a manner of speaking."

Nellie Gray watched his stern face and the play of emotions that flitted across his narrowed gray eyes. His hand raised slowly and rubbed the scar on his chin; pushed back his battered felt hat and touched a white streak of hair where the scalp showed pink. And she knew that the marks were the mementoes of battle.

"You tried and sentenced the robbers?" she prompted softly.

The gun-fighter nodded slowly. "I knew they were guilty," he growled. "Some of them I caught red-handed. Then I produced the evidence and asked the questions, but every man got his chance to prove that old Judge Colt was wrong!"

"You were also executioner," the woman whispered, and glanced at the two heavy guns riding low on his powerful legs.

"What else?" he asked sharply. "These bandits robbed and killed. The Courts couldn't do anything about it because the judges were afraid. If they convicted a man, some of his pards killed the judge and the officers who made the arrests!"

"You are an unusual man, Alamo Bowie," she said quietly, and there was no fault-finding in her soft voice. "And I know that you tempered Justice with mercy."

"Yes'm," he muttered. "I always shot dead center when the proof of guilt was established. But I gave up being a Wells Fargo lawyer when the case was closed!"

"Habit is a strange thing," the woman mused. "We are all creatures of habit, and you are following out the same general schedule here in Arizona. There are more than twenty in the gang of Three-finger Jack!"

The Texan shrugged with characteristic fatalism. "Twenty or a hundred, I have my work to do," he answered gruffly. "Shall we ride, Miss Nellie?"

Nellie Gray smiled and nodded her black head. "I would like to see you work," she confessed. "The Drew ranch is seven miles farther."

Shadows were slanting down from the Huacucas when they reined the horses to a stop in a sandy wash where the road crossed. Alamo Bowie slid to the ground and pointed to the wheel tracks and hoof marks. The woman followed when he made his way to a clump of desert willows and prickly pear. The tracks of two horses were plainly visible, and the Texan pointed to the frayed bark on a tree.

"A little red hoss was tied here with a hair rope," he muttered, and pointed to a few sorrel hairs caught in the bark. "This hoss likewise had his mane roached, cause you can see plain where he rubbed hisself."

"Big Enough Smith," the woman murmured. "He's the only man around here with a horse like that."

"Smith, eh?" Bowie repeated. "Little jigger with feet like a woman, and packs two cutters on his Bull-hide chaps!"

"You know him?" she asked in surprise.

The Texan shook his head. "Never laid eyes on the

jigger," he growled. "But he hunkered down there behind the thicket, and you can see the prints of six-guns. Nothing but Bullhide is stiff enough to cut in like them leather pants this gent wore, and he wasn't very wide across the narrows!"

Nellie Gray caught her breath sharply. "He is the most dangerous man in Tombstone, next to Three-finger," she whispered. "Fast as light with his guns, and deadly as a *vinegarone!*"

"The other gent was a barn-shouldered hombre wearing goose-necked rawls on number twelve boots," the Texan muttered, and traced the outlines on the sandy soil. "Packed a Spencer carbine and wore one gun on the off side. Chews snuff and spits through his front teeth!"

Nellie Gray stared at him in silent fascination while he read the descriptions with complete confidence. "It is uncanny," she whispered. "Bull Clanton has a front tooth missing, and he chews snuff. He has the biggest feet you ever saw, and he is left-handed!"

"Thanks, Miss Nellie," the special agent grunted. "I'm glad I broke over one time and brought you along. Where did you say these two varmints held forth?"

"I didn't say," and the woman shuddered. "But they usually stay in Diablo canyon where Clanton has a little spread. Poor old Pop Whipple."

"Yonder comes the sheriff and his posse," Bowie warned suddenly and levered to his feet. "Best not to say anything about what we discovered here. I want to watch Joe Blaine read the sign."

50

Nellie Gray nodded and waved her hand at the approaching posse. Sheriff Joe Blaine was in the lead with a saddle-gun across his knees. Fred Rutledge was behind him with three other riders circling close. Hard-faced men with the marks of the long trails scarred deep on their rigging and gear.

"Howdy, Bowie," the sheriff said pleasantly enough. "You find out something?"

Alamo Bowie was staring at a wide-shouldered man who carried an old Spencer carbine across the front of his saddle. A stubby black beard almost hid the little blue eyes slanting out from under a cuffed-down hat brim. The eyes of the Texan swung down to boot level and hardened when he saw the size.

"Meet up with Bull Clanton," the sheriff chuckled. "Bull offered to give us the lend of his gun."

"Howdy," Bowie grunted. "They ain't much to work on here."

"Them tracks there," the sheriff answered, and pointed toward the trees. "That's where the hold-ups hid out," and he sent his horse forward.

Bowie smiled when the other riders followed and clouded the sign. Only Fred Rutledge held back, and he was watching the Texan's face closely. He kneed his horse alongside and spoke in a whisper.

"You've read the sign, feller. What you aim to do about it?"

"Who, me?" and the Texan raised shaggy brows. "You can't noways do nothing without proof of guilt," he muttered carelessly.

"It ain't often you find one without the other," Rutledge remarked. "And the little feller is the worst of the pair."

Alamo Bowie smiled grimly while a light of admiration lighted his gray eyes. "You'll do, Mister," he praised quietly. "How come Big Enough to stay back in town?"

The deputy nodded this time. "I knew you was wise," he grunted. "And I'm giving you my word that Joe Blaine don't know anything about it. Joe ain't much of a tracker, and now-adays it's hard to press in a posse for a man-hunt."

"You shouldn't have come, Fred," the Texan muttered hoarsely. "Ed White is left back there on his lonesome!"

Fred Rutledge jerked in the saddle. "Hell," he swore softly. "Bull Clanton suggested to the sheriff about me coming. You reckon it means anything?"

Alamo Bowie turned to Nellie Gray who had been listening silently. "You mind hitting a high lope for town, Miss Nellie?" he asked softly.

"What is it, Alamo?" she asked quickly.

"Get to Ed White and warn him to be careful. Tell him to stay away from Big Enough Smith. I can't leave right now!"

"See you at supper," and Nellie Gray heeled her horse into a leaping run.

The two men watched her for a moment. "Never saw Nellie pay any mind to a man before," Rutledge mumbled. "She's the best there is, Bowie."

"Yeah," but the Texan's voice was careless. "Which away is Diablo canyon?" he asked slowly.

Fred Rutledge glanced at him sharply. "Just over the hog-back a matter of three miles," he answered. "There wouldn't be anyone there now."

"Well, I'll be seein' you," the Texan replied, and neck-reined the big red horse. "Get along, Snapper."

"Just a moment, Bowie," and Rutledge blocked the way. "That's where Bull Clanton has his spread. Runs three-four hundred head of scrub dogies back there in the tangles."

"Uh huh," the Texan murmured. "I just want to get the lay of the land while I got time. Tell the sheriff I hit out for town," and he scratched Snapper with his blunted spurs.

The deputy watched him lope over the rise and disappear on the other side. Then he joined the four men behind the trees and slid from the saddle to join the circle. Bull Clanton was pointing to some marks in the sandy soil while his deep voice rumbled and muttered.

"Star studded in the right heel," he told the sheriff. "That would be a Texan, Joe."

"Only Texan in these parts would be Bowie," Blaine answered, and scratched his head. "And he is special agent for Wells Fargo."

"Mebbe they don't pay him enough," Clanton suggested, and winked at his companions. "I bet dinero he was the hombre what stuck up the stage!"

"There's another set of tracks," Fred Rutledge interrupted. "And they were made by a woman."

The sheriff turned quickly. "Didn't see you, Fred," he answered. "You don't mean to let on that Nellie Gray had anything to do with the hold-up!"

The deputy repressed a sneer. "That big ox yonder," he grunted, and stared at Bull Clanton. "He knows as well as you and me that Bowie and Miss Nellie was back here trying to read the sign. He knows what would happen to him if the men back in town heard him making remarks about Nellie!"

"I'm reading it the way I see it," and Bull Clanton glared at the deputy with his big jaw thrust out. "If that star there fits the Texan's boot, it was him what shot old Pop Whipple!"

Fred Rutledge came to his feet and faced the big man with anger in his wide gray eyes. "Bowie was eating in the Russ House when Pop was killed," he snarled. "I saw him there myself."

"Get yore hackles down," Clanton warned, and dropped a hand to his gun. "You was seen and heard telling him about the sheriff turning Three-finger and the gang loose!"

The deputy swung his right fist from the hip and knocked the sneering outlaw kicking. Bull Clanton spilled the gun he was trying to draw, and Rutledge slapped his holster and got the drop. His voice was a grating whisper when he leveled down with the hammer dogged back.

"Get up and holster yore iron! I'm part of the law here in Tombstone!"

Bull Clanton staggered to his feet and turned to the sheriff. "You heard him," he growled. "Is he the law, or did I hear different?"

Sheriff Blaine stepped forward with a scowl on his beefy face. "Pouch yore cutter, Fred," he barked. "I'm the law here, and you take orders from me, or you can hand in yore star and take yore time!"

"Mebbe you better write it out," Rutledge muttered angrily. "That big long-rider done clouded the real sign back here to throw you off the trail. Then he tries to put Miss Nellie in a jam with his lying remarks. I should have killed him!"

"You didn't have the sand to draw me evens," Clanton snarled. "Wait till the boys hear about this!"

Fred Rutledge fumbled with his badge and threw it on the ground. Then he made a quick step and picked up Clanton's gun. Stuck it deep in the empty holster on the outlaw's left leg and stepped back.

"Show-down," he whispered. "Make yore pass, yuh swayed-back maverick!"

Joe Blaine stepped between the two men and pushed Rutledge back. His gun was in his right hand, and he slapped down when the deputy rapped down for the holster on his right leg. Flame spat out behind the sheriff when Bull Clanton dropped hammer, and Fred Rutledge went down with crimson spouting from under his Stetson.

Sheriff Blaine wheeled swiftly and faced the muttering gunman with his thumb slipping the hammer. Bull Clanton dropped his smoking gun and raised his hands. The sheriff held his shot and glared at the big man, and then he sighed with relief when Fred Rutledge stirred and came to his feet.

"I'd have killed you if Fred was done for," the sheriff told Clanton. "I don't go in for killing like you know, but the jigger don't live and keep on living that can gun down one of my men right under my eyes!"

"He asked for show-down," Clanton muttered. "You had no call to step between us. You might have got me killed!"

A thick voice whirled him around. Fred Rutledge was swaying unsteadily with his right hand hooked in his gunbelt. A trickle of blood ran down the deputy's face and dripped from his craggy chin, and his gray eyes were bleary with fog.

"Make yore pass, yuh curly wolf!"

Bull Clanton paled and began to tremble. "I ain't heeled," he whispered. "Don't shoot!"

"Get yoreself dressed," the deputy barked. "Or I'll let you have yore needin's right here and now!"

"Hold it, Fred!"

Joe Blaine shouted hoarsely with the gun hanging loosely in his hand. Fred Rutledge wabbled across the ground and again picked up the outlaw's weapon. He came forward slowly, swaying like a reed in a strong wind, and then he crashed forward on his face when he reached out to jam the gun in the scabbard on Clanton's thick leg.

Bull Clanton lashed out with his big boot and caught the falling man squarely on the chin. Then his huge hand ripped down to his holster while the red light of murder glowed in his little eyes. Joe Blaine came to life and jabbed his sixgun deep in the outlaw's belt while his voice snapped a warning.

"Unclutch or get killed!"

Bull Clanton scowled and backed away shaking his wide shoulders. The sheriff followed him with anger blazing from his eyes. Waved at the horse waiting with trailing reins.

"Hit leather and keep going," he barked. "I tried to work this ruckus out without a killing, but I'll drill you on sight for what you done to the law. Now git!"

Bull Clanton muttered under his breath and walked to his horse. "Three-finger will hear about this," he growled hoarsely. "And don't forget you said . . . *on sight!*"

He hit the saddle and roared away over the rise while the sheriff held the drop. Joe Blaine turned to the other posse men and holstered his gun.

"They say I'm yellow," he muttered. "They say I'm a pard to outlaws," and he shook himself angrily. "I'll kill that big hulk the next time I see him!"

"Knew it would happen one of the days, Joe," a slender rider said slowly, and stuck out his hand. "Shake, pard!"

"Yo're one of the town committee, Jed Swope," the sheriff answered slowly. "I was going to ask you to let Ed White go, but now I'm going to tell the marshal that he was right, and I was wrong. I'm telling Bowie the same thing!"

"Running the saddle-shop keeps me right busy," Swope answered. "But I'll tell Ed White what you said. Fred is beginning to stir yonder."

Joe Blaine was a different man when he hunkered down beside his deputy and lifted the wabbling head. His lips moved slowly until Rutledge opened his eyes and stared for a moment.

"I'm asking you to pin back that star, deputy,"

Blaine muttered huskily. "I'm picking Bull Clanton for my own cutter the next time him and me comes face to face!"

A happy light spread across the bloody face of deputy Fred Rutledge. He closed his eyes with a tired sigh, and made an effort to hold out his hand.

"Shake, sheriff," he murmured weakly. "I knew you'd get up yore mad one of the days. Now we can whip these wide-loopers without no trouble."

"Yore jaw," the sheriff muttered softly. "He kicked you when you fell."

Rutledge grinned faintly. "You can't kill a cowboy, Joe," he muttered. "Not unless you cut off his head and hide it from him."

"The dirty son," Blaine muttered. "He tried to let on that Alamo Bowie and Nellie Gray robbed the stage and killed old Pop Whipple!"

"She's gone, sher'ff," Rutledge whispered. "You and me was framed. Bowie sent her back to town to warn Ed White!"

"Framed? Ed White?"

Fred Rutledge sat up slowly. "Bowie read the sign the way it was," he explained. "Big Enough Smith and Bull Clanton robbed the stage. Bull wiped out the sign before you could see it, and then he pointed out the tracks Bowie and Nellie made!"

"And it was Clanton offered to come out with us while Big Enough stayed in town," he muttered slowly. "You reckon . . . ?"

"Ed White can't match that little side-winder with a hand-gun," Rutledge answered thickly. "So Bowie sent Nellie high-tailin' to tell Ed to watch himself."

"You reckon the Texan would work with me now?" the sheriff asked doubtfully. "You figger he might help us if I braced him like a man?"

"Looky, Joe," Rutledge answered eagerly. "Alamo Bowie would go all the way with any hombre who was big enough to admit he was wrong. You and him never shook hands, but the Texan will be the first to offer to touch skin!"

Sheriff Blaine rose slowly to his feet and sucked in a deep breath. Squared his shoulders and hitched up his gunbelt while a light of determination leaped to his eyes.

"I'll tell him," he announced softly. "Hey, Bowie!"

"He's gone," Rutledge interrupted. "He lit a shuck before I had that run-in with Clanton. Say! Where is that murdering rustler?"

He came upright and weaved on shaky legs while his eyes darted around the clearing. His right hand held poised above the worn scabbard on his leg, the only part of him that was steady.

"Gone," the sheriff muttered. "I sent him foggin' to keep from killing him. He high-tailed over the hump!"

Fred Rutledge stopped and dropped his hand. Wiped his face wearily and shook his head.

"You shouldn't have done it," he muttered. "He'll dry-gulch the Texan shore as sin."

"The Texan? You mean Bowie?" the sheriff shouted.

Rutledge nodded. "Bowie rode over to have a look in Diablo canyon while them two was away," he explained. "Said for me to tell you he was going back to town, but Bowie knew that Big Enough and Bull robbed the stage."

"Oh my God," the sheriff groaned. "Ed White and Big Enough in town, and that killer stalkin' the Texan back there in Devil canyon. Think fast, feller!"

Fred Rutledge staggered to his horse. "You and Jed burn the hocks off yore hosses gettin' back to Tombstone," he suggested. "I'll smoke it over to Clanton's spread, and if Clanton is alive . . . ?"

"I'll go to Clanton's," the sheriff growled. "I owe that big ox something!"

Rutledge shook his head while he pinned on his badge. "Bowie thinks you ain't friendly," he explained softly. "Better let me see him first and make medicine. Now you and Jed hit the breeze, and say a prayer on the way. And boss?"

"Yeah, Fred!"

"Three-finger Jack, he ain't going to like you no better after what you done to Clanton!"

The sheriff squared his shoulders. "To hell with Three-finger Jack," he barked. "I should have left him there in jail like the Texan figgered, but nohow, I'll do my duty the way I see it. C'mon, Jed!"

Fred Rutledge watched them thunder toward town while he climbed his saddle. Then he shook his head to clear the cobwebs of fog away. Struck sharply with his spurs to rocket his buckskin up the grade and over the rise toward Diablo canyon and the Clanton spread.

CHAPTER V

Alamo Bowie was rubbing the scar on his chin while he sent the big red horse swiftly across the mountain desert. Giant Sahuro and Cholla cactus cast weird shadows when the brassy sun turned to red and hovered above the distant Dragoons. Cattle branded with the old Jingle-bob grazed through the scant browse, and here and there a Box C steer rolled his eyes and boogered back into the tangles.

"The law says to get proof," the Texan muttered to himself. "I figger to find it!"

The desert narrowed away and came to an abrupt end where a deep file-sight canyon notched out between rolling hills. Here the grass was green and plentiful, and the Texan nodded his head when he sent Snapper through a sandy creek where the alders and alamosas bordered the banks through the canyon.

His keen eyes tallied the Box C cattle and checked off their points. Clanton had a natural protected range and needed few riders. The cattle would not wander far from such a paradise, and Bowie reined to a walk when he sighted a low adobe house on top of a little knoll. Corrals fronted the house with several well-grained saddle horses nickering over the rails.

The special agent dropped his hands and loosed his guns of riding crimp. The Twins, men called them in the Panhandle, and the walnut handles were worn smooth from daily practice. Bowie studied the house while he rode slowly across the yard, and he dropped off in front of the low porch with his shoulders stooped into a crouch.

For a moment he paused to listen with head cocked on one side. Then he moved cat-like across the gallery and pushed the front door open. Stepped in quickly and flashed his eyes across the dirty room before he relaxed.

"Nobody home," he grunted. "But I better work fast!"

Two bunks were built into the back wall, and covered with filthy quilts. The Texan studied them for a moment, and then his eyes lighted briefly. He crossed the room and ripped the soogans from the lower bunk. Reached down and spilled a heavy canvas sack to the floor.

"Gold," he whispered, and dumped the sack.

Small canvas pokes of dust and nuggets rolled soggily on the wide planking. A heavy silver watch blinked owlishly from the center of the heap. The Texan picked it up and turned it over in his hand. The hands had stopped at two o'clock. A pair of ornate initials were engraved on the back.

"P. W.," Bowie muttered. "Old Pop's name was Philip."

He pocketed the old time piece and sacked up the heavy pokes of gold. It took all his strength to drag the bag across the room, and the Texan hesitated while his eyes ran across the porch. Then he dragged the sack off the porch and stuffed it under the warped boards out of sight.

"Got to get more evidence," he muttered, and led the big red horse behind the house where the animal could not be seen from the lane. Then he climbed the porch and walked into the front room. A curtain hung from a window, and the special agent walked behind it and drew the cloth until it hung in loose folds.

He cocked his head again when hoof-beats pounded up the lane. A horse slid to a stop with boot heels racing across the porch floor. A man burst into the room shouting the Texan's name.

"Bowie! You here, feller?"

Alamo Bowie grimaced and answered before stepping out. He knew that Fred Rutledge would have his gun in hand, and the deputy might shoot by mistake.

"Coming out, pard," he muttered. "I thought you was Bull Clanton."

Fred Rutledge sighed with relief. "Ain't he here?" he asked, and gripped the Texan by the arm.

"He ain't been here since the hold-up," Bowie answered. "I was waiting for him. Now how did you get that nick in the skull?"

The deputy scowled angrily. "Clanton done that on a sneak," he growled. "Then he buffaloed me with his cutter when I fell on my face like a dang Pilgrim!"

The Texan's eyes narrowed. "The sheriff?" he asked softly. "What was he doin' all that time?"

"Trying to figger things out," Rutledge defended. "He got Clanton on the end of his cutter and sent him fogging. Threatened to smoke Clanton down the next time he saw him."

"Naw," and Bowie stared his unbelief. "Joe Blaine

never done that!"

"He done it," the deputy repeated, and a smile lighted his hard face. "He wants to tell you that he was wrong, and that you was right. He was wondering if you would give him some help to run out them outlaws!"

"Happy days," Bowie murmured. "You ain't trying to hooraw an old hand, are you?"

"Never saw him really mad before," Rutledge explained earnestly. "And he will kill Bull Clanton the next time they meet."

"What become of Clanton?" Bowie demanded. "I figgered him to hit a high lope over here."

"He must have doubled back to town," Rutledge answered. "First time I ever knowed him and Big Enough to separate."

"Big Enough Smith," Bowie muttered. "He will kill Ed White shore as sin!"

"Not now," Rutledge grinned. "The sheriff took it on the run with Jed Swope. He even asked Jed to keep Ed White on as Marshal, and they ought to be reaching Tombstone by now. You find anything?"

Bowie led the way outside and pulled the sack from under the porch. "There's the loot from the stage," he said simply, and reached to his vest pocket. "I found this old watch in the sack."

Rutledge took the watch and gasped. "That belonged to old Pop Whipple," he whispered. "You got yore proof now, Texan!"

Bowie shook his head. "Proof enough for you and me," he said slowly. "But a good lawyer in court could show how somebody else might have hid this stuff here to lay the blame on Clanton!"

"But them marks back there in the wash," Rutledge pointed out.

"Are them marks there now?"

"Clanton wiped them out," the deputy admitted.

"Could you take them marks into court?" Bowie persisted.

"And they call that law," Rutledge growled with disgust. "What you aim to do?"

"We'll take turns packing this stuff back to town," the Texan answered. "Must be close to two hundred pounds."

Alamo Bowie pursed his lips and whistled softly. The big red horse came tearing around the corner holding his head sideways so as not to step on the split reins. The Texan heaved the heavy sack behind the cantle and fastened it with saddle strings. Then he mounted Snapper and waited for Rutledge.

"There was bank notes in that shipment," he said quietly. "Mebbe so the robbers will spend a few tonight."

"Money is money," Rutledge shrugged. "You couldn't tell it."

"These was all fifties," Bowie explained. "Marty Williams has the numbers in his office."

"We're going to be late for supper," and the deputy scratched his horse lightly.

The twilight deepened and shut out the afterglow while they rode across the high desert. Two newly heaped mounds of earth bulked in Boot Hill graveyard when they topped the hill and started down the grade. Yellow lights glowing brightly on Allen street with winking red lights beckoning a welcome just beyond on Tough Nut street.

"Let's cut down to Fremont," and Rutledge avoided town and turned to the left. "Marty Williams will be in his office."

Bowie nodded and followed at a walk. The gold was still tied behind his saddle, and the horses crowded through the gate to the O K corral. Bowie edged the red horse to a platform and called softly.

"Marty? Come a-running, feller!"

The big Agent slid from his chair and piled out on the platform. He stared at Rutledge and Bowie, and then his eyes fastened to the sack behind the saddle.

"You got it," he whispered, and lifted the box easily to carry it inside.

The two officers followed him into the tiny office. "You see Big Enough Smith lately?" Bowie asked abruptly.

The big Agent sighed. "He killed a man this afternoon," he answered heavily. "One of the best men we had here in Tombstone."

Fred Rutledge leaped forward and grabbed his arm. "Not Ed White?"

Marty Williams nodded sadly. "It was after the posse rode out," he answered. "Big Enough kicked up a row in the Crystal Palace, and Ed White barged in to arrest him. Smith claims self defense, and he has a dozen witnesses!"

Alamo Bowie was rubbing the grips of his guns.

"Nellie Gray," he said slowly. "You see her?"

"Nellie come fogging into town with her hoss steaming," the Agent explained. "The shot rang out just as she passed the Crystal Palace, and Ed died in her arms."

"And Smith?"

"He laughed," Williams growled. "Nellie Gray stood up and told him to prepare to meet his God. Then she handed him a little prayer book she had in her pocket."

"Keep on talking," Bowie grunted. "She handed him a prayer book."

"Told him there was one man he couldn't beat with a gun," Williams recited. "The rest of us stood there and listened, and Big Enough wanted to know who this here magician was."

"I'll take him," Rutledge ground out angrily.

Alamo Bowie barred the door. "Wait," he whispered. "What did Nellie tell him?"

"Said there was a man who wore a star studded in the heel of his right boot," Williams continued slowly. "And she told him that this feller would square up for Ed White before the moon was high."

Alamo Bowie nodded his head slowly. "Guess I better get about my job of work," he said softly. "You got the numbers of those fifties that was stole with the loot?"

Marty Williams handed him a slip of paper. "Only twenty of them bills," he muttered. "Big Enough is gambling down in the Oriental."

Alamo Bowie hitched up his crossed belts and

cuffed the battered Stetson low over his gray eyes. "Askin' you gents to stay out," he muttered gruffly. "According to the law, he gets a chance!"

"The sheriff," Rutledge almost shouted. "We better hurry, Bowie!"

Alamo Bowie was already halfway across the Corral. Down the street gleamed the lights of the Oriental. High heels clicking rapidly on the wooden walks, and then the tall Texan slid through the slatted batwings and shouldered against the wall to blink his eyes against the light.

He saw Fred Rutledge come through the side door and jerk his head at Doc Holliday. The gambler left his case and sauntered slowly to the bar. Alamo Bowie came forward and joined the pair.

"Big Enough Smith; he gambling?" Bowie jerked.

"Not now," the gambler grinned. "I took him for five hundred in fifty-dollar bills. You like to see?"

He reached to his breast pocket and brought out a wallet. Handed some yellow bills to the Texan, and watched while Bowie compared the numbers with a slip of paper.

"That's them," the Texan said, and his hard face carried an expression of content. "You seen the sheriff?"

"He was around," Holliday answered carelessly. "Letting on like he was looking for Big Enough!"

"He was looking for him," Rutledge interrupted. "Joe Blaine has woke up at last, Doc."

"No!"

"Yes," Rutledge repeated. "And he served notice on

68

Bull Clanton that he would smoke him down on sight!"

"The damn fool," the gambler grunted. "That big killer will shoot him in the back shore as hell. Guess I better get back to my case," and he jerked his head toward the door.

Alamo Bowie followed the gesture with his eyes. A little slender man was swaggering along the bar with two guns tied low on his banty legs. Heavy Bullhide chaps with stiff batwings flapped loudly while he strutted. A pair of small boots peeped from under the leather, and Fred Rutledge left the bar and walked toward the rear.

Big Enough Smith was five-feet three, and forty years old. He would not weigh more than a hundred and ten, but the notches on the handles of his guns attested to the fact that he was gun-size. Long black mustaches hung down to frame his thin tight-lipped mouth, and he raised his little black eyes and stared insolently at the tall Texan.

"Heard you was looking for me," he sneered loudly.

Glasses thudded to the bar when his thin voice reached every corner of the room. Alamo Bowie studied the little gunman carefully before answering. He noted the handles of the heavy guns tilted out rustler-style for a speedy draw. His gray eyes lighted up when he saw the balanced weapons glowing dully against moulded scabbard leather.

"Might say I was," he answered slowly. "The stage was held up this afternoon."

"You finally found out about it," the little man

sneered. "I heard they found interesting sign out there in that dry wash. Some gent with a star studded in his right heel!"

"News travels fast," the Texan drawled, but his eyes were slitted and alert. "Mebbe it was a star like this one."

He raised his right foot slowly with his left hand close to his belt. The little man saw the movement and relaxed with a sigh while his eyes swiveled to the studded boot heel.

"That's the boot what made the tracks," he agreed. "And there was some prints made by a woman."

The Texan tensed his muscles and then relaxed. Anger slows up a man's gun-hand, and he knew that Big Enough Smith was a master with his tools.

"You learn to pray yet?" he countered softly.

Big Enough Smith bit his lips to control the sudden anger that flamed in his brain. "I traded that prayer book to a peon for a glass of tequila," he snarled. "So yo're the magician *she* was chinning about?"

"The same," Bowie answered. "Now we can get along without mentioning the lady any farther!"

The little gunman laughed loudly. "The great Alamo Bowie," he chuckled. "The Wells Fargo Lawyer taking up with a petticoat!"

"They don't die so quick when you shoot them through the belly," the Texan said thinly, and his deep voice was hard as steel. "I found yore tracks, little man!"

Big Enough Smith stopped laughing abruptly. "Little man, eh?" he snarled. "And you found my tracks!"

70

Alamo Bowie nodded his head. "Found them in that dry wash where you hid to kill pore old Pop Whipple," he said softly. "Then I found them in a filthy hawg-pen where I picked up this watch!"

His left hand raised slowly to his vest pocket while the outlaw stooped in a crouch with both hands taloned above his holsters. The Texan removed his hand slowly and laid the old silver watch on the long bar. Big Enough Smith took a look and sucked in his breath.

"So?" he breathed softly. "That all you found?"

The special agent shook his head slowly. "I brought the gold in with me," he said in his quiet drawl. "But I had to have more proof."

"You get it?"

Again the Texan nodded. "There were twenty bills in the shipment on the stage," he continued softly. "Ten of those fifty-dollar bills were lost right here in the Oriental this afternoon. We had the numbers, and now I have the bills."

Big Enough Smith raised his eyes and glanced at the gambling layout. "I'll settle with you later, Doc Holliday," he promised quietly, and returned his eyes to the craggy face of Alamo Bowie. "You got enough proof now?" he asked carelessly.

"Yeah," and the Texan sighed. "Guess I'll have to ask you to surrender for robbing the Wells Fargo stage, and for the murder of old Pop Whipple!"

Big Enough Smith rocked back on his high heels. "I've heard a lot about you," he said conversationally. "How you was the fastest gun-hand in Texas, and always gave a feller a chance."

"Right both times," Bowie agreed.

"Texas is a right big place," the little gunman said thoughtfully. "But it ain't the size that counts, and Arizona has her beat on fast straight shooting."

"Which I mis-doubts," Bowie contradicted. "Up to now I haven't seen any signs of speed to speak of."

"Ed White picked a ruckus with me this afternoon," the little killer taunted. "All the boys saw him go for his cutter, but none of them saw my hand move when I was forced to rub him out. Too bad you wasn't here."

"I'm here now," and the Texan's voice was thick with anger. "Elevate, you runty killer, or make yore pass!"

The little gunman skinned back his thin lips in a sardonic smile. "Three-finger sotter marked you for his own gun," he said with a chuckle. "But I guess there's enough witnesses to prove I couldn't help myself. You should have stayed in Texas."

Alamo Bowie steadied down and waited. He knew all the tricks of the game; knew the little killer was baiting him into a deadfall. His jaw jutted out with little ridges of muscle making hills in the shadows of his tanned face, and his gray eyes burned with a flaming light that nothing but gun-smoke could extinguish.

"I didn't stay in Texas," he remarked quietly. "And your trial is over as far as this court is concerned. I find you guilty!"

"So yo're the judge," Smith taunted. "Mebbe yo're the executioner too?"

Alamo Bowie nodded soberly. "I'm waiting," he clipped.

Big Enough Smith went into a crouch while the red killer light blazed in his little black eyes. He steadied for a bare pause, and then his taloned hands rapped down to pop leather with the speed of light. Alamo Bowie was balanced on wide-spread boots with both hands hooked in his belts, and then he made his magic.

Both hands shot down and twisted in a swivel with thumbs notching back the smooth filed hammers. Red flame splashed from gouting muzzles before the black powder put out the light, and Big Enough Smith was lifted from the floor and hurled on his shoulders with the guns spitting in his hands.

He landed heavily with the guns flying against the bar; tried to twist over and finally made it. Both hands gripping his middle while a crimson pool widened and spread into the thirsty sawdust. His beady little eyes held on the face of Alamo Bowie who was crouching above his smoking guns with the hammers eared back for a follow-up.

"You got me," the wounded man gasped. "Through the middle!"

"I hit where I shoot," the Texan answered coldly. You might live as long as an hour!"

The doors opened out front to admit the tall figure of a woman. Dressed in somber black with a small prayer book in one hand. She came slowly down the room until she reached Big Enough Smith. Then she knelt down beside him and opened the prayer book.

"A Mexican brought this to me," she said softly, and every man in the saloon removed his hat. "I thought maybe you might be needing it."

The wounded man snarled like a cornered rat. "I'll die the way I lived," he sneered. "Give it to him. He might want it when he meets Three-finger Jack!"

"I warned you," and Nellie Gray's voice was low with pity. "Can I do anything to make you easier?"

"Whiskey," he gasped. "I lived that away too!"

The woman nodded to the bar-dog and took a glass of whiskey. Held the wounded man's head up while she placed the glass to his lips. Big Enough gulped it down and smiled.

"My boots," he whispered. "I'd like to die with 'em off!"

Alamo Bowie reached down and turned around. Caught the left boot between his legs, and tugged it loose. Repeated with the right while the crowd watched in silence. Then he turned to watch the stricken man. Big Enough smiled gamely and closed his eyes.

"It won't be an hour, Texan," he murmured. "I thought I was Big Enough, but not big enough to buck two forty-five slugs in the same place. So long, feller. See yuh in Hell!"

Nellie Gray covered the pale face when the last rattle had died away. Then she rose slowly and turned to the Texan.

"Supper is ready," she whispered. "Will you walk home with me?"

CHAPTER VI

There was a difference in the hard-faced men of Tombstone when they glanced furtively at the tall Texan walking beneath the board awnings with Nellie Gray. With her black head held high, she took his arm and kept up with the measure of his stride. Alamo Bowie was uncomfortable because of the honor thrust upon him. Uncomfortable, but proud down in his heart.

"Your friend and mine will rest this night, Alamo Bowie," she said seriously. "The funeral is to be tomorrow morning at ten."

"Ed White felt it coming," the Texan muttered. "He knew it, but he wouldn't quit and run away."

"We live the time allotted to us," Nellie Gray murmured. "No more, no less, and nothing we can do will change it."

The Texan turned his head and studied her sweet face for a moment. "That's the way Doc Holliday feels," he answered thoughtfully. "And I reckon it's the way I feel too. I've faced many men, and always I had the feeling that my number wasn't up."

"I'm worried about Doc," she answered. "He wants to be appointed Town Marshal. You know how sick he is at times."

"Few people know that," the Texan murmured. "I've seen him call a killer with hell blazing deep in his green eyes. And all the time he knew he had the

75

other fellow beat . . . unless he started coughing. Some day Doc will cough at the wrong time, and then . . . ?"

Nellie Gray shuddered. "It will be murder," she said, and her throaty voice was low. "They will call it self defense."

She led the way up the steps to the boarding house; entered the long dining room and continued to a table in the corner. Then she smiled at Bowie and pointed to a little room offside.

"You will want to wash," she suggested. "Your dinner will be ready when you are."

Alamo Bowie bowed and caught himself with the hot blood rushing to his face. Nellie Gray brought out the best in men; reminded them of old forgotten customs of manner and speech. He almost ran to the wash room when she smiled and patted his arm.

In the wash room a sudden change swept over him. His hands moved swiftly and mechanically. The Twins flashed into view; smoke-grimed and deadly. The Texan wiped them carefully on an oiled rag, after which he ejected the empties and reloaded with fresh shells. Snugged the lethal weapons back in leather and carefully washed his brown hands in the crockery basin.

He frowned in the framed mirror when he caught sight of the white lock of hair in his brown head. A rifle bullet had creased him there; had deprived him of memory for three days and nights. The scar on his chin from the blade of an enemy in a Mexican Cantina below the line. One-shot Brady and his gang had died, and now there were others still living.

His gray eyes grew flinty when he thought of Three-finger Jack. Tagged the fastest and most deadly Colt-hand in wild and bloody Arizona, and the Texan rubbed the handles of his guns while his eyes grew eager with anticipation. Then he shrugged and brought himself back to the thought of dinner with the first woman who had caught his personal interest.

He smoothed his graying hair with steady hands and opened the door. Jed Swope was waiting at the little table along the wall, and Bowie stopped abruptly when he saw two other men staring at each other with surprise mirrored on their faces. Doc Holliday and sheriff Joe Blaine, with Nellie Gray standing between them.

"Doc, I want you to shake hands with my very good friend sheriff Blaine," and the woman smiled at the dapper gambler. "Joe proved himself today!"

The sheriff recovered his composure first and reached out his right hand with a smile. "Nellie is right in some ways, Doc," he said quietly. "Ed White was a friend of mine after all, and I'm asking you personal to take his place. Tombstone couldn't get a better man!"

The gambler stared with his peculiar eyes to detect some sign of insincerity. Then he extended his right hand and gripped the sheriff hard.

"Yo're a man, Joe Blaine," he said quietly. "You play yore cards different than I do, but the man strain is down there underneath, and I'll be glad to call you pard. I'll take the job!"

Alamo Bowie frowned and then smiled. He came forward and laid a hand on a shoulder of each man. Joe Blaine flushed with embarrassment until the tall Texan extended his hand.

"Proud to touch skin with you, sheriff," Bowie muttered. "Fred told me all about it. You can count on me to side you all the way!"

"That's why I arranged this little dinner," and Nellie Gray nodded at the gleaming table. "Won't you be seated, gentlemen?"

Doc Holliday bowed from the hips and stepped behind a chair. "After you, dear lady," he murmured, and seated her with the graceful chivalry of the old South.

The three men took chairs and watched their hostess. Nellie Gray raised her wine glass and waited for them to follow suit. Then she nodded at each in turn and gave the toast.

"To the confusion of our enemies," she whispered. "And may your shadows, and all of them, never grow less!"

They drank gravely and in silence. Sheriff Joe Blaine showed the inner happiness on his florid face. He had found a new world in the hearts of brave and honest men; had been accepted as one of them. It was the little saddle-maker who broke the silence.

"Now we really have law for Tombstone," he began. "Joe Blaine and Fred Rutledge in the sheriff's office. Doc Holliday as Town Marshal with Alamo Bowie and Marty Williams for Wells Fargo. Gentlemen, together you will make history that will never be forgotten!"

"And Nellie Gray made all this possible," Joe Blaine said quietly. "The old back-slapping days are gone for me, and for the first time since I took office I feel that I have a chance to do the work the citizens expected me to do. Just saying that there ain't another lady anywhere like . . . the Angel of Tombstone!"

Nellie Gray blushed with happiness. "In Union there is strength," she told them soberly. "Decent people will be able to sleep in their beds now!"

Joe Blaine frowned. "I'm afraid not, Nellie," he contradicted. "Not while Bull Clanton and Three-finger Jack are on the loose," and he squared his thick shoulders. "I heard that Clanton was in town tonight!"

"Must you?" and Nellie Gray pleaded with her brown eyes until the sheriff looked away.

"I'll take care of Bull Clanton," Doc Holliday interrupted grimly. "The sheriff ain't rightly what you'd call a gun-fighter. He's the law here in Cochise county, and he's too good a man to lose!"

The sheriff flushed with embarrassment. "I'll take him," and his usually pleasant voice was thick with determination. "I done served him notice, and you gents know what that means!"

"Dinner is served," Nellie Gray announced to change the subject. "I hope you will enjoy the food."

Alamo Bowie glanced at her and the hard look left his face to leave it softened with a strange wistfulness. Jed Swope and Doc Holliday exchanged glances, and sheriff Blaine nodded at Nellie Gray and attacked his plate.

They ate in silence like cowboys do, and finished off with apple pie and strong coffee. Alamo Bowie sighed and reached for the makings. Rolled a shuck quickly and fired it to fill his lungs full of pungent smoke. A waiter brought a small glass of brandy behind a napkin for the gambler, and he emptied the glass and sighed with content.

"It was a feast, Nellie," he told the hostess. "The way to a man's heart is through his stomach, and tonight you made yourself four abject slaves."

"Amen," the saddle-maker added. "Tombstone would be a dreary place without our Nellie."

"Go on with you," the woman murmured, but the color of happiness stained her gentle face and added to her beauty. "Like the sheriff, I am glad that you men allowed me to join you today," and she glanced at Alamo Bowie.

Alamo Bowie nodded slowly and took a slip of paper from his vest pocket. He handed it gravely to the sheriff while his gray eyes probed deep. Then he nodded again as though satisfied with what he found.

"We need a conviction against robbers to really break up that gang," he said bluntly. "None of those long-riders is afraid of dying, but doing time in that hell-hole over at Yuma is something else."

Sheriff Blaine stared at the numbers written on the slip. "I ain't so good at puzzles," he admitted at last. "Spell it out, Bowie."

"There was a thousand dollars in fifty-dollar bills in that loot taken from the stage today," the Texan explained. "Big Enough Smith lost half of them to

Doc Holliday. I figger the other ten bills will be on Bull Clanton."

"So," the sheriff whispered, and rubbed the grip of his gun. "I'll try not to spoil the evidence!"

"That's the point," Bowie answered slowly. "If we could take Bull Clanton alive, that evidence would send him to the Pen over on the two rivers. You never have made a conviction stick here yet!"

The sheriff rubbed his chin. "I'll see Fred Rutledge first," he muttered. "Fred is right rapid on the draw."

Bowie shook his head. "Not Fred," he cautioned. "Rutledge would ask for show-down and kill or get killed after what Clanton done to him. Better take Doc Holliday."

The gambler stared at his plate with two spots of color on his high cheek-bones. His right hand slipped under his long black coat and caressed the stock of his deadly sawed-off. Then he shook his head doubtfully.

"Ed White was a friend of mine," he said softly. "I'd want to drop both hammers on that varmint as soon as I caught the smell of skunk. If you want him alive, I reckon it's your job, Bowie. Not that you have had any practice taking prisoners," he added pointedly.

A suggestive cough sounded behind the Texan before he could answer. He kicked back his chair like a flash to face a tall stocky man whose deep brown eyes contrasted with the frost in his thick hair. A faint sneer curled the corners of his hard mouth.

"So you couldn't stay back there in El Paso and ride herd on the office," he sneered. "You had to come traipsin' up here to see was I doing the work I get paid for to do!"

The older man smiled crookedly and held out a fat hand. "Just wanted to give you Howdy, Alamo," he answered apologetically. "Was on my way to the San Francisco office, and I had a wire from Marty Williams. Nice work you've been doing."

The Texan smiled and relaxed. "Wants you gents to meet up with the squarest boss an old cowhand ever had," he began. "Gents, this here uncurried old son is Tom Scudder, general Manager of Wells Fargo for the southern district. Sheriff Joe Blaine on yore right, Tom. The little jigger is Jed Swope, and you mebbe know Doc Holliday. Overlook my manners for this one time, but the lady is Miss Nellie Gray what runs this here hotel."

Tom Scudder smiled and shook hands all around. Bowed gallantly to Nellie Gray with a knowing twinkle in his brown eyes. Then he slapped the Texan on the back.

"How's the Snapper hoss?" he asked with a grin. "Like as not both you and him is all wore out from yore labors!"

"Spoke like a prophet," Bowie agreed, and then his face changed. "Grab a chair, Tom. Old Pop Whipple was dry-gulched today!"

The Manager's face hardened while he swallowed a lump in his throat. "It can't be," he whispered. "I rode range many's the time with that old He, and Pop was the best driver we had. Who done for him?"

"A salty runt by the name of Big Enough Smith,"

the sheriff interrupted. "The funeral will be held tomorrow on Boot Hill!"

"Pop's funeral?" and Tom Scudder held his breath while he waited for the answer.

"Big Enough stopped two slugs not over an hour ago," Blaine answered dryly.

Tom Scudder glanced down at the two guns on the long legs of his special agent. "That would be the Twins," he murmured. "Smith work alone?"

The sheriff flushed and sighed deeply. "Big Enough had a pard," he explained. "Gent by the name of Bull Clanton. He was in the posse that rode out with me."

Tom Scudder stared at Alamo Bowie. "When are they planting Clanton?" he demanded grimly.

"They ain't," the Texan grunted. "We want a conviction for one time, and we aim to take Clanton alive. He's got cold evidence in his clothes in the shape of currency. The sheriff has the numbers of the bills."

"You wasn't told to take any prisoners," Tom Scudder grumbled under his breath. "Yore job is gunfighting these other lead-slingers who are plundering the stages. So fer you've been right lucky because these other hombres was slow on the draw!"

Alamo Bowie narrowed his eyes, and then a slow grin crept over his face when he glanced at the generous paunch on his chief. "Like always, yo're packing a lot of lard on yore skeleton," he sneered. "No one would ever believe that you was considerable heller when you was a yearling!"

Scudder flushed and then grinned. "Reckon yo're right, Alamo," he conceded. "I had to rib you up some, but now I'm ready to listen while you make medicine. About this Bull Clanton?"

"He's a big barn-shouldered killer with number twelve feet," the Texan answered descriptively. "One of Three-finger Jack's right-hand men. Pard to Big Enough Smith, and I found their sign out at the killing."

"You ride it down?"

Bowie nodded. "Me and Rutledge recovered the loot and turned it over to Marty Williams. We found that old silver watch in the bag; the one you gave Pop Whipple years ago."

"Prisoner hell," Scudder snapped. "You loose up the Twins and ride gun-sign on that bush-whacking bandit!"

"I want him alive," Bowie insisted stubbornly. "With Three-finger she's different!"

"Take him," Scudder shrugged. "What you waiting for?"

"Waiting for you to tell me about the next job," and Bowie grinned. "Looks like a man never can take his rest."

"Do the job you got on hand first," Scudder growled. "I just sotter dropped off this away to give you Howdy."

"Beggin' the lady's pardon, but yo're a hod danged liar," the Texan accused. "Right now yo're thinking about some tough spot where the Company is losing shipments!"

Tom Scudder allowed a grin to sweep his full face. "You see how it is, gents," he complained. "I hire me a gun-fighter, and he takes advantage of his ability. But there was a little matter I wanted to kinda go into," he admitted more seriously.

Bowie nodded. "I ought to be through here in a matter of a week or two," he said carelessly. "This other job?"

"Been having trouble up Flagstaff way," Scudder explained soberly. "Three stages stuck up last month. Three guards killed, and close to forty thousand taken from the boxes."

Alamo Bowie sighed. "Was figgering on a little rest for me and the Snapper hoss," he complained, but a steady light glowed in his gray eyes. "You got a line on the gang?"

Scudder shrugged. "Was some talk about it being Black Bart," he muttered. "Supposed to be the fastest Road Agent ever to come out of Californy."

"Black Bart," and the Texan's eyes glowed between slitted lids. "I've heard of the gent. Tall thin jigger, and chain lightning with both hands. Dresses in black and writes poetry when he makes a killing!"

"That's him," Scudder agreed. "But I ain't quite ready to lose you yet. I stopped over and had a talk with the sheriff up there."

Alamo Bowie glanced at Joe Blaine. "Might be the sheriff up there would want some help," he suggested. "Might be I could get done here a little sooner than I figgered."

"Take yore time," Scudder advised. "You ain't took Three-finger Jack up to now!"

"I taken him one time," the Texan growled, and

then bit his lip when the sheriff changed color.

"We had Jack in jail, Mister Scudder," Joe Blaine said softly. "I made a mistake and turned him loose. It won't happen again," he promised grimly.

"Had Jack in jail?" and Scudder stared his disbelief.

"Pass it for now," Bowie grunted. "We was talking about Black Bart."

"This Three-finger Jack gang," Scudder persisted. "Don't take any fool chances, Bowie. We never have got a conviction here, and we never will the way I see it. There is only one law they savvy, and you got two holsters full of the same!"

"We were talking about peace when you came in, Mister Scudder," Nellie Gray interrupted softly. "With all the forces of the law united, I thought it might really be a possibility."

Tom Scudder studied the tall woman before he answered. "Not in Tombstone," he said slowly. "Cattle coming up the trail from Texas and Mexico, and gold and silver being shoveled out of the mines. It's a free country, Miss Nellie, and nobody knows it any better than these outlaws!"

Nellie Gray pouted her full lips, and her sweet face was thoughtful. "There is such a very little difference between the men who ride for the law, and those who ride against it," she pointed out. "Both kind are paid gunmen, and they wouldn't be any different if they had their choice."

Tom Scudder glanced at his special agent and grinned. "That's right," he agreed. "You take Bowie for instance. Just mention an extra fast gun-hawk riding the long trail, and Bowie forgets how tired him and his Snapper hoss are. He always was that away, and he won't ever be no different!"

Alamo Bowie caught the hurt look in the deep brown eyes of Nellie Gray. "That's where you are wrong, boss," he contradicted stiffly. "Right now I'm saving against the day when me and Snapper will quit chousing around and settle down. I've thought about it several times!"

"You thought about it after you cleaned up the Big Four gang over at Deming," Scudder reminded. "You thought about it again when I sent you to Vegas to reason with the McCandless outfit. Now here you are getting ready to whittle for Three-finger, and casting longing glances toward Flagstaff to see what's over the hill!"

Alamo Bowie lowered his eyes and shuffled his feet. "After that Flagstaff job," he muttered. "That's when I'm turning Snapper out to pastures, and wrapping up the Twins for good!"

Tom Scudder laughed sneeringly. "Wahoo," he hoorawed. "And I doubt if you live long enough to ride gun-sign on Black Bart!"

Alamo Bowie whirled swiftly to face his chief. "That will do, Scudder," and his voice was raspy. "I taken just about all the slack I aim to stand. I come over here to do a job of work, and I aim to do it regardless of what you think!"

"Keep yore hackles down," Scudder soothed. "You was speaking about a chore when I busted in."

Alamo Bowie glowered and took a deep breath.

"Forgot about Bull Clanton there for a minute," he muttered. "Guess I'll be shaggin' along."

Tom Scudder winked at the sheriff and stepped back. "That's the ticket," he praised heartily. "And forget that nonsense about taking prisoners!"

Alamo Bowie stopped suddenly. "So that's the how come of all this hoorawing," he said quietly. "Wanted me to get up my mad so I'd track out yonder with my gun-hooks itching," and he sneered at the big manager with his lips curling.

Tom Scudder cursed under his breath. "Reckon I talked too much with my mouth," he growled, and laid a hand on the Texan's arm. "I'm serious this time, feller," he muttered. "Don't take no fool chances like you was figgering on!"

"Justice can be tempered with mercy," Nellie Gray interrupted softly. "I'm glad you remembered in time, Alamo!"

"I'll take Bull Clanton alive," and the Texan glared at his boss.

Tom Scudder sighed and turned to Doc Holliday. "Anything you can do?" he asked hopefully.

Doc Holliday stood up and stretched his long arms. "There is," he answered softly, and smothered a cough behind his white hand. "I can help Bowie take Clanton alive, but God help the rest of the gang if they cut in on the play," and he patted the deadly shotgun under his coat.

Alamo Bowie grinned and waved his hand. "See you in a couple weeks, Tom," he chuckled. "I come up here with some law for Tombstone, but yore job is riding herd on the office down Paso way. Be as good as you can, and stay off the hosses with that lard of yores!"

Tom Scudder watched the tall Texan walk from the room without looking back. He turned in time to catch the look on the face of Nellie Gray and shook his head.

"Might be something in what he says," he muttered under his breath. "He might settle down . . . but I still don't believe it!"

CHAPTER VII

The two men stalked silently away from the hotel on Tough Nut street. Up Fifth to Allen where the yellow coal-oil lamps winked in store fronts, and blazed a welcome in front of the saloons. Doc Holliday passed up the Oriental and continued on to the Crystal Palace.

"He ought to be here," he muttered. "Clanton likes to gamble, but he'd shy away from the Oriental because of my layout."

Alamo Bowie grunted and pushed through the swinging doors. He made a step to slide his shoulders along the wall before he noticed the sudden stillness in the crowded room. His hands made a swift movement down and then jerked to a stop when he saw the ring of grinning faces leering at him across leveled six-guns. Doc Holliday likewise stopped the movement toward the sawed-off under his coat.

"Reach upward, ever upward," a mocking voice purred softly. "This Court is about to sit on yore case!"

The tall Texan obeyed while his gray eyes narrowed slightly and locked glances with Three-finger Jack. The outlaw was watching him closely; the only man in the group with empty hands. Bull Clanton held a position in the center of the ring, and he turned his head to spit through the gap in his ugly front teeth.

"Turn slowly, Bowie," the tall outlaw whispered slowly.

The Texan turned his back with hands held shoulder high. "Get his guns, Pecos," Three-finger continued. "Might as well pull his stingers before we sit on his case."

A slender rider stepped out of the ring and lifted the Twins from their scabbards. Alamo Bowie twitched slightly and then held his pose. Pecos Traynor slipped the heavy guns through his own belts and stepped back.

"The prisoner will face the court," the tall outlaw ordered.

Bowie turned again with lines etched from nose to hard mouth. He counted ten men in the ring, not including Three-finger Jack. All were toughened riders of the long trails with the marks of their trade stamped plainly on their hard faces. Ready to kill if either man made a move.

"We won't take that sawed-off away from Doc," the outlaw said softly. "He just might forget and make a pass, and self defense is still a virtue in this camp!"

The gambler smiled and leaned back against the

walls. "I'll face you from scratch, Three-finger," he offered eagerly. "The sawed-off against yore cutters, and the devil take the hindmost!"

The outlaw shook his head and continued to stare at Alamo Bowie. "You killed Big Enough Smith," he accused sternly. "Big Enough was my best friend."

"Big Enough killed Ed White," the Texan answered in the same tone. "He was one of my best friends!"

A gleam of triumph filtered across the black eyes opposite. "This court heard yore admission," he answered promptly. "You killed him for personal reasons."

Alamo Bowie frowned. "I killed him in the line of duty," he corrected. "Gave him a chance to surrender to the law!"

"Make up yore mind," the outlaw taunted. "I heard you held a one-man trial!"

"The stage was held up," Bowie growled, and talked slowly to gain time. "Old Pop Whipple was killed, and I found his watch among the loot!"

"Yore tracks were found out there," the outlaw pointed out. "Along with other tracks that were made by the Angel!"

The Texan clenched his hands suddenly while the ridges of muscle leaped to his jaw. "Leave the lady out," he snapped. "Yo're crowding yore luck, feller!"

Three-finger Jack shrugged carelessly. *"Es no importante,"* he muttered. "Getting back to you, we figgered you held down too many jobs for one hombre!"

"Keep on talking," Bowie growled, and relaxed

again. "You was talking about holding Court!"

"You held up the stage, and you hid the loot out on the Box C," the outlaw accused boldly. "Then you bring it in to town to make yoreself a hero. You killed Pop Whipple to get Bull Clanton and Big Enough in bad!"

The Texan stared steadily. "The plunder was hid under Clanton's bunk," he grated.

"I suppose you have witnesses," and the outlaw raised his shaggy brows.

Bowie saw the trap and frowned. "Fred Rutledge saw the loot," he growled. "I was waiting for Clanton to come back to his hide-out!"

Three-finger Jack glanced around the ring of faces with a smile. "You heard the evidence, gentlemen," he said quietly. "We all know that Wells Fargo does not pay fortunes to their headhunters. What do you think, Bull?"

Bull Clanton stepped forward. "This jigger packed that loot out there to the Box C," he sneered. "Planted it under my bunk, and then showed it to Rutledge. He sent the Angel away when the posse rode up, and then he high-tailed while I was augering with Rutledge!"

Alamo Bowie stared at the big robber and waited. Three-finger Jack nodded his head and raised his right hand.

"You have heard the evidence, gentlemen of the jury," he said softly. "What is yore verdict?"

"Guilty as hell," the chorus shouted. "String him up for killing old Pop Whipple!"

Three-finger Jack shook his head. "I have another

plan," he answered. "Bull Clanton is the injured party, and Big Enough was his saddle-pard. I figger Bull is entitled to some satisfaction!"

Bull Clanton grinned and holstered his gun. "I'll take him with my maulies," and he spat through his teeth. "Turn him out and let him come apart!"

Three-finger Jack turned his head and stared at the Texan. "You heard what Clanton said," and a smile broke out on his thin face. "Prepare to meet yore God!"

Alamo Bowie saw the whole plan. The outlaw had used the same words Nellie Gray had used to warn Big Enough Smith. Bull Clanton chuckled and added his insult.

"Mebbe Bowie has his prayer book with him!"

"The sheriff is looking for you, Clanton," Doc Holliday interrupted softly.

All eyes were turned to the slender gambler. Three-finger Jack smiled and shook his black head.

"It don't work, Doc," he said softly. "The sentence of this Court is for Alamo Bowie to prove his innocence by meeting Bull Clanton man to man!"

"You do that and I'll take a chance," Holliday warned, and the twin spots of crimson leaped to his cheek-bones. "Clanton has fifty pounds on Bowie!"

"Fly at it," the outlaw purred, and his black eyes narrowed to pin-points of light. "After which the trial goes on just the same!"

Bull Clanton shucked off his gunbelts and flexed his huge arms. Alamo Bowie spoke to Doc Holliday without turning his head.

"Don't worry, pard. You and me have some law for Tombstone, and we might as well start now."

He stepped to the center of the ring with clenched fists held in front of his swelling chest. A hundred and eighty pounds of bone and toughened muscle, and his gray eyes flamed with the smoky light of battle. Bull Clanton dropped his belts and hunched his wide shoulders.

"Now I lay you down to sleep," he taunted, and rushed in with both arms flailing.

Alamo Bowie shifted quickly and thrust out his left boot. Bull Clanton stumbled and sprawled to the dirty floor with his chin plowing the sawdust. He twisted quickly and came up with a roar of rage, and the Texan met him with a left jab that pistoned like an engine driver. Then he brought over a straight right that rocked Clanton back on his rounded heels to stop his maddened rush.

Alamo Bowie stepped back and waited for his man to fall. His arm was numbed to the elbow, but Bull Clanton shook his head and charged again with a bellow. The Texan backed away and tried to shift. A gun bored into his spine with hands blocking escape. Bull Clanton landed a hay-maker, and the Texan went to his knees with lights exploding in his brain.

He looped instinctively into a roll and found himself against muscular legs. A boot thudded into his ribs, and he spread his arms wide while he launched himself forward. Bull Clanton was caught behind the knees and crashed back on his shoulders, and the Texan was on top of him like a panther. Three times

94

he battered the beefy face until the blood spurted under his fist. Then his steely fingers reached for the thick neck while low growls guttered from his lips.

A pair of hands fastened under his chin and jerked back. The Texan landed on his haunches and twisted his head to mark the new attacker. Pecos Traynor was reaching for his gun when the silky voice of Three-finger stopped the movement.

"Back, Pecos. Let 'em get on their pins and start all over. Bull ain't even started yet!"

Alamo Bowie came to his feet breathing easily. Bull Clanton lurched up and hunched his thick shoulders. Came weaving in like a giant grizzly blocking a one-way trail.

"Let me get my hands on him," he muttered. "Shooting is too good for a jigger like him!"

Alamo Bowie shifted sideways and avoided those clutching hands. He stepped forward again before the outlaws behind could touch him. Then he leaped toward Bull Clanton and drove straight lefts and rights to the battered face with all the weight of his body behind his blows.

Clanton bellowed and tried to cover up. His left eye was entirely closed, and the Texan danced and weaved while both fists hammered a shower of stiff punches at the left eye. The outlaw rushed blindly with both arms wide for a grip. The Texan saw the ring of men closing in behind him to give the blinded Clanton his only chance. A sullen silence hung over the smoke-filled room, but Alamo Bowie was conscious only of the man coming toward him.

He side-stepped like a dancer and shifted back when the ring closed in. Then he ducked low and leaped under the clutching arms before Clanton could come to grips. Whirling like a sun-fishing bucker, he put all his weight and strength behind his right arm. The blow landed behind the outlaw's ear with a thud that crashed loudly like an over-ripe melon, and Bull Clanton fell forward on his face and shivered like a stricken tree.

Alamo Bowie straightened up and faced Three-finger Jack with his right arm hanging limply at his side. "Guilty or not guilty?" he asked softly.

"Mis-trial," and Three-finger Jack allowed a smile to split his thin lips. "I've heard you was right fast with a cutter!"

Alamo Bowie stiffened and stared into the evil black eyes. His breath was wheezing heavily through his tired lungs. His right arm was limp and useless from the knock-out blow he had landed behind Bull Clanton's ear. And Three-finger Jack was reputed the fastest and most deadly gunman in Arizona!

"That's about yore style," he drawled softly. "But I'll take it. Five minutes to get my breath!"

"I'll make the terms," the outlaw sneered. "Pass him his guns right now!"

Pecos Traynor stepped behind the special agent and jammed the Twins down into the scabbards. Doc Holliday muttered until a bearded outlaw jabbed a gun against his ribs. The tall outlaw smiled thinly and spread his polished boots.

"Get set," he whispered, and now the red glow of

killer-light was dancing deep in his dark eyes. "I had you marked for my own cutter nohow!"

"Don't move, Three-finger," a throaty voice warned.

Alamo Bowie jerked up his head and stared at the masked man behind the tall outlaw. Two heavy forty-fives were pressing against the outlaw's back, and there was something vaguely familiar about that warning voice. Copper-studded Levis and heavy woolen shirt. Ten gallon hat pulled low to meet the red bandanna. Glittering black eyes shining through the slits of the cloth.

Three-finger Jack raised both hands slowly. Every outlaw in the gang was staring at the stranger. Then the voice of Doc Holliday cracked thinly from the front wall.

"Any of you skunks make a move, I'm blasting the lot of you to hell!"

"Hold yore guns on Bowie!"

Three-finger Jack barked the order when guns began to sag. Arms stiffened with sixguns lined down on the special agent. Then the stranger spoke again in a muffled voice.

"Back away slow, Three-finger. I'm droppin' hammer on you if you give the word to down the Texan!"

The outlaw cocked his head to listen. His brow furrowed in an effort to place the voice. Then he shrugged and backed up three steps with the guns holding him steady.

"A man dies when his time comes, and not before,"

Doc Holliday recited quietly. "Looks like no dice, Three-finger!"

"Spell it out," the outlaw growled. "I'll get the Texan nohow!"

Alamo Bowie leaned forward eagerly. "I'll draw you evens," he offered, and held his breath for the answer. "Just you and me for a show-down!"

"Not tonight," the stranger interrupted coldly. "Like Doc Holliday mentioned, it's No Dice!"

"You mean yo're trading me for him?" and the tall outlaw jerked a thumb at Alamo Bowie.

"That's what I mean," the stranger answered quietly. "You and yores get out and take that beast with you. I'll go good for Doc Holliday!"

Three-finger glanced at the gambler. "You heard?"

"I heard," Holliday muttered, and reached for the handkerchief in his breast pocket.

They watched when his shoulders commenced to shake. A violent fit of coughing doubled the slender gambler over, but the yawning tunnels of his gun continued to cover the crowd. Three-finger Jack glanced at Pecos Traynor and winked slightly. Bowie caught the signal and went into a crouch.

"He makes a move, I'm taking a chance," he warned softly.

"Hold it, Pecos," the outlaw sighed, and sneered when Doc Holliday straightened up and wiped a crimson froth from his bloodless lips.

Doc Holliday panted and then smiled. "Thanks, Bowie," he whispered weakly. "My finger nearly slipped when I heard Three-finger change his mind.

Keep on talking, stranger!"

"I'm taking Three-finger through that front door," the masked stranger muttered. "You keep yore sawed-off on the crowd. They can hold down on Bowie until Three-finger gives them the come-on. No shooting, because I passed my word!"

Doc Holliday straightened up with a smile. Three-finger Jack walked slowly to the door and passed through with the guns boring into his straight spine. Alamo Bowie turned slowly to face the door with his hands hooked in his gunbelts. Then the door swished softly.

"All right, men," and the steady voice of the outlaw came from the outside. "Like the stranger said, it's No Dice!"

The outlaws sidled to the door and passed through one at a time. Their guns were still trained on the special agent, and Doc Holliday slid between the batwings and took his position on the sidewalk with his back against the wall. Three-finger Jack was in the saddle on a big black horse, but both his holsters were empty.

"Yore guns, boss," Pecos Traynor growled.

"In my saddle-bags," the outlaw grunted. "Hit leather and take a hitch in yore jaw!"

His voice was vicious and strained now that the stalemate was past. Alamo Bowie came through the door last, and the Twins were cuddled against his palms. The right arm was cradled against his lean ribs for support.

"Some day I'll face you for show-down, Bowie,"

and Three-finger Jack rode his horse forward to cover his men. "You was lucky tonight!"

"Mebbe he said a prayer," Pecos Traynor sneered.

"Mebbe I did," Bowie answered softly. "Now you jiggers tie that barn-shouldered killer on his kak and make tracks!"

Two men lifted the limp form of Bull Clanton across a saddle and held him face down. Three-finger Jack tipped his hat mockingly and struck with his spurs. The band roared up Allen street with mocking jeers ringing from their lips, and Alamo Bowie turned to speak to the masked stranger.

"Want to thank you, feller," he began, and then he stared all about him.

"That stranger slid back there in the dark, Bowie," the gambler said quietly. "Reckon he didn't want to make himself known."

Three men came running across the street with six-guns in their hands. Sheriff Joe Blaine slid to a stop in front of the Texan with Fred Rutledge and Marty Williams at his heels.

"You get him?" he shouted.

Alamo Bowie shrugged. "We walked into a dead-fall," he admitted reluctantly. "Three-finger Jack had the trap all set."

"I knew I should have come along," the sheriff muttered. "How come you to spring the trap?"

"We had help," Doc Holliday interrupted dryly. "A stranger with a bandanna on his face got the drop on Three-finger. Then I unlimbered my Ace in the hole, but the gang had Bowie under their sights!"

"And nobody could shoot," Marty Williams interpreted.

"Doc called the play; No Dice," Bowie explained. "Sorry Bull Clanton got away, sheriff."

"We'll get him," the sheriff promised grimly. "Did Three-finger mention me?"

"Not a word," Bowie replied gruffly. "Bull Clanton told about the posse, and they held court on me. I proved my innocence by whipping Clanton, but Three-finger declared it a mis-trial. Reckon I'll be getting down to the Grand hotel!"

"Nellie sent word that she was holding a room for you at the Russ House," Fred Rutledge spoke up. "Yore war-bag is already in the room."

Alamo Bowie stared at the deputy for a long moment. "Any particular reason?" he asked bluntly.

"Some of them outlaws put up at the Grand," Rutledge explained. "Nellie and me both knew it, and so did the sheriff. We figgered the Russ house would be better in case you had to fort up against attack."

"Closer to the jail," Joe Blaine growled. "We don't aim to lose you yet, Bowie!"

"I might as well make my rounds," Doc Holliday chuckled. "My first night as town Marshal!"

Joe Blaine frowned uneasily. "Watch yoreself, Doc," he warned. "We done lost several good men. Shot in the back from some dark alley!"

The gambler laughed shortly. "I'll watch," he promised. "That's one good thing about having green eyes. Cat eyes, they used to call 'em when I was a button. You can see in the dark," and he strolled slowly down the street.

Fred Rutledge watched him for a moment. "Doc is going to cough at the wrong time some day," he muttered.

"He done it tonight," Bowie answered. "I'd like to know who that stranger was who bought chips in a closed game!"

"You got a few friends here, Alamo," Rutledge said jokingly. "And you can put Joe and me at the head of the list," and his voice changed to quiet sincerity. "You got any plans?"

The Texan shrugged. "Not for tonight," he muttered. "We lost that trick, you might say, but there will come another time," and he stared at Sheriff Blaine. "Better get off the streets tonight, Joe!"

Joe Blaine turned slowly. "Not me," he negatived. "I got a hunch something might come up before morning."

"Guess I'll turn in," the Texan answered. "Did Tom Scudder get away?"

"Went out on the evening stage," Rutledge answered. "I might look in on you before I call it a day."

"So long," and the tall Texan hitched up his belts and high-heeled across the street. Down Fifth to Tough Nut where the Russ House bulked on the corner as a place of security and rest.

CHAPTER VIII

lamo Bowie walked across the thick carpets and approached the desk. A Chinese boy grinned and handed him a key. The Texan took it and read the number.

"Missy, she make bed now," the Chinese chattered, and Alamo Bowie nodded and turned to the stairs.

"Number 12," he muttered, and tried the knob.

It turned under his hand, and he walked stiffly into the room. Nellie Gray was smoothing the counterpane, and she turned with a smile of greeting. The Texan hung his hat on the corner of the bed and took both of her hands.

"You shouldn't have done it, Nellie," he said sternly. "You might have got killed!"

"Killed just because I keep you here at my hotel?" and her brown eyes smiled with mischief.

"Killed because you bought chips in a closed game against the deadliest outlaw in the Territory," the Texan answered roughly. "I'd know yore voice anywhere, even if you did have a pebble rolled under yore tongue!"

Nellie Gray gripped his hands while her face drained of color. "So you recognized me," she whispered. "I wonder if anyone else did. I had on a big hat, and that bandanna completely covered my face!"

"Three-finger recognized you," the Texan answered quietly.

"No," the woman contradicted. "I'm sure he didn't!"

"Do you remember what he did just before he rode away?" and Bowie stared into her wide eyes. Eyes that now held a fleeting look of fear.

"He tipped his hat and waved his hand," the woman answered. "Oh, Alamo!"

"He wouldn't tip his hat to a man, now would he?" and the Texan shook his head slowly. "But you saved my life tonight, Nellie Gray!"

"I'd do it a dozen times to save your life, Alamo Bowie," and she cupped a hand under his stubborn chin and tilted his head. "I never felt it before, but now I just can't help it. I knew some day you would come. I knew that my heart would answer when you did!"

Alamo Bowie stared deep into the dark pools and drew her against his chest. His arms went around her full figure and held her tightly. Then he lowered his face slowly and kissed her full on the lips.

"Believe me, Nellie," he said huskily, "I never kissed a woman before in my life, except my mother. Yo're doing things to me, and I owe you my life!"

"Alamo! Is that why you kissed me?" and he caught the stricken look in her eyes.

His arms tightened. "I did it because we both wanted it," he muttered gruffly. "I kissed you because . . . because I knew your lips were mine. I'm saying I'd like to take care for you all the time, pard!"

Nellie Gray closed her eyes and snuggled against his shoulder. "We will talk about that when your work is done here, Alamo," she said softly. "Did you really say a prayer tonight when those outlaws had you under their guns?"

Alamo Bowie held her at arms length and smiled with his lips, while he looked into her eyes. Then he shook his head slowly.

"Never learned to pray, Nellie," he admitted honestly. "I didn't say any prayer."

"I like you better for telling the truth, Texan," she answered soberly. "I did enough praying for both of us, and my prayers were answered!"

"Reckon they was, Angel," he muttered. "I heard a sky-pilot orate one time. He said that Faith without works didn't get a jigger very far. So you backed up yore prayers with a pair of sixes, and that's the only talk them outlaws savvies."

The woman shuddered suddenly. "I was afraid for Doc Holliday when he started to cough," she whispered. "He looked so weak and white, and he doubled completely over!"

"Don't you worry about Doc," the Texan soothed. "I never saw a man in my life that packed the cold nerve he does. Right now he's out making his rounds as town Marshal."

"He shouldn't have taken the post," she murmured. "He has so many enemies."

"And he will kill a few of them if they cut his sign," Bowie said grimly. "I know Doc!"

The woman gripped him when a fusillade of shots roared out from the street. Then came the unmistakable roar of a shotgun, and Alamo Bowie released himself and pounded for the door. Down the stairs into the street with both guns spiking from his big hands.

A horse clattered away into the dark dragging its reins. A man was down in the street up near Allen, and the Texan raced toward him while he kept into the shadows. A slender figure stepped from the doorway and called softly.

"Slow down, Bowie. That's Joe Blaine laying in the street!"

"You hurt, Doc?" the Texan asked tensely.

"Not me," the gambler grunted. "But let's take a look back here in this alley. I just got me a jack rabbit on the fly!"

Joe Blaine came to his feet and staggered toward them. Alamo Bowie ran to meet him; steadied the sheriff when he saw the officer limp.

"Just a scratch on the leg," Blaine muttered. "Did Doc get Clanton?"

"He's back here," the gambler answered. "Watch out for a gun in his hand!"

"You back there," the sheriff called. "Keep yore hands up where we can see them!"

A groan answered them from back in the alley. "I'm done for," a hoarse voice shouted. "Through both legs!"

Alamo Bowie disappeared and raced between two buildings. Then he came out in the alley behind the wounded man. His voice barked sharply at Bull Clanton.

"Drop that cutter, Clanton. Yo're covered front and rear!"

Bull Clanton cursed, and they heard the clatter of

his gun. The Texan stepped forward and called to the sheriff and Doc Holliday.

"Come up and help pack him out!"

They dragged the prisoner to Fifth street where a light flickered from the corner. Doc Holliday held the crowd back that was collected from the saloons. Alamo Bowie stared at the thick legs and grunted.

"You'll live to swing," he said coldly. "Good thing Doc shot low!"

He leaned over and reached inside the faded vest. Bull Clanton snarled and gripped his hand. The sheriff whipped up his gun and held it against the outlaw's head while his voice barked a sharp order.

"Set tight before I drop hammer. Looks like you didn't get enough tonight!"

Alamo Bowie withdrew his hand and held out a sheath of bills. "Fifties," he told the sheriff. "Here's the evidence we wanted. You hold him here while I get Doc Kramer!"

"Call a couple of those loafers and make them carry him down to the jail," the sheriff suggested. "The Doc can see him there, and I hope he lives!"

"You said through the smoke," the outlaw muttered. "And I'd have drilled you center if Traynor's hoss hadn't shouldered me!"

"So Pecos Traynor was in on the play," Bowie grunted. "I'll remember that!"

He straightened up and approached the crowd. Pointed at two husky miners and jerked his head toward the wounded man.

"You two hard-rock fellers lend us a hand. We got

to get this jigger to jail so's the Doc can patch him up!"

The two miners came forward eagerly and made a cradle with their muscular hands. Hoisted Bull Clanton between them and followed the limping sheriff down the street. Alamo Bowie brought up the rear, and Doc Holliday joined him a moment later.

"One killer got away," the gambler apologized. "Wonder who he was?"

"Pecos Traynor," Bowie grunted. "You see anything of Three-finger?"

The gambler shook his head. "Never laid eyes on one of the gang," he answered positively. "Them two must have doubled back so's Bull could keep his promise to sheriff Blaine. And Bowie?"

"Yeah?"

"That Blaine has the guts of a tiger. Both them bandits opened up on him, and he went down first shot. Then he dragged his gun and cut loose until I pressed both triggers and cut the legs from under Clanton. Traynor hooked his hoss and high-tailed up the alley the back way, and then you come barging up the drag!"

"Tombstone has got her a sheriff now," Bowie agreed.

"Here comes the Croaker," the gambler whispered. "He never uses a knock-out when he works on a gent for gun-shot wounds," and the gambler grinned with anticipation. "I'm going to stick around and hear Bull beller!"

Doc Kramer was a small man with large powerful

hands. Little goatee trimmed to a point, and small blue eyes that twinkled from behind thick glasses. He nodded at Doc Holliday and held out a hand to Alamo Bowie.

"Glad to know you, Bowie," he said cordially, and the Texan winced at the strength in the doctor's hand. "Where's the victim?"

Bowie jerked his head to the rear. "In the back room," he answered. "We'll go along in case you need some help."

"I never need help," the Doctor answered with a smile. "I always carry a little persuader with me," and he drew a leather billy from his hip pocket. "One little tap on the skull in just the right place, and the patient goes to sleep while I do my work."

He opened the door and walked into the back room. Bull Clanton was lying on a low couch with the sheriff on guard. It was an inside room with no windows, and the wounded man looked up with a scowl.

"I don't want no Croaker," he muttered.

"Now, now," the Doctor said softly. "That scatter-gun runs nine balls to the barrel, and when you multiply that by two . . . ?"

"Some of them missed him," Doc Holliday said sadly. "Might be he stopped eight or ten of them!"

"We will have to take off his clothes," the Doctor said briskly. "Just lie still, Clanton."

The outlaw snarled and tried to draw up his legs. Then he lashed out with his fists and just missed Kramer. The little Doctor drew back, and his face stiffened and set in hard lines. His right hand went

109

back to his hip pocket and held there.

"We are going to fix you up," he grunted. "Take his feet, sheriff!"

Sheriff Blaine reached out a hand gingerly. Bull Clanton raised up and slapped viciously. Out came the Doctor's hand with the billy dangling limply. Then the little man stepped in swiftly and brought down his arm. A soft thud, and Bull Clanton groaned and relaxed.

"Strip him," the Doctor barked. "Cut them Levi's away from him!"

Alamo Bowie reached for his frogging knife and went to work. The Doctor got pans and hot water and poured some red pills for an antiseptic. Doc Holliday was busy with a rope, and when the Doctor was ready, the prisoner was bound to the couch.

"He only stopped seven buck-shot," the Doctor murmured after an examination. "And most of them are flesh wounds because you was so far away from the target."

"That ain't so good," the gambler murmured. "But old Brindle was meant for close work, and that reminds me that I forgot to reload."

He swiveled the sawed-off from under his coat and opened the breech. Alamo Bowie watched him with a half-smile on his tanned face, but the sheriff shuddered and waved his hand.

"Mighty glad I ain't out of friends with you no more, Doc," he said earnestly. "You and that dang scatter-gun."

Doctor Kramer was busy with his probes and

swabs. Bull Clanton groaned softly and opened his eyes. The Doctor fished for a ball and laid it on the couch, and the prisoner swore viciously.

"Hush yore fuss," the Medico grunted. "That was only the first one, and you've had all the anesthetic you are going to get!"

The sheriff watched the second operation and turned toward the door. "I'll go out and book him," he explained. "Kinda stuffy in here!"

"I'll see you later about that slug in your leg," the Doctor answered over his shoulder.

"It's just a scratch," Blaine explained hurriedly. "I've done washed it out myself!"

The Doctor winked at Bowie and returned to his work. Bull Clanton howled and bellowed, and got scant sympathy. Alamo Bowie watched for a while and returned to the jail office. He stopped abruptly when he saw a fat little man with a belly, talking to the sheriff.

"Judge Hart heard the ruckus and dropped in, Bowie," Blaine explained stiffly. "Mebbe you better talk to him some."

"You can't hold this man for murder," the judge almost shouted. "Three-finger Jack will kill us all in our beds!"

"He gets a fair trial for murder," the Texan answered coldly. "He was in that hold-up when Pop Whipple was killed, and I have enough evidence to swing him. Better hold the trial tomorrow morning."

"By what authority?" the judge roared.

"By authority of the U. S. Government," Bowie

answered. "If that ain't enough, I got this kind of law!"

His face was as hard as granite while he stared at the trembling little man and tapped the guns on his legs. The judge glanced at sheriff Blaine and shook a finger under his nose.

"It will mean your star if you live long enough," he threatened. "The wisest thing you ever did was turn that gang loose!"

"Set the trial for tomorrow at ten," sheriff Blaine answered softly. "I'll have the Jury all ready, and for one time they won't be outlaws. We aim to have decent law here in Tombstone!"

"I'll resign," the judge murmured weakly. "I'll go out on the early stage!"

Alamo Bowie glanced at the sheriff and nodded solemnly. "The judge better sleep with me tonight," he suggested quietly. "I'll see that nothing happens to him, and I'll see that he gets to court on time."

"I'll prosecute you in every court in the land," the little judge threatened. "You can't do this to me!"

"Now look, Judge," the Texan began quietly. "This man threatened to kill the sheriff. He robbed the stage, and I found the evidence in his bunk. Then he tried to kill me tonight, and I am an officer of the law. Are you listening?"

"You might have planted that plunder on the Box C yourself," the judge snarled.

"You have been talking to Three-finger Jack," Bowie clipped. "He made that same remark!"

"And what if I have?"

Bowie waved his hand. "Then Clanton and Pecos Traynor tried to dry-gulch the sheriff from the dark," he continued quietly. "His trial comes off at ten in the morning!"

Doc Holliday came out of the back room and took his stand facing the front door. The judge glanced at him uneasily, and the gambler nodded his head and patted the gun under his coat.

"Yeah, I was listening," he admitted. "The jury will bring in a verdict of guilty, and you better read it right!"

"You can't intimidate me, sir," the judge cried angrily. "I'll remove you men if I have to call in the troops from Fort Huachucua!"

"You have no authority to call in the troops," the sheriff interrupted quietly. "That falls to my office, and I don't figger we need them . . . yet!"

"Looky, Judge," Doc Holliday said softly, and his greenish eyes held steady on the little man. "I'm a private citizen any time I turn in my star. You try any shark tricks and yo're going to be in the same fix as Bull Clanton!"

The judge paled and turned to Alamo Bowie. "Can we retire now?" he asked weakly.

"Soon as I see the Doctor," the Texan answered, and walked into the back room.

Doctor Kramer was washing his instruments while he watched the prisoner. Bull Clanton was groaning while his huge muscles strained against the ropes that held him to the couch. His thick legs were neatly bandaged, and he shouted curses when he saw Bowie.

"You'll answer for this, Texan," he screamed. "Three-finger won't stand to see me dangle!"

"You'll hang and rattle," the Texan said coldly. "Three-finger is looking out for himself!"

"Don't try to reason with the swine," the Doctor advised. "Take this persuader and slap him to sleep if he goes on the prod!"

Bull Clanton clenched his jaws and watched the little Doctor. Alamo Bowie smiled and opened the door.

"I'll call you if we need help, Doc," he said pointedly, and stared at Clanton.

Doctor Kramer walked into the jail office and nodded curtly at Judge Hart. "When is the trial?" he asked Blaine.

"Ten in the morning," the sheriff answered. "I've got the jury picked out. Honest ranchers and miners we can trust for one time!"

"Be seeing you," and the Doctor walked out into the night.

Alamo Bowie turned to the judge and jerked his head toward the door. "Let's get going," he muttered. "See you tomorrow, sheriff. Night, Holliday."

Judge Hart walked outside and glanced up and down the deserted street. Then the Texan grinned and led the way to the Russ house. Up the broad stairs and into the lobby, and Nellie Gray handed him his key.

"Will he live?" she asked softly.

"He will live to hang," Bowie answered, and stared at the judge. "He's sleeping with me tonight, so he will be on hand for the trial in the morning."

"I'll take a room by myself," the judge snapped.

"I put an extra cot in your room," and Nellie Gray looked at Bowie. "I don't have an extra room."

"He can sleep on that," the Texan growled. "Good night, Miss Nellie."

He stepped aside and motioned to the stairs. The judge grumbled and walked ahead, and Bowie fitted his key to the lock and opened the door. The judge walked in first. Then he whirled suddenly with his right hand jerking from his pocket.

Alamo Bowie caught the hand and twisted sideways. A two-shot derringer spilled to the carpet and clattered under the bed. The Texan twisted and threw the fat little man away from him, and his gray eyes were blazing when he slapped down to his right holster.

"You wouldn't be missed much if you made another mistake," and his voice rasped like a file. "Now you get in that cot and shuck yore clothes before I do you a meanness!"

The judge puffed to his feet and sat down on the cot. Bowie sneered at the rolls of fat when the outer clothing fell away. The judge stripped down to his underwear and crawled under the covers, and the Texan went to bed by pulling off his boots.

"I sleep light," he warned. "And I shoot at anything that moves in the dark!"

He blew out the lamp and pushed the stand away from the bed. Closed his eyes and fell to sleep instantly while the judge laid awake and planned to escape. An hour passed, and the cot creaked when the judge sat up and reached for his pants.

"Stay where you are," a sharp voice barked. "I'll shoot at the next move!"

"I was just turning over," the judge whimpered.

Alamo Bowie smiled and holstered the gun that had leaped to his hand. This time he remained awake, and a few minutes later he heard a scraping sound on the floor. He opened one eye and saw the judge sky-lined against the window, but he made no move.

Judge Hart crept to the door and turned the key softly. His clothes were clutched in one fat hand, and then he stepped into the hall and closed the door behind him. A soft voice whirled him around with a muffled shout.

"Git back there, feller. You want me to run you in for indecent exposure?"

Doc Holliday was smiling as he blocked off escape. The judge turned the knob and opened the door. Alamo Bowie called sleepily from the big bed.

"You don't quit that tom-catting around, I aim to throw and hog-tie you like a yearling. Now you hit that bunk and stay put!"

Then he closed his eyes again and sank into deep slumber. The judge crawled between the blankets with goose-flesh pimpling his fat body. The Law had come to Tombstone.

CHAPTER IX

E agerness and anticipation wiped the sleep from the eyes of Tombstone when a brassy sun slanted over the rim of the distant Dragoons. Word of the capture of Bull Clanton and the impending trial had gone to Galeyville and Charleston on the San Pedro. Miners and cattlemen were arriving in the silver camp before breakfast, and every man was heavily armed.

Alamo Bowie was shaving clean before a small mirror near the double windows. Judge Hart had doused his face in cold water, but his florid jowls were stubby with gray bristles. The tall Texan offered his razor, and the judge groaned and held out his right hand.

"Look at me," he moaned. "Shaking like a leppy with the ticks in fly-time. It's my last day on earth, and it's all your fault!"

"Cheer up," Bowie muttered dryly. "Take a look out the window and see if you feel any better."

The judge creaked erect and waddled to the window. His pale blue eyes widened when he saw a group of blue-coated soldiers on the steps of the Court house. Bayonets fixed, with side arms gleaming and ready for instant use. The judge stared his unbelief, and drew a slow breath.

"The Trial is set for ten," he remarked, and his voice was once more strong, and tinged with the arrogance of judicial authority. "Can we have breakfast served here in our room?"

Alamo Bowie smiled when a knock sounded on the door. "That should be Wing now," he answered. "You mind letting him in?"

Judge Hart hopped to the door and threw it wide. The Chinese smiled blandly and came in with a steaming tray. Nellie Gray followed at his heels to clear the table, and her brown eyes were circled with rings of deep violet. Alamo Bowie laid his razor aside and took both her hands.

"You didn't sleep," he chided gently. "Tell the truth, Nellie."

"I was worried," and her throaty voice trembled slightly. "We fed the soldiers early this morning."

"Good for the sheriff," the Texan answered, and smiled at the judge. "My room-mate has taken a new lease on life."

"The food will get cold, Bowie," Judge Hart chuckled. "Wash the soap from your ugly face and grab yourself a chair. Ham and eggs, Mush, and hot cakes. We will make history in Tombstone this day!"

Nellie Gray smiled for the first time since she had held her guns on the outlaw chief. The color came back to her cheeks, and she hummed softly while she helped the Chinese prepare the table. The tall Texan washed his face and came around to put his big hands on her shoulders.

"You've met the Angel of Tombstone, Judge," he said soberly. "Like as not she spent the night praying for you, and for Bull Clanton. We've got to make this camp safe for folks like Nellie, and I'm hoping that you will remember that after the evidence is all in!"

"It would be collusion if I were to discuss the merits of the case with you," and the judge frowned heavily. "However, I might say that the ends of Justice will be served."

Nellie Gray held out her hand. "Thank you, Judge," she said earnestly. "Now if you will excuse me, I would like to speak to Alamo outside for a moment."

The Texan followed her to the hall when the judge bowed. Nellie Gray came to him with arms outstretched, and her head tilted back to look into his hard gray eyes. Alamo Bowie held her gently and waited.

"Be careful," she whispered tremulously. "The outlaws are gathering at the Crystal Palace. Fred Rutledge and Doc Holliday are watching them, but I know it means more trouble."

The Texan patted her shoulders awkwardly. "We will be ready," he answered quietly, and his deep voice held the old soft drawl. "The judge and I will stay here until ten o'clock."

She raised on her tip-toes and kissed him with a smile in her eyes. Bowie watched her go down the stairs, and his face was peaceful when he returned to the room and took his place at the table.

"Double order of ham and eggs," the judge remarked approvingly. "Nellie Gray certainly knows how to take care of her men-folks. Remarkable woman, Bowie!"

The Texan nodded. "In more ways than one," he agreed, and attacked his breakfast. "Mind telling me just what Three-finger said last night?"

The judge frowned. "Harumph," he muttered. "Three-finger Jack is not on trial." He studied his plate for a moment and raised his eyes slowly. "That stranger who helped you last night," he began slowly.

"I know," Bowie muttered. "Three-finger recognized the stranger!"

The judge nodded. "He recognized Nellie Gray," he admitted slowly. "Wanted to make a deal with me."

"You deal?"

The little judge squirmed uneasily. "That was last night," he answered irritably. "He wanted to trade Bull Clanton for Nellie Gray, and there was some other considerations involved."

"Bull Clanton is guilty," the Texan growled, and his face was like granite. "You told him . . . ?"

"I just nodded my head," Judge Hart murmured. "He had me, Bowie. My life was in danger, but as I remarked, that was last night!"

"Spoke like a man, Judge," the Texan praised quietly. "Stay off the streets until after round-up!"

"Round-up?" and the judge raised his eyebrows.

"Rustlers Round-up," Bowie snapped. "Outlaws either get out or get killed!"

The judge studied for a long moment and then returned to his food. "Tombstone will be a better place to live in," he murmured, and once more his fat hands were steady. "No longer will the forces of law and order be intimidated, and you can count on the co-operation of the bench!"

Alamo Bowie reached out his big right hand.

"Shake, pard," he said soberly, and smiled when the judge gripped his hand and beamed with pleasure.

"You have changed the whole course of my life, Bowie," the judge murmured. "United we stand!"

Bowie nodded and went back to his breakfast. He had said what was on his mind, and now he ate in silence, like a cowboy on the range. The judge finished his strong coffee and puffed on a long cheroot, and the Texan pushed back and reached for his saddle-bags. Brought out tools and proceeded to clean the Twins; the long-barreled forty-fives that seemed so much a part of him.

Judge Hart watched while the Texan washed his hands carefully and stood erect. A quick flashing pass at the moulded holsters; the regular daily practice of those who live by the speed of their draw, and the accuracy of their aim. With each successive move, the little Jurist gained confidence, and then he glanced under the bed when the Texan snugged the Twins low and turned to the window.

"You mind if I arm myself?" the judge asked hopefully.

"Yore derringer is under the bed," Bowie answered gravely. "But if I was you I'd get a man's-size cutter and use it for a gavel."

He reached under the bed and produced a heavy Colt from his saddle-bags. "Here's one Big Enough Smith won't be needing any more," and he handed the weapon to the judge.

Judge Hart took the sixgun and slipped it down in the band of his broadcloth trousers. "Once more I am a man, Alamo Bowie," he said soberly. "It is five minutes until ten!"

The Texan nodded and cuffed his battered Stetson low over his eyes. Together they walked down the stairs and through the lobby. Crossed the street to the Court House where the soldiers made a lane with rifles on their shoulders. The Captain saluted respectfully, and the Texan nodded his head. Sheriff Blaine met them at the door where he was presiding over a long table stacked with loaded sixguns.

Joe Blaine shot a quick glance at Judge Hart and gasped. He saw the butt of the heavy gun gleaming above the bulging pants band, and his hand shot out to grip the judge hard.

"Tombstone is breeding men fast here lately," he said softly. "The prisoner is in the box, yore Honor!"

The judge nodded and walked up the long aisle. Alamo Bowie took his stand against the back wall. His eyes lighted briefly when he saw Doc Holliday on the other side of the room. Three men were sitting close to the gambler, and the Texan recognized the town committee. Then his eyes swung to the back seats and hardened.

Three-finger Jack and twelve of his men held the entire back row. Empty holsters sagged on their legs, but the Texan knew about the hide-outs cleverly concealed in high cowboy boots. The outlaw leader caught his eye and smiled coldly, and Bowie started forward when he realized that Pecos Traynor was absent.

He stopped the move and turned toward the door

with a shrug of irritation when the outlaw smiled derisively. Then his gray eyes narrowed. Nellie Gray was coming through the door with big Marty Williams at her side. Bowie watched the outlaws, but only Three-finger showed emotion. The tall outlaw's eyes were blazing with anger while he stared at Nellie Gray, and then his thin lips set in a straight line.

He turned away and caught the Texan's eyes upon him. Shrugged carelessly and turned to speak to one of his men, and Bowie forgot about the incident when the judge rapped on the bench. Men craned forward to get a better view when they saw the new gavel in the hand of the judge. The heavy forty-five that had belonged to Big Enough Smith!

"Court will come to order! We are here to try the case of Bull Clanton; versus the people of the Territory of Arizona!"

The judge stared at Alamo Bowie and smiled confidently. Eight soldiers moved into the court room and took positions against the wall. Three-finger Jack scowled, and the judge began to read the charge.

"The prisoner will remain seated because of certain infirmities," he began sonorously. "You are charged with highway robbery and murder, among other things. Bull Clanton, are you guilty or not guilty?"

"Not guilty, Judge," the prisoner growled. "That damn Texan robbed the stage his ownself!"

"On what do you base your assertion?" the judge asked quietly.

"I was in the sheriff's posse," the prisoner answered sullenly. "We found Bowie's tracks out there, and there was a pair of tracks made by a woman who helped him do the job!"

Alamo Bowie's eyes narrowed dangerously. He controlled himself and glanced at the face of Nellie Gray. She was clenching her fists tightly while she stared at Bull Clanton as though she could not believe her ears. Then a low growl of anger ran through the crowd.

"String the buzzard up," a bearded man shouted. "Talkin' that away about the Angel!"

The troopers came forward with fixed bayonets and hammers eared back. The judge rapped for order and glared at the crowd.

"Order in the Court!" he bellowed. "Alamo Bowie will take the stand!"

His presence of mind attracted the attention of the crowd toward the Wells Fargo special agent. Bowie came up the aisle and raised his hand to take the oath. Bull Clanton glared piggishly and muttered under his breath. The judge nodded at the Texan.

"Tell your story," he barked sharply.

Alamo Bowie glanced at the prisoner and smiled. "I rode out to the Drew ranch when I heard that the stage had been robbed, and Pop Whipple killed," he began slowly. "Pop Whipple was the only witness who could have convicted Lantern-jaw Peters. I wanted a conviction, and Peters was a known outlaw. The outlaws did not want a conviction, and Pop Whipple was killed."

"Yo're a liar," Bull Clanton shouted. "Now tell about the woman!"

The Texan turned and stared at the prisoner. His gray eyes were blazing with a fury that could be felt over the room. His craggy jaw bulged with muscle while he fought to control his anger. Then he took a deep breath and cleared his throat.

"Miss Nellie Gray rode out to the scene of the crime with me," he began softly. "We found the marks of two pairs of boots where the killers hid in ambush. One was a pair of number twelves; the other pair were made by the boots of Big Enough Smith. Bull Clanton erased that sign while I was searching the house on the Box C where the plunder was hidden under the bunk of the defendant. And among the loot was found the silver watch Pop Whipple had carried on his run!"

"You planted the stuff there," Clanton shouted.

The judge rapped with the butt of his sixgun. "Another remark out of you and the sheriff will take measures," he warned. "Proceed, Mister Bowie!"

"There was a thousand dollars in fifty-dollar bills stolen in the hold-up," Bowie continued. "I have a witness to prove that Big Enough Smith lost ten of those marked bills in a gambling game. The other ten were taken from the prisoner when arrested last night!"

The crowd watched silently while the Texan made his way to the rear. The judge cleared his throat and called the name of John Holliday. The gambler took the stand and corroborated the testimony, and the crowd straightened up when sheriff Blaine took the stand.

"We found the money in the clothes of the prisoner

last night after he had tried to kill me from a dark alley," Joe Blaine testified sternly. "He had these marked bills inside his vest," and he passed the money to the judge. "Marty Williams marked the bills before Pop Whipple started his run!"

The judge nodded and stared at the crowd. "Three-finger Jack will represent the defendant," he said suddenly. "Take the witness!"

The tall outlaw came slowly up the aisle and paused to stare at the sheriff. "Did you get to the prisoner first last night, sheriff Blaine?" he asked quietly.

The sheriff flushed angrily. "I was there when Bowie searched him," he snapped.

"Then you could not be certain that Bowie did not plant that money," the outlaw answered with a smile. "That's all, sheriff."

Sheriff Blaine muttered to himself and stomped back to take his place by the door. The outlaw turned slowly and stared at Doc Holliday.

"I would like to question the temporary town Marshal," he said loudly.

The judge frowned. "The *permanent* town Marshal will take the stand," he corrected, but the crowd of outlaws guffawed loudly.

Doc Holliday took the stand and fastened his greenish eyes on the thin dark face of the outlaw. "Was Big Enough Smith a friend of yores?" Three-finger asked softly.

"He was not!" the gambler barked. "I'm no lily, but I don't pard up with outlaws!"

"Confine yore remarks to the answers," the outlaw

said coldly. "Have you any witnesses to prove that Big Enough Smith lost those bills at yore layout?"

"There was one," the gambler answered thinly. "And Big Enough killed him. I mean Ed White!"

"Then you have no actual witnesses," the outlaw answered with a smile. "The defense is through with the witness, yore Honor!"

The judge frowned and shook his head slightly. Three-finger Jack saw the gesture and winked at Bull Clanton. A cringing figure stood up near Alamo Bowie and raised his hand, and the judge rapped for silence.

"I'd like to testify," the ragged fellow announced shakily.

"Take the stand," and the judge stared at Three-finger Jack.

"I'm the swamper over at the Oriental," the man began.

"Just a moment," the judge interrupted. "Hold up your hand and take the oath. Your name?"

"My right name is Jack Whipple," the swamper answered, and his thin voice was stronger. "Pop Whipple was my Uncle, but he made me promise not to tell anyone."

"I object," Three-finger Jack interrupted. "Being a relative, he would be prejudiced!"

"Objection over-ruled," the judge barked. "Tell your story, Whipple!"

"I was sweeping up around the Faro layout when Big Enough Smith was gambling," the swamper began, and avoided the outlaw's piercing black eyes.

"I see him lose those fifty-dollar bills, because I heard Doc Holliday remark that they were the first he had seen in Tombstone. I didn't pay much attention at the time."

"How many were there?" the judge asked softly.

"Ten," Whipple answered, and his face paled when he glanced at the outlaw and read the promise of death glowing in the slitted black eyes. "I don't care if you kill me," he snarled at the outlaw. "Pop Whipple was good to me, and he was my only kin!"

"Any questions?" the judge asked the outlaw.

Three-finger Jack shrugged and returned slowly to his seat. The judge dismissed the witness and waited until the room was silent. He glanced at the jury box and cleared his throat.

"Gentlemen of the jury; you have heard the evidence and the testimony. You will retire to the jury room to arrive at a verdict. The penalty for conviction is well known by you all. You will elect a foreman who will bring the written verdict to me!"

Six stalwart miners and six cattlemen filed out of the box and closed the door to the jury room. Three-finger Jack talked in low tones with his men while the soldiers walked slowly back and forth. Bull Clanton slumped low in his seat with his thick legs on a chair in front of him. Then the murmur stilled instantly when the door of the jury room opened slowly.

A short heavy-set man took the lead and stood up while his eleven companions found their seats. Three-finger Jack stared at the cattleman and swore under his breath.

"John Slaughter," he whispered. "And he don't booger worth a hoot!"

"You have arrived at a verdict?" the judge asked clearly.

"We have, yore Honor," Slaughter answered, and passed over the folded paper he was holding in his left hand.

The judge waited for him to resume his seat. Then he unfolded the paper and read it silently. No expression on his fat face while he stared at the prisoner and cleared his throat.

"The prisoner will stand," he began, and then raised his right hand hastily. "Keep your seat; I forgot that you were wounded while making an attempt to kill a peace officer!"

His little blue eyes flicked to the rear of the room and locked glances with Three-finger Jack. Then the judge swiveled his eyes to the hard face of Alamo Bowie and held there as if to gain confidence. The soldiers sensed the Drama and stood stiffly at attention with rifles at the ready. The judge picked up the paper and read slowly.

"We the Jury, find the prisoner guilty of robbery and murder as charged.
John Slaughter, foreman."

Bull Clanton shrugged lower in his chair and turned to stare at Three-finger Jack with fear widening his little eyes. He gulped noisily and tugged at his lower lip until the judge rapped on the bench.

"It is now the duty of this court to pass sentence," Judge Hart said slowly, and his voice was a low whisper of sound that carried to every corner of the silent room.

Doc Holliday shifted his thin white hands and swiveled the deadly sawed-off from under his black coat. Alamo Bowie was crouching forward with both big hands hooked in the crossed gunbelts girding his lean hips. Nellie Gray was leaning forward with her hands clasped as though in prayer, and the judge stood up and spoke slowly.

"You have been found guilty of murder, Bull Clanton. I now sentence you to be hanged by the neck until you are dead . . . dead . . . dead! May God have mercy on your soul. The execution will take place at sunrise tomorrow. This court stands adjourned!"

Stunned silence in the room while men stared at the prisoner. Nellie Gray left her seat and walked slowly toward the doomed man. He stared at her with stricken eyes, and she held out a book to him.

"Take this prayer book and read it to give you courage," she said softly. "I am sorry because of your mother."

Bull Clanton reached out a trembling hand and took the book. His lips tried to frame words and failed. Three-finger Jack came up softly and sneered when he saw the book.

"Buck up, feller," he muttered. "You ain't hung yet!"

"Keep the book," a dry voice cut in sharply. "The carpenters are starting to build the scaffold now!"

Three-finger Jack turned slowly and faced Alamo Bowie. His lips pressed together while he stared for a moment, and then he shifted his eyes to the face of Nellie Gray. Without a word he lifted his hat and waved his hand before striding down the aisle and down the stairs.

"He tipped his hat like he did last night," and Nellie Gray clutched the Texan's arm. "He was telling me that he knew who the stranger was!"

Alamo Bowie waited until the sheriff and two husky miners removed the prisoner. Then he came to the bench and extended his hand to Judge Hart.

"Yo're all man, Judge," he said gravely. "I'll walk back to the hotel with you and Miss Nellie before I leave."

"Alamo! Where must you go?" and Nellie Gray watched his stern face anxiously.

"They are putting Ed White and old Pop Whipple away this morning," the Texan answered soberly. "I promised to tell 'em good-bye!"

CHAPTER X

A small group of hard-faced men uncovered their heads in the cemetery on top of the hill. Boot Hill played no favorites, and the Minister from the Universal church stood between the twin graves and read the simple service. Town Marshal Ed White, and old Pop Whipple had made the last long ride up the hill together; would sleep side by side in the wind-swept plot where Saint and Sinner found a common resting place.

Big Marty Williams and little Jed Swope. Doc Holliday clad immaculately in black broadcloth as always with ragged Jack Whipple at his side. Fred Rutledge and Alamo Bowie, with a handful of close friends who had come to pay their respects. Alamo Bowie picked up a clod and tossed it into the open graves.

"Vaya con Dios," he murmured, and said his farewells Indian fashion. "Go thou with God!"

Marty Williams nudged the tall Texan when he straightened up. A long procession was winding up the hill from town. Four black horses with somber pampas plumes tossing on their heads, were pulling the plate-glass hearse with Hunchy Domain in the driver's seat. Hunchy was one of the Undertakers, and he maintained a strict neutrality while he buried foe and friend alike.

The group beside the graves turned slowly and watched in silence. The coffin was visible inside the glass hearse. Just behind the wagon of the dead rode Three-finger Jack with Lantern-jaw Peters rubbing stirrups beside him. Twelve other outlaws followed by twos, and each was heavily armed, even to carbines in the saddle-boots under left legs.

The Universal Minister excused himself and walked slowly across the cemetery to take his stand at another open grave. They heard his deep sad voice begin his intonations before the cortège had reached the spot.

"Dust to dust," and then the hearse rolled past the

forces of the law.

Three-finger Jack turned his black eyes and stared at the shivering swamper who had added the word to convict Bull Clanton. Alamo Bowie put on his hat and cuffed the battered brim down over his smouldering gray eyes. The outlaw uttered two words when he passed at a slow walk.

"Buzzard bait," he said clearly.

Lantern-jaw Peters grinned openly while his left hand gripped the handle of his gun. His right arm was in a sling across his chest, and he passed without a word. The parade of horsemen passed and swung down to the tune of creaking saddle leather, and Three-finger Jack snapped a sharp command.

"Hats off!"

Alamo Bowie removed his head gear. No expression on his bleak face while the outlaws swept off their Stetsons. Marty Williams allowed the fleeting suggestion of a sardonic smile to twist his harsh features when the minister began his text.

"He who lives by the sword, shall die by the sword!"

He had used a different text for Ed White and old Pop Whipple. *"Greater love hath no man,"* had been his subject. Three-finger Jack was frowning while he stared coldly at Parson Gates, but the clergyman turned the pages of his little book and did his duty as he saw it.

Hunchy Domain stood beside his glittering showcase like a mis-shapen vulture that has finished his long vigil. The undertaker would have been a big man

133

except for the lump on his back. It thickened his enormous chest and caused his long arms to hang nearly to his knees, and his curved nose over-shadowed thick lips like the beak of a predatory bird. Glittering dark eyes that watched the face of Three-finger Jack without blinking. The outlaw chief was plainly the man who would pay the bill.

"Save trouble if we leave now," Fred Rutledge whispered to Bowie. "That gang is loaded for bear, and itching for grief!"

"It wouldn't be decent," the Texan muttered through stiff lips. "I don't see Pecos Traynor."

The little swamper leaned across and spoke in a shaking voice. "That's him there in the back," he whispered. "He's shaved off his whiskers and cowhorns!"

Doc Holliday heard and straightened stiffly. All eyes turned to the lanky figure of a rider who never removed his hands from the twin guns on his long legs. Shaved clean two days under the skin, but the black beard showed the plainer against dead white skin that had been protected from the desert sun.

"Not now," Bowie murmured. "Wait until they leave the grave-yard!"

The minister finished his reading and closed his book. Then he closed his eyes wearily and offered a short prayer. The law put on their hats and mounted their horses to ride slowly from Boot Hill. The outlaws remained behind until the mound was heaped high above the grave of their pard.

"Boots and saddles," Three-finger muttered, and

swung up on his big black horse. "We'll give 'em a chance right now!"

He hooked the spirited animal with the rowels and clattered across the rocky cemetery at a dead run. Lantern-jaw Peters waved his hand at the grave.

"See you in hell, Big Enough," he said in farewell.

Hunchy Domain turned slowly and watched the outlaws gallop across the graves and out of Boot Hill. His dark eyes gleamed knowingly while his big head nodded slowly, after which he climbed back on the seat and clucked to the four black horses. Tombstone had had her man for breakfast, and tomorrow was another day.

"Bull Clanton is a big jigger," he murmured with business-like calculation. "The other one won't take a very big box!"

Alamo Bowie was the first to hear the drumming beat of hoofs behind them. He spoke softly to his companions and pulled the big red horse to a halt. The others fanned out in a half circle with hands twitching guns loose in case of riding crimp. Then they waited for the thundering column to close the gap between them.

Three-finger Jack rode at a high lope and sat his horse down on its haunches with the cruel Spanish curb. Gravel flew under sliding hoofs to shower the forces of the law. The outlaws backed up their chief solidly with grins on their grimy faces. Only Three-finger Jack was immaculate and well-groomed.

"Talking to you, Bowie," he began without preamble. "You better turn Clanton loose if you pack any savvy!"

"Clanton swings at sunrise," the special agent answered harshly. "He had a fair trial!"

"That's final?"

"That's final!" the Texan barked, and returned the outlaw's steady gaze.

Three-finger shook his head arrogantly. "We have you out-numbered five to one," he pointed out.

The Texan shrugged carelessly. "I might as well tell you now, Jack," and his voice was low and clear. "Cochise County is going to be cleaned up. Outlaws either get out . . . or get killed!"

Three-finger glanced at his men and smiled. "You want to start now?" he asked softly.

Alamo Bowie drooped his shoulders into a crouch. "Now is a good time," he answered quietly. "But Bull Clanton will hang just the same!"

The tall outlaw changed expression as though he had just remembered something. "We've just buried the dead," he answered, and once more his voice was under control and quiet. "We'll wait!"

He swiveled his black eyes and stared at Jack Whipple with his upper lip curling into a sneer. Then he scratched the black and jerked his head at the band. Doc Holliday turned loose his grip on the sawed-off and shrugged the weapon under his black coat. Fred Rutledge broke the silence when he kneed his horse close to the Texan.

"We should have taken Traynor," he growled. "We proved he was guilty of trying to kill the sheriff!"

Alamo Bowie turned and stared at the rows of graves in Boot Hill. The deputy flushed and nodded his head. "Forgot about old Pop and Ed," he muttered.

The Texan turned to the little swamper. "I was you, I'd shake the dust of Tombstone from my feet, Jack," he said kindly. "That gang means to get you for what you done back there in the Court room."

Jack Whipple squared his thin shoulders. "I got a gun on me now," and his voice was suddenly strong and confident. "I don't aim to leave until I see Bull Clanton dance a hoe-down on thin air. Pop was the only kin I had!"

The Texan stared for a moment and then shrugged. "Yo're free, white, and twenty-one," he remarked. "Let's stop down at the Crystal Palace and irrigate. First-drink time, and I got a bad taste in my mouth."

"Better not all go in together," Marty Williams warned. "Just in case of."

The Texan nodded and touched Snapper with his blunted spur. Down the long hill and into Allen street just as the whistle across the gully blew to announce dinner time for the red-shirted miners in the *Lucky Cuss*. Horses tied at the scarred rail in front of the Crystal Palace Bar, and the tall Texan shouldered through the swinging doors with Jack Whipple at his side.

Marty Williams and Jed Swope turned and walked up to the side door. Fred Rutledge and Doc Holliday continued to the back and came in through the card room. Bowie looked over the crowded room and took a place at the end of the bar with his back to the door. The bar-dog raised his shaggy eyebrows while his hand reached for a bottle of Three Star.

"Straight, with a chaser of the same," the Texan grunted.

Jack Whipple was staring at a group of men half way up the bar. The face of Pecos Traynor made a picture of black and white where his shaven beard glowed through the pale skin. Alamo Bowie filled two glasses and made a swift pair of passes. Downed the first neat, and followed with a chaser of the same. Then he wiped his lips with the back of his hand and turned his head slightly to see what Whipple was doing.

The little swamper was staring steadily at Pecos Traynor. The saloon sensed the silent duel and became strangely quiet. A silence broken by the angry rasping voice of the outlaw who was sure of his disguise.

"You lookin' for somethin', hombre?"

"Pop Whipple was my only kin," and the swamper's voice was a thin ribbon of sound that cut the smoky air like a knife. "I'm going to watch Bull Clanton hang and rattle in the morning, and I'm going to laugh while he learns to dance!"

Three-finger Jack was not in sight, but the other outlaws mumbled under their breath. Pecos Traynor pushed away from the bar with his shoulders falling into a crouch, and the tips of his fingers brushed the handles of his guns to place them accurately. Jack Whipple faced him like a panther getting ready to spring, and Alamo Bowie stared steadily at Doc Holliday and shook his head slightly.

All the outlaws saw the signal except Pecos Traynor and Lantern-jaw Peters. They swiveled around and

138

dropped hands away from their guns when they saw Doc Holliday and big Marty Williams. The Texan stared at Peters, and his voice was brittle.

"You keep out of this, Lantern-jaw!"

Lantern-jaw Peters sneered and faced around squarely. "You got nothin' on me . . . now," he sneered.

Alamo Bowie thought swiftly. Perhaps he could steal the play and save the little swamper. No one who knew the code ever interfered when man met man and called for show-down. Jack Whipple had called Pecos Traynor, and the outlaw was fast on the draw. More than that, he placed his shots where he called them.

"We got enough on you, Peters," he answered slowly. "Don't forget it was me that put yore wing where it is!"

Peters flushed angrily and stretched out the wounded arm. "Yes, damn yuh," he growled. "But you won't ever get another chance!"

Jack Whipple lurched suddenly against the tall Texan and sent him off balance. A flashing roar exploded from among the bandages on the arm of Lantern-jaw Peters just as Alamo Bowie shifted his feet and caught his balance. His right hand slapped down and exploded in gun-flame like a sunbeam flashing from a mirror, and Peters was shocked back with a hide-out derringer spilling from the bandages.

The outlaw tried to catch himself against the shock of the heavy slug and failed. He sat down heavily on the floor with the white bandages turning to red. The arm dangled uselessly to show where the Texan's bullet had broken the bones above the elbow. Alamo Bowie swiveled his hand and pouched the smoking gun with a grunt, and then his gray eyes widened with wonder.

Jack Whipple was holding his crouch as though he had not heard the double shots. Pecos Traynor glanced sideways at Peters and curled his lips. His eyes held steadily on the little swamper's face while he hurled his challenge.

"With me it's different. That damn Texan don't dare cut into a closed game. Draw, you runty bantam!"

"Don't need no help," Whipple answered quietly. "I promised old Pop to hang up my guns as long as he was alive. Killed my own brother in a ruckus, and I kept my promise. Now Pop Whipple is dead and buried!"

Pecos Traynor cocked his head to one side. "So you picked on me," he said curiously. "It don't make no never-minds, but I'd like to know."

"I'd like to tell you," the little swamper answered coldly. "You can skin a skunk, but he's still a pole-cat. Even without the brush on yore map, yo're still Pecos Traynor!"

A deep sigh of expelling breath went up all over the room. Pecos Traynor jerked violently and shifted his eyes to the face of Alamo Bowie. The tall Texan shook his head slowly.

"It's between you and him," he drawled softly.

"So I'm Pecos Traynor," the outlaw muttered, and his hands twitched up with thumbs ratcheting the twin hammers. Jack Whipple concentrated on his right

140

hand gun and made his pass like a Master. He slipped the smooth filed hammer just as the long barrel tilted up over the lip of his mouldy old holster, and his face was a mask of hatred when the outlaw jerked back and triggered a pair of slugs into the floor between his wide-spread boots.

Gone was the cringing look of a beaten man while the little swamper caught the bucking gun on the recoil and eared back for a follow-up. Tense and deadly as a striking *vinegarone,* he crouched forward and watched his man swaying back and forth like a reed in the wind. A red circle widened on the left breast of the outlaw to smudge out the black hole in the dirty white cloth, and Pecos Traynor opened his mouth and gasped. Then he buckled his knees and sagged to the sawdust like a worn-out rope, and Jack Whipple holstered his gun while his little blazing eyes challenged the crowd.

"Any long-ridin' son taking up for the deceased?" he asked viciously.

Alamo Bowie allowed a smile of relief to flicker briefly across his hard face. "I reckon they've had enough, 'pard," he said softly. "But I might as well repeat what I told them up on the hill."

"Wait till Three-finger hears about this," and Lantern-jaw Peters staggered to his feet.

Alamo Bowie flicked his hands and palmed the Twins. "I'll do the talking, Peters," he snapped harshly. "Every man in the gang is a known outlaw. They either gets out, or they gets killed. Now don't you get any notions that I'm meaning you. Yo're

141

going to jail, and I let you live for a purpose."

"You got nothing on me," Peters snarled. "I was tried and acquitted."

"It's a felony to commit assault against the law with a deadly weapon," the Texan explained softly. "You tried to dry-gulch me on a gun-sneak, and you'll do at least ten years over Yuma way. Take him, Doc!"

Doc Holliday stepped out with the sawed-off cradled against his hip. "Get back here, Peters," and his voice was low and steady. "Yore pard got what was coming to him, and he'd have got it last night if he hadn't dogged it like a sneaking coyote!"

Lantern-jaw Peters turned slowly and looked at his friends. They avoided his eyes and kept their hands away from gun-butts, and the wounded man snarled like a cornered wolf.

"Pards," he sneered. "Yore still two-to-one, and you don't pack the sand to take a chance!"

"You know what the boss said," a bearded outlaw muttered softly. "You brought down the lightnin' on yore own head."

"Yeah? What did Three-finger say?" the Texan asked softly.

Peters swung around with a growl. "You'll find out soon enough," he taunted. "Now take me to yore lousy jail and try and keep me there!"

Alamo Bowie studied for a moment and jerked his head at Doc Holliday. "You and Marty take him down and book him," he told the gambler. "Fred and I want to talk with Jed Swope."

Doc Holliday prodded the prisoner with old Brindle

and shoved him through the batwings with the big Wells Fargo agent bringing up the rear. Alamo Bowie remained facing the outlaws with the Twins in his big hands, and he jerked his head toward the back door.

"You gents heard what I said," he began softly. "Yore hosses is rail-tied in the back, and you better hit leather and make tracks going away. Twenty-four hours is the deadline, and after that . . . ?"

They glared sullenly until the bearded spokesman shrugged and turned on his heel. Fred Rutledge stopped him and pointed to the corpse on the floor.

"Take him down to Hunchy," he barked. "Tell that old buzzard he made a mistake in the size of the box. We're going to make Jack Whipple shot-gun guard on the Benson stage old Pop used to drive. Now you rustlers drag Traynor out, and then fan the breeze!"

The outlaws carried Pecos Traynor through the back door where a low black wagon was waiting. Whiskers Compton scowled when he saw Hunchy Domain waiting with a stretcher already on the ground. The undertaker glanced at the body and raised his bushy brows.

"Not Whipple?" and his deep voice croaked like a frog.

"You take the corp and keep yore yap shut," Compton barked. "Three-finger will pay the freight!"

"Cash at the graveside, you tell him," Hunchy muttered. "I can't collect my pay from dead men!"

"Meaning what?" Whiskers Compton demanded.

"Meaning that the law is lining up a lot of dead shots," the undertaker answered clearly. "I want my dinero in advance, or the deceased can draw flies!"

Compton stared with a frown on his face. "I'll tell him," he muttered. "But if we didn't need you so bad shortly, I'd auger you down with the handle of my gun!"

"Any time, any time," and Hunchy Domain twitched back the tails of his long coat. Both his huge hands were wrapped around the ivory handles of a pair of forty-fives, and Compton smiled weakly.

"Can't you take a joke, feller," he muttered.

"It's my business to bury them," Hunch snapped, and jerked his head at the string of horses. "Now you gents load on and high-tail while I'm watching you!"

Alamo Bowie chuckled and turned back into the card room behind the saloon. Jack Whipple passed a thin hand across his face and glanced longingly at the bar. The Texan nodded and walked back to join Rutledge and Jed Swope. Shook his head when the little swamper invited him to drink, and smiled when Whipple ordered two glasses and downed the contents neat.

"You heard what Peters said?" and he glanced at Jed Swope.

"Said we wouldn't hold him in jail," the saddle-maker answered. "Say!"

The Texan nodded positively. "That's it," he agreed. "They plan a jail-break sometime tonight!"

Fred Rutledge smiled grimly. "I'll tell Joe Blaine," he promised. "We have plenty of rifles and shotguns in the jail office!"

"Better get the town committee to help as guards,"

the Texan suggested. "With Peters convicted, I don't look for much more trouble from the gang."

"Mebbe not from the gang," Jed Swope said softly. "But Three-finger won't give up until he matches you with his cutters!"

Alamo Bowie stared through a window with a far away look in his gray eyes. His hands touched the handles of the Twins, and then he rubbed the scar on his chin.

"They say he's the fastest," and his voice was a soft whisper. "They say he ain't never been bested in a show-down!"

Fred Rutledge frowned. "Yo're part of the law now, Alamo," he reminded.

"And I carry my part of it right here in my holsters," the Texan answered slowly. "Let's go and eat!"

CHAPTER XI

Nellie Gray watched Alamo Bowie climb the steps to his room after he had finished the noonday meal. The dining room was empty, but she waited a few minutes before following him to the second floor. A moment later she was facing him with a troubled look in her brown eyes.

"It's inhuman and cruel, Alamo," she almost sobbed. "You must help me to stop it!"

The Texan studied her face and patted her shoulder. "You wouldn't ask if it wasn't reasonable," he answered softly. "Spell it out, Nellie."

"It's Bull Clanton," she explained. "There is an empty lot next to the jail yard, and the owners are building a big grandstand to look down into the yard. They are going to charge five dollars a seat to see the hanging, and all the seats are already sold!"

"Like you say, it's inhuman," the Texan agreed. "But they ain't no law against it that I know of as long as those fellers own the property. What you want me to do?"

"Bull Clanton is reading the prayer book," and Nellie Gray smiled happily. "They will have to help him walk up the steps to the scaffold, and just think of all those inhuman beasts gloating at his agony."

"Bull should have thought of that," the Texan muttered. "Don't forget he helped kill Pop Whipple, and he tried to kill Joe Blaine!"

His voice was hard to match the expression on his craggy face. Nellie Gray watched him for a while and then put her hands on his shoulders.

"You are not hard down underneath, Alamo," she said gently. "I've watched you with that Snapper horse, and with people who are in trouble. That is why I love you."

"I can't say those kind of things like some fellers, but I think a heap of you," he murmured. "Kinda makes me dizzy at times when I think of an angel like you caring for a gun-fighter like me. Sometimes I misdoubts the wisdom of it, but I'd go plumb to hell for you."

"Then you will help me?"

He nodded somberly. "I'll get the boys lined up. We

figger the lightning will strike tonight nohow."

"Alamo! You mean Three-finger Jack?"

"Met him up in Boot Hill this morning," he answered carelessly. "He said we wouldn't hang Bull."

"That little swamper," Nellie Gray whispered and shuddered. "He really killed Pecos Traynor?"

"Deader than four o'clock in the morning," the Texan answered positively. "After which we throwed Lantern-jaw Peters in jail."

"Listen," and Nellie Gray sat on the bed beside the tall gaunt gun-fighter and took his hand. "The hanging takes place at sunrise. I'm not saying that Clanton don't deserve it. But I want those seats torn down before the sun comes up!"

Bowie nodded slowly. "I'll make medicine with the boys," he promised. "Now I want to get a little shut-eye, because I expect to be up all night."

She held him close and kissed him tenderly. Strong and mature like himself, with a wistful beauty that made him catch his breath while his arms closed about her until he could feel the steady pulsing of her heart.

"I will leave you now," she whispered. "And do be careful."

"It's you should be careful," and the Texan frowned. "You better stay in the hotel tonight."

"But I promised Clanton I would bring him a tray at midnight," she protested. "And he wants to talk to me . . . well, about the prayer book."

"I reckon it's yore job," he answered moodily, and shook his head. "But I don't like you to be out alone,

147

and I will be busy."

"No one ever bothers me," she answered with a smile. "I can go anywhere in Tombstone without fear of being molested."

"Nellie," and he was deadly serious. "You forget that Three-finger Jack tipped his hat to you twice!"

The woman caught his meaning and nodded soberly. "I'll be careful," she promised. "Now try to sleep."

Alamo Bowie thought deeply for a few moments after she had left the room. He had the outdoor man's knack of sleeping whenever he wanted to, and his deep breathing told of perfect relaxation. The afternoon heat gave way to a cooling breeze from the Dragoons when the sun went down, and twilight was merging with night when the Texan awoke suddenly and stretched to his feet.

Cold water in the stone basin freshened him for supper. He holstered his sixguns and made a few rapid passes. He told himself that he had never felt better, but his gray eyes hinted at a worry that he would not admit even to himself. He smoothed his hair and went down to the big dining room where Fred Rutledge and Doc Holliday were seated at the table back in a far corner.

"Howdy, Bowie," the deputy greeted. "Everything has been quiet this afternoon. Looks like Three-finger was bluffing."

The tall Texan grunted and took his seat. "He wasn't bluffing, and he don't work that away," he muttered dryly. "Now just put yoreself in his place for a spell of time. How would you figger it out?"

Fred Rutledge knitted his brows thoughtfully. "Be me, I'd strike just before daylight," he answered finally. "That's when folks is sleeping the heaviest, and they don't think so quick when they do wake up!"

"That's right good figgering," Bowie agreed quietly. "Not only that, but the white man learned that trick from the Apaches!"

"Me, I'm sleeping till about three A.M.," Doc Holliday cut in softly. "This outdoor life is agreeing with me."

"Guns," the Texan muttered. "How we fixed there in the jail?"

"A dozen riot guns loaded with buckshot," and the gambler smiled coldly. "As many rifles, and there will be nine of us altogether."

The Texan smiled crookedly with the corners of his hard mouth. Supper was served and eaten without further conversation. Then the three grim-faced men walked slowly from the hotel and down to the jail on Tough Nut street. Sheriff Joe Blaine sighed with relief when he saw them.

"Glad you come, Bowie," he muttered. "Jed Swope and I were just laying our plans. You reckon they'll strike?"

The Texan nodded positively. "They shore will," he answered. "You seen Marty Williams?"

"Marty will be here after he closes the office," the saddle-maker answered. "Bob Hatch and John Slaughter will be in shortly. Jack Whipple don't start his run till tomorrow after the hanging, and we have

149

plenty of ammunition for a stand!"

"Better go eat," Bowie suggested. "We don't look for anything until just before daybreak."

Doc Holliday inspected the shotguns and rifles while the Texan and Rutledge talked in low tones. When the sheriff returned, Holliday and Rutledge were sleeping soundly in the back room, and Bowie held up a warning hand.

"Better get some sleep, Joe," he suggested. "I've already had mine."

The sheriff nodded and went to his room. Marty Williams and Jack Whipple came in, followed by Slaughter and Bob Hatch. Hatch ran a billiard hall on Allen between Fourth and Fifth where he saw every man who entered town.

"Saw several of Three-finger's gang," he mentioned carelessly. "They walked too soft-like to suit me."

"There's a big show down at the Bird Cage tonight," Slaughter changed the subject. "I think I'll shag down there and listen to Lotta Crabtree sing."

Bob Hatch frowned. "The place will be full of rustlers," he muttered. "Better stay away, John."

Slaughter tapped the pearl-handled forty-five on his leg. "I know them all," he answered quietly. "And some of them might get careless and do some talking."

He smiled easily and left the room. The long night wore away with the forces of the law nodding in tilted chairs. Alamo Bowie straightened when the door opened to admit Nellie Gray, and his chair hit the floor when he hurried to take the steaming tray she carried.

"Cell six," he muttered, and led the way through the back room. "Looks like he's waiting up!"

Bull Clanton was a changed man. His heavy face was thinner and marked with deeply-etched lines. His thick legs were stretched out on the cot while he propped his shoulders against the head of the cell. He smiled at Nellie Gray and pointed to the open prayer book on his lap.

"Got a heap of comfort from that," he said slowly. "Been better off if I had read it before I came to the forks in the road and took the owl-hoot trail. You mind leavin' me talk to the Angel alone, Texan?"

Bowie nodded and left the cell. "Don't stay long," he whispered to the woman. "I've got reasons."

Nellie Gray came back to the office in fifteen minutes. Fred Rutledge roused up and went back to lock the cell. Alamo Bowie waited for the woman to speak, and she came close to his chair and whispered in a soft voice.

"Just before daylight. They think Clanton is in an outside cell."

"I'll walk home with you," Bowie answered as softly.

Nellie Gray shook her head. "You better stay here, Alamo," she told him. "I am not afraid, and you have your duty to do."

She pressed his hand and walked from the office as straight as an arrow. Tall for a woman, with the full rounded lines of mature beauty. He watched until the door closed softly, and when he turned, Jack Whipple

151

was watching him thoughtfully.

"I've knowed Nellie several years," the little swamper muttered. "Yo're lucky, Mister."

"About this raid," Bowie answered coldly. "Every man keeps a shotgun close to his hand. Slaughter and Hatch will get in a cell farther back where they can command the front door. Williams and you will watch the back. Rutledge and I will stay here in the front with the sheriff."

John Slaughter came in and smiled frostily. "Fifteen of them killers in town that I knows of," he reported crisply. "There was sixteen, but this other feller was sitting in a box right near the stage. He took a shot at an acrobat what was doing tricks on a bar, and Buckskin Frank cut down on him."

"Kill him?" Rutledge asked.

"You ever know Buckskin Frank Leslie to miss that close?"

Alamo Bowie shrugged. "You see Three-finger?" he asked carelessly, but his gray eyes were narrow slits.

The stocky cattleman shook his head. "Didn't see hide nor hair of him," he grunted. "Mebbe he's give up the idea."

"Not him," Marty Williams cut in quickly. "That big jigger is sitting back somewhere doing the thinking for the gang. You wait and see!"

Again conversation lagged as the hours dragged away. Alamo Bowie called the sheriff and stationed his men at their posts. Joe Blaine glanced through a window and reached for a shotgun.

"An hour before dawn," he said slowly. "Crowd coming down the street."

Alamo Bowie came to the window and counted the approaching horsemen. Fred Rutledge laid rifles and shotguns near each window and broke open boxes of shells. The Texan turned back with a grunt.

"Fourteen in that first bunch," he reported. "More following behind them, but I couldn't say for sure that they belong with the outlaws."

The outlaw gang were riding silently, and they disappeared in a gulch that ran down behind the jail. A shotgun roared out suddenly, and the darkness was split with jagged splashes of red and orange flame.

"Sounded like dynamite to me," the sheriff shouted, and raced through the cell blocks.

Four or five prisoners shouted and cursed to be released. Joe Blaine skidded to a stop on the stone floor in the rear where John Slaughter was triggering a shotgun at a group down in the gulch. Bob Hatch discarded his shotgun and reached for a rifle. Joe Blaine took a station and pressed trigger as fast as he could lever shells.

Three men were down among the attackers. The rest mounted their horses and took cover, and the sheriff turned back to the room and swore softly. One corner of the cell block was blown away, but Bob Hatch grinned through the powder smoke.

"They threw a bomb," he explained. "The jigger that did it is laying out there looking up at the stars."

"Something funny about this," Blaine muttered. "We figgered they would rush the front door."

Alamo Bowie came back and stared at the wreckage. Not a shot was being fired at the jail, and then Bob Hatch held up his hand for silence. Pick axes and sledges were battering loudly from the lot in back of the jail yard, and the sheriff swore under his breath.

"Somebody busting down that grand-stand," he muttered. "You reckon it's those outlaws?"

"Wouldn't be surprised," John Slaughter grinned. "Bowie and I had a talk about it just before I went up to see the show at the Bird Cage."

"Mebbe it's a secret," the sheriff growled.

"Well it was," Slaughter chuckled. "Nellie Gray thought it was inhuman to sell seats that away, and Bowie promised to do something about it. I just dropped a hint in Buckskin Frank's ear, and it sounds like he passed the word on to the gang."

The sheriff glanced at the Texan. "Didn't see how we could get out there and do it," Bowie explained. "So John and I made medicine and figgered that those outlaws would jump at the chance to cheat the public. Looks like they done a good job, and it's too late now for the owners to build a new one."

Doc Holliday came down the steps with Jack Whipple. The gambler shrugged his shotgun under his coat where it hung by a broad strap. Then he looked at his watch and pulled his black hat low.

"I'm taking a *pasear* up town to look things over before the hanging," he muttered. "There's something funny about this raid!"

"Better stay here, Doc," the sheriff advised. "There's fourteen of those rustlers on the loose."

154

"Eleven," Bob Hatch corrected, and jerked a thumb toward the three bodies in the gully. "But the rest of the gang might have come over from Charleston."

The gambler shrugged carelessly. Then he smiled and reached into his pocket while the others watched him. He took a thin sheath of bills from his wallet and passed them over to Bowie.

"There ought to be a thousand there," he said quietly. "The sheriff bet that much against yore red hoss that you wouldn't last forty-eight hours. It's past that now."

Joe Blaine smiled with sincere happiness. "Never paid off a bet more willing in my life," he chuckled. "No arguments, Texan. I never really began to live till you rode into Tombstone on that big red hoss."

Doc Holliday watched the two strong men grip hands, and walked out quietly while they were talking in low tones. He frowned when he stepped to the street and saw the thin figure of Jack Whipple up ahead in the gray gloom. The little swamper was heading for the Russ house, and the gambler twitched his hat and followed slowly.

His greenish eyes opened wide when he caught the moving shape of a horse in the alley behind the frame hotel. Cat-eyes that could see in the dark, and Holliday recognized the big black horse Three-finger Jack always used when speed was essential. His pace quickened in an effort to over-take Jack Whipple, but a sudden fit of coughing slowed him down and made him lean against a fence.

Doc Holliday whipped a hand to his breast pocket

and smothered the racking cough. His slender body bent at the middle while his eyes closed with weakness. All his will power was thrown into a titanic effort to control the paroxysm, but it was five minutes before he straightened up and wiped the crimson froth from his bloodless lips.

"A bullet will get me first," he muttered huskily. "Like I've always said!"

His steps were slow when he mounted the wide porch of the Russ House and entered the lobby. His eyes contracted to change with the light, and then he climbed the stairs to the second floor. A light was shining under the crack of Bowie's door, and Doc Holliday gripped the handle of his sixgun and pushed the door open with a jerk.

A woman's scream warned him too late. Blinding lights exploded in the gambler's brain when a heavy gun thudded down on his head to mash the four-X beaver flat. With the last ounce of his strength, the tall slender gambler buckled his knees and slumped to the heavy carpet like a piece of rubber hose, and he did not hear the grunt of satisfaction behind him.

Three-finger Jack swiveled the heavy gun in his hand to hold the drop on Jack Whipple who was just staggering to his feet with a ragged gash on the side of his head. Nellie Gray was seated on the bed with her arms tied to the posts. The outlaw closed the door behind him and waited for the little swamper to get his senses.

"I didn't hit you very hard," he said quietly. "I wanted you to see Doc Holliday fall on his face."

Jack Whipple took a deep breath and shook his head. His pale blue eyes stared at the outlaw while he swayed unsteadily on his thin legs. Glanced at Nellie Gray and down to the still figure on the floor, and his voice was a thin whistle of maddened passion when he screamed at Three-finger Jack.

"Tie her loose or you'll swing! Every man in Tombstone will ride gun-sign on you for what you done to the Angel!"

"The Angel hasn't been hurt . . . yet," the outlaw snarled, and then controlled himself. "I was hoping the Texan would come barging in here!"

"I had a hunch," and the little swamper was more composed. "I had a feeling you were hatching up a sneak!"

"You got yore hunch too late," the outlaw sneered. "I use my head for something else besides just a place to hang my Stetson."

"That raid was a blind," and Whipple sparred for time while he tuned his hearing for the sound of steps in the hall.

Three-finger Jack smiled sneeringly. "No one coming," he muttered. "And you killed Pecos Traynor!"

Jack Whipple straightened proudly. "I killed him," he boasted. "Just as easy as Bowie will kill you!"

"Pass Bowie for now," the outlaw answered, and holstered his gun. "You won't see Bull Clanton hang!"

The little swamper stared for a moment and became very still. With the jail not more than a block away, the sounds of gun-fire would be easily heard. Somebody was sure to investigate, and he studied the thin hard face and tried to solve the puzzle.

"A gent can't die but one time," and his voice was low and careless. "So I killed Pecos Traynor!"

"Pecos was fairly rapid with his hardware," the outlaw answered thoughtfully. "Nearly as fast as Big Enough Smith."

"And Big enough is out on Boot Hill," Whipple taunted.

"Don't do it, Jack," Nellie Gray pleaded earnestly. "He will kill you sure!"

Three-finger Jack smiled and hooked his hand in his belt under his black coat. "Right again," he agreed quietly. "That little rabbit said the word that caused all this grief. He testified in court, and it was him who recognized Pecos. He's lived too long!"

Jack Whipple crouched forward with his right hand hooked to fit the handle of his old gun. His pale eyes were tiny slits through which the glare-ice of cold anger glistened brightly. Rusty run-over boots planted wide apart for balance, and drops of thin bright blood dripping from his jutting chin.

"I'll take the chance," he whispered, and his voice was a keening whisper of grim determination. "Bull Clanton swings in another half hour!"

His hand slapped down and found familiar wood like the flick of a whip-lash. The tall outlaw brought his right hand from under the tails of his coat with a sweeping throw. A silver streak flashed through the yellow light from the coal-oil lamp, and Jack Whipple gurgled hoarsely and spilled his half-drawn gun to the carpet.

Nellie Gray stifled the scream that leaped to her full lips. The ivory handle of a throwing knife was gleaming against the throat of the little swamper, and he fell forward on top of his gun like a slender sapling that has been up-rooted by the silent rush of water. Nellie Gray closed her eyes with a soft moan and fainted for the first time in her life.

CHAPTER XII

Three-finger Jack nodded with no show of emotion on his dark face. He glanced at the limp body of Doc Holliday and sat down at the little table. Picked up a pencil and wrote a few lines in a fine Spencerian hand. Then he placed the note in the gambler's hand with a cold smile curling the corners of his hard mouth.

The gray of a new day was lighting to break through the shadows of night when the outlaw slipped through the back door of the hotel with Nellie Gray in his strong arms. A moment later he was in the saddle on the powerful Black, slipping silently through the shadows. The woman was strangely quiet and limp against his chest and Three-finger Jack smiled grimly and held his horse to a walk.

Back in the hotel, Doc Holliday coughed weakly and tried to sit up. The black Stetson was jammed tightly around his ears, and his left hand loosed it while he braced himself against the floor with his right. His eyes were closed from the blow that had felled him, but they opened slowly just a crack when the gambler realized where he was.

The room was oppressively quiet with that stillness which comes only with death. The gambler knew it; closed his eyes again until the fog had cleared enough to allow him to think. Then his right hand whipped suddenly under his coat and came out with thumb earing back the heavy hammers of the deadly sawed-off.

He jerked his body toward the spot where the outlaw had stood, and then the gun sagged in his white hands. Beautiful hands that could manipulate the paste-boards like a magician, or deal out death with the same careless indifference.

"Gone," he husked, and stared at the empty bed.

His eyes dropped to the huddle on the floor and stared intently. Then he became aware of the paper in his left hand. He dropped his eyes and studied for a moment; opened the note and squinted his eyes to read the beautiful writing.

"Alamo Bowie.
"One night I tipped my hat to a stranger. I am holding her as hostage. Nellie Gray for Bull Clanton in a fair exchange. You are the Judge.
"Three-finger Jack!"

"God!"

Doc Holliday forgot his throbbing head while he stared at the note. The first fingers of light were breaking through the curtains of night. The hanging would be held at sunrise, and Three-finger Jack was holding Nellie Gray as hostage for Bull Clanton.

"Bowie can't trade," the gambler whispered hoarsely. "The court has imposed sentence, and there is no repeal. Too late to reach the Governor!"

He crawled painfully to his feet and pressed a hand against his chest when a fit of coughing overtook him. When this passed, he turned the body of Jack Whipple over and stared at the handle of the throwing knife. The little swamper was dead, but he had died instantly. A half-smile still curved the corners of his lips.

Only the bartender was in the Oriental when Doc Holliday slipped through the back door and ordered a tall glass of brandy. The color leaped to his high cheek-bones while he sipped the potent liquor. His eyes narrowed slightly when he glanced in the mirror of the back-bar and caught a movement in the rear.

"Thanks, Yuma," he said carelessly to the bar-dog. "Be seeing you!"

He walked slowly down the long saloon and through the back door. A hand reached out and pulled him to the deeper shadows, and the gambler patted the hand on his arm.

"I saw you, Big-Nose," he said softly. "It will be sunrise in a few minutes," he added significantly.

Big-Nose Annie nodded her head grimly. She had the most beautiful figure in Tombstone, and the ugliest face. Hard coarse mouth with a tremendous nose spreading above it to give her the nick-name by which she was known. Queen of the most notorious red-light house on Tough Nut street, but loyal to her friends.

"It's the Angel, Doc," she whispered fiercely. "Three-finger Jack will kill me, but he brought her to the house just a few minutes ago. What's the matter with your head?"

"Three-finger slapped me to sleep," the gambler answered carelessly. "Just before he took Nellie."

"You got to tell the Texan," the woman said excitedly. "She loves him, and Nellie is a lady!"

"Who is with Nellie?"

"No one right now. Three-finger locked her in a back room and took the key. No window in that room. If they hang Bull Clanton, he is going to kill Nellie Gray!"

"He won't," the gambler snapped. "Slip in there and tell Yuma to give you a pint of brandy for me!"

"I don't want to be seen," Big-Nose Annie objected. "I have a pint down at the house."

The gambler took her arm and faded into the shadows. Keeping to the back streets, they made their way to the bawdy house and entered the back door. Doc Holliday followed the woman into her private apartment and drank deeply from the bottle of brandy.

"Tell the girls to keep to their rooms," he whispered, and walked out into the hall.

He picked up a fireman's ax standing in a corner. Facing the last door at the end of the hall, he struck a sharp blow that shattered the flimsy lock. Then he was inside with the door closed, and his greenish eyes pierced the gloom and saw Nellie Gray on the bed.

"Nellie," he called softly.

A soft moan answered him, and the gambler raced to the bed and cut the ropes that held her prisoner. A bandanna gag was torn away, and the Angel of Tombstone sat up and tried to straighten her black hair.

"Alamo! Is he all right?"

"Right as rain," Holliday answered. "I want you to come with me now."

He led her back to the apartment of Big-Nose Annie and shut the door. Annie ran forward and took Nellie Gray's hands.

"I'm not fit to wipe your shoes, Nell," she said huskily. "But I'd die willingly for a woman like you. Did he do you hurt, darlin'?"

Nellie Gray smiled gently. "Not a bit, Annie," she answered. "But he will kill you if he finds out."

"I'd be better off dead," Big-Nose Annie muttered. "And I'd be dead now if it wasn't for Doc yonder. What he can see in a tramp like me . . . ?"

"I can see the heart of a Saint underneath that ugly face of yours," the gambler said gruffly. "Pretty is as pretty does, and you are a square-shooter, old pard!"

Big-Nose Annie smiled happily. She did not resent being called ugly, and her blue eyes were tender when she put an arm around the gambler and held him close.

"You and me are just drift-wood in the tide of Life, gambling-man," she told him. "But we're better folks for having known Nellie Gray."

"I'm leaving Nellie with you," Holliday answered, and shrugged free. "I'll be back after the hanging, and you girls stay in here with the doors locked. Mind what I say!"

He left the apartment and closed the door behind him. Waited until he heard the key turn in the lock, and a sinister smile rode his thin lips when he walked out to Tough Nut street and made his way to the jail. A crowd was gathered outside the jail yard, and the sun was just peeping over the distant Dragoons when the gambler entered the office.

Alamo Bowie met him at the door. "Where you been, Doc? We thought something was wrong!"

"Jack Whipple is dead," the gambler answered calmly. "He was killed up in your room!"

The Texan stiffened. "Three-finger?" he whispered.

The gambler nodded. "Whipple must have had a hunch that the outlaw was laying for you. Three-finger threw a knife through his throat."

The Texan gripped the gambler with fingers that bit like steel. "Nellie?" he said hoarsely. "She all right?"

"Nellie is all right," the gambler answered with a smile. "I saw her not more than five minutes ago."

The Texan breathed a sigh of relief. "The sheriff is getting Bull Clanton ready," he said quietly, and glanced through the window. "It's sunrise!"

They walked back through the cell block to number six. The Parson from the Universal church was with the doomed man, and Clanton glanced up when he saw the gambler.

"Nellie," he said, and his blustering voice was soft. "Is the Angel all right?"

"She's all right, Bull," Holliday answered. "Sent you her best regards, and said for you to remember yore mother, and to keep yore head up."

Bull Clanton smiled happily. "I got it coming," he answered with emotion. "But I was afraid Three-finger would do something to the Angel."

He stared fixedly at the gambler, and Doc Holliday drooped his left eye-lid. "I left Nellie just five minutes ago," he answered quietly. "She is staying with friends until . . ."

"Let's go," Bull Clanton said to the sheriff. "And I don't need any help. I lived like an animal, but I can die like a man. No hard feelings from me, Bowie!"

He reached out a huge hand and waited for the Texan to speak. Alamo Bowie stared a moment and then gripped Clanton hard. Sheriff Blaine and Fred Rutledge looked away, and the sheriff muttered under his breath.

"Never felt like this about a job of law-work before. Mebbe he wants to talk."

Fred Rutledge shook his head, but the sheriff faced Clanton. "It's time, feller," Blaine said huskily. "You like to ease yore conscience any before you walk out yonder in the sunlight?"

Bull Clanton shrugged his huge shoulders. "I ain't never been a rat, sheriff," he answered quietly. "I'll pay for what I did just like Big Enough paid. He's waiting out there at the forks of the trail for me, and we always been saddle-pards. I ain't talking about nobody else!"

The sheriff nodded and stepped aside to clear the door. Bull Clanton closed his eyes for a moment while his lips moved silently. The prayer book was clutched tightly in one big hand, and then he walked from the cell and began the last slow march.

Alamo Bowie and the sheriff followed right behind him. Doc Holliday opened the back door and stepped outside. Perhaps fifty citizens were gathered in the yard where the grim gallows awaited with the hangman's noose dangling from the cross beam. Sheriff Blaine walked up the steps first and took his position near the trap.

Bull Clanton allowed his eyes to wander over the crowd while he slowed his steps as though enjoying the sunshine. Fred Rutledge reached out a hand and stopped him; tied the big hands firmly behind the massive back. Bull Clanton smiled a trifle and walked up the steps without help.

He glanced over the wall where the grand-stand had been erected. Nothing was left except a tangled mass of wreckage, and he turned to the sheriff and nodded his big head.

"Let 'er flicker, Joe," he said steadily. "A gent can't die but one time."

Sheriff Blaine slipped the noose over the doomed man's head and adjusted the knot behind the left ear. Doc Kramer waited with watch in hand, and the sheriff appealed once more to the prisoner.

"Any last word?" he asked shakily.

Bull Clanton smiled. "Yeah," he answered. "Just tell the Angel that I wasn't afraid . . . to meet my God. So long, sheriff!"

Sheriff Blaine stepped back and jerked the lever to spring the trap. Bull Clanton dropped suddenly before he could move his big number twelve boots. Then he hung limply with his head cocked to one side.

Silence from the crowd while they watched the gruesome scene. Alamo Bowie had turned his back while his gray eyes stared at the toes of his boots. He did not turn until Doc Kramer made his solemn announcement.

"The prisoner is dead. He died almost instantly. His heavy weight broke his neck!"

Deep sighs from the crowd as they stretched to their feet and turned silently away. Later there would be talk in plenty, but right now the spectre of death was too close for conversation. Fred Rutledge closed the gate and came back to the office where Bowie was talking quietly with Marty Williams and the sheriff.

"Where's Doc Holliday?" the deputy asked. "I didn't see him in the yard."

Alamo Bowie whirled with a frown. "I felt something was wrong all the time," he muttered. "We better get up to my room and make sure!"

The sheriff walked shoulder to shoulder with him to the hotel on the corner. Bowie leaped up the steps and through the lobby; tore out for the second floor with the sheriff running to keep up.

The Texan palmed his gun and slammed through the door with his gray eyes darting all about. Then he holstered the weapon and went to his knees beside the body of Jack Whipple just as the others came in.

"Dead," he whispered, and pointed to the haft of the knife. "I expected to find Doc here. You seen him?"

The sheriff shook his head. Then he reached down, suddenly and picked up a scrap of paper from the floor. Held the paper away to catch the light, and the Texan saw his name and snatched the note.

"God," he muttered hoarsely. "He's going to kill Nellie!"

The sheriff took the note and read it aloud. Marty Williams shook his head soberly.

"He just as good as says he will do to Nellie whatever we do to Bull," he whispered. "And we hung Bull!"

Alamo Bowie gripped his hands until the nails bit deep. "Let's figger this thing out," he said softly, but his face was pale. "Doc Holliday told me that Nellie was all right. Said he had left here just five minutes before the hanging."

"Three-finger was here while we were hanging Clanton," and Marty Williams shook his head.

"Wrong," Bowie snapped. "Whipple was killed before Doc came to the jail, and Doc was buffaloed over the skull by Three-finger!"

"And Doc told Bull that the Angel was staying with friends," Fred Rutledge added. "But Doc knew about this note!"

"He should have told me," Bowie gritted.

"Clanton had to hang," the sheriff interrupted quickly. "The question is, where's Doc Holliday? I figger he's gone where Nellie is hiding. Now why do you reckon he cut out so soon?"

The Texan was staring at the bed. "Nellie was a prisoner there," and his voice was a whisper. "Three-finger was here and killed Whipple, and he took Nellie with him!"

"Must have had a hoss out behind," Marty Williams offered. "Might be you could read the sign, Bowie."

The Texan raced from the room and down the back stairs. He was on hands and knees when the others reached the back yard, and Alamo Bowie was crawling along the ground like a hunting dog on the scent. No other marks in the thick dust, and the others followed silently while the grim-faced Texan followed the sign down the alley.

A horse roared away out in front on Tough Nut street. The Texan paused to listen with hands slipping to his guns. Then he lowered his head again and continued to follow the tracks. He paused at the back door of a house set well back, but fronting Tough Nut street, and Joe Blaine caught up with him there.

"Couldn't be here, Alamo," he muttered. "Big-Nose Annie runs this dive."

The Texan shook his hand loose. "That black hoss stopped here," and his deep voice was savage. "He was packin' double from the depth of his tracks."

"Might be yo're right," the sheriff admitted, but Alamo Bowie was paying no attention. Now he was pointing to the ground.

"Look," the Texan whispered. "Doc Holliday has been here. It must have been him brought Nellie."

The sheriff stared and shook his head. "Big-Nose Annie and Doc Holliday is just like that," he muttered, and crossed two fingers. "She'd die for Doc!"

"I'm going in," Bowie muttered. "Three-finger brought Nellie here and Doc followed. That's why he cut out the way he done at the hanging!"

He shouldered through the door with the Twins cuddled in his big hands. He paused for a moment when he saw a door standing open three steps beyond. Then he leaped swiftly through the opening with the hammers of his guns dogged back, and hell blazing from his narrowed gray eyes.

The hammers slipped slowly under his thumbs to ride on empties, and the tall Texan sheathed the weapons with the same move. Doc Holliday was lying face down in a pool of blood, and a ragged gash parted thin black hair almost in the middle. The Texan hunkered down and felt for a heart-beat, and a hoarse cry burst from his throat.

"Creased him! Doc is still alive!"

"Thank God! Oh, thank God!"

A pair of white hands tore the gambler away, and the Texan teetered back off balance. Big-Nose Annie was cradling the gambler's head against her breast; a breast that gleamed like white marble in the half light. She rocked slowly and crooned to the man in her arms, and Doc Holliday tried to sit up clawing for his gun.

"Don't move, sweetheart," the woman whispered in his ear, and kissed him tenderly. "I heard the shot, and I thought you were dead!"

The gambler pushed slowly erect and staggered until Big-Nose Annie steadied him. "I coughed at the wrong time," and he smiled weakly. "I was facing him for an even break, and then I started to cough!"

"That cough saved yore life, Doc," the Texan muttered. "Nellie! Is she all right?"

"She's in my apartment," Annie answered quickly, and pulled the silken robe about her full figure. "If you gentlemen will excuse me, I'll make myself more presentable."

Alamo Bowie restrained himself and turned to Doc Holliday. "That note?" he asked sharply. "We found it on the floor in my room!"

"I found it in my hand when I roused around back there after Three-finger had cold-cocked me," the gambler muttered. "Then Big-Nose saw me in the Oriental and brought me the news. Said the outlaw was holding Nellie here in this room."

"You should have told me," Bowie muttered, but his right hand gripped the gambler hard with sign-talk. "You come here?"

Doc Holliday nodded. "Three-finger was gone, so I broke down the door and put Nellie with Big Nose. I knew Three-finger would be right back here after the hanging, so I slipped away and hid here instead. He came!"

"That was his hoss I heard pounding away," Bowie muttered. "Funny for him to miss you that close!"

The gambler smiled wanly. "Like I said, I coughed at the wrong time," he murmured. "Doubled me over before I could get to my gun, and his shot creased me while I was going down. Head hurts like hell!"

"You should have let me know," the Texan growled. "He might have killed you!"

Doc Holliday smiled that thin-lipped smile. "I'm not much good in this world to anyone except Big Nose," he said quietly. "Five times now I've faced fast

171

gun-hawks thinking that mebbe a slug would beat the bugs. Looks like I can't win that away, pard."

Alamo Bowie winced and put an arm over the gambler's stooped shoulders. "I know, Doc," he said huskily. "It's hell to keep on waiting when you know yo're marked. I'm thanking you for both Nellie and myself for what you did for us."

"Someday I'll meet Three-finger again," the gambler muttered. "And when I do . . . ?"

"When you do you'll pass," the Texan clipped. "He's my man, and after what he done to Nellie, I got first show for shore!"

The gambler glanced at the hard face and blazing gray eyes. Then he nodded slowly and held out his hand.

"You got first show," he agreed. "But I'll take seconds if he tallies for you!"

CHAPTER XIII

Tombstone was strangely quiet when Alamo Bowie returned to the Russ house for breakfast. The streets were crowded with whispering men who seemed subdued and thoughtful while they discussed the hanging of Bull Clanton. The tall special agent washed his face and hands in the wash room, and Nellie Gray was waiting when he made his way to the table far back in the corner.

"Please don't, Alamo," she began softly, when he took his place without speaking. "I can see it in your eyes."

The Texan made no attempt to cloud the sign. "I'll get him," he promised grimly. "I've got him marked for my cutter."

"But he didn't hurt me," Nellie Gray insisted, and her brown eyes winked rapidly to keep back the tears. "He is deadly, Alamo. You might kill him, but he would also kill you!"

The Texan shrugged. "I come here to do a job of work," he muttered. "I'll do it like always!"

The woman sighed softly. "Don't I mean more to you than he does?" she whispered. "After what you told me?"

Alamo Bowie set his teeth. "You mean most everything to me now, Nellie," he answered, and his voice was dry and rasping. "But I couldn't go on living and holding my head up if I dogged it. Down Texas way we don't allow any man to put rough hands on our women folks!"

"I've been in some tough camps, honey," she said slowly. "And no one ever bothered me before. They won't again."

"That's right, they won't," he agreed, and his jaw thrust out pugnaciously. "I'll see to that!"

"He's gone," she said hopefully. "He rode over toward Charleston."

She bit her lip when the Texan raised his head quickly with an eager light shining in his gray eyes. "Charleston, eh?" he repeated. "Reckon I better ride over that away after I eat."

"Alamo! I'm sorry I told you," she whispered in deep distress. "I'm asking you not to go!"

Alamo Bowie grunted and attacked his breakfast.

Then he went up to his room which had been cleaned up during his absence. He was seated on the edge of the bed cleaning the Twins when the door opened to admit Nellie Gray. She came straight to him and took a seat with her arms about his muscled body.

"Please, Alamo," she pleaded. "I never needed a man before, but I do need you. Life would be mighty empty without you."

"Three-finger Jack put hands on you," the Texan muttered. "And he shot Doc Holliday."

"Annie is taking care of Doc," Nellie answered hopefully. "It was just a scalp wound!"

The Texan took her soft shoulders in his hard hands and stared deep in her brown eyes. "I never loved a woman before in all my born days," and his deep voice was husky. "Not till you came along and showed me what I have been missing. But I had a job to do that came ahead of meeting you, Nellie. I promised Tom Scudder, and the Wells Fargo Company. I likewise made a promise to Marshal Charley Dade when he made me a deputy U. S. Marshal."

"But you did meet me," and Nellie Gray laid her soft cheek against his hand. "You met me, and you said . . . you said you wanted to take care of me from now on out."

He nodded moodily. "I said that, and I meant it," he muttered. "But there's something pulls down inside me when a fast gun-slinger calls my hand. Something that is bigger than me, if you know what I mean!"

His voice was savage and angry; angry with himself. The woman studied his hard face and sighed with understanding. She did know what he meant, and a picture of the long years ahead brought a far-away look to her brown eyes and made them sad. Years when fast gun-slingers would challenge the speed of the only man she had ever loved.

"Alamo," she whispered softly, and leaned closer to him until the swell of her breasts brought a gentle expression of uneasiness to his craggy features. "Look at me, my dear."

The Texan turned his head and looked deep into her eyes. "Children," she began softly. "You want them some day, don't you?"

The Texan bit his lip. "I never did up to now," he muttered hoarsely. "Was always afraid they would be like me. Hard and deadly with killer instinct when some fast Colt-hand calls for show-down. And Life is full of show-downs, Nellie."

Fear flashed across her gentle face for a fleeting moment. "I couldn't bear that, Alamo," she whispered. "Better to leave them unborn for always!"

He nodded hopelessly. "That's what I augered with myself," he admitted moodily. "I've always been a gun-fighter; always will be!"

Nellie Gray took his right hand and held it against her breast. "I don't think so," she contradicted gently. "There's something about a baby that changes a man. Tiny tugging little fingers that seem so helpless and dependent. I've always wanted a baby, Alamo."

"I never did, but . . ." and his voice trailed away with wistfulness. "We could leave here when my work is finished."

"I could leave here, but I probably would stay," she corrected. "Three-finger Jack would be dead, but he would take you with him. He's fast, Alamo. There wouldn't be the flick of an eye-lash between the two of you. I'm sorry you came!"

"Nellie," and he twisted to face her squarely. "Unsay those words!"

She shook her head slowly. "I never cared before," she answered. "I kept busy looking after other folks who seemed to need me. It made me very happy, and then you rode into Tombstone on your big red horse. You looked so competent and strong, but you also looked hard as granite."

He shrugged uncomfortably. "I was just myself," he muttered. "Special agent for Wells Fargo, hired to keep the stage lines running."

"With the Twins tied low on your legs," she continued. "Every man in Tombstone knew you were a professional. Your hands kept brushing the handles of your guns. Your eyes stared at each face and looked right on through to their very souls. Then you looked at me, and did the same thing. I knew then that I loved you, and I knew that you would never be any different."

"I will be different," he answered earnestly. "As soon as this job of work is done."

Nellie Gray shook her head. "I heard you talking to Tom Scudder," she answered sadly. "I saw the eager look in your eyes when he mentioned Black Bart."

Alamo Bowie flushed and turned his head. Once more his gray eyes were flashing with the light of

176

battle. Black Bart was reported even faster than Three-finger Jack, and the tall Texan forgot himself and rubbed the handle of his guns. Nellie Gray sighed softly and recalled him to the present.

"You see," she muttered wearily. "It will always be like that."

Bowie shrugged angrily. "It won't," he growled savagely. "I'll hang up my guns after this job is done. I'll promise never to shoot it out with another man unless he brings it to me and crowds me close!"

"You mean that, Alamo?"

He nodded soberly. "I mean just that," he answered. "I'll only strap on the Twins in self defense!"

Nellie Gray drew him close and kissed him tenderly. "I believe you, Dear," she whispered happily. "Doc Holliday told me that you never broke a promise!"

Alamo Bowie patted her shoulder awkwardly. He could not make pretty speeches, and the years of self-restraint had trained him to cover up his emotions. Only his eyes showed the depth of his feeling, but now those wide gray eyes were an open book. A book which Nellie Gray could read and understand.

"I'll be a good father, Nellie," he stated proudly. "You won't ever be sorry."

Nellie Gray kissed him gently. "I belong to you now, Alamo," she whispered. "We will share all our troubles together."

"That's a contract," he answered quickly, as though some hidden intuition had made him speak. "We're pards for keeps no matter what happens."

Alamo Bowie jerked his head up when a soft knock sounded on the door. Nellie Gray opened the door and took a letter from Wing. Her eyes clouded when she read the postmark.

"San Francisco," she muttered. "I wonder if anything is wrong with Mary?"

Alamo Bowie was reloading his long-barreled guns. He glanced up after snugging the Twins down in the oiled scabbards on his long legs. Then he was on his feet when he saw the tears in Nellie's brown eyes. She bit her lips and held the letter toward him, and he took it gingerly and stepped back.

"Nellie," he whispered. "I understand, Pard," and he came forward and took her in his arms. "It's my job too!"

Nellie Gray sobbed softly and then wiped her eyes. "No, Alamo," she said firmly. "I won't let you assume such a burden!"

Alamo Bowie disregarded her. "Two little buttons all made to order," he whispered. "A little gal and a boy just big enough to straddle a kak. You reckon they will like a jigger like me?"

"They'd love you, Alamo," she answered promptly, and then her face clouded again. "Mary was my only sister, and they buried her last week. Those poor little orphans!"

"It's tough on them," the Texan answered softly, and his deep voice was a sympathetic drawl of sincerity. "But you and me can make them forget pretty soon. You reckon they will like it out on a cattle spread where they can have their own hosses to ride?"

"Cattle spread?" and she stared at him blankly.

"I got a pard over in New Mex," Bowie explained. "Sheriff Joe Grant of Luna county. Him and me saved our dinero and bought us some good land and cattle again the time when we quit riding for the law. The B Bar G is what I'm talking about, Nellie. I figgered you and me would live there when I finished my work."

"It wouldn't be fair to you, Alamo," and Nellie Gray shook her head firmly. "I release you from your promise. It's my duty to raise Mary's two chicks!"

The Texan took her shoulders in his hard hands and shook her gently. "You made a deal with me," and his voice was crisp. "You shook hands on it man-style, and I aim to hold you to yore promise. I ain't never had a chick nor child, and now you want to rob me just when something bobs up to make me happier than I've ever been before, 'ceptin' once."

"Alamo," and her throaty voice was a song. "You really mean it makes you happy to think of having Mary's two kiddies?"

"Way down inside," he murmured huskily. "Something keeps a jumpin' and a poundin' when I think of those little buttons. I never felt it when I was facing a killer," and his tone was one of awe.

"And the other time," she whispered. "What was that, Alamo?"

"That was the time you kissed me," he muttered, and turned his face away to hide the flush. "My heart stopped there for a spell of time and flopped clear over. I couldn't hardly breathe, and things just sotter spun around while you held me tight and talked soft-like till I quit boogering and bedded down."

"Alamo," and she turned him slowly to gaze deep into his eyes. "You are so big and fine down underneath that terrible hardness. A hardness that came from matching guns with the hardest outlaws in the southwest. And you really want Mary's little ones?"

"Want 'em? I'd eat my heart out now if I couldn't have 'em," and he glared at her like a mother bear about to lose her cubs. "When you going over to fetch 'em back?"

"I'm going to keep my promise, Alamo," she answered softly, and her face was lighted up with a deep happiness that vibrated through all the room. "At first I thought it was an imposition, but now I know that it would be wrong to keep them all for myself."

He seized her hands eagerly. "You go over there right away and get them," he almost shouted. "Tell 'em Alamo can't hardly wait till they get here!"

Nellie Gray smiled and turned over the letter. "You didn't read the back page," she chided. "It says here that the children will arrive at Fairbanks tomorrow morning!"

"A whole day to wait," he complained. "A gal and a boy chip!"

"Like as not they will need new clothes," Nellie smiled. "I'll get them some today."

Alamo Bowie dug down in his pocket and came out with a roll of paper money. "Use this," he suggested eagerly.

"I can't take your money," and Nellie Gray drew back.

The Texan chuckled. "Not my money," he explained. "Sheriff Joe Blaine and I had a little run-in the day I drifted to town. He bet me a thousand against my Snapper hoss that I wouldn't last forty-eight hours. Joe paid off last night, so you can take this dinero and get those chips fitted out in good shape."

Nellie Gray smiled and took the money. "You had no business to gamble that way," she scolded gently. "So I'll just take your winnings and use it for a good cause. You blessed old fraud!"

Alamo Bowie seized her around the waist and executed a giant swing. "Dossie Doe," he shouted. "Swing yore partner!"

"Alamo! You are mussing me all up, and I must meet my guests down stairs. But I love it," she admitted with a smile.

The Texan released her and became instantly serious. "I had forgot there for a time," and his voice was gruff. "Three-finger was lining out for Charleston over on the San Pedro."

"Wait until after tomorrow," Nellie pleaded. "As long as he stays away from Tombstone."

The Texan shook his head stubbornly. "I promised the sheriff to ride with him and Fred," he explained. "We figgered to keep those owl-hooters on the run now that we got them started. And Nellie?" and his eyes narrowed and swept down to a dark spot on the carpet.

"Yes, Alamo," she answered, and then followed his gaze.

"That's where Jack Whipple bled out," he told her

grimly. "And we owe something to that little swamper for what he done. He was thinking about you when he came back here, Nellie."

The woman shuddered. "Three-finger caught me when I returned from the jail," she whispered. "He drew his gun and made me come into your room. Then he tied me up and put that gag in my mouth."

"Keep on talking," Bowie grated. "I never asked you before."

"Then he sat down to wait," the woman continued. "Said he was going to kill you because you broke up his power. Said he was going to kill Joe Blaine for throwing him down."

"He tried," the Texan shrugged. "What else he say?"

"He said he had Blaine elected sheriff, and that he was going to put another man in that would shoot square. And all the time he stood there and practiced with those terrible guns!"

The Texan hunched his shoulders, and the tips of his fingers brushed the handles of his guns. "He fast?" he asked softly.

Nellie Gray shuddered violently. "I never saw anything so fast in my life," she whispered. "The guns just seemed to leap out of the holsters and into his hands. Both hands moved like lightning, like they were both pulled by the same string!"

"Sit down there," the Texan muttered. "Watch me close!"

Nellie Gray stared at him and sat on the edge of the bed. Alamo Bowie walked across the room and put his back against the door. Then his hands flicked down and up with effortless ease. The Twins leaped up and winked in the bright sunlight before they disappeared when the Texan waved his hands carelessly.

Nellie Gray came to her feet and nodded her black head emphatically. "Now I know why you have lived through these ten years you have rode for the law," she said positively. "I won't worry any more about you, Alamo."

The Texan smiled and opened the door. "I won't be back for dinner," he said carelessly. "We will eat over at Charleston."

"I didn't finish," and the woman's voice was once more serious. "Please close the door."

Bowie closed the door with a frown. "Three-finger sat there and watched the sky," she continued. "Sometimes he was fidgety, but he quieted down when a group of horsemen rode down the street."

"That was his gang," Bowie murmured. "Go on!"

"He bragged that they were going to tear down those seats so the people could not see the hanging," she whispered. "Then I knew that in some way you were working your plan to help me."

"Slaughter got the word to Buckskin Frank Leslie," the Texan admitted. "We saw the gang coming down the gulch behind the jail."

"They were going to blow up the jail even if it killed Peters and Bull Clanton," Nellie continued. "Three-finger laughed when that first bomb exploded."

"It cost them three men," the Texan said grimly.

"But we couldn't figure out why they didn't attack the front."

"We heard the shooting," the woman explained. "Then Three-finger looked to his guns and said it wouldn't be long. Said he knew you would be barging back here to see if I was all right!"

"I wanted to come," Bowie admitted. "But I had to stay right there. But we missed little Jack Whipple."

"He came so quiet we never heard him," Nellie whispered. "He knocked on the door, and Three-finger tiptoed and stood against the wall. Whipple opened the door and came in, and the outlaw hit him over the head with his gun!"

Alamo Bowie was muttering under his breath. "Jack fell on his face like he was dead," Nellie continued. "Three-finger dragged him back there and sat down to wait. Then Doc Holliday walked into the same trap."

"It wouldn't have been so bad if he had shot him," the Texan muttered. "But to throw that *cuchillo* clear through his neck!"

Nellie Gray bit her lips. "I tried to scream, but I couldn't," she whispered. "Doc Holliday was lying on the floor when Whipple roused around. He got to his feet and called Three-finger for show-down."

"We'd have heard the shot," Bowie agreed. "But Jack Whipple was fast!"

"Three-finger had his hand on the belt under his coat," Nellie explained. "He made a swing when Whipple rapped down for his gun . . ."

"Doc Holliday," Bowie muttered. "What about him?"

"I fainted," Nellie confessed, and blushed with shame. "But I know that Three-finger wrote a note to you and put it in Doc's hand. Then he carried me down the back way and took me to Big-Nose Annie's. He set another trap for you there, Alamo."

"Thanks to Doc, I didn't spring it," the Texan muttered. "I'll square up for Doc!"

"I'm afraid, Alamo," Nellie moaned. "Afraid because he is so treacherous, and he has brains. So far we have had all the luck!"

The Texan snugged his guns low and again opened the door. "I'll be seeing you come supper time," he muttered gruffly. "Don't you worry none."

Nellie Gray kissed him tenderly. "Do be careful, lover," she whispered. "You must, Alamo. You are a father now!"

"Dang if I ain't," he said happily, and then the old hard look rippled back to his face. "Be seeing you tonight!"

CHAPTER XIV

Three-finger Jack threw his tin dishes down beside the fire and glanced at the ring of men back in Skeleton Wash. Cowboys who had taken the wrong fork in the trail to ride outside the law under the leadership of the black-eyed killer facing them now with boots spread wide apart.

There was something compelling in the dark thin face with the black mustaches framing cruel lips that seldom smiled. Man after man shoved his dishes aside and glanced up uneasily. Glanced away just as quickly when they found those piercing black eyes studying them with cold calculation.

Only one man seemed at ease and unafraid, and he smiled behind the stubby beard that covered his pockmarked face. Two heavy guns and a throwing knife hung from his belts, and the heavy sombrero marked him as a man apart. A killer from across the border. He sneered at his companions and stroked the heavy mustachios with his left hand.

"It is as you have say, *mi Capitan,*" he remarked to Three-finger Jack. "These hombres they fear the law."

"But you don't, eh Chavez?" the tall outlaw asked softly.

"Me, I fear no man," the stocky Mexican answered swiftly. "This one you call the *Tejano.* I have hear of him, Senor!"

The tall outlaw watched the Mexican closely. Chavez was rubbing the haft of his throwing knife with a calloused palm while his dark eyes blazed with a sudden anger. Three-finger Jack nodded his head and spoke softly.

"You had a cousin, Chavez," he began. "Feller by the name of Sonora Lopez who figgered he was fast with a knife."

Carlos Chavez snapped his white teeth angrily. "This cousin of me could cut the head from a snake at ten paces, *Capitan,*" he purred softly. "*Por que?* It was I who have teach him!"

"And Alamo Bowie rubbed him out," the tall

outlaw added dryly.

Carlos Chavez growled deep in his throat and kicked a little hole in the dust with his boot. Iron-gray tinged his black hair to mark his age at forty-odd, but his muscular body was saddle-toughened and hard as rock. He nodded his head until the tall sombrero bobbed to set the silver bells tinkling on the brim.

"He kill Sonora," he admitted. "Some say he killed him on what you call the sneak. Me, I have waited to meet this so brave *Tejano!*"

"You will meet him," Three-finger said carelessly. "But don't carry the idea around in yore head that you can out-speed that Texan. There's only one man in Arizona can do that, and I'm him!"

Carlos Chavez pouted his full lips while his dark eyes flashed dangerously. "Me, I have heard what you call different," he grunted. "When this *Tejano* make for throw you in the *carcel!*"

Three-finger Jack waved his right hand while the fires of anger leaped to his black eyes. His gun appeared like magic and covered the Mexican's heart like a gaping tunnel. Chavez frowned and held both hands very still.

"Mebbe you don't know any better, Mex," the outlaw said softly. "But you mention that one more time, and you won't live to be hung!"

He shifted his hand again and the gun disappeared. Carlos Chavez sighed with relief and shifted his big feet. *"Pardone mio, Capitan,"* he murmured. "I am listen."

"You listen and I'll do the talking," the outlaw mur-

187

mured. "You know this Judge Hart that sentenced Bull Clanton?"

"*Si,*" the Mexican answered eagerly. "Leetle fat man; what we call *mucho gordo!*"

"I want that hombre," the outlaw muttered. "Before he sends Lantern-jaw Peters to the snakes den over at Yuma prison!"

"I listen, *Capitan,*" the little Mexican answered respectfully. "You have the plan?"

"Judge Hart lives in a little house behind the Bird Cage Theatre," the outlaw explained. "Tonight you will take two men and capture him. Bring him to the ranch house on the Box C, and don't hurt him too much!"

The Mexican smiled grimly. "Then our *compadre* Peters cannot be sentenced," and he shook his big head. "It shall be as you wish, Senor."

A shifty-eyed buscadero cleared his throat to gain attention. "You hear the latest, chief?" he asked with a grin.

"You mean about the morning stage carrying bullion?" the outlaw asked.

"Naw," and Squint Barrow shrugged his stooping shoulders. "That stage is bringing in something more valuable than gold!"

Three-finger Jack stared at the vicious face for a moment. "Spit it out," he growled impatiently. "You mean the stage is packing jewels?"

"Two of 'em," Squint Barrow chuckled. "A little gal and a button is coming to live with the Angel. Seems like her sister died up in Frisco and left Nellie the brats!"

The tall outlaw stared while he drew a deep breath. His black eyes flashed with eagerness while his mind raced with suddenly-formed plans. Squint Barrow thrust out his chest with newly acquired importance.

"That's the answer," Three-finger murmured softly. "With those kids in our power, we can crack the whip over Alamo Bowie. You can head the reception committee, Squint!"

"I ain't ready to die, boss," Barrow muttered. "You know yoreself that I can't match that Texan with a hand-gun!"

Three-finger Jack stiffened. "Get this straight, you jiggers," he snapped. "I've marked Bowie for my own personal cutter. You, Squint. What's that got to do with these kids?"

"Bowie is going to meet the stage," Barrow explained. "Thought you might want to know, boss."

"That's a right good place where we got Pop Whipple," the outlaw reminded coldly. "And far enough from town to be safe. You heard what I said!"

Squint Barrow shivered and glanced at his companions. "I'll take Chavez and Blackie Mann," he muttered. "But if that Texan shows . . . ?"

"He won't," the tall outlaw clipped. "Take the brats to the Box C and hold them there!"

Blackie Mann grunted and hitched up his crossed belts. "It won't be long now," he said meaningly. "I heard it said that Bowie was going to Dad those kids for his own!"

"Meaning what?" and Three-finger Jack stared until Mann dropped his shifty eyes.

"Meaning that Bowie won't rest until he rides gun-sign on the jigger that bothers those buttons," Mann muttered, and shook his bullet-shaped head.

Three-finger shrugged, and his voice was careless when he answered. "You get those kids and leave the rest of it to me like always. I swore to get even with Nellie Gray for what she done that night in the Crystal Palace, and this chance is made to order. And Squint?"

"Yeah, boss."

"You better save a shell for yoreself if you booger the job," and the tall outlaw glared like a killer-wolf.

"We will not fail, Senor," Carlos Chavez interrupted. "How Sonora Lopez would laugh if he were here."

Three-finger Jack stared coldly. "You gents take saddle-bags to pack the loot," he added. "Close to ten thousand on that stage, and we can use it in our business!"

"You go to Charleston, Senor?" the Mexican changed the subject quickly.

The tall outlaw frowned. "Sheriff Blaine is riding over there to collect taxes," he answered gruffly. "He won't get any taxes, but he might get something else!"

He motioned Squint Barrow and Chavez aside and turned to the waiting outlaws. He counted nine men and nodded with satisfaction. They watched him in silence while he stared thoughtfully.

"Tighten yore cinchas," he snapped. "John Slaughter has a small herd of beef-stuff bunched for the reservations. I know where I can sell that herd for cash, and it fits right in with my plans!"

190

Carlos Chavez shook his head. Three-finger Jack turned on him with a frown of impatience, and the Mexican shrugged his shoulders and lowered his eyes.

"Listen, Chavez," the tall outlaw said quietly. "I give the orders in this gang. Mebbe you don't like the way I figger?"

"This Slaughter is *malo hombre, Senor*," the Mexican muttered. "What you call the very bad man to fool with. We rustle the cattle, *Si*. But we never bother the herds of Senor Juan Slaughter!"

"You and me is different," the outlaw barked. "I take what I want, and Slaughter shoved in his bill where he had no business. On top of that, it gives me a chance to have a talk with sheriff Blaine!"

The Mexican smiled and nodded his head. "I did not know, Senor," he murmured. "And when you talk to the so brave shereef . . . ?"

He smiled again and tapped the handle of his gun. Three-finger Jack stared coldly and shook his head.

"I use my brains as often as my guns," he sneered. "I said I wanted to have a talk with Blaine!"

"Senor," and the Mexican's face was grave. "I have kill many men, and some day Carlos Chavez he will go the same way. Some of them I have face for what you call Show-down, but this *Tejano* is the *diablo!*"

"You worry about the judge and those brats," and the tall outlaw glared until the Mexican turned away with a shrug. "And don't forget, Chavez. We have no room in this gang for an hombre that falls down on the job!"

Chavez turned slowly and tipped his heavy sombrero to the back of his head. "Have not a fear, Senor," he murmured. "Like I have tell you, there are some men I face for show-down!"

The tall outlaw shifted his feet, and his hawk-like face hardened. "And there were several more you killed," he answered softly. "Several men you shot in the back when they were not looking!"

The Mexican nodded his head without blinking. "That is so, Senor," he agreed. "P'raps then we understand each the other."

Three-finger Jack stared for a moment and then turned his back squarely. Both hands were hooked in his gunbelts, and the watching band of outlaws swiveled their eyes on the Mexican and waited. Carlos Chavez raised his head and measured the straight back with appraising eyes. He caught the glint of sun on a nearby tree and smiled. A small mirror for shaving was propped in a low crotch, and he caught the reflection of those narrow black eyes watching him intently.

"You have shaved but recently, Senor Three-finger," he purred musically, and threw back his head to laugh. "It shall be as you have said. First the *Jefe Alcalde,* what you call the judge. Then the treasure which the stage bring in."

Three-finger Jack frowned but controlled his anger quickly. His eyes had caught the knowing expression on the Mexican's face in the mirror, and his right hand ripped down suddenly and flamed with roaring thunder. The mirror shattered and tinkled to the ground, but the smoking gun was back in leather before the pieces had touched earth.

"If that was Bowie . . . ?" and he turned to scowl at Carlos Chavez.

The Mexican crossed himself and returned the glance with a shake of his head. "To break the glass is *malo fortuna, Senor,*" he murmured soberly. "What you call the bad luck!"

The outlaw laughed shortly. "Bad luck for Alamo Bowie," he sneered, and then his face straightened. "Get after that beef-stuff," he growled at the watching outlaws. "Turn it over to Rattle-snake Bill Johnson up in San Luis Pass. What you waiting for?"

The silent outlaws swarmed on their horses and pounded across the alkali flats. Three-finger Jack smiled and nodded at Blackie Mann. Carlos Chavez watched him with brooding eyes and gently shook his head.

"You Blackie," the tall outlaw snapped. "Get into Charleston and leave word with Manuel in the Gold Dollar saloon. Tell him to get Blaine to one side and tell him I want to talk business, and I want to see him alone. He won't get hurt none!"

Blackie Mann forked his kak and lined out for Charleston without argument. He recognized the anger lurking behind those slitted black eyes, and he welcomed the opportunity to remove himself from the place where the mirror had been destroyed. The tall outlaw turned back to the Mexican with a smile.

"It don't pay to get mad, Chavez," he said softly. "It slows up the hand, and blinds the eye."

The Mexican shrugged. "You could kill me, Senor," he answered soberly. "But this *Tejano* he never gets mad. Sonora Lopez was very rapid with knife and gon, but Bowie . . . ?"

"You think Bowie is faster than me?" the outlaw demanded.

The Mexican shrugged and shook his head. "Only the good God knows," he murmured. "But Bowie met the great One-shot Brady, and the *Tejano* is still alive!"

Three-finger Jack bit his lip, and then smiled. "Brady lost his head," he answered slowly. "And even then his shot nicked the Texan on the shoulder. I never lose my head!"

Carlos Chavez glanced meaningly at the shattered mirror. The outlaw followed his glance and clicked his teeth.

"I saw you watching me in the glass," he growled. "Just wanted to show you how much chance you had to shoot me in the back!"

"I saw you watching me," the Mexican muttered softly. "And you saw me watching. You have said, *Amigo mio,* anger makes the hand slow."

The tall outlaw leaned forward suddenly and tapped the Mexican on his thick chest. "You heard my *habla,*" and his voice was vibrant with warning. "I've marked the Texan for my personal cutter, and I'll kill the man who bush-whacks him. *Comprende, hombre?*"

Carlos Chavez shrugged carelessly. "I understand, *Mi Capitan,*" he answered. "P'raps you have the plan when you talk to the shereef?"

The tall outlaw smiled and stepped back. "I have

the plan," he mimicked. "The Texan will be with sheriff Blaine over at Charleston. Bowie can read sign like an Apache, and he will follow the trail of the herd. I want the sheriff to stay at the Gold Dollar!"

Squint Barrow sighed his relief. "It's my job to see that Bowie finds out about the rustled herd," he suggested. "That it, chief?"

"Good head," the tall outlaw praised. "Cut on in and find some *paisano* you can trust. Have him carry the news to the sheriff."

Squint Barrow mounted his horse and rode away with his hat pulled down over his eyes. The outlaw watched him for a moment and then turned to Chavez.

"I don't trust you, Carlos," he admitted frankly. "I saw it in your face when I first mentioned Alamo Bowie. You meant to kill him!"

"Sonora Lopez was my cousin," the Mexican answered slowly. "I took what you call the oath. Someday p'raps, I shall keep that promise!"

"You won't," the outlaw contradicted bluntly. "Bowie answers to me!"

"But if he is lucky?" and the Mexican shrugged and spread his brown hands. "Then it is that I will remember Sonora Lopez!"

Three-finger Jack reached out quickly and seized the Mexican by the shoulder to swing him around. His black eyes were blazing furiously, and he made no attempt to conceal the anger that gripped him beyond all reason. His right hand whipped out and slapped Chavez full across the mouth while the Mexican was off balance. Then he threw the stocky gunman from him and grinned when Chavez tripped and fell to his haunches.

"I've told you for the last time," he gritted savagely, and taloned his right-hand above the open holster on his slender leg.

Carlos Chavez climbed slowly to his feet with his left hand rubbing his lips. The heavy sombrero had fallen to the back of his neck where the throat-latch held it, and his beady little eyes were boring into the outlaw's face without winking.

"You could shoot me, *Si*," the Mexican muttered. "To die is the reward of the brave hombre, but some day you will be sorry that you strike Carlos Chavez with the hand!"

His silky voice was quiet with a peculiar dignity that should have warned the outlaw. Three-finger Jack laughed carelessly and dropped his hand. The Mexican crouched suddenly with his right hand sliding to the back of his belt, and he made his throw with an under-hand cast to send the thin-bladed knife whistling through the air.

Three-finger Jack twitched his right shoulder. The long-barreled gun leaped to his hand and exploded before the sun-light could catch the sheen of polished metal. The singing knife stopped in mid-air and shattered to send a shower of tempered slivers around the crouching Mexican.

Carlos Chavez stared stupidly and picked a sliver from his cheek. His dark eyes regarded it dully before they raised to the face of Three-finger Jack. Then he drooped forward with a sigh and slowly raised his hands.

"I wait, Senor," he said with fatalistic calmness. "I only ask that you shoot straight and quickly!"

The tall outlaw smiled with his lips and holstered his gun. "I don't want to kill you, Chavez," he answered quietly. "But there is only room for one boss in any gang. Just wanted you to feel sure that I'm that feller."

The Mexican caught his breath with a sob. "You will not kill me?" he whispered. "I meant to kill you, Senor!"

"But you are so slow," the outlaw drawled. "Like Sonora Lopez was slow when he met a master. You forget that you taught him all he knew!"

"It is so," the Mexican admitted. "I listen, Senor."

Three-finger Jack nodded his head while a dreamy look came to his black eyes. "You wouldn't savvy, Chavez," he began. "But there is something that is more precious than money and jewels. Something that makes a man forget everything when he hears of another master."

"You speak of the Texan," Chavez murmured. "He is what you call the magician with the six-gon!"

The outlaw nodded. "He has met the best in his own country," he answered. "I have met the fastest over here. We ride on different sides of the law, but down underneath Alamo Bowie is no different than I am. He thinks he is the fastest with a gun, and I *know* that I am!"

"But he might kill you, Senor," the Mexican pointed out. "Better that you let me find him some dark night, and . . . ?"

"I let you live just now, Chavez," and the outlaw's voice was husky. "I'll kill the man who tallies for the Texan. He gets a chance according to the code!"

"The code, Senor?"

The outlaw shrugged. "You wouldn't savvy," he answered wearily. "It's that certain something that keeps a man honest when it comes to show-down. It burns in your heart like the brightest light in all the world. You know the other man is fast, but you know you have him beat. Life would be unbearable if you knew he was faster . . . and you still had to live!"

"Por Dios," the Mexican muttered. "I have hear of this thing you call the code. Sometimes I have stood up, but always when I was sure that I was the fastest. Life is sweet, Senor!"

The tall outlaw shrugged. "It is as bitter as gall sometimes," he muttered. "I would rather be dead now than know that Alamo Bowie had me beat with the tools of my trade!"

Carlos Chavez stared with a puzzled expression on his swarthy face. "It is as you have said, Senor," he admitted slowly. "Me, I do not understand."

Three-finger Jack stared at the toes of his boots before he answered. Then he smiled wistfully and held out his right hand.

"Sorry I lost my head and hit you, Chavez," and his voice was gruff from the effort it took to make the simple apology. "I had no call to go off half-cocked that away."

Carlos Chavez stared his unbelief, and then his dark eyes lighted happily. He grasped the extended hand

and gripped hard.

"That I do understand, Senor Jack," he said excitedly. "It take the brave man to make what you call the sorry. It is nothing, *amigo mio!*"

"We ride," the outlaw said shortly, and mounted the rangy black. "To the Gold Dollar at Charleston, and you shall guard my back."

"With my life, Senor," the Mexican promised earnestly, and Three-finger Jack knew that he had made a loyal friend.

CHAPTER XV

Alamo Bowie was thoughtful while he rode between sheriff Joe Blaine and deputy Fred Rutledge. Charleston on the San Pedro was one of the strongholds of the outlaw gang, and the tall Texan knew that Three-finger Jack had some definite purpose in mind; a purpose that had its inception in the hanging of Bull Clanton.

Joe Blaine was thinking the same thing when he turned to Bowie with a frown on his weathered face. "Me and Fred has to collect some taxes over here," and his voice was thoughtful. "We're bound to meet Three-finger and some of his gang."

Bowie nodded. "That's why we rode over," he growled. "Charleston is in Cochise county, and we passed the word that outlaws either get out, or get killed!"

No compromise in the stern set of his jaw while his

gray eyes burned with a steady glow of determination. Fred Rutledge studied both men, and he reached for the old Spencer under his left leg when they crossed the bridge over the San Pedro.

"Three-finger killed Jack Whipple," he reminded softly. "And he shot Doc Holliday."

Just the reminder they needed to stir the flames of anger to life. Events had moved so rapidly since Alamo Bowie had loped into Tombstone on his Snapper horse. The killings and robberies of the outlaw gang were like a great sore that had suddenly festered and come to a head, and the Texan voiced the thought of all three.

"We'll clean up once and for all," he announced grimly. "If you have a wound in yore body, the Doc burns out all the rotten flesh no matter how much it hurts. Three-finger and his crowd has got to go!"

"We will stop at the Gold Dollar first," Joe Blaine said casually. "Manuel can tell us what is going on."

They swung down in front of the saloon and rail-tied their horses with slip-knots. Joe Blaine shouldered through the swinging doors with Rutledge and Bowie right behind. Red-shirted miners glanced up indifferently and went on with their drinking. The sheriff walked to the end of the bar and jerked his head at the bartender.

"Howdy, Manuel," he greeted. "Just out collecting the taxes. You got it ready?"

The fat bartender was half Mexican with the dark hair and eyes of his mother's people. He smiled genially and slid a canvas bag of clinking coins across the bar to the sheriff.

"Figgered you would be here," he answered, and reached for a bottle. "Have one on the house."

He nodded to Rutledge and studied the tall Texan appraisingly. "Meet up with Alamo Bowie," Blaine introduced. "Bowie, make you used to Manuel Claiborne. Old cowhand what used to ride for Johnny Slaughter."

"Howdy, Claiborne," Bowie answered quietly. "Nice place you got here."

"Sometimes it is," the bartender answered frankly. "Then again it ain't so nice. I was held up about an hour ago. All they got was last night's take."

He shrugged indifferently while he wiped the mahogany bar. The sheriff put the bag of money in his coat pocket and watched the dark face for a moment.

"You recognize the fellers?" he asked.

"I pay tribute," and Claiborne shrugged. "I have a message for you, sheriff."

"Me? Spell it out, feller," the sheriff answered.

"Rustlers ran off about a hundred head of beef-stuff John Slaughter was gathering for the reservations," Claiborne recited like a pupil repeating a well-learned lesson. "Juan Ortega brought the word a few minutes ago."

The sheriff frowned. "Does Slaughter know?" he asked.

Claiborne shrugged. "Don't see how he could just yet. Thought mebbe you'd want to cut for sign while the trail was warm."

His left eye drooped slightly while he jerked his

head toward the end of the bar. The sheriff caught the signal and walked away to get a match. Leaned across the bar while Claiborne whispered under his breath.

"Three-finger wants to talk to you. Blackie Mann brought the word, and Jack wants to see you alone. Says you won't get hurt, but it might save trouble if you show good sense."

Joe Blaine bit the end from his cigar and thumbed the match to flame. He studied thoughtfully while he puffed slowly, and then he nodded his head and returned to his companions.

"Look, Rutledge," he said to his deputy. "You and Bowie take a jaunt out yonder toward Sulphur Springs valley and cut for sign if you don't mind. I'll finish my collecting and ride out to join you in an hour. Suit you, Alamo?"

Alamo Bowie watched the sheriff's face suspiciously. "You just want to get rid of us?" he asked softly.

Joe Blaine flushed. "I ain't worth shucks at reading sign," he admitted honestly. "While you can read it like a book. You and Fred find out how many they was in the gang and which way they went while I finish up my work here. That away we can tell how many men we need in the posse."

Alamo Bowie nodded slowly. "The trail ought to lead to Three-finger," he remarked gruffly. "Looks like we ought to get word to Slaughter, and the four of us would be the posse."

"I'll get word to John," the sheriff promised. "You fellers keep yore eyes skinned in case of ambush."

Fred Rutledge eyed his superior and followed the Texan from the saloon. They mounted their horses and crossed the river in silence, and it was Rutledge who spoke the thoughts of both.

"Joe got a message of some sort," he said quietly. "What you reckon, Bowie?"

"Joe is still a politician at heart," the Texan answered frankly. "He aims to settle a lot of this ruckus without bloodshed if he can. I figgered he was entitled to a try, seeing as he is sheriff."

"You mean this raid is a blind?"

"Not exactly," the Texan muttered. "John Slaughter helped us hold the jail back there in Tombstone, and Three-finger is a kind who would get even. The trail will lead to Box C unless I miss my guess."

Back at the bridge-head, sheriff Joe Blaine watched them ride away without looking back. He knew that the Texan was suspicious, but he also knew that the tall special agent respected his position. The sheriff sighed and hitched his gunbelt automatically before retracing his steps to the Gold Dollar.

Manuel was still standing at the head of the bar. The sheriff picked up his untasted glass and downed the liquor neat. His eyes raised to catch the slight jerk of the bartender's head, and he looked on past and stiffened slightly. Three-finger Jack was standing near the back door regarding him with a slight smile twitching the corners of his mouth.

Joe Blaine placed his glass on the bar and walked carelessly to the rear. His dark eyes were watchful when he stopped a few feet away from the tall outlaw and nodded carelessly.

"You wanted to see me?"

The outlaw nodded. "I helped elect you, Joe," and his voice was calm. "It will soon be time for election again."

"Yeah," Blaine agreed. "I figger to poll more votes this time."

"If you live that long," the outlaw corrected dryly. "The boys don't auger you gave us a square shake lately."

"Now see here, Three-finger," Blaine answered bluntly. "There was too much killing here abouts, and it had to stop. That's why I was elected!"

The outlaw ignored the change of tone. "You hung Bull Clanton after I sent you word," he continued in the same quiet voice. "You let this Texan tell you how to run yore office."

"He showed me my duty," Blaine muttered. "You've played out yore string here, Three-finger!"

The outlaw shrugged carelessly. "I never bothered you," he reminded. "And I gave orders to my men to make yore job easy."

"How about the night Bull dry-gulched me?" the sheriff barked.

"That was after you threw in with Bowie," the outlaw sneered, and now his eyes were flashing dangerously. "That was just a warning to remind you that it was healthier for you to play the game like you played it before that Texan rode in here on his red hoss!"

"This raid on Slaughter's stuff," and the sheriff

changed the subject. "That yore doin's, Three-finger?"

"Me? I'm right here talking to the law," the outlaw answered lightly. "Even you would have to swear to that on the stand if it ever came to court."

"If it comes to court things will be different," the sheriff growled. "Judge Hart would give you the limit now."

"Mebbe so; mebbe not," and the outlaw smiled knowingly. "Things will have to go back to the old way, Blaine. Just thought I would let you know. Being a man of judgment, chances are you can see the light."

Joe Blaine flushed angrily. "I stayed to meet you account of what you said," he grunted. "I can't match you with a hand-gun, but so far you have always kept yore word. Now I'm warning you to lay off the law!"

"Yo're warning me?"

"You heard me, Three-finger. You threw a knife through Jack Whipple's neck just to get even. Then you tried to kidnap Nellie Gray, and you shot Doc Holliday!"

"That's a black spot I will have to correct," the outlaw muttered. "He coughed just as I dropped hammer, and my slug only parted his hair. First time I ever missed a man I had marked for my meat cutter."

"He's part of the law," Blaine growled. "He was only doing his duty!"

"His duty was to case the games in the Oriental before Alamo Bowie rode into Tombstone," the outlaw muttered. "You know what it means to buck me, Joe."

Joe Blaine straightened his stocky shoulders and

faced the tall outlaw fearlessly. "Now I'll tell you, Jack," and his voice was firm. "I sent Bowie and Rutledge on ahead like you suggested. You are washed up here in Cochise County, and you better drift while you can!"

"Is that a threat?"

"It's a warning," the sheriff answered quietly. "Bowie came here to bring the law to Tombstone, and he ain't never left a job until it was finished. You know his record as well as I do."

The outlaw sneered. "He never met a real fast gunhawk yet," he answered thinly. "You might tell him I said so!"

Joe Blaine sighed. "I'll tell him," he answered. "I knew it had to come sooner or later."

"Cheer up," and Three-finger Jack smiled knowingly. "He might change his mind before it comes to Show-down!"

"Not Bowie," the sheriff answered promptly. "You and him will meet some day, Jack!"

He stared at the sudden change in the tall outlaw. Three-finger Jack was brushing the guns on his thighs with the tips of his long fingers. His nostrils flared wide while little flecks of red danced across his dark eyes. His whole body trembled with an eagerness he could not conceal, and his voice was a soft whisper when he spoke.

"I'd give all I have cached away to meet him. He thinks he is the fastest, but you know better!"

"I don't!"

The sheriff snapped the denial without winking. For

a moment he thought the tall outlaw was going to force the issue, and he sighed his relief when a change swept over the thin dark face. Three-finger Jack shrugged and reached for his glass with his left hand.

"Pass it for now," he muttered. "I have other plans I don't want to spoil."

"That's right good judgment," the sheriff answered dryly. "I saw Carlos Chavez hanging around town," he changed the subject.

"Better leave Chavez alone," the outlaw warned. "He's one Mex that ain't afraid of the law. Have a drink?"

Joe Blaine shook his head. "I ain't drinking. Is Chavez stringing along with you?"

The outlaw stared at him with a mocking light in his dark eyes. "And if he is?"

"Bowie is a U. S. deputy Marshal," Blaine answered. "He passed the word that known outlaws either get out or get killed!"

The outlaw snapped his fingers. "I'll meet Bowie some day," he muttered. "I'll meet him according to the code with no favors asked or given. Right now he's just another notch on the handle of my right-hand gun!"

The sheriff tried a new tack. "You and me used to be right friendly, Three-finger," he said softly. "Like you said, you helped elect me to office. You rode back in the tangles and helped me collect taxes, and I'm offering you the chance to ride on out before it's too late."

The outlaw laughed shortly. "I appreciate yore concern for the state of my health," he answered mockingly. "Which is why I sent word for you to meet me for a talk. You could easy find business some where else for the next two-three days!"

"You ever know me to run?" the sheriff asked grimly.

"You didn't have to run while you had me backing you up," the outlaw answered bluntly. "Tombstone has a town marshal she don't need, and Cochise county is a big place. I was you, I'd find business over at the other end. Like collecting taxes, for instance!"

He leaned forward and stared into the sheriff's face. Joe Blaine shrugged angrily and growled under his breath. The outlaw smiled gently and touched the handle of his gun, and Joe Blaine caught the significance of the move.

"Taxes can wait," he muttered. "You made one big mistake, Mister!"

"I've made lots of them," the outlaw admitted carelessly. "But I don't aim to make any more."

"When you took Nellie Gray," the sheriff continued. "Every man in Tombstone was mad about that!"

The outlaw smiled. "Wrong there," he corrected. "Bowie and Holliday was careful not to say anything. Outside the law, nobody but Hatch and Slaughter found it out, and you won't say anything!"

"I might," and the sheriff stared stubbornly. "You know damn well we don't make war on women out here, especially women like the Angel!"

"Now listen, Joe," and the outlaw scowled angrily.

"A woman is all the same man to me when she throws down on me with a sixgun. I knew who that stranger was all the time. Not only that, but she knew I was wise to her when I tipped my Stetson and rode away. I was winners until she bought chips in a man's game!"

"You set a trap for the law," Blaine argued stubbornly. "You figgered on killing Bowie right there!"

"And I'd have killed him," the outlaw growled savagely. "But we was talking about the Angel," and he sneered the last word.

"You robbed the stages," the sheriff said slowly. "You killed Pop Whipple to keep him from testifying. Yore men robbed the Gold Dollar this afternoon, and rustled Slaughter's cattle!"

"Can you prove it?" and the outlaw smiled mockingly.

The sheriff shrugged. "All them things don't amount to much in this country," he continued. "But when you do something to Nellie Gray, that there is a different matter. You better ride on out, Three-finger!"

"Why you . . ."

"I might be what you are thinking," the sheriff interrupted harshly. "But a gent can only die one time. I'm telling you not to bother Nellie Gray!"

Three-finger Jack stooped his shoulders into a crouch with the fires of hell blazing in his dark eyes. The fingers on his right hand flexed like writhing snakes, but Joe Blaine faced him with hand on his gun. For a long moment they stared at each other, and then the outlaw relaxed with a sneer.

"It would be murder," he muttered. "I could let you clear leather and kill you before you dropped hammer!"

"That's right," the sheriff agreed. "But you sent word that all you wanted was to make medicine. You all talked out?"

"Not quite," and the outlaw made no attempt to conceal his contempt. "You and the rest don't amount to shucks. It's the Texan I want, and I mean to tally for him. Tell him I said so. Arizona ain't big enough for both of us!"

"I'll tell him," the sheriff answered quietly. "Right now he's cutting for sign out in Sulphur Springs valley where the herd was rustled!"

"I'm riding the other way," the outlaw grinned. "So long, sheriff!"

He turned his back and walked slowly through the back door. Joe Blaine bit his mustache and frowned. Then he nodded to Manuel Claiborne and pointed at the bottle of whiskey. The bartender slid glass and bottle and followed slowly.

"Thought he was going to throw down on you for a minute," he remarked carelessly. "In spite of his promise he sent in by Blackie Mann!"

"Mann, eh?" the sheriff muttered. "I'll remember that name."

Claiborne looked worried. "Don't repeat me," he pleaded. "Being out here by my lonesome, they could rub me out, easy. I'd hate to be in that Texan's boots."

"Yeah? He's doing right well," the sheriff answered.

"Carlos Chavez is back," Claiborne whispered. "And Squint Barrow is saddle-pard to Blackie Mann. That tell you anything?"

"Tells me I better be riding," Blaine muttered. "What about Chavez?"

"He's a cousin to a feller named Sonora Lopez," the bartender whispered. "Bowie tallied for Lopez over Deming way."

"I know," Blaine muttered. "That's how come him to get that scar on his chin. Lopez threw a knife at him one time years ago. So Chavez is his cousin!"

"He's bad, Joe," Claiborne muttered. "And he taught Lopez all he knew about a knife. You might tell the Texan."

The sheriff finished his drink and nodded slowly. "I'll tell him," he promised, and walked slowly from the room.

He smiled to himself while he walked his horse across the heavy planking of the bridge. So far he had avoided bloodshed, and a feeling of content erased the worry and doubt that had gnawed at his mind. If Three-finger Jack followed the code in his inevitable meeting with Alamo Bowie, the best man would win. Neither could ask for more, and the sheriff spurred his horse and followed the tracks of the Texan and his deputy.

The sun was dropping behind the Dragoons when he overtook them in a grassy valley. Alamo Bowie nodded shortly and pointed to the plain trail leading toward the east.

"Seven riders pushing that jag of beef," he said quietly. "They met another bunch of riders back aways and turned over the herd. That tell you anything, sheriff?"

"The herd can wait," Blaine answered carelessly. "I met Three-finger back there in Charleston."

"So it was him," Bowie grunted. "I caught the sign, but figgered she was yore play."

"He's got something up his sleeve," Blaine muttered. "I couldn't figure what it was."

"He knew we was riding over here to collect taxes," Rutledge suggested. "And like as not he knew Bowie would be with us."

Alamo Bowie jerked around sharply. "That means he knew all three of us would be away from town," he barked. "We was tolled out here for a good reason, Joe!"

"That's what I figured," the sheriff answered with a frown. "He rustled this herd to get even with Slaughter, and to keep us busy. Then he sent word by Blackie Mann for me to meet him in the Gold Dollar for a pow wow. I don't like it!"

"We better make tracks back to Tombstone," Rutledge growled. "That jigger framed something up that won't do the law any good."

"Just a minute," Bowie interrupted. "What did he say, Joe?"

"Gent by the name of Chavez has joined up with them," the sheriff answered slowly. "He's a cousin to a feller what went by the name of Sonora Lopez!"

Alamo Bowie raised his left hand, rubbed the scar on his chin. "Glad to know about Chavez," he muttered. "But what did Three-finger tell you to tell me?"

"How'd you know?" Blaine asked with surprise showing on his face. "He said to tell you that there wasn't room enough in Arizona for the both of you. Said that some day you and him would meet up for Show-down . . . according to the Code!"

Alamo Bowie smiled happily. "That means a fair shake on both sides," he almost whispered. "Now we better split the breeze and get back to Tombstone. According to the Code," and his voice came back to them like a song.

CHAPTER XVI

Judge Hart sat in the front room of his little adobe house behind the Bird Cage Theatre. The little man carried himself with a new dignity, and one fat hand rubbed the handle of the old sixgun belted high under his light coat. He glanced out the open door toward the distant mountains, and the smile froze on his face when he saw the two men leaning against the door frame.

"Good evening, gentlemen," he said courteously. "Something I can do for you?"

Squint Barrow winked at his Mexican companion. "Going to kill the judge to straddle a hoss," he remarked with a grin.

"My riding days are over," the judge answered with quiet dignity. "And it is almost supper time."

Squint Barrow waved his hand and palmed a heavy

forty-five. "Yo're taking a ride for yore health," he growled. "Even if we have to slap you on the skull and pack you out like a side of beef. You come quiet and you won't get hurt none except saddle sores!"

"We better talk this matter over," the judge proposed hastily. "What is the purpose of this nocturnal ride?"

"Three-finger wants to have a little talk with you," Barrow grinned. "Make you acquainted with Carlos Chavez. You gave him a week in jail one time, and all he done was shoot a mouthy Pilgrim who wouldn't drink with him."

The judge shuddered. "I remember Chavez," he whispered. "In other places they would have called it murder. That tenderfoot didn't have a chance."

"But he drawed first," the Mexican interrupted softly. "I do nothing but protect me."

The judge frowned. "I have nothing to discuss with your leader," he growled. "I will do my talking in court!"

Squint Barrow shook his head. "That's what Three-finger was afraid of," he admitted. "You might do too much talking when pore old Lantern-jaw Peters comes up for trial. With you out of the way, there won't be any trial for a while."

"Now see here," Judge Hart muttered angrily. "I am appointed to sit on the bench. Peters will get a fair trial by his peers!"

"Three-finger don't believe in them kind of peers," Barrow answered. "Was a time when we fellers could get some decent law here in Tombstone, but all that sotter changed when that Texan come foggin' into town."

"He showed us our duty," and the judge squared his shoulders. "I refuse to go with you men!"

Squint Barrow narrowed his eyes and stepped forward to jab his gun in the fat paunch. "Up on yore hind legs," he growled. "It's dark enough now so we won't be recognized."

Judge Hart paled and swelled his chest. Squint Barrow slapped down with the barrel of his gun before the judge could shout. Carlos Chavez slid inside and caught the drooping figure under the arms, and he waited until Barrow sheathed his gun and caught the short fat legs.

Grunting under the load, they carried the judge outside where three horses waited. The unconscious man was laid face down across the saddle and tied ankle and wrist. Then the Mexican mounted his horse and reached for the lead reins. Walking their horses slowly in the dusk, they rode out of town and headed for the foothills.

Night settled down with a cool wind blowing across the wasteland. A groan brought the three horses to a stop, and Squint Barrow slid to the ground and threw off the ropes that bound the judge. He pushed the fat little man erect and pointed to the horn of the saddle. Then he made a few half-hitches and re-mounted.

"Holler yore head off," he said carelessly. "We will soon be at the Box C, and you better talk nice to Three-finger!"

"My word on it, gentlemen," the judge whispered

hoarsely. "Release me and I will return to Tombstone and keep a still tongue."

"You'll keep a still tongue nohow," Barrow sneered.

"I'll prosecute every member of the gang for this outrage," the judge sputtered. "I'll see you all rot in Yuma prison!"

Carlos Chavez dropped back and held a gleaming knife in his right hand. "You make for talk too much," he muttered. "One little cut and you will bleed like the peeg!"

The judge stared at the knife and shuddered. Carlos Chavez smiled and replaced the knife in the scabbard between his shoulder blades. Squint Barrow pointed to lights ahead, and the three horses continued on to the Box C and stopped before the low porch.

Squint Barrow threw off his ties and pulled the judge from the high saddle. "In the house," he grunted. "And you better talk pretty!"

Judge Hart swayed and almost fell. His legs ached from the long ride, and his head throbbed from the blow he had received. The Mexican pushed him through the wide door, and the little man blinked in the light when a chorus of laughter greeted him.

Ten men were lounging in the long room along the log walls. Three-finger Jack was seated near a scarred desk, and he looked the judge over and waited.

"You will go to prison for this, Three-finger Jack," the judge shouted angrily. "You have insulted and assaulted the dignity of the law!"

"That's only a start," the tall outlaw sneered. "I

wanted to talk to you about Peters. His trial comes up tomorrow!"

"I never discuss a case out of court," and the little judge straightened proudly. "It is against all the ethics of jurisprudence!"

"Might be it is," the outlaw answered with a shrug. "But we figured you might listen to reason. There's a thousand dollars in it for you to decide this case the right way!"

"Those days are passed," the judge muttered. "Your day is done here, Jack!"

"Stubborn, eh?" the outlaw muttered. "Mebbe you think more of yore duty than you do yore worthless life!"

The judge nodded his head. "I do," he said clearly. "You can kill me if you like, but you can't regulate the decisions of my Court!"

"Was a time when I did," the outlaw reminded. "And we both made money!"

"That was before I learned the error of my ways," the little man answered fearlessly. "That was before Alamo Bowie brought a new kind of law for Tombstone. I've started a new page in the book of life!"

"And you can tear it out," the outlaw chuckled. "So far you haven't done much writing on that new page!"

"At least I have made a start," the judge answered firmly. "Don't forget that Bull Clanton was hanged by the neck!"

Squint Barrow stepped forward with an oath and slapped the little man across the face. The other outlaws growled threats until Three-finger Jack drew his gun and forced them back.

"You, Squint!" he barked. "You do that again and you won't live long enough to talk about it. I'll handle this case!"

Squint Barrow paled and slid back to the wall. The other outlaws muttered under their breath and watched their tall leader. Three-finger Jack pouched his gun and turned to the judge.

"How long would you last?" he asked softly. "Mebbe you've changed yore mind about that trial!"

Judge Hart rubbed his face and shook his head. "You can kill me," he answered quietly. "And I will try to die like a man!"

The tall outlaw glared for a moment. "Tie him up and throw him in the back room," he growled. "They can't hold a trial without the judge nohow!"

Carlos Chavez smiled while he tied the hands of Judge Hart behind his back. Then he led the little man to a back room and fastened the fat ankles. His voice was a silky purr when he held the gleaming knife close to the trembling throat.

"One leetle move and *el cuchillo* will drink your blood," he whispered. "*Adios,* my fat one."

"*Hasta la vista,*" the judge answered softly.

"So you think we shall meet again, eh?" the Mexican chuckled. "P'raps it will be as you say," and he left the room and closed the door behind him.

Three-finger Jack was frowning when the Mexican returned to the front room. The rest of the men were eating wolfishly, and Carlos Chavez filled his plate from the kettles on the big wood stove. The tall outlaw stabbed at him with a finger when he took his place at the long table.

"Good work, Chavez," the leader praised quietly. "And don't forget what you have to do in the morning. Better turn in early tonight."

"Gracias, Capitan mio," and Chavez beamed with pride. "You think they will come here tonight?"

The outlaw shook his head. "I don't expect them," he said quietly. "But we will post guards to make sure. I will wait back in my cabin as usual. I want to think things out!"

They watched his straight back as he walked to the door and mounted the big black horse. The outlaw rode swiftly until he came to a screen of brush concealing a small canyon, and he slid from the saddle and held the nose of his horse when three bobbing shapes were sky-lined on a distant rise.

"It won't be so funny when they find out," he muttered softly, and led the black through the screen to the little clearing where a neat cabin nestled against the rocky hill.

Alamo Bowie raised his head and stared through the darkness with a frown on his tanned face. "Thought I heard a hoss's hoofs," he muttered.

"Must have been a steer," Rutledge answered. "You getting jumpy, pard?"

The Texan shrugged. "I'll feel better when that trial is over tomorrow," he admitted honestly. "A conviction will hurt that gang more than a dozen killings!"

"I hope Nellie has saved supper for us," sheriff Blaine said eagerly. "I'm hungry enough to eat mutton."

"I never could get that hungry," the Texan muttered. "Let's line out for grub!"

Silence while they rode under the stars at a high lope. They swung back to Tough Nut street when they reached town, and all three tied their horses behind the Russ house. After washing on the back porch, they trooped into the dining room and took their regular table. Nellie Gray smiled and brought a steaming tray of food.

"Expected you," she said quietly. "I knew you boys would be hungry as bears."

"Yo're an Angel, Nellie," the sheriff praised, and cut into his thick steak.

Nellie Gray went back to her desk and watched the three men devour their food. Her dark eyes were fastened on the Texan, and several times he raised his head and smiled at her. When the coffee and pie was finished, she came over to the table and laid her hand on Bowie's shoulder.

"Feel better?" she asked.

"I could start all over and work all night on that grub, Nellie," Bowie answered with a grin. "That green apple pie is the best I ever put in my mouth."

He glanced up and stared at her face with a frown. "You might have to work all night," she said softly. "Judge Hart has not been in for his supper yet!"

"The judge? Why, he's always first man at the table," the sheriff answered. "What you trying to tell us, Nellie?"

"You better ride up there to his house and see if he is all right," she murmured. "I am worried about him, what with that trial tomorrow and all."

"I felt that something was up," Bowie muttered. "That's why I left my Snapper hoss behind the hotel. You should have told us sooner, Nellie!"

"I wanted you to enjoy your suppers first," and Nellie Gray clasped her hands tightly. "I know something is wrong, Alamo!"

"Don't say anything to anyone else," and the tall Texan raced from the room. He was in the saddle speeding up the street when the sheriff and Fred Rutledge bolted through the back door and hit their saddles to follow closely.

Bowie was facing the door of the little adobe house with the Twins in his hands when Joe Blaine swung down in the tidy yard. The Texan called softly and waited.

"Judge? You all right, Judge?"

"He ain't there," Blaine muttered. "Let's go on in!"

Bowie shouldered through the door and slid his shoulders along the wall. He listened for a moment and then flicked a match with his thumb nail. The other two officers came in while he was lighting the lamp, and the Texan snapped a sharp order.

"Stand where you are so's not to cloud the sign. We might find out something!"

His eyes darted to the floor and stared intently. "An old-country Mex has been here," he whispered, and picked up a twisted cigarette.

"Carlos Chavez," the sheriff said positively. "I remember when he rolled them corn husks down at the jail. The judge gave him a week one time for rubbing out a Pilgrim!"

Alamo Bowie held his place and glanced around the little room. "Two men were here," he said briefly. "A white man and the Mex. Slender jigger with pointed toes on his boots and crosses studded in the heels!"

"Squint Barrow," Rutledge breathed softly. "He's one of Three-finger's gang!"

"They stood there at the door for a while," the Texan continued softly and pointed to the scuffed dust on the boards. "Then they both came inside."

"They wanted to fix that trial in the morning," the sheriff growled, and shook his head. "They couldn't do that now since you came into Tombstone, Bowie!"

The Texan frowned, pointed to the floor. "A heavy man dropped right there," he said positively. "He broke the arm of that chair before he hit the floor. Like as not they knocked him over the head with a gun-barrel!"

He left the room and carried the light to examine the ground beyond the little porch. Sheriff Blaine and Fred Rutledge followed slowly with hands on their guns. They knew the habits of the outlaws, but the tall Texan ignored the fact that he made a perfect target if ambushers were hidden in the dark.

"Three horses," he grunted, and pointed to the tracks. "They dragged him out here and roped him across the saddle. Then the Mex mounted up and led his horse. You gents got any ideas?"

"Lower that lamp and let's get inside," the sheriff muttered. "Wonder where Doc Holliday is right now?"

Alamo Bowie followed inside and shut the door. "Doc wouldn't be up this far," he answered soberly. "I warned the judge not to stay down here alone!"

Sheriff Blaine spread his hands hopelessly. "There's our trial," he muttered. "We will have to hold Peters until we can bring a new judge over from Phoenix. Now I know what Three-finger meant when he said that mebbe Lantern-jaw wouldn't be convicted!"

Alamo Bowie was thinking deeply while the little ridges of muscle stood out on his craggy jaw. "Can't follow that sign in the dark," he muttered. "Not unless you gents has some idea where they would hold the judge."

"There's a dozen places," Blaine answered with a frown. "And on top of that, the stage comes in from Benson at six in the morning!"

"Yeah," and Alamo Bowie jerked up his head. "Now we know why that damn outlaw wanted us out of town this afternoon. We fell right into it like a crowd of sheep!"

"What else could we do?" Rutledge asked. "You reckon they took him to Skeleton Canyon?"

"Skeleton Canyon or Buffalo Wash," the sheriff muttered angrily. "Sulphur Springs, or back in the badlands where you couldn't find yore own shadow on a dark night!"

"We got the judge into this ruckus, and we got to get him out," Bowie grunted. "And the way to do it is to get some sleep and start reading sign come daylight."

"They might kill him," Blaine whispered. "You reckon, Bowie?"

"Not if I read Three-finger right," the Texan grunted. "He will hold the judge to force our hands with Peters. I'm going back to the hotel. See you gents come daylight."

Nellie Gray was waiting when he returned from the O K Corral where he kept Snapper. She met him at the door and put her white hands on his shoulders when he avoided her eyes.

"Did you find him?"

The Texan shook his head. "Kidnapped," he muttered. "Carlos Chavez and Squint Barrow did the job!"

"You found out that?"

Bowie nodded. "The sign was plain," he explained. "Then they took him away on a lead hoss. We couldn't follow the sign in the dark."

"But Alamo," and Nellie Gray was close to tears. "They might kill him!"

"I don't think so. I'm getting back there to follow the sign as soon as it gets light."

"Alamo?"

The Texan raised his head and frowned. "I know what you are thinking," he growled. "So I'm riding out to meet the stage early in the morning. And God help that owl-hoot outfit if they lay a hand on the kids!"

"I'm afraid, Alamo," she whispered. "They strike in so many different places at the same time. You didn't see Three-finger at Charleston?"

224

"Joe Blaine saw him while Fred and I were following a rustled herd," the Texan growled savagely. "It was just a plant to get us away from town. You seen Doc Holliday?"

"He was here after you left," and Nellie Gray shook her head. "He looked awfully sick, Alamo."

"He better rest up a few days," the Texan muttered. "But I wish I had him at my side in the morning."

"That's why he came," she answered with a sigh. "Said to tell you he had a hunch, and that he was riding out with you in the morning to meet the stage!"

The Texan smiled for the first time since supper. "A feller couldn't ask for a better pard," he answered thankfully. "I look for trouble tomorrow, Nell!"

"I want to go with you," and the woman clung to him while her eyes searched his face. "I couldn't stand it if anything happened to the children!"

Alamo Bowie held her for a moment and patted her shoulders. "You have a good breakfast ready," and he tried to make his voice quiet and natural. "Like as not they will be hungry as well as tired. I can hardly wait to see the little buttons."

Nellie Gray sighed and kissed him with the tears standing in her eyes. "They couldn't have a better father," she whispered. "Oh Alamo; I'll be so glad when this trouble is all settled!"

"Don't you worry yore pretty head none," the Texan whispered. "Three-finger knows he is wrong, and he knows he can't win. It won't be long before you and me and the kids slide out of here and go over to the new ranch."

"The judge," and Nellie Gray shuddered. "Three-finger threatened to get even because he sentenced Bull Clanton to be hanged!"

Alamo Bowie sighed. "I'll do the best I can in the morning," he promised. "Now I'm going to turn in and get some sleep."

"Just one," she pleaded softly, and the hard-faced Texan put his arms around her and kissed the full soft lips. Then he released himself and raced up the stairs to his room with a flush of happiness staining his bronzed face.

CHAPTER XVII

The first finger of false dawn raised the curtain of night temporarily when Alamo Bowie slipped from the back door of the old Russ house. The streets were deserted except for a slender figure up near the Crystal Palace, and the Texan nodded grimly when he recognized Doc Holliday. The new Town Marshal was taking his duties seriously in spite of the scalp wound that had almost closed his career.

His eyes were bright and feverish when he greeted Bowie, and he emptied a brandy flask and tossed it away in an empty lot. Then the gambler sighed softly and wiped his pale lips, but the Texan knew that a coughing spell had again taken its toll.

"Better turn in and get some rest, Doc," he said gruffly. "Looks like you've been up all night."

Doc Holliday shrugged. "Had my ear to the ground," he remarked carelessly. "Sometimes the ears are better than the eyes when a feller is riding a blind trail!"

Alamo Bowie stopped and levelled his gray eyes. "I was going up to gear my Snapper hoss," he said quietly. "Was going out there to Judge Hart's shack to read sign. That what you mean?"

The gambler nodded. "We know they took him out in the hills, Alamo. They ain't a man living could follow the sign through town and on out in the tangles. I never cared too much for His Honor, but he turned out to have the makings of a man in him since you rode up the trail."

"Keep on talking, pard," Bowie muttered. "You had yore ear to the ground."

"Just got the word an hour ago," Holliday replied, and leaned closer as he lowered his voice. "Judge Hart is out on the old Box C!"

Bowie's face hardened, but he showed no sign of excitement. "Somebody got to talking with his mouth," he guessed shrewdly. "Some of the gang rode in and lickered up."

Again the gambler nodded. "It was Dick Bardwell," he muttered. "He left town not more than an hour ago. Three-finger would kill him if he knew."

Alamo Bowie hitched his crossed belts and cuffed the battered Stetson low over his eyes. Darkness fell again to dissipate the faint light, but both men knew that the sun would peep over the Dragoons in another half hour. The Texan was once more the man-hunter with the eager light of battle glowing in his deep-set gray eyes.

"Slip down to the jail, Doc," he clipped. "Tell the sheriff and Fred Rutledge to gear their tops and meet me at the O K Corral. The four of us ought to be able to handle that gang at the Box C!"

"Five," the gambler corrected. "Johnny Slaughter heard about that jag of beef, and right now he's waiting up at the barn. I'll get Blaine and Fred."

He started slowly down the deserted street under the board awnings. Walking slowly so as not to set off the cough that threatened his life, and the tall Texan watched him and shook his head.

"He ought to be in bed, but you can't stop him," he muttered, and continued on to the barn.

Big Marty Williams came out of his shack while the Texan was cinching his double-rigged saddle. Texas-man from Stetson to high heels with a tie-fast maguey looped to the left side of the nubbin. The big red horse was whickering softly and nudging his master, and Bowie palmed him a cube of sugar while his deep voice crooned endearments. Love-talk that he could not use to a woman, and the big Wells Fargo Agent smiled in the gloom.

"Howdy, Alamo," he greeted softly. "Anything special to get you up in the middle of the night?"

Bowie frowned and pretended to inspect his latigo. "The judge is being held out on the Box C," he growled. "We're going out there to cut him loose!"

Marty Williams stepped into the box stall. "I'll get my sawed-off and join up," he offered eagerly.

228

Alamo Bowie shook his head vigorously. "You stay here and look after yore runs," he grunted. "Get word to Jed Swope and Bob Hatch in case we run into grief, but we won't need any help!"

"You might," the big man argued. "The Kids come in on the early stage from Benson. You forget about that?"

He stopped when he saw the misery in the hard gray eyes. "I haven't forgotten, Marty," and the Texan's voice was brittle. "I'm riding out the trail to meet the stage after we spring Judge Hart!"

"Damn Judge Hart," Williams growled savagely. "I know about you and Nellie, and the store you set by those buttons. Better meet the stage first!"

"Looky, Marty," the Texan answered evenly. "Judge Hart done a big thing when he sentenced Bull Clanton, and we got to stand behind him. I made him that promise!"

Marty Williams nodded slowly. He knew what a promise meant to the gaunt gunman who had the reputation of never breaking his word. It seemed incredible that one man could exert the influences Alamo Bowie held over so many people. Then the big Agent glanced down the street with a grim smile curving his lips.

"Looks like Hunchy Domain is in for a busy day," he remarked quietly. "Yonder comes the Sheriff with Fred Rutledge and Doc Holliday. John Slaughter was sleeping back yonder when I turned in."

A short, wide-shouldered man of forty slid down from the loft and high-heeled across the barn.

"Howdy, Bowie," he called softly. "Be with you in a shake!"

"Howdy, Slaughter," and the Texan watched the cattleman lead out a tall gray. "I see you heard the news."

John Slaughter threw his heavy saddle on and drew back the saddle-blanket so as not to curl the hair on the gray's back. "Doc told me," he answered over his shoulder. "They sold that jag of beef, but I figger to make 'em pay."

"We're riding on law business," the Texan remarked softly. "We haven't any real proof about the cattle rustling."

"I say, I say," Slaughter muttered, and rubbed the grip of his pearl-handled sixgun. "I aim to help the law, but every time I trigger a slug, I figger on collecting for them beef critters. Howdy, sher'ff!"

Joe Blaine rubbed his eyes sleepily. "Howdy, Slaughter," he grunted. "Heard you was riding with us."

"Riding and a-shootin'," Slaughter muttered grimly. "Them owl-hooters has played high-hand too long in this camp. My idea is to shoot first and tell 'em to throw up their hands afterwards!"

He glared at Bowie and shoved a heavy Spencer carbine deep in the saddle boot. Doc Holliday mounted a little sorrel gelding a sleepy hostler brought from the rear. Blaine and Rutledge sat their saddles just inside the barn and watched the tall Texan. Alamo Bowie caught the gleam in Slaughter's dark eyes and shrugged his shoulders.

"Keno," he agreed softly. "They had their warning, and they wouldn't take it. Shoot on sight, but if any of them jiggers surrenders, they get a fair shake."

"That's talking, Texan," sheriff Blaine seconded. "We don't want any more killing than we can help," and he watched the face of John Slaughter.

The cattleman mounted his gray horse without answering. A veteran of the long trail-drives, he had the reputation of never losing a steer to rustlers. The sheriff sighed and gigged his horse into the big corral. Down in his heart he knew that Johnny Slaughter would collect for his beef.

The sun was just peeping over the Dragoons when the little party left town quietly and headed for the foothills. Doc Holliday rode with Alamo Bowie just behind Slaughter. Rutledge and Joe Blaine rode in the drag and glanced at each other. Again the sheriff sighed and shook his head sadly.

"Tombstone will have her man for breakfast," he muttered.

Alamo Bowie heard and smiled grimly while he drew closer to Doc Holliday. The gambler glanced up and neck-reined his sorrel up to rub stirrups with his head cocked to one side.

"Listen, Doc," the Texan whispered. "After the ruckus is over, you cut out and foller me. The sheriff and Fred might be busy, and you and me is meeting the stage up near the Pass!"

The gambler nodded, not changing expression. Two spots of vivid color rode high on his cheek-bones to show that the brandy had taken effect. Once more he was steady eyed and calm, and the bulge under his coat told the story of the deadly sawed-off he called "Brindle."

"If we're both in the saddle," he remarked dryly. "Must be eight or ten of them long-riders at the Box C."

Alamo Bowie did not answer, and the little group rode across the high desert at a swift lope. John Slaughter drew up in front of a heap of bleached bones that almost blocked the entrance to Buffalo Wash. His left hand drew the Spencer from the boot, and his eyes were hard and bright when he saw his companions follow the move.

"I say," he muttered and glared at sheriff Blaine. "We'll get the jump on those jaspers all same Apache. Like the Texan mentioned, she's Rustlers Round-up!"

"The judge is in the back room," Doc Holliday interrupted. "Better throw yore shots off that away."

"This wash makes a bend yonder," Bowie cut in. "We will walk the hosses up to there for a look-see. No shooting till I give the word!"

Five horses walking softly through the loose sand in the eerie light of the early dawn. No sound except the soft creak of well-oiled saddle-leather, and the dry whisper of hoof-deep sand. Alamo Bowie touched his Snapper horse and took the lead away from Slaughter, and he checked the big red horse at the bend of the trail. Then he edged his head around the rocky wall and sucked in his breath.

"Five men at the corrals," he whispered over his shoulder. "Take as many prisoners as you can!"

He straightened his horse and jerked his head for the others to come up and fan out. John Slaughter scowled and glanced at Doc Holliday. Both were dark-eyed with coal black hair, and the gambler smiled and nodded at the cattleman. No mercy in those hard black eyes, and then the Texan dug with his spurs and started the wild stampede toward the corrals.

Five horses thundering across the packed ground before the startled outlaws sensed the danger. Two men dropped down behind the bars and reached for their guns while their companions made a run for the house. John Slaughter brought up his Spencer and fired between jumps, and one of the men in the corrals threw up his hands and fell forward.

Alamo Bowie swept down his big hands and palmed the Twins with thumbs dogging back the heavy hammers. Two reports roared out sullenly, and two of the fleeing outlaws went down with bullets in their legs. The second man in the corral snapped a shot from his sixgun to slap the black Stetson from the gambler's head, and Doc Holliday shifted old Brindle and pressed trigger.

The outlaw was picked up and slammed to the center of the corral by the force of the buckshot, and John Slaughter smiled grimly and slid his gray to a stop. The Spencer came to his shoulder and spouted orange flame to cut down the outlaw leaping to the porch of the log house. Then the cattleman kneed his horse into a lope and circled the house with the gambler right behind him.

Alamo Bowie roared up to the porch and lit off a-running with his boots ploughing furrows in the splintered planking. A shot blasted out from the front room to knock Fred Rutledge from the saddle, but the deputy rolled over and came up with both guns in his hands, and sent a shower of lead through the open door.

Joe Blaine was coming up behind the Texan with gun eared back for a shot. He made an easy target from the house, and a bullet jerked his left arm back and spun the sheriff around before he reached the porch. Then the sullen roar of a shotgun blasted from inside the house and Alamo Bowie leaped through the door to face Doc Holliday. The gambler was thumbing fresh shells into the breech of his sawed-off while he watched a man writhing on the floor.

"Six," he said quietly, and grinned at John Slaughter who came through the back room with his Spencer at the ready.

"Four," the cattleman muttered. "Bowie just winged two of those owl-hooters through the legs!"

"That's the gent did the talking," and Doc Holliday pointed to the man on the floor.

"That's Dick Bardwell," Slaughter grunted. "He was lining down on the sheriff when Doc pressed trigger. Is Joe hurt bad?"

Alamo Bowie pointed through the open door. "Him and Fred is holding the prisoners," he answered quietly. "We wanted somebody that was able to talk!"

He shouldered past the cattleman and entered the back room. Then he reached for his skinning knife and hunkered down to cut the ropes that held the little judge. Doc Holliday came back and slid the sawed-off under his coat with a deft shrug, and Judge Hart sat up and tried to smile.

"Knew you'd come, Bowie," he croaked hoarsely. "Gimme a drink!"

Doc Holliday reached to a bucket and dipped up a cup of water. "You owe something to Doc Holliday, Judge," the Texan said softly. "He heard Bardwell talking in the Crystal Palace just before he left town. They hurt you any?"

The little man drank deeply and shook his head. "None to speak," he answered more strongly. "But part of the gang rode away at day-break."

"Carlos Chavez, and Squint Barrow," Bowie muttered. "And Blackie Mann."

"That Mexican," the judge shuddered. "He threatened to cut my throat from ear to ear!"

"He rode away," Bowie prompted. "You hear them say what for?"

"It was something about the stage," Judge Hart answered slowly. "But I couldn't make out just what."

Alamo Bowie straightened suddenly and glanced at the gambler. "You hear that, Doc?" he asked quietly, but his gray eyes were blazing with an inner excitement. "It was something about the stage!"

Doc Holliday nodded and rubbed the stock of his sawed-off. "They aim to mebbe stick up the stage," he answered, and lowered his left eye-lid slightly. "Looks like you and me ought to take a *pasear* out that away, seeing that you are drawing yore pay from Wells Fargo!"

The judge was rubbing his ankles and wrists to restore circulation. "I missed my supper last night," he complained irritably, and then his pale eyes widened. "Did you see Three-finger Jack?"

The Texan shook his head. "He wasn't here when we rode in. Thought mebbe he rode out with the Mex and Squint Barrow."

"He left last night right after they brought me in," the judge explained. "He's got a cabin hid away somewhere close to town."

"We better get out and see how bad Fred and Joe is hurt," Doc Holliday suggested. "I saw Rutledge go down while we were taking the house."

Fred Rutledge was sitting against the porch with his right leg stretched in front of him. Both guns were in his hands covering the two wounded outlaws, and sheriff Joe Blaine was leaning against the porch with his left arm dangling while he questioned the prisoners. John Slaughter had both feet planted wide apart, and the heavy Spencer cradled against his hip with the hammer eared back.

"Better talk, McLowery," Blaine said slowly. "What did you jiggers do with that herd of beef-stuff you rustled last night?"

"G'wan and shoot," the bearded rustler growled. "Me and Butch ain't doin' any wind-jamming!"

"You and Butch is due to swing by the neck," Slaughter growled viciously. "Was me that brought you jiggers down, the Territory would have saved trial money," and he jerked his head toward the two dead outlaws in the corral.

"The sheriff always was soft-hearted that away," McLowery sneered. "Account of him and Three-finger being pards before that damn Texan rode in here!"

John Slaughter reached to his saddle and took down his rope. His hand shot out with a finicky loop to snare the blustering prisoner, and McLowery gulped and showed fear for the first time.

"That beef-herd," Slaughter demanded, and his deep voice was thick with anger. "Talk fast before I cut off yore wind!"

"I'm yore prisoner, sheriff," McLowery whined. "I demand the protection of the law!"

"It was you shot my deputy through the leg," the sheriff answered gruffly. "And yore pard like to got me from the house!"

"Dick would have got you if he hadn't been drunk," the prisoner snarled. "That's what he gets for riding to town against the chief's orders!"

"Yeah," the Texan added. "He talked with his mouth before he left town!"

McLowery skinned back his thick lips. "I heard a shotgun in the house," he barked. "You get Bard-well?"

Doc Holliday shoved forward a step. "You ever hear of me missing with old Brindle?" he asked softly.

McLowery grinned like a wolf. "Glad you got that mouthy hairpin," he gloated. "Three-finger would have killed him nohow, only he would have shot him through the belly so's he wouldn't die so fast!"

"Mebbe you'd like some of the same," and John

Slaughter glared at the lanky prisoner. "I've been watching you and yore saddle-pard for quite a spell of time."

McLowery glanced appealing at the sheriff. "Keep him off me, Sheriff," he pleaded. "I done surrendered to the law!"

Judge Hart waddled down the steps and held up a fat hand to John Slaughter. "He'll get a fair trial, Slaughter," he promised grimly. "You ever been over to Yuma prison?"

The stocky cattleman loosed the rope with a grin. "Didn't see you before, Judge," he answered. "You reckon him and Butch will do time over on the forks of the Gila and the Colorado?"

"Count on it," the judge answered gruffly. "I don't often discuss a case out of court, and you can't prove rustling on these men. But I can prove that they assaulted and kidnapped a presiding judge, and the limit for such a felony is twenty years!"

McLowery sneered arrogantly. "You ain't got Three-finger, and you won't ever take him," he boasted. "On top of that, there's Chavez, Barrow and Blackie Mann. Me and Butch won't do no time in that Yuma hell-hole!"

Alamo Bowie walked over and faced the stocky cattleman. "Asking you to do me something, Slaughter," he said gruffly. "And you can't noways refuse!"

"Give it a name, Texan," Slaughter answered promptly, and tapped the stock of his carbine.

"Me and Doc has to ride fast to meet that stage," the

Texan said softly. "Both the sheriff and Fred is wounded some, not including those two owl-hooters. I'm asking you to see that they get to jail!"

"I say, I say," Slaughter demurred. "I was aiming to ride along with you and Doc. I ain't no where's near satisfied!"

"Can't you see, cowboy," the Texan said slowly. "We got to split the job, and Three-finger might strike at the jail. I'm asking it, pard!"

John Slaughter sighed and shook his shoulders angrily. "Got it to do," he muttered. "But looky, Bowie. You see any of them killers out yonder, shoot first and ask questions afterwards. Remember those two kids riding the Overland!"

Alamo Bowie smiled and held out his hand. "That makes it easier for me," he murmured. "I'll leave you to explain to Joe and Fred!"

He nodded at Doc Holliday and walked to his big red horse. The gambler climbed his own saddle with an eager light in his black eyes. Sheriff Blaine shouted excitedly, but the Texan waved his hand and roared across the yard with his rowels biting deep.

"He's got to meet the stage," John Slaughter told the sheriff. "That tall jigger just can't wait no longer to see those two kids he's taken under his wing!"

CHAPTER XVIII

Bud Philpot was tooling his four-horse hitch up the long grade through the pass. Bob Paul was riding shotgun on top of the stage just behind the lean old driver, and both men were watchful when they topped the rise and started down into a sandy wash.

"Cutest kids I ever see," the driver remarked with a chuckle. "Both of 'em sound asleep down there in the stage!"

"G'wan," the shotgun guard bantered. "You taken a shine to that button because his name is Bud."

Bud Philpot laughed softly. "And the little gal," he added. "Mary Jane fits her like a cowboy's hand-made boot."

Bob Paul glanced back over his shoulder toward the leather boot. "I'd feel better if we wasn't hauling that cash in," he muttered. "Ten thousand is a lot of temptation to these road Agents here abouts."

"Ain't been a stick-up since the Texan got here," the old driver answered carelessly. "He's shore played hell with Three-finger and his gang."

"Hands up, gents!"

A nasal voice twanged the stick-up command sharply from the roadside brush just as the stage rumbled through the deep sand of the wash. Bob Paul swung around and jumped his sawed-off to his shoulder when a slender rider rode out on a strawberry

240

roan. The robber pressed trigger and threw himself from the saddle just as the shotgun roared, and Bob Paul pitched over the edge of the high roof with a bullet through his heart. The strawberry roan floated to the side of the road with the full charge of buck-shot through its body, and the robber slid behind the kicking horse and levelled down on old Bud.

The old driver held the leather ribbons in his right hand while his left slapped for the old Peacemaker on his leg. Two other men spurred to the middle of the road with sixguns spiking from their hands. Old Bud sighed and raised both hands while he muttered curses under his breath.

"The cash is back there in the boot," he snarled.

"We take the *Dinero, Si,*" one of the bandits answered. "But we also take the *muchacho* and *la muchacha!*"

Old Bud raised his voice angrily. "Don't you touch that boy and gal," he shrilled. "You can kill me, but don't you bother them buttons none!"

"Shoot him offen that box," another bandit sneered. "Like as not he knows us nohow!"

"You dang right I do, Squint Barrow," the old driver shouted. "And that other *banditto* is Carlos Chavez. On top of that, I'd know Blackie Mann even if he was white-washed!"

Blackie Mann was unfastening the straps on the leather boot. He stopped suddenly and came around the stage to glare at Bud Philpot.

"So you know me, eh?" he snarled, and flames spurted from his right hand.

The old driver was slapped back on the roof where he clawed for a hold. Blood spurted from his left shoulder, and Squint Barrow shouted at Blackie Mann and knocked the levelled gun aside.

"Let him go," Barrow bellowed. "Get the kids out of the stage!"

"I get, Senor," the Mexican answered softly, and opened the door.

An eight-year old boy with round blue eyes glared at the swarthy face while he held the hand of his sister. "You go away and leave me and Mary Jane alone," he shouted. "Lessen you want that I should tell my new Dad about you!"

Carlos Chavez threw back his head and laughed. His heavy sombrero hung from the chin strap at the back of his curly black head, and his white teeth gleamed between his parted lips.

"This new *Padre* of yours," he purred. "His name, my leetle *caballero!*"

"He means Alamo Bowie," the little girl interrupted. "Me and Buddy loves him already."

"Ees too bad," and Chavez shook his head sadly. "P'raps you weel not see the new *Pappacita.* Now you come with me. No?"

"We won't come," and the nine-year-old Mary Jane clung to her chubby brother. "Now you go way and leave us alone!"

"Drag them brats out of there," Squint Barrow snarled. "We ain't got all day to auger with them!"

Carlos Chavez reached in a brown hand and caught the boy by the arm. Mary Jane flew at him like a tiger and clawed at the swarthy face just as racing hoofs pounded down the slope toward the wash. The Mexican drew back with scratches on his cheek. Then he whirled like a great cat and dropped to the ground when a gun exploded up the slope.

Squint Barrow went down before he could press trigger. Blackie Mann whirled to face the charging horsemen and cursed under his breath.

"That damn Texan! Get him, Carlos!"

He raised his guns with thumbs dropping the filed hammers. Doc Holliday was riding free-handed with the reins looped over the horn. The deadly sawed-off roared suddenly and nearly kicked the gambler from the saddle, and Blackie Mann did a hoolihan and flopped on his back in the trail-side sage.

Carlos Chavez slapped for his gun and crawled back into the brush. His forty-five levelled on the charging Texan, and then the Mexican lowered the hammer gently and jumped for his horse. He was racing through the catclaw riding low on the neck of his horse when Alamo Bowie slid to a stop with the Twins in his hands.

"Daddy," a voice called excitedly. "It's me and Buddy waiting for you!"

The heavy guns sagged in the strong brown hands. Alamo Bowie slid from the saddle with the color mounting high beneath the leathery skin of his tanned face. A slender body leaped out at him and fastened chubby arms around his neck, and the Texan swallowed a lump in his throat while his arms closed around the warm little body.

"Me and Mary Jane knew you'd come, Alamo. My name is Buddy Bowie!"

"Sho nuff," the tall Texan mumbled and held the boy off at arms' length. "Glad to meet up with you, son, but you shore work fast. So yo're Buddy Bowie!"

"I'd tell uh man," the youngster answered solemnly. "And me and Mary Jane loves you a heap. Don't we, Sis?"

"Yes sir, we do," and the little girl stepped down from the stage and ran to the tall Texan. "Please can I have a kiss so's me and Buddy will know you are glad to see us?"

"Bless my heart," Alamo Bowie gulped, and buckled his knees to the dust of the road. "You really want to kiss an old booger like me?"

Mary Jane put her arms around his neck and kissed him squarely on the lips. "You ain't a ole booger," she contradicted. "Bud Philpot told me and Buddy how handsome you was. Didn't he, Buddy?"

"I'd tell uh man," Buddy answered promptly. "You reckon them men is stone dead over yonder?"

Alamo Bowie glanced at the bodies of the two bandits. "Reckon they are, son," he answered gravely. "I'm sorry you and Mary Jane had to see them."

"Shucks, feller," the small boy boasted. "I saw three men get rubbed out one day back in Frisco. The cops killed 'em for robbin' a bank!"

The Texan recalled himself when Doc Holliday coughed. "The Mex got away," the gambler muttered. "You got a swell family, Bowie."

"Make you acquainted with Bud Bowie, Mister

Holliday," the Texan answered soberly. "And Miss Mary Jane. This is Mister Doc Holliday."

"Mary Jane Bowie," the little girl corrected, and smiled at the gambler. "I've heard a lot about you, Doc!"

The gambler smiled in spite of himself. "Make me a promise, honey," he begged softly. "Promise you will always call me . . . Doc!"

"I promise, Doc," the little girl answered. "Can Buddy call you Doc too?"

Buddy walked across the wash and held out his hand. "Put it there, pard," and his voice was blustering. "Any pard of Alamo's is high-card with me. T'meetcha!"

Doc Holliday shook hands without smiling. Alamo Bowie turned his head to hide a grin, and his arms held Mary Jane hungrily while her small fingers played with the handles of his guns.

"You killed that one man, didn't you, Daddy?"

"Reckon I did, Mary Jane," the Texan grunted. "But you haven't said anything about yore new Mother."

"She's an Angel," Buddy interrupted. "She stayed with us for a week one time. It's going to be swell with you and Nellie."

"And Doc killed that squinty-eyed robber," Mary Jane interrupted. "But you let that other man get away. I scratched his face when he tried to take Buddy!"

"Listen Daddy," a cracked voice called sarcastically. "You mind giving me a hand down before I bleed out here on this roof?"

Alamo Bowie scowled and glanced to the top of the

stage. "Thought you was dead, you ole pelican," and climbed up to help Bud Philpot to the ground. "You hurt bad, old raw-hider?" he asked anxiously.

"Hurt bad enough so's I might live a while longer," and the old driver pointed to a wound high in his left shoulder. "That there's my gun-hook, and I won't be taking any more fool chances for a while," he explained dryly.

His little blue eyes twinkled when he tongued the huge chew of tobacco from his mouth and plastered it poultice-fashion over the bullet hole. Buddy watched the operation gravely and glanced at the old stage coach. Then he peered under the high body and shook his head.

"Can't find none," he muttered with disappointment.

Old Bud Philpot grinned knowingly and winked at Bowie. "Can't find what, button?" he asked innocently.

"Spider webs," the boy answered promptly. "An old sailor back home told me that spider webs was just the thing to stop bleeding."

"That there's a right good idea, feller," the old driver chuckled. "But you won't never find no setch on my stage. We don't let 'em set still long enough to draw no fly-catchers."

Alamo Bowie grinned and cut the heavy wool shirt-sleeve away from the wounded arm. Then he made a tight bandage while Mary Jane wrinkled her nose and turned her face away. Bud Philpot gritted his teeth against the pain until Doc Holliday swung down and began to talk to the little girl.

"You was right lucky, Texan," he whispered to Bowie. "I thought there for a minute you was a goner."

Alamo Bowie grunted. "Missed me clean," he answered carelessly. "And then Doc cut loose with old Brindle."

"Yeah," the driver grunted. "And Doc got Blackie Mann dead center. But I was talking about Carlos Chavez."

The Texan shrugged. "He high-tailed to save his skin," he grunted. "I'll come up on Chavez one day!"

"I was laying up there on the roof," Philpot pointed out. "Where I could see the whole show. Chavez lined down and had you under his sights where you couldn't see him back there in the bresh. Then he lowered his hammer and hit saddle without firing a shot."

Alamo Bowie stared at the little driver. "Meaning that Chavez could have dropped me?" he muttered hoarsely.

Bud Philpot nodded his head. "You was wide open," he answered. "Chavez couldn't have missed you."

Alamo Bowie shook his head while his left hand rubbed the scar on his chin. "I can't figger that one out," he admitted slowly. "Chavez is kin to a gent I had a ruckus with over in New Mex, and he was pard to them two," and he jerked his head toward the stiffening bodies.

"It's Three-finger," and Bud Philpot glanced around at the trail-side brush. "Three-finger figgers to whittle

247

yore notch on the handle of his own cutter!"

"Say!" and the Texan narrowed his gray eyes. "I got the word from him just like you said. Straight showdown according to the Code, with no edges on either side!"

"That's why the Mex didn't drop hammer," the old driver muttered, and stared at the gaunt Texan. "You can't gun fight that owl-hooter now, Bowie."

Alamo Bowie turned quickly. "What's the reason I can't?" he demanded, and his eyes glowed feverishly. "I'll meet him any time and any place he puts a name to!"

Old Bud shook his head. "You can't cut 'er, feller," he repeated stubbornly. "Not since you become a father," and he jerked his head toward the two children.

Little Bud tugged at Bowie's long right leg. "Don't pay him no mind, Alamo," he piped shrilly. "You go ahead and kill that feller with the Twins!"

Alamo Bowie studied the chubby face gravely. "Reckon I got it to do one of the days," he answered soberly. "But I made that promise before I knowed about you and Mary Jane."

The little girl was staring at his hard face, and her lips began to tremble. Then she began to sob and ran toward him with her arms spread wide. Alamo Bowie hunkered down and caught her in his long arms, and Mary Jane cried on his shoulder while her little fingers tangled in his hair.

"I heard you," she sobbed. "I don't want you to get killed!"

"Sho now, honey," the big man murmured. "You shouldn't ought to take on that away. I ain't never been killed yet up to now. Yo're goin' spoil them pretty blue eyes crying that away!"

"I want you for my Daddy," and Mary Jane cuddled closer to him while her arms tightened about his neck. "Me and Buddy come all the way here account of because we like you so much."

Alamo Bowie held her tenderly while a bewildered expression swept across his hard tanned face. Old Bud Philpot dug a hole in the sand with the toe of his rusty boot and covered it again. Doc Holliday coughed and looked away, but little Bud dug his fists down in his pockets and grunted like only a small boy can.

"That's the way all wimmin is, Alamo," he growled. "Always uh cryin' and caterwaulin' when a feller gets in a tight. Don't you pay her no mind!"

Mary Jane raised her head to listen and then turned on her brother furiously. "You can talk," she screamed. "But when that man was pulling you out of the stage, you held on to me and squalled like a baby!"

"I never," the boy replied hotly. "And besides, he was way bigger than me. I was only afraid he was going to take you!"

"You fibber," and Mary Jane withered him with a glance. "You was hollering yore head off for Daddy Bowie, and you know it!"

"Well, what if I was," Buddy growled. "Didn't he come uh foggin' down the road with both the Twins bangin' in his fists?"

Mary Jane glanced away and her shoulders began to

shake again. "Poor Mister Paul," she whimpered. "He was such a nice man, and I saw him fall off the roof. Is he dead, Daddy Bowie?"

The Texan glanced at the body of the shotgun guard and nodded slowly. "I'm afraid he is, Mary Jane," he admitted reluctantly. "But he died doing his duty, and the Wells Fargo Company won't forget it."

"Will they bury him in Boot Hill?" and Mary Jane held her breath for the answer.

The Texan nodded again. "Reckon they will, honey."

"Gee, that's swell," little Buddy interrupted. "Me and Mary Jane has heard a lot about Boot Hill. Can we all go to the funeral?"

"Buddy!" and the little girl began to cry again. "Please, Daddy; take me to Angel!"

Alamo Bowie jerked erect with a queer look in his eyes. He had forgotten about Nellie Gray during the excitement, but now a flush of color stained his cheeks and softened the fire in his gray eyes. His big hands patted the little girl, and his voice was soft and tender when he answered.

"She's waiting for us, honey. Now you stop crying and look after Buddy. We'll be getting right along to Tombstone!"

"Reckon you'll have to handle the ribbons, Bowie," and old Bud pointed to his shoulder. "I ain't feelin' quite so peart as I was a spell back."

"I want to ride Snapper," and Buddy waited while his blue eyes watched the Texan's face. "Kin I, Daddy Bowie?"

Alamo Bowie swung Mary Jane up on the driver's seat before he answered. "You promise not to cut him up none with the rowels?" he asked the boy seriously. "You give me yore word not to saw his mouth lessen he gets to boogerin'?"

"I'd tell uh man," Buddy promised eagerly. "And us Bowies never go back on our spoken word!"

Alamo Bowie whistled for the big red horse. Snapper came mincing toward him with head held sideways to keep the reins clear of his feet. The Texan took the soft muzzle in his big hands and talked softly while the two children watched his every move.

"You got work to do, Snapper. Wants you to bring Buddy Bowie in without no fireworks. He's our chip now, old hoss."

Snapper nodded his head and muzzled his master. Alamo Bowie picked Buddy up and placed him in the high saddle. Handed the split reins to the boy and patted the satiny neck while Buddy hooked his shoes in the loops of the fenders. Then the Texan glanced at Doc Holliday and jerked his head toward the bodies.

"We got to take 'em," he muttered. "Only place is inside the stage!"

Doc Holliday nodded and swung down. The two bandits were loaded between the seats, with the shotgun-guard propped against the back cushion. Then the Texan climbed up the wheel and held a hand to swing old Bud Philpot up beside him. Mary Jane snugged close while Bowie unwrapped the long reins and kicked the brake loose.

"Stay close to the button, Doc," he called softly.

"Not that Snapper won't look out for him, but just in case," and he swung his eyes out over the brush.

Doc Holliday gigged his horse close to Buddy and tapped the stock of his shotgun. "I'll ride herd on him, pard," he promised, and the old stage rattled across the wash and started the climb up the grade.

Old Bud Philpot swayed weakly and held to the iron rail on the roof. "You reckon he will ride out, Bowie?" he whispered softly.

"He won't," the Texan answered gruffly. "Three-finger don't work that away, and besides it wouldn't be what you call a fair shake."

"I wouldn't trust him too far," and the old driver shook his head. "Course I don't know much about what you gun-fanning jiggers calls the Code," he admitted.

"She calls for an even break," Bowie explained, and his face was ridged with the deeply-etched lines of battle. "A gent who cheated in a show-down wouldn't be fit to live with himself. On top of that, Three-finger don't know yet that he lost this hand."

"Yo're forgetting about Carlos Chavez," Philpot grunted. "He lit out at a high lope, fanning his braunk down the hind laigs at every jump. Right now Three-finger is looking to his cutters!"

He shuddered when he saw the eager light that flashed across the narrowed gray eyes. Alamo Bowie was driving with one hand while his right loosed the long-barreled gun on his long leg. Then the Texan saw the small boy on the red horse and relaxed with a sigh.

"The Angel will be waiting," he muttered, and his

252

craggy face broke into a smile when little Mary Jane clutched him tightly. "Yonder's Tombstone," and he sent the four horses down the long hill on a dead run.

CHAPTER XIX

Carlos Chavez spurred his lathered horse through the deep brush that screened the hidden canyon in the shadow of Sheephead mountain. Three-finger Jack dropped back behind a tree with hands slapping for his holsters. Then he relaxed and stepped out when he recognized the Mexican.

"You got that hoss smokin'," and his voice was sharp. "The boys coming here with the kids?"

Carlos Chavez slid from the saddle and shook his head slowly. "Squint Barrow and Blackie Mann," he muttered. "She both *muerto;* what you call dead!"

The tall outlaw stiffened. "Dead," he repeated softly, and the little red lights glowed deep in his black eyes. "You said they was both dead!"

The Mexican nodded. "We have hold up the stage like you say," he murmured softly, and his brown eyes watched the long-fingered hands of the tall outlaw. "Blackie is back getting the dinero. Me, I try for take these Keeds from the stage after we have kill the guard."

"Keep on talking," the outlaw grunted, but now the flames were leaping high in his eyes. "You was dragging the kids out."

Carlos Chavez bobbed his head. "We hear horses coming fast, and then Squint Barrow fall," and the Mexican shrugged expressively. "Blackie shoot fast at that one who looks like the skeleton, and then Senor Death shoot his terrible gon!"

"Senor Death," Three-finger sneered. "You mean Doc Holliday cut down on Blackie Mann with that damned sawed-off?"

The Mexican nodded. "It ees like you have say," he agreed. "Blackie jump back long way and fall in the brush," and Carlos Chavez crossed himself and shuddered.

Three-finger Jack stared for a long moment while his fingers twisted like snakes. "What you doing all this time?" he demanded sharply. "Quit that shaking and talk straight!"

"I see this *Tejano* charging on the big red *caballo*," Chavez whispered. "I jump back in the brush and make for shoot him with this," and he patted the sixgun in his holster.

"You had him under yore sights and didn't pull trigger?" and Three-finger Jack stared angrily.

"But no, Senor," the Mexican answered, and his brown eyes were open wide. "I remember what you have say that day when we have our little talk," and he rubbed his bruised lips. "You tell me about this thing you have call the Code. Me, Carlos Chavez, put the gon away and mount my 'orse *andale*. In the big quick. I come ver' fast, Senor!"

Three-finger Jack showed his surprise when he stared at the Mexican with his lips parted.

254

"They ain't a white man would do it," he whispered. "You took yoreself a vow account of yore cousin, and you had the Texan under yore gun. Then you holsters yore smoke-pole and hit leather when you could have killed the Texan!"

"*Si, Senor,*" the Mexican answered with a twisted smile. "You have do me the great honor when we shake the hands. That day I make to you the promise, and Carlos Chavez he never forgets!"

Three-finger Jack stepped forward and gravely offered his hand. "Yo're the squarest pard I ever had," he grunted. "From now on out she's a fifty-fifty shake between you and me. Yo're a man, Carlos Chavez!"

The Mexican gripped the hard fingers while a smile spread across his swarthy face. "Ees the happiest day of my life," he almost shouted. "We live together, Senor. Mebbe so we die together, but *por Dios,* Carlos Chavez never forget!"

Three-finger nodded and whistled for his horse. The big Black came to him and reached for the cube of sugar on the outlaw's extended palm. Carlos Chavez mounted his own horse and waited while he watched the dark face. Three-finger swung up to the saddle and jerked his head toward the brush screen.

"We ride to the Box C," he grunted. "I have something to say to Judge Hart!"

The two men loped their horses across the salt grass toward the distant foothills. Tombstone was a sprawling blot to the East, and the tall outlaw pulled his horse into the brush when they crossed the dusty stage road. Wheels were rattling behind a rise, and the two watched when the bobbing ears of horses topped the crest.

"He comes," Chavez whispered with excitement. "We get them now, Senor?"

The outlaw shook his head. "Too close to town," he muttered. "And I promised to face him according to the Code!"

The Mexican shook his head. "This code," he complained. "I do not like. The Texan sits high on the stage with the reins in his hand. The old one is wounded. We have rifles, Senor Three-finger!"

Again the outlaw shrugged irritably. "That is not the way of the code," he growled. "On top of that, we'd bring the lightning down on our heads from town. We couldn't get away with the two kids on our saddles. I have a better plan!"

Alamo Bowie shook out the long whip and rattled down the grade without a glance at the brush. Three-finger Jack watched until the stage was a dust-cloud before he continued his ride to the Box C. Carlos Chavez shook his head sadly until they came to the huddle of corrals back in Buffalo Wash, and he reined in sharply when he saw the tall outlaw stop the big black.

Three-finger Jack was staring at the dead bodies in the trampled dust of the yard. He swung down with a muttered curse and identified each corpse. Then he raced for the log house with both guns spiking out from his fists.

"Dick!" he shouted. "Dick Bardwell!"

His polished boots hit the porch and slid to a stop in front of the open door. The guns drooped slowly, and then the outlaw walked inside and stared at the body of Dick Bardwell.

"Dead," he muttered. "Filled full of buck-shot at short range. That cursed gambler!"

Carlos Chavez was peering over his shoulder. "We make mistake, Senor," he murmured softly. "Senor Death he ride by the boy beside the stage. Him we should have kill!"

"I'll kill him," the outlaw muttered savagely. "I won't miss again!"

His boot-heels beat a tattoo as he raced to the back room and saw the cut ropes on the floor. "Gone," he muttered, and read the sign as though he had seen the rescue of Judge Hart.

"They take the judge," Chavez whispered. "Now they hold the trial, Senor!"

Three-fingered Jack nodded. "They must have took Butch and McLowery alive," he grunted. "And Lantern-jaw Peters is down there in the jail!"

"We ride, Senor?" Chavez asked softly. "We have been insult, and mebbe so we die one time!"

The outlaw shrugged angrily. "Somebody talked," he growled. "A posse was here, and they must have found out we were holding the judge. Who left here last night after I rode away?"

The Mexican lowered his eyes and glanced at the body of Dick Bardwell. "Senor Ricardo go to Tombstone," he answered softly. "He return at day-break mucho *baracha;* what you call ver' drunk."

The tall outlaw growled in his throat and kicked the stiffened body on the floor. "He talked with his mouth, the dirty son. That's one killing I won't hold again Doc Holliday!"

"You are dark, Senor," the Mexican whispered softly. "In a little time, I make you look like the *Mexicano. Es no?*"

Three-finger Jack turned swiftly. "You mean a disguise," he snapped. "You have the extra clothes, Chavez?"

"*Si, Senor.* I have the fine clothes from old *Mejico.* Mebbe so you ride to Tombstone, no?"

"You should have come sooner," the outlaw muttered. "Two weeks ago I had the biggest gang in the Territory. Now look at them," and he jerked his head at the bodies in the yard. "Go get the clothes!"

Carlos Chavez ran across the yard to a long low bunk house. He returned with tight-laced pantalones and bolero jacket; silken sash and brilliant *serape.* Then he took off his own high-crowned sombrero and handed it to the outlaw.

"Make for change," he smiled. "You will shave the mustachios, Senor Three-finger?"

The tall outlaw nodded and began to strip off his black broadcloth. A few minutes later he stared at his face in a small mirror. Smooth-shaven to roll the years away with the cunning lines Carlos Chavez had added and erased with brown stain and grease pencil.

Three-finger Jack straightened to his full six-feet-one. The laced pantalones cased his strong slender legs like gloves. White silk shirt with crimson sash under the tight bolero jacket. Silver bells tinkled musically from the brim of the black sombrero, and the

Mexican folded the *serape,* and draped it across the left shoulder.

"You are the *caballero Mexicano,*" Chavez murmured pridefully. "What we call the Mexican gentleman in my country."

The slender outlaw smiled and bowed from the hips. "I go now to Tombstone, my fren'," he said softly, and the Mexican smiled.

"You speak the ver' good Spanish, Senor," he praised. *"Vaya con Dios!"*

"Go thou with God," the outlaw repeated softly, but his black eyes blazed with the fires of hell. "You will wait here for me!"

He strode from the room and down the porch steps. Chavez had roped out his own horse from the cavvy; a deep-chested little Spanish horse with slender ankles and small head. A heavy silver saddle was bolted tight; light bridle studded with silver conchas. Three-finger Jack placed a polished boot in the long *tapadero* and swung up like an old-country *vaquero.* Then he sent the grulla roaring across the yard with a touch of his drop-shanked spurs.

Carlos Chavez watched him go with a look of sadness in his brown eyes. After a while he turned away and shrugged when his eyes flicked across the bodies on the ground. A shovel was leaning against a corral post, and he picked out a soft spot under the tamarinds and began to dig a deep hole.

Three-finger Jack hummed a Spanish song and sent the fast little grulla across the alkali flats. He raced down the long hill into Allen street just as the heavy stage made the turn toward the O K corral on Fremont. Sombrero pulled low over his eyes when he edged his horse up close to the platform where Alamo Bowie was swinging his teams with a flourish.

A crowd was gathered around the stage depot, and all eyes were watching the tall Texan and his small passenger. Mary Jane caught her breath when she saw Nellie Gray on the platform, and she tugged at Alamo Bowie's arm in her excitement.

"There's Angel," she cried happily.

Nellie Gray held out her arms and caught the little girl. "I'm so glad you got here safe, darling," she crooned, and held the little body to her breast. "Where is Buddy?"

"Yere I am, Angel," and Buddy gigged the big red horse close to the platform and stepped off. "Ain't Alamo a great feller?"

Nellie Gray smiled and hugged the youngster hungrily. "He sure is, Buddy," she agreed. "But why are you riding Snapper?"

She raised her eyes and saw Bud Philpot for the first time. She caught her breath sharply when she saw the blood-stained bandage, and Alamo Bowie climbed down from the stage and shook hands with sheriff Joe Blaine.

"Better send for Hunchy Domain," the Texan whispered. "Blackie Mann and Squint Barrow are on the floor inside. Bob Paul is propped against the seat."

He explained briefly while the crowd milled around the old Concord for a look at the bandits. His lips pulled down a trifle at the corners when a low black wagon pulled up beside the stage. A thick-chested man with a huge hump on his back swung down and came forward nodding his head.

"Figgered there would be work with ten thousand riding in the boot," he explained in his deep voice. "How many you get?"

"Now looky, Hunchy," the sheriff protested. "You must have eye-sight like a buzzard. We just found out about them killings!"

"Heard the Texan was riding out," the undertaker answered quietly. "He don't often take prisoners when he holds court on them that robs the Wells Fargo!"

Alamo Bowie frowned and turned aside when a soft hand touched his arm. Nellie Gray was standing between the two children, and her brown eyes were brimming with the tears of happiness.

"I won't try to thank you, dear," she said softly. "But Mary Jane told me what you and Doc did. I am only sorry you had to use the Twins again!"

The Texan held her eyes for a long moment and sighed. "I owe a debt," he answered quietly. "Carlos Chavez had me under his gun and refused to drop hammer."

"Alamo! He could have killed you," and Nellie Gray shuddered.

The Texan continued to gaze into her eyes. "He saved me for a pard of his," and his voice was harsh. "He made a promise to Three-finger Jack!"

He looked away to avoid the tears in the brown eyes so close to him. Then he stiffened and stared at a tall Mexican sitting a deep-chested grulla not more than ten paces away. The Mexican was smiling mockingly from under the brim of a black sombrero. Even as he watched, a crowd of cowboys surrounded the little Spanish horse.

"Lynch the Mex," a hoarse voice shouted. "He's a stranger in town!"

Black eyes snapped viciously until their owner saw the menacing guns pointed at him. Then he shrugged carelessly and raised his long-fingered hands shoulder-high.

"I have do nothing, Senors," he protested softly. "I but ride through to my home in Chihuahua!"

A red-shirted miner reached for the Mexican when Alamo Bowie stepped forward with Doc Holliday at his side. "No lynch law in Tombstone," and the Texan's voice was gruff. "You gents slide back there away and holster yore irons!"

He waved his hands as he spoke, and the crowd gasped when the Twins leaped to his calloused palms. Joe Blaine stared at the angry crowd over the top of his gun, and the men fell back with muttered curses.

"This feller ain't done you no hurt," Bowie continued. "He is a gent from the cut of his riggings, which is more than I can say for some of you fellers. Now scatter before you miss that trial coming off in about an hour!"

The big miner crowded forward. "You say trial, Texan?" he demanded loudly.

Alamo Bowie nodded. "Judge Hart is holding court on Lantern-jaw Peters," he announced. "I'm thanking you gents for not making us no more trouble than we got!"

Once more the crowd was grinning as they discussed the trial among themselves. The tall Texan turned back to the Mexican and spoke softly in Spanish.

"Pardone, Senor. Vaya con Dios!"

The Mexican raised his sombrero and wheeled his horse. *"Gracias, Senor Tejano,"* he said politely. *"Hasta la vista!"*

The Texan stared at the straight back racing down the street toward the court house. He turned thoughtfully when Nellie Gray touched his shoulder.

"You wished him to go with God," and her throaty voice was a soft whisper. "Then he thanked you and said something else!"

"Till we meet again," the Texan interrupted. "I wonder what he meant by that?"

"Look at me, Alamo," Nellie Gray commanded sharply.

The Texan turned his face and locked glances. "You recognized him," Nellie Gray accused. "You knew who he was the same as I did!"

"Like you say," and the Texan made no attempt to lie. "But I'm asking you to keep that secret to yoreself. I have good reasons!"

"If you ask it, Alamo," she agreed with a puzzled frown. "But you could have stopped this whole business by taking him prisoner. You might never get another chance!"

"But I made a promise," Bowie muttered softly, and

263

refused to meet her eyes. "Now you better take the younguns home account they are hungry!"

"Alamo; promise me you won't meet him!"

The Texan shook his head stubbornly. "Can't promise that, Nellie," he said miserably. "I made a promise before I met you or heard about the buttons."

"What promise, Daddy?" and Mary Jane tugged at his holster.

"I promised to see a man about a dog," the Texan lied quickly, and tried to smile at the little girl.

"What kind of a dog?" Mary Jane persisted.

"When are you going to shoot it out with that outlaw, Alamo?" Buddy asked loudly.

"He ain't," Mary Jane answered quickly. "He is going to come home and eat breakfast with us."

"Breakfast," Buddy scoffed. "Alamo has more important things than eating to do. Ain't you, pard?"

"I'd tell uh man," Bowie muttered, and frowned when the boy grinned impudently.

"Me and Alamo would both tell uh man," he boasted to his sister. "We got to grain that Snapper account he ain't et yet!"

"That there's an idea," Bowie agreed eagerly. "I got to take Snapper back and let him feed. I'll be down to eat as soon as I get through."

"Before the trial?" and Nellie Gray held the Texan's eyes.

Alamo Bowie smiled and bobbed his head. "Before the trial," he promised. "Save me a seat between them weaners."

Doc Holliday was waiting back in the barn when

Bowie led Snapper inside. Hunchy Domain was driving down the street with the same quiet smile on his heavy face. The gambler watched the black wagon while the Texan stripped his riding gear and turned Snapper into a box stall.

"That Mexican," the gambler began abruptly. "I don't like that *caballero,* Bowie!"

The Texan turned swiftly. "Meaning what?" he demanded.

"Meaning that I never forget a gent once I've seen him make a pass for his irons," Holliday answered softly. "You savvy the burro?"

The Texan sighed and nodded his head. "I get you, Doc," he growled. "Glad you stayed out and let the play go by!"

"She wasn't my deal," the gambler muttered. "But you should have slipped the bracelets on that owl-hooter when you had the chance!"

"I made him a promise," Bowie answered, and his voice was quietly serious. "You ever know me to break my spoken word, Doc?"

The gambler shook his head. "Like Buddy said back there at the hold-up," he agreed. "Us Bowies never break our word!"

"See you at the court house in an hour," and Bowie turned on his heel and stomped out of the barn and across the O K corral. He had promised to eat breakfast with his family.

CHAPTER XX

Nellie Gray smiled happily while she arranged the breakfast table for her new family. Buddy swaggered importantly and told Wing how he had mastered the big red horse, Snapper. Mary Jane sat demurely at the table with hands folded, and her big blue eyes followed every move of her new mother.

"I wish Daddy Bowie would hurry," she fretted. "I'm hungry."

Nellie Gray stopped and stared at the child. "Who told you about Alamo?" she asked curiously.

"The lady we were staying with told us all about him," the little girl answered. "She read us your letter to Mamma, and then we saw Mister Scudder while we were waiting for the stage."

"Bud Philpot told us too," Buddy interrupted loudly. "He said Alamo was going to take us to a big cattle ranch. Is he, Angel?"

Nellie Gray frowned for a moment. "I had no idea so many folks knew about it," she murmured. "Are you going to like riding horses, Buddy?"

"I'd tell uh man," Buddy shouted. "And I'm goin' to get Alamo to show me how to shoot a gun," and his eyes flashed with excitement. "Then I won't be afraid like I was this morning," he added in a whisper.

"I'm glad Chavez got away," Nellie Gray answered softly. "To think of you little children seeing what you did this morning!"

"Alamo will get that feller," Buddy boasted. "Him or Doc Holliday one!"

"Buddy," Nellie reproved gently. "You should call him Mister Holliday."

"No'm," Buddy contradicted. "He made me and Mary Jane promise to call him Doc," and the small boy grinned impudently. "You ought to have seen how mean he looked when he shot that bandit with the shotgun!"

Nellie Gray shuddered. "Buddy, please," she murmured. "You mustn't talk like that!"

"Shucks," the youngster grunted. "That wasn't nothin'. Alamo told me nobody but him had ever rode Snapper before, and Doc Holliday said Alamo was the fastest gun-slinger in these parts!"

"Mister Holliday said that?"

Buddy bobbed his head. "Doc said somebody would have to rub that Mexican feller out account of him being kin-folks to some jigger Alamo killed over in New Mex!"

"Buddy," Mary Jane wailed. "If you don't stop talking like that I'm going to slap you. I ain't hungry no more."

"I am," Buddy grunted. "I wish Alamo would hurry so's we could eat."

"Hush, Buddy," and Nellie Gray held a finger to his lips. "Here he comes now. Please don't talk so much while we eat."

The tall Texan was smiling when he came into the big dining room. Mary Jane ran to him and held out her arms. Bowie swung her up and grinned at Buddy.

"Riding that Snapper hoss before breakfast gives a man an appetite, don't it, pard?" he chuckled.

"I'd tell uh man," Buddy boasted proudly. "When you going to show me how to handle a hog-leg, Alamo?"

The smile faded from the tall Texan's face. "That's one thing I don't aim to teach you, son," he answered gravely. "You and me won't be wearing hardware over there on the cattle spread where we're going!"

Nellie Gray smiled with relief, but Buddy showed his disappointment. "Me a cowboy and no sixgun?" he scowled.

"Cowboys don't have much time for gun-fighting as a rule," and the Texan placed Mary Jane in her chair.

"But you was a cowboy, because Doc told me so," Buddy insisted. "He said you was a ring-tailed snorter down there in Texas when you was a yearlin'!"

Alamo Bowie sighed and glanced at Nellie Gray. "That's what I was afraid of," he murmured softly. "Riding on the stage with Bud Philpot, and then rubbing stirrups with Doc Holliday after the hold-up. They didn't mean nothing by it, but I wish they had bridled their tongues."

"Don't worry, Alamo," Nellie answered quietly, but he caught the look of anxiety in her brown eyes. "Buddy is only eight, and he will forget it when we leave here. But I'll be glad when that trial is over this morning."

The Texan remained silent while Wing brought hot cakes with ham and eggs. Nellie Gray was seated at the head of the table, with Mary Jane and Buddy on each side of Bowie. He stared at his plate until the Chinaman had returned to the kitchen, and his low voice carried a warning when he spoke.

"You stay right here with the children, Nellie. I don't like it with Carlos Chavez on the loose."

"You mean that Mex what tried to take us out of the stage?" Buddy demanded. "The one what got away when you and Doc come faunchin' down the hill?"

Bowie nodded. "You and Mary Jane stay in the house," he murmured, and his deep voice was stern.

"I'll look after Mary Jane if you'll lend me one of yore cutters," and Buddy waited hopefully while his blue eyes watched the Texan's face.

Nellie Gray caught her breath quickly, but Alamo Bowie turned to the boy and shook his head. "You wouldn't have a chance, little pard," he explained. "Carlos Chavez is mighty fast with his tools, so I want yore promise to stay inside and look after Mary Jane."

"I could hold a gun if I took both hands," and Buddy refused to give up his original idea. "That away I could look after Mary Jane and the Angel better."

"You better start on them hot cakes," and Bowie changed the subject. "This grub shore smells good."

He buttered his cakes and poured syrup while the small boy stared sulkily. "I hope that Mexican comes," Buddy muttered.

"Cowboys don't talk while they are eating," Bowie grunted. "You better start shovelin' it in!"

Nellie Gray's brown eyes narrowed a trifle at the

sharpness of his voice. Buddy also caught the change and started to eat. Mary Jane snuggled close to the Texan until the harsh lines softened around his mouth.

"You won't ever go away and leave me and Buddy, will you, Daddy Bowie?" she whispered.

Bowie glanced across the table and smiled at Nellie Gray. "Not never," he promised softly. "Only when I have work to do, and then I won't stay long."

"Cowboys don't talk when they eat," Buddy growled sullenly. "You better feed yore face, Mary Jane!"

Alamo Bowie grinned and attacked his food. Even Nellie Gray was silent until the meal was finished, but the look of worry came back to her pretty face when the door opened to admit Doc Holliday. The gambler came straight to the table and whispered to Bowie.

"Court is about to start, Alamo. Judge Hart wants you down there just in case of."

The Texan was instantly alert, but he forgot the presence of the children. "How's Fred and the sheriff making it?" he asked.

"Rutledge can't walk account of that wound in his leg," the gambler answered. "Sheriff Blaine is getting around with his arm in a sling, but he looks pretty shaky. Marty Williams and Jed Swope are on hand, and Slaughter is sticking close to the jail guarding the prisoners."

"Good for him," Bowie muttered. "We won't have to worry about a jail delivery while Lantern-jaw stands trial. Have Butch and McLowery been arraigned?"

270

Doc Holliday nodded. "Judge Hart issued a pair of warrants for each of them," he answered quietly. "For rustling that herd of Slaughter's, and for kidnap and assault on himself. Then he granted a change of venue so's he could be the prosecuting witness. He heard them talking about the herd while they was holding him prisoner out there on the Box C!"

"There won't be any trouble," Bowie said thoughtfully. "But I wish you would keep an eye on them," and he jerked his head toward the children. "Carlos Chavez is still on the loose."

Doc Holliday nodded and looked down when a small hand tugged at his long coat. "I'll look after the women if you'll give me the lend of a gun," and Buddy scowled at Alamo Bowie. "I can hold it with two hands!"

Alamo Bowie's face grew stern while his left hand rubbed the scar on his chin. Doc Holliday glanced at the Texan and back to the small boy. Then he shook his head gravely.

"Best you wait till you get the velvet off yore horns, yearlin'," he said slowly. "Alamo knows what is best for you, and a good hand don't never make no fuss when the Ramrod gives orders for the day's work."

Buddy's face clouded up, and he turned away to hide the tears of disappointment. Alamo Bowie reached down a big hand and patted the shaking shoulders.

"She's this away, little pard," he explained softly. "I'm counting on you big to look after Angel and Mary Jane. You was a few years older, I'd give you one of my own guns, but the Twins kick back like a pair of buckin' mules."

Buddy stiffened and raised his head. Then he turned slowly and stuck out his right hand. "Shake, feller," he said soberly. "I'll watch out for 'em, and I won't kick up no more fuss!"

"Spoke like a man," and the tall Texan gripped the small hand firmly. "And don't forget that us Bowies don't never break a promise!"

Nellie Gray smiled and then covered her mouth with her hand. She came around the table and turned Bowie to face her with both hands on his square shoulders.

"You just said a Bowie never breaks his promise," and her throaty voice held a note of fear. "Does that mean . . . ?"

The Texan stared deep into her eyes and nodded slowly. "You mean Three-finger?" he asked.

"Yes, and we need you now!"

"Don't worry," he whispered. "I came here to do a job of work, and the job is almost finished. Now I must get down to the Court house."

Nellie Gray released his shoulders and sighed. She knew that nothing could change the tall hard-faced man who had ridden so suddenly into her life, and Doc Holliday turned quickly and started for the door. Alamo Bowie kissed Mary Jane and patted Buddy on the shoulder.

"See you at dinner," and then he swung on his heel and followed the gambler down the street.

"We got us a jury," Holliday said carelessly.

272

"Mostly all miners from the Lucky Cuss and the Contention mines. This trial won't take long."

Alamo Bowie did not answer. At one time it had seemed very important to get a conviction against one of the outlaws, but now his thoughts were with Nellie Gray and the two children. His hands touched the handles of his gun, and the Texan shrugged irritably. Guns and a family did not go together, and Bowie had never been broke to harness. Doc Holliday glanced at his moody face and spoke soothingly.

"That button will forget all about guns when you get him on the ranch," he murmured. "But I know how you feel, feller."

"I've played lone wolf most of my life," Bowie grunted. "Seems like everybody knows about Nellie and me, and most of them think I won't make a go of it."

The gambler stopped in front of the Court house. "About Three-finger," and his voice was harsh and low. "You can down him, Alamo, but it's a dead cinch he'll take you with him. Better let me auger it out with him!"

The Texan straightened while swift anger leaped to his gray eyes and ridged the muscles of his jaw. His shoulders drooped forward with both hands shadowing the Twins, and his voice was a rasping snarl against tightly clenched teeth.

"It might be my last show-down, Doc. Like you said, Three-finger might take me with him. But up to now I ain't never broke my word, and I'd rather be dead than accused of dogging it. I'm going through with the play!"

The gambler nodded and sighed softly. "Knew you would," and he stuck out his hand. "But like I said, I'm taking seconds if that big owl-hooter gets the luck!"

Alamo Bowie gripped hard and shrugged his anger away. "Let's get on in," he growled. "The bullet ain't been made yet with my name on it!"

Sheriff Joe Blaine was checking hardware at the front door. Alamo Bowie's eyes lighted up when he saw Fred Rutledge seated on a bench with his legs stretched out in front of him. The deputy had a riot gun across his lap, and a wide grin on his face.

"Howdy, Texan," he chuckled. "Heard you was having yore first meal with yore family."

"That's right," Bowie answered softly. "But you should have stayed in bed, feller."

"Joe ain't in bed," Rutledge answered gruffly. "You showed us something about the law when you rode that Snapper horse to Tombstone, and we're having too much fun to quit now. Howdy, Doc."

"Howdy, Fred," and Holliday turned to Bowie. "Reckon I better stay back here and keep my eyes on the street," he muttered. "As long as Fred and Joe are on the job. Yonder is Jed Swope and Marty Williams calling you."

He eased out through the door when Bowie made his way up the aisle. Then he was almost running toward the Russ house on the corner. A rangy black horse had entered the alley and was tied in back of the kitchen, and the gambler's greenish eyes narrowed to slits when he climbed the steps and slid through the back door.

He paused in the pantry when a soft purring voice came from the other side of the kitchen door. Left hand reaching for the handkerchief in his breast pocket when his shoulders began to twitch from the exertion of his run. The slight body shook while the gambler pressed the cloth to his lips to muffle the sound of his coughing.

"Do not make the move, Senora," the purring voice warned. "Permit me to introduce myself. I am Carlos Chavez, and I take the Keeds for my amigo, Three-finger!"

Nellie Gray faced the square-shouldered Mexican with an arm around each of the children. Her oval face was dead white with fright, but she shook her head and stared at him with steady brown eyes.

"I know you," she answered in a whisper. "I am glad that you did not kill Alamo Bowie!"

The Mexican's dark eyes widened, and then he shrugged. A heavy gun was held steady in his right hand, and he clicked his white teeth and laughed grimly.

"I allow him to live because I make the promise," he answered softly. "Three-finger he have save the *Tejano* for his own gon!"

Nellie Gray shook her head. "You cannot take the children," she said firmly. "Not unless you kill me first!"

"No kill; just put to sleep," and the Mexican shrugged carelessly.

He took a quick step forward and stopped suddenly when a soft cough sounded behind him. He jerked his head around and stared at the slender gambler in the doorway.

"Senor Death!" he whispered, and his eyes swung down to the empty hands.

Nellie Gray shielded the two children with her body and bit her lip. Carlos Chavez whirled like a cat with thumb earing back the hammer of the gun in his hand. The white-fingered hand of Doc Holliday slapped down to his right leg. The long-tailed coat was ripped aside when red gunlight flamed like a flash of lightning. Lightning followed by the sullen roar of thunder that beat against the low ceiling while Carlos Chavez was falling to the floor.

The gun exploded and flew from his hand before he had completed his turn, and Doc Holliday crouched across the smoking old Peacemaker and waited until the rattling boots had finished their rapid tattoo. Then he slumped back against the wall and doubled over when a fit of coughing shook him like a reed in the wind.

Nellie Gray went to a cupboard and reached for a bottle of brandy. She poured a tall glass and braced the gambler with her right arm while he drank jerkily between spasms. At last he straightened up with a wan smile and holstered his gun.

"I saw the black come in the alley," he explained softly. "Started me to coughing when I ran up here."

"I don't know how to thank you, Doc," and Nellie Gray gripped his hand. "He was going to take the children!"

"I heard him," the gambler nodded. "Looks like I wasn't meant to go out by the gun."

"Please lie down a spell," and Nellie Gray pointed to a side room. "You will feel stronger in a few minutes."

Doc Holliday shook his head stubbornly and reached for the bottle of brandy. He saw Buddy watching him and turned his back while he drained the bottle. Then he straightened up with a smile.

"Never felt better in my life," he announced strongly. "And you, Buddy; that was shore brave the way you faced that big jigger and never batted an eye."

"I'd have drilled him center if I'd have had a cutter," and Buddy glared at the body on the floor. "He had it comin', I'd tell uh man!"

"Better take 'em upstairs," the gambler whispered to Nellie Gray. "I got to be getting back there for that trial."

He nodded and stepped out the back door. A long black wagon was just drawing up, and Doc Holliday muttered under his breath. Hunchy Domain stopped his team and slid to the ground facing the gambler.

"Saw him come a-foggin', and then I see you hittin' the high-spots," the undertaker explained. "He in the kitchen?"

"Yeah, yuh dang buzzard," the gambler growled, and stomped down the alley to the Court house.

CHAPTER XXI

Judge Hart took his seat behind the bench and rapped with the handle of his gun.

"This court will come to order," he barked sharply, and glared at the man in the prisoner's box. "Lantern-jaw Peters, versus the Territory of Arizona!"

Alamo Bowie snugged his shoulders deep in his seat and stared at the tall Mexican across the room. He noted the empty holsters on the long slender legs, and he sat up suddenly and twisted his head when a shot echoed from up the street. A strange feeling clutched at his heart, and then he noticed the absence of Doc Holliday.

"Alamo Bowie will take the stand!"

The Texan arose when the judge called his name. He took the oath and gave his evidence impassively. The red-shirted miners in the jury box watched and listened closely, and several nudged each other when Bowie concluded his testimony, and walked down the aisle. Sheriff Blaine jerked his head toward the sound of the shot, and Bowie nodded and walked outside.

Doc Holliday was coming down the alley, and the two men stopped halfway and stared at each other. The Texan spoke first.

"Carlos Chavez?" he asked.

The gambler nodded carelessly and jerked a thumb toward the black wagon at the end of the alley.

"Hunchy Domain is taking him up to the morgue," he grunted. "That feller can spot a corpse further than a buzzard!"

Alamo Bowie put out a hand and gripped Holliday by the fore-arm. "Nellie?" and his deep voice was a staccato whisper. "Is Nellie and the kids all right?"

"He didn't have time to hurt them any," the gambler answered grimly. "He was going to slap Nellie to sleep with the barrel of his gun when she told him he would have to take Buddy and Mary Jane over her dead body. I didn't throw off my shot none!"

Alamo Bowie took a deep breath, and there was an unusual light of affection and gratitude in his gray eyes. "I won't ever forget, pard," he murmured, and then his mood changed. "That trial back yonder," he grunted. "Looks like Peters will get all of fifteen years."

"That means work for you, Bowie," the slender gambler remarked quietly. "That just about cleans up Three-finger's gang except for some stragglers. If I was you, I'd do some talking to a tall Mex that rode in here on a grulla hoss with silver trappings."

Alamo Bowie glanced at the back of the Russ house and shifted uneasily. "I don't want to go back there until I have finished my work," he muttered. "But Nellie will think it funny that I don't run in after that killing."

"Angel has uncommon good sense," Holliday said sincerely. "She will savvy, feller."

"We better get back to the trial," Bowie answered with a nod of his head. "Not that they need me any more, but both Fred and Joe are crippled up some."

The two men walked slowly down the alley while the wagon of Hunchy Domain rolled away in the other direction. A ten-year-old Mexican boy detached himself from the top bar of a corral and slid to the dust. He eyed Alamo Bowie for a moment and then shuffled forward. The Texan paid no attention until the boy planted himself on his bare feet and spoke softly.

"Senor Bowie?"

"*Si, muchacho,*" Bowie answered. "What you got on yore mind, little feller?"

"*Un carta,*" the boy murmured, and held out a piece of paper. "*El Caballero* he give to me *por* you. Then he ride away swiftly!"

Alamo Bowie glanced sharply at the grimy face and took the note. He stiffened when he saw the fine Spencerian writing. Doc Holliday also recognized that writing and nodded slowly.

"I figgered he would slope while you was gone," he murmured. "Spell it out, pard."

Alamo Bowie threw a coin to the boy and swept his eyes up the street. No sign of a horseman in either direction, and he could hear the drone of voices coming from the Court room. Then he scanned the note and read aloud.

"*Alamo Bowie.*
"*Peters will go to Yuma. You and me made a promise. I hold you brought too much law for Tombstone. I will wait in Skeleton if you come alone, as I am alone. Show-down at ten paces*

280

and an even break according to the code. I will be waiting.

"Three-finger Jack."

"He writes a nice hand," Doc Holliday commented. "And he can see for three miles in any direction to make shore you come alone. Adios, pard," and he held out his hand.

Alamo Bowie gripped firmly with a light of admiration in his eyes. He knew that the gambler understood; knew he would ask no questions or make any objections. A promise was a promise, and both knew the conditions of the gunman's code.

"Snapper is geared up and waiting," he said softly. "And I have been waiting for this chance a long time."

The flame of battle once more glowed fiercely in his gray eyes to erase all suggestion of sentiment. Once more he was the man-hunter; an Ace among Aces with the tools of his trade. Doc Holliday gripped hard and nodded.

"I'll ride out in half an hour," he promised. "Good luck, Texan!"

Alamo Bowie brushed the handles of his guns with sensitive finger tips and strode up the alley with long eager steps. Big Marty Williams was back in the court room, and the Texan spoke softly to the big red horse waiting in the box stall at the O K corral. A moment later he was in the high saddle riding toward the foothills of the purple Dragoons, with the battered black Stetson cuffed low above his eyes.

No fear in his heart. Nothing but the eager anticipation he always felt when another master challenged his skill. He promised himself that he would hang up the Twins after this one last Show-down. Nellie and the Kids needed him, and he was getting along in years. Thirty his next birthday, if he lived to observe it.

Skeleton Canyon was perhaps six miles from town, and the tall Texan knew the short-cuts across the dry flats and through the rolling hills. He drew the Twins one at a time and checked them carefully. Five loads in each with the filed hammers riding on an empty. Men had shot themselves by packing sixes full if a gun spilled from the holster, and Bowie snugged the heavy forty-fives back in oil-moulded leather with a grunt of satisfaction.

His chest swelled out with the happiness that comes only to those in the top rank. Not that he discounted the speed of his foe, but self-confidence was one of the Texan's chief characteristics. It would be close, with a three-by-seven waiting on Boot Hill for the loser . . . or losers. And then the Texan saw the bone-choked entrance to Skeleton Canyon.

He turned in the saddle and scanned the back trail. Smiled with content when no dust-cloud showed against the sky-line. Snapper was loping easily to keep the rendezvous of death. The strange duel which still might mark the difference between law and out-lawry. Single-handed, Three-finger Jack had built up his dreaded gang, and the Texan knew that he could do it again. What man has done, man can do.

His hands dropped and loosed the heavy guns

against riding crimp that might jam them deep in holster leather to slow up the draw. Snapper single-footed through the narrow opening between great piles of gleaming white bones. Tall rows of upright stones stretching back into the canyon like guarding sentinels. The sentinels of the dead.

Now the Texan's face was craggy and hard when he checked the big red horse and dropped the split reins to the ground. A soft word sent Snapper back among the burned lava rocks, and his master sucked in a great breath of air and tilted the handles of his guns with a careless but expert sweep of his big hands. His eyes read the sign on the ground where the deep-chested grulla had marked a course. Alamo Bowie waited.

A high-crowned sombrero appeared suddenly above a row of stones and moved slowly to the clearing. Three-finger Jack stepped out empty-handed and nodded his head. His black eyes held a look of admiration for the man who came alone to keep his promise. A man who lived, and would die . . . by the code.

He came forward slowly with eyes calculating the distance. When he stopped, the tall Texan took a forward step and spread his big boots wide.

"Ten paces," he said quietly.

"You knew me, Texan," Three-finger remarked positively. "You knew me back there in Tombstone when the miners wanted to string me up!"

"I knew you," Bowie agreed softly. "But that would leave the question unanswered. I got yore *carta,* and I came alone!"

"No hurry," the outlaw said calmly. "This morning you were marked for death, but Carlos Chavez lowered his hammer because he had made me a promise."

"In some ways, Chavez had the makings of a man," the Texan answered in his deep drawl.

"Had?"

Alamo Bowie nodded slowly. "That shot you heard back in Tombstone when we were in the Court room," he said slowly, and shook his head. "That slug had yore pard's name on it."

Three-finger Jack straightened suddenly and stared. "Doc Holliday?" he asked, and his voice was a biting whisper.

Alamo Bowie nodded. "Chavez went to the Russ house and tried to take the kids. He rode in on yore hoss, and Doc saw the Black in the back alley."

For a moment the tall outlaw bit his lips to control his emotions. "Senor Death," he muttered harshly. "I should have let Chavez bush-whack him this morning when he had the gambler under his sights!"

"That Mex wouldn't have had a show," Bowie contradicted dryly.

"You were driving the stage," and the outlaw's voice was husky. "The button was in yore saddle on the red hoss with Holliday rubbing stirrups beside him. Me and Carlos were a hundred yards away. Hiding there in the brush just before you come to the grade leading into town."

"Yeah," Bowie murmured. "But that ain't the white man's way, and yo're a white man, Jack. Carlos Chavez is dead!"

The outlaw scowled and stared from under the brim of his heavy sombrero. "He had you tagged for his own cutter," he growled. "Account of what you did to Sonora Lopez, his cousin. He'd have killed you, Bowie. Mebbe not according to the code, but he'd have tallied just the same!"

"And he made you a promise?" the Texan murmured.

The outlaw nodded. "I told him I had first chance. He had a knife in the air before you could wink, but it didn't strike!"

Alamo Bowie watched in silence, but his gray eyes wandered down to the ivory-handled Colts on the slender legs. "How come?" he muttered.

Three-finger Jack smiled. "I made my pass and faded him," he said quietly. "My slug stopped the *cuchillo* in the air. After which me and Chavez decided to be pards."

"And now he is dead," Bowie reminded. "Hunchy Domain was taking him away when I high-loped out of town!"

Three-finger Jack bit his lower lip and glared while the angry color stained his dark face. His black eyes glowed redly with killer-light while the Texan waited for him to control his temper. His soft voice spoke a gentle warning.

"Getting mad slows up a gent's gun-hand, Three-finger. I don't want any edges!"

The outlaw controlled himself and smiled. "This One-Shot Brady over in New Mex?" he asked. "I figgered on taking it to him one of the days. Was he fast?"

A reminiscent gleam flicked across the narrowed gray eyes. "He was fast," the Texan admitted. "His slug made that hole in my vest when he dropped," and he pointed to a tear in the left side of his calf-skin vest.

"I knew I had him beat," and the outlaw's voice expressed his confidence and satisfaction.

Alamo Bowie shrugged. "How you figger?"

"Account of now," the outlaw murmured, and smiled with his thin lips. "My mark will be right over yore heart when the smoke clears off!"

Alamo Bowie crouched forward with shoulders stooped. His face was hard and unsmiling while he stared at the man he knew was trying to make him lose his head. Then he sighed softly and relaxed.

"You talked out?" he asked quietly, but his voice rasped like metal.

Three-finger Jack shook his head one time. "Not quite," he answered. "You wasn't cut out to be a family man, Bowie. You won't never be anything but a gun-fighter. I feel sorry for the kids!"

Alamo Bowie stared steadily. "Yo're the fastest gun-dog I ever faced, Three-finger," he admitted honestly. "The fastest . . . and the last!"

"That's right," the outlaw agreed. "I'll cut yore notch on the handle of my gun when you stop kicking!"

The Texan ignored the boast. "I'm hanging up the Twins after you ride to Boot Hill," he continued in the same tone. "I made a promise to Nellie, and I always keep my word. I brought the Law for Tombstone, and my work is almost finished!"

Three-finger Jack smiled broadly. "I'm saving you grief, Bowie," he said softly. "If you hadn't promised to face me for show-down, you might have got married. Blood will always tell, and you might have had a chip of yore own."

The Texan growled deep in his throat. "It's yore last talk," he muttered. "You was saying?"

"The button would be a gun-slammer like you and me," and the outlaw nodded positively. "This away you won't have to worry. You won't have no more family than you got right now!"

"I'm telling you because yore time is about up," the Texan answered thoughtfully. "I figgered on all that. I'll have a button of my own, and he won't be a Colt-hand!"

"That's right, he won't," the outlaw agreed. "The sun is getting high. You ready?"

Alamo Bowie stared for a moment and nodded. "You could have been somebody with yore brains, Three-finger," he answered. "Make yore fight!"

The tall outlaw under-went a startling change. The easy smile ripped from his face like a mask. Now his nostrils were flaring while his black eyes narrowed to pin-points. His long-fingered hands taloned out above the tilted handles of his guns, and he caught his balance easily on wide-spread polished boots.

"Yore deal," he whispered.

The Texan shook his head slowly. "I'll say the word," he murmured. "According to the code!"

Three-finger Jack nodded slightly without relaxing his vigilance. The tall Texan crouched toward him with elbows against lean ribs. Blue eyes watching the corners of those black eyes, and then he took a deep breath. The outlaw stiffened slightly and waited, and Alamo Bowie smiled with the corners of his mouth.

"When!"

He saw the tell-tale V wrinkles leap suddenly under the impetus of the outlaw's brain. Then he twitched his right shoulder with fingers shaped to fit the handle of his tally-gun. Three-finger Jack was making his strike like a hawk coming for the kill, and gun-metal hissed against oiled leather before the word had died away.

Alamo Bowie caught the worn handle with thumb dogging back the delicately-filed hammer. Up came the long barrel with flame gouting above the holster lip. A flame that was reflected from gleaming metal ten paces away before the twin muzzle-blooms were snuffed out by widening rings of black powder smoke.

The tall Texan was slapped into a turn when a giant hammer dealt him a blow in the left arm below the shoulder. He stomped his boot to stop the turn, and the muzzle of his gun was sagging toward the sand when he squared around. Three-finger Jack was leaning toward him empty-handed with the smoking gun between his polished boots.

Alamo Bowie stopped the twitch that was snapping his gun up in line. A wave of sickness and pain swept across his brain, and he watched dully until the outlaw buckled his knees to break his fall.

The Texan stared as in a daze and tried to bring up his left hand to eject the shell from his gun. A soft groan escaped from his lips when the arm refused to move. His eyes widened when the outlaw's boots rattled for a brief minute against the lava rocks, and then all was strangely still.

It seemed an Eternity since he had made his pass for the last show-down, but the smoke was still curling slowly from the muzzle of his gun when he holstered it and swayed weakly. Not more than the space of two heart-beats, and Alamo Bowie removed his hat and whispered softly.

"Law for Tombstone," he muttered. "I better be getting back to Nellie and the kids."

He took a step and sprawled on the ground with both hands reaching out to break his fall. For a moment he braced himself before his body sank slowly until he rested on the ground.

Silence for a long moment. Two black dots wheeled high in the blue above the Dragoons and circled closer on wings that did not move. They banked sharply and wheeled away when a dust-cloud appeared on the dim trail and grew larger with the speed of a horse, but Alamo Bowie did not hear the pounding hoofs. He had faced show-down, and Three-finger Jack had made *El Jornado del Muerto*. The journey of Death!

CHAPTER XXII

Doc Holliday glanced up at the black dots in the sky and scratched his horse with the rowels. A sneering smile twisted his thin lips at the corners while his greenish eyes glared savagely.

"Damn buzzards," he muttered under his breath, and sent his horse through the narrow opening between the piles of bleached bones. "I knew it would be close to a stand-off!"

Row after row of upright lava rocks stretching back into the Devil's kitchen. Two long-legged bodies sprawled on the ground about ten paces apart. The big red horse watching with ears pricked back, waiting for the familiar whistle to call him forward. The deep-chested grulla farther back with the gleaming silver saddle catching the rays of the noonday sun. While the two black dots poised high in the blue as though to watch.

The gambler reined in and slid from the saddle to ground-hitch his horse with trailing reins. He stared for a brief moment at Three-finger Jack and shrugged with careless fatalism. The outlaw had finished his reign of terror and had come to the forks of the trail. Every detail about his posture spoke plainly of death, and Doc Holliday shrugged and turned at last to Alamo Bowie.

He did not touch the body, but his eyes brightened suddenly when a slight movement caught his attention. Just the slow rise and fall of the deeply-arched chest to tell of respiration. The Texan was breathing! Then the slender gambler threw back his head and laughed up at the circling dots.

"You can have him," he muttered. "I thought they was both done for, but you can't fool a buzzard!"

A black team was racing madly across the Alkali stretch beyond the mouth of the draw. The gambler jerked his head and stared at the careening black wagon and shook his head. He shrugged angrily and hunkered down beside the Texan while he reached to his hip pocket for the bottle of brandy he always carried.

"Get a snort of this, pard," he murmured tenderly, and forced open the pallid lips. "It's Doc, feller. You got to be sittin' up before Hunchy Domain rattles in!"

Alamo Bowie swallowed and coughed loudly. Then he sat up suddenly and clutched at the gambler. His gray eyes opened wide; blinked uncertainly and then cleared up. Then the gaunt Texan smiled at the gambler and drank deeply of the proffered bottle.

"The trial?" he whispered. "How'd it go?"

"Lantern-jaw drew fifteen years at Yuma," Holliday answered quietly. "Butch and McLowery will get the same when their time comes. Looks like yore chore is all finished."

Alamo Bowie nodded and stiffened when the black wagon rattled across the rocky ground and pulled up with a flourish. Hunchy Domain wrapped the reins around the stock of his whip and stepped down gravely. No excitement on his big heavy face when he glanced at the Texan and then walked toward the body of Three-finger Jack.

"He made a slight mistake," he remarked quietly in his deep rumble. "He paid me a thousand in advance to bury Bowie. That included the glass hearse with four black horses," and the undertaker chuckled without mirth. "He was paying for his own job, and he didn't know it!"

Doc Holliday turned slowly with a frown of anger on his thin face. "You take that corpse and light a shuck, you dang buzzard," he growled. "All the time you was figgering on *two* cases!"

"Sooner or later, I get 'em all," Hunchy Domain answered without emotion, and opened the back of his wagon. "You mind giving me a hand with his boots?"

The gambler stared without moving. "So far I haven't started coughing," and he skinned back his thin lips in a savage grin. "Better handle him by yore lonesome!"

Hunchy Domain shrugged and bent his powerful shoulders. A moment later the remains of the dreaded outlaw were traveling slowly toward Tombstone. Doc Holliday watched the wagon through the opening of the draw, and when he turned, Alamo Bowie was on his feet.

"Can you ride?" he asked quietly.

"Better tie a rag tight on this arm," and the Texan pointed to the injured member. "His slug broke the bone, but Doc Kramer can fix it up!"

Doc Holliday knew something of surgery, and he shook his head while he bandaged the broken arm. A forty-five slug makes a nasty wound, and Alamo Bowie gritted his teeth and managed a wan smile.

"You might lose that arm, pard," the gambler muttered.

The Texan stiffened angrily. "I'll die first," he snarled. "It won't be much good to me, but I aim to keep all I got. Lead Snapper close and give me a hand!"

The big red horse seemed to know that his master was hurt. He picked his steps carefully over the rocky ground, and Alamo Bowie swayed weakly in the high saddle. Doc Holliday rode up close and offered the brandy bottle without a word, and after a stiff pull, the Texan sat erect and grinned at the gambler.

"Never felt better," he lied. "Let's get back to Nellie and the kids!"

He scratched Snapper into a high lope and rode easily when the big red horse racked along swiftly over the back trail. The gambler watched closely and reined away from Allen street when they loped into town. Down Fifth and through the alley to the back door of the Russ house where the tall Texan slid from the saddle and staggered up the steps to his room.

"Pull my boots off, Doc," he whispered, and his gray eyes were bright with fever. "Then get Doc Kramer up here on the run. Better leave me the brandy!"

The gambler nodded silently and turned his back. Caught the hand-made boots between his legs and tugged them off while Bowie laid back on the bed with a tired sigh. Then Doc Holliday stepped into the hall and jerked back when he saw Nellie Gray coming toward him. He put a finger to his lips and went to meet her.

"He's all right except for a broken arm," he whispered, and steadied the brown-eyed woman when she swayed weakly. "He's in there, and I'm sending Doc Kramer up."

"Three-finger Jack?" and Nellie Gray held her breath.

"Hunchy Domain brought him to town in his wagon," the gambler answered harshly. "You better stay with Bowie!"

The tall Texan jerked his eyes open when she opened the door softly and stepped inside. Then he smiled and held out his right hand. Nellie Gray stifled a sob and fell to her knees beside the bed to wrap him in her arms.

"My Dear," she sobbed, and he patted the black curls and sighed contentedly. "I saw you ride away, and I prayed!"

"Reckon yore prayers were answered, honey," he whispered, and closed his eyes.

The throbbing pain in his arm grew less when he drifted into a hazy stupor. He could hear voices from a great distance, but nothing mattered except the nearness of the woman he loved. The only woman he had ever loved in his stormy life. Figures moved like shadowy silhouettes against the bright light from the window, but Alamo Bowie was lost in the anesthesia of unconsciousness.

Nellie Gray watched the square-shouldered Doctor

as he probed for the bullet. Doc Kramer worked impassively and cauterized the angry wound. After making a temporary dressing, he sat on the side of the bed and whittled a pair of splints with his jack knife.

"That arm will have to come off," he whispered soberly. "To save his life!"

"You ain't goin' to cut off Daddy Bowie's arm," a fierce childish voice contradicted.

Nellie Gray and the Doctor turned to Buddy who stood at the foot of the bed. The chubby youngster was holding one of the Texan's heavy guns in both hands with the barrel resting on the foot of the bed. Tears of anger and determination rolled down the red cheeks while the boy braced his short legs wide apart and glared at the Medico.

"Buddy," and the voice of Nellie Gray was a wail of fear. "Put that gun down at once!"

"I won't," the boy barked. "I heard Daddy Bowie say he would rather be dead than lose his arm. I'll kill the Croaker lessen he promises not to do what he said!"

Doc Holliday stood against the door and smiled. He was behind the boy, but a sudden movement might drop the heavy hammer. Doc Kramer paled slightly and stared into the black muzzle. Then he shrugged his shoulders and nodded his head.

"She's a promise, feller," he answered dryly. "That arm stays right where it is till Bowie gives the word. I ain't never broke my word up to now!"

Buddy carefully lowered the hammer with both thumbs and laid down the gun. Then he came around the bed and held out his right hand gravely.

"Put it there, Doc," he muttered. "I taken yore word!"

Doc Kramer did not smile as he shook hands. Nellie Gray shook her head slowly, and then a low chuckle came from the man on the bed.

"Thanks, little pard. Just for that I'm giving you a little Spanish hoss with a silver saddle. I'll do the same for you sometime!"

Alamo Bowie was smiling at them with the old careless grin on his hard face. A face that was somewhat more pale, and softened by the unseen alchemy of love. Nellie Gray lowered her face and kissed him tenderly, and Buddy began to sob with reaction.

The Texan reached out his hand and gripped the little fellow hard. "I believe you would have shot the Doc," he said seriously.

"I'd tell uh man," the boy sniffed jerkily, and wiped his face on the sleeve of his jacket. "You and me is pards, and I'll side you all the way down the river!"

"Knew it all the time, feller," and the Texan's voice was husky with happiness. "Where's my little sweetheart?"

"You mean Mary Jane?"

The Texan nodded. "She said she couldn't stand to see you suffer," and Buddy allowed a faint sneer to tinge his voice. "She high-tailed down the hall when Doc commenced to fish for that slug!"

"I'm here, Daddy Bowie," a tearful voice wailed, and Mary Jane threw herself down beside the bed while her chubby arms went around the wounded man's neck. "I hurt almost as bad as you do, and I want you to get well real quick!"

"Shore, honey," and Alamo Bowie smoothed her long brown curls. "I don't aim to leave you all no more."

"Alamo!" and Nellie Gray caught his hand. "Is that a promise?"

The Texan nodded slowly. "It's a promise, Nellie," he answered slowly. "I've faced my last show-down unless it's brought to me!"

A dry cough sounded from the door. All eyes turned to stare at the stranger, and Doc Holliday smiled coldly and dropped the sawed-off back under his long-tailed coat. Tom Scudder stepped in and came to the foot of the bed where he stared at his special agent.

"You hurt bad, feller?" he whispered hoarsely.

Alamo Bowie smiled. "Just a scratch," he answered. "Broken arm, but it will mend in a few days."

"Yeah, in about six months," the Doctor corrected dryly. "Unless blood-poison sets in."

"I heard about Three-finger," Tom Scudder said quietly. "The Company had rewards posted on several of them owl-hooters, and you've earned yoreself another stake!"

"My last one," and Alamo Bowie glared at his superior. "Me and Snapper aims to settle down now, Tom."

Tom Scudder laughed. "I've heard that many's the time," he scoffed. "Just as soon as you get yore legs, under you, it will be all different."

The Texan stared with his gray eyes and then

glanced at Nellie Gray. A smile erased the hard look on his weathered face when he patted her hand and shook his head.

"You heard what I said when you come through the door," he answered quietly. "I've shucked the Twins for good, Tom!"

Tom Scudder stared with his mouth open. He turned his eyes on Nellie Gray; swiveled his head for a better look at Buddy and Mary Jane. Then he shook his head again.

"Just a minute, feller," he said quietly. "You forgotten about Black Bart over Prescott way?"

Alamo Bowie twisted uneasily. Once more the old eager light of contest flamed in his steady gray eyes. The fingers of his right hand began to flex rapidly, and Nellie Gray watched him with a sinking feeling in her heart. Tom Scudder read the sign and smiled triumphantly.

"Black Bart made his brags," he continued. "Said no long-haired Texan could cut his sign and live to whittle a notch!"

"He said that?" and the Texan tried to sit up.

Tom Scudder nodded. "Said he would be waiting up in the high hills until you got up nerve enough to face a real man. He robbed the stage day before yesterday, and left some poetry pinned to the driver's chest. You like to hear it?"

"Please," Nellie Gray whispered pleadingly. "Can't you see what you are doing, Mister Scudder?"

"That poetry," Bowie interrupted harshly. "What'd it say?"

"I got it here," and Tom Scudder reached to his inside pocket.

"Read it," the Texan growled. "The mouthy son!"

Tom Scudder smoothed out the soiled paper and faced the light from the window. Doc Holliday and the Doctor locked glances and shook their heads. Little Buddy crowded forward with his blue eyes wide, and Nellie Gray sighed deeply. Tom Scudder began to read slowly.

> *"I take the gold and call it fun*
> *I make the other feller run.*
> *If Alamo Bowie packs a gun,*
> *It's show-down with the setting sun.*
> *I'll be waiting. Black Bart."*

All eyes turned to watch the face of Alamo Bowie. Once more the ridges of muscles were making his jaws craggy with determination. Once more the old reckless killer-light blazed fiercely in the deep gray eyes. Then the light faded as the Texan shook his head.

"I ain't never cut his sign," he said slowly. "I never started on his trail. That makes a difference, Tom Scudder!"

"Difference, how come?" the Wells Fargo Manager demanded. "We talked about him when I passed through here ten days ago. And I always hired you to carry the law in yore holsters!"

"Up to now," and Alamo Bowie closed his eyes and clenched his teeth. "I made a promise to my family!"

"Promise?" and Tom Scudder threw back his head and laughed. "You always was a gun-fighter, and you always will be!"

"That's what Three-finger said," the Texan muttered. "And Three-finger is dead!"

"Black Bart is fast," Tom Scudder whispered. "He's so fast no one has ever seen his hand move. Just wished his hardware out of the air, and he can shoot the eye from a striking snake and call which eye!"

"That's tolerable fast," and Alamo Bowie kept his eyes closed. "That's faster than most, but One-shot Brady or Three-finger both had it shaded!"

Nellie Gray held her breath and watched the play of emotions on his tanned face. Lines of pain had etched deeply, and the gray was more prominent in the thick hair. Tom Scudder nodded, and Nellie Gray pressed the Texan's hand under the cover.

"They was both fast," the big manager admitted. "But neither one of them wanted any truck with Black Bart. Mebbe yo're right at that, Alamo. Like as not he'd shoot first was you to meet up with him!"

Alamo Bowie opened his eyes and stared coldly. "Don't hooraw me, Tom," he growled, and his deep voice was stronger. "Sooner or later the law will catch up with Black Bart, but I found something stronger than the wish to match irons with a fast gun-passer. It's no good, boss!"

Tom Scudder stared. "Meaning you won't take up his challenge?" he almost shouted.

Alamo Bowie nodded and drew his hand from under the covers. His big fingers were wrapped

around the small hand of Nellie Gray, and his gun-fighting gray eyes were soft with a new light when he spoke.

"I made a promise," he said quietly. "I faced my last show-down when I met Three-finger out there in Skeleton Canyon. Back there in the Devil's Kitchen where Doc found us both. I'm handing you my resignation, Tom!"

"You can't do it," Scudder shouted. "The Wells Fargo can't get along without you!"

Alamo Bowie shook his head. "Times are changing, Tom," he answered quietly. "Things ain't like they was when you was helling down along the border. The law is coming in like I told you it would, and you ain't never knowed me to break my spoken word. I promised to get Three-finger Jack, and right now he's waiting for the glass hearse to take him on his last ride. He paid for it in advance!"

Running feet coming up the hall stopped what ever answer Tom Scudder was framing. Sheriff Joe Blaine rushed in with a smile on his florid face. Came straight to the bed and gripped Alamo Bowie by the hand.

"They caught Black Bart yesterday," he shouted. "They're taking him back to California on an old warrant!"

Tom Scudder sighed and came forward slowly. "I reckon you mean it this time, Alamo," and his voice sounded tired. "I'm wishing you all the good luck and none of the bad. Take good care of him, Angel!"

Nellie Gray smiled happily and shook hands. "We need him more than the Wells Fargo does, Mister

Scudder," she answered softly, and pointed at the two little orphans. "I don't think they could love him any more than they do right now."

"I'm leaving tonight," Tom Scudder growled. "I'll drop in before I leave!"

Alamo Bowie jerked his head for Nellie Gray to lean closer. Then he whispered in her ear, and a slow flush of color spread across his pretty face. When she nodded her head, the Texan grinned at Tom Scudder.

"Come up about eight, will you Tom?" he asked, and waited eagerly for the answer.

Tom Scudder scowled and nodded. "Any particular reason?" he demanded gruffly.

"I'd tell uh man," the Texan chuckled. "My good friend Judge Hart will be here then with his book. Nellie and me are going to get hitched!"

Center Point Publishing
600 Brooks Road ● PO Box 1
Thorndike ME 04986-0001 USA

(207) 568-3717

US & Canada:
1 800 929-9108

"P. D. James . . . writes the most lethal, erudite, people-complex novels of murder and detection since Michael Innes first began and Dorothy Sayers left us."

—*Vogue*

"The best practitioner of the mystery novel writing today."

—*The Boston Globe*

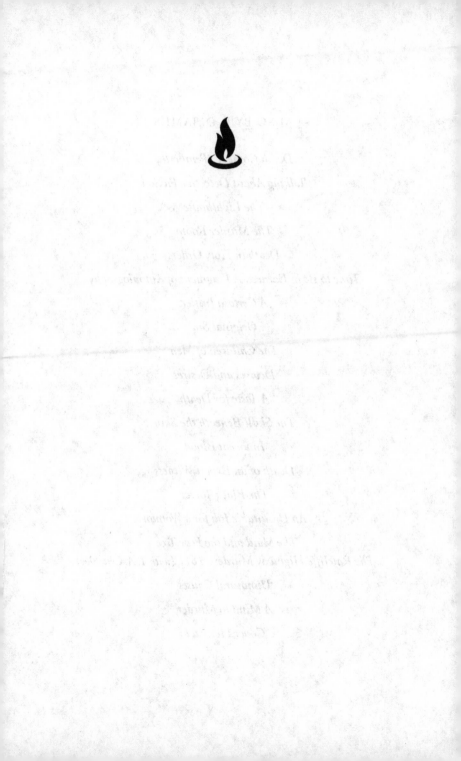

ALSO BY P. D. JAMES

P. D. JAMES

———— ✳ ————

Shroud
for a Nightingale

SCRIBNER

New York London Toronto Sydney New Delhi

Scribner
An Imprint of Simon & Schuster, Inc.
1230 Avenue of the Americas
New York, NY 10020

This Scribner trade paperback edition February 2020

SCRIBNER and design are registered trademarks of The Gale Group, Inc., used under license by Simon & Schuster, Inc., the publisher of this work.

For information about special discounts for bulk purchases, please contact Simon & Schuster Special Sales at 1-866-506-1949 or business@simonandschuster.com.

The Simon & Schuster Speakers Bureau can bring authors to your live event. For more information or to book an event, contact the Simon & Schuster Speakers Bureau at 1-866-248-3049 or visit our website at www.simonspeakers.com.

Interior design by Erich Hobbing

Manufactured in the United States of America

23 25 27 29 30 28 26 24

Library of Congress Control Number: 2001032260

ISBN 978-0-7432-1960-0
ISBN 978-1-4516-9779-7 (ebook)

For J.M.C.

Shroud for a Nightingale

CHAPTER ONE

Demonstration of Death

I

ON THE MORNING of the first murder Miss Muriel Beale, Inspector of Nurse Training Schools to the General Nursing Council, stirred into wakefulness soon after 6 o'clock and into a sluggish early morning awareness that it was Monday, 12th January, and the day of the John Carpendar Hospital inspection. Already she had half-registered the first familiar sounds of a new day: Angela's alarm silenced almost before she was conscious of hearing it; Angela herself padding and snuffling about the flat like a clumsy but benevolent animal; the agreeably anticipatory tinklings of early tea in preparation. She forced open her eyelids, resisting an insidious urge to wriggle down into the enveloping warmth of the bed and let her mind drift again into blessed unconsciousness. What on earth had prompted her to tell Matron Taylor that she would arrive shortly after 9 a.m. in time to join the third-year students' first teaching session of the day? It was ridiculously, unnecessarily early. The hospital was in Heatheringfield on the Sussex/Hampshire border, a drive of nearly fifty miles, some of which would have to be done before daybreak. And it was raining, as it had rained with dreary insistence for the past week. She could hear the faint hiss of car tyres on the Cromwell Road and an occasional spatter against the window-pane. Thank

11

God she had taken the trouble to check the map of Heatheringfield to find out exactly where the hospital lay. A developing market town, particularly if it were unfamiliar, could be a time-wasting maze to the motorist in the snarl of commuter traffic on a wet Monday morning. She felt instinctively that it was going to be a difficult day and stretched out under the bedclothes as if bracing herself to meet it. Extending her cramped fingers, she half-relished the sharp momentary ache of her stretched joints. A touch of arthritis there. Well, it was to be expected. She was forty-nine after all. It was time she took life a little more gently. What on earth had led her to think she could get to Heatheringfield before half past nine?

The door opened, letting in a shaft of light from the passage. Miss Angela Burrows jerked back the curtains, surveyed the black January sky and the rain-spattered window and jerked them together again. "It's raining," she said with the gloomy relish of one who has prophesied rain and who cannot be held responsible for the ignoring of her warning. Miss Beale propped herself on her elbow, turned on the bedside lamp, and waited. In a few seconds her friend returned and set down the early morning tray. The tray cloth was of starched embroidered linen, the flowered cups were arranged with their handles aligned, the four biscuits on the matching plate were precisely placed, two of a kind, the teapot gave forth a delicate smell of freshly made Indian tea. The two women had a strong love of comfort and an addiction to tidiness and order. The standards which they had once enforced in the private ward of their teaching hospital were applied to their own comfort, so that life in the flat was not unlike that in an expensive and permissive nursing home.

Miss Beale had shared a flat with her friend since they had both left the same training school twenty-five years ago.

Miss Angela Burrows was the Principal Tutor at a London teaching hospital. Miss Beale had thought her the paradigm of nurse tutors and, in all her inspections, subconsciously set her standard by her friend's frequent pronouncements on the principle of sound nurse teaching. Miss Burrows, for her part, wondered how the General Nursing Council would manage when the time came for Miss Beale to retire. The happiest marriages are sustained by such comforting illusions and Miss Beale's and Miss Burrow's very different, but essentially innocent, relationship was similarly founded. Except in this capacity for mutual but unstated admiration they were very different. Miss Burrows was sturdy, thick-set and formidable, hiding a vulnerable sensitivity under an air of blunt common sense. Miss Beale was small and birdlike, precise in speech and movement and threatened with an out-of-date gentility which sometimes brought her close to being thought ridiculous. Even their physiological habits were different. The heavy Miss Burrows awoke to instantaneous life at the first sound of her alarm, was positively energetic until teatime, then sank into sleepy lethargy as the evening advanced. Miss Beale daily opened her gummed eyelids with reluctance, had to force herself into early morning activity and became more brightly cheerful as the day wore on. They had managed to reconcile even this incompatibility. Miss Burrows was happy to brew the early morning tea and prepare breakfast and Miss Beale washed up after dinner and made the nightly cocoa.

Miss Burrows poured out both cups of tea, dropped two lumps of sugar in her friend's cup and took her own to the chair by the window. Early training forbade Miss Burrows to sit on the bed. She said: "You need to be off early. I'd better run your bath. When does it start?"

Miss Beale muttered feebly that she had told Matron that she would arrive as soon as possible after nine o'clock.

The tea was blessedly sweet and reviving. The promise to start out so early was a mistake but she began to think that she might after all make it by 9:15.

"That's Mary Taylor, isn't it? She's got quite a reputation considering she's only a provincial matron. Extraordinary that she's never come to London. She didn't even apply for our job when Miss Montrose retired." Miss Beale muttered incomprehensibly which, since they had had this conversation before, her friend correctly interpreted as a protest that London wasn't everybody's choice and that people were too apt to assume that nothing remarkable ever came out of the provinces.

"There's that, of course," conceded her friend. "And the John Carpendar's in a very pleasant part of the world. I like that country on the Hampshire border. It's a pity you're not visiting it in summer. Still, it's not as if she's matron of a major teaching hospital. With her ability she easily could be; she might have become one of the Great Matrons." In their student days she and Miss Beale had suffered at the hands of one of the Great Matrons but they never ceased to lament the passing of that terrifying breed.

"By the way, you'd better start in good time. The road's up just before you strike the Guildford by-pass."

Miss Beale did not inquire how she knew that the road was up. It was the sort of thing Miss Burrows invariably did know. The hearty voice went on:

"I saw Hilda Rolfe, their Principal Tutor, in the Westminster Library this week. Extraordinary woman! Intelligent, of course, and reputedly a first-class teacher, but I imagine she terrified the students."

Miss Burrows frequently terrified her own students, not to mention most of her colleagues on the teaching staff, but would have been amazed to be told it. Miss Beale asked:

"Did she say anything about the inspection?"

"Just mentioned it. She was only returning a book and was in a hurry so we didn't talk long. Apparently they've got a bad attack of influenza in the school and half her staff are off with it."

Miss Beale thought it odd that the Principal Tutor should find time to visit London to return a library book if staffing problems were so difficult, but she didn't say so. Before breakfast Miss Beale reserved her energy for thought rather than speech. Miss Burrows came round the bed to pour out the second cups. She said:

"What with this weather and with half the training staff off sick, it looks as if you're in for a pretty dull day."

As the two friends were to tell each other for years to come, with that cosy predilection for re-stating the obvious which is one of the pleasures of long intimacy, she could hardly have been more wrong. Miss Beale, expecting nothing worse of the day than a tedious drive, an arduous inspection, and a possible tussle with those members of the Hospital Nurse Education Committee who took the trouble to attend, dragged her dressing-gown around her shoulders, stubbed her feet into her bedroom slippers and shuffled off into the bathroom. She had taken the first steps on her way to witness a murder.

II

Despite the rain, the drive was less difficult than Miss Beale had feared. She made good time and was in Heatheringfield just before 9 o'clock in time to meet the last surge of the morning rush to work. The wide Georgian High Street was blocked with vehicles. Women were driving their commuter husbands to the station or their children to school, vans were delivering goods, buses were discharging and loading their passengers. At the three sets of traffic lights the pedestrians streamed across the road, umbrellas slanted against the soft drizzle. The young had the spruce, over-uniformed look of the private-school child; the men were mostly bowler-hatted and carrying briefcases; the women were casually dressed with that nice compromise between town smartness and country informality, typical of their kind. Watching for the lights, the pedestrian crossings and the signpost to the hospital, Miss Beale had only a brief chance to notice the elegant eighteenth-century guildhall, the carefully preserved row of timber-fronted houses and the splendid crocketed spire of Holy Trinity church, but she gained an impression of a prosperous community which cared about preserving its architectural heritage even if the row of modern chain stores at the end of the High Street suggested that the caring might well have begun thirty years earlier.

But here at last was the signpost. The road to the John Carpendar Hospital led upward from the High Street between a broad avenue of trees. To the left was a high stone wall which bounded the hospital grounds.

Miss Beale had done her homework. Her briefcase, plump on the back seat of the car, contained a comprehensive note on the hospital's history as well as a copy of the last General Nursing Council Inspector's report and the comments of the Hospital Management Committee on how far it had been possible to implement the inspector's optimistic recommendations. As she knew from her researches, the hospital had a long history. It had been founded in 1791 by a wealthy merchant who had been born in the town, had left it in youthful penury to seek his fortune in London, and had returned there in his retirement to enjoy patronizing and impressing his neighbours. He could have purchased fame and ensured his salvation by succouring the widows and fatherless or by rebuilding the church. But the age of science and reason was succeeding the age of faith and it had become fashionable to endow a hospital for the sick poor. And so, with the almost obligatory meeting in a local coffee house, the John Carpendar Hospital was born. The original house, of some architectural interest, had long since been replaced, first by a solid Victorian monument to ostentatious piety and then by the more functional gracelessness of the twentieth century.

The hospital had always flourished. The local community was predominantly middle-class and prosperous, with a well-developed charitable sense and too few objects on which to indulge it. Just before the Second World War a well-equipped private patients' wing had been added. Both before and after the advent of the National Health Service it had attracted wealthy patients, and consequently eminent consultants, from London and further afield. Miss Beale reflected that it was all very well for Angela to talk about the prestige of a London teaching hospital, but the John Carpendar had its own reputation. A woman might well think there were worse jobs than being Matron of a developing district general hospital, well thought of by the community it served, agreeably placed and fortified by its own local traditions.

She was at the main gates now. There was a porter's lodge on the left, an ornate doll's house in tessellated brick, a relic of the Victorian hospital, and—on the right—the doctor's car park. Already a third of the marked plots were occupied by the Daimlers and the Rolls. It had stopped raining and the dawn had given way to the grey normality of a January day. The lights were full on in the hospital. It lay before her like a great ship at anchor, brightly lit, latent with activity and power. To the left stretched the low glass-fronted buildings of the new out-patient department.

Already a thin stream of patients was making its dispirited way to the entrance.

Miss Beale drew up alongside the inquiry hatch of the lodge, wound down the car window, and announced herself. The porter, ponderous and uniformed in self-importance, deigned to come out to present himself.

"You'll be the General Nursing Council, Miss," he stated grandiloquently. "What a pity you decided to come in this gate. The Nurse Training School is in Nightingale House, only 100 yards or so from the Winchester Road entrance. We always use the back entrance for Nightingale House."

He spoke with reproachful resignation, as if deploring a singular lack of judgement which would cost him dear in extra work.

"But presumably I can get to the school this way?"

Miss Beale had no stomach for a return to the confusion of the High Street or intention of circling the hospital grounds in search of an elusive back entrance.

"Well you can, Miss." The porter's tone implied that only the wilfully obstinate would try, and he settled himself against the car door as if to deliver confidential and complicated directions. They proved, however, remarkably simple. Nightingale House was in the hospital grounds at the rear of the new out-patient department.

"Just take this road to the left, Miss, and keep straight on past the mortuary till you get to the resident medical quarters. Then turn to the right. There's a signpost where the road forks. You can't miss it."

For once this notoriously unpropitious assertion seemed justified. The grounds of the hospital were extensive and well wooded, a mixture of formal garden, grass, and clumped unkempt trees which reminded Miss Beale of the grounds of an old mental hospital. It was rare to find a general hospital so well endowed with space. But the several roads were well signposted and only one led to the left of the new out-patient department. The mortuary was easily identified, a squat, ugly little building tactfully sited among the trees and made more sinister by its strategic isolation. The medical officers' residence was new and unmistakable. Miss Beale had time to indulge her usual, frequently quite unjustified, resentment that Hospital Management Committees were always more ready to rehouse their doctors than to provide adequate accommodation for the nurse training school, before noting the promised sign. A white painted board pointed to the right and read "Nightingale House, Nurse Training School."

She changed gear and turned carefully. The new road was narrow and winding, banked high on each side with sodden leaves so that there was barely room for the single car. Everywhere was dampness and desolation. The trees grew close to the path and knitted themselves above it, ribbing the dark tunnel with their strong black boughs. From time to time a gust of wind brought down a spatter of raindrops on the car roof or flattened a falling leaf against the windscreen. The grass verge was scarred with flower beds, regular and oblong as graves and spiked with stunted bushes. It was so dark under the trees that Miss Beale switched on her side lamps. The road shone before her like an oiled ribbon. She had left the car window down and could smell, even above the inevitable car smell of petrol and warm vinyl, a sweet fungoid stench of decay. She felt strangely isolated in the dim quietness and suddenly she was touched with an irrational unease, a bizarre sensation of journeying out of time into some new dimension, borne onwards towards an uncomprehended and inescapable horror. It was only a second's folly and she quickly shook it off, reminding herself of the cheerful bustle of the High Street less than a mile away and the nearness of life and activity. But it had been an odd and disconcerting experience. Angry at herself at this lapse into morbid folly, she wound up the car window and stepped on the accelerator. The little car leaped forward.

Suddenly she found she had turned the last corner and Nightingale House was before her. She nearly stood on the brakes in surprise. It was an extraordinary house, an immense Victorian edifice of red brick, castellated and ornate to the point of fancy, and crowned with four immense turrets. It was brightly lit in the dark January morning and after the gloom of the road it blazed at her like the castle from some childhood mythology. An immense conservatory was grafted onto the right side of the house, looking, thought Miss Beale, more appropriate to Kew Gardens than to what had obviously once been a private residence. It was less brightly lit than the house but through the faintly luminous glass she could discern the sleek green leaves of aspidistras, the harsh red of poinsettias and the yellow and bronze blobs of chrysanthemums.

Miss Beale's recent moment of panic under the trees was completely forgotten in her amazement at Nightingale House. Despite her normal confidence in her own taste, she was not entirely immune to the vagaries of fashion and she wondered uneasily whether in certain company it might not be proper to admire it. But it had become a habit with her to look at every building with an eye to its suitability as a nurse training school—she had once, on a Paris holiday, found herself to her horror rejecting the Elysée Palace as unworthy of further notice—and as a nurse training school Nightingale House was obviously quite impossible. She had only to look at it for the objections to spring to mind. Most of the rooms would be far too large. Where, for instance, would one find cosy offices for the principal tutor, clinical instructor or school secretary?

Then the building would be extremely difficult to heat adequately and those oriel windows, picturesque no doubt if one liked that sort of thing, would keep out a great deal of light. Worse still, there was something forbidding, even frightening, about the house. When the Profession (Miss Beale, in defiance of an unfortunate comparison, always thought of it with a capital P) was climbing so painfully into the twentieth century, kicking away the stones of out-worn attitudes and methods—Miss Beale was frequently required to make speeches and certain pet phrases tended to stick in her mind—it really was a pity to house young students in this Victorian pile. It would do no harm to incorporate a strong comment about the need for a new school in her report. Nightingale House was rejected even before she set foot in it.

But there was nothing to criticize in her welcome. As she reached the top step, the heavy door swung open letting out a gust of warm air and a smell of fresh coffee. A uniformed maid stood deferentially aside and behind her down the wide oak staircase, gleaming against the dark panelling like a Renaissance portrait in grey and gold, came the figure of Matron Mary Taylor, hand out-stretched. Miss Beale assumed her bright professional smile, compounded of happy expectation and general reassurance, and stepped forward to meet her. The ill-fated inspection of the John Carpendar Training School had begun.

III

Fifteen minutes later, four people made their way down the main staircase to the demonstration room on the ground floor where they were to watch the first teaching session of the day. Coffee had been served in Matron's sitting room in

one of the turret blocks where Miss Beale had been introduced to the principal tutor, Miss Hilda Rolfe, and to a senior consultant surgeon, Mr. Stephen Courtney-Briggs. She
knew both by reputation. Miss Rolfe's presence was necessary and expected, but Miss Beale was a little surprised that
Mr. Courtney-Briggs was prepared to devote so much of his
morning to the inspection. He had been introduced as
Vice-Chairman of the Hospital Nurse Education Committee and she would normally have expected to meet him
with other members of the committee for the summing-up
discussion at the end of the day. It was unusual for a senior
surgeon to sit in at a teaching session and it was gratifying
that he took such a personal interest in the school.

There was room for three to walk abreast in the wide
wood-panelled corridors and Miss Beale found herself
escorted by the tall figures of Matron and Mr. Courtney-
Briggs rather, she felt, like a diminutive delinquent. Mr.
Courtney-Briggs, stoutly impressive in the formal striped
trousers of a consultant, walked on her left. He smelt of
after-shave lotion. Miss Beale could discern it even above
the pervading smell of disinfectant, coffee and furniture
cream. She thought it surprising but not disagreeable. The
Matron, tallest of the three, walked in serene silence. Her
formal dress of grey gaberdine was buttoned high to the
neck with a thin band of white linen around the throat and
cuffs. Her corn-gold hair, almost indistinguishable in
colour from her skin, was combed back from the high
forehead and bound tight by an immense triangle of
muslin, its apex reaching nearly to the small of her back.
The cap reminded Miss Beale of those worn during the last
war by Sisters of the Army Nursing Service. She had seldom seen it since. But its simplicity suited Miss Taylor.
That face, with its high cheekbones and large, slightly
protuberant eyes—they reminded Miss Beale irreverently

of pale veined gooseberries—could have looked grotesque under the fripperies of a more orthodox head-dress. Behind the three of them Miss Beale could sense the disturbing presence of Sister Rolfe, uncomfortably close on their heels.

Mr. Courtney-Briggs was talking:

"This influenza epidemic has been a thorough nuisance. We've had to defer taking the next set off the wards and we thought at one time that this set would have to go back. It was a close thing."

"It would be," thought Miss Beale. Whenever there was a crisis in the hospital the first people to be sacrificed were the student nurses. Their training programme could always be interrupted. It was a sore point with her, but now was hardly the time to protest. She made a vaguely acquiescent noise. They started down the last staircase. Mr. Courtney-Briggs continued his monologue:

"Some of the training staff have gone down with it too. The demonstration this morning is being taken by our clinical instructor, Mavis Gearing. We've had to recall her to the school. Normally, of course, she would be doing nothing but ward teaching. It's a comparatively new idea that there should be a trained instructor to teach the girls on the wards, using the patients as clinical material. Ward sisters just haven't the time these days. Of course the whole idea of the block system of training is relatively new. When I was a medical student the probationers, as we called them then, were taught entirely on the wards with occasional lectures in their own free time from the medical staff. There was little formal teaching and certainly no taking them off the wards each year for a period in the nurse training school. The whole concept of nurse training has altered."

Miss Beale was the last person to require an explanation of the function and duties of a clinical instructor or the development of nurse training methods. She wondered whether Mr. Courtney-Briggs had forgotten who she was. This elementary instruction was more suitable for new members of a Hospital Management Committee, who were generally as ignorant of nurse training as they were of anything else to do with hospitals. She had the feeling that the surgeon had something on his mind. Or was this merely the aimless chatter, unrelated to its hearer, of an egotist who could not tolerate even a moment without the comforting resonance of his own voice? If so, the sooner he got back to his out-patient session or ward round and let the inspection proceed without the benefit of his presence, the better for all concerned.

The little procession passed across the tessellated hall to a room at the front of the building. Miss Rolfe slipped forward to open the door and stood aside as the others entered. Mr. Courtney-Briggs ushered Miss Beale in before him. Immediately she was at home. Despite the anomalies of the room itself—the two great windows with their spatter of coloured panes, the immense fireplace of carved marble with its draped figures supporting the chimney-piece, the high moulded ceiling desecrated with the three tubes of fluorescent light—it was happily evocative of her own student days, an utterly acceptable and familiar world. Here was all the paraphernalia of her profession; the rows of glass-fronted cabinets, with their instruments placed in shining precision; the wall charts showing in lurid diagram the circulation of the blood and the improbable processes of digestion; the wall-mounted blackboard smeared with the dust of past lecture notes imperfectly erased; the demonstration trolleys with their linen-covered trays; the two demonstration beds, one containing a life-sized doll propped among the pillows; the inevitable skeleton hanging from its gibbet in forlorn decrepitude. Pervading all was the astringent and potent smell of disinfectant. Miss Beale breathed it in like an addict. Whatever faults she might later find with the room itself, the adequacy of the teaching equipment, the lighting or the furniture, she never felt other than at home in this intimidating atmosphere.

She bestowed on students and teacher her brief smile of reassurance and encouragement and perched herself on one of the four chairs placed ready at the side of the room. Matron Taylor and Miss Rolfe seated themselves on each side of her as quietly and unobtrusively as possible in the face of Mr. Courtney-Briggs's determination to be fussily gallant over pulling out the ladies' chairs. The arrival of the little party, however tactfully arranged, seemed temporarily to have disconcerted the nurse tutor. An inspection was hardly a natural teaching situation, but it was always interesting to see how long it took a tutor to re-establish *rapport* with her class. A first-class teacher, as Miss Beale knew from personal experience, could hold a class's interest even through a heavy bombing raid let alone the visit of a General Nursing Council Inspector; but she did not feel that Mavis Gearing was likely to prove one of that rare and dedicated band. The girl—or woman rather—lacked authority. She had a propitiatory air; she looked as though she might easily simper. And she was a great deal too heavily made up for a woman who should have her mind on less ephemeral arts. But she was, after all, merely the clinical instructor, not a qualified nurse tutor. She was taking the session at short notice and under difficulties. Miss Beale made a mental resolution not to judge her too harshly.

The class, she saw, were to practise feeding a patient by intra-gastric tube. The student who was to act as patient was already in one of the demonstration beds, her check dress protected by a mackintosh bib, her head supported by the back rest and a bank of pillows. She was a plain girl with a strong, obstinate and oddly mature face, her dull hair drawn back unbecomingly from a high nobbly forehead. She lay there immobile under the harsh strip lighting, looking a little ridiculous but strangely dignified as if concentrating on some private world and dissociating herself from the whole procedure by an effort of will. Suddenly it occurred to Miss Beale that the girl might be frightened. The thought was ridiculous but it persisted. She found herself suddenly unwilling to watch that resolute face. Irritated by her own unreasonable sensitivity, she turned her attention to the nurse tutor.

Sister Gearing cast an apprehensive and interrogative glance at the Matron, received a confirmatory nod and resumed her lesson.

"Nurse Pearce is acting the part of our patient this morning. We have just been going through her history. She is Mrs. Stokes, the fifty-year-old mother of four children, wife of a council refuse collector. She has had a laryngectomy for the treatment of cancer." She turned to a student sitting on her right.

"Nurse Dakers, will you please describe Mrs. Stokes's treatment so far."

Nurse Dakers dutifully began. She was a pale, thin girl who blushed unbecomingly as she spoke. It was difficult to hear her but she knew her facts and presented them well. A conscientious little thing, thought Miss Beale, not outstandingly intelligent, perhaps, but hard working and reliable. It was a pity that no one had done anything about her acne. She retained her air of bright professional interest whilst Nurse Dakers propounded the fictional medical history of Mrs. Stokes and took the opportunity of a close look at the remaining students in the class, making her customary private assessment of their characters and ability.

The influenza epidemic had certainly taken its toll.

There was a total of seven girls only in the demonstration room. The two who were standing one on each side of the demonstration bed made an immediate impression. They were obviously identical twins, strong, ruddy-faced girls, with copper-coloured hair clumped in a thick fringe above remarkable blue eyes. Their caps, the pleated crowns as small as saucers, were perched well forward, the two immense wings of white linen jutting behind. Miss Beale, who knew from her own student days what could be done with a couple of white-tipped hat pins, was nevertheless intrigued by the art which could so firmly attach such a bizarre and unsubstantial edifice on such a springing bush of hair. The John Carpendar uniform struck her as interestingly out of date. Nearly every hospital she visited had replaced these old-fashioned winged caps with the smaller American-type which were easier to wear, quicker to make up, and cheaper to buy and launder. Some hospitals, to Miss Beale's regret, were even issuing disposable paper caps. But a hospital's nurse uniform was always jealously defended and changed with reluctance and the John Carpendar was obviously wedded to tradition. Even the uniform dresses were slightly old fashioned. The twins' plump and speckled arms bulged from sleeves of check pink gingham which reminded Miss Beale of her own student days. Their skirt lengths paid no concession to modern fashion and their sturdy feet were planted in low-heeled black lace-up shoes.

She glanced quickly at the remaining students. There was a calm, bespectacled girl with a plain intelligent face. Miss Beale's immediate reaction was that she would be glad to have her on any ward. Next to her sat a dark, sulky-looking girl, rather over-made-up and assuming an air of careful disinterest in the demonstration. Rather common, thought Miss Beale. Miss Beale, to her superiors' occasional embarrassment, was fond of such unfashionable adjectives, used them unashamedly and knew precisely what she meant by them. Her dictum "Matron recruits a very nice type of girl" meant that they came of respectable middle-class families, had received the benefit of grammar school education, wore their skirts knee length or longer, and were properly aware of the privilege and responsibilities of being a student nurse. The last student in the class was a very pretty girl, her blonde hair worn in a fringe as low as her eyebrows above a pert, contemporary face. She was attractive enough for a recruiting poster, thought Miss Beale, but somehow it was the last face one would choose. While she was wondering why, Nurse Dakers came to the end of her recital.

"Right, Nurse," said Sister Gearing. "So we are faced with the problem of a post-operative patient, already seriously under-nourished and now unable to take food by mouth. That means what? Yes, Nurse?"

"Intra-gastric or rectal feeding, Sister."

It was the dark sulky-looking girl who answered, her voice carefully repressing any note of enthusiasm or even interest. Certainly not an agreeable girl, thought Miss Beale.

There was a murmur from the class. Sister Gearing raised an interrogative eyebrow. The spectacled student said:

"Not rectal feeding, Sister. The rectum can't absorb sufficient nourishment. Intra-gastric feeding by the mouth or nose."

"Right, Nurse Goodale, and that's what the surgeon has ordered for Mrs. Stokes. Will you carry on please, Nurse. Explain what you are doing at each step."

One of the twins drew the trolley forward and demonstrated her tray of requirements: the gallipot containing sodium bicarbonate mixture for cleaning mouth or nostrils; the polythene funnel and eight inches of tubing to fit it; the connector; the lubricant; the kidney bowl with the tongue spatula, tongue forceps and gag. She held up the Jacques oesophageal tube. It dangled from her freckled hand obscenely like a yellow snake.

"Right, Nurse," encouraged Sister Gearing. "Now the feed. What are you giving her?"

"Actually, it's just warm milk, Sister."

"But if we were dealing with a real patient?"

The twin hesitated. The spectacled student said with calm authority: "We could add soluble protein, eggs, vitamin preparations and sugar."

"Right. If tube feeding is to continue for more than forty-eight hours we must ensure that the diet is adequate in calories, protein and vitamins. At what temperature are you giving the feed, Nurse?"

"Body temperature, Sister, 38° C."

"Correct. And as our patient is conscious and able to swallow we are giving her this feed by mouth. Don't forget to reassure your patient, Nurse. Explain simply to her what you are going to do and why. Remember this, girls, never begin any nursing procedure without telling your patient what is to happen."

They were third-year students, thought Miss Beale. They should know this by now. But the twin, who no doubt would have coped easily enough with a real patient, found it embarrassingly difficult to explain her procedure to a fellow student. Suppressing a giggle she muttered a few words at the rigid figure in the bed and almost thrust the oesophageal tube at her. Nurse Pearce, still gazing fixedly ahead, felt for the tube with her left hand and guided it into her mouth. Then shutting her eyes she swallowed. There was a convulsive spasm of the throat muscles. She paused to take breath, and then swallowed again. The tube shortened. It was very silent in the demonstration room. Miss

Beale was aware that she felt unhappy but was unsure why. It was a little unusual perhaps for gastric feeding to be practised on a student in this way but it was not unknown. In a hospital it might be more usual for a doctor to pass the tube but a nurse might well have to take the responsibility; it was better to learn on each other than on a seriously ill patient and the demonstration doll wasn't really a satisfactory substitute for a living subject. She had once acted as the patient in her own training school and had found swallowing the tube unexpectedly easy. Watching the convulsive movements of Nurse Pearce's throat and swallowing in an unconscious sympathy she could almost recall, after thirty years, the sudden chill as the tube slid over the soft palate and the faint shock of surprise at the ease of it all. But there was something pathetic and disturbing about that rigid white-faced figure on the bed, eyes tight closed, bibbed like a baby, the thin tube dragging and wriggling like a worm from the corner of her mouth. Miss Beale felt that she was watching gratuitous suffering, that the whole demonstration was an outrage. For a second she had to fight an urge to protest.

One of the twins was now attaching a 20-ml. syringe to the end of the tube, ready to aspirate some of the gastric juices to test that the end of the tube had reached the stomach. The girl's hands were quite steady. Perhaps it was just Miss Beale's imagination that the room was preternaturally silent. She glanced across at Miss Taylor. The Matron had her eyes fixed on Nurse Pearce. She was frowning slightly. Her lips moved and she shifted in her seat. Miss Beale wondered if she were about to expostulate. But the Matron made no sound. Mr. Courtney-Briggs was leaning forward in his chair, his hands clasping his knees. He was gazing intently, not at Nurse Pearce, but at the drip as if mesmerized by the gentle swing of the tubing. Miss

Beale could hear the heavy rasp of his breathing. Miss Rolfe sat bolt upright, her hands folded loosely in her lap, her black eyes expressionless. But Miss Beale saw that they were fixed, not on the girl in the bed, but on the fair and pretty student. And for a fleeting second the girl looked back at her, equally expressionless.

The twin who was administering the feed, obviously satisfied that the end of the oesophageal tube was safely in the stomach, lifted the funnel high over Nurse Pearce's head and began slowly to pour the milky mixture down the tube. The class seemed to be holding its breath. And then it happened. There was a squeal, high-pitched, horribly inhuman, and Nurse Pearce precipitated herself from the bed as if propelled by an irresistible force. One second she was lying, immobile, propped against her mound of pillows, the next she was out of bed, teetering forward on arched feet in a parody of a ballet dancer, and clutching ineffectually at the air as if in frantic search of the tubing. And all the time she screamed, perpetually screamed, like a stuck whistle. Miss Beale, aghast, had hardly time to register the contorted face, the foaming lips, before the girl thudded to the floor and writhed there, doubled like a hoop, her forehead touching the ground, her whole body twitching in agony.

One of the students screamed. For a second no one moved. Then there was a rush forward. Sister Gearing tugged at the tube and tore it from the girl's mouth. Mr. Courtney-Briggs moved resolutely into the mêlée, his arms wide. Matron and Sister Rolfe bent over the twitching figure hiding her from view. Then Miss Taylor rose and looked round at Miss Beale.

"The students . . . could you look after them please? There's an empty room next door. Keep them together."

She was trying to keep calm but urgency made her voice sharp. "Quickly please."

Miss Beale nodded. The Matron bent again over the convulsed figure. The screaming had stopped now. It was succeeded by a piteous moaning and a dreadful staccato drumming of heels on the wooden floor. Mr. Courtney-Briggs took off his coat, threw it to one side, and began to roll up his sleeves.

IV

Muttering gentle encouragement, Miss Beale shepherded the little group of students across the hall. One of them, she was not sure which, said in a high-pitched voice: "What happened to her? What happened? What went wrong?" But no one replied. They moved in a shocked daze into the room next door. It was at the back of the house, a small, odd-shaped room which had obviously been partitioned from the original high-ceilinged drawing-room and which now served as the Principal Tutor's office. Miss Beale's first glance took in a business-like desk, a bank of green steel filing cabinets, a crowded notice board, a small pegboard fitted with hooks from which hung a variety of keys, and a chart along the whole of one wall showing the teaching programme and the progress of each individual student. The partition wall cut the mullioned window in half so that the office, unpleasing in its proportions, was also inconveniently dark. One of the students clicked down the switch and the central bar of fluorescence began to flicker into light. Really, thought Miss Beale, her mind clutching desperately at the comfort of its normal preoccupations, it was a most unsuitable room for a Principal Tutor, or for any other tutor, come to that.

This brief remembrance of the purpose of her visit brought a second's comfort. But almost immediately the awful reality of the moment reasserted itself. The students—a pathetic and disorganized little bunch—had crowded together in the middle of the room as if incapable of action. Glancing quickly around Miss Beale saw that there were only three chairs. For a moment she felt as embarrassed and nonplussed as a hostess who is not sure how she is going to seat all her guests. The concern wasn't altogether irrelevant. She would have to get the girls comfortable and relaxed if there were to be any chance of keeping their minds off what was happening next door; and they might be incarcerated for a long time.

"Come along," she said brightly. "Let's move Sister's desk back against the wall, then four of you can perch there. I'll take the desk chair and two of you can have the easy chairs."

At least it was activity. Miss Beale saw that the thin, fair student was shaking. She helped her into one of the easy chairs and the dark, sulky-looking girl promptly took the other. Trust her to look after number one, thought Miss Beale. She busied herself helping the other students to clear the desk and push it back against the wall. If only she could send one of them to make some tea! Despite her intellectual assent to more modern methods of combating shock, Miss Beale still put her faith in warm strong sweet tea. But there wasn't a chance of any. It wouldn't do to upset and alert the kitchen staff.

"Now suppose we introduce ourselves," she said encouragingly. "My name is Miss Muriel Beale. There's no need to tell you I'm a G.N.C. Inspector. I know some of your names but I am not really sure who is who."

Five pairs of eyes gazed at her with startled incomprehension. But the efficient student—as Miss Beale still thought of her—quietly identified them.

"The twins are Maureen and Shirley Burt. Maureen is the elder by about two minutes and has the most freckles. Otherwise we don't find it easy to tell them apart. Next to Maureen is Julia Pardoe. Christine Dakers is in one armchair and Diane Harper in the other. I'm Madeleine Goodale."

Miss Beale, never good at remembering names, made her customary mental recapitulation. The Burt twins. Bonny and bouncing. It would be easy enough to remember their name, although impossible to decide which was which. Julia Pardoe. An attractive name for an attractive girl. Very attractive if one liked that blonde, rather feline prettiness. Smiling into the unresponsive violet-blue eyes, Miss Beale decided that some people, and not all of them men, might like it very much indeed. Madeleine Goodale. A good sensible name for a good sensible girl. She thought she would have no difficulty in remembering Goodale. Christine Dakers. Something very wrong there. The girl had looked ill throughout the brief demonstration and now seemed close to collapse. She had a poor skin, unusually so for a nurse. It was now drained of colour so that the spots around the mouth and over the forehead stood out in an angry rash. She was huddled deep into the armchair, her thin hands alternately smoothing and plucking at her apron. Nurse Dakers was certainly the most affected of all the group. Perhaps she had been a particular friend of Nurse Pearce. Miss Beale superstitiously made a quick mental amendment of tense. Perhaps she was a particular friend. If only they could get the girl some hot reviving tea!

Nurse Harper, her lipstick and eye shadow garish on the whitened face, said suddenly: "There must have been something in the feed."

The Burt twins turned to her simultaneously. Maureen said:

"Of course there was! Milk."

"I mean something beside the milk." She hesitated. "Poison."

"But there couldn't be! Shirley and I took a fresh bottle of milk out of the kitchen fridge first thing this morning. Miss Collins was there and saw us. We left it in the demo room and didn't pour it into the measuring jug until just before the demonstration, did we, Shirley?"

"That's right. It was a fresh bottle. We took it at about 7 o'clock."

"And you didn't add anything by mistake?"

"Like what? Of course we didn't."

The twins spoke in unison, sounding sturdily confident, almost unworried. They knew exactly what they had done and when, and no one, Miss Beale saw, was likely to shake them. They weren't the type to be tormented by unnecessary guilt or fretted by those irrational doubts which afflict less stolid, more imaginative personalities. Miss Beale thought that she understood them very well.

Julia Pardoe said: "Perhaps someone else mucked about with the feed."

She looked round at her fellow students from under lowered lids, provocative, a little amused.

Madeleine Goodale said calmly: "Why should they?"

Nurse Pardoe shrugged and pursed her lips into a little secret smile. She said: "By accident. Or it might have been a practical joke. Or perhaps it was done on purpose."

"But that would be attempted murder!" It was Diane Harper who spoke. She sounded incredulous. Maureen Burt laughed.

"Don't be daft, Julia. Who would want to murder Pearce?"

No one replied. The logic was apparently unassailable. It was impossible to imagine anyone wanting to murder Pearce. Pearce, Miss Beale realized, was either of the company of the naturally inoffensive or was too negative a personality to inspire the tormenting hatred which can lead to murder. Then Nurse Goodale said drily: "Pearce wasn't everyone's cup of tea."

Miss Beale glanced at the girl, surprised. It was an odd remark to come from Nurse Goodale, a little insensitive in the circumstances, disconcertingly out of character. She noted, too, the use of the past tense. Here was one student who didn't expect to see Nurse Pearce alive again.

Nurse Harper reiterated stoutly: "It's daft to talk about murder. No one would want to kill Pearce."

Nurse Pardoe shrugged: "Perhaps it wasn't meant for Pearce. Jo Fallon was supposed to act as patient today, wasn't she? It was Fallon's name next on the list. If she hadn't been taken ill last night, it would have been Fallon in that bed this morning."

They were silent. Nurse Goodale turned to Miss Beale.

"She's right. We take it in strict turn to act as patient; it wasn't really Pearce's turn this morning. But Josephine Fallon was taken into the sick bay last night—you've probably heard that we have an influenza epidemic—and Pearce was next on the list. Pearce was taking Fallon's place."

Miss Beale was momentarily at a loss. She felt that she ought to put a stop to the conversation, that it was her responsibility to keep their minds off the accident, and surely it could only have been an accident. But she didn't know how. Besides, there was a dreadful fascination in getting at the facts. For her, there always had been. Perhaps, too, it was better that the girls should indulge this detached, investigatory interest, rather than sit there making unnatural and ineffective conversation. Already she saw that shock was giving way to that half-ashamed excitement which can follow tragedy, so long, of course, as it is someone else's tragedy.

Julia Pardoe's composed, rather childish voice went on: "So if the victim was really meant to be Fallon, it couldn't have been one of us, could it? We all knew that Fallon wouldn't be acting the patient this morning."

Madeleine Goodale said: "I should think that everyone knew. Everyone at Nightingale House anyway. There was enough talk about it at breakfast."

They were silent again, considering this new development. Miss Beale noted with interest that there were no protestations that no one would want to murder Fallon. Then Maureen Burt said:

"Fallon can't be all that sick. She was back here in Nightingale House this morning, just after eight-forty. Shirley and I saw her slipping out of the side door just before we went into the demo room after breakfast."

Nurse Goodale asked sharply: "What was she wearing?" Maureen was unsurprised at this apparently irrelevant question.

"Slacks. Her top coat. That red headscarf she wears. Why?"

Nurse Goodale, obviously shaken and surprised, made an attempt to conceal it. She said:

"She slipped those on before we took her to the sick bay last night. I suppose she came back to fetch something she wanted from her room. But she shouldn't have left the ward. It was stupid. She had a temperature of 103.8 when she was warded. Lucky for her that Sister Brumfett didn't see her."

Nurse Pardoe said maliciously: "Funny though, isn't it?" No one replied. It was indeed funny, thought Miss Beale. She recalled her long damp drive from the hospital to the nurse training school. The road was a winding one; obviously there would be a short cut through the trees. But it was a strange journey for a sick girl to make on an early January morning. There must have been some compelling reason to bring her back to Nightingale House. After all, if she did want something from her room there was nothing to prevent her asking for it. Any of the students would gladly have taken it across to the sick bay. And this was the girl who should have played the patient that morning, who should, logically, be lying next door among the tangle of tubes and linen.

Nurse Pardoe said: "Well, there's one person who knew that Fallon wouldn't be acting patient this morning. Fallon herself."

Nurse Goodale, white-faced, looked across at her.

"If you want to be stupid and malicious I suppose I can't stop you. But, if I were you, I would stop short of slander."

Nurse Pardoe looked unconcerned, even a little pleased. Catching sight of her sly, gratified smile, Miss Beale decided that it was time this talking stopped. She was searching for a change of topic when Nurse Dakers said faintly from the depths of her chair: "I feel sick."

There was immediate concern. Only Nurse Harper made no move to help. The rest gathered around the girl, glad of the chance to be doing something. Nurse Goodale said: "I'll take her to the downstairs cloakroom."

She supported the girl out of the room. To Miss Beale's surprise Nurse Pardoe went with her, their recent antagonism apparently forgotten as they supported Nurse Dakers between them. Miss Beale was left with the Burt twins and Nurse Harper. Another silence fell. But Miss Beale had learned her lesson. She had been unforgivably irresponsible. There was to be no more talk of death or murder. While they were here and in her charge they might as well work. She gazed sternly at Nurse Harper and invited her to describe the signs, symptoms and treatment of pulmonary collapse.

Ten minutes later the absent three returned. Nurse Dakers still looked pale but was composed. It was Nurse

Goodale who looked worried. As if unable to keep it to herself, she said:

"The bottle of disinfectant is missing from the lavatory. You know the one I mean. It's always kept there on the little shelf. Pardoe and I couldn't find it."

Nurse Harper interrupted her bored but suprisingly competent recital and said:

"You mean that bottle of milky-looking mixture? It was there after supper last night."

"That's a long time ago. Has anyone been in that loo this morning?"

Apparently no one had. They looked at each other in silence.

It was then that the door opened. Matron came quietly in and shut it behind her. There was a creak of starched linen as the twins slipped from the desk and stood to attention. Nurse Harper rose gracelessly from her chair. All of them turned towards Miss Taylor.

"Children," she said, and the unexpected and gentle word told them the truth before she spoke.

"Children, Nurse Pearce died a few minutes ago. We don't yet know how or why, but when something inexplicable like this happens we have to call the police. The Hospital Secretary is doing that now. I want you to be brave and sensible as I know you will be. Until the police arrive, I think it would be better if we don't talk about what has happened. You will collect your textbooks and Nurse Goodale will take you to wait in my sitting-room. I shall be ordering some strong hot coffee and it will be brought up to you soon. Is that understood?"

There was a subdued murmur of, "Yes, Matron."

Miss Taylor turned to Miss Beale.

"I'm so very sorry, but it will mean your waiting here too."

"Of course, Matron, I quite understand."

Across the heads of the students their eyes met in bewildered speculation and wordless sympathy.

But Miss Beale was a little horrified to remember afterwards the banality and irrelevance of her first conscious thought.

"This must be the shortest inspection on record. What on earth will I say to the General Nursing Council?"

V

A few minutes earlier the four people in the demonstration room had straightened up and looked at each other, white-faced, utterly exhausted. Heather Pearce was dead. She was dead by any criteria, legal or medical. They had known it for the last five minutes but had worked on, doggedly and without speaking, as if there were still a chance that the flabby heart would pulse again into life. Mr. Courtney-Briggs had taken off his coat to work on the girl and the front of his waistcoat was heavily stained with blood. He started at the thickening stain, brow creased, nose fastidiously wrinkled, almost as if blood were an alien substance to him. The heart massage had been messy as well as ineffectual. Surprisingly messy for Mr. Courtney-Briggs, the Matron thought. But surely the attempt had been justified? There hadn't been time to get her over to the theatre. It was a pity that Sister Gearing had pulled out the oesophageal tube. It had, perhaps, been a natural reaction but it might have cost Pearce her only chance. While the tube was in place they could at least have tried an immediate stomach wash-out. But an attempt to pass another tube by the nostril had been frustrated by the girl's agonized spasms and, by the time these had ceased, it was too late and Mr. Courtney-Briggs had been forced to open the chest wall and try the only measure left to him. Mr. Courtney-Briggs's heroic efforts were well known. It was only a pity that they left the body looking so pathetically mangled and the demonstration room stinking like an abattoir. These things were better conducted in an operating theatre, shrouded and dignified by the paraphernalia of ritual surgery.

He was the first to speak.

"This wasn't a natural death. There was something other than milk in that feed. Well, that's obvious to all of us I should have thought. We'd better call the police. I'll get on to the Yard. I know someone there, as it happens. One of the Assistant Commissioners."

He always did know someone, thought the Matron. She felt the need to oppose him. Shock had left an aftermath of irritation and, irrationally, it focused on him. She said calmly:

"The local police are the ones to call and I think that the Hospital Secretary should do it. I'll get Mr. Hudson on the house telephone now. They'll call in the Yard if they think it necessary. I can't think why it should be. But that decision is for the Chief Constable, not for us."

She moved over to the wall telephone, carefully walking round the crouched figure of Miss Rolfe. The Principal Tutor was still on her knees. She looked, thought the Matron, rather like a character from a Victorian melodrama with her smouldering eyes in a deathly white face, her black hair a little dishevelled under the frilly cap, and those reeking hands. She was turning them over slowly and studying the red mass with a detached, speculative interest as if she, too, found it difficult to believe that the blood was real. She said:

"If there's a suspicion of foul play ought we to move the

body?" Mr. Courtney-Briggs said sharply: "I have no intention of moving the body."

"But we can't leave her here, not like this!" Miss Gearing was almost weeping in protest. The surgeon glared at her.

"My dear woman, this girl's dead! Dead! What does it matter where we leave the body? She can't feel. She can't know. For God's sake don't start being sentimental about death. The indignity is that we die at all, not what happens to our bodies."

He turned brusquely and went over to the window. Sister Gearing made a movement as if to follow him, and then sank into the nearest chair and began to cry softly like a snuffling animal. No one took any notice of her. Sister Rolfe got stiffly to her feet. Holding her hands raised in front of her in the ritual gesture of an operating theatre nurse she walked over to a sink in the corner, nudged on the tap with her elbow, and began to wash her hands. At the wall-mounted telephone the Matron was dialling a five-digit number. They heard her calm voice.

"Is that the Hospital Secretary's office? Is Mr. Hudson there? It's Matron." There was a pause. "Good morning, Mr. Hudson. I am speaking from the ground floor demonstration room in Nightingale House. Could you please come over immediately? Yes. Very urgent. I'm afraid something tragic and horrible has happened and it will be necessary for you to telephone the police. No, I'd rather not tell you on the telephone. Thank you." She replaced the receiver and said quietly: "He's coming at once. He'll have to put the Vice-Chairman in the picture, too—it's unfortunate that Sir Marcus is in Israel—but the first thing is to get the police. And now I had better tell the other students."

Sister Gearing was making an attempt to control herself. She blew loudly into her handkerchief, replaced it in her uniform pocket, and raised a blotched face.

"I'm sorry. It's the shock, I suppose. It's just that it was all so horrible. Such an appalling thing to happen. And the first time I've taken a class too! And everyone sitting and watching it like that. The other students as well. Such a horrible accident."

"Accident, Sister?" Mr. Courtney-Briggs turned from the window. He strode over to her and bent his bull-like head close to hers. His voice was harsh, contemptuous as he almost spat the words into her face. "Accident? Are you suggesting that a corrosive poison found its way into that feed by accident? Or that a girl in her right mind would choose to kill herself in that particularly horrible way? Come, come, Sister, why not be honest for once? What we've just witnessed was murder!"

CHAPTER TWO

Cease Upon the Midnight

I

IT WAS LATE in the evening of Wednesday, 28th January, sixteen days after the death of Nurse Pearce and, in the students' sitting-room on the first floor of Nightingale House, Nurse Dakers was writing her mid-week letter to her mother. It was usual for her to finish it in time for the Wednesday evening post but, this week, she had lacked the energy and inclination to settle down to the task. Already the waste-paper basket at her feet held the screwed-up copies of the first two rejected drafts. And now she was trying again.

She was sitting at one of the twin writing-desks in front of the window, her left elbow almost brushing the heavy curtains which shut out the dank blackness of the night, her forearm curled protectively around the writing-pad. Opposite to her, the desk lamp shone on the bent head of Madeleine Goodale, so close that Nurse Dakers could see the clean white scalp at the hair parting and smell the almost imperceptible antiseptic tang of shampoo. Two textbooks were open before Goodale and she was making notes. Nothing, thought Nurse Dakers with resentful envy, was worrying her; nothing in the room or beyond it could disturb her quiet concentration. The admirable and secure Goodale was making sure that the John Carpendar Gold

Medal for top marks in the final examination would eventually be pinned on her immaculate apron.

Frightened by the strength of this sudden and shaming antagonism, which she felt must communicate itself to Goodale, Nurse Dakers slid her eyes from the bent head so disconcertingly close to hers and gazed around the room. It was so familiar to her after nearly three years of training that normally she hardly noticed the details of architecture or furnishing. But tonight she saw it with an unexpected clarity, as if it had nothing to do with her or with her life. It was too large to be cosy and was furnished as if it had acquired odd items over the years and taken them to itself. It must once have been an elegant drawing-room, but the walls had long since lost their paper and were now painted and scruffy, due—it was rumoured—for redecoration when money allowed. The ornate fireplace of carved marble and surrounding oak was fitted with a large gas stove, old and ugly in design but still remarkably efficient, hissing a strong heat even into the dark corners of the room. The elegant mahogany table against the far wall with its jumble of magazines might have been bequeathed by John Carpendar himself. But it was scratched and dull now, dusted regularly but rarely polished, its surface scarred and ringed. To the left of the fireplace, in incongruous contrast, stood a large, modern television set, the gift of the Hospital League of Friends. In front of it was an immense cretonne-covered sofa with sagging springs, and a single matching armchair. The rest of the chairs were similar to those in the hospital out-patient department but were now too old and shabby to be tolerated for the use of patients. The arm-rests of pale wood were grubby; the coloured vinyl seats were stretched and dented and now smelt unpleasantly in the heat from the fire. One of the chairs was empty. It was the red-seated one which Nurse Pearce had invariably used. Scorning the intimacy of the sofa, she would sit there, a little apart from the huddle of students around the television set, watching the screen with careful disinterest as if it were a pleasure she could easily forgo. Occasionally she would drop her eyes to a book in her lap as if the folly presented for her entertainment had become too much to bear. Her presence, thought Nurse Dakers, had always been a little unwelcome and oppressive. The atmosphere of the students' sitting-room had always been lighter, more relaxed without that upright and censorious figure. But the empty chair, the dented seat, was almost worse. Nurse Dakers wished that she had the courage to walk over to it, to swing it into line with the other chairs around the television set and settle herself nonchalantly into its sagging curves, exorcizing once and for all that oppressive ghost. She wondered if the other students felt the same. It was impossible to ask. Were the Burt twins, bunched together in the depths of the sofa, really as absorbed as they appeared by the old gangster film they were watching? They were each knitting one of the heavy sweaters which they invariably wore in winter, their fingers clicking away, their eyes never leaving the screen. Beside them Nurse Fallon lolled in the armchair, one trousered leg swung casually over the arm. It was her first day back in the school after her sick leave and she still looked pale and drawn. Was her mind really on the sleek-haired hero with his tall wide-ribboned and ridiculous trilby, his over-padded shoulders, whose raucous voice, punctuated with gunshots, filled the room? Or was she, too, morbidly conscious of that empty red chair, the dented seat, the rounded ends of the arm-rests polished by Pearce's hand?

Nurse Dakers shivered. The wall clock showed that it was already after nine-thirty. Outside the wind was rising. It was going to be a wild night. In the rare intervals of quiet from the television set she could hear the creaking and sighing of the trees and could picture the last leaves falling softly on grass and path, isolating Nightingale House in a sludge of silence and decay. She forced herself to pick up her pen. She really must get on! Soon it would be time for bed and, one by one, the students would say their good nights and disappear, leaving her to brave alone the poorly-lit staircase and the dark corridor beyond. Jo Fallon would still be here of course. She never went to bed until the television programme closed for the night. Then she would make her lonely way upstairs to prepare her nightly hot whisky and lemon. Everyone knew Fallon's invariable habit. But Nurse Dakers felt that she could not face being left alone with Fallon. Hers was the last company she would choose, even in that lonely, frightening walk from the sitting-room to bed.

She began writing again.

"Now please, Mummy, don't keep on worrying about the murder."

The impossibility of the sentence struck her as soon as she saw the words on the paper. Somehow she must avoid the use of that emotive, blood-stained word. She tried again. "Now please, Mummy, don't start worrying about the things you read in the papers. There really isn't any need. I'm perfectly safe and happy and no one really believes that Pearce was deliberately killed."

It wasn't true of course. Some people must think that Pearce had been deliberately killed or why would the police be here? And it was ridiculous to suppose that the poison could have got into the feed by accident or that Pearce, the god-fearing, conscientious and essentially dull Pearce, would have chosen to kill herself in that agonizing and spectacular way. She wrote on:

"We still have the local C.I.D. here, but they don't come

in so often now. They have been very kind to us students and I don't think they suspect anyone. Poor Pearce wasn't very popular, but it's ridiculous to think that anyone here would want to harm her."

Had the police really been kind? she wondered. They had certainly been very correct, very polite. They had produced all the usual reassuring platitudes about the importance of co-operating with them in solving this terrible tragedy, telling the truth at all times, keeping nothing back however trivial and unimportant it might seem. Not one of them had raised his voice; not one had been aggressive or intimidating. And all of them had been frightening. Their very presence in Nightingale House, masculine and confident, had been, like the locked door of the demonstration room, a constant reminder of tragedy and fear. Nurse Dakers had found Inspector Bailey the most frightening of them all. He was a huge, ruddy, moon-faced man whose encouraging and avuncular voice and manner were in unnerving contrast to his cold pig-like eyes. The questioning had gone on and on. She could still recall the interminable sessions, the effort of will necessary to meet that probing gaze.

"Now I'm told that you were the most upset of them all when Nurse Pearce died. She was a particular friend of yours perhaps?"

"No. Not really. Not a particular friend. I hardly knew her."

"Well, there's a surprise! After nearly three years of training with her? Living and working so closely together, I should have thought that you all got to know each other pretty well."

She had struggled to explain.

"In some ways we do. We know each other's habits. But I didn't really know what she was like; as a person, I mean." A silly reply. How else could you know anyone except as a person? And it wasn't true. She had known Pearce. She had known her very well.

"But you got on well together? There hadn't been a quarrel or anything like that? No unpleasantness?"

An odd word. Unpleasantness. She had seen again that grotesque figure, teetering forward in agony, fingers scrabbling at the ineffectual air, the thin tubing stretching the mouth like a wound. No, there had been no unpleasantness.

"And the other students? They got on well with Nurse Pearce, too? There had been no bad blood as far as you know?"

Bad blood. A stupid expression. What was the opposite she wondered? Good blood? There was only good blood between us. Pearce's good blood. She had answered:

"She hadn't any enemies as far as I know. And if anyone did dislike her, they wouldn't kill her."

"So you all tell me. But someone did kill her, didn't they? Unless the poison wasn't intended for Nurse Pearce. She only played the part of the patient by chance. Did you know that Nurse Fallon had been taken ill that night?"

And so it had gone on. Questions about every minute of that last terrible demonstration. Questions about the lavatory disinfectant. The empty bottle, wiped clean of fingerprints, had been quickly found by the police lying among the bushes at the back of the house. Anyone could have thrown it from a bedroom window or bathroom window in the concealing darkness of that January morning. Questions about her movements from the moment of first awakening. The constant reiteration in that minatory voice that nothing should be held back, nothing concealed.

She wondered whether the other students had been as frightened. The Burt twins had seemed merely bored and resigned, obeying the Inspector's sporadic summons with a shrug of the shoulders and a weary, "Oh, God, not again!" Nurse Goodale had said nothing when she was called for questioning and nothing afterwards. Nurse Fallon had been equally reticent. It was known that Inspector Bailey had interviewed her in the sick bay as soon as she was well enough to be seen. No one knew what had happened at that interview. It was rumoured that Fallon had admitted returning to Nightingale House early in the morning of the crime but had refused to say why. That would be very like Fallon. And now she had returned to Nightingale House to rejoin her set. So far she hadn't even mentioned Pearce's death. Nurse Dakers wondered if and when she would; and, morbidly sensitive to the hidden meaning in every word, struggled on with her letter:

"We haven't used the demonstration room since Nurse Pearce's death but otherwise the set is continuing to work according to plan. Only one of the students, Diane Harper, has left school. Her father came to fetch her two days after Nurse Pearce died and the police didn't seem to mind her leaving. We all thought it was silly of her to give up so near to her finals but her father has never been keen on her training as a nurse and she is engaged to be married anyway, so I suppose she thought it didn't matter. No one else is thinking of leaving and there really isn't the slightest danger. So please, darling, do stop worrying about me. Now I must tell you about tomorrow's programme."

There was no need to go on drafting now. The rest of the letter would be easy. She read over what she had written and decided that it would do. Taking a fresh sheet of paper from the pad she began to write the final letter. With any luck she would just get it finished before the film ended and the twins put away their knitting and went to bed.

She scribbled quickly on and, half an hour later, her

letter finished, saw with relief that the film had come to the last holocaust and the final embrace. At the same moment Nurse Goodale removed her reading spectacles, looked up from her work, and closed her book. The door opened and Julia Pardoe appeared.

"I'm back," she announced, and yawned. "It was a lousy film. Anyone making tea?" No one answered but the twins stubbed their knitting-needles into the balls of wool and joined her at the door, switching off the television on their way. Pardoe would never bother to make tea if she could find someone else to do it and the twins usually obliged. As she followed them out of the sitting-room Nurse Dakers looked back at the silent, immobile figure of Fallon alone now with Madeleine Goodale. She had a sudden impulse to speak to Fallon, to welcome her back to the school, to ask after her health, or simply to say good night. But the words seemed to stick in her throat, the moment passed, and the last thing she saw as she closed the door behind her was Fallon's pale and individual face, blank eyes still fixed on the television set as if unaware that the screen was dead.

II

In a hospital, time itself is documented, seconds measured in a pulse beat, the drip of blood or plasma; minutes in the stopping of a heart; hours in the rise and fall of a temperature chart, the length of an operation. When the events of the night of 28th–29th January came to be documented there were few of the protagonists at the John Carpendar Hospital who were unaware what they had been doing or where they were at any particular moment of their waking hours. They might not choose to tell the truth, but at least they knew where the truth lay.

It was a night of violent but erratic storm, the wind varying in intensity and even in direction from hour to hour. At ten o'clock it was little more than a sobbing *obbligato* among the elms. An hour later it suddenly reached a crescendo of fury. The great elms around Nightingale House cracked and groaned under the onslaught, while the wind screamed among them like the cachinnation of devils. Along the deserted paths, the banks of dead leaves, still heavy with rain, shifted sluggishly then broke apart into drifts and rose in wild swirls like demented insects, to glue themselves against the black barks of the trees. In the operating theatre at the top of the hospital Mr. Courtney-Briggs demonstrated his imperturbability in the face of crisis by muttering to his attendant registrar that it was a wild night before bending his head again to the satisfying contemplation of the intriguing surgical problem which throbbed between the retracted lips of the wound. Below him in the silent and dimly lit wards the patients muttered and turned in their sleep as if conscious of the tumult outside. The radiographer, who had been called from home to take urgent X-rays of Mr. Courtney-Briggs's patient, replaced the covers on the apparatus, switched out the lights and wondered whether her small car would hold the road. The night nurses moved silently among their patients testing the windows, drawing the curtains more closely as if to keep out some threatening and alien force. The porter on duty in the main gate lodge shifted uneasily in his chair then rose cramped to his feet and put a couple more chunks of coal on the fire. He felt in need of warmth and comfort in his isolation. The little house seemed to shake with every gust of the wind.

But shortly before midnight the storm abated, as if sensing the approach of the witching hour, the dead of night when the pulse of man beats slowest and the dying patient slips most easily into the last oblivion. There was an eerie silence for about five minutes, succeeded by a soft rhythmic moaning as the wind swooped and sighed among the trees as if exhausted by its own fury. Mr. Courtney-Briggs, the operation completed, peeled off his gloves and made his way into the surgeons' changing-room. As soon as he was disrobed he made a telephone call from the wall instrument to the Sisters' floor at Nightingale House and asked Sister Brumfett, the Sister in charge of the private ward, to return to the ward to supervise the care of his patient for the first critical hour. He noted with satisfaction that the wind had dropped. She could make her own way through the grounds as she had done at his bidding countless times before. He need feel under no obligation to fetch her in his car.

Less than five minutes later Sister Brumfett plodded resolutely through the trees, her cloak folded around her like a flag whipped close to a flag pole, her hood drawn down over the frilly Sister's cap. It was curiously peaceful in this brief interlude of the storm. She moved silently over the sodden grass, feeling the pull of the rain-soaked earth through the thick soles of her shoes while, from time to time, a thin branch, torn by the storm, broke loose from its last thread of bark and thudded with gentle inadvertence at her feet. By the time she had gained the peace of the private ward and was helping the third-year student make up the post-operative bed and prepare the stand ready for the blood drip, the wind was rising again. But Sister Brumfett, absorbed in her task, no longer noticed it.

Shortly after half past twelve Albert Colgate, the porter on night duty in the main lodge, who was nodding over his evening paper, was jerked into consciousness by a band of light sweeping across the lodge window and the purr of an approaching car. It must, he thought, be Mr. Courtney-

Briggs's Daimler. So the operation was over. He expected the car to sweep out of the main gate but unexpectedly it stopped. There were two peremptory hoots on the horn. Muttering, the porter thrust his arms into his overcoat and made his way out of the lodge door. Mr. Courtney-Briggs wound down the window and shouted at him through the wind.

"I tried to get out of the Winchester gate but there's a tree down across the path. I thought I'd better report it. Get it seen to as soon as you can."

The porter thrust his head through the car window encountering an immediate and luxurious smell of cigar smoke, after-shave lotion and leather. Mr. Courtney-Briggs recoiled slightly from his nearness. The porter said:

"That'll be one of those old elms no doubt, sir. I'll report it first thing in the morning. There's nothing I can do tonight, sir, not in this storm."

Mr. Courtney-Briggs began to wind up the window. Colgate's head made a sudden withdrawal.

The surgeon said: "There's no need to do anything tonight. I've tied my white scarf on one of the boughs. I doubt whether anyone else will use that road until the morning. If they do, they'll see the scarf. But you might warn anyone who drives in this way. Good night, Colgate."

The large car purred out of the front gate and Colgate made his way back into the lodge. Meticulously he noted the time by the wall clock over the fireplace and made a record in his book. "12:32 Mr. Courtney-Briggs reports fallen tree across the Winchester Road path."

He had settled again into his chair and taken up his paper before the thought struck him that it was odd that Mr. Courtney-Briggs should have tried to drive out through the Winchester gate. It wasn't on his quickest route home and it was a road he seldom used. Mr. Courtney-Briggs invariably used the front entrance. Presumably, thought Colgate, he had a key to the Winchester Road gate. Mr. Courtney-Briggs had a key to most parts of the hospital. But it was odd all the same.

Just before 2 o'clock on the silent second floor of Nightingale House, Maureen Burt stirred in her sleep, muttered incoherently through her moist pursed lips and awoke to the disagreeable awareness that three cups of tea before bed had been two too many. She lay still for a moment, sleepily aware of the groaning of the storm, wondered whether she might not after all manage to get to sleep again, realized that her discomfort was too great to be reasonably borne and felt for the switch of her bedside lamp. The light was instantaneous and blinding, shocking her into full consciousness. She wriggled her feet into her bedroom slippers, threw her dressing-gown around her shoulders and padded out into the corridor. As she quietly closed her bedroom door behind her a sudden gust of wind billowed out the curtains at the far corridor window. She went across to shut it. Through the agitated tracery of boughs and their leaping shadows on the window-pane she could see the hospital riding the storm like a great ship at anchor, the ward windows only faintly luminous in comparison with the vertical line of brightly lit eyes marking the Sisters' offices and ward kitchens. She shut down the window carefully and, reeling slightly with sleep, felt her way down the passage to the cloakroom. Less than a minute later she came out again into the corridor, pausing momentarily to accustom her eyes to the gloom. From the confusion of shadows at the top of the stairs a deeper shadow detached itself, moved forward and was revealed as a cloaked and hooded figure. Maureen was not a nervous girl and in her somnolent state was conscious only of surprise that someone else should be awake and about. She saw at once that it was Sister Brumfett. Two piercing bespectacled eyes peered at her through the gloom. The Sister's voice was unexpectedly sharp.

"It's one of the Burt twins, isn't it? What are you doing here? Is anyone else up?"

"No, Sister. At least I don't think so. I've just been to the lavatory."

"Oh I see. Well, as long as everyone's all right. I thought that the storm might have disturbed you all. I've just come back from my ward. One of Mr. Courtney-Briggs's patients had a relapse and he had to operate urgently."

"Yes, Sister," said Nurse Burt, uncertain what else was expected of her. She was surprised that Sister Brumfett should bother to explain her presence to a mere student nurse, and she watched a little uncertainly as the Sister drew her long cloak more firmly around her and stumped briskly down the corridor towards the far stairs. Her own room was on the floor above, immediately next to Matron's flat. When she reached the bottom of the stairs, Sister Brumfett turned and seemed about to speak. It was at that moment that Shirley Burt's door opened slowly, and a tousled red head appeared.

"What's up?" it inquired sleepily.

Sister Brumfett walked towards them.

"Nothing, Nurse. I'm just on my way back to bed. I've come from my ward. And Maureen had to get up to go to the lavatory. There's nothing to worry about."

Shirley gave no impression that she was or ever had been worried. She now trotted out on to the landing, pulling her dressing-gown around her. Resigned and a little complacent, she said:

"When Maureen wakes up I do too. We've always been like that ever since we were babies. You ask Mum!" A little unsteady with sleep but not ungratified that the family theurgy still worked, she closed her bedroom door behind her with the finality of one who, being up, intends to stay up.

"No use trying to get off again in this wind. I'm going to brew some cocoa. Can we bring you up a mug, Sister? It'd help you to sleep."

"No thank you, Nurse. I don't think I shall have any trouble in sleeping. Be as quiet as you can. You don't want to disturb the others. And don't get cold." She turned again towards the stairs. Maureen said: "Fallon's awake. At least her bedside lamp's still on."

The three of them looked down the corridor to where an eye of light from Nurse Fallon's keyhole pierced the darkness and threw a small luminous shadow on the linenfold panelling opposite.

Shirley said: "We'll take her a mug then. She's probably awake and reading. Come on, Maureen! Good night, Sister."

They shuffled off together down the corridor to the small utility room at the end. After a second's pause Sister Brumfett, who had been looking steadily after them, her face rigid and expressionless, turned finally towards the stairs and made her way up to bed.

Exactly one hour later but unheard and unrecorded by anyone in Nightingale House, a weakened pane of glass in the conservatory which had rattled spasmodically throughout the night, fell inwards to explode into splinters on the tessellated floor. The wind rushed in through the aperture like a questing animal. Its cold breath rustled the magazines on the wicker tables, lifted the fronds of the palms and sent the fern leaves gently waving. Finally it found the long white cupboard centred under the plant shelves. Early in the evening, the door had been left ajar by the desperate and hurried visitor who had last thrust a hand into the cupboard depths. All night the door had stayed open, motionless on its hinges. But now the wind set it gently swinging to and fro, then as if wearying of the game, finally closed it with a soft, decisive thud.

And everything living under the roof of Nightingale House, slept.

III

Nurse Dakers was awoken by the whirr of the bedside alarm clock. The faintly luminous dial showed the time as 6:15. Even with the curtains drawn back the room was still completely dark. The square of faint light came, as she knew, not from the door but from the distant lights of the hospital where already the night staff would be taking round the first morning cups of tea. She lay still for a moment, adjusting to her own wakefulness, putting out tentative feelers to the day. She had slept well despite the storm of which she had been only briefly aware. She realized with a spring of joy that she could actually face the day with confidence. The misery and apprehension of the previous evening, of the previous weeks, seemed to have lifted. It seemed now no more than the effect of tiredness, and temporary depression. She had passed down a tunnel of misery and insecurity since Pearce's death but this morning, miraculously, she had come out into daylight again. It was like Christmas morning in childhood. It was the beginning of a summer holiday from school. It was waking refreshed at the end of a febrile illness with the comfortable knowledge that Mummy was there and that all the solaces of convalescence lay ahead. It was familiar life restored.

The day shone before her. She catalogued its promises and pleasures. In the morning there would be the materia-medica lecture. This was important. She had always been weak on drugs and dosages. Then, after the coffee break,

Mr. Courtney-Briggs would give his third-year surgery seminar. It was a privilege that a surgeon of his eminence should take so much trouble with the student nurse training. She was a little afraid of him, particularly of his sharp staccato questions. But this morning she would be brave and speak up confidently. Then in the afternoon the hospital bus would take the set to the local maternity and child welfare clinic to watch the local authority staff at work. This, too, was important to someone who hoped in time to become a district nurse. She lay for a few moments contemplating this gratifying programme, then she got out of bed, shuffled her feet into her slippers, struggled into her cheap dressing-gown and made her way along the passage to the students' utility room.

The Nightingale nurses were called promptly at seven each morning by one of the maids, but most students, accustomed to early waking when on the wards, set their alarm clocks at 6:30 to give themselves time for tea-making and gossip. The early arrivals were already there. The little room was brightly lit, cheerfully domestic, smelling, as always, of tea, boiled milk and detergent. The scene was reassuringly normal. The Burt twins were there, faces still puffy from sleep, each twin stoutly cocooned into a bright red dressing-gown. Maureen was carrying her portable wireless tuned to Radio 2 and was gently jerking hips and shoulders to the rhythm of the B.B.C.'s early morning syncopation. Her twin was setting their two immense mugs on a tray and rummaging in a tin for biscuits. The only other student present was Madeleine Goodale who, clad in an ancient plaid dressing-gown, was watching, teapot in hand, for the first spurt of steam from the kettle. In her mood of optimism and relief, Nurse Dakers could have hugged them all.

"Where's Fallon this morning?" asked Maureen Burt with no great interest.

Nurse Fallon was a notoriously late riser, but she was usually one of the first to make tea. It was her habit to carry it back to enjoy at leisure in bed, where she would stay until the last possible moment consistent with presenting herself at breakfast on time. But this morning her personal teapot and the matching cup and saucer were still on the cupboard shelf beside the canister of china tea which Fallon preferred to the strong brown brew which the rest of the set considered necessary before they could face the day.

"I'll give her a call," suggested Nurse Dakers, happy to be of use and longing to celebrate her release from the strain of the last few weeks by general benevolence.

"Wait a moment, then you can take her a cuppa out of my pot," suggested Maureen.

"She won't like Indian tea. I'll see if she's awake and just let her know the kettle's on the boil."

For a moment it occurred to Nurse Dakers to make Fallon's tea for her. But the impulse faded. It was not that Fallon was particularly temperamental or unpredictable, but somehow people did not interfere with her personal things nor expect her to share them. She had few possessions but they were expensive, elegant, carefully chosen and so much part of her *persona* that they seemed sacrosanct.

Nurse Dakers almost ran along the passage to Fallon's room. The door was unlocked. That did not surprise her. Ever since one of the students had been taken ill in the night some years ago and had been too weak to creep across the room to unlock the door, there had been a rule forbidding girls to lock themselves in at night. Since Pearce's death one or two had taken to turning their keys, and if the Sisters suspected it they said nothing. Perhaps they, too, slept more soundly behind locked doors. But Fallon had not been afraid.

The curtains were closely drawn. The bedside lamp

was on but with the adjustable shade tilted so that it threw a pale moon on the far wall and left the bed in shadow. There was a tangle of black hair on the pillow. Nurse Dakers felt along the wall for the light switch and paused before clicking it on. Then she pressed it down very gently as if it were possible softly and gradually to illuminate the room and spare Fallon the first fierce wakening. The room blazed into light. She blinked in the unexpected glare. Then she moved very quietly across to the bed. She didn't scream or faint. She stood absolutely still for a moment looking down at Fallon's body, and smiling a little as if surprised. She had no doubt that Fallon was dead. The eyes were still wide open but they were cold and opaque, like the eyes of dead fish. Nurse Dakers bent down and stared into them as if willing them into brightness or seeking in vain some trace of her own reflection. Then she slowly turned and left the room, switching off the light and closing the door behind her. She swayed like a sleepwalker along the passage, steadying her hands against the wall.

At first the students didn't notice her return. Then three pairs of eyes were suddenly fixed on her, three figures stood frozen in a tableau of puzzled inquiry. Nurse Dakers leaned against the door post and opened her mouth soundlessly. The words wouldn't come. Something seemed to have happened to her throat. Her whole jaw was trembling uncontrollably and her tongue was stuck to the roof of her mouth. Her eyes pleaded with them. It seemed minutes while they watched her struggle. When the words did come she sounded calm, gently surprised.

"It's Fallon. She's dead."

She smiled like someone waking from a dream, patiently explaining: "Someone's murdered Fallon."

The room emptied. She wasn't aware of their concerted dash down the corridor. She was alone. The kettle was screeching now, the lid rattling under the force of the steam. Carefully she turned down the gas, frowning with concentration. Very slowly, like a child entrusted with a precious task, she took down the canister, the elegant teapot, the matching cup and saucer, and humming gently to herself, made Fallon's early morning tea.

CHAPTER THREE

Strangers in the House

I

"THE PATHOLOGIST is here, sir."

A detective constable put his cropped head round the bedroom door and raised an interrogative eyebrow.

Chief Superintendent Adam Dalgliesh turned from his examination of the dead girl's clothes, his six feet two inches uncomfortably trapped between the foot of the bed and the wardrobe door. He looked at his watch. It was eight minutes past ten. Sir Miles Honeyman, as always, had made good time.

"Right, Fenning. Ask him to be good enough to wait for a moment, will you? We'll be finished in here in a minute. Then some of us can clear out and make room for him."

The head disappeared. Dalgliesh closed the wardrobe door and managed to squeeze himself between it and the foot of the bed. Certainly there was no room for a fourth person at present. The huge bulk of the finger-print man occupied the space between the bedside table and the window as, bent almost double, he brushed charcoal carefully on to the surface of the whisky bottle, turning it by its cork. Beside the bottle stood a glass plate bearing the dead girl's prints, the whorls and composites plainly visible.

"Anything there?" asked Dalgliesh.

The print man paused and peered more closely.

"A nice set of prints coming up, sir. They're hers all right. Nothing else, though. It looks as if the chap who sold it gave the bottle the usual wipe over before wrapping. It'll be interesting to see what we get from the beaker."

He cast a jealously possessive glance at it as it lay where it had fallen from the girl's hand, lightly poised in a curve of the counterpane. Not until the last photograph had been taken would it be yielded up for his examination.

He bent again to his task on the bottle. Behind him the Yard photographer manœuvred his tripod and camera—a new Cambo monorail, Dalgliesh noticed—to the right-hand foot of the bed. There was a click, an explosion of light, and the image of the dead girl leapt up at them and lay suspended in air, burning itself on Dalgliesh's retina. Colour and shape were intensified and distorted in that cruel, momentary glare. The long black hair was a tangled wig against the whiteness of the pillows; the glazed eyes were exophthalmic marbles, as if rigor mortis were squeezing them out of their sockets; the skin was very white and smooth, looking repulsive to the touch, an artificial membrane, tough and impermeable as vinyl. Dalgliesh blinked, erasing the image of a witch's plaything, a grotesque puppet casually tossed against the pillow. When he next looked at her she was again a dead girl on a bed; no more and no less. Twice more the distorted image leapt up at him and lay petrified in air as the photographer took two pictures with the Polaroid Land camera to give Dalgliesh the immediate prints for which he always asked. Then it was over. "That was the last. I'm through, sir," said the photographer. "I'll let Sir Miles in now." He put his head around the door while the print man, grunting with satisfaction, lovingly lifted the drinking beaker from the counterpane with a pair of forceps and set it alongside the whisky bottle.

Sir Miles must have been waiting on the landing for he

trotted in immediately, a familiar rotund figure with his immense head of black curling hair and eager beady eyes. He brought with him an air of music hall *bonhommie* and, as always, a faint smell of sour sweat. He was unfretted by the delay. But then Sir Miles, God's gift to forensic pathology or an amateur mountebank as you chose to take him, did not easily take offence. He had gained much of his reputation and also, possibly, his recent knighthood by adhering to the principle that you should never willingly offend anyone, however humble. He greeted the departing photographer and the fingerprint officer as if they were old friends, and Dalgliesh by his Christian name. But the socialities were perfunctory; his preoccupation preceded him like a miasma as he wriggled up close to the bed.

Dalgliesh despised him as a ghoul; hardly, he admitted, a rational cause for dislike. In a perfectly organized world, foot fetishists would, no doubt, become chiropodists; hair fetishists, hairdressers; and ghouls, morbid anatomists. It was surprising that so few of them did. But Sir Miles laid himself open to the implication. He approached each new corpse with eagerness, almost with glee; his macabre jokes had been heard at half the dining clubs in London; he was an expert in death who obviously enjoyed his work. Dalgliesh felt inhibited in his company by the consciousness of his dislike for the man. Antipathy seemed to crackle from him. But Sir Miles was oblivious of it. He liked himself too well to conceive that other men might find him less lovable, and this endearing naïvety gave him a kind of charm. Even those colleagues who most deplored his conceit, his publicity seeking, and the irresponsibility of most of his public utterances, found it hard to dislike him as much as they felt they should. Women were said to find him attractive. Perhaps he had a morbid fascination for them. Certainly his was the infectious good nature of a man who necessarily finds the world an agreeable place since it contains himself.

He always tut-tutted over a body. He did so now, plucking back the sheet with a curiously mincing gesture of his pudgy fingers. Dalgliesh walked over to the window and gazed out at the tracery of boughs through which the distant hospital, still lit up, gleamed like an insubstantial palace suspended in air. He could hear the faint rustling of bed linen. Sir Miles would only be making a preliminary examination, but even to think of those pudgy fingers insinuating themselves into the body's tender orifices was enough to make one hope for a peaceful death in one's own bed. The real job would be done later on the mortuary table, that aluminium sink with its grim accessories of drains and sprays on which Josephine Fallon's body would be systematically dismembered in the cause of justice, or science, or curiosity, or what you will. And afterwards, Sir Miles's mortuary attendant would earn his guinea by stitching it up again into a decent semblance of humanity so that the family could view it without trauma. If there were a family. He wondered who, if anyone, would be Fallon's official mourners. Superficially there was nothing in her room—no photographs, no letters—to suggest that she had close ties with any living soul.

While Sir Miles sweated and muttered, Dalgliesh made a second tour of the room, carefully avoiding watching the pathologist. He knew this squeamishness to be irrational and was half ashamed of it. Post-mortem examinations did not upset him. It was this impersonal examination of the still warm female body which he couldn't stomach. A few short hours ago she would have been entitled to some modesty, to her own choice of doctor, free to reject those unnaturally white and eagerly probing fingers. A few hours ago she was a human being. Now she was dead flesh.

It was the room of a woman who preferred to be unencumbered. It contained the necessary basic comforts and one or two carefully chosen embellishments. It was as if she had itemized her needs and provided for them expensively but precisely and without extravagance. The thick rug by the bed was not, he thought, the kind provided by the Hospital Management Committee. There was only one picture but that was an original water colour, a charming landscape by Robert Hills, hung where the light from the window lit it most effectively. On the window-sill stood the only ornament, a Staffordshire pottery figure of John Wesley preaching from his pulpit. Dalgliesh turned it in his hands. It was perfect; a collector's piece. But there were none of the small trivial impedimenta which those living in institutions often dispose about them to provide comfort or reassurance.

He walked over to the bookcase beside the bed and again examined the books. They, too, seemed chosen to minister to predictable moods. A collection of modern poetry, his own last volume included; a complete set of Jane Austen, well worn but in a leather binding and printed on India paper; a few books on philosophy nicely balanced between scholarship and popular appeal; about two dozen paper-backs of modern novels, Greene, Waugh, Compton Burnett, Hartley, Powell, Cary. But most of the books were poetry. Looking at them, he thought, we shared the same tastes. If we had met we should at least have had something to say to each other. "Everyman's death diminishes me." But, of course, Doctor Donne. The over-exploited dictum had become a fashionable catch phrase in a crowded world where non-involvement was practically a social necessity. But some deaths still held their power to diminish more than others. For the first time in years he was conscious of a sense of waste, of a personal irrational loss.

He moved on. At the foot of the bed was a wardrobe with a chest of drawers attached, a bastard contraption in pale wood, designed, if anyone had consciously designed an object so ugly, to provide the maximum of space in the minimum of room. The top of the chest was meant to serve as a dressing-table and held a small looking-glass. In front of it were her brush and comb. Nothing else.

He opened the small left-hand drawer. It held her make-up, the jars and tubes neatly arranged on a small papier mâché tray. There was a great deal more than he had expected to find: cleansing cream, a box of tissues, foundation cream, pressed powder, eye shadow, mascara. She had obviously made up with care. But there was only one of each item. No experiments, no impulse buying, no half used and discarded tubes with the make-up congealed round the stopper. The collection said: "This is what suits me. This is what I need. No more and no less."

He opened the right-hand drawer. It held nothing but a concertina file, each compartment indexed. He thumbed through the contents. A birth certificate. A certificate of baptism. A post office savings account book. The name and address of her solicitor. There were no personal letters. He tucked the file under his arm.

He moved on to the wardrobe and examined again the collection of clothes. Three pairs of slacks. Cashmere jumpers. A winter coat in bright red tweed. Four well-cut dresses in fine wool. They all spoke of quality. It was an expensive wardrobe for a student nurse.

He heard a final satisfied grunt from Sir Miles and turned round. The pathologist was straightening himself and peeling off his rubber gloves. They were so thin that it looked as if he were shedding his epidermis. He said:

"Dead, I should say, about ten hours. I'm judging mainly by rectal temperature and the degree of rigor in the lower limbs. But it's no more than a guess, my dear fellow. These things are chancy, as you know. We'll have a look at the stomach contents; that may give us a clue. At present, and on the clinical signs, I should say she died about midnight give or take an hour. Taking a common sense view, of course, she died when she drank that nightcap."

The finger-print officer had left the whisky bottle and beaker on the table and was working now on the door handle. Sir Miles trotted round to them and without touching the beaker bent his head and placed his nose close to the rim.

"Whisky. But what else? That's what we're asking ourselves, my dear fellow. That's what we're asking ourselves. One thing, it wasn't a corrosive. No carbolic acid this time. I didn't do the P.M. on that other girl by the way. Rikki Blake did that little job. A bad business. I suppose you're looking for a connection between the two deaths?"

Dalgliesh said: "It's possible."

"Could be. Could be. This isn't likely to be a natural death. But we'll have to wait for the toxicology. Then we may learn something. There's no evidence of strangulation or suffocation. No external marks of violence come to that. By the way, she was pregnant. About three months gone, I'd say. I got a nice little *ballottement* there. Haven't found that sign since I was a student. The P.M. will confirm it of course."

His little bright eyes searched the room. "No container for the poison apparently. If it were poison, of course. And no suicide note?"

"That's not conclusive evidence," said Dalgliesh.

"I know. I know. But most of them leave a little *billet doux*. They like to tell the tale, my dear fellow. They like to tell the tale. The mortuary van's here by the way. I'll take her away if you're finished with her."

"I've finished," said Dalgliesh.

He waited and watched while the porters manœuvred their stretcher into the room and with brisk efficiency dumped the dead weight onto it. Sir Miles fretted around them with the nervous anxiety of an expert who has found a particularly good specimen and must carefully supervise its safe transport. It was odd that the removal of that inert mass of bone and tightening muscle, to which each in his different way had been ministering, should have left the room so empty, so desolate. Dalgliesh had noticed it before when the body was taken away; this sense of an empty stage, of props casually disposed and bereft of meaning, of a drained air. The recently dead had their own mysterious *charisma;* not without reason did men talk in whispers in their presence. But now she was gone, and there was nothing further for him to do in the room. He left the fingerprint man annotating and photographing his finds, and went out into the passage.

II

It was now after eleven o'clock but the corridor was still very dark, the one clear window at the far end discernible only as a square haze behind the drawn curtains. Dalgliesh could at first just make out the shape and colour of the three red fire buckets filled with sand and the cone of a fire extinguisher gleaming against the carved oak panelling of the walls. The iron staples, driven brutally into the woodwork, on which they were supported, were in incongruous contrast to the row of elegant light fittings in convoluted brass which sprang from the centres of the quatrefoil carvings. The fittings had obviously originally been designed for gas, but had been crudely adapted without imagination or skill to the use of electricity. The brass was unpolished and most of the delicate glass shades, curved in a semblance of flower petals, were missing or broken. In each of the deflowered clusters a single socket was now monstrously budded with one grubby and low-powered bulb whose faint and diffused light threw shadows across the floor and served only to accentuate the general gloom. Apart from the one small window at the end of the corridor there was little other natural light. The huge window over the well of the staircase, a pre-Raphaelite representation in lurid glass of the expulsion from Eden, was hardly functional.

He looked into the rooms adjacent to that of the dead girl. One was unoccupied, with the bed stripped, the wardrobe door ajar and the drawers, lined with fresh newspaper, all pulled out as if to demonstrate the room's essential emptiness. The other was in use but looked as if it had been hurriedly left; the bedclothes were carelessly thrown back and the bedside rug was rumpled. There was a little pile of textbooks on the bedside table and he opened the flyleaf of the first to hand and read the inscription, "Christine Dakers." So this was the room of the girl who had found the body. He inspected the wall between the two rooms. It was thin, a light partition of painted hardboard which trembled and let out a soft boom as he struck it. He wondered whether Nurse Dakers had heard anything in the night. Unless Josephine Fallon had died instantly and almost soundlessly some indication of her distress must surely have penetrated this insubstantial partition. He was anxious to interview Nurse Christine Dakers. At present she was in the nurses' sick bay suffering, so he was told, from shock. The shock was probably genuine enough, but even if it were not, there was nothing he could do about it. Nurse Dakers was for the moment effectively protected by her doctors from any questioning by the police.

He explored a little further. Opposite the row of nurses' bedrooms was a suite of bathroom cubicles and lavatories leading out of a large square cloakroom fitted with four wash-basins, each surrounded by a shower curtain. Each of the bath cubicles had a small sash window fitted with opaque glass, inconveniently placed but not difficult to open. They gave a view of the back of the house and of the two short wings, each built above a brick cloister, which were incongruously grafted on to the main building. It was as if the architect, having exhausted the possibilities of Gothic revival and baroque, had decided to introduce a more contemplative and ecclesiastical influence. The ground between the cloisters was an overgrown jungle of laurel bushés and untended trees which grew so close to the house that some of the branches seemed to scrape the downstairs windows. Dalgliesh could see dim figures searching among the bushes and could hear the faint mutter of voices. The discarded bottle of disinfectant which had killed Heather Pearce had been found among these bushes and it was possible that a second container, its contents equally lethal, might also have been hurled in the dark hours from the same window. There was a nail brush on the bath rack and, reaching for it, Dalgliesh hurled it in a wide arc through the window and into the bushes. He could neither see nor hear its fall but a cheerful face appeared among the parted leaves, a hand was waved in salute and the two searching constables moved back deeper into the undergrowth.

He next made his way along the passage to the nurses' utility room at the far end. Detective Sergeant Masterson was there with Sister Rolfe. Together they were surveying a motley collection of objects laid out before them on the working surface rather as if they were engaging in a private Kim's game. There were two squeezed lemons; a bowl of granulated sugar; an assortment of mugs containing cold tea, the surface of the liquid mottled and puckered; and a delicate Worcester teapot with matching cup and saucer and milk jug. There was also a crumpled square of thin white wrapping paper bearing the words "Scunthorpe's Wine Stores, 149, High Street, Heatheringfield" and a scribbled receipt smoothed out and held flat by a couple of tea canisters.

"She bought the whisky yesterday morning, sir," Masterson said. "Luckily for us, Mr. Scunthorpe is punctilious about receipts. That's the bill and that's the wrapping paper. So it looks as if she first opened the bottle when she went to bed yesterday."

Dalgliesh asked: "Where was it kept?"

It was Sister Rolfe who replied. "Fallon always kept her whisky in her bedroom."

Masterson laughed.

"Not surprising with the stuff costing nearly three quid a bottle."

Sister Rolfe looked at him with contempt.

"I doubt whether that would worry Fallon. She wasn't the type to mark the bottle."

"She was generous?" asked Dalgliesh.

"No, merely unconcerned. She kept her whisky in her room because Matron asked her to."

But brought it in here yesterday to prepare her late night drink, thought Dalgliesh. He stirred the sugar gently with his finger.

Sister Rolfe said: "That's innocent. The students tell me that they all used it when they made their morning tea. And the Burt twins, at least, drank some of theirs."

"But we'll send it and the lemon to the lab just the same," said Dalgliesh.

He lifted the lid from the little teapot and looked inside. Answering his unspoken question, Sister Rolfe said:

"Apparently Nurse Dakers made early tea in it. The pot is Fallon's of course. No one else has early tea in antique Worcester."

"Nurse Dakers made tea for Nurse Fallon before she knew that the girl was dead?"

"No, afterwards. It was a purely automatic reaction, I imagine. She must have been in shock. After all, she had just seen Fallon's body. She could hardly expect to cure rigor mortis with hot tea, even with the best China blend. I suppose you'll want to see Dakers, but you'll have to wait. She's in the sick bay at the moment. I think they told you. It's part of the private wing and Sister Brumfett is looking after her. That's why I'm here now. Like the police, we're a hierarchical profession and when Matron isn't in Nightingale House, Brumfett is next in the pecking order. Normally she would be dancing attendance on you, not I. You've been told, of course, that Miss Taylor is on her way back from a conference in Amsterdam. She had to deputise unexpectedly for the Chairman of the Area Nurse Training Committee, luckily for her. So at least there's one senior member of the staff with an alibi."

Dalgliesh had been told, and more than once. The absence of the Matron seemed to be a fact which everyone he had met, however briefly, had found it necessary to mention, explain or regret. But Sister Rolfe was the first to make a snide reference to the fact the it gave Miss Taylor an alibi, at least for the time of Fallon's death.

"And the rest of the students?"

"They're in the small lecture room on the floor below. Sister Gearing, our clinical instructor, is taking them for a private study period. I don't suppose they're doing much reading. It would have been better to set them something more active but it's not easy at a moment's notice. Will you see them there?"

"No, later. And in the demonstration room where Nurse Pearce died."

She glanced at him and then turned her eyes away quickly, but not so quickly that he missed the look of surprise and, he thought, disapproval. She had expected him to show more sensitivity, more consideration. The demonstration room had not been used since Nurse Pearce's death. To interview the students there so soon after this second tragedy would reinforce memory with fresh horror. If any of them were ready to be unnerved, this might do it and he had never considered using any other room. Sister Rolfe, he thought, was like all the rest of them. They wanted their murderers caught but only by the most gentlemanly means. They wanted them punished, but only if the punishment did not outrage their own sensibility.

Dalgliesh asked: "How is this place locked at night?"

"Sister Brumfett, Sister Gearing, and myself take responsibility for a week at a time. It's Gearing's turn this week. We're the only three Sisters who are resident here. We lock and bolt the front door and the kitchen door at eleven o'clock promptly. There's a small side door with a Yale lock and an inside bolt. If any student or member of the staff has a late pass she is issued with a key to that door and bolts it when she comes in. Sisters have a key in their possession permanently. There's only one other door and that leads from Matron's flat on the third floor. She has a private staircase and, of course, her own key. Apart from that, there are the fire escape doors but they are all kept locked on the inside. The place wouldn't be difficult to break into. I imagine that few institutions are. But we've never had a burglar so far as I know. Incidentally, there's a pane of glass out in the conservatory. Alderman Kealey, the Vice-Chairman, seems to think that Fallon's murderer got in that way. He's a great man for finding comfortable explanations for all life's embarrassing problems. It looks to me as if the pane blew in with the wind, but you'll no doubt form your own opinion."

She's talking too much, he thought. Loquacity was one of the commonest reactions to shock or nervousness and one which any interrogating officer made the most of. Tomorrow she would despise herself for it, and become that much more difficult, that much less co-operative. In the meantime she was telling him more than she realized.

The broken pane would, of course, have to be looked at, the woodwork examined for marks of entry. But he thought it unlikely that Nurse Fallon's death had been the work of any intruder. He asked: "How many people slept here last night?"

"Brumfett, Gearing and myself. Brumfett was out for part of the night. I understand she was recalled to the ward by Mr. Courtney-Briggs. Miss Collins was here. She's the house-keeper. And there were five student nurses: Nurse Dakers, the Burt twins, Nurse Goodale, and Nurse Pardoe. And Fallon slept here of course. That is, if Fallon had time to sleep! Incidentally, her bedside light was on all night. The Burt twins were up brewing cocoa shortly after two and nearly took a cup in to Fallon. If they'd done so you might have got a clearer idea of the time of death. But it occurred to them that she might have fallen asleep with the light on and wouldn't exactly welcome being woken, even to the sight and smell of cocoa. The twins' invariable solace is food and drink, but at least they've lived long enough to realize that not everyone shares their preoccupation and that Fallon, in particular, might prefer sleep and privacy to cocoa and their company."

"I shall be seeing the Burt twins. What about the hospital grounds? Are they left open at night?"

"There's always a porter on duty at the front lodge. The main gates aren't locked because of the accident ambulances but he keeps an eye on anyone else who comes in or leaves. Nightingale House is much closer to the rear entrance to the grounds, but we don't usually go that way by foot because the path is ill-lit and rather frightening. Besides, it leads into the Winchester Road which is almost two miles from the main part of the town. The back gate is locked at dusk summer and winter by one of the porters but all the Sisters and Matron have keys."

"And the nurses with late passes?"

"They're expected to use the front gate and walk along the main path which skirts the hospital. There's a much shorter cut through the trees which we use in the daytime— it's only about two hundred yards—but not many people choose to come that way at night. I daresay Mr. Hudson, he's the Hospital Secretary, can let you have a plan of the grounds and of Nightingale House. Incidentally, he and the Vice-Chairman are waiting for you now in the library. The Chairman, Sir Marcus Cohen, is in Israel. Even so, it's quite a reception committee. Even Mr. Courtney-Briggs has deferred his out-patient session to welcome the Yard to Nightingale House."

"Then," said Dalgliesh, "perhaps you'll be good enough to let them know that I'll be with them shortly."

It was a dismissal. Sergeant Masterson, as if to soften it, said suddenly and loudly: "Sister Rolfe has been very helpful."

The woman gave a guttural snort of derision.

"Helping the police!Isn't there a sinister connotation about that phrase? Anyway, I don't think I can be particularly helpful. I didn't kill either of them. And last night I was at a film at the new arts cinema here. They're showing an Antonioni series. This week it's *L'Avventura*. I didn't get in until just before eleven and went straight to bed. I didn't even see Fallon."

Dalgliesh asked: "Did you go to the cinema alone?"

Sister Rolfe hesitated for a second and said curtly: "Yes."

Dalgliesh recognized with weary resignation the first lie and wondered how many more, important and unimportant, would be spoken before the investigation was complete. But this wasn't the time to interrogate Sister Rolfe. She wasn't going to be an easy witness. She had answered his questions fully but with undisguised resentment. He wasn't sure whether it was he or his job which she disliked, or whether any man would have provoked this tone of angry contempt. Her face matched her personality, rebarbative and defensive. It was strong and intelligent but without softness or feminity. The deep-set and very dark eyes might have been attractive but they were set under a pair of perfectly straight black eyebrows, so dark and bushy that they gave to the face a faint suggestion of deformity. Her nose was large and open pored, her lips a thin uncompromising line. It was the face of a woman who had never learnt to come to terms with life, and had, perhaps, given up trying. He thought suddenly that, if she proved to be a murderess and her photograph were at last published, other women, avidly searching that uncompromising mask for the marks of depravity, would profess themselves unsurprised. Suddenly he felt sorry for her with a mixture of irritation and compassion one might feel for the inadequate or the physically deformed. He turned quickly away so that she should not catch that sudden spasm of pity. To her it would, he knew, be the ultimate insult. And when he turned again to thank her formally for her help, he saw that she had gone.

III

Sergeant Charles Masterson was six feet three inches tall and broad shouldered. He carried his bulk easily and all his movements were surprisingly controlled and precise for such an assertively masculine and heavy man. He was generally considered handsome, particularly by himself, and with his strong face, sensual lips and hooded eyes looked remarkably like a well-known American film actor of the guts-and-guns school. Dalgliesh occasionally suspected that the sergeant, aware, as he could hardly fail to be, of the resemblance, was helping it along by assuming a trace of an American accent.

"All right, Sergeant. You've had a chance to look at the place, you've talked to some of the people. Tell me about it."

This invitation had been known to strike terror into the hearts of Dalgliesh's subordinates. It meant that the Superintendent now expected to hear a brief, succinct, accurate, elegantly phrased but comprehensive account of the crime which would give all the salient facts so far known to someone who came to it freshly. The ability to know what you want to say and to say it in the minimum of appropriate words is as uncommon in policemen as in other members of the community. Dalgliesh's subordinates were apt to complain that they hadn't realized that a degree in English was the new qualification for joining the C.I.D. But Sergeant Masterson was less intimidated than most. He had his weaknesses, but lack of confidence was not one of them. He was glad to be working on the case. It was well known at the Yard that Superintendent Dalgliesh couldn't tolerate a fool and that his definition of folly was individual and precise. Masterson respected him because Dalgliesh was one of the Yard's most successful detectives and for Masterson success was the only real criterion. He thought him very able, which is not to say that he thought Adam Dalgliesh as able as Charles Masterson. Most of the time, and for reasons which it seemed to him unprofitable to explore, he disliked him heartily. He suspected that the antipathy was mutual, but this didn't particularly worry him. Dalgliesh wasn't a man to prejudice a subordinate's career because he disliked him and was known to be meticulous, if judicious, in ascribing credit where it was due. But the situation would need watching, and Masterson intended to watch it. An ambitious man on his carefully planned climb to senior rank was a fool if he didn't early recognize that it was bloody daft to antagonize a senior officer. Masterson had no intention of being that kind of a fool. But a little co-operation from the Super in this campaign of mutual goodwill wouldn't be unwelcome. And he wasn't sure he was going to get it. He said:

"I'll deal with the two deaths separately, sir. The first victim. . . ."

"Why talk like a crime reporter, Sergeant? Let's be sure we have a victim before we use the word."

Masterson began: "The first deceased . . . the first girl to die was a twenty-one-year-old student nurse, Heather Pearce." He went on to recite the facts of both girls' deaths, as far as they were known, taking care to avoid the more blatant examples of police jargon, to which he knew his Super to be morbidly sensitive, and resisting the temptation to display his recently acquired knowledge of intra-gastric feeding about which he had taken trouble to extract from Sister Rolfe a comprehensive, if grudging, explanation. He ended: "So we have, sir, the possibilities that one or both of the deaths was suicide, that one or both was accidental, that the first was murder but that the wrong victim was killed, or that there were two murders with two intended victims. An intriguing choice, sir."

Dalgliesh said: "Or that Fallon's death was due to natural causes. Until we get the toxicology report we're theorizing in advance of the facts. But for the present we treat both deaths as murder. Well, let's go to the library and see what the Vice-Chairman of the Hospital Management Committee has to say to us."

IV

The library, easily identified by a large painted sign above the door, was a pleasant high-ceilinged room on the first floor, next to the student nurses' sitting-room. One wall was entirely taken up with three ornate oriel windows, but the other three were book-lined to the ceiling, leaving the centre of the room bare. It was furnished with four tables ranged in front of the windows and two shabby sofas, one on each side of the stone fireplace, where now an ancient gas fire hissed its sinister welcome. In front of it, under the two strips of fluorescent lighting, a group of four men, muttering together conspiratorially, turned in one movement at the entrance of Dalgliesh and Masterson and watched them with wary curiosity. It was a familiar moment to Dalgliesh, compounded as always of interest, apprehension and hope—this first confrontation of the protagonists in a murder case with the outsider, the alien expert in violent death who has come among them, an unwelcome guest, to demonstrate his invidious talents.

Then the silence broke, the rigid figures relaxed. The two men Dalgliesh had already met—Stephen Courtney-Briggs and Paul Hudson, the Hospital Secretary—moved forward with formal welcoming smiles. Mr. Courtney-Briggs, who apparently took charge of any situation dignified by his presence, made the introductions. The Group Secretary,

Raymond Grout, shook hands damply. He had a gently lugubrious face, puckered now with distress like that of a child on the verge of crying. His hair lay in strands of silver silk over a high-domed forehead. He was probably younger than he appeared, thought Dalgliesh, but even so, he must be very near retirement.

Beside the tall, stooped figure of Grout, Alderman Kealey looked as perky as a terrier . He was a ginger-haired, foxy little man, bandy as a jockey and wearing a plaid suit, the awfulness of its pattern emphasized by the excellence of its cut. It gave him an anthropomorphic appearance, like an animal in a child's comic; and Dalgliesh almost expected to find himself shaking a paw.

"It was good of you to come, Superintendent, and so promptly," he said.

The folly of the remark apparently struck him as soon as he had made it, for he darted a keen glance from under spiky ginger eyebrows at his companions, as if defying them to smirk. No one did, but the Group Secretary looked as humiliated as if the solecism had been his, and Paul Hudson turned his face away to hide an embarrassed grin. He was a personable young man who, on Dalgliesh's first arrival at the hospital, had shown himself as both efficient and authoritative. Now, however, the presence of his Vice-Chairman and the Group Secretary seemed to have inhibited his speech and he had the apologetic air of a man present on sufferance. Mr. Courtney-Briggs said:

"It's too much to hope for any news yet, I suppose? We saw the mortuary van leaving, and I had a few words with Miles Honeyman. He couldn't commit himself at this stage, of course, but he'll be surprised if this was a natural death. The girl killed herself. Well, I should have thought that was obvious to anyone."

Dalgliesh said: "Nothing is obvious yet."

There was a silence. The Vice-Chairman seemed to find it embarrassing for he cleared his throat noisily and said:

"You'll want an office, of course. The local C.I.D. worked from the police station here. They were really very little trouble to us. We hardly knew they were in the place." He looked with faint optimism at Dalgliesh, as if hardly sanguine that the flying squad would be equally accommodating. Dalgliesh replied shortly:

"We shall want a room. Is it possible to make one available in Nightingale House? That would be the most convenient."

The request seemed to disconcert them. The Group Secretary said tentatively: "If Matron were here ... it's difficult for us to know what's free. She shouldn't be long now."

Alderman Kealey grunted. "We can't let everything wait for Matron. The Superintendent wants a room. Find him one."

"Well there's Miss Rolfe's office on the ground floor, just next to the demonstration room." The Group Secretary bent his sad eyes on Dalgliesh. "You've met Miss Rolfe, our Principal Tutor, of course. Now if Miss Rolfe can move temporarily into her secretary's room ... Miss Buckfield is off with flu, so it's free. It's rather cramped, only a cupboard really, but if Matron ..."

"Get Miss Rolfe to move out any of her things she'll need. The porters can shift the filing cabinets." Alderman Kealey turned and barked at Dalgliesh: "Will that do?"

"If it's private, reasonably soundproof, has a lock on the door, is large enough to take three men and has a direct telephone to the exchange, it will do. If it also has running water, so much the better."

The Vice-Chairman, chastened by this formidable list of

requirements, said tentatively: "There's a small cloakroom and lavatory on the ground floor opposite Miss Rolfe's room. That could be put at your disposal."

Mr. Grout's misery deepened. He glanced across at Mr. Courtney-Briggs as if seeking an ally but the surgeon had been unaccountably silent for the last few minutes and seemed reluctant to meet his eyes. Then the telephone rang. Mr. Hudson, apparently glad of a chance of activity, sprang to answer it. He turned to his Vice-Chairman.

"It's the *Clairon,* sir. They're asking for you personally."

Alderman Kealey grasped the receiver resolutely. Having decided to assert himself he was apparently ready to take command of any situation, and this one was well within his capabilities. Murder might be outside his normal pre-occupations but dealing tactfully with the local Press was something he understood.

"Alderman Kealey here. The Vice-Chairman of the Management Committee. Yes, we've got the Yard here. The victim? Oh, I don't think we want to talk about a victim. Not yet anyway. Fallon. Josephine Fallon. Age?" He placed his hand over the mouthpiece and turned to the Group Secretary. Oddly enough, it was Mr. Courtney-Briggs who replied.

"She was thirty-one years, ten months," he said. "She was precisely twenty years younger than me to the day."

Alderman Kealey, unsurprised by the gratuitous information, returned to his listener.

"She was thirty-one. No, we don't know yet how she died. No one knows. We are awaiting the post mortem report. Yes, Chief Superintendent Dalgliesh. He's here now but he's too busy to talk. I hope to issue a Press statement this evening. We ought to have the autopsy report by then. No, there's no reason to suspect murder. The Chief Constable has called in the Yard as a precautionary meas-

ure. No, as far as we're aware, the two deaths aren't connected in any way. Very sad. Yes, very. If you care to telephone about six I may have some more information. All
we know at present is that Nurse Fallon was found dead in
her bed this morning shortly after seven. It could very well
have been a heart attack. She was just recovering from flu.
No, there wasn't a note. Nothing like that."

He listened for a moment then again placed his hand
over the mouthpiece and turned to Grout.

"They're asking about relatives. What do we know
about them?"

"She hadn't any. Fallon was an orphan." Again it was
Mr. Courtney-Briggs who replied.

Alderman Kealey passed on this information and replaced the receiver. Smiling grimly he gave Dalgliesh a look
of mingled self-satisfaction and warning. Dalgliesh was
interested to hear that the Yard had been called in as a precautionary measure. It was a new conception of the flying
squad's responsibilities and one which he felt was unlikely
to deceive the local Press boys, still less the London
reporters who would soon be on the scent. He wondered
how the hospital was going to cope with the publicity.
Alderman Kealey was going to need some advice if the
inquiry were not to be hampered. But there was plenty of
time for that. Now all he wanted was to get rid of them, to
get started with the investigation. These social preliminaries were always a time-consuming nuisance. And soon
there would be a Matron to propitiate, to consult, possibly
even to antagonize. From the Group Secretary's unwilling-
ness to move a step without her consent, it looked as if she
were a strong personality. He didn't relish the prospect of
making it clear to her, tactfully, that there would be room
for only one strong personality in this investigation.

Mr. Courtney-Briggs, who had been standing at the

window, staring out at the storm-wrecked garden, turned, shook himself free of his preoccupations and said:

"I'm afraid I can't spare any more time now. I have a patient to see in the private wing and then a ward round. I was due to lecture to the students here later this morning but that'll have to be cancelled now. You'll let me know, Kealey, if there's anything I can do."

He ignored Dalgliesh. The impression given, and no doubt intended, was that he was a busy man who had already wasted too much time on a triviality. Dalgliesh resisted the temptation to delay him. Agreeable as it would be to tame Mr. Courtney-Briggs's arrogance, it was an indulgence which he couldn't afford at present. There were more pressing matters.

It was then that they heard the sound of a car. Mr. Courtney-Briggs returned to the window and looked out, but did not speak. The rest of the little group stiffened and turned as if pulled by a common force to face the door. A car door slammed. Then there was silence for a few seconds followed by the clip of hurried footsteps on a tessellated floor. The door opened and Matron came in.

Dalgliesh's first impression was of a highly individual yet casual elegance and a confidence that was almost palpable. He saw a tall slender woman, hatless, with pale honey-gold skin and hair of almost the same colour, drawn back from a high forehead and swathed into an intricate coil at the nape of her neck. She was wearing a grey tweed coat with a bright green scarf knotted at her neck and carrying a black handbag and a small travelling case. She came into the room quietly and, placing her case on the table, drew off her gloves and surveyed the little party silently. Almost instinctively, as if watching a witness, Dalgliesh noticed her hands. The fingers were very white, long and tapering but with unusually bony joints. The nails were clipped short. On the third finger of the right hand an immense sapphire ring in an ornate setting gleamed against the knuckle. He wondered irrelevantly whether she took it off when she was on duty and, if so, how she forced it over those nodular joints.

Mr. Courtney-Briggs, after a brief, "Good morning, Matron," made his way to the door and stood there like a bored guest, demonstrating his anxiety to make a quick get-away. But the others crowded around her. There was an immediate sense of relief. Muttered introductions were made.

"Good morning, Superintendent." Her voice was deep, a little husky, a voice as individual as herself. She seemed hardly aware of him, yet he was conscious of a swift appraisal from the green exophthalmic eyes. Her handshake was firm and cool, but so momentary that it seemed a fleeting meeting of palms, nothing more.

The Vice-Chairman said: "The police will want a room. We thought perhaps Miss Rolfe's office?"

"Too small, I think, and not private enough, so close to the main hall. It would be better if Mr. Dalgliesh had the use of the visitors' sitting-room on the first floor and the cloakroom next door to it. The room has a key. There's a desk with lockable drawers in the general office and that can be moved up. That way the police will get some privacy and there'll be a minimum of interference with the work of the school."

There was a murmur of assent. The men looked relieved. The Matron said to Dalgliesh: "Will you need a bedroom? Do you want to sleep in the hospital?"

"That won't be necessary. We shall be staying in the town. But I would prefer to work from here. We shall probably be here late every night so that it would be helpful if we could have keys."

"For how long?" asked the Vice-Chairman suddenly. It

was on the face of it, a stupid question, but Dalgliesh noticed that all their faces turned to him as if it were one he could be expected to answer. He knew his reputation for speed. Did they perhaps know it too?

"About a week," he said. Even if the case dragged on for longer, he would learn all he needed from Nightingale House and its occupants within seven days. If Nurse Fallon had been murdered—and he believed she had—the circle of suspects would be small. If the case didn't break within a week it might never break. He thought there was a small sigh of relief.

Matron said: "Where is she?"

"They took the body to the mortuary, Matron."

"I didn't mean Fallon. Where is Nurse Dakers? I understood it was she who found the body."

Alderman Kealey replied. "She's being nursed in the private ward. She was pretty shaken up so we asked Dr. Snelling to take a look at her. He's given her a sedative and Sister Brumfett's looking after her."

He added: "Sister Brumfett was a little concerned about her. On top of that she's got rather a sick ward. Otherwise she would have met you at the airport. We all felt rather badly about your arriving with no one to meet you, but the best thing seemed to be to telephone a message for you, asking you to ring us here as soon as you landed. Sister Brumfett thought that the shock would be less if you learnt it in that way. On the other hand it seemed wrong not to have someone there. I wanted to send Grout but. . . ."

The husky voice broke in with its quiet reproof: "I should have thought that sparing me shock was the least of your worries." She turned to Dalgliesh:

"I shall be in my sitting-room here on the third floor in about forty-five minutes' time. If it's convenient for you, I should be glad to have a word with you then."

Dalgliesh, resisting the impulse to reply with a docile, "Yes, Matron," said that it would. Miss Taylor turned to Alderman Kealey.

"I'm going to see Nurse Dakers now. Afterwards the Superintendent will want to interview me and then I shall be in my main office in the hospital if you or Mr. Grout want me. I shall, of course, be available all day."

Without a further word or look she gathered up her travelling case and handbag and went out of the room. Mr. Courtney-Briggs perfunctorily opened the door for her, then prepared to follow. Standing in the open doorway, he said with jovial belligerence:

"Well, now that Matron's back and the important matter of accommodation for the police has been settled, perhaps the work of the hospital can be permitted to continue. I shouldn't be late for your interview if I were you, Dalgliesh. Miss Taylor isn't accustomed to insubordination."

He shut the door behind him. Alderman Kealey looked for a moment perplexed, then he said:

"He's upset, of course. Well, naturally. Wasn't there some kind of rumour. . . ."

Then his eyes lit on Dalgliesh. He checked himself suddenly, and turned to Paul Hudson:

"Well, Mr. Hudson, you heard what Matron said. The police are to use the visitors' sitting-room on this floor. Get on with it, my dear fellow. Get on with it!"

V

Miss Taylor changed into uniform before she went over to the private ward. At the time it seemed an instinctive thing to do, but, wrapping her cloak tightly around her as she walked briskly along the small footpath leading from

Nightingale House to the hospital, she realized that the instinct had been prompted by reason. It was important to the hospital that Matron was back, and important that she should be seen to be back.

The quickest way to the private wing was through the out-patients' hall. The department was already buzzing with activity. The circles of comfortable chairs, carefully disposed to give an illusion of informality and relaxed comfort, were filling quickly. Volunteers from the ladies' committee of the League of Friends were already presiding at the steaming urn, serving tea to those regular patients who preferred to attend an hour before their appointments for the pleasure of sitting in the warmth, reading the magazines and chatting to their fellow habitués. As Matron passed she was aware of heads turning to watch her. There was a brief silence, followed by the customary murmur of deferential greeting. She was conscious of the white-coated junior medical staff standing briefly to one side as she passed, of the student nurses pressing themselves back against the wall.

The private ward was on the second floor of what still was called the new building, although it had been completed in 1945. Miss Taylor went up by the lift, sharing it with two radiographers and a young houseman. They murmured their formal, "Good morning, Matron," and stood in unnatural silence until the lift stopped, then stood back while she went out before them.

The private ward consisted of a suite of twenty single rooms, opening each side of a wide central corridor. The Sister's office, the kitchen, and the utility room were just inside the door. As Miss Taylor entered, a young first-year student nurse appeared from the kitchen. She flushed when she saw Matron and muttered something about fetching Sister.

"Where is Sister, Nurse?"

"In room 7 with Mr. Courtney-Briggs, Matron. His patient isn't too well."

"Don't disturb them: just tell Sister when she appears that I've come to see Nurse Dakers. Where is she?"

"In room 3, Matron." She hesitated.

"It's all right, Nurse, I'll find my own way. Get on with what you are doing."

Room 3 was at the far end of the corridor, one of six single rooms, usually reserved for sick nurses. Only when these rooms were all occupied were the staff nursed in the side rooms of the wards. It was not, Miss Taylor noted, the room in which Josephine Fallon had been nursed. Room 3 was the sunniest and most pleasant of the six rooms reserved for nurses. A week ago it had been occupied by a nurse with pneumonia, a complication of influenza. Miss Taylor, who visited every ward in the hospital once a day and who received daily reports on every sick nurse, thought it unlikely that Nurse Wilkins was fit enough yet to be discharged. Sister Brumfett must have moved her to make room 3 available for Nurse Dakers. Miss Taylor could guess why. The one window gave a view of the lawns and smoothly forked flower beds at the front of the hospital; from this side of the ward it was impossible to glimpse Nightingale House even through the bare tracery of the winter trees. Dear old Brumfett! So unprepossessingly rigid in her views, but so imaginative when it came to the welfare and comfort of her patients. Brumfett, who talked embarrassingly of duty, obedience, loyalty, but who knew exactly what she meant by those unpopular terms and lived by what she knew. She was one of the best ward sisters that the John Carpendar had, or ever would have. But Miss Taylor was glad that devotion to duty had kept Sister Brumfett from meeting the plane at Heathrow. It was bad enough to come home to this further tragedy without the added burden of Brumfett's doglike devotion and concern.

She drew the stool from under the bed and seated herself beside the girl. Despite Dr. Snelling's sedative, Nurse Dakers was not asleep. She was lying very still on her back gazing at the ceiling. Now her eyes turned to look at Matron. They were blank with misery. On the bedside locker there was a copy of a textbook, *Materia Medica for Nurses*. The Matron picked it up.

"This is very conscientious of you, Nurse, but just for the short time you are in here, why not have a novel from the Red Cross trolley or a frivolous magazine? Shall I bring one in for you?"

She was answered by a flood of tears. The slim figure twisted convulsively in the bed, buried her head in the pillow and clasped it with shaking hands. The bed shook with the paroxysm of grief. The Matron got up, moved over to the door and clicked across the board which covered the nurses' peephole. She returned quickly to her seat and waited without speaking, making no move except to place her hand on the girl's head. After a few minutes the dreadful shaking ceased and Nurse Dakers grew calmer. She began to mutter, her voice hiccuping with sobs, half muffled by the pillow:

"I'm so miserable, so ashamed."

The Matron bent her head to catch the words. A chill of horror swept over her. Surely she couldn't be listening to a confession of murder? She found herself praying under her breath.

"Dear God, please not. Not this child! Surely not this child?"

She waited, not daring to question. Nurse Dakers twisted herself round and gazed up at her, her eyes reddened and swollen like two amorphous moons in a face blotched and formless with misery.

"I'm wicked, Matron, wicked. I was glad when she died."

"Nurse Fallon?"

"Oh no, not Fallon! I was sorry about Fallon. Nurse Pearce."

The Matron placed her hands on each of the girl's shoulders, pressing her back against the bed. She held the trembling body firmly and looked down into the drowned eyes.

"I want you to tell me the truth, Nurse. Did you kill Nurse Pearce?"

"No, Matron."

"Or Nurse Fallon?"

"No, Matron."

"Or have anything at all to do with their deaths?"

"No, Matron."

Miss Taylor let out her breath. She relaxed her hold on the girl and sat back.

"I think you'd better tell me all about it."

So, calmly now, the pathetic story came out. It hadn't seemed like stealing at the time. It had seemed like a miracle. Mummy had so needed a warm winter coat and Nurse Dakers had been saving thirty shillings from her monthly salary cheque. Only the money had taken so long to save and the weather was getting colder; and Mummy, who never complained, and never asked her for anything, had to wait nearly fifteen minutes for the bus some mornings, and caught cold so easily. And if she did catch cold she couldn't stay away from work because Miss Arkwright, the buyer in the department store, was only waiting for an opportunity to get her sacked. Serving in a store wasn't really the right job for Mummy, but it wasn't easy to find a job when you were over fifty and unqualified, and the young assistants in the department weren't very kind. They kept hinting that Mummy wasn't pulling her weight, which wasn't true. Mummy might not be as quick as they were but she really took trouble with the customers.

Then Nurse Harper had dropped the two crisp new £5 notes almost at her feet. Nurse Harper who had so much pocket money from her father that she could lose £10 without really worrying about it. It had happened about four weeks ago. Nurse Harper had been walking with Nurse Pearce from the Nurses' Home to the hospital dining-room for breakfast, and Nurse Dakers had been following a few feet behind. The two notes had fallen out of Nurse Harper's cape pocket and had lain there fluttering gently. Her first instinct had been to call after the other two students, but something about the sight of the money had stopped her. The notes had been so unexpected, so unbelievable, so beautiful in their pristine crispness. She had just stood looking at them for a second, and then she had realized that she was really looking at Mummy's new coat. And, by then, the other two students had passed almost out of sight, the notes were folded in her hand, and it was too late.

The Matron asked: "How did Nurse Pearce know that you had the notes?"

"She said that she'd seen me. She just happened to glance round when I was bending to pick up the notes. It meant nothing to her at the time, but when Nurse Harper told everyone that she'd lost the money and that the notes must have fallen out of her cape pocket on the way over to breakfast, Nurse Pearce guessed what had happened. She and the twins went with Nurse Harper to search the path to see if they could find the money. I expect that was when she remembered about my stooping down."

"When did she first talk to you about it?"

"A week later, Matron, a fortnight before our set came into block. I expect she couldn't bring herself to believe it before then. She must have been trying to make up her mind to speak to me."

So Nurse Pearce had waited. The Matron wondered why. It couldn't have taken her a whole week to clarify her suspicions. She must have recalled seeing Dakers stoop to pick up the notes as soon as she heard that they were missing. So why hadn't she tackled the girl at once? Had it perhaps been more satisfying to her twisted ego to wait until the money was spent and the culprit safely in her power?

"Was she blackmailing you?" she demanded.

"Oh no, Matron!" The girl was shocked.

"She only took back five shillings a week, and that wasn't blackmail. She sent the money every week to a society for discharged prisoners. She showed me the receipts."

"And did she, incidentally, explain why she wasn't repaying it to Nurse Harper?"

"She thought it would be difficult to explain without involving me and I begged her not to do that. It would have been the end of everything, Matron. I want to take a district nurse training after I'm qualified so that I can look after Mummy. If I could get a country district we could have a cottage together and perhaps even a car. Mummy will be able to give up the store. I told Nurse Pearce about that. Besides, she said that Harper was so careless about money that it wouldn't hurt her to learn a lesson. She sent the payments to the society for discharged prisoners because it seemed appropriate. After all, I might have gone to prison if she hadn't shielded me."

The Matron said drily: "That, of course, is nonsense and you should have known it was nonsense. Nurse Pearce seems to have been a very stupid and arrogant young woman. Are you sure that she wasn't making any other demands on you? There is more than one kind of blackmail."

"But she wouldn't do that, Matron!" Nurse Dakers struggled to lift her head from the pillow. "Pearce was . . . well, she was good." She seemed to find the word inadequate and puckered her brow as if desperately anxious to explain.

"She used to talk to me quite a lot and she gave me a card with a passage out of the Bible which I had to read every day. Once a week she used to ask me about it."

The Matron was swept by a sense of moral outrage so acute that she had to find relief in action. She got up from the stool and walked over to the window, cooling her flaring face against the pane. She could feel her heart bumping and noticed with almost clinical interest that her hands were shaking. After a moment she came back again to the bedside.

"Don't talk about her being good. Dutiful, conscientious, and well-meaning if you like, but not good. If ever you meet real goodness you will know the difference. And I shouldn't worry about being glad that she is dead. In the circumstances you wouldn't be normal if you felt differently. In time you may be able to pity her and forgive her."

"But Matron, it's me who ought to be forgiven. I'm a thief." Was there a suggestion of masochism in the whine of the voice, the perverse self-denigration of the born victim? Miss Taylor said briskly:

"You're not a thief. You stole once; that's a very different thing. Every one of us has some incident in our lives that we're ashamed and sorry about. You've recently learned something about yourself, about what you're capable of doing, which has shaken your confidence. Now you have to live with that knowledge. We can only begin to understand and forgive other people when we have learned to understand and forgive ourselves. You won't steal again. I know that, and so do you. But you did once. You are capable of stealing. That knowledge will save you from being too pleased with yourself, from being too self-satisfied. It can make you a much more tolerant and understanding person and a better nurse. But not if you go on indulging in guilt and remorse and bitterness. Those insidious emotions may be very enjoyable but they aren't going to help you or anyone else."

The girl looked up at her.

"Will the police have to know?"

That, of course, was the question. And there could be only one answer.

"Yes. And you will have to tell them, just as you've told me. But I shall have a word first with the Superintendent. He's a new detective, from Scotland Yard this time, and I think he's an intelligent and understanding man."

Was he? How could she possibly tell? That first meeting had been so brief, merely a glance and a touching of hands. Was she merely comforting herself with a fleeting impression that here was a man with authority and imagination who might be able to solve the mystery of both deaths with a minimum of harm to the innocent and guilty alike. She had felt this instinctively. But was the feeling rational? She believed Nurse Dakers's story; but then she was disposed to believe it. How would it strike a police officer faced with a multiplicity of suspects but no other discernible motive? And the motive was there all right. It was Nurse Dakers's whole future, and that of her mother. And Dakers had behaved rather oddly. True she had been most distressed of all the students when Pearce had died, but she had pulled herself together remarkably quickly. Even under intense police questioning she had kept her secret safe.

What then had precipitated this disintegration into confession and remorse? Was it only the shock of finding Fallon's body? And why should Fallon's death be so cataclysmic if she had had no hand in it?

Miss Taylor thought again about Pearce. How little one really knew about any of the students. Pearce, if one thought about her at all, had typified the dull, conscientious, unattractive student who was probably using nursing to compensate for the lack of more orthodox satisfactions. There was usually one such in every nurse training school. It was difficult to reject them when they applied for training since they offered more than adequate educational qualifications and impeccable references. And they didn't on the whole make bad nurses. It was just that they seldom made the best. But now she began to wonder. If Pearce had possessed such a secret craving for power that she could use this child's guilt and distress as fodder for her own ego, then she had been far from ordinary or ineffective. She had been a dangerous young woman.

And she had worked it all out very cleverly. By waiting a week until she could be reasonably certain that the money had been spent, she had left Dakers no option. The child could hardly claim then that she had yielded to a sudden impulse but intended to return the money. And even if Dakers had decided to confess, perhaps to the Matron, Nurse Harper would have had to be told: Pearce would have seen to that. And only Harper could decide whether or not to prosecute. It might have been possible to influence her, to persuade her to mercy. But suppose it had not been possible? Nurse Harper would almost certainly have confided in her father, and the Matron couldn't see Mr. Roland Harper showing mercy to anyone who had helped herself to his money. Miss Taylor's acquaintance with him had been brief but revealing. He had arrived at the hospital two days after Pearce's death, a large, opulent-looking and aggressive man, top heavy in his fur-lined motoring coat. Without preliminaries or explanation he had launched into his prepared tirade, addressing Matron as if she were one of his garage hands. He wasn't going to let his girl stay another minute in a house with a murderer at large, police or no police. This nurse training had been a damn fool idea in the first place, and now it was going to stop. His Diane didn't need a career anyway. She was engaged, wasn't she? A bloody good match too! His partner's son. They could put the marriage forward instead of waiting until the summer and, in the meantime, Diane could stay at home and help in the office. He was taking her away with him now, and he'd like to see anyone try to stop him.

No one had stopped him. The girl had made no objection. She had stood meekly in the Matron's office overtly demure, but smiling a little as if gratified by all the fuss, by her father's assertive masculinity. The police could not prevent her leaving, nor had they seemed concerned to try. It was odd, thought the Matron, that no one had seriously suspected Harper; and if the two deaths were the work of one hand, their instinct had been right. She had last seen the girl stepping into her father's immense and ugly car, legs spindly beneath the new fur coat he had bought her to compensate for her disappointment at cutting short her training, and turning to wave good-bye to the rest of the set like a film star condescending to her assembled fans. No, not a particularly attractive family: Miss Taylor would be sorry for anyone who was in their power. And yet, such were the vagaries of personality, Diane Harper had been an efficient nurse, a better nurse in many ways than Pearce.

But there was one more question which had to be asked, and it took her a second to summon the courage to ask it.

"Did Nurse Fallon know about this business?"

The girl answered at once, confident, a little surprised.

"Oh no, Matron! At least I don't think so. Pearce swore that she wouldn't tell a soul, and it wasn't as if she was particularly friendly with Fallon. I'm sure she wouldn't have told Fallon."

"No," said the Matron. "I don't suppose she would."

Gently she lifted Nurse Dakers's head and smoothed the pillows.

"Now I want you to try and get some sleep. You'll feel a great deal better when you wake up. And try not to worry."

The girl's face relaxed. She smiled up at the Matron and, putting out her hand, briefly touched Miss Taylor's face. Then she snuggled down into the sheets as if resolute for sleep. So that was all right. But of course it was. It always worked. How easy and how insidiously satisfying was this doling out of advice and comfort, each portion individually flavoured to personal taste! She might be a Victorian vicar's wife presiding over a soup kitchen. To each according to her need. It happened in the hospital every day. A ward Sister's brightly professional voice. "Here's Matron to see you, Mrs. Cox. I'm afraid Mrs. Cox isn't feeling quite so well this morning, Matron." A tired pain-racked face smiling bravely up from the pillow, mouth avid for its morsel of affection and reassurance. The Sisters bringing their problems, the perpetual unsolvable problems over work and incompatible personalities.

"Are you feeling happier about it now, Sister?"

"Yes, thank you, Matron. Much happier."

The Group Secretary, desperately coping with his own inadequacies.

"I should feel better if we could have just a word about the problem, Matron." Of course he would! They all wanted to have just a word about the problem. They all went away feeling better. Hear what comfortable words our Matron saith. Her whole working life seemed a blasphemous liturgy of reassurance and absolution. And how much easier both to give and to accept was this bland milk of human kindness than the acid of truth. She could imagine the blank incomprehension, the resentment with which they would greet her private credo.

"I haven't anything to offer. There isn't any help. We are all alone, all of us from the moment of birth until we die. Our past is our present and our future. We have to live with ourselves until there isn't any more time left. If you want salvation look to yourself. There's nowhere else to look."

She sat for a few more minutes and then quietly left the room. Nurse Dakers gave a brief valedictory smile. As she entered the corridor she saw Sister Brumfett and Mr. Courtney-Briggs coming out of his patient's room. Sister Brumfett bustled up.

"I'm sorry, Matron. I didn't know you were on the ward."

She always used the formal title. They might spend the whole of their off-duty together driving or golfing; they might visit a London show once a month with the cosy, boring regularity of an old married couple; they might drink their early morning tea and late night hot milk together in indissoluble tedium. But in the hospital Brumfett always called her Matron. The shrewd eyes searched hers.

"You've seen the new detective, the man from the Yard?"

"Only briefly. I'm due for a session with him as soon as I get back."

Mr. Courtney-Briggs said: "I know him as a matter of fact; not well but we have met. You'll find him reasonable and intelligent. He's got quite a reputation of course. He's said to work very quickly. As far as I'm concerned, that's a considerable asset. The hospital can stand only so much disruption. He'll want to see me I suppose, but he'll have to wait. Let him know that I'll pop across to Nightingale House when I've finished my ward round, will you Matron?"

"I'll tell him if he asks me," replied Miss Taylor calmly. She turned to Sister Brumfett.

"Nurse Dakers is calmer now, but I think it would be better if she were not disturbed by visitors. She'll probably manage to get some sleep. I'll send over some magazines for her and some fresh flowers. When is Dr. Snelling due to see her?"

"He said he would come in before lunch, Matron."

"Perhaps you would ask him to be good enough to have a word with me. I shall be in the hospital all day."

Sister Brumfett said: "I suppose that Scotland Yard detective will want to see me too. I hope he isn't going to take too long about it. I've got a very sick ward."

The Matron hoped that Brum wasn't going to be too difficult. It would be unfortunate if she thought she could treat a Chief Superintendent of the Metropolitan Police as if he were a recalcitrant House Surgeon. Mr. Courtney-Briggs, no doubt, would be his usual arrogant self, but she had a feeling that Superintendent Dalgliesh would be able to cope with Mr. Courtney-Briggs.

They walked to the door of the ward together. Miss Taylor's mind was already busy with fresh problems. Something would have to be done about Nurse Dakers's mother. It would be some years before the child was fully qualified as a district nurse. In the meantime she must be relieved of the constant anxiety about her mother. It might be helpful to have a word with Raymond Grout. There might be a clerical job somewhere in the hospital which would suit her. But would that be fair? One couldn't indulge one's own urge to help at someone else's expense. Whatever problems of staff recruitment the hospital service might have in London, Grout had no difficulty in filling his clerical jobs. He had a right to expect efficiency; and the Mrs. Dakerses of this world, dogged by their own inadequacy as much as by ill-luck, could seldom offer that. She supposed she would have to telephone the woman; the parents of the other students too. The important thing was to get the girls out of Nightingale House. The training schedule couldn't be disrupted; it was tight enough as it was. She had better arrange with the House Warden for them to sleep in the Nurses' Home—there would be room enough with so many nurses in the sick bay—and they could come over each day to use the library and lecture room. And then there would be the Vice-Chairman of the Hospital Management Committee to consult and the Press to cope with, the inquest to attend and the funeral arrangements to be discussed. People would be wanting to get in touch with her continually. But first, and most important, she must see Superintendent Dalgliesh.

CHAPTER FOUR

Questions and Answers

I

THE MATRON and the Sisters had their living-quarters on the third floor of Nightingale House. When he reached the top of the staircase Dalgliesh saw that the south-west wing had been cut off from the rest of the landing by a specially constructed partition in white-painted wood in which a door, meanly proportioned and insubstantial in contrast to the high ceiling and oak-lined walls, bore the legend "Matron's Flat." There was a push bell, but before pressing it he briefly explored the corridor. It was similar to the one below but fitted with a red carpet which, although faded and scuffed, gave an illusion of comfort to the emptiness of this upper floor.

Dalgliesh moved silently from door to door. Each bore a handwritten name card slotted into the brass holder. He saw that Sister Brumfett occupied the room immediately adjacent to Matron's flat. Next was a bathroom, functionally divided into three mean cubicles, each with its bath and lavatory. The slot on the next door bore Sister Gearing's name; the next two rooms were empty. Sister Rolfe was at the north end of the corridor immediately next to the kitchen and utility room. Dalgliesh had no authority to enter any of the bedrooms but he tentatively turned the handles on each of the doors. As he expected, they were locked.

The Matron herself opened the door of her flat to him within seconds of his ring, and he followed her into the sitting-room. Its size and magnificence caught the breath. It occupied the whole of the south-west turret, an immense white-painted octagonal room, the ceiling starred in patterns of gold and pale blue, and with two huge windows facing out towards the hospital. One of the walls was lined from ceiling to floor with white bookcases. Dalgliesh resisted the impertinence of walking casually towards them in the hope of assessing Mary Taylor's character by her taste in literature. But he could see from where he stood that there were no textbooks, no bound official reports or sloping banks of files. This was a living-room, not an office.

An open fire burnt in the grate, the wood still crackling with its recent kindling. It had as yet made no impression on the air of the room which was cold and very still. Matron was wearing a short scarlet cape over her grey dress. She had taken off her head-dress and the huge coil of yellow hair lay like a burden on the frail, etiolated neck.

She was fortunate, he thought, to have been born in an age which could appreciate individuality of feature and form, owing everything to bone structure and nothing to the gentle nuances of femininity. A century ago she would have been called ugly, even grotesque. But today most men would think her interesting, and some might even describe her as beautiful. For Dalgliesh she was one of the most beautiful women he had ever met.

Placed precisely in the middle of the three windows was a sturdy oak table bearing a large black-and-white telescope. Dalgliesh saw that this was no amateur's toy but an expensive and sophisticated instrument. It dominated the room. The Matron saw his eyes upon it and said:

"Are you interested in astronomy?"

"Not particularly."

She smiled. " 'Le silence éternel de ces espaces infinis m'affraie'?"

"Discomforts rather than terrifies. It's probably my vanity. I can't interest myself in anything which I not only don't understand but know that I have no prospect of ever understanding."

"That for me is the attraction. It's a form of escapism, even of voyeurism, I suppose—this absorption in an impersonal universe which I can't do anything to influence or control and, better still, which no one expects me to. It's an abdication of responsibility. It restores personal problems to their proper proportion."

She motioned Dalgliesh towards the black leather sofa in front of the fire. Before it, a low table held a tray with a coffee percolator, hot milk, crystal sugar and two cups.

As he seated himself, he smiled and said: "If I want to indulge in humility or speculate on the incomprehensible, I prefer to look at a primrose. The expense is nugatory, the pleasure is more immediate, and the moral just as valid."

The mobile mouth mocked him.

"And at least you restrict your indulgence in these dangerous philosophical speculations to a few short weeks in the spring."

The conversation is, he thought, a verbal pavane. If I'm not careful I shall begin to enjoy it. I wonder when she will get down to business. Or is she expecting me to make the first move? And why not? It is I who am the suppliant, the intruder.

As if reading his thoughts, she said suddenly:

"It's odd that they should both have been such friendless girls, both orphans. It makes my task less onerous. There aren't any desolated parents to be comforted, thank God. Nurse Pearce only had the grandparents who brought her up. He's a retired miner and they live in some poverty in a cottage just outside Nottingham. They belong to a very puritanical religious sect and their only reaction to the child's death was to say, 'God's Will Be Done.' It seemed an odd response to a tragedy which was so obviously the will of man."

"So you think Nurse Pearce's death was murder then?"

"Not necessarily. But I don't accuse God of tampering with the intra-gastric drip."

"And Nurse Fallon's relatives?"

"None, as far as I know. She was asked for her next of kin when she first became a student and told us she was an orphan with no blood relations living. There was no reason to question it. It was probably true. But her death will be in the papers tomorrow and if there are any relatives or friends no doubt we shall be hearing from them. You've spoken to the students, I expect?"

"I've just had a preliminary talk with them as a group. I saw them in the demonstration room. It's been useful in giving me a background to the case. They've all agreed to be fingerprinted and that's being done now. I shall need the prints of everyone who was in Nightingale House last night and this morning, if only for elimination purposes. And I shall, of course, need to interview everyone separately. But I'm glad of this chance to see you first. After all, you were in Amsterdam when Nurse Fallon died. That means there's one less suspect for me to worry about."

He saw with surprise her knuckles whiten around the handle of the coffee pot. Her face flushed. She closed her eyes and he thought he heard her sigh. He watched her a little disconcerted. What he had said must surely be obvious to a woman of her intelligence. He hardly knew why he had bothered to say it. If this second death were murder, then anyone with an alibi covering the whole of yesterday evening and night must be free of suspicion. As if sensing his surprise, she said:

"I'm sorry. I must seem obtuse. I know it's foolish to feel such relief at not being under suspicion when one knows anyway that one is innocent. Perhaps it's because none of us is innocent in any real sense. A psychologist could explain it, I'm sure. But ought you to be so confident? Couldn't the poison—if it were poison—have been put into Fallon's whisky bottle any time after she bought it, or another and poisoned bottle substituted for the one she purchased? That could have been done before I left for Amsterdam on Tuesday evening."

"I'm afraid you must resign yourself to innocence. Miss Fallon bought this particular bottle of whisky from Scunthorpe's wine shop in the High Street yesterday afternoon, and took her first and only drink from it on the night she died. The bottle is still almost full, the whisky remaining is perfectly good whisky as far as we know, and the only prints on the bottle are Miss Fallon's own."

"You've worked very fast. So the poison was put either into the glass after she'd poured her hot drink or into the sugar?"

"If she were poisoned. We can't be sure of anything till we get the P.M. report and perhaps not even then. The sugar is being tested but that is really only a formality. Most of the students helped themselves from that bowl when they had their early morning tea and at least two of the girls drank theirs. So that leaves us with the beaker of whisky and hot lemon. Miss Fallon made it very easy for a murderer. Apparently the whole of Nightingale House knew that, if she didn't go out in the evening, she watched the television until the programme closed down. She was a poor sleeper and never went to bed early. When the television ended she would go to her room and undress. Then in her bedroom slippers and dressing-gown she would go to the little pantry on the second floor and make her nightcap. She kept the whisky in her room but she couldn't make the drink there because there's no water laid on and no means of heating it. So it was her habit to take the insulated tumbler with the whisky poured out ready and add the hot lemon in the pantry. A supply of lemons was kept there in the cupboard with the cocoa, coffee, chocolate and other items with which the nurses used to make their late night drinks. Then she would take the tumbler back to her room and leave it on the bedside locker while she had her bath. She always bathed quickly and she liked to get into bed immediately afterwards while she was still warm. I expect that's why she made her drink before she went into the bathroom. By the time she got back to her room and into bed, the drink was precisely the right temperature. And apparently the routine never varied."

The Matron said: "It's rather frightening how much people get to know about each other's habits in a small closed community like this. But, of course, it's inevitable. There's no real privacy. How can there be? I knew about the whisky, of course, but it hardly seemed my business. The girl certainly wasn't an incipient alcoholic and she wasn't handing it out to the younger students. At her age she was entitled to her own choice of nightcap."

Dalgliesh asked how the Matron had learned about the whisky.

"Nurse Pearce told me. She asked to see me and gave me the information in a spirit of 'I don't want to tell tales but I think you ought to know.' Drink and the devil were one and the same to Nurse Pearce. But I don't think Fallon made any secret of the whisky drinking. How could she? As I said, we know about each other's little habits. But there are some things, of course, that we don't know. Josephine Fallon was a very private person. I can't give you any information about her life outside the hospital and I doubt whether anyone here can."

"Who was her friend here? She must have had someone she confided in, surely? Isn't that necessary for any woman in this kind of closed community?"

She looked at him a little strangely.

"Yes. We all need someone. But I think Fallon needed a friend less than most. She was remarkably self-sufficient. If she confided in anyone it would be Madeleine Goodale."

"The plain one with the round face and large spectacles?"

Dalgliesh recalled her. It was not an unattractive face, mainly because of the good skin and the intelligence of those large grey eyes behind the thick horn rims. But Nurse Goodale could never be other than plain. He thought he could picture her future; the years of training willingly endured, the success in examinations; the gradually increasing responsibility until, at last, she too was a Matron. It was not unusual for such a girl to be friendly with a more attractive woman. It was one way of gaining at least a vicarious share in a more romantic, less dedicated life. As if reading his thoughts, Miss Taylor said:

"Nurse Goodale is one of our most efficient nurses. I was hoping that she would stay on after her training to take a post as staff nurse. But that is hardly likely. She's engaged to our local vicar and they want to marry next Easter."

She glanced across at Dalgliesh a little maliciously.

"He is considered a most eligible young man. You seem surprised, Superintendent."

Dalgliesh laughed: "After over twenty years as a policeman I should have learnt not to make superficial judgements. I think I had better see Nurse Goodale first. I understand the room you're making available isn't ready yet. I suppose we could go on using the demonstration room. Or are you likely to be needing it?"

"I would prefer you to see the girls somewhere else if you would. That room has very unhappy and dramatic memories for them. We're not even using it yet for teaching demonstrations. Until the small visitors' room on the first floor is ready I'd be happy for you to interview the students here."

Dalgliesh thanked her. He replaced his coffee cup on the table. She hesitated, then said:

"Mr. Dalgliesh, there's one thing I want to say. I feel— I am—*in loco parentis* to my students. If ever any question . . . if you should begin to suspect that any one of them is involved, I can rely on you to let me know? They would then need protection. There would surely be the question of getting a solicitor." She hesitated again:

"Please forgive me if I'm being offensive. One has so little experience in these matters. It's just that I shouldn't like them . . ."

"To be trapped?"

"To be rushed into saying things which might quite wrongly incriminate them or other members of the staff."

Dalgliesh found himself unreasonably irritated.

"There are rules laid down, you know," he said.

"Oh, rules! I know there are rules. But I'm sure you are both too experienced and too intelligent to let them hinder you over much. I'm just reminding you that these girls are less intelligent and in such matters not experienced at all."

Fighting his irritation, Dalgliesh said formally:

"I can only tell you that the rules are there and that it's in our interests to keep them. Can't you imagine what a gift to the defending counsel any infringement would be? A young unprotected girl, a student nurse, bullied by a senior police officer with years of experience in trapping the unwary. Enough difficulties are placed in the path of the police in this country; we don't voluntarily add to them."

She flushed and he was interested to see the wave of colour sweep from her neck over the pale honey glowing skin making her look momentarily as if the veins ran with fire. Then, instantaneously, it passed. The change was so sudden that he couldn't be sure that he had actually seen that tell-tale metamorphosis. She said composedly:

"We both have our responsibilities. We must hope that they don't conflict. In the meantime you must expect me to be as concerned with mine as you are with yours. And that brings me to some information which I have to give you. It concerns Christine Dakers, the student who discovered Nurse Fallon's body."

She described briefly and succinctly what had happened during her visit to the private ward. Dalgliesh noted with interest that she made no comment, offered no opinion, and attempted no justification of the girl. He didn't ask her whether she believed the story. She was a highly intelligent woman. She must know that what she had handed him was the first motive. He asked when he would be able to interview Nurse Dakers.

"She's sleeping now. Dr. Snelling, who is in charge of the nurses' health, is to see her later this morning. He will then report to me. If he agrees, it should be possible for you to see her this afternoon. And now I'll send for Nurse Goodale. That is, if there is nothing more I can tell you?"

"I shall need a great deal of information about people's ages, backgrounds and the time they've been at the hospital. Won't that be on their personal records? It would be helpful if I could have those."

The Matron thought. Dalgliesh noticed that when she did so her face fell into absolute repose. After a moment she said:

"All the staff here have personal dossiers, of course. Legally these are the property of the Hospital Management Committee. The Chairman won't be back from Israel until tomorrow evening but I'll consult the Vice-Chairman. I imagine that he will ask me to look through the records, and if they contain nothing private which is irrelevant to your inquiry, to pass them over."

Dalgliesh decided that it would be prudent not to press for the moment the question of who should decide what was irrelevant to his inquiry.

He said: "There are personal questions I shall have to ask, of course. But it would be a great deal more convenient and would save time if I could get the routine information from the records."

It was strange that her voice could be so agreeable and yet so obstinate.

"I can see that it would be a great deal more convenient; it would also be a check on the truth of what you are told. But the records can only be handed over under the conditions I have just stated."

So she was confident that the Vice-Chairman would accept and endorse her view of what was right. And undoubtedly he would. Here was a formidable woman. Faced with a tricky problem she had given the matter thought, come to a decision and had stated it firmly without apology or wavering. An admirable woman. She would be easy to deal with as long, of course, as all her decisions were as acceptable as this.

He asked if he might use the telephone; recalled Sergeant Masterson from his supervision of the preparation of the small visitor's room to serve as an office; and prepared himself for the long tedium of the individual interviews.

II

Nurse Goodale was summoned by telephone and arrived within two minutes looking unhurried and composed. Miss Taylor seemed to think that neither explanation nor reassurance was necessary to this self-possessed young woman but simply said:

"Sit down, Nurse. Superintendent Dalgliesh wants to talk to you."

Then she took up her cloak from the chair, swung it over her shoulders, and went out without another glance at either of them. Sergeant Masterson opened his notebook. Nurse Goodale seated herself in an upright chair at the table but when Dalgliesh motioned her to an armchair before the fire, moved without demur. She sat stiffly on the very edge of the chair, her back straight, her surprisingly shapely and elegant legs planted modestly side by side. But the hands lying in her lap were perfectly relaxed and Dalgliesh, seated opposite, found himself confronting a pair of disconcertingly intelligent eyes. He said:

"You were probably closer to Miss Fallon than anyone else in the hospital. Tell me about her."

She showed no surprise at the form of his first question, but paused for a few seconds before replying as if marshalling her thoughts. Then she said:

"I liked her. She tolerated me better than she did most of the other students but I don't think her feeling for me was much stronger than that. She was thirty-one after all, and we must all have seemed rather immature to her. She had a rather sarcastic tongue which didn't help, and I think some of the girls were rather afraid of her.

"She seldom spoke to me about her past but she did tell me that both her parents were killed in 1944 in a bombing raid on London. She was brought up by an elderly aunt and educated at one of those boarding-schools where they take children from an early age and keep them until they're ready to leave. Provided the fees are paid of course, but I got the impression that there wasn't any difficulty about that. She always wanted to be a nurse but she got tuberculosis after she left school and had to spend two years in a sanatorium. I don't know where. After that, two hospitals turned her down on grounds of health, so she took a number of temporary jobs. She told me soon after we began our training that she had once been engaged but that it didn't work out."

"You never asked her why?"

"I never asked her anything. If she had wanted to tell me she would have done so."

"Did she tell you that she was pregnant?"

"Yes. She told me two days before she went sick. She must have suspected before then but the confirming report came that morning. I asked her what she intended doing about it and she said that she would get rid of the baby."

"Did you point out that this was probably illegal?"

"No. She didn't care about legality. I told her that it was wrong."

"But she still intended to go ahead with the abortion?"

"Yes, she said that she knew a doctor who would do it and that there wouldn't be any real risk. I asked her if she needed money and she said that she would be all right, that money was the least of her problems. She never told me who she was going to, and I didn't ask."

"But you were prepared to help her with money had she needed it, even though you disapproved of getting rid of the baby?"

"My disapproval wasn't important. What was important was that it was wrong. But when I knew that she had made up her mind I had to decide whether to help her. I was afraid that she might go to some unqualified back street abortionist and risk her life and health. I know that the law has changed, that it's easier now to get a medical recommendation, but I didn't think she would qualify. I had to make a moral decision. If you are proposing to commit a sin it is as well to commit it with intelligence. Otherwise you are insulting God as well as defying Him, don't you think?"

Dalgliesh said gravely: "It's an interesting theological point which I'm not competent to argue. Did she tell you who was the father of the child?"

"Not directly. I think it may have been a young writer she was friendly with. I don't know his name or where you can find him but I do know that Jo spent a week with him in the Isle of Wight last October. She had seven days' holiday due and she told me that she'd decided to walk in the island with a friend. I imagine he was the friend. It certainly wasn't anyone from here. They went during the first week and she told me that they'd stayed in a small inn about five miles south of Ventor. That's all she did tell me. I suppose it's possible that she became pregnant during that week?"

Dalgliesh said: "The dates would fit. And she never confided in you about the father of the child?"

"No. I asked her why she wouldn't marry the father and she said that it would be unfair to the child to burden it with two irresponsible parents. I remember her saying: 'He would be horrified at the idea, anyway, unless he had a sudden urge to experience fatherhood just to see what it was like. And he might like to see the baby born so that he could write a lurid account of childbirth some day. But he really isn't committed to anyone but himself.' "

"But did she care for him?"

The girl paused a full minute before replying. Then she said:

"I think she did. I think that may have been why she killed herself."

"What makes you think that she did?"

"I suppose because the alternative is even more unlikely. I never thought that Jo was the type to kill herself—if there is a type. But I really didn't know her. One never does really know another human being. Anything is possible for anyone. I've always believed that. And it's surely more likely that she killed herself than that someone murdered her. That seems absolutely incredible. Why should they?"

"I was hoping you might be able to tell me."

"Well, I can't. She hadn't any enemies at the John Carpendar as far as I know. She wasn't popular. She was too reserved, too solitary. But people didn't dislike her. And even if they did, murder surely suggests something more than ordinary dislike. It seems so much more probable that she came back to duty too soon after influenza, was overcome by psychological depression, felt she couldn't cope with getting rid of the baby, and yet couldn't face up to having an illegitimate child and killed herself on impulse."

"You said when I questioned you all in the demonstration room that you were probably the last person to see her alive. What exactly happened while you were together last night? Did she give you any idea that she might be thinking of suicide?"

"If she had, I should hardly have left her to go to bed alone. She said nothing. I don't think we exchanged more than half a dozen words. I asked her how she felt and she replied that she was all right. She obviously wasn't in the mood to chat so I didn't make myself a nuisance. After about twenty minutes I went up to bed. I never saw her again."

"And she didn't mention her pregnancy?"

"She mentioned nothing. She looked tired, I thought,

and rather pale. But then, Jo always was rather pale. It's distressing for me to think that she might have needed help and that I left her without speaking the words that might have saved her. But she wasn't a woman to invite confidences. I stayed behind when the others left because I thought she might want to talk. When it was plain that she wanted to be alone, I left."

She talked about being distressed, thought Dalgliesh, but she neither looked nor sounded it. She felt no self-reproach. Why indeed should she? He doubted whether she felt particular grief. She had been closer to Josephine Fallon than any of the students. But she had not really cared. Was there anyone in the world who had? He asked:

"And Nurse Pearce's death?"

"I think that was essentially an accident. Someone put the poison in the feed as a joke or out of vague malice without realizing that the result would be fatal."

"Which would be odd in a third-year student nurse whose programme of lectures presumably included basic information on corrosive poisons."

"I wasn't suggesting that it was a nurse. I don't know who it was. I don't think you'll ever find out now. But I can't believe that it was wilful murder."

That was all very well, thought Dalgliesh, but surely it was a little disingenuous in a girl as intelligent as Nurse Goodale. It was, of course, the popular, almost the official view. It exonerated everyone from the worst crime and indicted no one of anything more than malice and carelessness. It was a comforting theory, and unless he were lucky it might never be disproved. But he didn't believe it himself, and he couldn't accept that Nurse Goodale did. But it was even harder to accept that here was a girl to comfort herself with false theories or deliberately to shut her eyes to unpalatable facts.

Dalgliesh then asked her about her movements on the morning of Pearce's death. He already knew them from Inspector Bailey's notes and her previous statement and was not surprised when Nurse Goodale confirmed them without hesitation. She had got up at 6:45 and had drunk early morning tea with the rest of the set in the utility room. She had told them about Fallon's influenza since it was to her room that Nurse Fallon had come when she was taken ill in the night. None of the students had expressed particular concern but they had wondered how the demonstration would go now that the set was so decimated and had speculated, not without malice, how Sister Gearing would acquit herself in the face of a G.N.C. inspection. Nurse Pearce had drunk her tea with the rest of the set and Nurse Goodale thought that she remembered Pearce saying:

"With Fallon ill, I suppose I shall have to act the patient." Nurse Goodale couldn't recall any comment or discussion about this. It was well accepted that the next student on the list substituted for anyone who was ill.

After she had drunk her tea, Nurse Goodale had dressed and had then made her way to the library to review the treatment of laryngectomy in preparation for the morning's session. It was important that there should be a quick and lively response to questions if the seminar were to be a success. She had settled herself to work at about 7:15 and Nurse Dakers had joined her shortly afterwards, sharing a devotion to study which, thought Dalgliesh, had at least been rewarded by an alibi for most of the time before breakfast. She and Dakers had said nothing of interest to each other while they had been working and had left the library at the same time and gone into breakfast together. That had been at about ten minutes to eight. She had sat with Dakers and the Burt twins, but had left the breakfast room before them. That was at 8:15. She had returned to her bedroom to make the bed, and then gone to the library to write a couple of letters. That done, she had paid a brief visit to the cloakroom and had made her way to the demonstration room just before a quarter to nine. Only Sister Gearing and the Burt twins were already there, but the rest of the set had joined them shortly afterwards; she couldn't remember in what order. She thought that Pearce had been one of the last to arrive.

Dalgliesh asked: "How did Nurse Pearce seem?"

"I noticed nothing unusual about her, but then I wouldn't expect to. Pearce was Pearce. She made a negligible impression."

"Did she say anything before the demonstration began?"

"Yes, she did as a matter of fact. It's odd that you should ask that. I haven't mentioned it before, I suppose because Inspector Bailey didn't ask. But she did speak. She looked round at us—the set had all assembled by then—and asked if anyone had taken anything from her bedroom."

"Did she say what?"

"No. She just stood there with that accusing rather belligerent look she occasionally had and said: 'Has anyone been to my room this morning or taken anything from it?'"

"No one replied. I think we just all shook our heads. It wasn't a question we took particularly seriously. Pearce was apt to make a great fuss about trifles. Anyway, the Burt twins were busy with their preparations and the rest of us were chatting. Pearce didn't get a great deal of attention paid to her question. I doubt whether half of us heard her even."

"Did you notice how she reacted? Was she worried or angry or distressed?"

"None of those things. It was odd really. I remember now. She looked satisfied, almost triumphant, as if something she suspected had been confirmed. I don't know why I noticed that, but I did. Sister Gearing then called us to order and the demonstration began."

Dalgliesh did not immediately speak at the end of this recital and, after a little time, she took his silence for dismissal and rose to go. She got out of the chair with the same controlled grace as she had seated herself, smoothed her apron with a scarcely discernible gesture, gave him a last interrogatory glance and walked to the door. Then she turned as if yielding to an impulse.

"You asked me if anyone had a reason to kill Jo. I said I knew of no one. That is true. But I suppose a legal motive is something different. I ought to tell you that some people might think I had a motive."

Dalgliesh said: "Had you?"

"I expect you'll think so. I am Jo's heir, at least I think I am. She told me about three months ago that she had made her will and that she was leaving me all she had. She gave me the name and address of her solicitor. I can let you have the information. They haven't yet written to me but I expect they will, that is if Jo really made her will. But I expect she did. She wasn't a girl to make promises she didn't fulfil. Perhaps you would prefer to get in touch with the solicitors now? These things take time, don't they?"

"Did she say why she was making you her legatee?"

"She said that she had to leave her money to someone and that I would probably do most good with it. I didn't take the matter very seriously and neither, I think, did she. After all she was only thirty-one. She wasn't expecting to die. And she warned me that she'd probably change her mind long before she got old enough to make the legacy a serious prospect for me. After all she'd probably marry. But she felt she ought to make a will and I was the only person at the time who she cared to remember: I thought that it was only a formality. It never occurred to me that she might have much to leave. It was only when we had our talk about the cost of an abortion that she told me how much she was worth."

"And was it—is it—much?"

The girl answered calmly: "About £16,000 I believe. It came from her parents' insurances."

She smiled a little wryly.

"Quite worth having you see, Superintendent. I should think it would rank as a perfectly respectable motive, wouldn't you? We shall be able to put central heating in the vicarage now. And if you saw my fiancé's vicarage—twelve rooms, nearly all of them facing north or east— you would think I had quite a motive for murder."

III

Sister Rolfe and Sister Gearing were waiting with the students in the library; they had moved from the nurses' sitting-room in order to occupy the waiting time with reading and revision. How much the girls were really taking in was problematic but the scene certainly looked peaceful and studious enough. The students had seated themselves at the desks in front of the window and sat, books open before them, in apparent absorption. Sister Rolfe and Sister Gearing, as if to emphasize their seniority and solidarity, had withdrawn to the sofa in front of the fire and were seated side by side. Sister Rolfe was marking with green biro a pile of first-year students' exercises, picking up each notebook from a stack on the floor at her feet, and adding it, when dealt with, to the growing pile which rested against the back of the sofa. Sister Gearing was ostensibly making notes for her next lecture, but seemed unable to keep her eyes from her colleague's decisive hieroglyphics.

The door opened and Madeleine Goodale returned. Without a word she went back to her desk, took up her pen and resumed work.

Sister Gearing whispered: "Goodale seems calm enough. Odd, considering she was supposed to be Fallon's best friend."

Sister Rolfe did not raise her eyes. She said drily:

"She didn't really care about Fallon. Goodale has only a limited emotional capital and I imagine she expends it all on that extraordinarily dull person she's decided to marry."

"He's good-looking, though. Goodale's lucky to get him, if you ask me."

But the subject was of a secondary interest to Sister Gearing and she didn't pursue it. After a minute she said peevishly:

"Why haven't the police sent for someone else?"

"They will." Sister Rolfe added another exercise book, liberally embellished in green, to a completed pile by her side. "They're probably still discussing Goodale's contribution."

"They ought to have seen us first. After all, we're Sisters. Matron should have explained. And why isn't Brumfett here? I don't see why she should be treated any differently from us."

Sister Rolfe said: "Too busy. Apparently a couple of the second-year students on the ward have now gone down with flu. She sent over some sort of note to Mr. Dalgliesh by a porter, presumably giving information about her movements last night. I met him bringing it in. He asked me where he could find the gentlemen from Scotland Yard."

Sister Gearing's voice became petulant:

"That's all very well, but she ought to be here. God knows, we're busy too! Brumfett lives in Nightingale House; she had as much opportunity to kill Fallon as anyone."

Sister Rolfe said quietly: "She had more chance."

"What do you mean, more chance?"

Sister Gearing's sharp voice cut into the silence and one of the Burt twins lifted her head.

"She's had Fallon in her power in the sick bay for the last ten days."

"But surely you don't mean . . . ? Brumfett wouldn't!"

"Precisely," said Sister Rolfe coldly. "So why make stupid and irresponsible remarks?"

There was a silence broken only by the rustle of paper and the hiss of the gas fire. Sister Gearing fidgeted.

"I suppose if Brumfett's lost another two nurses with flu she'll be pressing Matron to recall some of this block. She's got her eyes on the Burt twins, I know."

"Then she'll be unlucky. This set have had their training disrupted enough already. After all, it's their last block before their finals. Matron won't let it be cut short."

"I shouldn't be too sure. It's Brumfett, remember. Matron doesn't usually say no to her. Funny though, I did hear a rumour that they aren't going on holiday together this year. One of the pharmacists' assistants had it from Matron's secretary that Matron plans to motor in Ireland on her own."

My God, thought Sister Rolfe. Isn't there any privacy in this place? But she said nothing, only shifting a few inches from the restless figure at her side.

It was then that the wall telephone rang. Sister Gearing leapt up and went across to answer it. She turned to the rest of the group, her face creased with disappointment.

"That was Sergeant Masterson. Superintendent Dalgliesh would like to see the Burt twins next please. He's moved to the visitors' sitting-room on this floor."

Without a word and with no signs of nervousness, the Burt twins closed their books and made for the door.

IV

It was half an hour later and Sergeant Masterson was making coffee. The visitors' sitting-room had been provided with a miniature kitchen, a large recess fitted with a sink and Formica-covered cupboard, on which stood a double gas-ring. The cupboard had been cleared of all its paraphernalia except for four large beakers, a canister of sugar and one of tea, a tin of biscuits, a large earthenware jug and strainer, and three transparent air-tight packets of fresh-ground coffee. By the side of the sink were two bottles of milk. The cream-line was easily discernible, but Sergeant Masterson prised the cap away from one of the bottles and sniffed at the milk suspiciously before heating a quantity in a saucepan. He warmed the earthenware jug with hot water from the tap, dried it carefully in the tea towel which hung by the side of the sink, spooned in a generous quantity of coffee and stood waiting for the kettle's first burst of steam. He approved of the arrangements that had been made. If the police had to work in Nightingale House this room was as convenient and comfortable as any and the coffee was an unexpected bonus which mentally, he credited to Paul Hudson. The Hospital Secretary had struck him as an efficient and imaginative man. His couldn't be an easy job. The poor devil probably had one hell of a life, sandwiched between those two old fools, Kealey and Grout, and that high-handed bitch of a Matron.

He strained the coffee with meticulous care and carried a beaker over to his chief. They sat and drank companionably together, eyes straying to the storm-wrecked garden. Both of them had a strong dislike of badly cooked food or synthetic coffee and Masterson thought that they never got closer to liking each other than when they were eating and drinking together, deploring the inadequacies of the meals at the inn, or as now, rejoicing in good coffee. Dalgliesh comforted his hands around the beaker and thought that it was typical of Mary Taylor's efficiency and imagination to ensure that they had real coffee available. Hers couldn't be an easy job. That ineffectual couple, Kealey and Grout, wouldn't be much help to anyone, and Paul Hudson was too young to give much support.

After a moment of appreciative sipping, Masterson said: "That was a disappointing interview, sir."

"The Burt twins? Yes, I must say I had hoped for something more interesting. After all, they were at the centre of the mystery; they administered the fatal drip; they glimpsed the mysterious Nurse Fallon on her way out of Nightingale House; they met Sister Brumfett on her perambulations in the early hours. But we knew all that already. And we don't know any more now."

Dalgliesh thought about the two girls. Masterson had drawn up a second chair on their entrance and they had sat there side by side, freckled hands ritualistically disposed in their laps, legs modestly crossed, each girl a mirror image of her twin. Their polite antiphonal answers to his questions, spoken in a West Country burr, were as agreeable to the ear as their shining good health to the eye. He had rather taken to the Burt twins. He might, of course, have been facing a couple of experienced accomplices in evil. Anything was possible. Certainly they had had the best opportunity to poison the drip and as good a chance as anyone in Nightingale House to doctor Falon's nightcap. Yet they had seemed perfectly at ease with him, a little bored perhaps at having to repeat much of their story, but neither frightened nor particularly worried. From time to time they had gazed at him with a gentle speculative concern rather as if he were a difficult patient whose condition was beginning to give rise to some anxiety. He had noticed this intent and compassionate regard on the faces of the other nurses during their first encounter in the demonstration room and had found it disconcerting.

"And you noticed nothing odd about the milk?"

They had answered almost in unison, rebuking him in the calm voice of common sense.

"Oh no! Well, we wouldn't have gone ahead with the drip if we had, would we?"

"Can you remember taking the cap off the bottle; was it loose?"

Two pairs of blue eyes looked at each other, almost as if in signal. Then Maureen replied:

"We don't remember that it was. But even if it had been, we wouldn't have suspected that someone had been at the milk. We would just have thought that the dairy put it on like that."

Then Shirley spoke on her own:

"I don't think we would have noticed anything wrong with the milk anyway. You see, we were concentrating on the procedures for giving the drip, making sure that we had all the instruments and equipment we needed. We knew that Miss Beale and Matron would arrive at any minute."

That, of course, was the explanation. They were girls who had been trained to observe, but their observation was specific and limited. If they were watching a patient they would miss nothing of his signs or symptoms, not a flicker of the eyelids or a change of pulse; anything else happening in the room, however dramatic, would probably be unnoticed. Their attention had been on the demonstration, the apparatus, the equipment, the patient. The bottle of milk presented no problems. They had taken it for granted. And yet they were farmer's daughters. One of them—it had been Maureen—had actually poured the stuff from the bottle. Could they really have mistaken the colour, the texture, the smell of milk?

As if reading his thoughts Marueen said:

"It wasn't as if we could smell the carbolic. The whole demo room stinks of disinfectant. Miss Collins throws the stuff around as if we're all lepers."

Shirley laughed: "Carbolic isn't effective against leprosy!"

They looked at each other, smiling in happy complicity.

And so the interview had gone on. They had no theories to propound, no suggestions to offer. They knew no one who could wish Pearce or Fallon dead, and yet both deaths—since they had occurred—seemed to cause them no particular surprise. They could recall every word of the conversation between Sister Brumfett and themselves in the small hours of that morning, yet the encounter apparently had made little impression on them. When Dalgliesh asked if the Sister had seemed unusually worried or distressed, they gazed at him simultaneously, brows creased in perplexity, before replying that Sister had seemed just the same as usual.

As if following his chief's thoughts, Masterson said:

"Short of asking them outright if Sister Brumfett looked as if she'd just come straight from murdering Fallon you couldn't have put it much plainer. They're an odd uncommunicative couple."

"At least they're sure of the time. They took that milk shortly after seven o'clock and went straight into the demonstration room with it. They stood the bottle unopened on the instrument trolley while they made preliminary preparations for the demonstration. They left the demonstration room at seven twenty-five for breakfast and the bottle was still on the trolley when they returned at about twenty-to-nine to complete their preparations. They then stood it, still unopened, in a jug of hot water to bring it to blood heat and it remained there until they poured the milk from the bottle into a measuring jug about two minutes before Miss Beale and Matron's party arrived. Most of the suspects were at breakfast together from eight until eight twenty-five, so that the mischief was either done between seven twenty-five and eight o'clock or in the short period between the end of breakfast and the twins' return to the demonstration room."

Masterson said: "I still find it strange that they noticed nothing odd about that milk."

"They may have noticed more than they realize at present. After all, this is the umpteenth time they've told their story. During the weeks since Pearce's death, their first statements have become fixed in their minds as the immutable truth. That's why I haven't asked them the crucial question about the milk bottle. If they gave me the wrong answer now they'd never change it. They need to be shocked into total recall. They're not seeing anything that happened with fresh eyes. I dislike reconstructions of the crime; they always make me feel like a fictional detective. But I think there may be a case for reconstruction here. I shall have to be in London early tomorrow, but you and Greeson can see to it. Greeson will probably enjoy himself."

He told Masterson briefly what he proposed and ended:

"You needn't bother to include the Sisters. I expect you can get a supply of the disinfectant from Miss Collins. But for God's sake keep an eye on the stuff and chuck it away afterwards. We don't want another tragedy."

Sergeant Masterson took up the two beakers and carried them over to the sink. He said:

"Nightingale House does seem to be touched with ill-luck, but I can't see the killer having another go while we're around."

It was to prove a singularly unprophetic remark.

V

Since her encounter with Dalgliesh in the nurses' utility room earlier that morning Sister Rolfe had had time to recover from shock and to consider her position. As Dalgliesh had expected she was not far less forthcoming. She had already given to Inspector Bailey a clear and unambiguous statement about the arrangements for the demonstration and the intra-gastric feeding and about her own movements on the morning that Nurse Pearce died. She confirmed the statement accurately and without fuss. She agreed that she had known that Nurse Pearce was to act the part of the patient and pointed out sarcastically that there would be little point in denying the knowledge since it was she whom Madeleine Goodale had called when Fallon was taken ill.

Dalgliesh asked: "Did you have any doubt of the genuineness of her illness?"

"At the time?"

"Then or now."

"I suppose you're suggesting that Fallon could have feigned influenza to ensure that Pearce took her place, and then sneaked back to Nightingale House before breakfast to doctor the drip? I don't know why she did come back, but you can put any idea that she was pretending to be ill out of your head. Even Fallon couldn't simulate a temperature of 103.8, a minor rigor and a racing pulse. She was a very sick girl that night, and she remained sick for nearly ten days."

Dalgliesh pointed out that it was all the more odd that she should have been well enough to make her way back to Nightingale House next morning. Sister Rolfe replied that it was so odd that she could only assume that Fallon had had an imperative need to return. Invited to speculate on what that need could have been she replied that it wasn't her job to propound theories. Then, as if under a compulsion, she added:

"But it wasn't to murder Pearce. Fallon was highly intelligent, easily the most intelligent of her year. If Fallon came back to put the corrosive in the feed she would know perfectly well that there was a considerable risk of her being seen in Nightingale House even if she weren't missed on the ward, and she'd have taken good care to have a story ready. It wouldn't have been difficult to think of something. As it is, I gather she merely declined to give Inspector Bailey any explanation."

"Perhaps she was clever enough to realize that this extraordinary reticence would strike another intelligent woman in exactly that way."

"A kind of double bluff? I don't think so. It would be banking too heavily on the intelligence of the police."

She admitted calmly that she had no alibi for any of the time from seven o'clock when the twins had collected the bottle of milk from the kitchen until ten minutes to nine when she had joined the Matron and Mr. Courtney-Briggs in Miss Taylor's sitting-room to await the arrival of Miss Beale, except for the period from eight to eight twenty-five when she had breakfasted at the same table as Sister Brumfett and Sister Gearing. Sister Brumfett had left the table first and she had followed at about eight twenty-five. She had gone first to her office next door to the demonstration room, but finding Mr. Courtney-Briggs in occupation, had made her way at once to her bed-sitting-room on the third floor.

When Dalgliesh asked whether Sister Gearing and Sister Brumfett had appeared their usual selves at breakfast she replied drily that they exhibited no signs of impending homicidal mania if that was what he meant. Gearing had read the *Daily Mirror* and Brumfett the *Nursing Times,* if that were of any significance, and the conversation had been minimal. She regretted she could offer no witnesses to her own movements before or after the meal but that was surely understandable; for some years now she had preferred to wash and go to the lavatory in private. Apart from that, she valued the free time before the day's work and preferred to spend it alone.

Dalgliesh asked: "Were you surprised to find Mr. Court-ney-Briggs in your office when you went there after breakfast?"

"Not particularly. I took it for granted that he had spent the night in the medical officers' quarters and had come over early to Nightingale House to meet the G.N.C. Inspector. He probably wanted somewhere to write a letter. Mr. Courtney-Briggs assumes the right to use any room in the John Carpendar as his private office if the fancy takes him."

Dalgliesh asked her about her movements the previous night. She repeated that she had been to the cinema alone but added this time that she had met Julia Pardoe on the way out and that they had walked back to the hospital together. They had come in through the Winchester Road gate to which she had a key and had got back to Nightingale House shortly after eleven. She had gone immediately to her room and had seen no one. Nurse Pardoe, she assumed, had either gone straight to bed or had joined the rest of the set in the student nurses' sitting-room.

"So you have nothing to tell me, Sister? Nothing that can help?"

"Nothing."

"Not even why, unnecessary surely, you lied about going to the cinema alone?"

"Nothing. And I shouldn't have thought my private affairs were any concern of yours."

Dalgliesh said calmly: "Miss Rolfe, two of your students are dead. I'm here to find out how and why they died. If you don't want to co-operate, say so. You don't have to answer my questions. But don't try to tell me what questions I am to ask. I'm in charge of this investigation. I do it my way."

"I see. You make up the rules as you go along. All we can do is say when we don't want to play. Yours is a dangerous game, Mr. Dalgliesh."

"Tell me something about these students. You're the Principal Nurse Tutor; you must have a good many girls through your hands. I think you're a good judge of character. We'll start with Nurse Goodale."

If she felt surprise or relief at his choice she concealed it.

"Madeleine Goodale is confidently expected to take the Gold Medal as the best nurse of her year. She is less intelligent than Fallon—than Fallon was—but she's hard working and extremely conscientious. She's a local girl. Her father is well known in the town, an extremely successful estate agent who inherited a long established family business. He's a member of the Town Council and was on the Hospital Management Committee for a number of years. Madeleine went to the local grammar school and then came to us. I don't think she ever considered any other nurse training school. The whole family has a strong local loyalty. She is engaged to the young vicar of Holy Trinity and I understand they plan to marry as soon as she completes her training. Another good career lost to the profession, but she knows her own priorities I suppose."

"The Burt twins?"

"Good sensible kindly girls, with more imagination and sensitivity than they are usually credited with. Their people are farmers near Gloucester. I'm not sure why they chose this hospital. I have an idea a cousin trained here and was happy enough. They are the kind of girls who would chose a training school on that kind of family basis. They aren't particularly intelligent but they aren't stupid. We don't have to take stupid girls here, thank God. Each of them has a steady boy friend and Maureen is engaged. I don't think either of them looks on nursing as a permanent job."

Dalgliesh said: "You're going to have trouble finding leaders for the profession if this automatic resignation on marriage becomes the rule."

She said drily: "We're having trouble now. Who else are you interested in?"

"Nurse Dakers."

"Poor kid! Another local girl, but with a very different background from Goodale. Father was a minor local government officer who died of cancer when she was twelve. Mother has been struggling on ever since with a small pension. The girl was educated at the same school as Goodale but they were never friendly as far as I know. Dakers is a conscientious hard-working student with a great deal of ambition. She'll do all right but she won't do better than all right. She tires easily, isn't really robust. People think of her as timid and highly strung, whatever that euphemism means. But Dakers is tough enough. She's a third-year student, remember. A girl doesn't get this far with her training if she's fundamentally weak, physically or mentally."

"Julia Pardoe?"

Sister Rolfe had herself well under control now and there was no change in her voice as she went on.

"The only child of divorced parents. Mother is one of

those pretty but selfish women who find it impossible to
stay long with one husband. She's on her third now, I
believe. I'm not sure that the girl really knows which is her
father. She hasn't been often at home. Mother sent her off
to prep. school when she was five. She had a stormy school
career and came here straight from the sixth form of one of
those independent girls' boarding-schools, where the girls
are taught nothing but manage to learn a great deal. She
first applied to one of the London teaching hospitals. She
didn't quite measure up to their standard of acceptance
either socially or academically but the Matron referred her
here. Schools like ours have this kind of arrangement with
the teaching hospitals. They get a dozen applications for
every place. It's mostly snobbery and the hope of catching
a husband. We're quite happy to take a number of their
rejects; I suspect that they often make better nurses than
the girls they accept. Pardoe was one of them. An intelligent but untrained mind. A gentle and considerate nurse."

"You know a great deal about your students."

"I make it my business to. But I take it I'm not expected
to give an opinion of my colleagues."

"Sister Gearing and Sister Brumfett? No. But I'd be
glad of your opinion of Nurse Fallon and Nurse Pearce."

"I can't tell you much about Fallon. She was a reserved,
almost a secretive girl. Intelligent, of course, and more
mature than the majority of students. I think I only had one
personal conversation with her. That was at the end of
her first year when I called her for an interview and asked
her for her impressions of nursing. I was interested to
know how our methods here struck a girl who was so different from the ordinary run of the straight-from-school
student. She said that it wasn't fair to judge while one was
still an apprentice and treated as if one were a sub-normal
kitchen maid but that she still thought nursing was her job.

I asked her what had attracted her to the profession and she said that she wanted to acquire a skill which would make her independent anywhere in the world, a qualification which would always be in demand. I don't think she had any particular ambition to get on in the profession. Her training was just a means to an end. But I could be wrong. As I said, I never really knew her."

"So you can't say whether she had enemies?"

"I can't say why anyone should want to kill her, if that's what you mean. I should have thought that Pearce was a much more likely victim."

Dalgliesh asked her why.

"I didn't take to Pearce. I didn't kill her, but then I'm not given to murdering people merely because I dislike them. But she was a strange girl, a mischief maker and a hypocrite. It's no use asking me how I know. I haven't any real evidence and, if I had, I doubt whether I should give it to you."

"So you didn't find it surprising that she should have been murdered?"

"I found it astonishing. But I never for one moment thought her death was suicide or an accident."

"And who do you suppose killed her?"

Sister Rolfe looked at him with a kind of grim satisfaction.

"You tell me, Superintendent. You tell me!"

VI

"So you went to the cinema last night and on your own?"

"Yes, I told you."

"To see a revival of *L'Avventura*. Perhaps you felt that the subtleties of Antonioni could best be experienced without a companion? Or perhaps you couldn't find anyone willing to go with you?"

She couldn't, of course, resist that.

"There are plenty of people to take me to the movies if I want them to."

The movies. It had been the flicks when Dalgliesh was her age. But the generation chasm was deeper than a matter of mere semantics, the alienation more complete. He simply didn't understand her. He hadn't the slightest clue to what was going on behind that smooth and childish forehead. The remarkable violet blue eyes, set wide apart under curved brows, gazed at him, wary but unconcerned. The cat's face with its small rounded chin and wide cheek bones expressed nothing but a vague distaste for the matter in hand. It was difficult, Dalgliesh thought, to imagine finding a prettier or more agreeable figure than Julia Pardoe beside one's sick bed; unless, of course, one happened to be in real pain or distress, when the Burt twins' sturdy common sense or Madeleine Goodale's calm efficiency would be a great deal more acceptable. It might be a personal prejudice, but he couldn't imagine any man willingly exposing his weakness or physical distress to this pert and self-absorbed young woman. And what precisely, he wondered, was she getting out of nursing? If the John Carpendar had been a teaching hospital he could have understood it. That trick of widening the eyes when she spoke so that the hearer was treated to a sudden blaze of blue, of slightly parting moist lips above the neat eburnean teeth would go down very well with a gaggle of medical students.

It was not, he noticed, without its effect on Sergeant Masterson.

But what was it that Sister Rolfe had said of her?

"An intelligent but untrained mind; a gentle and considerate nurse."

Well, it could be. But Hilda Rolfe was prejudiced. And so, in his own way, was Dalgliesh.

He pressed on with his interrogation, resisting the impulse to sarcasm, to the cheap jibes of antipathy.

"Did you enjoy the film?"

"It was all right."

"And you returned to Nightingale House from this all right film when?"

"I don't know. Just before eleven, I suppose. I met Sister Rolfe outside the cinema and we walked back together. I expect she's told you."

So they must have talked since this morning. This was their story and the girl was repeating it without even the pretence that she cared whether she were believed. It could be checked of course. The girl in the cinema box office might remember whether they had arrived together. But it was hardly worth the trouble of inquiry. Why indeed should it matter, unless they had spent the evening concocting murder as well as imbibing culture? And if they had, here was one partner in iniquity who wasn't apparently worried.

Dalgliesh asked: "What happened when you got back?"

"Nothing. I went to the nurses' sitting-room and they were all watching the telly. Well, actually they switched it off as I came in. The Burt twins came to make tea in the nurses' kitchen and we took it into Maureen's room to drink it. Dakers came with us. Madeleine Goodale was left with Fallon. I don't know what time they came up. I went to bed as soon as I'd had my tea. I was asleep before twelve."

So she might have been. But this had been a very simple murder. There had been nothing to prevent her waiting, perhaps in one of the lavatory cubicles, until she heard Fallon running her bath. Once Fallon was in the bathroom, Nurse Pardoe would know what all the other students knew; that a beaker of whisky and lemon would be waiting on Fallon's bedside table. How simple to slip into her room and add something to the drink. Add what? It was maddening, this working in the dark with its inevitable tendency to theorize in advance of the facts. Until the autopsy was completed and the toxicology result available he couldn't even be sure that he was investigating a murder.

He suddenly changed tack, reverting to a previous course of questioning.

"Are you sorry about Nurse Pearce's death?"

Again the wide opened eyes, the little *moue* of consideration, the suggestion that it was really rather a silly question.

"Of course." A little pause. "She never did me any harm."

"Did she do anyone any harm?"

"You'd better ask them." Another pause. Perhaps she felt that she had been imprudently foolish and rude. "What harm could Pearce do to anyone?"

It was spoken with no tinge of contempt, almost with disinterest, a mere statement of fact.

"Someone killed her. That doesn't suggest that she was innocuous. Someone must have hated her enough to want her out of the way."

"She could have killed herself. When she swallowed that tube she knew what was coming to her all right. She was terrified. Anyone watching her could see that."

Julia Pardoe was the first student to have mentioned Nurse Pearce's fear. The only other person present to have noticed it had been the General Nursing Council Inspector who, in her statement, had stressed the girl's look of apprehension, almost of endurance. It was interesting and surprising that Nurse Pardoe should have been so perceptive. Dalgliesh said:

"But do you really believe that she put a corrosive poison into the feed herself?"

The blue eyes met his. She gave her little secret smile.

"No. Pearce was always terrified when she had to act as patient. She hated it. She never said anything, but anyone could see what she was feeling. Swallowing that tube must have been particularly bad for her. She told me once that she couldn't bear the thought of a throat examination or operation. She'd had her tonsils out as a child and the surgeon—or it may have been a nurse—was rough with her and hurt her badly. Anyway, it had been a horrible experience and had left her with this phobia about her throat. Of course, she could have explained to Sister Gearing and one of us would have taken her place. She didn't have to act the patient. No one was forcing her. But I suppose Pearce thought it was her duty to go through with it. She was a great one for duty."

So anyone present could have seen what Pearce was feeling. But in fact, only two of them had seen. And one of them had been this apparently insensitive young woman.

Dalgliesh was intrigued, but not particularly surprised, that Nurse Pearce should have chosen to confide in Julia Pardoe. He had met it before, this perverse attraction which the pretty and popular often held for the plain and despised. Sometimes it was even reciprocated; an odd mutual fascination which, he suspected, formed the basis of many friendships and marriages that the world found inexplicable. But if Heather Pearce had been making a pathetic bid for friendship or sympathy by a recital of childhood woes she had been unlucky. Julia Pardoe respected strength, not weakness. She would be impervious to a plea for pity. And yet—who knew?—Pearce might have got something from her. Not friendship, or sympathy, or pity even; but a modicum of understanding.

He said on a sudden impulse:

"I think you probably knew more about Nurse Pearce than anyone else here, probably understood her better. I don't believe her death was suicide, neither do you. I want you to tell me everything about her which would help me to a motive."

There was a second's pause. Was it his imagination or was she really making up her mind to something? Then she said in her high, unemphatic, childish voice:

"I expect she was blackmailing someone. She tried it with me once."

"Tell me about it."

She looked up at him speculatively as if assessing his reliability or wondering whether the story was worth the trouble of telling. Then her lips curved in a little reminiscent smile. She said calmly:

"My boy friend spent a night with me about a year ago. Not here; in the main nurses' home. I unlocked one of the fire escape doors and let him. We did it for a lark really."

"Was he someone from the John Carpendar?"

"Um, um. One of the surgical registrars."

"And how did Heather Pearce find out about it?"

"It was the night before our preliminary—the first examination for State Registration. Pearce always got a stomachache before exams. I suppose she was prowling down the corridor to the loo and saw me letting Nigel in. Or she may have been on her way back to bed and listened at the door. Perhaps she heard us giggling or something. I expect she listened as long as she could. I wonder what she made of it. No one has ever wanted to make love to Pearce so I suppose she got a thrill just out of listening to someone else in bed with a man. Anyway, she tackled me about it next morning and then threatened to tell Matron and have me chucked out of the nurse training school."

She spoke without resentment, almost with a touch of amusement. It hadn't bothered her at the time. It didn't bother her now.

Dalgliesh asked: "And what price was she asking for her silence?"

He had no doubt that, whatever the price, it hadn't been paid.

"She said she hadn't made up her mind about that; she would have to think about it. It would have to be appropriate. You should have seen her face. It was all mottled and red like a disgusted turkey cock. I don't know how I kept a straight face. I pretended to be terribly worried and contrite and asked if we should talk about it that night. That was just to give me time to get in touch with Nigel. He lived with his widowed mother just outside the town. She adores him and I knew she wouldn't make any difficulty about swearing that he spent the night at home. She wouldn't even mind that we'd been together. She thinks that her precious Nigel's entitled to take just what he likes. But I didn't want Pearce to talk before I got that fixed up. When I saw her that evening I told her that both of us would deny the story absolutely and that Nigel would back it up with an alibi. She'd forgotten about his mother. There was something else she'd forgotten too. Nigel is Mr. Courtney-Briggs's nephew. So if she talked, all that would happen would be that Mr. Courtney-Briggs would get her chucked out, not me. Pearce was terribly stupid, really."

"You seem to have coped with admirable efficiency and composure. So you never learned what punishment Pearce had in store for you?"

"Oh yes I did! I let her talk about that before I told her. It was more amusing that way. It wasn't a question of punishment; it was more like blackmail. She wanted to come in with us, be one of my crowd."

"Your crowd?"

"Well, me, Jennifer Blain and Diane Harper really. I was going with Nigel at the time and Diane and Jennifer had his friends. You haven't met Blain; she's one of the students who are off with the flu. Pearce wanted us to fix her up a man for her so that she could make up a fourth."

"Didn't you find that surprising? From what I've heard of her, Heather Pearce wasn't exactly the type to be interested in sex."

"Everyone is interested in sex, in their own way. But Pearce didn't put it like that. She made out that the three of us weren't to be trusted and that we ought to have someone reliable to keep an eye on us. No prizes for guessing who! But I knew what she really wanted. She wanted Tom Mannix. He was the paediatric registrar at the time. He was spotty and rather a drip really, but Pearce fancied him. They both belonged to the hospital Christian Fellowship and Tom was going to be a missionary or something after his two years here were up. He'd have suited Pearce all right, and I daresay I could have made him go out with her once or twice if I'd pressed him. But it wouldn't have done her any good. He didn't want Pearce; he wanted me. Well, you know how it is."

Dalgliesh did know. This, after all, was the commonest, the most banal of personal tragedies. You loved someone. They didn't love you. Worse still, in defiance of their own best interests and to the destruction of your peace, they loved another. What would half the world's poets and novelists do without this universal tragicomedy? But Julia Pardoe was untouched by it. If only, thought Dalgliesh, her voice had held a trace of pity, or even interest! But Pearce's desperate need, the longing for love which had led her to this pathetic attempt at blackmail, provoked in her victim nothing, not even an amused contempt. She couldn't even be bothered to ask him to keep the story a secret. And then, as if reading his thoughts, she told him why.

"I don't mind your knowing about it now. Why should I? After all, Pearce is dead. Fallon too. I mean, with two murders in the place, Matron and the Hospital Management Committee have something more important to worry about than Nigel and me in bed together. But when I think of that night! Honestly, it was hilarious. The bed was far too narrow and it kept creaking and Nigel and I were giggling so much we could hardly.... And then to think of Pearce with one eye to the keyhole!"

And then she laughed. It was a peal of spontaneous and reminiscent joy, innocent and infectious. Looking up at her, Masterson's heavy face coruscated into a wide indulgent grin and, for one extraordinary second, he and Dalgliesh had to restrain themselves from laughing aloud with her.

VII

Dalgliesh hadn't summoned the members of the little group in the library in any particular order and it wasn't with malice aforethought that he had left Sister Gearing to the last. But the long wait had been unkind to her. She had obviously found time, earlier in the morning, to make up her face with lavish care; an instinctive preparation, no doubt, for whatever traumatic encounters the day might bring. But the make-up had worn badly. The mascara had run and was now smudged into the eye shadow, there were beads of sweat along the forehead and a trace of lipstick in the cleft of the chin. Perhaps she had been unconsciously fiddling with her face. Certainly, she was finding it difficult now to keep her hands still. She sat twisting her handkerchief through her fingers and crossing and recrossing her legs in fidgety discomfort. Without waiting for Dalgliesh to speak she broke into a high frenetic chatter.

"You and your sergeant are staying with the Maycrofts at the Falconer's Arms, aren't you? I hope they're making you comfortable. Sheila's a bit of a drag but Bob's good value when you get him on his own."

Dalgliesh had taken very good care not to get Bob on his own. He had chosen the Falconer's Arms because it was small, convenient, quiet, and half empty; it had not taken long to understand why. Group Captain Robert Maycroft and his wife were more concerned to impress visitors with their own gentility than to minister to the comfort of their guests, and Dalgliesh fervently hoped to be out of the place by the end of the week. In the meantime he had no intention of discussing the Maycrofts with Sister Gearing and he guided her politely but firmly towards more relevant subjects.

Unlike the other suspects she found it necessary to waste the first five minutes in expressing her horror at the deaths of the two girls. It had been all too horrible, tragic, awful, ghastly, beastly, unforgettable, inexplicable. The emotion, thought Dalgliesh, was real enough even if its expression wasn't original. The woman was genuinely distressed. He suspected that she was also very frightened.

He took her through the events of Monday, 12th January. She had little new of interest to say and her account tallied with that already on the file. She had woken very late, dressed in a hurry, and had only just managed to get down to the dining-room by eight o'clock. There she had joined Sister Brumfett and Sister Rolfe for breakfast and had first heard from them that Nurse Fallon had been taken ill in the night. Dalgliesh asked her if she remembered which of the Sisters had given her the news.

"Well, I can't say I do really. I think it was Rolfe but I can't be sure. I was in a bit of a tizzy that morning what with one thing and another. It hadn't helped oversleeping like that, and I was naturally a bit nervous about the General Nursing Council inspection. After all, I'm not a qualified Sister Tutor. I was only deputizing for Sister Manning. And it's bad enough taking the first demonstration of a set without Matron and the G.N.C. Inspector, Mr. Courtney-Briggs and Sister Rolfe all sitting there with their beady eyes on every move you make. It struck me that with Fallon absent, there would only be about seven students left in the set. Well, that suited me all right; the fewer the better as far as I was concerned. I only hoped the little beasts would answer up and show some intelligence."

Dalgliesh asked her who had left the dining-room first.

"Brumfett did. Dead keen as usual to get back to her ward, I suppose. I left next. I took my papers through into the conservatory with a cup of coffee and sat down for ten minutes' read. Christine Dakers, Diane Harper and Julia Pardoe were there. Harper and Pardoe were chatting together and Dakers was sitting on her own reading a magazine. I didn't stay long and they were still there when I left. I went up to my room at about half past eight, collecting my post on the way, and then came down again and went straight into the demonstration room just before quarter to nine. The Burt twins were already there finishing their preparations and Goodale arrived almost immediately. The rest of the set came in together at about ten to nine, except Pearce, who didn't arrive until last. There was the usual girlish chatter before we got down to work but I can't remember any of it. The rest you know."

Dalgliesh did know. But although he thought it unlikely that there was anything new to learn from Sister Gearing he took her again through the events of that traumatic demonstration. But she had nothing fresh to reveal. It had all been too awful, terrible, ghastly, frightful, unbelievable. She would never forget it as long as she lived.

Dalgliesh then turned to the death of Fallon. But here Sister Gearing had a surprise for him. She was the first suspect to produce an alibi, or what she obviously hoped was one, and she put it forward with understandable satisfaction. From eight o'clock until after midnight she had been entertaining a friend in her room. She gave Dalgliesh his name with coy reluctance. He was Leonard Morris, the chief pharmacist of the hospital. She had invited him to dinner, had produced a simple meal of spaghetti bolognaise in the Sisters' kitchen on the third floor and had served it in her sitting-room at eight o'clock, shortly after his arrival. They had been together for the whole of the four hours except for the few minutes when she had fetched the supper dish from the kitchen, and for a couple of minutes at about midnight when he had visited the lavatory, and a similar period earlier in the evening when she had left him for the same purpose. Apart from that they had never been out of each other's sight. She added eagerly that Len—Mr. Morris that was—would be only too happy to confirm her story. Len would remember the times perfectly well. Being a pharmacist he was precise and accurate about details. The only difficulty was that he wasn't in the hospital this morning. He had telephoned the pharmacy just before nine to say that he was sick. But he would be back at work tomorrow, she was sure of it. Len hated taking time off.

Dalgliesh asked at what hour he had actually left Nightingale House.

"Well, it couldn't have been long after midnight. I remember that when my clock struck twelve Len said that it was really time he was off. We went out about five minutes later, down the back staircase, the one leading from

Matron's flat. I left the door open: Len collected his bicycle from where he'd left it and I walked with him to the first turn in the path. It wasn't exactly a night for a stroll but we'd still one or two matters about the hospital to discuss— Len lectures in pharmacology to the second-year students—and I thought I could do with a breath of air. Len didn't like to leave me to walk back alone so he came back as far as the door. I suppose it was about twelve fifteen when we finally parted. I came in through Matron's door and locked it behind me. I went straight back to my room, took the supper things into the kitchen to wash them up, went to the bathroom, and was in bed by a quarter to one. I didn't see Fallon all the evening. The next thing I knew was Sister Rolfe dashing in to wake me up with the news that Dakers had found Fallon dead in bed."

"So you went out and returned through Miss Taylor's flat. Was her door left unlocked then?"

"Oh, yes! Matron usually leaves it open when she's away. She knows we find it convenient and more private to use her staircase. After all we're grown women. We're not exactly forbidden to entertain friends in our rooms and it isn't particularly nice to have to show them out through the main house with every little student watching with her eyes out on stalks. Matron's awfully good like that. I think she even leaves her sitting-room unlocked when she's not in Nightingale House. I suppose that's so that Sister Brumfett can use it if she feels inclined. Brumfett, in case you hadn't heard, is Matron's spaniel. Most Matrons keep a little dog you know. Mary Taylor has Brumfett."

The note of bitter cynicism was so unexpected that Masterson's head came up from his note-taking with a jerk and he looked at Sister Gearing as if she were an unpromising candidate who had suddenly revealed unexpected potentialities. But Dalgliesh let it pass. He asked:

"Was Sister Brumfett using Miss Taylor's flat last night?"

"At midnight! Not Brumfett! She goes to bed early unless she's in town gallivanting with Matron. She's usually brewing her last cuppa by ten-fifteen. Anyway, she was called out last night. Mr. Courtney-Briggs rang her to go over to the private ward and receive one of his patients back from the theatre. I thought everyone knew. That was just before twelve."

Dalgliesh asked if Sister Gearing had seen her.

"No, but my friend did. Len, I mean. He popped his head out of the door to see if the coast was clear to go to the loo before we left and saw Brumfett wrapped in her cloak, carrying that old bag of hers, disappearing down the staircase. It was obvious that she was going out, and I guessed that she had been called back to the ward. That's always happening to Brumfett. Mind you, it's partly her own fault. There's such a thing as being too conscientious."

It was not, thought Dalgliesh, a fault to which Sister Gearing was likely to be prone. It was difficult to imagine her tramping through the grounds at midnight in the depth of winter at the casual summons of any surgeon, however eminent. But he felt rather sorry for her. She had given him a depressing glimpse into the stultifying lack of privacy, and of the small pettinesses and subterfuges with which people living in unwelcome proximity try to preserve their own privacy or invade that of others. The thought of a grown man peeping surreptitiously around the door before coming out, of two adult lovers creeping furtively down a back staircase to avoid detection, was grotesque and humiliating. He remembered the Matron's words. "We do get to know things here; there's no real privacy." Even poor Brumfett's choice of nightcap and her usual hour for bed were common knowledge. Small wonder that Nightingale House bred its own brand of neurosis, that Sister

Gearing felt it necessary to justify a walk with her lover in the grounds, their obvious and natural wish to prolong the final good night, with unconvincing twaddle about the need to discuss hospital business. He found it all profoundly depressing and he wasn't sorry when it was time to let her go.

VIII

Dalgliesh rather enjoyed his half hour with the housekeeper, Miss Martha Collins. She was a thin, brown-skinned woman, brittle and nobbly as a dead branch, who looked as if the sap had long since dried in her bones. She gave the appearance of having gradually shrunk in her clothes without having noticed it. Her working overall of thick fawn cotton hung in long creases from her narrow shoulders to mid-calf and was bunched around her waist by a schoolboy's belt of red and blue stripes clasped with a snake buckle. Her stockings were a concertina around her ankles, and either she preferred to wear shoes at least two sizes too large, or her feet were curiously disproportionate to the rest of her body. She had appeared as soon as summoned, had plonked herself down opposite Dalgliesh, her immense feet planted firmly astride, and had eyed him with anticipatory malevolence as if about to interview a particularly recalcitrant housemaid. Throughout the interview she didn't once smile. Admittedly there was nothing in the situation to provoke amusement but she seemed incapable of raising even the briefest smile of formal recognition. But despite these inauspicious beginnings the interview hadn't gone badly. Dalgliesh wondered whether her acidulated tone and perversely unattractive appearance were part of a calculated *persona*. Perhaps some forty years earlier she had decided to become a hospital character, the beloved tyrant of fiction, treating everyone from the matron to the junior maid with equal irreverence, and had found the characterization so successful and satisfying that she had never managed to drop it. She grumbled incessantly but it was without malice, a matter of form. He suspected that, in fact, she enjoyed her work and was neither as unhappy nor discontented as she chose to appear. She would hardly have stayed in the job for forty years if it were as intolerable as she made it sound.

"Milk! Don't talk to me about milk. There's more trouble about milk in this house than about the rest of the catering put together and that's saying something. Fifteen pints a day we're getting through even with half the house down with the flu. Don't ask me where it's all going. I've stopped being responsible for it and so I told Matron. There's a couple of bottles go up first thing each morning to the Sisters' floor so that they can make their own early tea. Two bottles between three I send up. You'd think that'd be enough for everyone. Matron's is separate, of course. She gets a pint and not a drop grudged. But the trouble that milk causes! The first Sister to get at it takes all the cream, I suppose. Not very considerate, and so I told Matron. They're lucky to get a bottle or two of Channel Island milk; no one else in the house does. There's nothing but complaints. Sister Gearing going on because it's too watery for her and Sister Brumfett because it's not all Channel Island and Sister Rolfe wanting it sent up in half-pint bottles which she knows as well as I do you can't get any more. Then there's the milk for the students' early tea and that cocoa and stuff they brew themselves at night. They're supposed to sign for the bottles which they take from the fridge. The stuff isn't grudged, but that's the rule. Well, you take a look at the record book yourself! Nine times out of

ten they can't be troubled. And then there are the empties.
They're supposed to rinse them out and return them to the
kitchen. You wouldn't think that would be too much bother.
Instead they leave the bottles about the house, in their
rooms, in the cupboards, and in the utility room—half-
rinsed too—until the place stinks. My girls have got enough
to do without running around after the students and their
empties, and so I told Matron.

"What do you mean, was I in the kitchen when the Burt
twins took their pint? You know I was. I said so to the other
policeman. Where else would I be at that hour of the day?
I'm always in my kitchen by quarter to seven and it was
nearly three minutes past when the Burt twins came in.
No, I didn't hand the bottle to them. They helped themselves from the fridge. It's not my job to wait hand and foot
on the students and so I told Matron. But there was nothing wrong with that milk when it left my kitchen. It wasn't
delivered until six thirty and I've got enough to do before
breakfast without messing about putting disinfectant into
the milk. Besides, I've got an alibi. I was with Mrs. Muncie
from six forty-five onwards. She's the daily woman who
comes in from the town to lend a hand when I'm short.
You can see her any time you like but I don't suppose you'll
get much out of her. The poor soul hasn't got much
between the ears. Come to think of it, I doubt whether
she'd notice if I spent the whole morning poisoning the
milk. But she was with me for what it's worth. And I was
with her all the time. No popping out every other minute
to the lavatory for me, thank you. I do all that sort of thing
at the proper time.

"The lavatory disinfectant? I thought you'd be asking
about that. I fill up the bottles myself from the big tin they
send over once a week from the main hospital store. It's not
really my job but I don't like to leave it to the housemaids.

They're so careless. They'd only get the stuff slopped all over the lavatory floors. I refilled that bottle in the downstairs W.C. the day before Nurse Pearce died so it must have been nearly full. Some of the students bother to put a little down the bowl when they've finished with the lavatory but most of them don't. You'd think student nurses would be particular about little things like that, but they're no better than other young people. The stuff is mostly used by the maids when they've cleaned the W.C. bowl. All the lavatories get cleaned once a day. I'm very particular about having clean lavatories. The downstairs one was due to be cleaned by Morag Smith after lunch, but Nurse Goodale and Nurse Pardoe noticed that the bottle was missing before then. I'm told that the other policeman found it empty among the bushes at the back of the house. And who put it there, I'd like to know?

"No, you can't see Morag Smith. Didn't they tell you? She's on a day's leave. She went off after tea yesterday, lucky for her. They can't pin this latest spot of bother on Morag. No. I don't know whether she went home. I didn't inquire. The maids are enough responsibility when they're under my nose in Nightingale House. I don't concern myself with what they do on their days off. Just as well from some of the things I hear. She'll be back late tonight more than likely and Matron has left instructions that she's to move to the Resident Staff Hostel. This place is too dangerous for us now apparently. Well, no one's shifting me. I don't know how I'm supposed to manage in the mornings if Morag doesn't show her face until just before breakfast. I can't control my staff if they're not under my eyes and so I told Matron. Not that Morag's much bother. She's as obstinate as they come but she's not a bad worker once you get her started. And if they try to tell you that Morag Smith interfered with the dripfeed, don't you believe them. The girl may be a bit dense but she's not a raving lunatic. I'll not have my staff slandered without cause.

"And now I'll tell you something, Mr. Detective." She raised her thin rump from her chair, leaned forward across the desk and fixed Dalgliesh with her beady eyes. He willed himself to meet them without blinking and they stared at each other like a couple of wrestlers before a bout.

"Yes, Miss Collins?"

She stuck out a lean nodular finger and prodded him sharply in the chest. Dalgliesh winced.

"No one had any right to take that bottle out of the lavatory without my permission or to use it for any other purpose except for cleaning the lavatory bowl. Nobody!"

It was apparent where in Miss Collins's eyes the full enormity of the crime had lain.

IX

At twenty minutes to one, Mr. Courtney-Briggs appeared. He knocked briskly at the door, came in without waiting for an invitation, and said curtly:

"I can give you a quarter of an hour now, Dalgliesh, if it's convenient."

His tone assumed that it would be. Dalgliesh assented and indicated the chair. The surgeon looked across at Sergeant Masterson sitting impassively with his notebook at the ready, hesitated, then turned the chair so that its back was to the sergeant. Then he seated himself and slipped his hand into his waistcoat pocket. The cigarette case he drew out was of finely tooled gold and so slim that it looked hardly functional. He offered a cigarette to Dalgliesh but not to Masterson and seemed neither surprised nor particularly interested at the Superintendent's refusal.

He lit his own. The hands cupped around the lighter were large, square-fingered; not the sensitive hands of a fictional surgeon, but strong carpenter's hands, beautifully cared for.

Dalgliesh, overtly busy with his papers, observed the man. He was big but not yet fat. The formal suit fitted him almost too well, containing a sleek well-fed body and enhancing the effect of latent power only imperfectly controlled. He could still be called handsome. His long hair brushed straight back from a high forehead was strong and dark, except for one single white strand. Dalgliesh wondered whether it were bleached. His eyes were too small for the large, rather florid face, but were well shaped and set wide apart. They gave nothing away.

Dalgliesh knew that it had been Mr. Courtney-Briggs who had been mainly responsible for the Chief Constable calling in the Yard. From Inspector Bailey's somewhat bitter account during their brief colloquy when Dalgliesh had taken over the case, it was easy to understand why. The surgeon had made himself a nuisance from the beginning and his motives, if they were capable of rational explanation, raised interesting speculations. At first he had asserted vigorously that Nurse Pearce had obviously been murdered, that it was unthinkable that anyone connected with the hospital could have been concerned with the crime, and that the local police had a duty to proceed on this assumption and to find and arrest the killer with a minimum of delay. When their investigations yielded no immediate results, he became restive. He was a man used to exercising power and he was certainly not without it. There were eminent people in London who owed their lives to him and some of them had considerable nuisance value. Telephone calls, some tactful and half-apologetic, others frankly critical, were made both to the Chief Constable and to the Yard. As the

Inspector in charge of the investigation became more convinced that Nurse Pearce's death was the result of a practical joke which had tragically misfired, so Mr. Courtney-Briggs and his co-agitators proclaimed more loudly that she had been murdered, and pressed more strongly for the case to be handed over to the Yard. And then Nurse Fallon had been found dead. It could be expected that the local C.I.D. would be galvanized into fresh activity, that the diffuse light which had played over the first crime would sharpen and focus on this second death. And it was at this moment that Mr. Courtney-Briggs had chosen to telephone the Chief Constable to announce that no further activity was necessary, that it was obvious to him that Nurse Fallon had committed suicide, that this could only have been in remorse at the tragic result of the practical joke which had killed her colleague, and that it was now in the hospital's interest to close the case with the minimum of fuss before nurse recruitment and indeed the whole future of the hospital was jeopardized. The police are not unused to these sudden quirks of temperament, which is not to say that they welcome them. Dalgliesh thought that it must have been with considerable satisfaction that the Chief Constable decided that, in all the circumstances, it would be prudent to call in the Yard to investigate both the deaths.

During the week following Nurse Pearce's death, Courtney-Briggs had even rung up Dalgliesh, who had been his patient three years earlier. It had been a case of uncomplicated appendicitis, and although Dalgliesh's vanity was gratified by the smallness and neatness of the resultant scar, he felt that the surgeon's expertise had been adequately rewarded at the time. He had certainly no wish to be used for Courtney-Briggs's private ends. The telephone call had been embarrassing and he had resented it. He was interested to see that the surgeon had apparently decided that this was an incident it would be advisable for both of them to forget.

Without lifting his eyes from his papers, Dalgliesh said:

"I understand that you take the view that Miss Fallon killed herself?"

"Of course. It's the obvious explanation. You're not suggesting that someone else put stuff into her whisky? Why should they?"

"There's the problem, isn't there, of the missing container? That is, if it were poison. We shan't know until we get the autopsy report."

"What problem? There's no problem. The beaker was opaque, heat insulated. She could have put the stuff into it earlier that evening. No one would have noticed. Or she could have carried a powder in a slip of paper and flushed it down the lavatory. The container's no problem. Incidentally, it wasn't a corrosive this time. That much was evident when I saw the body."

"Were you the first doctor on the scene?"

"No. I wasn't in the hospital when they found her. Dr. Snelling saw her. He's the general physician who looks after the nurses here. He realized at once that there was nothing to be done. I went across to have a look at the body as soon as I heard the news. I arrived at the hospital just before nine. By then the police had arrived, of course. The local people, I mean. I can't think why they weren't left to get on with it. I rang the Chief Constable to make my views known. Incidentally, Miles Honeyman tells me that she died about midnight. I saw him just as he was leaving. We were at medical school together."

"So I understand."

"You were wise to call him in. I gather that he's generally considered to be the best."

He spoke complacently, success condescending to recognize success. His criteria were hardly subtle, thought Dalgliesh. Money, prestige, public recognition, power. Yes, Courtney-Briggs would always demand the best for himself, confident of his ability to pay for it.

Dalgliesh said: "She was pregnant. Did you know?"

"So Honeyman told me. No, I didn't know. These things happen, even today when birth control is reliable and easily obtained. But I should have expected a girl of her intelligence to be on the Pill."

Dalgliesh remembered the scene that morning in the library when Mr. Courtney-Briggs had known the girl's age to a day. He asked his next question without apology.

"Did you know her well?"

The implication was plain and the surgeon did not reply for a moment. Dalgliesh had not expected him to bluster or threaten and he did neither. There was an increased respect in the sharp look which he gave his interrogator.

"For a time, yes." He paused. "You could say I knew her intimately."

"Was she your mistress?"

Courtney-Briggs looked at him, impassive, considering. Then he said:

"That's putting it rather formally. We slept together fairly regularly during her first six months here. Are you objecting?"

"It's hardly for me to object if she didn't. Presumably she was willing?"

"You could say that."

"When did it end?"

"I thought I told you. It lasted until the end of her first year. That's a year and a half ago."

"Did you quarrel?"

"No. She decided she'd, shall we say, exhausted the possibilities. Some women like variety. I do myself. I wouldn't have taken her on if I'd thought she was the type to make trouble. And don't get me wrong. I don't make it a practice to sleep with student nurses. I'm reasonably fastidious."

"Wasn't it difficult to keep the affair secret? There's very little privacy in a hospital."

"You have romantic ideas, Superintendent. We didn't kiss and cuddle in the sluice room. When I said I slept with her I meant just that. I don't use euphemisms for sex. She came to my Wimpole Street flat when she had a night off and we slept there. I haven't a resident man there and my house is near Selborne. The porter at Wimpole Street must have known, but he can keep his mouth shut. There wouldn't be many tenants left in the building if he couldn't. There wasn't any risk, provided that she didn't talk, and she wasn't a talker. Not that I would have minded particularly. There are certain areas of private behaviour in which I do as I like. You too no doubt."

"So it wasn't your child?"

"No. I'm not careless. Besides the affair was over. But if it hadn't been I should hardly have killed her. That kind of solution causes more embarrassment than it prevents."

Dalgliesh asked: "What would you have done?"

"That would have depended on the circumstances. I should have had to be sure it was my child. But this particular problem is hardly uncommon and not insoluble if the woman is reasonable."

"I've been told that Miss Fallon planned to get an abortion. Did she approach you?"

"No."

"She might have done?"

"Certainly she might have done. But she didn't."

"Would you have helped her if she had?"

The surgeon looked at him.

"That question is hardly within your terms of reference, I should have thought."

Dalgliesh said: "That's for me to judge. The girl was pregnant; she apparently intended to get an abortion; she told a friend that she knew someone who would help her. I'm naturally interested to know who she had in mind."

"You know the law. I'm a surgeon not a gynaecologist. I prefer to stick to my own speciality and to practise it legally."

"But there are other kinds of help. Referring her to an appropriate consultant, helping with the fees."

A girl with £16,000 to bequeath was hardly likely to want help with the fees for an abortion. But Miss Goodale's legacy was not being made public and Dalgliesh was interested to learn whether Courtney-Briggs knew about Fallon's capital. But the surgeon gave no sign.

"Well, she didn't come to me. She may have had me in mind but she didn't come. And if she had, I wouldn't have helped. I make it my business to assume my own responsibilities; but I don't take on other people's. If she chose to look elsewhere for her satisfaction she could look elsewhere for her help. I didn't impregnate her. Someone did. Let him look after her."

"That would have been your response?"

"Certainly it would. And rightly."

His voice held a note of grim satisfaction. Looking at him, Dalgliesh saw that his face was flushed. The man was controlling his emotion with difficulty. And Dalgliesh had little doubt of the nature of that emotion. It was hate. He went on with his interrogation.

"Were you in the hospital last night?"

"Yes. I was called to operate on an emergency. One of my patients relapsed. It wasn't altogether unexpected, but very serious. I finished operating at eleven forty-five p.m. The time will be noted in the theatre register. Then I rang Sister Brumfett at Nightingale House to ask her to be good enough to return to her ward for an hour or so. My patient was a private patient. After that I rang my home to say that I would be returning that night instead of sleeping here in the medical officers' quarters as I do occasionally after a late operation. I left the main building shortly after twelve. I intended driving out by the Winchester Road gate. I have my own key. However, it was a wild night, as you probably noticed, and I discovered that there was an elm down over the path. I was lucky not to drive into it. I got out of the car and knotted my white silk scarf round one of the branches to warn anyone else who might be driving that way. It wasn't likely that anyone would, but the tree was an obvious danger and there was no chance of getting it moved before daylight. I reversed the car and left by the main entrance, reporting the fallen tree to the gate porter on my way out."

"Did you notice the time then?"

"I didn't. He may have done. But, at a guess, it was probably about twelve fifteen, maybe later. I wasted a bit of time at the tree."

"You would have had to drive past Nightingale House to reach the back gate. You didn't go in?"

"I had no reason to go in and I didn't go in, either to poison Nurse Fallon or for any other reason."

"And you saw no one in the grounds?"

"After midnight and in the middle of a storm? No, I saw no one."

Dalgliesh switched his questioning.

"You saw Nurse Pearce die, of course. I suppose there was never a real chance of saving her?"

"Never, I should say. I took pretty vigorous measures, but it isn't easy when you don't know what you're treating."

"But you knew it was poison?"

"Pretty soon. Yes. But I didn't know what. Not that it would have made any difference. You've seen the post-mortem report. You knew what that stuff did to her."

Dalgliesh asked: "You were in Nightingale House from eight o'clock onwards on the morning that she died?"

"You know perfectly well that I was if, as I assume, you've taken the trouble to read my original statement. I arrived in Nightingale House shortly after eight. My contract here is for six notional halfdays a week; I'm in the hospital all day on Monday, Thursday and Friday; but it's not uncommon for me to be called in to operate on an emergency, particularly if it's a private patient, and I occasionally do a Saturday morning session in the theatre if the lists are long. I'd been called out shortly after eleven o'clock on Sunday night for an emergency appendicectomy—one of my private patients—and it was convenient to spend the night in the medical officers' quarters."

"Which are where?"

"In that deplorably designed new building near the out-patients' department. They serve breakfast at the ungodly hour of seven thirty."

"You were here rather early surely. The demonstration wasn't due to begin until nine."

"I wasn't here merely for the demonstration, Superintendent. You're really rather ignorant of hospitals, aren't you? The Senior Consultant Surgeon doesn't normally attend nurse training sessions unless he's actually lecturing the students. I only attended on January 12th because the G.N.C. Inspector was to be there and I'm Vice-Chairman of the Nurse Education Committee. It was a courtesy to Miss Beale to be here to meet her. I came in early because I wanted to work on some clinical notes which I had left in Sister Rolfe's office after a previous lecture. I also wanted to have a chat with Matron before the inspection began to be sure that I was there in time to receive Miss Beale. I went up to Matron's flat at eight thirty-five and found her finishing breakfast. And, if you're thinking that I could have put the corrosive in the milk bottle any time between eight and eight thirty-five, you're perfectly right. As it happens, I didn't."

He looked at his watch.

"And now if there's nothing else you need to ask I must get my lunch. I've another out-patients' session this afternoon and time's pressing. If it's really necessary, I can probably give you a few more minutes before I leave but I hope it won't be. I've already signed one statement about Pearce's death and I've nothing to add or to alter. I didn't see Fallon yesterday. I didn't even know she was discharged from the sick-bay. She wasn't carrying my child, and even if she had been, I shouldn't have been foolish enough to kill her. Incidentally, what I told you about our previous relationship was naturally in confidence."

He looked across meaningly at Sergeant Masterson.

"Not that I care whether it's made public. But, after all, the girl is dead. We may as well try to protect her reputation."

Dalgliesh found it difficult to believe that Mr. Courtney-Briggs was interested in anyone's reputation but his own. But, gravely, he gave the necessary assurance. He saw the surgeon leave without regret. An egotistical bastard whom it was agreeable, if childish, to provoke. But a murderer? He had the hubris, the nerve and the egotism of a killer. More to the point, he had had the opportunity. And the motive? Hadn't it been a little disingenuous of him to have confessed so readily to his relationship with Josephine Fallon? Admittedly he couldn't have hoped to keep his secret for long; a hospital was hardly the most discreet of institutions. Had he been making a virtue of necessity, ensuring that

Dalgliesh heard the version of the affair before the inevitable gossip reached his ears? Or had it been merely the candour of conceit, the sexual vanity of a man who wouldn't trouble to conceal any exploit which proclaimed his attraction and virility?

Putting his papers together, Dalgliesh became aware that he was hungry. He had made an early start to the day and it had been a long morning. It was time to turn his mind from Stephen Courtney-Briggs and for him and Masterson to think about luncheon.

CHAPTER FIVE

Table Talk

I

THE RESIDENT SISTERS and students from Nightingale House took only their breakfast and afternoon tea in the dining-room at the school. For their main midday and evening meal they joined the rest of the staff in the hospital cafeteria where all but the consultants ate in institutionalized and noisy proximity. The food was invariably nourishing, adequately cooked, and as varied as was compatible with the need to satisfy the differing tastes of several hundred people, avoid outraging their religious or dietary susceptibilities, and keep within the catering officer's budget. The principles governing the menu planning were invariable. Liver and kidneys were never served on days when the urinary surgeon operated, and the nurses were not faced with the same menu as that which they had just served to the patients.

The cafeteria system had been introduced at the John Carpendar hospital against strong opposition from all grades of staff. Eight years ago there had been separate dining-rooms for the Sisters and nurses, one for the administrative and lay professional staff, and a canteen for the porters and artisans. The arrangements had suited everyone as making a proper distinction between grades and ensuring that people ate in reasonable quietness and in the company of those with whom they preferred to spend their lunch break. But now only the senior medical staff enjoyed the peace and privacy of their own dining-room. This privilege, jealously defended, was under perpetual attack from Ministry auditors, Government catering advisers and work study experts who, armed with costing statistics, had no difficulty in proving that the system was uneconomical. But so far the doctors had won. Their strongest argument was their need to discuss the patients in privacy. This suggestion that they never stopped working, even for meals, was greeted with some scepticism but was difficult to refute. The need to keep the patients' affairs confidential touched on that area of patient-doctor relationship which the doctors were always quick to exploit. Before this mystique even the Treasury auditors were powerless to prevail. Furthermore, they had had the support of Matron. Miss Taylor had made it known that she considered it eminently reasonable that the senior medical staff should continue to have their own dining-room. And Miss Taylor's influence over the Chairman of the Hospital Management Committee was so obvious and of such long standing that it had almost ceased to excite comment. Sir Marcus Cohen was a wealthy and personable widower and the only surprise now was that he and Matron hadn't married. This, it was generally accepted, was either because Sir Marcus, an acknowledged leader of the country's Jewish community, chose not to marry outside his faith or because Miss Taylor, wedded to her vocation, chose not to marry at all.

But the extent of Miss Taylor's influence over the Chairman and thus over the Hospital Management Committee was beyond speculation. It was known to be particularly irritating to Mr. Courtney-Briggs since it considerably diminished his own. But in the matter of the consultants' dining-room it had been exercised in his favour and had proved decisive.

But if the rest of the staff had been forced into proximity they had not been forced into intimacy. The hierarchy was still apparent. The immense dining-room had been divided into smaller dining areas separated from each other by screens of lattice work and troughs of plants, and in each of these alcoves the atmosphere of a private dining-room was recreated.

Sister Rolfe helped herself to plaice and chips, carried her tray to the table which, for the past eight years, she had shared with Sister Brumfett and Sister Gearing, and looked around at the denizens of this strange world. In the alcove nearest the door were the laboratory technicians in their stained overalls, noisily animated. Next to them was old Fleming, the out-patient pharmacist, rolling bread pellets like pills in his nicotine-stained fingers. At the next table were four of the medical stenographers in their blue working overalls. Miss Wright, the senior secretary, who had been at the John Carpendar for twenty years, was eating with furtive speed as she always did, avid to get back to her typewriter. Behind the adjacent screen was a little clutch of the lay professional staff—Miss Bunyon the head radiographer, Mrs. Nethern, the head medical social worker and two of the physiotherapists, carefully preserving their status by an air of calm unhurried efficiency, an apparent total disinterest in the food they were eating and the choice of a table as far removed as possible from that of the junior clerical staff.

And what were they all thinking about? Fallon probably. There couldn't be anyone in the hospital from the consultants to the ward maids who didn't know by now that a second Nightingale student had died in mysterious circumstances and that Scotland Yard had been called in.

Fallon's death was probably the subject of gossip at most of the tables this morning. But it didn't prevent people from eating their lunch or from getting on with their job. There was so much to do; there were so many other pressing concerns; there was even so much fresh gossip. It wasn't just that life had to go on; in hospital that cliché had particular relevance. Life did go on, carried forward by the imperative momentum of birth and death. New booked admissions came in; ambulances daily disgorged the emergencies; operation lists were posted; the dead were laid out and the healed discharged. Death, even sudden and unexpected death, was more familiar to these young fresh-faced students than it was to even the most experienced senior detective. And there was a limit to its power to shock. You either came to terms with death in your first year, or you gave up being a nurse. But murder? That was different. Even in this violent world, murder still held its macabre and primitive power to shock. But how many people in Nightingale House really believed that Pearce and Fallon had been murdered? It would take more than the presence of the Yard's wonder boy and his retinue to give credence to such an extraordinary idea. There were too many other possible explanations, all of them simpler and more believable than murder. Dalgliesh might believe as he chose; proving it would be another matter.

Sister Rolfe bent her head and began unenthusiastically to dissect her plaice. She felt no particular hunger. The strong smell of food was heavy on the air, stifling appetite. The noise of the cafeteria beat against her ears. It was ceaseless and inescapable, a confused continuum of discord in which individual sounds were scarcely distinguishable.

Next to her, her cloak folded neatly at the back of her chair and the shapeless tapestry bag which accompanied her everywhere dumped at her feet, Sister Brumfett was eating steamed cod and parsley sauce with belligerent intensity as if she resented the need to eat and was venting her irritation on the food. Sister Brumfett invariably chose steamed fish; and Sister Rolfe felt suddenly that she couldn't face another lunch hour of watching Brumfett eat cod.

She reminded herself that there was no reason why she should. There was nothing to prevent her sitting someplace else, nothing except this petrification of the will which made the simple act of carrying her tray three feet to a different table seem impossibly cataclysmic and irrevocable. On her left, Sister Gearing toyed with her braised beef, and chopped her wedge of cabbage into neat squares. When she actually began to eat she would shove the feed in avidly like a greedy schoolgirl. But always there were these finicky and salivatory preliminaries. Sister Rolfe wondered how many times she had resisted the urge to say, "For God's sake Gearing, stop messing about and eat it!" One day, no doubt, she would say it. And another middle-aged and unlikeable Sister would be pronounced "getting very difficult. It's probably her age."

She had considered living out of the hospital. It was permissible and she could afford it. The purchase of a flat or a small house would be the best investment for her retirement. But Julia Pardoe had disposed of that idea in a few half-interested, destructive comments dropped like cold pebbles into the deep pool of her hopes and plans. Sister Rolfe could still hear that high, childish voice.

"Live out. Why should you want to do that? We shouldn't see so much of each other."

"But we should, Julia. And in much greater privacy and without all this risk and deceit. It would be a comfortable and agreeable little house. You'd like it."

"It wouldn't be as easy as slipping upstairs to see you when I feel like it."

When she felt like it? Felt like what? Sister Rolfe had desperately fought off the question she never dared to let herself ask.

She knew the nature of her dilemma. It wasn't, after all, peculiar to herself. In any relationship there was one who loved and one who permitted himself or herself to be loved. This was merely to state the brutal economics of desire; from each according to his ability, to each according to his need. But was it selfish or presumptuous to hope that the one who took knew the value of the gift; that she wasn't wasting love on a promiscuous and perfidious little cheat who took her pleasure wherever she chose to find it? She had said:

"You could probably come twice or three times a week, perhaps more often. I wouldn't move far."

"Oh, I don't see how I could manage that. I don't see why you want the work and bother of a house. You're all right here."

Sister Rolfe thought: "But I'm not all right here. This place is souring me. It isn't only the long-stay patients who become institutionalized. It's happening to me. I dislike and despise most of the people I'm required to work with. Even the job is losing its hold. The students get more stupid and worse educated with every intake. I'm not even sure any more of the value of what I'm supposed to be doing."

There was a crash near the counter. One of the maids had dropped a tray of used crockery. Looking instinctively across, Sister Rolfe saw that the detective had just come in and taken up his tray at the end of the line. She watched the tall figure, disregarded by the chattering queue of nurses, as he began to move slowly down the line between a white-coated houseman and a pupil midwife, helping himself to roll and butter, waiting for the girl to hand out his choice of main course. She was surprised to see him there. It had never occurred to her that he would eat in the hospital dining-hall or that he would be on his own. Her eyes followed him as he reached the end of the line, handed over his meal ticket and turned to look for a vacant seat. He seemed utterly at ease and almost oblivious of the alien world around him. She thought that he was probably a man who could never imagine himself at a disadvantage in any company since he was secure in his private world, possessed of that core of inner self-esteem which is the basis of happiness. She wondered what kind of a world his was, then bent her head to her plate irritated at this unusual interest he aroused in her. Probably he would be thought handsome by most women, with that lean bony face, at once arrogant and sensitive. It was probably one of his professional assets, and being a man he would make the most of it. No doubt it was one of the reasons why he had been given this case. If dull Bill Bailey could make nothing of it, let the Yard's wonder boy take over. With a house full of women and three middle-aged spinsters as his chief suspects, no doubt he fancied his chances. Well, good luck to him!

But she was not the only one at the table to notice his arrival. She felt rather than saw Sister Gearing stiffen and a second later heard her say:

"Well, well. The handsome sleuth! He'd better feed with us or he may find himself in a gaggle of students. Someone should have told the poor man how the system works."

And now, thought Sister Rolfe, she'll give him one of her street corner come-hither looks and we shall be burdened with him for the rest of the meal. The look was given and the invitation not refused. Dalgliesh, carrying his tray nonchalantly and apparently completely at ease, threaded his way across the room and came up to their table. Sister Gearing said:

"What have you done with that handsome sergeant of yours? I thought policemen went about in pairs like nuns."

"My handsome sergeant is studying reports and lunching on sandwiches and beer in the office while I enjoy the fruits of seniority with you. Is this chair taken?"

Sister Gearing moved her own chair closer to Sister Brumfett and smiled up at him:

"It is now."

II

Dalgliesh sat down, well aware that Sister Gearing wanted him, that Sister Rolfe didn't, and that Sister Brumfett, who had acknowledged his arrival with a brief nod, didn't care whether he joined them or not. Sister Rolfe looked across at him unsmilingly and said to Sister Gearing:

"Don't imagine Mr. Dalgliesh is sharing our table for the sake of your *beaux yeux*. The Superintendent plans to take in information with his braised beef."

Sister Gearing giggled: "My dear, it's no use warning me! I couldn't keep a thing to myself if a really attractive man set his mind to wangle it out of me. It would be quite useless for me to commit a murder. I haven't the brain for it. Not that I think for one moment that anyone has—committed murder I mean. Anyway, let's leave the grisly subject during lunch. I've had my grilling, haven't I, Superintendent?"

Dalgliesh disposed his cutlery around the plate of braised beef and tilting back his chair to save himself the trouble of rising, added his used tray to the stack on the nearby stand. He said:

"People here seem to be taking Nurse Fallon's death calmly enough."

Sister Rolfe shrugged: "Did you expect them to be wearing black arm bands, talking in whispers, and refusing their lunch? The job goes on. Anyway, only a few will have known her personally, and still fewer knew Pearce."

"Or liked her apparently," said Dalgliesh.

"No, I don't think they did on the whole. She was too self-righteous, too religious."

"If you can call it religious," said Sister Gearing.

"It wasn't my idea of religion. *Nil nisi* and all that, but the girl was just a prig. She always seemed to be a damn sight more concerned with other people's shortcomings than she was with her own. That's why the other kids didn't like her. They respect genuine religious conviction. Most people do, I find. But they didn't like being spied on."

"Did she spy on them?" asked Dalgliesh.

Sister Gearing seemed half to regret what she had said.

"Perhaps that's putting it a bit strongly. But if anything went wrong in the set you can bet Nurse Pearce knew all about it. And she usually managed to bring it to the notice of authority. Always with the best motives, no doubt."

Sister Rolfe said drily: "She had an unfortunate habit of interfering with other people for their own good. It doesn't make for popularity."

Sister Gearing pushed her plate to one side, drew a bowl of plums and custard towards her and began to extract the stones from the fruit as carefully as if it were a surgical operation. She said:

"She wasn't a bad nurse, though. You could rely on Pearce. And the patients seemed to like her. I suppose they found that holier than thou attitude reassuring."

Sister Brumfett looked up from her plate and spoke for the first time.

"You're not in a position to give an opinion on whether she was a good nurse. Nor is Rolfe. You only see the girls in the training school. I see them on the wards."

"I see them on the wards too. I'm the clinical instructor remember. It's my job to teach them on the ward."

Sister Brumfett was unrepentant.

"Any student teaching that's done on my ward is done by me, as you know very well. Other ward Sisters can welcome the clinical instructor if they like. But on the private ward I do the teaching. And I prefer it that way when I see some of the extraordinary ideas you seem to put into their heads. And, by the way, I happen to know—Pearce told me, as a matter of fact—that you visited my ward when I was off duty on 7th January and conducted a teaching session. In future, please consult me before using my patients as clinical material."

Sister Gearing flushed. She tried to laugh but her amusement sounded artificial. She glanced across at Sister Rolfe as if enlisting her aid but Sister Rolfe kept her eyes firmly on her plate. Then, belligerently and rather like a child determined to have the last word, she said with apparent irrelevance:

"Something happened to upset Pearce while she was on your ward."

Sister Brumfett's sharp little eyes glared up at her.

"On my ward? Nothing upset her on my ward!"

The sturdy assertion conveyed unmistakably that no nurse worthy of the name could be upset by anything that happened on the private ward; that upsetting things just weren't permitted when Sister Brumfett was in charge.

Sister Gearing shrugged.

"Well, something upset her. It could have been something totally unconnected with the hospital, I suppose, but one never quite believes that poor Pearce had any real life outside these walls. It was the Wednesday of the week before this block went into school. I visited the chapel just after five o'clock to do the flowers—that's how I remember which day it was—and she was sitting there alone. Not kneeling or praying, just sitting. Well, I did what I had to do and then went out without speaking to her. After all, the chapel's open for rest and meditation and if one of the students wants to meditate that's all right by me. But when I went back nearly three hours later because I'd left my scissors in the sacristy she was still there, sitting perfectly still and in the same seat. Well, meditation's all very well, but four hours is a bit excessive. I don't think that the kid could have had any supper. She looked pretty pale too, so I went up to her and asked her if she was all right, if there was anything I could do for her. She didn't even look at me as she replied. She said: 'No thank you, Sister. There was something troubling me which I had to think over very carefully. I did come here for help but not from you.' "

For the first time during the meal Sister Rolfe sounded amused.

She said: "Caustic little beast! Meaning, I suppose, that she'd come to consult a higher power than the clinical instructor."

"Meaning mind your own business. So I did."

Sister Brumfett said, as if feeling that her colleague's presence at a place of worship needed some explanation:

"Sister Gearing is very good at arranging flowers. That's why Matron asked her to look after the chapel. She sees to the flowers every Wednesday and Saturday. And she does very charming arrangements for the Annual Sisters' Dinner." Sister Gearing stared at her for a second and then laughed.

"Oh, little Mavis isn't just a pretty face. But thanks for the compliment."

A silence fell. Dalgliesh addressed himself to his braised beef. He wasn't disconcerted by the lack of conversation and had no intention of helping them out by introducing a fresh subject. But Sister Gearing seemed to feel that silence was reprehensible in the presence of a stranger. She said brightly:

"I see from the minutes that the Hospital Management Committee have agreed to introduce the Salmon Committee proposals. Better late than never. I suppose that means that Matron will be head of the nursing services over all the hospitals in the group. Chief Nursing Officer! It'll be a big thing for her, but I wonder how C.B. will take it. If he had his way, Matron would be given less authority not more. She's a big enough thorn in his flesh as it is."

Sister Brumfett said: "It's time something was done to wake up the psychiatric hospital and the geriatric units. But I don't know why they want to change the title. If Matron was good enough for Florence Nightingale it's good enough for Mary Taylor. I don't suppose she particularly wants to be called Chief Nursing Officer. It sounds like an army rank. Ridiculous."

Sister Rolfe shrugged her thin shoulders.

"Don't expect me to get enthusiastic about the Salmon Report. I'm beginning to wonder what's happening to nursing. Every report and recommendation seems to take us further away from the bedside. We have dieticians to see to the feeding, physiotherapists to exercise the patients, medical social workers to listen to their troubles, ward orderlies to make the beds, laboratory technicians to take blood, ward receptionists to arrange the flowers and interview the relatives, operating theatre technicians to hand the surgeon the instruments. If we're not careful nursing will become a residual skill, the job which is left when all the technicians have had their turn. And now we have the

Salmon Report with all its talk of first, second and third tiers of management. Management for what? There's too much technical jargon. Ask yourself what is the function of the nurse today. What exactly are we trying to teach these girls?"

Sister Brumfett said: "To obey orders implicitly and be loyal to their superiors. Obedience and loyalty. Teach the students those and you've got a good nurse."

She sliced a potato in two with such viciousness that the knife rasped the plate. Sister Gearing laughed.

"You're twenty years out of date, Brumfett. That was good enough for our generation, but these kids ask whether the orders are reasonable before they start obeying and what their superiors have done to deserve their respect. A good thing too on the whole. How on earth do you expect to attract intelligent girls into nursing if you treat them like morons? We ought to encourage them to question established procedures, even to answer back occasionally."

Sister Brumfett looked as if she, for one, would willingly dispense with intelligence if its manifestations were so disagreeable.

"Intelligence isn't the only thing. That's the trouble nowadays. People think it is."

Sister Rolfe said: "Give me an intelligent girl and I'll make a good nurse of her whether she thinks she has a vocation or not. You can have the stupid ones. They may minister to your ego but they'll never make good professional women." She looked at Sister Brumfett as she spoke and the undertone of contempt was unmistakable. Dalgliesh dropped his eyes to his plate and pretended more interest than he could feel in the careful separation of meat from fat and gristle. Sister Brumfett reacted predictably:

"Professional women! We're talking about nurses. A good nurse thinks of herself as a nurse first and last. Of course she's a professional woman! I thought we'd all accepted that by now. But there's too much thinking and talking of status nowadays. The important thing is to get on with the job."

"But what job exactly? Isn't that precisely what we're asking ourselves?"

"You may be. I'm perfectly clear what I'm doing. Which, at the moment, is coping with a very sick ward."

She pushed her plate to one side, flicked her cloak around her shoulders with brisk expertise, gave them a valedictory nod which was as much a warning as a good-bye, and strutted out of the dining-room with her brisk ploughman's waddle, the tapestry bag swinging at her side. Sister Gearing laughed and watched her go.

"Poor old Brum! According to her, she's always got a very sick ward."

Sister Rolfe said drily: "She invariably has."

III

They finished the meal almost in silence. Then Sister Gearing left, first murmuring something about a clinical teaching session on the E.N.T. ward. Dalgliesh found himself walking back to Nightingale House with Sister Rolfe. They left the dining-room together and he retrieved his coat from the rack. They then passed down a long cor-ridor and through the out-patients' department. It had obviously only recently been opened and the furniture and decoration were still bright and new. The large waiting-hall with its groups of Formica-topped tables and easy chairs, its troughs of pot plants and unremarkable pictures was cheer-ful enough, but Dalgliesh had no wish to linger. He had the healthy man's dislike and disgust of hospitals, founded partly on fear and partly on repugnance, and he found this atmosphere of determined cheerfulness and spurious normality unconvincing and frightening. The smell of disinfectant, which to Miss Beale was the elixir of life, infected him with the gloomier intimations of mortality. He did not think that he feared death. He had come close to it once or twice in his career and it had not unduly dismayed him. But he did grievously fear old age, mortal illness and disablement. He dreaded the loss of independence, the indignities of senility, the yielding up of privacy, the abomination of pain, the glimpses of patient compassion in the faces of friends who knew that their indulgences would not be claimed for long. These things might have to be faced in time unless death took him quickly and easily. Well, he would face them. He was not arrogant enough to suppose himself secure from the lot of other men. But in the meantime, he preferred not to be reminded.

The out-patients' department was next to the casualty department entrance and as they passed it a stretcher was wheeled in. The patient was an emaciated old man; his moist lips spewed feebly above the rim of a vomit bowl, his immense eyes rolled uncomprehendingly in the skull-like head. Dalgliesh became aware that Sister Rolfe was looking at him. He turned his head in time to catch her glance of speculation and, he thought, contempt.

"You don't like this place, do you?" she asked.

"I'm not very happy in it, certainly."

"Neither am I at present, but I suspect for very different reasons."

They walked on for a minute in silence. Then Dalgliesh asked if Leonard Morris lunched in the staff dining-room when he was in the hospital.

"Not often. I believe he brings sandwiches and eats them in the pharmacy office. He prefers his own company."

"Or that of Sister Gearing?"

She laughed contemptuously.

"Oh, you've got on to that have you? But of course! She was entertaining him last night, I hear. Either the food or the subsequent activity seems to have been rather more than the little man could take. What thorough little scavengers the police are! It must be a strange job, sniffing around for evil like a dog round trees."

"Isn't evil a strong word for Leonard Morris's sexual preoccupations?"

"Of course. I was just being clever. But I shouldn't let the Morris-Gearing affair worry you. It's been hiccuping on for so long now that it's become almost respectable. It isn't even good for a gossip. She's the kind of woman who must have someone in tow, and he likes someone to confide in about the awfulness of his family and the beastliness of the hospital medical staff. They don't exactly take him at his own evaluation as an equal professional man. He's got four children, by the way. I imagine that if his wife decided to divorce him and he and Gearing were free to marry nothing would disconcert them more. Gearing would like a husband no doubt, but I don't think she's cast poor little Morris for the role. It's more likely . . ."

She broke off. Dalgliesh asked:

"You think she has a more eligible candidate in mind?"

"Why not try asking her? She doesn't confide in me."

"But you are responsible for her work? The clinical instructor comes under the senior nurse tutor?"

"I'm responsible for her work not her morals."

They had reached the far door of the casualty department and as Sister Rolfe put out her hand to push it open Mr. Courtney-Briggs swept in. He was followed by a half-dozen chattering junior staff, white-coated and with stethoscopes slung round their necks. The two on each side of him were nodding in deferential attention as the great man spoke. Dalgliesh thought that he had the conceit, the patina of vulgarity and the slightly coarse *savoir-faire* which he associated with one type of successful professional man. As if reading his thoughts, Miss Rolfe said:

"They're not all alike, you know. Take Mr. Molravey, our ophthalmic surgeon. He reminds me of a dormouse. Every Tuesday morning he patters in and stands for five hours in the theatre without speaking an unnecessary word, whiskers twitching and picking away with fastidious little paws at a succession of patients' eyes. Then he thanks everyone formally down to the most junior theatre nurse, peels off his gloves and patters away again to play with his collection of butterflies."

"A modest little man, in fact."

She turned towards him and he detected again in her eyes that uncomfortable elliptical flicker of contempt.

"Oh no! Not modest! He gives a different performance, that's all. Mr. Molravey is just as convinced as is Mr. Court-ney-Briggs that he's a very remarkable surgeon. They are both vain in a professional sense. Vanity, Mr. Dalgliesh, is a surgeon's besetting sin as subservience is a nurse's. I've never yet met a successful surgeon who wasn't convinced that he ranked only one degree lower than Almighty God. They're all infected with hubris." She paused:

"Isn't that supposed to be true also of murderers?"

"Of one type of murderer. You must remember that murder is a highly individual crime."

"Is it? I should have thought that the motives and the means would be monotonously familiar to you. But you, of course, are the expert."

Dalgliesh said: "You have little respect for men apparently, Sister?"

"A great deal of respect. I just don't happen to like them.

But you have to respect a sex that has brought selfishness to such an art. That's what gives you your strength, this ability to devote yourselves entirely to your own interest."

Dalgliesh said, a little maliciously, that he was surprised that Miss Rolfe, since she obviously resented the subservience of her job, hadn't chosen a more masculine occupation. Medicine perhaps? She laughed bitterly.

"I wanted to do medicine but I had a father who didn't believe in educating women. I'm forty-six, remember. When I was at school we didn't have universal free grammar school education. Father earned too much for me to get a free place, so he had to pay. He stopped paying as soon as he decently could, when I was sixteen."

Dalgliesh found nothing appropriate to say. The confidence surprised him. She was hardly the woman, he would have thought, to expose a personal grievance to a stranger and he didn't flatter himself that she found him sympathetic. She would find no man sympathetic. The outburst was probably a spontaneous release of pent up bitterness, but whether against her father, men in general or the limitations and subservience of her job it was hard to say.

They had left the hospital now and were passing along the narrow path which led to Nightingale House. Neither of them spoke another word until the house was reached. Sister Rolfe wrapped her long cloak tightly around her and pulled up her hood as if it could protect her from more than the bite of the wind. Dalgliesh was immersed in his private thoughts. And thus, with the width of the path between them, they paced together in silence under the trees.

IV

In the office Detective Sergeant Masterson was typing a report. Dalgliesh said:

"Immediately before she came into the school, Nurse Pearce was working on the private ward under Sister Brumfett. I want to know if anything significant happened there. And I want a detailed account of her last week's duty and an hour-by-hour account of what she did on her last day. Find out who the other nursing staff were, what her duties were, when she was off duty, how she appeared to the other staff. I want the names of the patients who were on the ward while she was nursing there and what happened to them. Your best plan is to talk to the other nurses and to work from the nursing reports. They're bound to keep a book which is written up daily."

"Shall I get it from Matron?"

"No. Ask Sister Brumfett for it. We deal directly with her, and for God's sake be tactful. Have you those reports ready yet?"

"Yes, sir. They've been typed. Do you want to read them now?"

"No. Tell me if there's anything I ought to know. I'll look at them tonight. I suppose it's too much to expect that any of our suspects has a police record?"

"If they have, sir, it isn't noted on the personal dossiers. There's remarkable little information in most of them. Julia Pardoe was expelled from school, though. She seems to be the only delinquent among them."

"Good God! What for?"

"Her dossier doesn't say. Apparently it was something to do with a visiting maths master. Her headmistress felt it right to mention it when she sent Matron a reference before the girl started here. It isn't very specific. She writes that

Julia was more sinned against than sinning and that she hoped the hospital would give her the chance of training for the only career she has ever shown any interest in, or signs of being suited for."

"A nice double edged comment. So that's why the London teaching hospitals wouldn't take her. I thought Sister Rolfe was being a little disingenuous about the reasons. Anything about the others? Any previous connections between them?"

"Matron and Sister Brumfett trained together in the north at Nethercastle Royal Infirmary, did their midwifery training at the Municipal Maternity Hospital there and came here fifteen years ago, both as ward Sisters. Mr. Courtney-Briggs was in Cairo during 1946–7 and so was Sister Gearing. He was a major in the R.A.M.C. and she was a nursing sister in the Q.A.R.N.S. There's no suggestion that they knew each other there."

"If they did, you'd hardly expect to find the fact recorded on their personal records. But they probably did. Cairo in '46 was a chummy place, so my army friends tell me. I wonder if Miss Taylor served in the Q.A.R.N.S. That's an army nursing service cap which she wears."

"If she did, sir, it isn't on her dossier. The earliest document is her reference from her training school when she came here as a Sister. They thought very highly of her at Nethercastle."

"They think very highly of her here. Have you checked on Courtney-Briggs?"

"Yes, sir. The lodge porter makes a note of every car in and out after midnight. Mr. Courtney-Briggs left at twelve thirty-two a.m."

"Later than he led us to believe. I want a check on his schedule. The precise time he finished the operation will be in the operating theatre book. The junior doctor assisting him will probably know when he left—Mr. Courtney-Briggs is the kind of man who gets escorted to his car. Then drive over the route and time him. They will have moved the tree by now but it should be possible to see where it came down. He can't have wasted more than a few minutes at the most tying on his scarf. Find out what happened to that. He'd hardly lie about something so easily disproved, but he's arrogant enough to think he can get away with anything, including murder."

"Constable Greeson can do the checking, sir. He likes these reconstruction jobs."

"Tell him to curb his urge for verisimilitude. There's no need for him to don an operating gown and go into the theatre. Not that they'd let him. Is there any news yet from Sir Miles or the lab?"

"No, sir, but we've got the name and address of the man Nurse Fallon spent that week in the Isle of Wight with. He's a G.P.O. night telephonist and lives in North Kensington. The local people got on to them almost at once. Fallon made it very easy for them. She booked in her own name and they had two single rooms."

"She was a woman who valued her privacy. Still, she hardly got pregnant by staying in her own room. I'll see the man tomorrow morning after I've visited Miss Fallon's solicitor. Is Leonard Morris in the hospital yet, do you know?"

"Not yet, sir. I checked at the pharmacy that he telephoned this morning and said he wasn't well. Apparently he suffers from a duodenal ulcer. They assume that it's playing him up again."

"It will play him up a great deal worse if he doesn't come back soon and get the interview over. I don't want to embarrass him by visiting his house, but we can't wait indefinitely to get Sister Gearing's story verified. Both these murders, if they were murders, hinge on the question of timing. We must know everyone's movements, if possible, to the minute. Time is crucial."

Masterson said: "That's what surprises me about the poisoned drip. The carbolic couldn't have been added to the milk without a great deal of care, particularly in replacing the bottle seal and making sure that the concentration was right and that the stuff had the texture and colour of milk. It couldn't have been done in a hurry."

"I've no doubt a great deal of care and time were taken. But I think I know how it was done."

He described his theory. Sergeant Masterson, cross with himself for having missed the obvious, said:

"Of course. It must have been done that way."

"Not must, Sergeant. It was probably done that way."

But Sergeant Masterson had seen an objection and voiced it.

Dalgliesh replied: "But that wouldn't apply to a woman. A woman could do it easily and one woman in particular. But I admit it would be more difficult for a man."

"So the assumption is that the milk was doctored by a woman?"

"The probability is that both girls were murdered by a woman. But it's still only a probability. Have you heard yet whether Nurse Dakers is well enough to be interviewed? Dr. Snelling was supposed to be seeing her this morning."

"Matron rang just before lunch to say that the girl is still asleep, but that she'll probably be fit enough once she wakes up. She's under sedation, so God knows when that'll be. Shall I take a look at her while I'm in the private wing?"

"No. I'll see her later. But you might check on this story

that Fallon returned to Nightingale House on the morning of 12th January. Someone might have seen her leave. And where were her clothes kept while she was warded? Could anyone have got hold of them and impersonated her? It seems unlikely but it ought to be checked."

"Inspector Bailey did check, sir. No one saw Fallon leave but they admit that she could have got out of the ward undetected. They were very busy and she had a private room. If it were found empty they would probably have assumed that she'd gone to the bathroom. Her clothes were hung in the wardrobe in her room. Anyone who had a right to be in the ward could have got at them, provided, of course, that Fallon was asleep or out of the room. But no one thinks it likely that anyone did."

"Nor do I. I think I know why Fallon came back to Nightingale House. Nurse Goodale told us that Fallon had received the pregnancy confirmation only two days before she went sick. It's possible that she didn't destroy it. If so, it's the one possession in her room which she wouldn't want to leave for someone else to find. It certainly isn't among her papers. My guess is that she came back to retrieve it, tore it up, and flushed it down the lavatory."

"Couldn't she have telephoned Nurse Goodale and asked her to destroy it?"

"Not without exciting suspicion. She couldn't be sure that she'd get Goodale herself when she rang and she wouldn't want to give anyone else a message. This insistence to speak to one particular nurse and the reluctance to accept help from anyone else would look rather odd. But it's no more than a theory. Is the search of Nightingale House completed?"

"Yes, sir. They've found nothing. No trace of poison and no container. Most of the rooms contain bottles of aspirin and Sister Gearing, Sister Brumfett and Miss Taylor all have a small supply of sleeping tablets. But surely Fallon didn't die of hypnotic or soporific poisoning?"

"No. It was quicker than that. We shall just have to possess ourselves in patience until we get the laboratory report."

V

At two thirty-four p.m. precisely, in the largest and most luxurious of the private rooms, Sister Brumfett lost a patient. She always thought of death in that way. The patient was lost; the battle was over; she, Sister Brumfett, had been personally defeated. The fact that so many of her battles were foredoomed to failure, that the enemy even if repulsed in the present skirmish, was always assured of final victory, never mitigated her sense of failure. Patients did not come into Sister Brumfett's ward to die; they came in to get better, and with Sister's indomitable will to fortify them, they usually did get better, often to their own surprise and occasionally despite their own wishes.

She had hardly expected to win this particular battle but it was only when Mr. Courtney-Briggs lifted his hand to turn off the blood drip that she accepted failure. The patient had certainly fought well; a difficult patient, a demanding patient, but a good fighter. He had been a wealthy business man whose meticulous plans for his future certainly didn't include dying at forty-two. She recalled the look of wild surprise, almost of outrage, with which he had greeted the realization that death was something neither he nor his accountant could fix. Sister Brumfett had seen too much of his young widow on that lady's daily visits to suppose that she would suffer much grief or inconvenience. The patient was the only one who would have been furious at the failure of Mr. Courtney-Briggs's heroic and expensive efforts to save him, and happily for the surgeon, the patient was the one person in no position to demand either explanation or excuse.

Mr. Courtney-Briggs would see the widow and offer her his customary carefully phrased condolences, his assurance that everything humanly possible had been done. In this case, the size of the bill would be a guarantee of that and a powerful antidote, no doubt, to the inevitable guilt of bereavement. Courtney-Briggs was really very good with the widows; and to do him justice, the poor as well as the rich received the consolation of his hand on their shoulder, of the stereotyped phrases of comfort and regret.

She drew the fold of the sheet up over the suddenly vacant face. Closing the dead eyes with practised fingers, she felt the eyeballs still warm under the wrinkled lids. She was conscious neither of grief nor anger. There was only, as always, this dragging weight of failure tugging like a physical load at the tired muscles of her stomach and back.

They turned away from the bed together. Glancing at the surgeon's face, Sister Brumfett was struck by his look of weariness. For the first time he, too, appeared threatened with failure and with age. It was, of course, unusual for a patient to die when he was there to see it happen. Still less frequently did they die on the operating table, even if the scramble from the theatre to the ward was sometimes a little undignified. But, unlike Sister Brumfett, Mr. Courtney-Briggs did not have to watch over his patients to the last gasp. All the same, she did not believe that this particular death had depressed him. It was, after all, not unexpected. He had nothing with which to reproach himself even if he had been given to self-criticism. She felt that he was stressed by some subtler worry, and she wondered whether it was something to do with Fallon's death. He's lost some of his bounce, thought Sister Brumfett. He looks suddenly ten years older.

He preceded her down the passage to her office. As they neared the ward kitchen there was the sound of voices. The door was open. A student nurse was setting a trolley with the afternoon tea trays. Sergeant Masterson was leaning against the sink and watching her with the air of a man completely at home. As the Sister and Mr. Courtney-Briggs appeared in the doorway the girl flushed, muttered a low "good afternoon, sir" and pushed her trolley past them into the corridor with clumsy haste. Sergeant Masterson gazed after her with tolerant condescension, then transferred his level gaze to the Sister. He appeared not to notice Mr. Courtney-Briggs.

"Good afternoon, Sister, could I have a word with you?"

Baulked of the initiative, Sister Brumfett said repressively:

"In my office if you please, Sergeant. That is where you should have waited in the first place. People do not wander in and out of my ward just as they please, and that includes the police."

Sergeant Masterson, unchastened, looked slightly gratified at this speech as if it confirmed something to his satisfaction. Sister Brumfett bustled into her office, tight-lipped and ready for battle. Rather to her surprise Mr. Courtney-Briggs followed.

Sergeant Masterson said: "I wonder, Sister, if I could see the ward report book covering the period when Nurse Pearce was on this ward? I'm particularly interested in her last week here."

Mr. Courtney-Briggs broke in roughly:

"Aren't they confidential medical records, Sister? Surely

the police will have to apply for a subpoena before they can make you produce them?"

"Oh, I don't think so, sir." Sergeant Masterson's voice, quiet, almost too respectful, yet held a tinge of amusement which wasn't lost on his hearer. "Ward nursing records surely aren't medical documents in the proper sense. I merely want to see who was being nursed here during that period and whether anything happened which might be of interest to the Superintendent. It's been suggested that something occurred to upset Nurse Pearce while she was nursing on your ward. She went from here straight to the school, remember."

Sister Brumfett, mottled and shaking with an anger which left small room for fear, found her voice.

"Nothing happened on my ward. Nothing! It's all stupid, malicious gossip. If a nurse does her job properly and obeys orders there's no need for her to be upset. The Superintendent is here to investigate a murder not to interfere with my ward."

Mr. Courtney-Briggs broke in blandly:

"And even if she were—upset is the word I think you used, Sergeant—I don't see what relevance that has to her death."

Sergeant Masterson smiled at him as if humouring a wilfully obstinate child.

"Anything that happened to Nurse Pearce in the week immediately before she was killed may have relevance, sir. That's why I'm asking to see the ward report book."

As neither Sister Brumfett nor the surgeon made any move to comply, he added:

"It's only a matter of confirming information we already have. I know what she was doing on the ward during that week. I'm told she was devoting all her time to nursing one particular patient. A Mr. Martin Dettinger. 'Specializing' him, I think you call it. My information is that she seldom left his room while she was on duty here during the last week of her life."

So, thought Sister Brumfett, he had been gossiping with the student nurses. But of course! That was how the police worked. It was pointless to try to keep anything private from them. Everything, even the medical secrets of her ward, the nursing care of her own patients, would be nosed out by this impertinent young man and reported to his superior officer. There was nothing in the ward report book which he couldn't find out by more devious means; discover, magnify, misinterpret and use to make mischief. Inarticulate with anger and something close to panic she heard Mr. Courtney-Briggs's bland and reassuring voice.

"Then you'd better hand the book over, Sister. If the police insist on wasting their own time there's no need for us to encourage them to waste ours."

Without another word, Sister Brumfett went to her desk and, bending down, opened the deep right-hand drawer and took out a large, hard-backed book. Silently and without looking at him, she handed it to Sergeant Masterson. The Sergeant thanked her profusely and turned to Mr. Courtney-Briggs:

"And now, sir, if the patient's still with you, I'd like to have a word with Mr. Dettinger."

Mr. Courtney-Briggs made no attempt to keep the satisfaction out of his voice.

"I think that is likely to challenge even your ingenuity, Sergeant. Mr. Martin Dettinger died on the day Nurse Pearce left this ward. If I remember rightly, she was with him when he died. So both of them are safely out of reach of your inquisition. And now, if you'd be good enough to excuse us, Sister and I have work to do."

He held open the door and Sister Brumfett strutted out

before him. Sergeant Masterson was left alone, holding the ward record book in his hand.

"Bloody bastard," he said aloud.

He stood for a moment, thinking. Then he went in search of the medical record department.

VI

Ten minutes later he was back in the office. Under his arm was the ward report book and a buff-coloured file, stamped with a warning in black capital letters that it was not to be handed to the patient, and bearing the name of the hospital and Martin Dettinger's medical record number. He placed the book on the table and handed the file to Dalgliesh.

"Thank you. You got it without trouble?"

"Yes, sir," said Masterson. He saw no reason to explain that the Medical Records Officer had been out of his department and that he had half persuaded, half bullied the junior clerk on duty into handing over the file on the grounds, which he didn't for a moment believe, that the rules about the confidentiality of medical records no longer applied when the patient was dead and that when a Superintendent of the Yard asked for a thing he was entitled to get it without fuss and without delay. They studied the file together. Dalgliesh said:

"Martin Dettinger. Aged forty-six. Gave his address as his London Club. C. of E. Divorced. Next-of-kin, Mrs. Louise Dettinger, 23 Saville Mansions, Marylebone. Mother. You had better see the lady, Masterson. Make an appointment for tomorrow evening. I shall need you here during the day while I'm in town. And take trouble with her. She must have visited her son pretty frequently when he was in hospital. Nurse Pearce was specializing him. The two women probably saw quite a lot of each other. Something happened to upset Pearce while she was working on the private ward during the last week of her life and I want to know what it was."

He turned back to the medical record.

"There's a lot of paper here. The poor chap seems to have had a stormy medical history. He suffered from colitis for the past ten years, and before that there's a record of long spells of undiagnosed ill health, perhaps a forerunner of the condition which killed him. He was in hospital for three periods during his army service, including a spell of two months in an army hospital in Cairo in 1947. He was invalided out of the army in 1952 and emigrated to South Africa. That doesn't seem to have done him much good. There are notes here from a hospital in Johannesburg. Courtney-Briggs wrote for them; he certainly takes trouble. His own notes are pretty copious. He took over the case a couple of years ago and seems to have been acting as a kind of general practitioner to Dettinger as well as his surgeon. The colitis became acute about a month ago, and Courtney-Briggs operated to remove a large part of the bowel on Friday, 2nd January. Dettinger survived the operation, although he was in a pretty bad state by then, and made some progress until the early morning of Monday, 5th January, when he relapsed. After that he was seldom conscious for long, and he died at five thirty p.m. on Friday, 9th January."

Masterson said: "Nurse Pearce was with him when he died."

"And apparently she nursed him almost single-handed for the last week of his life. I wonder what the nursing record tells us."

But the nursing record was far less informative than the

medical file. Nurse Pearce had entered in her careful school-girl's hand the details of her patient's temperature, respiration and pulse, his restlessness and brief hours of sleep, his medication and food. It could not be faulted as a meticulous record of nursing care. Beyond that it told them nothing.

Dalgliesh closed the book.

"You'd better return this to the ward and the medical folder to the proper department. We've learnt all we can from them. But I feel in my bones that Martin Dettinger's death has something to do with this case."

Masterson did not reply. Like all detectives who had worked with Dalgliesh, he had a healthy respect for the old man's hunches. Inconvenient, perverse and far-fetched they might seem, but they had been proved right too often to be safely ignored. And he had no objection to an evening trip to London. Tomorrow was Friday. The time-table on the hall notice-board showed that the students' sessions ended early on Friday. They would be free soon after five. He wondered whether Julia Pardoe would fancy a drive to town. After all, why not? Dalgliesh wouldn't be back by the time he was due to set out. It could be arranged with care. And there were some suspects it would be a positive pleasure to interview on their own.

VII

Just before half past four Dalgliesh, in defiance of convention and prudence, took tea alone with Sister Gearing in her bed-sitting-room. She had met him casually passing across the ground floor hall as the students were filing out of the lecture room after the last seminar of the day. She had given the invitation spontaneously and without coyness, although Dalgliesh noted that Sergeant Masterson was not included. He would have accepted the invitation even had it been delivered on highly scented and pink writing-paper and accompanied by the most blatant of sexual innuendoes. What he wanted after the formal interrogation of the morning was to sit in comfort and listen to a flow of artless, candid and slightly malicious gossip; to listen with the surface of his mind soothed, uninvolved, even a little cynically amused, but with the sharp claws of the intelligence sharpened for their pickings. He had learned more about the Nightingale House Sisters from their conversation at luncheon than he had in all his formal interviews, but he couldn't spend all his time tagging along behind the nursing staff, picking up scraps of gossip like so many dropped handkerchiefs. He wondered whether Sister Gearing had something to tell or something to ask. Either way he didn't expect an hour in her company to be wasted.

Dalgliesh hadn't yet been in any of the rooms on the third floor except Matron's flat and he was struck by the size and pleasant proportions of Sister Gearing's room. From here, even in winter, the hospital couldn't be seen, and the room had a calm of its own, remote from the frenetic life of wards and departments. Dalgliesh thought that in summer it must be very pleasant with nothing but a curdle of tree tops breaking the view of the far hills. Even now, with the curtains drawn against the fading light and the gas fire giving out a merry hiss, it was welcoming and warm. Presumably the divan bed in the corner with its cretonne cover and carefully arranged bank of cushions had been provided by the Hospital Management Committee, as had the two comfortable armchairs similarly covered and the rest of the uninteresting but functional furniture. But Sister Gearing had imposed her own personality on the room. There was a long shelf along the far wall on which she had arranged a collection of dolls in different national costumes. On another wall was a smaller shelf holding an assortment of china cats of different sizes and breeds. There was one particularly repulsive specimen in spotted blue, bulging of eye and adorned with a bow of blue ribbon; and propped beside it was a greetings card. It showed a female robin, the sex denoted by a frilly apron and flowered bonnet, perched on a twig. At her feet, a male robin was spelling out the words "Good luck" in worms. Dalgliesh hastily averted his eyes from this abom-ination and continued his tactful examination of the room.

The table in front of the window was presumably intended as a desk but about half a dozen photographs in silver frames effectively took up most of the working space. There was a record player in a corner with a cabinet of records beside it and a poster of a recent pop idol pinned on the wall above. There was a large number of cushions of all sizes and colours, three pouffes of unattractive design, an imitation tiger rug in brown-and-white nylon, and a coffee table on which Sister Gearing had set out the tea. But the most remarkable object in the room, in Dalgliesh's eyes, was a tall vase of winter foliage and chrysanthemums, beauti-fully arranged, standing on a side table. Sister Gearing was reputably good with flowers, and this arrangement had a simplicity of colour and line which was wholly pleas-ing. It was odd, he thought, that a woman with such an instinctive taste in flower arrangement should be content to live in this vulgarly overfurnished room. It suggested that Sister Gearing might be a more complex person than one would at first suppose. On the face of it, her character was easily read. She was a middle-aged, uncomfortably pas-sionate spinster, not particularly well educated or intelligent, and concealing her frustrations with a slightly spurious gai-ety. But twenty-five years as a policeman had taught him

that no character was without its complications, its incon-
sistencies. Only the young or the very arrogant imagined
that there was an identikit to the human mind.

Here in her own place Sister Gearing was less overtly
flirtatious than she was in company. Admittedly she had
chosen to pour the tea while curled on a large cushion at
his feet, but he guessed from the number and variety of
these cushions plumped around the room that this was
her usual comfortable habit, rather than a kittenish invitation for him to join her. The tea was excellent. It was hot
and freshly brewed, and accompanied by lavishly buttered
crumpets with anchovy paste. There was an admirable
absence of doilys and sticky cakes, and the cup handle
could be comfortably held without dislocating one's fingers. She looked after him with quiet efficiency. Dalgliesh
thought that Sister Gearing was one of those women who,
when alone with a man, consider it their duty to devote
themselves entirely to his comfort and the flattering of his
ego. This may arouse fury in other less dedicated women,
but it is unreasonable to expect a man to object.

Relaxed by the warmth and comfort of her room and
stimulated by tea, Sister Gearing was obviously in a mood
for talk. Dalgliesh let her chatter on, only occasionally
throwing in a question. Neither of them mentioned
Leonard Morris. The artless confidences for which Dalgliesh hoped would hardly spring from embarrassment or
restraint.

"Of course, what happened to that poor kid Pearce is
absolutely appalling, however it was caused. And with the
whole set looking on like that! I'm surprised that it hadn't
upset their work completely, but the young are pretty tough
these days. And it isn't as if they liked her. But I can't
believe any one of them put that corrosive into the feed.
After all, these are third-year students. They know that

carbolic acid taken straight into the stomach in that concentration is lethal. Damn it all, they had a lecture about poisons in their previous block. So it couldn't have been a practical joke that misfired."

"All the same, that seems to be the general view."

"Well, it's natural, isn't it? No one wants to believe that Pearce's death was murder. And if this were a first-year block I might believe it. One of the students might have tampered with the feed on impulse, perhaps with the idea that Lysol is an emetic and that the demonstration might be enlivened by Pearce sicking up all over the G.N.C. Inspector. An odd idea of humour, but the young can be pretty crude. But these kids must have known what that stuff would do to the stomach."

"And what about Nurse Fallon's death?"

"Oh, suicide I should think. After all, the poor girl was pregnant. She probably had a moment of intense depression and didn't see the point of going on. Three years of training wasted and no family to turn to. Poor old Fallon! I don't think she was really the suicidal type, but it probably happened on impulse. There has been a certain amount of criticism about Dr. Snelling—he looks after the students' health—letting her come back to the block so soon after her influenza. But she hates being off and it isn't as if she were on the wards. This is hardly the time of the year to send people away for convalescence. She was as well off in school as anywhere. Still, the flu couldn't have helped. It probably left her feeling pretty low. This epidemic is having some pretty nasty after-effects. If only she'd confided in someone. It's awful to think of her putting an end to herself like that with a houseful of people who would have been glad to help if only she'd asked. Here, let me give you another cup. And try one of those shortbreads. They're home made. My married sister sends me them from time to time."

Dalgliesh helped himself to a piece of shortbread from the proffered tin and observed that there were those who thought that Nurse Fallon might have had another reason for suicide, apart from her pregnancy. She could have put the corrosive in the feed. She had certainly been seen in Nightingale House at the crucial time.

He put forward the suggestion slyly, awaiting her reaction. It wouldn't, of course, be new to her; it must have occurred to everyone in Nightingale House. But she was too simple to be surprised that a senior detective should be discussing his case so frankly with her, and too stupid to ask herself why.

She dismissed this theory with a snort.

"Not Fallon! It would have been a foolish trick and she was no fool. I told you, any third-year nurse would know that the stuff was lethal. And if you're suggesting that Fallon intended to kill Pearce—and why on earth should she?—I'd say that she was the last person to suffer remorse. If Fallon decided to do murder she wouldn't waste time repenting afterwards, let alone kill herself in remorse. No, Fallon's death is understandable enough. She had post-flu depression and she felt she couldn't cope with the baby."

"So you think they both committed suicide?"

"Well, I'm not so sure about Pearce. You'd have to be pretty crazy to choose that agonizing way of dying, and Pearce seemed sane enough to me. But it's a possible explanation, isn't it? And I can't see you proving anything else however long you stay."

He thought he detected a note of smug complacency in her voice and glanced at her abruptly. But the thin face showed nothing but its usual look of vague dissatisfaction. She was eating shortbread, nibbling at it with sharp, very white teeth. He could hear them rasping against the biscuits. She said:

"When one explanation is impossible, the improbable must be true. Someone said something like that. G. K. Chesterton wasn't it? Nurses don't murder each other. Or anyone else for that matter."

"There was Nurse Waddingham," said Dalgliesh.

"Who was she?"

"An unprepossessing and unpleasant woman who poisoned with morphine one of her patients, a Miss Baguley. Miss Baguley had been so ill advised as to leave Nurse Waddingham her money and property in turn for life-long treatment in the latter's nursing home. She struck a poor bargain. Nurse Waddingham was hanged."

Sister Gearing gave a frisson of simulated distaste.

"What awful people you do get yourself mixed up with! Anyway, she was probably one of those unqualified nurses. You can't tell me that Waddingham was on the General Nursing Council's Register."

"Come to think of it, I don't believe she was. And I wasn't mixed up with it. It happened in 1935."

"Well, there you are then," Sister Gearing said as if vindicated.

She stretched across to pour him a second cup of tea, then wriggled herself more comfortably into her cushion and leaned back against the arm of his chair, so that her hair brushed his knee. Dalgliesh found himself examining with mild interest the narrow band of darker hair each side of the parting where the dye had grown out. Viewed from above, her foreshortened face looked older, the nose sharper. He could see the latent pouch of skin under the bottom eyelashes and a spatter of broken veins high on the cheekbones, the purple threads only half disguised by make-up. She was no longer a young woman; that he knew. And there was a great deal more about her that he had gleaned from her dossier. She had trained at a hospital in the East End of

London after a variety of unsuccessful and unprofitable office jobs. Her nursing career had been chequered and her references were suspiciously non-committal. There had been a doubt about the wisdom of seconding her for training as a clinical instructor, a suggestion that she had been motivated less by a desire to teach than by the hope of an easier job than that of ward Sister. He knew that she was having difficulty with the menopause. He knew more about her than she realized, more than she would think he had any right to know. But he didn't yet know whether she was a murderess. Intent for a moment on his private thoughts, he hardly caught her next words.

"It's odd your being a poet. Fallon had your last volume of verse in her room, didn't she? Rolfe told me. Isn't it difficult to reconcile poetry with being a policeman?"

"I've never thought of poetry and police work as needing to be reconciled in that ecumenical way."

She laughed coyly.

"You know very well what I mean. After all it is a little unusual. One doesn't think of policemen as poets."

He did, of course, know what she meant. But it wasn't a subject he was prepared to discuss. He said:

"Policemen are individuals like people in any other job. After all, you three nursing Sisters haven't much in common have you? You and Sister Brumfett could hardly be more different personalities. I can't see Sister Brumfett feeding me on anchovy crumpets and home-made shortbread."

She reacted at once, as he had known she would.

"Oh, Brumfett's all right when you get to know her. Of course she's twenty years out of date. As I said at lunch, the kids today aren't prepared to listen to all that guff about obedience and duty and a sense of vocation. But she's a marvellous nurse. I won't hear a word against Brum. I had an appendicectomy here about four years ago. It went a bit wrong and the wound burst. Then I got an infection which was resistant to antibiotics. The whole thing was a mess. Not one of our Courtney-Briggs's most successful efforts. Anyway I felt like death. One night I was in ghastly pain and couldn't sleep and I felt absolutely sure I wouldn't see the morning. I was terrified. It was sheer funk. Talk about the fear of death! I knew what it meant that night. Then Brumfett came round. She was looking after me herself; she wouldn't let the students do a thing for me when she was on duty. I said to her: 'I'm not going to die, am I?' She looked down at me. She didn't tell me not to be a fool or give me any of the usual comforting lies. She just said in that gruff voice of hers: 'Not if I can help it you aren't.' And immediately the panic stopped. I knew that if Brumfett was fighting on my side I'd win through. It sounds a bit daft and sentimental put like that, but that's what I thought. She's like that with all the really sick patients. Talk about confidence! Brumfett makes you feel that she'd drag you back from the edge of the grave by sheer will-power, even if all the devils in hell were tugging the other way; which in my case they probably were. They don't make them like that any more."

Dalgliesh made appropriately assenting noises and paused briefly before picking up the references to Mr. Courtney-Briggs. He asked rather naïvely whether many of the surgeon's operations went so spectacularly wrong. Sister Gearing laughed:

"Lord, no! Courtney-Briggs's operations usually go the way he wants. That's not to say they go the way the patient would choose if he knew the whole of it. C.B. is what they call a heroic surgeon. If you ask me, most of the heroism has to be shown by the patients. But he does an extraordinary good job of work. He's one of the last remaining great general surgeons. You know, take anything on, the more hopeless the better. I suppose a surgeon is rather like a lawyer. There's no glory to be had in getting someone off if he's obviously innocent. The greater the guilt the greater the glory."

"What is Mrs. Courtney-Briggs like? I presume he's married. Does she show herself at the hospital?"

"Not very often, although she's supposed to be a member of the League of Friends. She gave the prizes away last year when the Princess couldn't come at the last moment. Blonde, very smart. Younger than C.B. but beginning to wear a bit now. Why do you ask? You don't suspect Muriel Courtney-Briggs surely? She wasn't even in the hospital the night Fallon died. Probably tucked up in bed in their very nice little place near Selborne. And she certainly hadn't any motive for killing poor Pearce."

So she did have a motive for getting rid of Fallon. Mr. Courtney-Briggs's liaison had probably been more noticed than he had realized. Dalgliesh wasn't surprised that Sister Gearing should know about it. Her sharp nose would be adept at smelling out sexual scandal.

He said: "I wondered if she were jealous."

Sister Gearing, unaware of what she had told, rambled happily on.

"I don't suppose she knew. Wives don't usually. Anyway, C.B. wasn't going to break up his marriage to wed Fallon. Not him! Mrs. C.B. has plenty of money of her own. She's the only child of Price of Price and Maxwell, the building firm—and what with C.B.'s earnings and Daddy's ill-gotten gains, they're very comfortable. I don't think Muriel worries much what he does as long as he behaves himself properly to her and the money keeps rolling in. I know I wouldn't. Besides, if rumour's correct, our Muriel doesn't exactly qualify for the League of Purity."

"Anyone here?" asked Dalgliesh.

"Oh no, nothing like that. It's just that she goes around with quite a smart set. She usually gets her picture in every third issue of the social glossies. And they're in with the theatrical crowd too. C.B. had a brother who was an actor, Peter Courtney. He hanged himself about three years ago. You must have read about it."

Dalgliesh's job gave him few opportunities to see a play and theatre going was one of the pleasures he missed most. He had seen Peter Courtney act only once but it had been a performance not easily forgotten. He had been a very young Macbeth, as introspective and sensitive as Hamlet, in thrall sexually to a much older wife, and whose physical courage was compounded of violence and hysteria. It had been a perverse but interesting interpretation, and it had very nearly succeeded. Thinking of the performance now, Dalgliesh imagined that he could detect a likeness between the brothers, something to do with the set of the eyes perhaps. But Peter must have been the younger by nearly twenty years. He wished he knew what the two men, so widely separated in age and talent, had made of each other.

Suddenly and irrelevantly Dalgliesh asked:

"How did Pearce and Fallon get on together?"

"They didn't. Fallon despised Pearce. I don't mean she hated her or would have harmed her; she just despised her."

"Was there any particular reason?"

"Pearce took it upon herself to tell Matron about Fallon's little tipple of whisky at nights. Self-righteous little beast. Oh, I know she's dead and I ought not to have said that. But really, Pearce could be insufferably self-righteous. Apparently what happened was that Diane Harper—she's left the training school now—had a bad cold about a fortnight before the set came into the block, and Fallon fixed her a hot whisky and lemon. Pearce could smell the stuff half-way along the corridor and concluded that Fallon was now attempting to seduce her juniors with the demon drink. So she appeared in the utility room—they were in the main nurses' home then, of course—in her dressing-gown, sniffing the air like an avenging angel, and threatened to report Fallon to Matron unless she promised more or less on her knees never to touch the stuff again. Fallon told her where to go and what to do with herself when she got there. She had a picturesque turn of phrase when roused, had Fallon. Nurse Dakers burst into tears, Harper lost her temper and the general noise brought the House Sister on to the scene. Pearce reported it to Matron all right, but no one knows with what result, except that Fallon started keeping her whisky in her own room. But the whole thing caused a great deal of feeling in the third year. Fallon was never popular with the set, she was too reserved and sarcastic. But they liked Pearce a damn sight less."

"And did Pearce dislike Fallon?"

"Well, it's difficult to say. Pearce never seemed to concern herself with what other people thought of her. She was an odd girl, pretty insensitive too. For example, she might disapprove of Fallon and her whisky-drinking but that didn't prevent her from borrowing Fallon's library ticket."

"When did this happen?"

Dalgliesh leaned across and replaced his teacup on the tray. His voice was level, unconcerned. But he felt again that spring of excitement and anticipation, the intuitive sense that something important had been said. It was more than a hunch; it was, as always, a certainty. It might happen several times during a case if he were lucky, or not at all. He couldn't will it to happen and he was afraid to examine its roots too closely since he suspected that it was a plant easily withered by logic.

"Just before she came into block, I think. It must have

been the week before Pearce died. The Thursday, I think.
Anyway, they hadn't yet moved into Nightingale House. It
was just after supper time in the main dining-room. Fallon
and Pearce were walking out of the door together and I was
just behind them with Goodale. Then Fallon turned to
Pearce and said: 'Here's the library token I promised you.
I'd better give it to you now as I don't suppose we'll see each
other in the morning. You'd better take the reader's ticket
too, or they may not let you have the book.' Pearce mumbled something and grabbed the token rather ungraciously
I thought, and that was that. Why? It isn't important, is it?"

"I can't think why it should be," said Dalgliesh.

VIII

He sat through the next fifteen minutes in exemplary
patience. Sister Gearing couldn't have guessed from his
courteous attention to her chattering and the leisurely way
in which he drank his third and last cup of tea, that every
moment was now grudged. When the meal was over, he
carried the tray for her into the small Sisters' kitchen at the
end of the corridor while she fretted at his heels, bleating her
protests. Then he said, "Thank you," and left.

He went at once to the cell-like bedroom which still held
nearly all the possessions Nurse Pearce had owned at the
John Carpendar. It took him a moment to select the correct
key from the heavy bunch in his pocket. The room had
been locked after her death and was still locked. He went in,
switching on the light. The bed was stripped and the whole
room was very tidy and clean as if it, too, had been laid out
for burial. The curtains were drawn back so that, from
outside, the room would look no different from any other.
The window was open but the air held a faint tang of dis-

infectant as if someone had tried to obliterate the memory of Pearce's death by a ritual purification.

He had no need to refresh his memory. The detritus of this particular life was pathetically meagre. But he went through her leavings again, turning them in careful hands as if the feel of cloth and leather could transmit their own clues. It didn't take long. Nothing had altered since his first inspection. The hospital wardrobe, identical to that in Nurse Fallon's room, was more than adequate for the few woollen dresses, unexciting in colour and design, which, under his questing hands, swung from their padded hangers and gave out a faint smell of cleaning fluid and mothballs. The thick winter coat in fawn was of good quality but obviously old. He sought once more in the pockets. There was nothing except the handkerchief which had been there on his first examination, a crumpled ball of white cotton smelling of sour breath.

He moved to the chest of drawers. Here again the space provided had been more than sufficient. The two top drawers were filled with underclothes, strong sensible vests and knickers, comfortably warm no doubt for an English winter but with no concessions to glamour or fashion. The drawers were lined with newspaper. The sheets had been taken out once already, but he ran his hand under them and felt nothing but the gritty surface of bare unpolished wood. The remaining three drawers held skirts, jumpers and cardigans; a leather handbag, carefully wrapped in tissue paper; a pair of best shoes in a string bag; an embroidered handkerchief sachet with a dozen handkerchiefs carefully folded; an assortment of scarves; three pairs of identical nylon stockings still in their wrappers.

He turned again to the bedside locker, and the small shelf fixed above it. The locker held a bedside lamp, a small alarm clock in a leather case which had long since

run down, a packet of paper handkerchiefs with one crumpled tissue half-pulled through the slit, and an empty
water carafe. There was also a leather-bound Bible and a
writing-case. Dalgliesh opened the Bible at the flyleaf and
read again the inscription in careful copper plate. "Awarded
to Heather Pearce for attendance and diligence. St. Mark's
Sunday School." Diligence. An unfashionable, intimidating word, but one, he felt, of which Nurse Pearce would
have approved.

He opened the writing-case, but with little hope of finding what he sought. Nothing had changed since his first
examination. Here still was the half-finished letter to her
grandmother, a dull recital of the week's doings written as
impersonally as a ward report, and a quarto-sized envelope, posted to her on the day of her death and obviously
slipped into the writing-case by someone who, having
opened it, couldn't think of what else to do with it. It was
an illustrated brochure on the work of a home in Suffolk
for German war refugees apparently sent in the hope of a
donation.

He turned his attention to the small collection of books
on the wall shelf. He had seen them before. Then, as now,
he was struck by the conventionality of her choice and by
the meagreness of this personal library. A school prize for
needlework. *Lamb's Tales from Shakespeare.* Dalgliesh had
never believed that any child read them and there was no
evidence that Nurse Pearce had done so. There were two
travel books, *In the Steps of St. Paul* and *In the Steps of the
Master.* In both the girl had carefully inscribed her name.
There was a well-known but out-of-date edition of a nursing textbook. The date on the flyleaf was nearly four years
old. He wondered whether she had bought it in anticipation of her training, only to find that its advise on applying
leeches and administering enemas had become out of date.

There was a copy of Palgrave's *Golden Treasury,* also a school prize, but this time inappropriately for deportment. This, too, showed little sign of having been read. Lastly there were three paperbacks—novels by a popular woman writer, each advertised as "The Book of the Film"— and a fictional and highly sentimental account of the wanderings across Europe of a lost dog and cat which Dalgliesh remembered had been a best-seller some five years previously. This was inscribed, "To Heather, with love from Auntie Edie, Christmas 1964." The whole collection told him little about the dead girl, except that her reading had apparently been as restricted as her life. And nowhere he found what he was seeking.

He didn't go again to look in Nurse Fallon's room. The scene-of-crime officer had searched every inch of it, and he himself could have described the room in minute detail and given an accurate inventory of all its contents. Wherever the library ticket and the token were, he could be sure that they weren't there. Instead he ran lightly up the wide staircase to the floor above where he had noticed a wall-mounted telephone when carrying Sister Gearing's tea tray to the utility room. A card listing the internal extensions hung beside it and, after a moment's thought, he rang the nurses' sitting-room. Maureen Burt answered. Yes, Nurse Goodale was still there. Almost immediately Dalgliesh heard her voice and he asked her to come up to see him in Nurse Pearce's room.

She came so promptly that he had hardly reached the door before he saw the self-assured, uniformed figure at the top of the stairs. He stood aside and she moved into the room before him and silently surveyed the stripped bed, the silent bedside clock, the closed Bible, letting her gaze rest briefly on each object with gentle uninquisitive interest. Dalgliesh moved to the window and, both standing, they regarded each other wordlessly across the bed. Then he said:

"I'm told that Nurse Fallon lent a library ticket to Nurse Pearce sometime during the week before she died. You were leaving the dining-room with Sister Gearing at the time. Can you remember what happened?"

Nurse Goodale was not given to showing surprise.

"Yes, I think so. Fallon had told me earlier that day that Pearce wanted to visit one of the London libraries and had asked to borrow her reader's ticket and the token. Fallon was a member of the Westminster library. They've got a number of branches in the City but you aren't really supposed to belong unless you either live or work in Westminster. Fallon had a flat in London before she became a student here and had kept her reader's card and token. It's an excellent library, much better than we've got here, and it's useful to be able to borrow books. I think Sister Rolfe is a member too. Fallon took her reader's ticket and one of the tokens across to lunch and handed them to Pearce as we were leaving the dining-room."

"Did Nurse Pearce say why she wanted them?"

"Not to me. She may have told Fallon. I don't know. Any of us could borrow one of Fallon's tokens if we wanted to. Fallon didn't require an explanation."

"What precisely are these tokens like?"

"They're small oblongs of pale blue plastic with the City Arms stamped on them. The library usually gives four to every reader and you hand one in every time you take out a book, but Jo only had three. She may have lost the fourth. There's also the reader's ticket. That's the usual small piece of cardboard with the name, address and date of expiry. Sometimes the assistant asks to see the reader's ticket and I suppose that's why Jo handed it over with the token."

"Do you know where the other two are?"

"Yes, in my room. I borrowed them about a fortnight ago when I went up to town with my fiancé to attend a special service in the Abbey. I thought we might have time to visit the Great Smith Street branch to see whether they had the new Iris Murdoch. However, we met some friends from Mark's theological college after the service and never got to the library. I meant to return the tokens to Jo but I slipped them in my writing-case and forgot about them. She didn't remind me. I can show them to you if it would be helpful."

"I think it would. Did Heather Pearce use her token, do you know?"

"Well, I assume she did. I saw her waiting for the Green Line bus to town that afternoon. We were both off duty so it must have been the Thursday. I imagine that she had it in mind to visit the library."

She looked puzzled.

"Somehow I feel quite sure that she did take out a library book but I can't think why I should be so certain."

"Can't you? Think very hard."

Nurse Goodale stood silently, her hands folded composedly as if in prayer over the white stiffness of her apron. He did not hurry her. She gazed fixedly ahead then turned her eyes to the bed and said quietly:

"I know now. I saw her reading a library book. It was the night when Jo was taken ill, the night before Pearce herself died. I went into her bedroom just after half past eleven to ask her to go and look after Jo while I fetched Sister. She was sitting up in bed with her hair in two plaits and she was reading. I remember now. It was a large book, bound in a dark colour, dark blue I think, and with a reference number stamped in gold at the foot of the spine. It looked an old and rather heavy book. I don't think it was fiction. She was holding it propped up against her knees I remember. When I appeared she closed it quickly and slipped it under her pillow. It was a strange thing to do but it didn't mean anything to me at the time. Pearce was always oddly secretive. Besides, I was too concerned about Jo. But I remember it now."

She stood again in silence for a few moments. Dalgliesh waited. Then she said quietly:

"I know what's worrying you. Where's that book now? It wasn't among her things when Sister Rolfe and I tidied her room and made a list of her belongings after her death. The police were with us and we didn't find a book anything like it. And what happened to the ticket? It wasn't among Fallon's things either."

Dalgliesh asked:

"What exactly happened that night? You said you went in to Nurse Fallon shortly after eleven thirty. I thought she didn't go to bed before midnight."

"She did that night. I suppose it was because she wasn't feeling well and hoped that an early bed would put her right. She didn't tell anyone she was ill. Jo wouldn't. And I didn't go in to her. She came in to me. Shortly after eleven thirty she woke me up. She looked ghastly. She was obviously in a high fever and she could hardly stand. I helped her back to her bed, went in to ask Pearce to stay with her, and then rang Sister Rolfe. She's generally responsible for us when we're in Nightingale House. Sister came to look at Jo and then telephoned the private wing and asked for an ambulance to come over for her. Then she rang Sister Brumfett to let her know what had happened. Sister Brumfett likes to know what's happening on her ward even when she's off duty. She wouldn't have been pleased to arrive in the hospital next morning and find that Jo had been warded without her being told. She came down to have a look at Jo but didn't go over in the ambulance with her. It wasn't really necessary."

"Who did accompany her?"

"I did. Sister Rolfe and Sister Brumfett went back to their rooms and Pearce returned to hers."

So the book could hardly have been removed that night, thought Dalgliesh. Pearce would certainly have noticed its absence. Even if she had decided not to continue reading it, she would hardly settle to sleep with a heavy book under her pillow. So the probability was that someone had taken it after her death. One thing was certain. A particular book had been in her possession late on the night before she died yet was not in her room when the police, Miss Rolfe and Nurse Goodale examined it for the first time at about ten past ten the next morning. Whether or not that book had come from Westminster library, it was missing, and if the book wasn't from the library, then what had happened to the token and the reader's ticket? Neither was among her things. And if she had decided not to use them and handed them back to Fallon, why weren't they among Fallon's possessions?

He asked Nurse Goodale what had happened immediately after Nurse Pearce's death.

"Matron sent us students up to her sitting-room and asked us to wait there. Sister Gearing joined us after about half an hour and then some coffee came and we drank that. We stayed there together talking and trying to read until Inspector Bailey and Matron arrived. That must have been about eleven o'clock, perhaps a little earlier."

"And were you all together in that room for the whole of that time?"

"Not all the time. I went out to the library to fetch a book I wanted and was away about three minutes. Nurse Dakers left the room too. I'm not sure why but I think she muttered something about going to the lavatory. Otherwise, as far as I can remember, we all stayed together. Miss Beale, the G.N.C. Inspector, was with us."

She paused.

"You think that this missing library book has something to do with Pearce's death, don't you? You think it's important."

"I think that it may be. That's why I want you to say nothing about our conversation."

"Of course, if that's what you want." She paused.

"But couldn't I try to find out what has happened to the book? I could ask the other students quite casually if they had the ticket and token. I could pretend that I wanted to use them."

Dalgliesh smiled: "Leave the detecting to me. I'd much prefer you to say nothing."

He saw no reason to suggest to her that in a murder investigation too much knowledge could be dangerous. She was a sensible girl. She would think it out for herself soon enough. Taking his silence for dismissal she turned to go. When she reached the door she hesitated and turned:

"Superintendent Dalgliesh, forgive me if I'm interfering. I can't believe that Pearce was murdered. But if she was, then surely the library book could have been taken from her room any time after five to nine when Pearce went into the demo room. The murderer would know that she wouldn't come out of that room alive and that it would be safe for him, or her, to remove it. If the book were taken after Pearce's death it could have been taken by anyone and for a perfectly innocent reason. But if it were taken before she died then it was taken by her killer. That would be true even if the book itself had nothing to do with the reason why she was killed. And Pearce's question to us all about something missing from her room suggests that the book was taken before she died. And why should the murderer bother to remove it if it wasn't in some way connected with the crime?"

"Exactly," said Dalgliesh. "You're a very intelligent young woman."

For the first time he saw Nurse Goodale disconcerted. She blushed, looking at once as pink and pretty as a young bride, then smiled at him, turned quickly and was gone. Dalgliesh, intrigued by the metamorphosis, decided that the local vicar had shown much sense and discernment in choosing his wife. What the parochial church council would make of her uncompromising intelligence was another matter. And he hoped that he wouldn't have to arrest her for murder before they had a chance to make up their minds.

He followed her into the corridor. As usual it was gloomily obscure, lit only by the two bulbs high in a cluster of entwined brass. He had reached the top of the staircase when instinct made him pause and then retrace his steps. Switching on his torch he bent low and moved the beam slowly over the surface of sand in the two fire buckets. The nearer one was caked and grey with dust; it had obviously not been disturbed since it was filled. But the surface of the second one bore a fresher look. Dalgliesh put on his thin cotton searching gloves, fetched from Nurse Pearce's bedroom a sheet of newspaper from one of the drawers, spread it on the corridor floor and slowly tipped out the sand in a rising pyramid. He found no hidden library ticket. But there tumbled out a squat, screw-topped tin, with a stained label. Dalgliesh brushed off the grains of sand to reveal the black print of a skull and the word POISON in capitals. Underneath were the words: "Plant Spray. Death to Insects, Harmless to Plants. Use carefully in accordance with instructions."

He did not need to read the instructions to know what he had found. The stuff was almost pure nicotine. The poison which had killed Nurse Fallon was at last in his hands.

CHAPTER SIX

Long Day's Ending

I

FIVE MINUTES LATER Dalgliesh, having spoken to the forensic science laboratory director and to Sir Miles Honeyman, looked up at a sulkily defensive Sergeant Masterson.

"I'm beginning to see why the Force is so keen on training civilian searchers. I told the scene-of-crime officer to stick to the bedroom, that we'd see to the rest of the house. I thought for some reason that policemen could use their eyes."

Sergeant Masterson, the more furious because he knew the rebuke to be justified, controlled himself with difficulty. He found any criticism difficult to take; from Dalgliesh it was almost impossible. He stiffened to attention like an old soldier on a charge, knowing full well that Dalgliesh would be exasperated rather than mollified by this punctilio, and contrived to sound at the same time both aggrieved and contrite.

"Greeson is a good searcher. I haven't known Greeson miss anything before. He can use his eyes all right, sir."

"Greeson has excellent eyesight. The trouble is that there's no connection between his eyes and his brain. And that's where you come in. The damage is done now. There's no point in holding a post mortem. We don't know whether this tin was in the bucket or not when Fallon's body was discovered this morning. But at least we've found it now. The laboratory has the viscera by the way. Sir Miles called in with it about an hour ago. They're already putting some of the stuff through the gas chromatograph. Now that they know what they're looking for it should speed things. We'd better get this tin off to them as soon as possible. But we'll have a look at it first."

He went over to his murder bag for the finger-print powder, insufflator and lens. The squat little tin became sooty under his careful hands. But there were no prints, only a few amorphous smudges on the faded label.

"Right," he said. "Find the three Sisters, will you Sergeant? They're the ones most likely to know where this tin came from. They live here. Sister Gearing is in her sitting-room. The others should be somewhere around. And if Sister Brumfett is still on her ward she'll have to leave it. Anyone who dies in the next hour must do so without her assistance."

"Do you want to see them separately or together?"

"Either. It doesn't matter. Just get them. Gearing's the one most likely to help. She looks after the flowers."

Sister Gearing arrived first. She came in jauntily, her face perked with curiosity and flushed with the lingering euphoria of a successful hostess. Then her eyes lit on the tin. The transformation was so immediate and startling that it was almost comic. She gasped, "Oh, no!", shot her hand to her mouth and sank into the chair opposite Dalgliesh, deadly pale.

"Where did you . . . ? Oh my God! You're not telling me that Fallon took nicotine?"

"Took, or was given. You recognize this tin, Sister?"

Sister Gearing's voice was almost inaudible.

"Of course. It's my . . . isn't it the tin of rose spray? Where did you find it?"

"Somewhere about the place. Where and when did you see it last?"

"It's kept in that white cupboard under the shelf in the conservatory, just to the left of the door. All my gardening stuff is there. I can't remember when I saw it last."

She was on the edge of tears; happy confidence completely disolved.

"Honestly, it's just too awful! It's frightful! I feel dreadful about it. I really do. But how was I to tell that Fallon would know the stuff was there and use it? I didn't even remember about it myself. If I had, I'd have gone to check that it was still there. I suppose there's no doubt about it? She did die of nicotine poisoning?"

"There's a great deal of doubt until we get the toxicology report. But taking the common-sense view, it looks as if this stuff killed her. You bought it when?"

"Honestly, I can't remember. Sometime early last summer, just before the roses were due. One of the other Sisters might remember. I'm responsible for most of the plants in the conservatory here. At least, I'm not really responsible; it's never been an official arrangement. But I like flowers and there's no one else to bother so I do what I can. I was trying to establish a small rose bed outside the dining-room, too, and I needed the stuff to kill pests. I bought it from Bloxham's Nurseries on the Winchester Road. Look, you can see the address stamped on the label. And I kept it with my other gardening things, gloves and string and the watering cans and trowels and so on, in the corner cupboard in the conservatory."

"Can you remember when you last saw it?"

"Not really. But I went to the cupboard for my gloves last Saturday morning. We had a special service at the chapel on Sunday and I wanted to do the flowers. I thought I might be able to find some interesting boughs, bits of autumn foliage or seed pods in the garden to help the decoration. I don't remember seeing the tin there on Saturday but I think I might have noticed if it were actually missing. But I'm not sure. I haven't used it for months."

"Who else knew that it was there?"

"Well, anyone could have known. I mean, the cupboard isn't locked and there was nothing to stop people looking inside. I suppose I ought to have locked it but one doesn't expect . . . I mean if people are going to kill themselves they'll find a way somehow. I feel absolutely awful but I won't be made to feel responsible. I won't! It isn't fair! She could have used anything. Anything!"

"Who could?"

"Well, Fallon. If Fallon did kill herself. Oh, I don't know what I'm saying."

"Did Nurse Fallon know about the nicotine?"

"Not unless she looked in the cupboard and found it. The only people I can say for certain who did know are Brumfett and Rolfe. I remember that they were sitting in the conservatory when I put the tin into the cupboard. I held it up and said something daft about having enough poison there to kill the lot of them, and Brumfett told me that I ought to lock it up."

"But you didn't?"

"Well, I put it straight away in the cupboard. There isn't a lock so I couldn't do anything about it. Anyway, the tin's labelled clearly enough. Anyone can see that it's poison. And one doesn't expect people to kill themselves. Besides, why the nicotine? Nurses have plenty of opportunity to get hold of drugs. It's not fair to blame me. After all, the disinfectant which killed Pearce was just as lethal. No one complained because that was left in the lavatory. You can't run a nurse training school like a psychiatric unit. I'm not going to be blamed. People here are supposed to be sane, not homicidal maniacs. I won't be made to feel guilty. I won't!"

"If you didn't use the stuff on Nurse Fallon there's no reason why you should feel guilty. Did Sister Rolfe say anything when you brought in the tin?"

"I don't think so. Just looked up from her book. But I can't really remember. I can't even tell you exactly when it was. But it was a warm sunny day. I do remember that. I think it was probably in late May or early June. Rolfe may remember, and Brumfett certainly will."

"We'll ask them. In the meantime I'd better have a look at this cupboard."

He left the tin of nicotine for Masterson to pack for despatch to the laboratory, told him to send Sister Brumfett and Sister Rolfe to the conservatory, and followed Sister Gearing out of the room. She led him down to the ground floor, still muttering her indignant protests. They passed into the empty dining-room. The discovery that the door into the conservatory was locked shook Sister Gearing from her mood of frightened resentment.

"Damn! I'd forgotten. Matron thought we'd better keep it locked after dark because some of the glass isn't too secure. You remember that a pane fell out during the storm? She's afraid someone could get in this way. Usually we don't bother to lock it until we do the final locking up last thing at night. The key will be on the board in Rolfe's office. Wait here. I won't be a jiffy."

She returned almost immediately and fitted the large old-fashioned key into the lock. They passed into the warm fungoid smell of the conservatory. Sister Gearing unerringly reached for the switch, and the two long tubes of fluorescent light, suspended from the high concave ceiling, flickered erratically, then burst into brilliance, revealing the arboreal jungle in all its lushness. The conservatory was a remarkable sight. Dalgliesh had thought so on his first tour of the house, but now, dazzled by the fierce glare on leaves and glass, he blinked in wonder. Around him a minor forest of greenery twined, sprouted, crept and burst in menacing profusion while, outside, its pale reflection hung in the evening air and stretched, motionless and insubstantial, into a green infinity.

Some of the plants looked as if they had flourished in the conservatory since the day it was built. They sprang like mature if miniature palm trees from ornate urns, spreading a canopy of glistening leaves under the glass. Others, more exotic, sprouted bursts of foliage from their scarred and dentate stalks or, like giant cacti, lifted rubber lips, spongy and obscene, to suck the humid air. Between them the ferns sprayed a green shadow, their fragile fronds moving in the draught from the door. Around the sides of the great room were white shelves on which stood pots of the more domestic and agreeable plants which were Sister Gearing's care—red, pink and white chrysanthemums, and African violets. The conservatory should have evoked a tender scene of Victorian domesticity, of fluttering fans and whispered confidences behind the palms. But for Dalgliesh, no corner of Nightingale House was free of the oppressive atmosphere of evil; the very plants seemed to be sucking their manna from a tainted air.

Mavis Gearing went straight over to a low, four-foot-long cupboard in white-painted wood, fitted underneath the wall shelf to the left of the door and hardly visible behind the curtain of waving ferns. It had one inadequate door fitted with a small knob and no lock. Together they crouched to look in it. Although the overhead fluorescent lights were unpleasantly garish, the recesses of the cupboard were dim and their view obstructed by the shadow of their heads. Dalgliesh switched on his torch. Its beam revealed the usual paraphernalia of the indoor gardener. He made a mental inventory. There were balls of green twine, a couple of watering cans, a small spray, packets of seed, some opened and half-used with their tops pressed back, a small plastic bag of potting compost and one of fertilizer, about two dozen flower pots of varying sizes, a small stack of seed trays, pruning shears, a trowel and small fork, a disorderly pile of seedmen's catalogues, three clothbound books on gardening, their covers stained and dirty, an assortment of flower vases, and bundles of tangled wire.

Mavis Gearing pointed to a space in the far corner.

"That's where it was. I put it well back. It couldn't have been a temptation to anyone. You wouldn't even notice it, just opening the door. It was quite hidden really. Look, that's the space—you can see where it was."

She spoke with urgent self-justification, as if the empty space acquitted her of all responsibility. Then her voice changed. It dropped a tone and became huskily pleading like an amateur actress playing a seduction scene.

"I know it looks bad. First, I was in charge of the demonstration when Pearce died. And now this. But I haven't touched the stuff since I used it last summer. I swear I haven't! I know some of them won't believe me. They'll be glad—yes glad—and relieved if suspicion falls on me and Len. It'll let them out. Besides they're jealous. They've always been jealous. It's because I've got a man and they haven't. But you believe me don't you? You've got to believe me!"

It was pathetic and humiliating. She pressed her shoulder against his, as they knelt huddled together in a ridiculous parody of prayer. He could feel her breath against his cheek. Her right hand, the fingers twitching nervously, crept across the floor towards his hand.

Then her mood broke. They heard Sister Rolfe's cold voice from the door.

"The Sergeant told me to meet you here. Am I interrupting anything?"

Dalgliesh felt the pressure on his shoulder immediately released, and Sister Gearing scrambled gracelessly to her feet. He got up more slowly. He neither felt nor looked embarrassed, but he was not sorry that Miss Rolfe had chosen that moment to appear.

Sister Gearing broke into explanation:

"It's the rose spray. That stuff containing nicotine. Fallon must have taken it. I feel absolutely ghastly about it, but how was I to know? The Superintendent has found the tin."

She turned to Dalgliesh.

"You didn't say where?"

"No," Dalgliesh said. "I didn't say where." He spoke to Miss Rolfe.

"Did you know the stuff was kept in this cupboard?"

"Yes, I saw Gearing put it there. Some time last summer wasn't it?"

"You didn't mention this to me."

"I didn't think of it until now. It never occurred to me that Fallon might have taken nicotine. And, presumably, we don't yet know that she did."

Dalgliesh said: "Not until we get the toxicology report."

"And even then, Superintendent, can you be sure that the drug came from this tin? There are other sources of nicotine at the hospital surely? This could be a blind."

"Of course, although it seems to me highly unlikely. But the forensic science laboratory should be able to tell us that. This nicotine is mixed with a proportion of concentrated detergent. It will be identifiable by gas chromatography."

She shrugged.

"Well, that should settle it then."

Mavis Gearing cried out: "What do you mean, other sources of supply? Who are you getting at? Nicotine isn't kept in the pharmacy, as far as I know. And anyway Len had left Nightingale House before Fallon died."

"I wasn't accusing Leonard Morris. But he was on the spot when both of them died, remember, and he was here in this room when you put the nicotine in the cupboard. He's a suspect like the rest of us."

"Was Mr. Morris with you when you bought the nicotine?"

"Well, he was as a matter of fact. I'd forgotten it or I would have told you. We'd been out together that afternoon and he came back here to tea."

She turned angrily to Sister Rolfe.

"It's nothing to do with Len, I tell you! He hardly knew Pearce or Fallon. Pearce hadn't anything on Len."

Hilda Rolfe said calmly: "I wasn't aware that she had anything on anyone. I don't know whether you're trying to put ideas into Mr. Dalgliesh's head, but you're certainly putting them into mine."

Sister Gearing's face disintegrated into misery. Moaning, she jerked her head from side to side as if desperately seeking help or asylum. Her face, sickly and surrealist, was suffused with the green light of the conservatory.

Sister Rolfe gave Dalgliesh one sharp look, then ignoring him, moved over to her colleague and said with unexpected gentleness:

"Look Gearing, I'm sorry. Of course I'm not accusing Leonard Morris or you. But the fact that he was here would have come out anyway. Don't let the police fluster you. It's how they work. I don't suppose the Superintendent cares a damn whether you or I or Brumfett killed Pearce and Fallon so long as he can prove someone did. Well, let him get on with it. Just answer his questions and keep calm. Why not get on with your job and let the police get on with theirs?"

Mavis Gearing wailed like a child seeking reassurance: "But it's all so awful!"

"Of course it is! But it won't last for ever. And in the meantime, if you must confide in a man, find yourself a solicitor, a psychiatrist or a priest. At least you can be reasonably sure they'll be on your side."

Mavis Gearing's worried eyes moved from Dalgliesh to Rolfe. She looked like a child hesitating to decide where her allegiance lay. Then the two women moved imperceptibly together and gazed at Dalgliesh, Sister Gearing in puzzled reproach and Sister Rolfe with the tight satisfied smile of a woman who has just brought off a successful piece of mischief.

II

At that moment Dalgliesh caught the sound of approaching footsteps. Someone was moving across the dining-room. He turned to the door, expecting to find that Sister Brumfett had at last come to be interviewed. The conservatory door opened but, instead of her squat figure, he saw a tall bare-headed man wearing a belted raincoat and with a gauze patch taped across his left eye. A peevish voice spoke from the doorway:

"What's happened to everyone? This place is like a morgue."

Before anyone could reply, Miss Gearing had darted forward and seized his arm. Dalgliesh saw with interest his frown and twitch of involuntary recoil.

"Len, what is it? You're hurt! You never told me! I thought it was your ulcer. You never said anything about hurting your head!"

"It was my ulcer. But this didn't help it."

He spoke directly to Dalgliesh:

"You must be Chief Superintendent Dalgliesh of New Scotland Yard. Miss Gearing told me that you wanted to see me. I'm on my way to my general practitioner's surgery but I'm at your disposal for half an hour."

But Sister Gearing was not to be diverted from her concern.

"But you never said anything about an accident! How did it happen? Why didn't you tell me about it when I rang?"

"Because we had other things to discuss and because I didn't want you to fuss."

He shook off her detaining arm and sat himself down in a wicker chair. The two women and Dalgliesh moved in close to him. There was a silence. Dalgliesh revised his unreasonably preconceived notions of Miss Gearing's lover. He should have looked ridiculous, sitting there in his cheap raincoat with his patched eye and bruised face and speaking in that grating sarcastic voice. But he was curiously impressive. Sister Rolfe had somehow conveyed the impression of a little man, nervous, ineffectual and easily intimidated. This man had force. It might be only the manifestation of pent-up nervous energy; it might be the obsessive resentment born of failure or unpopularity. But his was certainly not a comfortable or negligible personality.

Dalgliesh asked: "When did you learn that Josephine Fallon was dead?"

"When I rang my pharmacy office just after nine thirty this morning to say that I wouldn't be in. My assistant told me. I suppose the news was all over the hospital by then."

"How did you react to the news?"

"React? I didn't react. I hardly knew the girl. I was surprised, I suppose. Two deaths in the same house and so close together in time; well, it's unusual to say the least of it. It's shocking really. You could say I was shocked."

He spoke like a successful politician condescending to express an attributable opinion to a cub reporter.

"But you didn't connect the two deaths?"

"Not at the time. My assistant just said that another Nightingale—we call the students Nightingales when they are in block—that another Nightingale student, Jo Fallon, had been found dead. I asked how and he said something about a heart attack following influenza. I thought it was a natural death. I suppose that's what everyone thought at first."

"When did you think otherwise?"

"I suppose when Miss Gearing rang me about an hour later to say that you were here."

So Sister Gearing had telephoned Morris at his home. She must have wanted to reach him urgently to have risked that. Was it perhaps to warn him, to agree their story? While Dalgliesh was wondering what excuse, if any, she had given to Mrs. Morris, the pharmacist answered the unspoken question.

"Miss Gearing doesn't usually ring me at home. She knows that I like to keep my professional and my private life absolutely separate. But she was naturally anxious about my health when she rang the laboratory after breakfast and was told that I wasn't in. I suffer from a duodenal ulcer."

"Your wife, no doubt, was able to reassure her."

He replied calmly but with a sharp glance at Sister Rolfe, who had moved to the periphery of the group:

"My wife takes the children to her mother's all day on Fridays."

As Mavis Gearing would no doubt have known. So they had, after all, had a chance to consult each other, to decide on their story. But if they were concocting an alibi, why fix it for midnight? Because they knew for the best or worst of reasons that Fallon had died at that hour? Or because, knowing her habits, they judged that midnight was the most likely time? Only the killer, and perhaps not even he, could know precisely when Fallon had died. It could have been before midnight. It could have been as late as two thirty. Even Miles Honeyman with his thirty years' experience couldn't time the death precisely from clinical signs alone. The only certain thing was that Fallon was dead and that she had died almost immediately after drinking her whisky. But when exactly had that been? It was her usual habit to prepare her late night drink as soon as she went upstairs to bed. But no one admitted to having seen her after she left the nurses' sitting-room. Fallon could, just possibly, have been alive when Sister Brumfett and the Burt twins saw her light shining through the keyhole just after two a.m. And if she had been alive then what had she been doing between midnight and two o'clock? Dalgliesh had been concentrating on those people who had access to the school. But suppose Fallon had left Nightingale House that night, perhaps to keep an assignation. Or suppose she had deferred making her nightly drink of whisky and lemon because she was expecting a visitor. The front and back doors of Nightingale House had been found bolted in the morning, but Fallon could have let her visitor out any time during the night and bolted the door behind him.

But Mavis Gearing was still preoccupied with her lover's damaged head and bruised face.

"What happened to you, Len? You've got to tell me. Did you come off your bicycle?"

Sister Rolfe laughed unkindly. Leonard Morris bestowed on her a measured glance of intimidating contempt, then turned to Sister Gearing.

"If you must know Mavis, yes I did. It happened after I left you last night. There was one of the big elms down across the path and I cycled right into it."

Sister Rolfe spoke for the first time.

"Surely you could see it in the light of your bicycle lamp?"

"My bicycle lamp, Sister, not unreasonably, is fixed to shine on the road. I saw the tree trunk. What I didn't see in time was one of the high jutting boughs. I was lucky not to lose an eye."

Sister Gearing, predictably, gave an anguished yelp.

Dalgliesh asked: "What time did this happen?"

"I've just told you. Last night after I had left Nightingale House. Oh, I see! You're asking what time precisely? As it happens I can answer that. I came off my bicycle under the impact and was afraid that my watch had been broken. Fortunately it hadn't. The hands stood at twelve seventeen a.m. precisely."

"Wasn't there some warning—a white scarf—tied to the branch?"

"Of course not, Superintendent. If there had been I should hardly have ridden straight into it."

"If it were tied high up on a bough you might not have noticed it."

"It wasn't there to notice. After I'd picked up my bicycle and recovered a little from the shock I inspected the tree carefully. My first thought was that I might be able to shift it at least slightly and leave part of the road clear. That was obviously impossible. The job was going to need a tractor and tackle. But there was no scarf on any part of that tree at twelve seventeen a.m."

"Mr. Morris," said Dalgliesh, "I think it's time you and I had a little talk."

But Sister Brumfett was waiting for him outside the interview room. Before Dalgliesh could speak she said accusingly:

"I was summoned to see you in this room. I came promptly at some inconvenience to my ward. When I arrive I'm told that you're not in your room and will I please go down to the conservatory. I don't propose to chase around Nightingale House for you. If you want to see me I can spare you half an hour now."

"Miss Brumfett," said Dalgliesh, "you seem determined by your behaviour to give me the impression that you killed these girls. It's possible you did. I shall come to a conclusion about that as soon as I reasonably can. In the meantime, please curb your enthusiasm for antagonizing the police and wait until I can see you. That will be when I've finished talking to Mr. Morris. You can wait here outside the office or go to your own room, whichever suits you. But I shall want you in about thirty minutes and I, too, have no intention of chasing over the house to find you."

He had no idea how she would take this rebuke. Her reaction was surprising. The eyes behind the thick spectacles softened and twinkled. Her face broke into a momentary grin and she gave a satisfied little nod as if she had at least succeeded in provoking a particularly docile student into showing a flash of spirit.

"I'll wait here." She plonked herself down on the chair outside the office door then, nodded towards Morris.

"And I shouldn't let him do all the talking or you'll be lucky to be through in half an hour."

III

But the interview took less than thirty minutes. The first couple were spent by Morris making himself comfortable. He took off his shabby raincoat, shaking it and smoothing down the folds as if it had somehow become contaminated in Nightingale House, then folded it with fussy precision over the back of his chair. Then he seated himself opposite Dalgliesh and took the initiative.

"Please don't fire questions at me, Superintendent. I don't like being interrogated. I prefer to tell my story in my own way. You needn't worry about it being accurate. I'd hardly be chief pharmacist of an important hospital if I hadn't the head for detail and a good memory for facts."

Dalgliesh said mildly: "Then could I have some facts please, starting perhaps with your movements last night."

Morris continued as if he hadn't heard this eminently reasonable request.

"Miss Gearing has given me the privilege of her friendship for the past six years. I've no doubt that certain people here, certain women living in Nightingale House, have placed their own interpretation on that friendship. That is to be expected. When you get a community of middle-aged spinsters living together you're bound to get sexual jealousy."

"Mr. Morris," said Dalgliesh gently. "I'm not here to investigate your relationship with Miss Gearing or hers with her colleagues. If those relationships have anything to do with the deaths of these two girls, then tell me about them. Otherwise let's leave out the amateur psychology and get down to the material facts."

"My relationship with Miss Gearing is germane to your inquiry in that it has brought me into this house at about the time Nurse Pearce and Nurse Fallon died."

"All right. Then tell me about those two occasions."

"The first was the morning when Nurse Pearce died. You are, no doubt, aware of the details. Naturally I reported my visit to Inspector Bailey since he caused a notice to be appended to all the hospital notice-boards inquiring the names of people who had visited Nightingale House on the morning on which Nurse Pearce died. But I have no objection to repeating the information. I called in here on my way to the pharmacy to leave Miss Gearing a note. It was in fact a card, one of those 'good luck' cards which it is customary to send friends before some important event. I knew that Miss Gearing would have to take the first demonstration of the day, indeed the first demonstration of this school, as Sister Manning, who is Miss Rolfe's first assistant, is sick with flu. Miss Gearing was naturally nervous, particularly as the General Nursing Council Inspector was to be present. Unfortunately I missed the previous evening's post. I was anxious for her to get my card before she went into the demonstration so I decided to slip it into her cubby hole myself. I came to work especially early, arrived at Nightingale House shortly after eight, and left almost immediately. I saw no one. Presumably the staff and students were at breakfast. I certainly didn't enter the demonstration room. I wasn't particularly keen to draw attention to myself. I merely inserted the card in its envelope into Miss Gearing's cubby hole and withdrew. It was rather an amusing card. It showed two robins, the male bird forming the words 'good luck' in worms at the feet of the female. Miss Gearing may well have kept the card; she has a fancy for such trifles. No doubt she would show it to you on request. It would corroborate my story of what I was doing in Nightingale House."

Dalgliesh said gravely: "I have already seen the card. Did you know what the demonstration would be about?"

"I knew that it was on intra-gastric feeding but I didn't know that Nurse Fallon had been taken ill in the night or who was to act the part of the patient."

"Have you any idea at all how the corrosive poison got into the drip?"

"If you would just let me take my own time. I was about to tell you. I have none. The most likely explanation is that someone was playing a stupid joke and didn't realize that the result would be fatal. That, or an accident. There are precedents. A new-born baby was killed in the maternity wing of a hospital—not happily one of ours—only three years ago when a bottle of disinfectant was mistaken for milk. I can't explain how the accident here could have occurred or who in Nightingale House could have been so ignorant and stupid as to think that the result of putting a corrosive poison in the milk feed would entertain anyone."

He paused as if defying Dalgliesh to interrupt with another question. Meeting only a bland interrogatory gaze, he went on:

"So much for Nurse Pearce's death. I can't help you further there. It's rather a different matter with Nurse Fallon."

"Something that happened last night; someone you saw?"

The irritation snapped out: "Nothing to do with last night, Superintendent, Miss Gearing has already told you about last night. We saw no one. We left her room immediately after twelve o'clock and went out down the back stairs through Miss Taylor's flat. I retrieved my bicycle from the bushes at the rear of the house—I see no reason why my visits here should be advertised to every mean-minded female in the neighbourhood—and we walked together to the first turn in the path. Then we paused to talk and I escorted Miss Gearing back to Nightingale House and watched her in through the back door. She had left it open. I finally rode off and as I have told you, got to the fallen elm at twelve seventeen a.m. If anyone passed that way after me and fixed a white scarf to a branch, I can only say that I didn't see him. If he came by car it must have been parked at the other side of Nightingale House. I saw no car."

Another pause. Dalgliesh made no sign, but Masterson permitted himself a sigh of weary resignation as he rustled over a page of his note pad.

"No, Superintendent, the event which I am about to relate took place last spring when this present set of students, including Nurse Fallon, were in their second-year block. As was customary, I gave them a lecture on poisons. At the end of my talk all the students except Nurse Fallon had gathered up their books and left. She came up to the desk and asked me for the name of a poison which could kill painlessly and instantaneously and which an ordinary person might be able to obtain. I thought it an unusual question but saw no reason why I should refuse to answer it. It never occurred to me for one moment that the question had any personal application and, in any case, it was information she could have obtained from a book in the hospital library on materia medica or forensic medicine."

Dalgliesh said: "And what exactly did you tell her, Mr. Morris?"

"I told her that one such poison was nicotine and that it could be obtained from an ordinary rose spray."

Truth or a lie? Who could tell? Dalgliesh fancied that he could usually detect lying in a suspect; but not this suspect. And if Morris stuck to his story, how could it ever be disproved? And if it were a lie, its purpose was plain—to suggest that Josephine Fallon had killed herself. And the obvious reason why he should wish to do that was to protect Sister Gearing. He loved her. This slightly ridiculous, pedantic man; that silly, flirtatious, ageing woman—they loved each other. And why not? Love wasn't the prerogative of the young and desirable. But it was a complication in any investigation—pitiable, tragic or ludicrous, as the case might be, but never negligible. Inspector Bailey, as he knew from the notes on the first crime, had never fully believed in the story of the greetings card. It was in his opinion a foolish and childish gesture for a grown man, and particularly out of character for Morris; therefore he distrusted it. But Dalgleish thought differently. It was one with Morris's lonely, unromantic cycle rides to visit his mistress; the machine hidden ignominiously in the bushes behind Nightingale House; the slow walk together through the cold of a January midnight prolonging those last precious minutes; his clumsy but strangely dignified defence of the woman he loved. And this last statement, true or false, was inconvenient to say the least. If he stuck to it it would be a powerful argument for those who preferred to believe that Fallon had died by her own hand. And he would stick to it. He looked at Dalgliesh now with the steadfast, exalted gaze of a prospective martyr, holding his adversary's eyes, daring him to disbelieve. Dalgliesh sighed:

"All right," he said. "We won't waste time in speculation. Let's go once again over the timing of your movements last night."

IV

Sister Brumfett, true to her promise, was waiting outside the door when Masterson let Leonard Morris out. But her previous mood of cheerful acquiescence had vanished and she settled herself down opposite Dalgliesh as if to do battle. Before that matriarchal glare he felt something of the inadequacy of a junior student nurse newly arrived on the private ward; and something stronger and horribly familiar. His mind traced the surprising fear unerringly to its source. Just so had the Matron of his prep. school once looked at him, producing in the homesick eight-year-old the same inadequacy, the same fear. And for one second he had to force himself to meet her gaze.

It was the first opportunity he had had to observe her closely and on her own. It was an unattractive and yet an ordinary face. The small shrewd eyes glared into his through steel spectacles, their bridge half embedded in the deep fleshy cleft above the mottled nose. Her iron grey hair was cut short, framing in ribbed waves the plump marsupial cheeks and the obstinate line of the jaw. The elegant gophered cap which on Mavis Gearing looked as delicate as a meringue of spun lace and which flattered even Hilda Rolfe's androgynous features was bound low on Sister Brumfett's brow like a pie frill circling a particularly unappetizing crust. Take that symbol of authority away and replace it by an undistinguished felt hat, cover the uniform with a shapeless fawn coat, and you would have the prototype of a middle-aged suburban housewife strutting through the supermarket, shapeless bag in hand, eyes shrewd for this week's bargain. Yet here, apparently, was one of the best ward Sisters John Carpendar had ever had. Here, more surprisingly, was Mary Taylor's chosen friend.

Before he could begin to question her, she said:

"Nurse Fallon committed suicide. First she killed Pearce and then herself. Fallon murdered Pearce. I happen to know that she did. So why don't you stop worrying Matron and let the work of the hospital go on? There's nothing you can do to help either of them now. They're both dead."

Spoken in that authoritative and disconcertingly evocative tone the statement had the force of a command. Dalgliesh's reply was unreasonably sharp. Damn the woman! He wouldn't be intimidated.

"If you know that for certain, you must have some proof. And anything you know ought to be told. I'm investigating murder, Sister, not the theft of a bedpan. You have a duty not to withhold evidence."

She laughed; a sharp, derisive hoot like an animal coughing.

"Evidence! You wouldn't call it evidence. But I know!"

"Did Nurse Fallon speak to you when she was being nursed on your ward? Was she delirious?"

It was no more than a guess. She snorted her derision.

"If she did, it wouldn't be my duty to tell you. What a patient lets out in delirium isn't gossip to be bandied about. Not on my ward anyway. It isn't evidence either. Just accept what I tell you and stop fussing. Fallon killed Pearce. Why do you think she came back to Nighingale House that morning, with a temperature of 103? Why do you think she refused to give the police a reason? Fallon killed Pearce. You men like to make things so complicated. But it's all so simple really. Fallon killed Pearce, and there's no doubt she had her reasons."

"There are no valid reasons for murder. And even if Fallon did kill Pearce, I doubt whether she killed herself. I've no doubt your colleagues have told you about the rose spray. Remember that Fallon hadn't been in Nightingale House since that tin of nicotine was placed in the conservatory cupboard. Her set haven't been in Nightingale House since the spring of last year and Sister Gearing bought the rose spray in the summer. Nurse Fallon was taken ill on the night that this block began and didn't return to Nightingale House until the evening before she died. How do you account for the fact that she knew where to find the nicotine?"

Sister Brumfett looked surprisingly disconcerted. There was a moment's silence and then she muttered something unintelligible. Dalgliesh waited. Then she said defensively:

"I don't know how she got hold of it. That's for you to discover. But it's obvious that she did."

"Did you know where the nicotine had been put?"

"No. I don't have anything to do with the garden or the conservatory. I like to get out of the hospital on my free days. I usually play golf with Matron or we go for a drive. We try to arrange our off duty together."

Her tone was smug with satisfaction. She made no attempt to hide her complacency. What was she trying to convey, he wondered. Was this reference to the Matron her way of telling him that she was teacher's pet, to be treated with deference?

He said: "Weren't you in the conservatory that evening last summer when Miss Gearing came in with the stuff?"

"I don't remember."

"I think you'd better try to remember, Sister. It shouldn't be difficult. Other people remember perfectly well."

"If they say I was there, I probably was."

"Miss Gearing says that she showed you all the bottle and made a facetious remark about being able to poison the whole school with a few drops. You told her not to be childish and to make sure the tin was locked away. Do you remember now?"

"It's the sort of silly remark Mavis Gearing would make and I daresay I did tell her to be careful. It's a pity she didn't take notice of me."

"You take these deaths very calmly, Sister."

"I take every death very calmly. If I didn't I couldn't do my job. Death is happening all the time in a hospital. It's probably happening now on my ward as it did this afternoon to one of my patients!"

She spoke with sudden and passionate protest, stiffening as if in outrage that the dread finger could touch anyone for whom she was responsible. Dalgliesh found the sudden change of mood disconcerting. It was as if this thickening, unattractive body housed the temperament of a *prima donna,* passionate and irrational. At one moment the eyes, small and unremarkable behind their thick lenses, met his in dull resentment, the obstinate little mouth snapped out its grievances. And then, suddenly, there was this metamorphosis. She blazed at him, her face flaming with indignation so that it came fiercely alive. He had a glimpse of that fervent and possessive love with which she encompassed those in her care. Here was a woman, outwardly unremarkable, who had dedicated her life to a single aim with formidable determination. If something—or someone—got in the way of what she regarded as the greater good, how far would that determination carry her? She seemed to Dalgliesh a fundamentally unintelligent woman. But murder was frequently the last resort of the unintelligent. And were these murders, for all their complexity, the work of a clever woman? A bottle of disinfectant quickly seized; a tin of nicotine readily available. Didn't both these deaths speak of a sudden uncontrolled impulse, an unthinking reliance on the easiest means? Surely in a hospital there were more subtle methods of disposal?

The shrewd eyes were regarding him with watchful dislike. The whole interrogation was an outrage to her. It was hopeless to try to propitiate such a witness and he had no stomach to try. He said:

"I want to go through your movements on the morning Nurse Pearce died, and last night."

"I've already told Inspector Bailey about the morning Pearce died. And I've sent you a note."

"I know. Thank you for it. Now I want you to tell me yourself."

She made no further protest but recited the sequence of her movements and actions as if they were a railway timetable.

Her account of her movements on the morning of Heather Pearce's death agreed almost exactly with the written statement she had already given to Inspector Bailey. She described only her own actions, put forward no theories, gave no opinion. After that first revealing outburst she had apparently decided to stick to facts.

She had woken at six thirty on the Monday the twelfth of January, and had then joined the Matron for early morning tea which it was their habit to drink together in Miss Taylor's flat. She had left Matron at seven fifteen and had then bathed and dressed. She had stayed in her own room until about ten minutes to eight when she had collected her paper from the rack in the hall and had gone in to breakfast. She had seen no one on the stairs or in the hall. Sister Gearing and Sister Rolfe had joined her in the dining-room and they had breakfasted together. She had finished her breakfast and had left the room first; she was unable to say precisely when but it was probably not later than twenty past eight, had returned briefly to her sitting-room on the third floor, and had then walked over to the hospital where she had arrived on her ward shortly before nine o'clock. She had known about the General Nursing Council Inspection since, obviously, Matron had talked to her about it. She had known about the demonstration since details of the nurse training programme were on the hall notice-board. She had known about Josephine Fallon's illness since Sister Rolfe had telephoned her during the night. She had not, however, known that Nurse Pearce was to take Fallon's place. She agreed that she could have discovered this easily by a glance at the notice-board, but she had not troubled to look. There was no reason why she should be concerned. Taking an interest in the general nurse training programme was one thing, bothering to check on who was to act as the patient was quite another.

She had not known that Nurse Fallon had returned to Nightingale House that morning. Had she done so, she would have reprimanded the girl severely. By the time she had reached the ward Nurse Fallon was in her room and in bed. No one in the ward had noticed her absence. Apparently the Staff Nurse had thought she was in the bathroom or the lavatory. It was reprehensible of the Staff Nurse not to have checked, but the ward was particularly busy and one did not expect patients, particularly student nurses, to behave like idiots. Nurse Fallon had probably only left the ward for about twenty minutes. Her walk through the dark morning had apparently done her no harm. She had made a quick recovery from the influenza and there had been no complications. She had not seemed particularly depressed while she was in the ward, and if there was anything worrying her, she had not confided in Sister Brumfett. In Sister Brumfett's opinion, the girl had been perfectly well enough on discharge from the ward to rejoin her set in Nightingale House.

Next she went through her movements on the previous night, in the same dull, unemphatic voice. Matron had been in Amsterdam at the International Conference so she had spent the evening alone watching television in the Sisters' sitting-room. She had gone to bed at ten p.m. and had been awakened at about quarter to twelve by Mr. Courtney-Briggs's telephone call. She made her way across to the hospital by a short cut through the trees and had helped the student nurse on duty to prepare the bed for the patient's return. She had stayed with her patient until satisfied that the oxygen and drip were being satisfactorily administered and that his general condition was as good as could be expected. She had returned to Nightingale House shortly after two a.m. and on her way up to her room had seen Maureen Burt coming out of the lavatory. The other twin had appeared almost immediately and she had had a brief conversation with them. She had declined their offer to make her cocoa and had gone straight up to her room. Yes, there was a light shining through Fallon's keyhole at that time. She had not gone into Fallon's room and had no way of knowing whether the girl was alive or dead. She had slept well and had awoken just after seven o'clock when Sister Rolfe had come rushing in with the news that Fallon's body had been discovered. She hadn't seen Fallon since the girl was discharged from her ward after supper on the Tuesday.

At the end of the recital there was a silence, then Dalgliesh asked:

"Did you like Nurse Pearce, Sister? Or Nurse Fallon?"

"No. I didn't dislike them either. I don't believe in having personal relationships with the student nurses. Like and dislike don't come into it. They're either good nurses or they aren't."

"And were they good nurses?"

"Fallon was better than Pearce. She had more intelligence and more imagination. She wasn't an easy colleague but the patients liked her. Some people thought her callous but you wouldn't find a patient who said so. Pearce tried too hard. She went about looking like a young Florence Nightingale, or so she thought. Always thinking of the impression she was making. A silly girl fundamentally. But you could rely on her. She always did what was correct.

Fallon did what was right. That takes instinct as well as training. Wait until you're dying, my good man. You'll know the difference."

So Josephine Fallon had been both intelligent and imaginative. He could believe it. But these were the last two qualities he would have expected Sister Brumfett to praise. He recalled the conversation at luncheon, her insistence on the need for unquestioning obedience. He said carefully:

"I'm surprised that you should rank imagination among the virtues of a student nurse. I thought that you valued absolute obedience above all. It's difficult to reconcile imagination, which is surely individual, even iconoclastic, with the submission to authority of the good subordinate. I'm sorry if I sound presumptuous. This conversation hasn't much to do with my business here, I know. But I'm curious."

It had a great deal to do with his business there; his curiosity wasn't irrelevant. But she wasn't to know that. She said gruffly:

"Obedience to rightful authority comes first. You're in a disciplined service; you shouldn't need telling. It's only when the obedience is automatic, when the discipline is accepted and even welcomed, that one learns the wisdom and courage that can safely step outside the rules when the moment comes. Imagination and intelligence are dangerous in nursing if they aren't founded on discipline."

So she wasn't as simple or as obstinately conformist as she appeared, or chose to appear to her colleagues. And she, too, had imagination. Was this the Brumfett, he wondered, that Mary Taylor knew and valued. And yet, he was convinced that his first impressions hadn't been wrong. Fundamentally, she wasn't an intelligent woman. Was she, even now, voicing the theory, the very words perhaps, of another? "The wisdom and courage to step outside the rules." Well, someone in Nightingale House had stepped outside them, someone hadn't lacked the courage. They looked at each other. He was beginning to wonder if Nightingale House had put some kind of spell on him, if its threatening atmosphere had begun to affect his judgement. For behind the thick spectacles he thought he saw the eyes change, thought he detected an urgency to communicate, to be understood, even a plea for help. And then the illusion passed. He was facing again the most ordinary, the most uncompromising, the least complex of all his suspects. And the interview was at an end.

V

It was now after nine o'clock but Dalgliesh and Masterson were still together in the office. There were at least a couple of hours' work ahead before they could break for the night, checking and comparing statements, searching for the tell-tale discrepancy, planning tomorrow's activity. Dalgliesh decided to let Masterson get on with it and dialling the internal number of Matron's flat, he asked if she could give him twenty minutes of her time. Courtesy and policy both dictated that he should keep her informed, but there was another reason for seeing her before he left Nightingale House.

She had left the door of the flat open for him and he passed straight down the corridor to the sitting-room, knocked and entered. He walked into peace, quietness, light. And coldness. The room was surprisingly chilly. A bright fire was burning in the grate but its warmth hardly reached the far corners of the room. As he went across to her he saw that she was appropriately dressed, her long legs encased in brown velvet slacks topped by a high necked cashmere sweater in pale fawn, the sleeves pushed back from brittle wrists. A silk scarf in bright green was knotted around her throat.

They sat down together on the sofa. Dalgliesh saw that she had been working. There was an open briefcase propped against the leg of the coffee table and a spread of papers across its surface. A coffee pot stood in the grate, and the comforting scent of warm wood and coffee pervaded the room.

She offered him coffee or whisky; nothing else. He accepted the coffee and she rose to fetch a second cup. When she had returned, the coffee poured, he said:

"They've told you, I expect, that we've found the poison."

"Yes. Gearing and Rolfe both came to see me after you'd finished questioning them. I suppose this means that it must be murder?"

"I think so, unless Nurse Fallon hid the tin herself. But somehow that seems unlikely. To make a deliberate mystery of suicide with the object of causing the maximum of trouble would be the action of an exhibitionist or a neurotic. This girl seems to me to have been neither, but I wanted your view."

"I agree with you. Fallon, I would have said, was essentially a rational person. If she decided to kill herself it would be for reasons which seemed good to her at the time and I would expect her to leave a brief but lucid note explaining them. A great many suicides kill themselves to make trouble for other people. But not Fallon."

"That would be my assessment, but I wanted to ask someone who had actually known her."

She asked: "What does Madeleine Goodale say?"

"Nurse Goodale thinks that her friend killed herself; but that was before we found the nicotine."

He didn't say where and she didn't ask. He had no

intention of telling anyone in Nightingale House where the tin had been found. But one person would know where it had been hidden and with luck might inadvertently reveal their guilty knowledge.

He went on: "There is another matter. Miss Gearing tells me she entertained a friend in her room last night; she says that she let him out through your door. Does that surprise you?"

"No. I leave the flat open when I'm not here so that the Sisters can use the back staircase. It gives them at least the illusion of privacy."

"At the cost, surely, of your own?"

"Oh, I think it's understood that they don't come into the flat. I trust my colleagues. Even if I didn't there's nothing here to interest them. I keep all official papers in my office over at the hospital."

She was right of course. There was nothing here to interest anyone except him. The sitting-room for all its individuality was almost as plain as his own flat high above the Thames at Queenhithe. Perhaps that was one reason why he felt so at home. Here were no photographs to invite speculation; no bureau bursting with its accumulated hoard of trivia; no pictures to betray a private taste; no invitations to advertise the diversity, the existence even, of a social life. He held his own flat inviolate; it would have been intolerable to him to think that people could walk in and out at will. But here was an even greater reticence; the self-sufficiency of a woman so private that even her personal surroundings were permitted to give nothing away.

He said: "Mr. Courtney-Briggs tells me that he was Josephine Fallon's lover for a short period during her first year. Did you know that?"

"Yes. I knew it in the same way that I know Mavis Gearing's visitor yesterday was almost certainly Leonard Morris. In a hospital, gossip spreads by a kind of osmosis. One can't always remember being told the latest scandal; one just gets to know."

"And is there much to know?"

"More perhaps than in less sensational institutions. Is that so very surprising? Men and women who have to watch daily what the body can suffer in agony and degradation aren't likely to be too scrupulous about availing themselves of its solace."

When, and with whom, he wondered, did she find her consolation? In her job; in the power which that job undoubtedly gave her? In astronomy, tracing through long nights the paths of the movable stars? With Brumfett? Surely to God not with Brumfett!

She said: "If you're thinking that Stephen Courtney-Briggs might have killed to protect his reputation, well, I don't believe it. I got to know about the affair. So did half the hospital, I've no doubt. Courtney-Briggs isn't particularly discreet. Besides, such a motive would only apply to a man vulnerable to public opinion."

"Every man is vulnerable in some way to public opinion."

She gave him a sudden keen glance from those extraordinary exophthalmic eyes.

"Of course. No doubt Stephen Courtney-Briggs is as capable of killing to prevent personal disaster or public disgrace as any of us. But not, I think, to prevent people knowing that a young and attractive woman was willing to go to bed with him; or that, middle-aged as he may be, he is still able to take his sexual pleasure where he finds it."

Was there a trace of contempt, of resentment almost, in her voice? For a moment he caught an echo of Sister Rolfe.

"And Hilda Rolfe's friendship with Julia Pardoe? You knew about that?"

She smiled a little bitterly.

"Friendship? Yes, I know, and I think that I understand. But I'm not sure that you do. The orthodox reaction, if the affair became known, would be that Rolfe is corrupting Pardoe. But if that young woman has been corrupted, I suspect that it happened before she came to the John Carpendar. I don't propose to interfere. The affair will settle itself. Julia Pardoe should qualify as a State Registered Nurse in a few months' time. I happen to know that she has plans for her future and they certainly don't include staying on here. I'm afraid there is a great deal of unhappiness ahead for Sister Rolfe. But we must meet that when it comes."

Her voice told him that she knew, that she was watching, that she had the situation under control. And that it was not a matter for further discussion.

He finished his coffee in silence, then rose to go. There was nothing else he needed to ask at present and he found himself disagreeably sensitive to every nuance in her voice, every silence which might imply that his presence was irksome. It could hardly be welcome, he knew that. He was used to being the harbinger, at best of ill news, at worst of disaster. But at least he could avoid forcing his company on her a minute more than was necessary.

As she rose to accompany him to the door he made a casual reference to the architecture of the house and asked how long it had been in the possession of the hospital. She said:

"It's a tragic and rather horrible story. The place was built in 1880 by a Thomas Nightingale, a local string and rope manufacturer who had come up in the world and wanted a house to dignify his new position. The name is fortuitously appropriate; it has nothing to do with Florence or with the bird. Nightingale lived here with his wife, they had no children, until 1886. In the January of that year the body

of one of the maidservants, a nineteen-year-old girl called
Nancy Gorringe, who had been taken by Mrs. Nightingale
from an orphanage, was found hanging from one of the
trees in the grounds. When the body was cut down it was
apparent that she had been systematically ill-treated, beaten,
tortured even, over a period of months. It had been calculated sadism. One of the most horrible features of the case
was that the other members of the staff must have had some
idea what was going on, but did nothing. They were apparently well treated; they paid touching tribute at the trial to
Nightingale as a just and considerate master. It must have
been similar to some of these modern cases of child cruelty
where only one member of the family is singled out for violence and neglect and the others acquiesce in the ill treatment. A taste for vicarious sadism, I suppose, or just the
desperate hope of preserving their own safety. And yet it's
odd. Not one of them turned against Nightingale, not
even when local feeling was at its height in the weeks following the trial. He and his wife were both convicted and
spent many years in prison. I have an idea that they died
there. Anyway, they never returned to Nightingale House.
It was sold to a retired boot manufacturer who lived here for
only two years before deciding that he didn't like it. He sold
it to one of the governors of the hospital who spent the last
twelve years of his life here and bequeathed it to the John
Carpendar. It has always been something of an embarrassment to the hospital; no one has been quite sure what
to do with it. It's not really suitable as a nurse training
school, but it's difficult to see what exactly it would be
suitable for. There's a story that Nancy Gorringe's ghost can
be heard weeping in the grounds after dark at this time of
year. I've never heard her and it's a tale we try to keep from
the students. But it's never been a happy house."

And it was less happy than ever now, thought Dalgliesh,

as he made his way back to the office. Now there were two murders to add to the history of the violence and hate.

He told Masterson that he could go off duty, then settled down for a last solitary study of the papers. Hardly had the Sergeant left when the outside telephone rang. It was the director of the forensic science laboratory to say that the tests were complete. Josephine Fallon had died of nicotine poisoning and the nicotine had come from the tin of rose spray.

VI

It was two hours before he finally locked the side door of Nightingale House behind him and set out to walk back to the Falconer's Arms.

The path was lit by the old-fashioned type of street lamp, but the lamps were widely spaced and dim so that for most of the time he walked in darkness. He met no one and could well believe that this lonely path was unpopular with the students once night had fallen. The rain had stopped but the wind was rising, shaking down the last drops from the interlocking branches of the elms. He could feel them spitting against his face and seeping under the collar of his coat, and felt a momentary regret that he had decided that morning not to use his car. The trees grew very close to the path, separated from it by a narrow verge of sodden turf. It was a warm night despite the rising wind, and a light mist moved among the trees and coiled around the lamps. The pathway was about ten feet wide. It must have been once a main drive to Nightingale House, but it wound inconsequently among the clumps of elms and birch as if the original owner of the house had hoped to increase his self-importance by the length of his drive.

As he walked he thought about Christine Dakers. He had seen the girl at three forty-five p.m. The private ward had been very quiet at that time and, if Sister Brumfett were about, she had taken care to keep out of his way. The Staff Nurse had received him and had shown him into Nurse Dakers's room. The girl had been sitting up against the pillows looking as flushed and triumphant as a newly-delivered mother and had welcomed him as if she expected congratulations and an offering of flowers. Someone had already supplied her with a vase of daffodils and there were two pots of chrysanthemums beside the tea tray on the overbed table, and a spatter of magazines strewn over the bed cover.

She had tried to appear unconcerned and contrite as she told her story but the acting had been unconvincing. In truth she had been radiant with happiness and relief. And why not? Matron had visited her. She had confessed and had been forgiven. She was filled now with the sweet euphoria of absolution. More to the point, he thought, the two girls who might have menaced her had gone for good. Diane Harper had left the hospital. And Heather Pearce was dead.

And to what exactly had Nurse Dakers confessed? Why this extraordinary liberation of spirit? He wished he knew. But he had come out of her room little wiser than when he went in. But at least, he thought, she had confirmed Madeleine Goodale's evidence of their study time together in the library. Unless there was collusion, which seemed unlikely, they had given each other an alibi for the time before breakfast. And, after breakfast, she had taken her final cup of coffee into the conservatory where she had sat reading the *Nursing Mirror* until it was time to join the demonstration. Nurse Pardoe and Nurse Harper had been with her. The three girls had left the conservatory at the same time, had paid a brief visit to the bathroom and lavatories on the second floor, and had then made their way straight to the demonstration room. It was very difficult to see how Christine Dakers could have poisoned the feed.

Dalgliesh had covered about fifty yards when he stopped in mid-stride, frozen into immobility by what, for one unbelievable second, he thought was the sound of a woman crying. He stood still, straining to distinguish that desperate alien voice. For a moment all was silent, even the wind seemed to have dropped. Then he heard it again, this time unmistakably. This wasn't the night cry of an animal or the figment of a tired but over-stimulated brain. Somewhere in the cluster of trees to his left a woman was howling in misery.

He was not superstitious, but he had the imaginative man's sensitivity to atmosphere. Standing alone in the darkness and hearing that human voice wailing in descant to the rising wind he felt a frisson of awe. The terror and helplessness of that nineteenth-century maidservant touched him briefly as if with her own cold finger. He entered for one appalling second into her misery and hopelessness. The past fused with the present. Then the moment passed. This was a real voice, a living woman. Pressing on his torch, he turned from the path into the utter darkness of the trees.

About twenty yards from the edge of the turf he could see a wooden hut about twelve feet square, its one dimly lit window casting a square of light on the bark of the nearest elm. He strode over to it, his feet soundless on the sodden earth, and pushed open the door. The warm, rich smell of wood and of paraffin wafted out to meet him. And there was something else. The smell of human life. Sitting huddled in a broken wicker chair, with a storm lantern on the upturned box beside her, was a woman.

The impression of an animal trapped in its lair was immediate and inevitable. They gazed at each other soundlessly. Despite her wild crying, cut off instantaneously at his entrance as if it had been simulated, the eyes which peered keenly into his were unclouded and bright with menace. This animal might be in distress but it was on its own ground and all its senses were alert. When she spoke she sounded gloomily belligerent but with no trace of curiosity or fear.

"Who are yer?"

"My name's Adam Dalgliesh. What's yours?"

"Morag Smith."

"I've heard about you, Morag. You must have got back to the hospital this evening."

"That's right. And told by Miss Collins to report to the resident staff hostel if yer please. I asked to go back to the medical officers' quarters if I couldn't stay in Nightingale House. But oh no! No bloody fear! Got on too well with the doctors I did. So it's off to the 'ostel. They bugger you about properly in this place, they do. I asked to see Matron but Sister Brumfett said she wasn't to be worried."

She paused in her recital of woes to fiddle with the wick of the lantern. The light increased. She screwed up her eyes at him.

"Adam Dalgliesh. Funny name. You're new around 'ere, aren't yer?"

"I only arrived this morning. I expect they've told you about Nurse Fallon. I'm a detective. I'm here to find out how she and Nurse Pearce died."

At first he thought that the news was going to precipitate another bout of wailing. She opened her mouth wide but then, thinking better of it, gave a little gasp and closed it sharply again. She said gruffly:

"I never killed 'er."

"Nurse Pearce? Of course not. Why should you?"

"That's not what the other one thought."

"What other one?"

"That Inspector, Inspector bloody Bill Bailey. I could see what 'e was thinking. Asking all them questions, and his eyes fixed on yer all the bleeding time. What were yer doing from the moment you got up? What the 'ell did he think I was doing? Working! That's what I was doing. Did you like Nurse Pearce? Was she ever unkind to you? I'd 'ave like to see 'er try. Anyway, I never even knew 'er. Well, I 'adn't been over Nightingale 'ouse for more than a week. But I could see what 'e was after. It's always the same. Blame the poor bloody maid."

Dalgliesh moved into the hut and seated himself on a bench against the wall. He would have to question Morag Smith and this seemed as good a time as any. He said:

"I think you're wrong, you know. Inspector Bailey didn't suspect you. He told me so."

She gave a derisive snort.

"Yer don't want to believe everything the police tell yer. Blimey, didn't yer dad tell yer that? 'e suspected me all right. Bloody Bugger Bailey. My God, my dad could tell you some things about the police."

No doubt the police could tell a lot about dad, thought Dalgliesh, but rejected that line of conversation as unlikely to be profitable. The inspector's name lent itself to alliterative abuse and Morag was in the mood to relish it. Dalgliesh hastened to defend his colleague.

"Inspector Bailey was only doing his job. He didn't mean to upset you. I'm a policeman too, and I shall have to ask questions. We all do. I shan't get anywhere unless you help. If Nurse Pearce and Nurse Fallon were killed, then I'm going to find out who did it. They were young, you know. Nurse Pearce was about your age. I don't suppose they wanted to die."

He was not sure how Morag would react to this nicely judged appeal to justice and sentiment but he could see the sharp little eyes probing through the semi-darkness.

"'elp yer!" Her voice was full of scorn. "Don't kid me. Your sort don't need 'elp. Yer know 'ow the milk got into the coconut all right."

Dalgliesh considered this startling metaphor and decided, in the absence of contrary evidence, that it was intended as a compliment. He balanced his torch upright on the bench so that it threw one bright pool of light on the roof, wriggled his thighs more firmly against the wall, and cushioned his head against a thick bundle of raffia which hung from a nail above him. He was surprisingly comfortable. He asked conversationally:

"Do you come here often?"

"Only when I'm upset." Her tone suggested that this was an eventuality for which any reasonable woman would make provision.

"It's private 'ere." She added defensively: "It used to be private, anyway."

Dalgliesh felt rebuked.

"I'm sorry. I won't come here again."

"Oh, I don't mind you. You can come again if you like."

The voice might be ungracious but the compliment was unmistakable. They sat for a moment in curiously companionable silence.

The stout walls of the hut enclosed them, insulating them in an unnatural silence from the moaning of the wind. Inside, the air was cold but musty, smelling pungently of wood, paraffin and humus. Dalgliesh looked around him. The place was not uncomfortable. There was a bale of straw in the corner, a second old cane chair similar to that in which Morag was curled, and an upturned packing-case covered with oilcloth which served as a table. On it he could just make out the shape of a Primus oil stove. One of the wall shelves held a white aluminium teapot and a couple of mugs. He guessed that the gardener had once used the place as a comfortable retreat from the ardours of work as well as a potting and storage shed. In spring and summer, isolated in the quiet of the trees and surrounded by bird song, it must, Dalgliesh thought, be an agreeable hiding place. But this was mid-winter. He said:

"Forgive my asking, but wouldn't it be more comfortable to be upset in your own room? And more private?"

"It isn't cosy over in Nightingale 'ouse. And it isn't cosy in the resident staff 'ostel either. I like it 'ere. It smells like my dad's shed on the allotment. And nobody comes after dark. They're all afraid of the ghost."

"And you aren't?"

"I don't believe in 'em."

It was, thought Dalgliesh, the ultimate vindication of sturdy scepticism. You didn't believe in a thing, therefore it didn't exist. Untortured by imagination, you could enjoy the reward of your own certainty even if it were only the undisputed possession of a garden shed when you were feeling upset. He found this admirable. He wondered whether he ought to inquire the cause of her grief, suggest perhaps that she should confide in Matron. Had that wild crying really been caused by nothing more than Bill Bailey's passionately resented attentions? Bailey was a good detective, but not particularly subtle with people. One couldn't afford to be critical. Every detective, however competent, knew what it was unwittingly to antagonize a witness. Once this happened it was the devil to get anything useful out of her— and it usually was a woman—even if the antipathy were partly subconscious. Success in a murder investigation depended largely on making people want to help you, getting them to talk. Bill Bailey had singularly failed with Morag Smith. Adam Dalgliesh, too, had failed in his time.

He remembered what Inspector Bailey, in that brief hour's colloquy when the case had been handed over, had told him about the two maids.

"They're out of it. The old one, Miss Martha Collins, has been at the hospital for forty years and if she had homicidal tendencies would have shown them before now. She's mainly concerned about the theft of the lavatory disinfectant. Seems to regard it as a personal affront. Probably takes the view that the lavatory is her responsibility and the murder isn't. The young girl, Morag Smith, is half dotty if you ask me, and as obstinate as an army mule. She might have done it, I suppose, but I can't for the life of me see why. Heather Pearce hadn't done anything to upset her as far as I know. And in any case she hardly had the time. Morag was only transferred from the doctors' residence to Nightingale House on the day before Pearce died. I gather that she wasn't too pleased about the change, but that's scarcely a motive for starting to kill off the student nurses. Besides, the girl isn't frightened. Obstinate, but not frightened. If she did it, I doubt whether you'll ever prove it."

They sat on in silence. He wasn't anxious to probe into her grief and suspected that she had been indulging an irrational need for a good cry. She had chosen her secret place for it and was entitled to emotional privacy even if her physical privacy had been invaded. He was too reticent himself to have any stomach for the emotional prying which gives so many people the comforting illusion that they care. He seldom did care. Human beings were perpetually interesting to him, and nothing about them surprised him any more. But he didn't involve himself. He wasn't surprised that she should like the shed, smelling as it did of home.

He became aware of a confused background mumbling. She had returned to a recital of her grievance.

"Kept looking at me all the time 'e did. And asking the same old thing over and over again. Stuck up too. You could see that he fancied himself."

Suddenly she turned to Dalgliesh.

"You feeling sexy?"

Dalgliesh gave the question serious attention.

"No. I'm too old to feel sexy when I'm cold and tired. At my age you need the creature comforts if you're to perform with any pleasure to your partner or credit to yourself."

She gave him a look in which disbelief struggled with commiseration.

"You're not that old. Thanks for the 'anky anyway."

She gave one last convulsive blow before handing it back. Dalgliesh slipped it quickly into his pocket, resisting the temptation to drop it unobtrusively behind the bench. Stretching his legs ready to move, he only half heard her next words.

"What did you say?" he asked, careful to keep his voice level, uninquisitorial.

She answered sulkily.

"I said that 'e never found out about me drinking the milk anyway, bugger 'im. I never told 'im."

"Was that the milk used for the demonstration feed? When did you drink it?"

He tried to sound conversational, only mildly interested. But he was aware of the silence in the hut and the two sharp eyes staring at him. Could she really be unaware of what she was telling him?

"It was at eight o'clock, maybe a minute before. I went

into the demo room to see if I'd left my tin of polish there. And there was this bottle of milk on the trolley and I drank some of it. Just a bit off the top."

"Just out of the bottle?"

"Well, there wasn't any cup 'andy was there? I was thirsty and I saw the milk and I just fancied a bit. So I took a swig."

He asked the crucial question.

"You just had the cream off the top?"

"There wasn't no cream. It wasn't that kind of milk."

His heart leapt.

"And what did you do then?"

"I didn't do nothing."

"But weren't you afraid that Sister Tutor would notice that the bottle wasn't full?"

"The bottle was full. I filled it up with water from the tap. Anyway, I only took a couple of gulps."

"And replaced the seal on top of the bottle?"

"That's right. Careful like so as they wouldn't notice."

"And you never told anyone?"

"No one asked me. That Inspector asked me if I'd been in the demo room and I said only before seven o'clock when I did a bit of cleaning. I wasn't going to tell 'im nothing. It wasn't 'is bloody milk anyway; 'e never paid for it."

"Morag, are you quite, quite sure of the time?"

"Eight o'clock. The demo clock said eight anyway. I looked at it because I was supposed to help serve the breakfasts, the dining-room maids being off with flu. Some people think you can be in three places at once. Anyway, I went into the dining-room where the Sisters and the students had all started eating. Then Miss Collins gave me one of 'er looks. Late again Morag! So it must 'ave been eight. The students always start breakfast at eight."

"And were they all there?"

"Of course they was all there! I told yer! They was at their breakfast."

But he knew that they had been there. The twenty-five minutes from eight until eight twenty-five was the only time in which all the female suspects had been together, eating under the eye of Miss Collins and full in each other's gaze. If Morag's story were true, and he didn't for one moment doubt it, then the scope of the inquiry had been dramatically narrowed. There were only six people who had no firm alibi for the whole of the period from eight o'clock until the class assembled at eight forty. He would have to check the statements of course, but he knew what he would find. This was the sort of information he had been trained to recall at will and the names came obediently to mind. Sister Rolfe, Sister Gearing, Sister Brumfett, Nurse Goodale, Leonard Morris and Stephen Courtney-Briggs.

He pulled the girl gently to her feet.

"Come on, Morag, I'm going to see you back to the hostel. You're a very important witness and I don't want you to get pneumonia before I've had a chance to take your statement."

"I don't want to write nothing down. I'm no scholar."

"Someone will write it down for you. You'll only have to sign it."

"I don't mind doing that. I'm not daft. I can sign my name I 'ope."

And he would have to be there to see that she did. He had a feeling that Sergeant Masterson would be no more successful than Inspector Bailey in dealing with Morag. It would be safer to take her statement himself even if it meant a later start than he had planned for his journey to London.

But it would be time well spent. As he turned to pull the shed door firmly closed behind them—it had no lock—he felt happier than at any time since the finding of the nicotine. Now he was making progress. On the whole, it hadn't been too bad a day.

CHAPTER SEVEN

Danse Macabre

I

IT WAS FIVE MINUTES to seven the next morning. Sergeant
Masterson and Detective Constable Greeson were in the
kitchen at Nightingale House with Miss Collins and Mrs.
Muncie. It seemed like the middle of the night to Masterson, dark and cold. The kitchen smelt agreeably of new
baked bread, a country smell, nostalgic and comforting. But
Miss Collins was no prototype of the buxom and welcoming country cook. She watched, lips tight and arms akimbo,
as Greeson placed a filled milk bottle in the front of the
middle shelf of the refrigerator, and said:

"Which one are they supposed to take?"

"The first bottle to hand. That's what they did before,
didn't they?"

"So they say. I had something better to do than sit and
watch them. I've got something better to do now."

"That's okay by us. We'll do the watching."

Four minutes later the Burt twins came in together. No
one spoke. Shirley opened the refrigerator door and Maureen took out the first bottle to hand. Followed by Masterson and Greeson the twins made their way to the
demonstration room through the silent and echoing hall.
The room was empty and the curtains drawn. The two fluorescent lights blazed down on a semicircle of vacant chairs

and on the high narrow bed where a grotesque demonstration doll, round mouthed, nostrils two black and gaping apertures, was propped against the pillows. The twins
set about their preparations in silence. Maureen set down
the bottle on the trolley, then dragged out the drip-feed
apparatus and positioned it by the side of the bed. Shirley
collected instruments and bowls from the various cupboards and set them out on the trolley. The two policemen
watched. After twenty minutes Maureen said:

"That's as much as we did before breakfast. We left the
room just like it is now."

Masterson said: "Okay. Then we'll put forward our
watches to eight forty when you came back here. There's no
point in hanging about. We can call the rest of the students
in now."

Obediently the twins adjusted their pocket watches
while Greeson rang the library where the remaining students were waiting. They came almost immediately and in
the order of their original appearance. Madeleine Goodale
first, followed by Julia Pardoe and Christine Dakers who
arrived together. No one made any attempt to talk and
they took their places silently on the semicircle of chairs,
shivering a little as if the room were cold. Masterson noticed
that they kept their eyes averted from the grotesque doll in
the bed. When they had settled themselves he said:

"Right, Nurse. You can go ahead with the demonstration now. Start heating the milk."

Maureen looked at him puzzled.

"The milk? But no one's had a chance to . . ." Her voice
died away.

Masterson said: "No one's had a chance to poison it?
Never mind. Just go ahead. I want you to do precisely
what you did last time."

She filled a large jug with hot water from the tap then

stood the unopened bottle in it for a few seconds to warm the milk. Receiving Masterson's impatient nod to get on with it, she prised the cap off the bottle and poured the liquid into a glass measuring jug. Then she took a glass thermometer from the instrument trolley and checked the temperature of the liquid. The class watched in fascinated silence. Maureen glanced at Masterson. Receiving no sign, she took up the oesophageal tube and inserted it into the rigid mouth of the doll. Her hand was perfectly steady. Lastly she lifted a glass funnel high over her head and paused. Masterson said:

"Go ahead, Nurse. It isn't going to hurt the doll to get a bit damp. That's what it's made for. A few ounces of warm milk isn't going to rot its guts."

Maureen paused. This time the fluid was visible and all their eyes were on the white curving stream. Then suddenly the girl paused, arm still poised high, and stood motionless, like a model awkwardly posed.

"Well," said Masterson: "Is it or isn't it?"

Maureen lowered the jug to her nostrils, then without a word passed it to her twin. Shirley sniffed and looked at Masterson.

"This isn't milk, is it? It's disinfectant. You wanted to test whether we really could tell!"

Maureen said: "Are you telling us that it was disinfectant last time; that the milk was poisoned before we took the bottle out of the fridge?"

"No. Last time the milk was all right when you took it out of the fridge. What did you do with the bottle once the milk had been poured into the measuring jug?"

Shirley said: "I took it over to the sink in the corner and rinsed it out. I'm sorry I forgot. I should have done that earlier."

"Never mind. Do it now."

Maureen had placed the bottle on the table by the side of the sink, its crumpled cap at its side. Shirley picked it up. Then she paused. Masterson said very quietly:

"Well?"

The girl turned to him, perplexed.

"There's something different, something wrong. It wasn't like this."

"Wasn't it? Then think. Don't worry yourself. Relax. Just relax and think."

The room was preternaturally silent. Then Shirley swung round to her twin.

"I know now, Maureen! It's the bottle top. Last time we took one of the homogenized bottles from the fridge, the kind with the silver cap. But when we came back into the demonstration room after breakfast it was different. Don't you remember? The cap was gold. It was Channel Island milk."

Nurse Goodale said quietly from her chair: "Yes. I remember too. The only cap I saw was gold."

Maureen looked across at Masterson in puzzled inquiry.

"So someone must have changed the cap?"

Before he had a chance to reply they heard Madeleine Goodale's calm voice.

"Not necessarily the cap. Somebody changed the whole bottle."

Masterson did not reply. So the old man had been right! The solution of disinfectant had been made up carefully and at leisure and the lethal bottle substituted for the one from which Morag Smith had drunk. And what had happened to the original bottle? Almost certainly it had been left in the small kitchen on the Sisters' floor. Wasn't it Sister Gearing who had complained to Miss Collins that the milk was watery?

II

Dalgliesh's business at the Yard was quickly completed and by eleven o'clock he was in North Kensington.

Number 49 Millington Square, W.10, was a large dilapidated Italianate house fronted with crumbling stucco. There was nothing remarkable about it. It was typical of hundreds in this part of London. It was obviously divided into bed-sitting-rooms since every window showed a different set of curtains, or none, and it exuded that curious atmosphere of secretive and lonely over-occupation which hung over the whole district. Dalgliesh saw that there was no bank of bell pushes in the porch and no neat list of the tenants. The front door was open. He pushed through the glass panelled door which led to the hall and was met at once by a smell of sour cooking, floor polish and unwashed clothes. The walls of the hall had been papered with a thick encrusted paper, now painted dark brown, and glistening as if it exuded grease and perspiration. The floor and staircase were laid with a patterned linoleum, patched with a brighter newer design where the tears would have been dangerous, but otherwise torn and unmended. The paintwork was an institutional green. There was no sign of life but, even at this time of the day, he felt its presence behind the tightly closed and numbered doors as he made his way unchallenged to the upper floors.

Number 14 was on the top floor at the back. As he approached the door he heard the sharp staccato clatter of typing. He knocked loudly and the sound stopped. There was a wait of more than a minute before the door half opened and he found himself facing a pair of suspicious and unwelcoming eyes.

"Who are you? I'm working. My friends know not to call in the mornings."

"But I'm not a friend. May I come in?"

"I suppose so. But I can't spare you much time. And I don't think it'll be worth your while. I don't want to join anything; I haven't the time. And I don't want to buy anything because I haven't the money. Anyway, I've got everything I need." Dalgliesh showed his card.

"I'm not buying or selling; not even information which is what I'm here for. It's about Josephine Fallon. I'm a police officer and I'm investigating her death. You, I take it, are Arnold Dowson."

The door was opened wider.

"You'd better come in." No sign of fear but perhaps a certain wariness in the grey eyes.

It was an extraordinary room, a small attic with a sloping roof and a dormer window, furnished almost entirely with crude and unpainted wooden boxes, some still stencilled with the name of the original grocer or wine merchant. They had been ingeniously fitted together so that the walls were honeycombed from floor to ceiling with pale wooden cells, irregular in size and shape and containing all the impedimenta of daily living. Some were stacked close with hard-backed books; others with orange paper-backs. Another framed a small two-bar electric fire, perfectly adequate to heat so small a room. In another box was a neat pile of clean but unironed clothes. Another held blue-banded mugs and other crockery, and yet another displayed a group of *objets trouvés,* sea-shells, a Staffordshire dog, a small jam jar or bird feathers. The single bed, blanket-covered, was under the window. Another upturned box served as a table and desk. The only two chairs were the folding canvas type sold for picnicking. Dalgliesh was reminded of an article once seen in a Sunday colour supplement on how to furnish your bed-sitting-room for under £50. Arnold Dowson had probably done it for half the price.

But the room was not unpleasing. Everything was functional and simple. It was perhaps too claustrophobic for some tastes and there was something obsessional in the meticulous tidiness and the way in which every inch of space had been used to the full which prevented it from being restful. It was the room of a self-sufficient, well-organized man who, as he had told Dalgliesh, plainly had everything he wanted.

The tenant suited the room. He looked almost excessively tidy. He was a young man, probably not much over twenty, Dalgliesh thought. His fawn polo-neck sweater was clean, with each cuff neatly turned back to match its fellow, and the collar of a very white shirt visible at the neck. His blue jeans were faded but unstained and had been carefully washed and ironed. There was a crease down the centre of each leg and the ends had been turned up and stitched carefully into place. It gave an oddly incongruous effect to such an informal outfit. He wore leather sandals of the buckled style normally seen on children, and no socks. His hair was very fair and was brushed into a helmet which framed his face in the manner of a medieval page. The face beneath the sleek fringe was bony and sensitive, the nose crooked and too large, the mouth small and well shaped with a hint of petulance. But his most remarkable feature were his ears. They were the smallest Dalgliesh had ever seen on a man, and were without colour even at the tips. They looked as if they were made of wax. Sitting on an upturned orange box with his hands held loosely between his knees and his watchful eyes on Dalgliesh, he looked like the centrepiece of a surrealist painting; singular and precise against the multi-cellular background. Dalgliesh pulled out one of the boxes and seated himself opposite the boy. He said:

"You knew that she was dead, of course?"

"Yes. I read about it in this morning's papers."

"Did you know that she was pregnant?"

This at least produced emotion. The boy's tight face whitened. His head jerked up and he stared at Dalgliesh silently for a moment before replying.

"No. I didn't know. She didn't tell me."

"She was nearly three months' pregnant. Could it have been your child?"

Dowson looked down at his hands.

"It could have been, I suppose. I didn't take any precautions, if that's what you mean. She told me not to worry, that she'd see to that. After all, she was a nurse. I thought she knew how to take care of herself."

"That was something I suspect she never did know. Hadn't you better tell me about it?"

"Do I have to?"

"No. You don't have to say anything. You can demand to see a solicitor and make any amount of fuss and trouble and cause a great deal of delay. But is there any point? No one is accusing you of murdering her. But someone did. You knew her and presumably you liked her. For some of the time, anyway. If you want to help you can best do it by telling me everything you knew about her."

Dowson got slowly to his feet. He seemed as slow-moving and clumsy as an old man. He looked round as if disoriented. Then he said:

"I'll make some tea."

He shuffled over to a double gas ring, fitted to the right of the meagre and unused fireplace, lifted the kettle as if testing by weight that it held sufficient water, and lit the gas. He took down two of the mugs from one of the boxes and set them out on a further box which he dragged between himself and Dalgliesh. It held a number of neatly folded newspapers which looked as if they hadn't been read. He spread one over the top of the box and set out the blue mugs and a bottle of milk as formally as if they were about to drink from Crown Derby. He didn't speak again until the tea was made and poured. Then he said:

"I wasn't her only lover."

"Did she tell you about the others?"

"No, but I think one of them was a doctor. Perhaps more than one. That wouldn't be surprising in the circumstances. We were talking once about sex and she said that a man's nature and character were always completely revealed when he made love. That if he were selfish or insensitive or brutal he couldn't conceal it in bed whatever he might do with his clothes on. Then she said that she had once slept with a surgeon and it was only too apparent that most of the bodies he came into contact with had been anaesthetized first; that he was so busy admiring his own technique that it never occurred to him that he was in bed with a conscious woman. She laughed about a great many things."

"But you don't think she was happy?"

He appeared to be considering. Dalgliesh thought: And for God's sake don't answer, "who is?"

"No, not really happy. Not for most of the time. But she did know how to be happy. That was the important thing."

"How did you meet her?"

"I'm learning to be a writer. That's what I want to be and I've never wanted to be anything else. I have to earn some money to live while I get my first novel finished and published, so I work at night as a continental telephone operator. I know enough French to make it possible. The pay isn't bad. I don't have many friends because there isn't time and I never went to bed with any woman until I met Jo. Women don't seem to like me. I met her last summer in St. James's Park. She was there on one of her off-duty days and I was there to watch the ducks and see what the park looked like. I wanted to set one of the scenes in my book in St. James's Park in July, and I went there to make some notes. She was lying on her back on the grass staring at the sky. She was quite alone. One of the pages of my notebook got detached and blew across the grass into her face. I went after it and apologized, and we chased it together."

He was holding the mug of tea looking at it as if staring again into the summer surface of the lake.

"It was an odd day—very hot, sunless and blustery. The wind blew in warm gusts. The lake looked heavy like oil."

He paused for a moment, and when Dalgliesh didn't speak, went on:

"So we met and talked, and I asked her to come back for tea. I don't know what I expected. After tea we talked more and she made love to me. She told me weeks later that she didn't have that in mind when she came here but I don't know. I don't even know why she came back. Perhaps she was bored."

"Did you have it in mind?"

"I don't know that either. Perhaps. I know that I wanted to make love to a woman. I wanted to know what it was like. That's one experience you can't write about until you know."

"And sometimes not even then. And how long did she continue to provide you with copy?"

The boy seemed unaware of the irony. He said:

"She used to come here about once a fortnight on her day off. We never went out together except to a pub occasionally. She would bring in some food and cook a meal and afterwards we would talk and go to bed."

"What did you talk about?"

"I suppose I did most of the talking. She didn't tell me much about herself, only that both her parents had been killed while she was a child and that she had been brought up in Cumberland by an elderly aunt. The aunt is dead now. I don't think Jo had a very happy childhood. She always wanted to be a nurse but she got T.B. when she was seventeen. It wasn't very bad and she spent eighteen months in a sanatorium in Switzerland and was cured. But the doctors advised her not to train as a nurse. So she did a number of other jobs. She was an actress for about three years; but that wasn't much of a success. Then she was a waitress and a shop assistant for a time. Then she became engaged but nothing came of it. She broke it off."

"Did she say why?"

"No, except that she found something out about the man which made it impossible to marry him."

"Did she say what it was or who the man was?"

"No, and I didn't ask. But I think he may have been some kind of sexual pervert."

Seeing Dalgliesh's face he added quickly:

"I don't really know. She never told me. Most of the things I know about Jo just came up casually in conversation. She never really talked about herself for long. It's just an idea I have. There was a kind of bitter hopelessness about the way she spoke of her engagement."

"And after that?"

"Well, apparently she decided that she might as well go back to her original idea of being a nurse. She thought she could get through the medical examination with luck. She chose the John Carpendar Hospital because she wanted to be near London but not actually in it, and thought that a small hospital would be less arduous. She didn't want her health to break down, I suppose."

"Did she talk about the hospital?"

"Not much. She semed happy enough there. But she spared me the intimate details of the bedpan rounds."

"Do you know whether she had an enemy?"

"She must have had, mustn't she, if somebody killed her? But she never told me about it. Perhaps she didn't know."

"Do these names mean anything to you?"

He went through the names of all the people, students, sisters, surgeon, pharmacist, who had been in Nightingale House the night Josephine Fallon had died.

"I think she mentioned Madeleine Goodale to me. I've a feeling they were friendly. And the Courtney-Briggs name seems familiar. But I can't remember any details."

"When did you last see her?"

"About three weeks ago. She came on her night off and cooked supper."

"How did she seem then?"

"She was restless and she wanted to make love rather badly. Then just before she left she said that she wouldn't see me again. A few days later I got a letter. It merely said, 'I meant what I said. Please don't try to get in touch. It's nothing you've done so don't worry. Good-bye and thank you. Jo.'"

Dalgliesh asked if he had kept the letter.

"No. I only keep important papers. I mean, there isn't room here to hoard letters."

"And did you try to get in touch with her again?"

"No. She'd asked me not to and there didn't seem much point in it. I suppose if I'd known about the child I might have done. But I'm not sure. There's nothing I could have done. I couldn't have had a child here. Well, you can see that. How could I? She wouldn't want to marry me and I never considered marrying her. I don't want to marry anyone. But I don't think she killed herself because of the baby. Not Jo."

"All right. You don't think she killed herself. Tell me why."

"She wasn't the type."

"Oh, come now! You can do better than that."

The boy said belligerently: "It's true enough. I've known two people in my life who killed themselves. One was a boy in my last year at school when we were sitting for our G.C.E. The other was a manager of a dry cleaning firm I worked for. I drove the delivery van. Well, in both cases, everyone said all the usual things about how dreadful and how surprising it was. But I wasn't really surprised. I don't mean that I was expecting it or anything like that. I just wasn't really surprised. When I thought about both deaths I could believe that they had actually done it."

"Your sample is too small."

"Jo wouldn't kill herself. Why should she?"

"I can think of reasons. She hadn't made much success of her life so far. She hadn't any relatives to care about her, and very few friends. She didn't sleep easily at night, wasn't really happy. She had at last succeeded in training to be a nurse and was within a few months of her final examination. And then she finds herself pregnant. She knows that her lover won't want the child, that it's no use looking to him for comfort or support."

Dowson cried out in vehement protest.

"She never looked to anyone for comfort or support! That's what I'm trying to tell you! She slept with me because she wanted to. I'm not responsible for her. I'm not responsible for anyone. Anyone! I'm only responsible for myself. She knew what she was doing. It wasn't as if she were a young, inexperienced girl who needed kindness and protection."

"If you believe that the young and innocent need comfort and protection you're thinking in clichés. And if you begin by thinking in clichés you end by writing them."

The boy said sullenly: "Maybe. But that's what I believe."

Suddenly he got up and went over to the wall. When he came back to the centre box Dalgliesh saw that he held a large smooth stone. It fitted snugly into his curved palm, a perfect ovoid. It was a pale grey, flecked like an egg. Dowson let it slide from his hand on to the table where it rocked gently into stillness. Then he sat down again and bent forward, his head in his hands. Together they looked at the stone. Dalgliesh did not speak. Suddenly the boy said:

"She gave it to me. We found it together on the beach at Ventnor, in the Isle of Wright. We went there together last October. But of course you know. That must have been how you traced me. Lift it. It's surprisingly heavy."

Dalgliesh took the stone in his hands. It was satisfying to touch, smooth and cool. He took pleasure in the sea-washed perfection of its shape, in the hard unyielding roundness of it which yet fitted with such gentleness into the palm of his hand.

"I never had a holiday by the sea when I was a boy. Dad died before I was six and the old woman hadn't the money. So I missed out on the seaside. Jo thought it would be fun to go there together. It was very warm last October. Remember? We took the ferry from Portsmouth and there were only half a dozen people on it besides ourselves. The island was empty too. We could walk from Ventor to St. Catherine's Lighthouse without meeting a soul. It was warm enough and deserted enough to bathe naked. Jo found this stone. She thought it would do as a paper-weight. I wasn't going to tear my pocket carrying that weight home but she did. Then, when we got back here, she gave it to me as a keepsake. I wanted her to have it but she said that I'd forget the holiday long before she did. Don't you see? She knew how to be happy. I'm not sure that I do. But Jo did. If you're like that you don't kill yourself. Not when you know how marvellous living can be. Colette knew about that. She wrote about 'a compelling fierce and secret *rapport* with the earth and everything that gushes from its breasts.' " He looked at Dalgliesh.

"Colette was a French writer."

"I know. And you believe that Josephine Fallon could feel that?"

"I know she could. Not for long. Not often. But when she was happy she was marvellous. If you once know that kind of happiness you don't kill yourself. While you live there's a hope it could happen again. So why cut yourself off from the hope of it for ever?"

Dalgliesh said: "You cut yourself off from the misery too. That might seem more important. But I think you're right. I don't believe Josephine Fallon killed herself. I believe she was murdered. That's why I'm asking if there's anything else you can tell me."

"No. I was on duty at the Exchange the night she died. I had better give you the address. I suppose you'll want to check."

"There are reasons why it's extremely unlikely to have been anyone who wasn't familiar with Nightingale House. But we shall check."

"Here's the address then."

He tore a corner from the newspaper covering the table and taking a pencil from his trouser pocket, wrote down the address in a crabbed hand, his head nearly touching the paper. Then he folded it as if the message were secret, and pushed it across the table.

"Take the stone too. I'd like you to have it. No, take it. Please take it. You think I'm heartless, that I'm not grieving for her. But I am. I want you to find out who killed her. It won't do any good to her or to the man, but I want you to find out. And I am sorry. It's just that I can't let myself feel too much. I can't let myself get involved. You understand?"

Dalgliesh took the stone in his hand and rose to go.
"Yes," he said: "I understand."

III

Mr. Henry Urquhart of Messrs. Urquhart, Wimbush and
Portway was Josephine Fallon's solicitor. Dalgliesh's appointment with him was for twelve twenty-five p.m., a time
disobligingly chosen, he felt, to intimate that every minute
of the solicitor's time was valuable and that he was prepared to spare the police no more than half an hour before
lunch. Dalgliesh was admitted immediately. He doubted
whether a detective sergeant would have been received so
promptly. This was one of the minor advantages for his
passion of doing the job himself, for resisting the pressures
to make him into a desk detective, controlling the investigation from his office with a small army of detective constables, scenes-of-crime men, photographers, finger-print
experts and scientists ministering to his ego and effectively
cutting him off from all but the main protagonists of the
crime. He knew that he had a reputation for solving his
cases very fast, but he never grudged time on jobs which
some of his colleagues thought more appropriate to a
detective constable. As a result he was sometimes given
information which a less experienced interrogator would
have missed. He hardly expected this happy bonus from
Mr. Henry Urquhart. This interview was likely to be little
more than the formal and punctilious exchange of relevant
facts. But it had been necessary for him to visit London.
There were matters which he had to attend to at the Yard.
And it was always a pleasure to visit on foot and in the fitful
sunlight of a winter morning these secluded corners of the
City.

Messrs. Urquhart, Wimbush and Portway were one of the most respected and successful of the City's firms of solicitors. Dalgliesh felt that few of Mr. Urquhart's clients could have been mixed up in a murder investigation. They might have their little difficulties from time to time with the Queen's proctor; they might, against all advice, indulge in imprudent litigation or obstinately persist in devising unwise wills; they might require their solicitor's services to devise technical defences to the drink and driving laws; it might indeed be necessary to extricate them from all manner of folly and imprudence. But their killing would be done legally.

The room into which he was shown could have served as a stage set for a successful solicitor's office. The coal fire was banked high in the grate. From above the mantel shelf the portrait of the founder gazed down in approval on his great-grandson. The desk at which the great-grandson sat was of the same period as the portrait and displayed the same qualities of durability, fitness for the task in hand, and a sturdy opulence which stopped just short of ostentation. On the other wall there was a small oil. Dalgliesh thought that it looked very like a Jan Steen. It proclaimed to the world that the firm knew a good picture when it saw one and could afford to display it on the wall.

Mr. Urquhart, tall, ascetic, discreetly grey at the temples and with the air of a reserved dominie, was well cast for the role of a successful solicitor. He was wearing an exceedingly well-cut suit, but in lovat tweed as if the more orthodox pin stripe would have verged on caricature. He received Dalgliesh without apparent curiosity or concern but the Superintendent noted with interest that Miss Fallon's box was already on the table before him. Dalgliesh stated his business briefly and ended:

"Can you tell me anything about her? In a murder inquiry anything we can learn about the past life and personality of the victim is helpful."

"And this, you are now confident, is murder?"

"She was killed by taking nicotine in her late night beaker of whisky. As far as we know, she wasn't aware that the tin of rose spray was in the conservatory cupboard, and if she knew and it occurred to her to use it, I doubt whether she would subsequently have hidden the tin."

"I see. And there is, too, the suggestion that the poison administered to the first victim—Heather Pearce wasn't it—was intended for my client?"

Mr. Urquhart sat for a moment finger to finger with his head slightly bent as if consulting either his own subconscious, a higher power, or the ghost of his former client before divulging what he knew. Dalgliesh thought that he could have saved the time. Urquhart was a man who knew perfectly well how far he was prepared to go, professionally or otherwise. The pantomime was unconvincing. And his story, when it came, did nothing to clothe the dry bones of Josephine Fallon's life. The facts were there. He consulted the papers in front of him, and presented them logically, unemotionally, lucidly. The time and place of her birth; the circumstances of her parents' death; her subsequent upbringing by an elderly aunt, who together with him had been a trustee until Miss Fallon's majority; the date and circumstance of that aunt's death from cancer of the uterus; the money left to Josephine Fallon and the exact way in which it had been invested; the girl's movements after her twenty-first birthday in so far, as he pointed out drily, she had troubled to inform him of them.

Dalgliesh said: "She was pregnant. Did you know?"

It could not be said that this news disconcerted the

solicitor although his face creased into the vaguely pained look of a man who can never quite reconcile himself to the messiness of the world.

"No. She didn't tell me. But then I would not expect her to do so, unless, of course, she was thinking of applying for an affiliation order. I gather that was not in question."

"She told her friend, Madeleine Goodale, that she intended to have an abortion."

"Indeed. An expensive and to my mind, despite the recent legislation, a dubious business. I speak morally, of course, not legally. The recent legislation . . ."

Dalgliesh said: "I am aware of the recent legislation. So there is nothing else you can tell me?"

The solicitor's tone held a tinge of reproof.

"I have already told you a great deal about her background and financial position in so far as they were known to me. I am afraid I can't supply you with any more recent or intimate information. Miss Fallon consulted me seldom. Indeed she had no reason to do so. The last time was about her will. You are, I believe, already appraised of its terms. Miss Madeleine Goodale is the sole legatee. The estate is likely to amount to approximately twenty thousand pounds."

"Was there a previous will?"

Was it Dalgliesh's imagination, or did he detect the slight stiffening of facial muscles, the almost imperceptible frown which greeted an unwelcome question.

"There were two, but the second of these was never signed. The first, made soon after her majority, left everything to medical charities, including cancer research. The second she proposed to execute on the occasion of her marriage. I have the letter here."

He handed this across to Dalgliesh. It was addressed

from a flat in Westminster and was written in a confident upright and unfeminine hand.

"Dear Mr. Urquhart, This is to let you know that I shall be married on 14th March at St. Marylebone Registry Office to Peter Courtney. He is an actor; you may have heard of him. Will you please draw up a will for me to sign on that date. I shall leave everything to my husband. His full name incidentally is Peter Albert Courtney Briggs. No hyphen. I expect you'll need to know that to draw up the will. We shall be living at this address.

"I shall also need some money. Could you please ask Warranders to make two thousand pounds available to me by the end of the month? Thank you. I hope that you and Mr. Surtees are keeping well. Yours sincerely, Josephine Fallon."

A cool letter, thought Dalgliesh. No explanations. No justification. No expressions of happiness or hope. And come to that, no invitation to the wedding.

Henry Urquhart said: "Warranders were her stockbrokers. She always dealt with them through us, and we kept all her official papers. She preferred us to do so. She said she preferred to travel unencumbered."

He repeated the phrase, smiling complacently as if he found it in some way remarkable, and glanced at Dalgliesh as if expecting him to comment.

He went on: "Surtees is my clerk. She always asked after Surtees."

He seemed to find that fact more puzzling than the terms of the letter itself.

Dalgliesh said: "And Peter Courtney subsequently hanged himself."

"That is so, three days before the wedding. He left a note for the coroner. It wasn't read out at the inquest, I'm thankful to say. It was quite explicit. Courtney wrote that he had planned to marry to extricate himself from certain financial and personal difficulties, but at the last moment had found he couldn't face it. He was a compulsive gambler apparently. I am informed that uncontrolled gambling is, in fact, a disease akin to alcoholism. I know little of the syndrome but can appreciate that it could be tragic in its consequences, particularly for an actor whose earnings, although larger, are erratic. Peter Courtney was very heavily in debt and totally unable to extricate himself from a compulsion which daily made that debt worse."

"And the personal difficulties? I believe he was a homosexual. There was gossip about it at the time. Do you know whether your client knew?"

"I have no information. It seems unlikely that she should not have known since she committed herself so far as to become engaged. She may, of course, have been so sanguine or so unwise as to suppose that she could help to cure him. I should have advised her against the marriage had she consulted me, but as I have said she did not consult me."

And shortly afterwards, thought Dalgliesh, a matter of months only, she had begun her training at the John Carpendar and was sleeping with Peter Courtney's brother. Why? Loneliness? Bordom? A desperate need to forget? Payment for services rendered? What services? Simple sexual attraction, if physical need were ever simple, for a man who physically was a coarse edition of the fiancé she had lost? The need to reassure herself that she could attract heterosexual desire? Courtney-Briggs himself had suggested that it was she who had taken the initiative. It was certainly she who had brought the affair to an end. There had been no mistaking the surgeon's bitter resentment of a woman who had had the temerity to reject him before he had chosen to reject her.

As he rose to go Dalgliesh said: "Peter Courtney's brother is a consultant surgeon at the John Carpendar Hospital. But perhaps you knew?"

Henry Urquhart smiled his tight, unamused smile.

"Oh yes, I know. Stephen Courtney-Briggs is a client of mine. Unlike his brother, he has acquired a hyphen to his name and a more permanent success." He added with apparent irrelevance:

"He was holidaying in a friend's yacht in the Mediterranean when his brother died. He came home immediately. It was, of course, a great shock as well as being a considerable embarrassment."

It must have been, thought Dalgliesh. But Peter dead was decidedly less embarrassing than Peter living. It would no doubt have suited Stephen Courtney-Briggs to have had a well-known actor in the family, a younger brother who, without competing in his own field, would have added his lustre to the patina of success and given Courtney-Briggs an entrée to the extravagantly egotistical world of the stage. But the asset had become a liability; the hero an object of derision or, at best, of pity. It was a failure his brother would find hard to forgive.

Five minutes later Dalgliesh shook hands with Urquhart and left. As he passed through the hall the girl at the switchboard, hearing his footsteps, glanced round, flushed, and paused in momentary confusion, plug in hand. She had been well trained but not quite well enough. Unwilling to embarrass her further, Dalgliesh smiled and passed swiftly out of the building. He had no doubt that, on Henry Urquhart's instructions, she was ringing Stephen Courtney-Briggs.

IV

Saville Mansions was a block of late Victorian flats close to Marylebone Road, respectable, prosperous but neither ostentatious nor opulent. Masterson had the expected trouble in finding a vacant lot to park his car and it was after seven thirty before he entered the building. The entrance hall was dominated by a grille-encased lift of ornate design and a reception desk presided over by a uniformed porter. Masterson, who had no intention of stating his business, nodded to him casually and ran up the stairs. Number 23 was on the second floor. He pressed the bell and prepared for a brief wait.

But the door opened immediately and he found himself almost embraced by an extraordinary apparition, painted like the caricature of a stage whore and wearing a short evening dress of flame-coloured chiffon which would have looked incongruous on a woman half her age. The bodice was so low that he could glimpse the fold between the sagging breasts bunched high into the cups of her brassière, and could see where the powder lay caked in the cracks of dry yellow skin. Her lashes were weighted with mascara; the brittle hair, dyed an improbable blonde, was dressed in lacquered swathes around the raddled face; her carmine-painted mouth hung open in incredulous dismay. Their surprise was mutual. They stared at each other as if unable to believe their eyes. The change in her face from relief to disappointment was almost comic.

Masterson recovered first and announced himself:

"You remember," he said, "I telephoned early this morning and made an appointment?"

"I can't see you now. I'm just going out. I thought you were my dancing partner. You said you'd come early in the evening."

A shrill nagging voice made sharper by disappointment. She looked as if she might close the door in his face. Quickly he slid one foot across the threshold.

"I was unavoidably detained. I'm sorry."

Unavoidably detained. Too right, he had been. That frantic but ultimately satisfying interlude in the back of the car had occupied more of the evening than he had anticipated. It had taken longer, too, to find a sufficiently secluded spot even on a dark winter's evening. The Guildford Road had offered few promising turnings into open country with its prospect of grass verges and unfrequented lanes. Julia Pardoe had been fussy too. Every time he slowed the car at a likely spot he had been met with her quiet, "not here." He had first seen her as she was about to step off the pavement on to the pedestrian crossing which led to the entrance of Heatheringfield station. He had slowed the car for her but, instead of waving her on, had leaned over and opened the passenger door. She had paused for only a second before walking over to him, coat swinging above the knee-length boots, and had slipped into the seat beside him without a word or glance. He had said:

"Coming up to town?"

She had nodded and had smiled secretively, eyes fixed on the windscreen. It had been as simple as that. She had hardly spoken a dozen words throughout the drive. The tentative or more overt preliminaries which he felt the game demanded of him had met with no response. He might have been a chauffeur with whom she was driving in unwelcome proximity. In the end, pricked by anger and humiliation, he had begun to wonder whether he could have been mistaken. But there had been the reassurance of that concentrated stillness, the eyes which, for minutes at a time, had watched with blue intensity his hands stroking the wheel or busy with the gears. She had wanted it all right.

She had wanted it as much as he. But you could hardly call it a quick lay. One thing, surprisingly, she had told him. She was on her way to meet Hilda Rolfe; they were going to a theatre together after an early dinner. Well, either they would have to go without dinner or miss the first act; she was apparently unconcerned either way.

Amused and only slightly curious he had asked:

"How are you going to explain your lateness to Sister Rolfe? Or won't you bother now to turn up?"

She had shrugged.

"I shall tell her the truth. It might be good for her." Seeing his sudden frown she had added with contempt:

"Oh, don't worry! She won't sneak to Mr. Dalgliesh. Hilda isn't like that."

Masterson hoped she was right. This was something Dalgliesh wouldn't forgive.

"What will she do?" he had asked.

"If I tell? Chuck in her job I imagine; leave the John Carpendar. She's pretty fed up with the place. She only stays on because of me."

Wrenching his mind from the memory of that high, merciless voice into the present, Masterson forced himself to smile at the very different woman now confronting him and said in a propitiatory tone:

"The traffic you know. . . . I had to drive from Hampshire. But I shan't keep you long."

Holding out his warrant card with that slightly furtive air inseparable from the gesture he edged himself into the flat. She didn't try to stop him. But her eyes were blank, her mind obviously elsewhere. As she closed the door, the telephone rang. Without a murmur she left him standing in the hall and almost ran into a room to the left. He could hear her voice rising in protest. It seemed to be expostulating, then pleading. Then there was a silence. He moved quietly up the hall and strained his ears to hear. He thought he detected the clicking of the dial. Then she was speaking again. He couldn't hear the words. This time the conversation was over in seconds. Then came another click of the dial. Another wail. In all she rang four numbers before she reappeared in the hall.

"Is anything wrong?" he asked. "Can I help?"

She screwed up her eyes and regarded him intently for a second like a housewife assessing the quality and price of a piece of beef. Her reply when it came was peremptory and astonishing.

"Can you dance?"

"I was the Met. police champion for three years running," he lied. The Force, not surprisingly, held no dancing championships but he thought it unlikely that she would know this and the lie, like most of his lies, came easily and spontaneously.

Again that speculative, intent gaze.

"You'll need a dinner-jacket. I've still got Martin's things here. I'm going to sell them but the man hasn't come yet. He promised he'd come this afternoon but he didn't. You can't rely on anyone these days. You look about the same size. He was quite broad before his illness."

Masterson resisted the temptation to laugh aloud. He said gravely:

"I'd like to help you out if you're in a difficulty. But I'm a policeman. I'm here to get information not to spend the night dancing."

"It isn't the whole night. The ball stops at eleven thirty. It's the Delaroux Dancing Medal Ball at the Athenaeum Ballroom off the Strand. We could talk there."

"It would be easier to talk here." Her sullen face set in obstinacy.

"I don't want to talk here."

She spoke with the peevish insistence of a whining child. Then her voice hardened for the ultimatum.

"It's the ball or nothing."

They faced one another in silence. Masterson considered. The idea was grotesque, of course, but he wasn't going to get anything out of her tonight unless he agreed. Dalgliesh had sent him to London for information and his pride wouldn't let him return to Nightingale House without it. But would his pride permit him to spend the rest of the evening escorting this painted hag in public? There was no difficulty about the dancing. That was one of the skills, although not the most important, that Sylvia had taught him. She had been a randy blonde, ten years older than himself, with a dull bank manager husband whom it had been a positive duty to cuckold. Sylvia had been crazy on ballroom dancing and they had progressed together through a series of bronze, silver and gold medal competitions before the husband had become inconveniently menacing, Sylvia had begun to hint about divorce, and Masterson had prudently decided that the relationship had outlasted its usefulness, not to say his capacity for indoor exercise, and that the police service offered a reasonable career for an ambitious man who was looking for an excuse for a period of comparative rectitude. Now his taste in women and dancing had changed and he had less time for either. But Sylvia had had her uses. As they told you at Detective Training School, no skill is ever wasted in police work.

No, there would be no difficulty about the dancing. Whether she was equally expert was another matter. The evening would probably be a fiasco and whether he went with her or not she would probably talk in time. But when would that be? Dalgliesh liked to work fast. This was one of those cases where the number of suspects was limited to a small, closed community and he didn't normally expect to spend more than a week on them. He wouldn't exactly thank his subordinate for a wasted evening. And then there was that time in the car to be accounted for somehow. It wouldn't be a good night to return empty-handed. And what the hell! It would make a good story for the boys. And if the evening became too impossible he could always ditch her. He'd better remember to take his own clothes in the car in case he needed to make a quick escape.

"All right," he said. "But it's got to be worth my while."

"It will be."

Martin Dettinger's dinner-jacket fitted him better than he had feared. It was strange, this ritual of dressing up in another man's clothes. He found himself searching in the pockets as if they too could hold some kind of clue. But he found nothing. The shoes were too small and he made no effort to force them on his feet. Luckily he was wearing black shoes with leather soles. They were too heavy for dancing and looked incongruous with the dinner-jacket but they would have to do. He bundled his own suit in a cardboard box reluctantly provided by Mrs. Dettinger and they set off.

He knew that there would be little chance of finding a space for the car in or near the Strand so drove over the South Bank and parked next to County Hall. Then they walked to Waterloo Station and hired a taxi. That part of the evening wasn't too bad. She had wrapped herself in a voluminous, old-fashioned fur coat. It smelt strong and sour as if a cat had got at it, but at least it was concealing. For the whole of the journey neither of them spoke a word.

The dance had already started when they arrived shortly after eight and the great hall was unpleasantly full. They made their way to one of the few remaining empty tables under the balcony. Masterson noticed that each of the male instructors sported a red carnation; the women a white one.

There was a great deal of promiscuous kissing and caressing pats of shoulders and arms. One of the men minced up to Mrs. Dettinger with little bleats of welcome and congratulation.

"You're looking marvellous Mrs. D. Sorry to hear that Tony's ill. But I'm glad you found a partner."

The glance at Masterson was perfunctorily curious. Mrs. Dettinger received this greeting with a clumsy jerk of the head and a slight leer of gratification. She made no attempt to introduce Masterson.

They sat out the next two dances and Masterson contented himself with looking round the hall. The whole atmosphere was drearily respectable. A huge bunch of balloons hung from the ceiling, ready no doubt to descend for some orgiastic climax to tonight's festivities. The band wore red jackets with gold epaulettes and had the gloomily resigned look of men who have seen it all before. Masterson looked forward to an evening of cynical uninvolvement, the gratification of observing the folly of others, the insidious pleasure of disgust. He recalled the description of a French diplomat of the English dancing "avec les visages si tristes, les derrières si gais." Here the bottoms were positively staid, but the faces were fixed in grins of simulated delight so unnatural that he wondered whether the school had taught the approved facial expression with the correct steps. Away from the dance floor all the women looked worried, their expressions ranging from slight apprehension to almost frantic anxiety. They greatly outnumbered the men and some of them were dancing together. The majority were middle-aged or older and the style of dress was uniformly old-fashioned, the bodices tight and low cut, the immense circular skirts studded with sequins.

The third dance was a quick step. She turned to him suddenly and said, "We'll dance this." Unprotesting, he led her on to the floor and clasped her rigid body with his left arm. He resigned himself to a long and exhausting evening. If this old harpy had anything useful to tell—and the old man seemed to think she had—then, by God, she would tell it even if he had to jangle her round this bloody floor until she dropped. The notion was pleasing and he indulged it. He could picture her, disjointed as a puppet loosed from its cords, the brittle legs sprawled awkwardly, the arms swinging into the final exhaustion. Except that he would probably drop first. That half-hour with Julia Pardoe hadn't been the best possible preparation for a night on the dance floor. But the old bitch had plenty of life in her. He could taste and feel the beads of sweat tickling the corners of his mouth, but she was hardly breathing faster and her hands were cool and dry. The face close to his was intent, the eyes glazed, the lower lip sagging open. It was like dancing with an animated bag of bones.

The music crashed to a stop. The conductor swung round and flashed his artificial smile over the floor. The players relaxed, permitting themselves a brief smile. The kaleidoscope of colour in the middle of the floor coalesced then flowed into new patterns as the dancers disengaged and minced back to their tables. A waiter was hovering for orders. Masterson crooked his finger.

"What will you have?"

He sounded as ungracious as a miser forced into standing his round. She asked for a gin and tonic and when it came accepted it without thanks or apparent gratification. He settled for a double whisky. It was to be the first of many. Spreading the flame-coloured skirt around her chair, she began to survey the hall with that look of disagreeable intensity which he was beginning to know so well. He might not have been there. Careful, he thought, don't get impatient. She wants to keep you here. Let her.

"Tell me about your son," he said quietly, careful to keep his voice even and unemphatic.

"Not now. Some other evening. There's no hurry."

He nearly shouted aloud with exasperation. Did she really think that he planned to see her again? Did she expect him to dance with her for ever on the half promise of a titbit of information? He pictured them, capering grotesquely through the years, involuntary participants in a surrealist charade. He put down his glass.

"There won't be another time. Not unless you can help me. The Superintendent isn't keen on spending public money when there's nothing to be learned. I have to justify every minute of my time."

He instilled into his voice the right degrees of resentment and self-righteousness. She looked at him for the first time since they had sat down.

"There might be something to be learned. I never said there wasn't. What about the drinks?"

"The drinks?" He was momentarily nonplussed.

"Who pays for the drinks?"

"Well, normally they are on expenses. But when it's a question of entertaining friends, like tonight for example, naturally I pay myself."

He lied easily. It was one of the talents which he thought helped most in his job.

She nodded as if satisfied. But she didn't speak. He was wondering whether to try again when the band crashed into a cha-cha. Without a word she rose and turned towards him. They took the floor again.

The cha-cha was succeeded by a mambo, the mambo by a waltz, the waltz by a slow fox-trot. And still he had learned nothing. Then there was a change in the evening's programme. The lights suddenly dimmed and a sleek man, glistening from head to toe as if he had bathed in hair oil, appeared in front of the microphone and adjusted it for his height. He was accompanied by a languid blonde, her hair elaborately dressed in a style already five years out of date. The spotlight played upon them. She dangled a chiffon scarf negligently from her right hand and surveyed the emptying dance floor with a proprietorial air. There was an anticipatory hush. The man consulted a list in his hand.

"And now, ladies and gentlemen, the moment we have all been waiting for. The exhibition dances. Our medallists for the year will demonstrate for our delight the dances which won them their awards. We begin with our silver medallist, Mrs. Dettinger, dancing"—he consulted the list—"dancing the tango."

He swept a chubby hand around the floor. The band crashed into a discordant fanfare. Mrs. Dettinger rose, dragging Masterson with her. Her claw was like a vise round his wrist. The spotlight swung round and settled on them. There was a little burst of applause. The sleek man continued:

"Mrs. Dettinger is dancing with—could we have the name of your new partner Mrs. Dettinger?" Masterson called out loudly:

"Mr. Edward Heath."

The sleek man paused, then decided to take it at its face value. Forcing enthusiasm into his voice, he proclaimed:

"Mrs. Dettinger, silver medallist, dancing the tango with Mr. Edward Heath."

The cymbals clashed, there was a further spatter of applause. Masterson led his partner on to the floor with exaggerated courtesy. He was aware that he was slightly drunk and was glad of it. He was going to enjoy himself.

He clasped his hand to the small of her back and assumed an expression of lecherous expectancy. It won an immediate giggle from the nearest table. She frowned and he watched fascinated while an unbecoming crimson flowed over her face and neck. He realized with delight that she was intensely nervous, that this pathetic charade actually mattered to her. It was for this moment that she had dressed so carefully, painted her raddled face. The Delaroux Medal Ball. The demonstration tango. And then her partner had failed her. Lost courage probably, the poor sap. But fate had provided her with a personable and competent substitute. It must have seemed like a miracle. It was for this moment that he had been enticed to the Athenaeum Hall, kept dancing here hour after tedious hour. The knowledge was exhilarating. By God, he had her now. This was to be her big moment. He would see that she didn't forget it in a hurry.

The slow rhythm began. He noted with irritation that it was the same old tune for this dance that they had played most of the evening. He hummed the words in her ear. She whispered:

"We're supposed to be dancing the Delaroux tango."

"We're dancing the Charles Masterson tango, sweetheart."

Clasping her tightly he marched her belligerently across the floor in a strutting parody of the dance, swung her viciously around so that her lacquered hair nearly brushed the floor and he heard her bones cracking, and held her in the pose while he bestowed a smile of surprised gratification on the party at the nearest table. The giggle was louder now, more prolonged. As he jerked her upright and waited for the next beat she hissed:

"What do you want to know?"

"He recognized someone, didn't he? Your son. When he was in the John Carpendar Hospital. He saw someone he knew?"

"Will you behave yourself and dance properly?"

"Perhaps."

They were moving again in an orthodox tango. He could feel her relaxing a little in his arms, but he still kept a firm hold on her.

"It was one of the Sisters. He'd seen her before."

"Which Sister?"

"I don't know, he didn't tell me."

"What did he tell you?"

"After the dance."

"Tell me now if you don't want to end on the floor. Where had he seen her before?"

"In Germany. She was in the dock. It was a war trial. She got off but everybody knew she was guilty."

"Where in Germany?"

He mouthed the words through lips stretched into the fatuous smile of a professional dancing partner.

"Felsenheim. It was a place called Felsenheim."

"Say it again. Say that name again!"

"Felsenheim."

The name meant nothing to him but he knew he would remember it. With luck he would get the details later but the salient facts must be torn from her now while he had her in his power. It might not be true, of course. None of it might be true. And if true it might not be relevant. But this was the information he had been sent to get. He felt a surge of confidence and good humour. He was even in danger of enjoying the dance. He decided that it was time for something spectacular and led her into a complicated routine beginning with a progressive link and ending with a close promenade that took them diagonally across the hall. It was faultlessly executed and the applause was loud and sustained. He asked:

"What was her name?"

"Irmgard Groble. She was only a young girl then, of

course. Martin said that was why she got off. He never had any doubt she was guilty."

"Are you sure he didn't tell you which Sister it was?"

"No. He was very ill. He told me about the trial when he came home from Europe, so I already knew about it. But he was unconscious most of the time in hospital. And when he wasn't he was mostly delirious."

So he could have made a mistake, thought Masterson. It was an unlikely enough story. And surely it would be hard to recognize a face after over twenty-five years; except that he must have watched that particular face with fascinated intensity all through the trial. It must have made an impression on a young and probably sensitive man. Enough, perhaps, for him to relive it in his delirium and delude himself that one of the faces bending over him in those few moments of consciousness and lucidity was the face of Irmgard Grobel. But supposing, just supposing, he had been right. If he had told his mother he might well have told his special nurse or blurted it out in his delirium. And what use had Heather Pearce made of her knowledge?

He whispered softly into her ear: "Who else have you told?"

"Nobody. I haven't told anybody. Why should I?"

Another rock swing. Then an over swing. Very nice. More applause. He tightened his hold on her and made his voice husky with menace beneath the fixed grin.

"Who else? You must have told someone."

"Why should I?"

"Because you're a woman."

It was a lucky reply. The mulish obstinacy on her face softened. She glanced up at him for a second, then fluttered her sparse mascara-coated eyelashes in a travesty of flirtation. Oh God, he thought, she's going to be coy.

"Oh well . . . perhaps I did tell just one person."

"I know bloody well you did. I'm asking who?"

Again the deprecatory glance, the little moo of submission. She had decided to enjoy this masterful man. For some reason, perhaps the gin, perhaps the euphoria of the dance, her resistance had crumbled. It was going to be hunky-dory from now on.

"I told Mr. Courtney-Briggs, Martin's surgeon. Well, it seemed only right."

"When?"

"Last Wednesday. The Wednesday of last week, I mean. At his consulting rooms in Wimpole Street. He had just left the hospital on the Friday when Martin died so I couldn't see him earlier. He's only at the John Carpendar on Monday, Thursday and Friday."

"Did he ask to see you?"

"Oh no! The staff nurse who was taking Sister's place said that he would be very glad to have a talk with me if I thought it would be helpful and that I could phone Wimpole Street to make an appointment. I didn't then. What was the use? Martin was dead. But then I got his bill. Not very nice, I thought, so soon after Martin had passed away. Two hundred guineas! I thought it was monstrous. After all, it's not as if he did any good. So I thought I'd just pop into Wimpole Street and see him and mention what I knew. It wasn't right for the hospital to employ a woman like that. A murderess really. And then to charge all that money. There was a second bill from the hospital for his maintenance you know, but it wasn't anything like Mr. Courtney-Briggs's two hundred guineas."

The sentences were disjointed. She spoke them close into his ear as opportunity offered. But she was neither breathless nor incoherent. She had plenty of energy for both the dance and the talk. And it was Masterson who was feeling the strain. Another progressive link leading into the *doré* and ending with a close promenade. She didn't put a foot wrong. The old girl had been well taught even if they couldn't give her grace or *élan*.

"So you trotted along to tell him what you knew and suggested that he took a slice off his profits?"

"He didn't believe me. He said that Martin was delirious and mistaken and that he could personally vouch for all the Sisters. But he took £50 off the bill."

She spoke with grim satisfaction. Masterson was surprised. Even if Courtney-Briggs had believed the story there was no reason why he should deduct a not inconsiderable amount from his bill. He wasn't responsible for recruiting or appointing the nursing staff. He had nothing to worry about. Masterson wondered whether he had believed the story. He had obviously said nothing, either to the Chairman of the Hospital Management Committee or to the Matron. Perhaps it was true that he could vouch personally for all the Sisters and the £50 deduction had merely been a gesture to keep a tiresome woman quiet. But Courtney-Briggs hadn't struck Masterson as the kind of man to submit himself to blackmail or to relinquish a penny of what he thought was due to him.

It was at that moment that the music crashed to a finish. Masterson smiled benevolently on Mrs. Dettinger, and led her back to their table. The applause lasted until they reached it and then was cut off abruptly as the sleek man announced the next dance. Masterson looked around for the waiter and beckoned.

"Well, now," he said to his partner, "that wasn't so bad, was it? If you behave yourself nicely for the rest of the evening I might even take you home."

He did take her home. They left early but it was well past midnight before he finally left the Baker Street flat. By then he knew that he had as much of the story as she could tell him. She had grown maudlin after their return, a reaction, he felt, to triumph and gin. He had kept her supplied with the latter through the rest of the evening, not enough to make her unmanageably drunk but sufficient to keep her talkative and pliable. But the journey home had been a nightmare, not made easier by the cab driver's glances of mingled amusement and contempt as he drove them from the hall to the South Bank car park, and by the disapproving superciliousness of the hall porter when they arrived at Saville Mansions. Once in the flat he had coaxed, comforted and bullied her into coherence, making black coffee for them both in the unbelievably squalid kitchen—a slut's kitchen he thought, glad of one more reason to despise her—and giving it to her with promises that, of course, he wouldn't leave her, that he would call for her again the following Saturday, that they would be permanent dancing partners. By midnight he had got out of her all he wanted to know about Martin Dettinger's career and his stay in the John Carpendar Hospital. There wasn't a great deal to be learned about the hospital. She hadn't visited often during the week he was there. Well, what was the point of it? There wasn't anything she could do for him. He was unconscious most of the time and didn't really know her even when he woke. Except that once, of course. She had hoped then for a little word of comfort and appreciation, but all she had got was that odd laugh and the talk about Irmgard Grobel. He had told her that story years before. She was tired of hearing it. A boy ought to be thinking of his mother when he was dying. It had been a terrible effort to sit there watching. She was a sensitive person. Hospitals upset her. The late Mr. Dettinger hadn't understood how sensitive she was.

There was apparently a great deal that the late Mr. Dettinger hadn't understood, his wife's sexual needs among them. Masterson listened to the story of her marriage without interest. It was the usual story of an unsatisfied wife, a hen-pecked husband and an unhappy and sensitive child. Masterson heard it without pity. He wasn't particularly interested in people. He divided them into two broad groups, the law-abiding and the villains and the ceaseless war which he waged against the latter fulfilled, as he knew, some inarticulate need of his own nature. But he was interested in facts. He knew that, when anybody visited the scene of a crime, some evidence was left behind or some was taken away. It was the detective's job to find that evidence. He knew that finger-prints hadn't yet been known to lie and that human beings did frequently, irrationally, whether they were innocent or guilty. He knew that facts stood up in court and people let you down. He knew that motive was unpredictable although he had honesty enough sometimes to recognize his own. It had struck him at the very moment of entering Julia Pardoe that his act, in its anger and exaltation, was in some way directed against Dalgliesh. But it never occurred to him to ask why. That would have seemed profitless speculation. Nor did he wonder whether, for the girl also, it had been an act of malice and private retribution.

"You'd think a boy would want his mother when he was dying. It was terrible to sit there and hear that dreadful breathing, first soft and then dreadfully loud. Of course he had a private room. That's why the hospital was able to charge. He wasn't National Health. But the other patients must have heard the noise all over the ward."

"Cheyne-Stoke's breathing," said Masterson. "It comes before the death rattle."

"They should have done something about it. It upset me dreadfully. That special nurse he had should have done something about it. The plain one. I suppose she was doing her duty, but she never gave a thought to me. After all, the living need some attention. There wasn't anything else she could do for Martin."

"That was Nurse Pearce. The one who died."

"Yes, I remember you told me. So she's dead too. I hear of nothing but death. It's all around me. What did you call that breathing?"

"Cheyne-Stoke's. It means that you're going to die."

"They should have done something about it. Did she breathe like that before she died?"

"No, she screamed. Someone poured disinfectant into her stomach and burned it out."

"I don't want to hear about it! I don't want to hear about it any more! Tell me about the dance. You will come back next Saturday, won't you?"

And so it had gone on. It had been tedious and exhausting and, in the end, almost frightening. The triumphant glow of getting what he wanted had faded before midnight and he was aware only of hatred and disgust. While he listened to her babblings he toyed with imagined violence. It was easy to see how these things happened. A handy poker. The silly face smashed into pulp. Blow on blow on blow. The bones splintering. A gush of blood. An orgasm of hatred. Imagining it, he found it hard to keep his breathing even. He took her hand gently.

"Yes," he said. "Yes, I'll come again. Yes. Yes."

The flesh was dry and hot now. She might have been in a fever. The painted nails were ridged. On the back of the hand the veins stood out like purple cords. He traced with a caressing finger the brown stains of age.

Shortly after midnight her voice burbled into incoherency, her head sank forward, and he saw that she was asleep. He waited for a moment, then disengaged his hand and tiptoed into the bedroom. It took him only a couple of minutes to change his clothes. Then he tiptoed into the bathroom and washed his face and the hand which had touched hers, washed them over and over again. Finally he left the flat, shutting the door quietly behind him as if afraid to wake her, and went out into the night.

V

Fifteen minutes later, Masterson's car passed the flat where Miss Beale and Miss Burrows, cosily dressing-gowned, were sipping their late night cocoa before the dying fire. They heard it as one brief crescendo in the intermittent flow of traffic, and broke off their chatter to speculate with desultory interest on what brought people out in the small hours of the morning. It was certainly unusual for them to be still up at this hour, but tomorrow was Saturday and they could indulge their fondness for late-night conversation in the comforting knowledge that they could lie in next morning.

They had been discussing the visit that afternoon of Chief Superintendent Dalgliesh. Really, they agreed, it had been a success, almost a pleasure. He had seemed to enjoy his tea. He had sat there, deep in their most comfortable armchair, and the three of them had talked together as if he were as harmless and familiar as the local vicar.

He had said to Miss Beale: "I want to see Nurse Pearce's death through your eyes. Tell me about it. Tell me everything you saw and felt from the moment you drove through the hospital gates."

And Miss Beale had told him, taking a shameful pleasure in her half-hour of importance, in his obvious appreciation that she had observed so carefully and could describe with such clarity. He was a good listener, they conceded. Well, that was part of his job. He was clever, too, at making

people talk. Even Angela, who had sat in watchful silence
for most of the time, couldn't explain why she had felt
drawn to mention her recent encounter with Sister Rolfe in
the Westminster library. And his eyes had flickered with
interest, interest which had faded into disappointment
when she told him the date. The friends agreed that they
couldn't have been mistaken. He had been disappointed.
Sister Rolfe had been seen in the library on the wrong day.

VI

It was after eleven o'clock when Dalgliesh turned the key
in his desk drawer, locked the office behind him and let
himself out of the side door of Nightingale House to walk
back to Falconer's Arms. At the turn of the path where it
narrowed before losing itself in the dark shadows of the
trees, he looked back at the gaunt pile of the house, enormous and sinister, with its four turrets black against the
night sky. The house was in almost total darkness. There
was only one lighted window and it took him a minute to
identify the room. So Mary Taylor was in her bedroom but
not yet asleep. The light was merely a faint glow, perhaps
from a bedside lamp, and as he watched it went out.

He made his way towards the Winchester Gate. The
trees here were very close to the path. Their black boughs
arched over his head shutting out the faint light from the
nearest lamp. For about fifty yards he walked in absolute
darkness, treading swiftly and silently over the mush of
dead leaves. He was in that state of physical tiredness
when the mind and body seem detached, the body, condi-
tioned to reality, moving half consciously in the familiar
physical world, while the liberated mind swings into
uncontrolled orbit in which fantasy and fact show an

equally ambiguous face. Dalgliesh was surprised that he was so tired. This job was no more arduous than any other. He was working long hours, but then a sixteen-hour day was normal for him when he was on a case. And this extraordinary weariness wasn't the exhaustion of frustration or failure. The case would break by tomorrow morning. Later tonight Masterson would be back with another piece of the jigsaw and the picture would be complete. In two days at the latest he would have left Nightingale House. In two days' time he would have seen the last of that gold and white room in the south-west turret.

Moving like an automaton he heard, too late, the sudden muted footfall at his back. Instinctively, he threw himself round to face his adversary and felt the blow glance from his left temple to his shoulder. There was no pain, only a crack as if his whole cranium had split, a numbness of his left arm, and after a second which seemed an eternity, the warm, almost comforting, gush of blood. He gave one gasp and crumpled forward. But he was still conscious. Blinded by blood and fighting against nausea, he tried to rise, feeling for the earth with both hands, willing himself to get up and fight. But his feet scrabbled ineffectively in the moist earth and there was no strength in his arms. His eyes were blinded by his own blood. The suffocating smell of damp humus pressed against his nose and mouth, pungent as an anaesthetic. He lay there, helplessly retching, waking pain with every spasm, and waited in angry impotence for the final annihilating blow.

But nothing happened. He sank, unresisting, into unconsciousness. A few seconds later he was recalled to reality by a hand gently shaking his shoulder. Someone was bending over him. He heard a woman's voice.

"It's me. What's 'appened? Somebody cosh yer?"

It was Morag Smith. He struggled to answer, to warn her

to get away quickly. The two of them would be no match for a determined killer. But his voice seemed incapable of forming words. He was aware that somewhere very close a man was groaning, then realized with bitter humour, that the voice was his. He seemed to have no control over it. He was aware of hands moving around his head. Then she shuddered like a child.

"Ugh! Yer all over blood!"

Again he tried to talk. She bent her head nearer. He could see the dark strands of hair and the white face hovering in front of him. He struggled to rise and this time managed to get to his knees.

"Did you see him?"

"Not really—'e 'eard me coming through. Made off towards Nightingale 'ouse. Blimey, you don't 'alf look a bloody mess. 'ere, lean on me."

"No. Leave me and get help. He may be back."

"Not 'im. Anyway, we're better together. I don't fancy going it alone. Ghosts is one thing, bloody murderers is another. Come on, I'll give yer a 'and."

He could feel the sharp bones in her thin shoulders, but the fragile body was remarkably wiry and she stood his weight well. He forced himself to his feet and stood there swaying. He asked:

"Man or woman?"

"Didn't see. Could've been either. Never mind about that now. Think yer can make it to Nightingale 'ouse? That'd be the nearest."

Dalgliesh felt remarkably better now that he was on his legs. He could scarcely see the path but he took a few tentative steps forward, his hand supported by her shoulder.

"I think so. The back door would be the nearest. It can't be more than fifty yards. Ring the bell of Matron's flat. I know she's there."

Together they shuffled slowly along the path obliterating, as Dalgliesh realized bitterly, any footprints as he might otherwise have hoped to find next morning. Not that these sodden leaves would yield many clues. He wondered what had happened to the weapon. But this was pointless speculation. He could do nothing until it was light. He felt a wave of gratitude and affection for the tough little person whose brittle arm lay weightless as a child's around his hip. We must look an odd pair, he thought. He said:

"You probably saved my life, Morag. He only ran off because he heard you coming."

He, or was it she? If only Morag had been in time to glimpse whether it were a man or a woman. He could scarcely catch her reply.

"Don't talk bloody daft."

He heard, without surprise, that she was crying. She made no attempt to suppress or check her sobbing and it didn't impede their progress. Perhaps, to Morag, crying was almost as natural as walking. He made no effort to comfort her except to press on her shoulders. She took that as a plea for more support and tightened her arm around his hips, leaning against him, helping him on his way. And thus incongruously entwined they passed under the shadows of the trees.

VII

The light in the demonstration room was bright, too bright. It pierced even his gummed eyelids and he moved his head restlessly from side to side to escape the shaft of pain. Then his head was being steadied by cool hands. Mary Taylor's hands. He heard her speaking to him, telling him that Courtney-Briggs was in the hospital. She had sent for

Courtney-Briggs. Then the same hands were taking off his tie, undoing the buttons of his shirt, slipping his arms out of his jacket with practised skill.

"What happened?"

It was Courtney-Briggs's voice, harsh and masculine. So the surgeon had arrived. What had he been doing in the hospital? Another emergency operation? Courtney-Briggs's patients seemed curiously prone to relapse. What alibi had he for the last half-hour? Dalgliesh said:

"Someone was lying in wait for me. I've got to check who's in Nightingale House."

A firm grip was on his arm. Courtney-Briggs was pressing him back into his chair. Two swinging blobs of grey hovered over him. Her voice again.

"Not now. You can hardly stand. One of us will go."

"Go now."

"In a minute. We've locked all the doors. We shall know if anyone returns. Rely on us. Just relax."

So reasonable. Rely on us. Relax. He gripped metal arms on the chair, taking hold on reality.

"I want to check for myself."

Half blinded by blood, he sensed rather than saw their mutual glance of concern. He knew that he sounded like a petulant child, beating his insistence against the implacable calm of the grown-ups. Maddened with frustration, he tried to rise from the chair. But the floor tipped sickeningly, then rose up to meet him through whorls of screaming colour. It was no good. He couldn't stand.

"My eyes," he said. Courtney-Briggs's voice, annoyingly reasonable:

"In one moment. I must look first at your head."

"But I want to see!" His blindness infuriated him. Were they doing this to him deliberately? He put up a hand and began to pick at the caked eyelids. He could hear them talking together, low voiced, in the muttered idiom of their craft from which he, the patient, was excluded. He was conscious of new sounds, the hiss of a sterilizer, a jingle of instruments, the closing of a metal lid. Then the smell of disinfectant sharpened. Now she was cleaning his eyes. A pad, deliciously cool, was wiped across each lid, and he opened them blinking to see more clearly the sheen of her dressing-gown and the long plait of hair falling over her left shoulder. He spoke to her directly.

"I must know who's in Nightingale House. Could you check now, please?"

Without another word or a further glance at Courtney-Briggs, she slipped out of the room. As soon as the door was closed, Dalgliesh said:

"You didn't tell me that your brother was once engaged to Josephine Fallon."

"You didn't ask me."

The surgeon's voice was deliberate, uninterested, the response of a man with his mind on his job. There was a snip of scissors, a momentary chill of steel against the skull. The surgeon was clipping Dalgliesh's hair around the wound.

"You must have known that I should be interested."

"Oh, interested! You'd be interested all right. Your kind have an infinite capacity for taking an interest in other people's affairs. But I confined myself to satisfying your curiosity only so far as the deaths of these two girls were concerned. You can't complain that I've held anything relevant back. Peter's death isn't relevant—merely a private tragedy."

Not so much a private tragedy thought Dalgliesh as a public embarrassment. Peter Courtney had violated his brother's first principle, the necessity of being successful. Dalgliesh said:

"He hanged himself."

"As you say, he hanged himself. Not a very dignified or pleasant way to go, but the poor boy hadn't my resources. The day when they make the final diagnosis I shall have more appropriate measures available than doing myself to death on the end of a rope."

His egotism, thought Dalgliesh, was astounding. Even his brother's death had to be seen in relationship to himself. He stood complacently secure at the hub of his private universe while other people—brother, mistress, patient— revolved round that central sun existing by virtue of its warmth and light, obedient to its centripetal force. But wasn't that how most people saw themselves? Was Mary Taylor less self-absorbed? Was he himself? Wasn't it merely that she and he pandered more subtly to their essential egotism?

The surgeon moved over to his black instrument case and took out a mirror mounted on a metal band which he clipped around his head. He came back to Dalgliesh, ophthalmoscope in hand and settled himself into a chair opposite his patient. They sat confronting each other, foreheads almost touching. Dalgliesh could sense the metal of the instrument against his right eye. Courtney-Briggs commanded:

"Look straight ahead."

Dalgliesh stared obediently at the pinpoint of light. He said:

"You left the main hospital building at about midnight. You spoke to the porter at the main gate at twelve thirty- eight a.m. Where were you between those times?"

"I told you. There was a fallen elm blocking the back path. I spent some minutes examining the scene and making sure that other people didn't injure themselves on it."

"One person did precisely that. That was at twelve seventeen a.m. There was no warning scarf tied on the branches at that time."

The ophthalmoscope moved to the other eye. The surgeon's breathing was perfectly regular.

"He was mistaken."

"He doesn't think so."

"So you deduce that I arrived at the fallen tree later than twelve seventeen a.m. It may have been so. As I wasn't concocting an alibi, I didn't check the time every two minutes."

"But you're not suggesting that it took you over seventeen minutes to drive from the main hospital to that particular place."

"Oh, I think I could make out quite a case for the delay, don't you know. I could claim that I needed, in your deplorable police jargon, to obey a call of nature and left my car to meditate among the trees."

"And did you?"

"I may have done. When I've dealt with your head, which incidentally is going to need about a dozen stitches, I'll give some thought to the matter. You'll forgive me if I concentrate now on my own job."

The matron had quietly returned. She took up her stance next to Courtney-Briggs like an acolyte waiting for orders. Her face was very white. Without waiting for her to speak the surgeon handed her the ophthalmoscope. She said:

"Everyone who should be in Nightingale House is in her room."

Courtney-Briggs was running his hands over Dalgliesh's left shoulder causing pain with every thrust of the strong probing fingers. He said:

"The collar-bone seems all right. Badly bruised but not

fractured. Your attacker must have been a tall woman. You're over six feet yourself."

"If it were a woman. Or she may have had a long weapon, a golf club perhaps."

"A golf club. Matron, what about your clubs? Where do you keep them?"

She answered dully: "In the hall at the bottom of my staircase. The bag is usually left just inside the door."

"Then you'd better check them now."

She was gone for less than two minutes and they waited her return in silence. When she came back she spoke directly to Dalgliesh.

"One of the irons is missing."

The news seemed to hearten Courtney-Briggs. He said almost jovially:

"Well, there's your weapon for you! But there's not much point in searching for it tonight. It'll be lying about somewhere in the grounds. Your men can find it and do everything necessary to it tomorrow; test it for finger-prints, look for blood and hair, all the usual tricks. You're not in any fit state to bother yourself tonight. We've got to get this wound sutured. I shall have to get you over to the out-patient theatre. You'll need an anaesthetic."

"I don't want an anaesthetic."

"Then I can give you a local. That just means a few injections around the wound. We could do this here, Matron."

"I don't want any anaesthetic. I just want it stitched."

Courtney-Briggs explained patiently as if to a child:

"It's a very deep cut and it's got to be sutured. It's going to hurt badly if you won't accept an anaesthetic."

"I tell you I don't want one. And I don't want a prophy-lactic injection of penicillin or anti-tetanus. I just want it sutured."

He felt them look at each other. He knew that he was being obstinately unreasonable but he didn't care. Why couldn't they get on with it? Then Courtney-Briggs spoke, curiously formal:

"If you'd prefer another surgeon. . . ."

"No, I just want you to get on with it."

There was a moment's silence. Then the surgeon spoke: "All right. I'll be as quick as I can."

He was aware that Mary Taylor had moved behind him. She drew his head back against her breast, supported in between cold, firm hands. He shut his eyes like a child. The needle felt immense, an iron rod simultaneously ice cold and red hot which pierced his skull time and time again. The pain was an abomination, made bearable only by anger and by his obstinate determination not to betray weakness. He set his features into a rigid mask. But it was infuriating to feel the involuntary tears seeping under his eyelids.

After an eternity he realized that it was over. He heard himself say:

"Thank you. And now I'd like to get back to my office. Sergeant Masterson has instructions to come on here if I'm not in the hotel. He can drive me home."

Mary Taylor was winding a crêpe bandage around his head. She didn't speak. Courtney-Briggs said:

"I'd prefer you to go straight to bed. We can let you have a room in the Medical Officers' quarters for tonight. I'll arrange for an X-ray first thing in the morning. Then I'd like to see you again."

"You can arrange what you like for tomorrow. Just now I'd like to be left alone."

He got up from the chair. She put a hand on his arm, supporting him. But he must have made some kind of gesture for she dropped her arm. He felt surprisingly light on his feet. It was odd that such an insubstantial body could support the weight of so heavy a head. He put up an exploring hand and felt the scrape of the bandage; it seemed an immense distance from his skull. Then, focusing his eyes carefully, he walked unhindered across the room to the door. As he reached it, he heard Courtney-Briggs's voice.

"You will want to know where I was at the time of the attack. I was in my room in the Medical Officers' quarters. I'm staying there for tonight ready for an early operating session. I'm sorry I can't oblige you with an alibi. I can only hope that you realize that, if I want to put anyone out of the way, I have subtler methods at my disposal than a golf iron."

Dalgliesh didn't reply. Without looking round and without a further word he left them and closed the door of the demonstration room quietly behind him. The stairs looked a formidable climb and, at first, he was afraid that he wouldn't be able to make it. But he grasped the banister resolutely and, step by careful step, made his way back to the office and settled down to wait for Masterson.

CHAPTER EIGHT

A Circle of Burnt Earth

I

IT WAS NEARLY two in the morning when the gate porter waved Masterson through the main entrance of the hospital. The wind was rising steadily as he drove along the twisting path to Nightingale House between an avenue of black rumbustious trees. The house was in darkness except for the one lit window where Dalgliesh was still working. Masterson scowled at it. It had been irritating and disconcerting to discover that Dalgliesh was still at Nightingale House. He expected to have to give his report on the day's activities; the prospect wasn't unpleasing since he was fortified by success. But it had been a long day. He hoped that they weren't in for one of the Superintendent's all-night sessions.

Masterson let himself in at the side door, double locking it behind him. The silence of the vast entrance hall received him, eerie and portentous. The house seemed to be holding its breath. He smelt again the alien but now familiar amalgam of disinfectant and floor polish, unwelcoming and faintly sinister. As if afraid to stir the sleeping house—half empty as it was—he did not switch on the light but made his way across the hall by the beam of his electric torch. The notices on the hall board gleamed white reminding him of mourning cards in the vestibule of some foreign cathedral. Of your charity pray for the soul of Josephine Fallon. He found himself tiptoeing up the stairs as if afraid to wake the dead.

In the first-floor office Dalgliesh was sitting at his desk with the file open before him. Masterson stood stock-still in the doorway, concealing his surprise. The Superintendent's face was drawn and grey under an immense cocoon of white crêpe bandage. He was sitting bolt upright, forearms resting on the desk, palms spread lightly each side of the page. The pose was familiar. Masterson reflected, not for the first time, that the Superintendent had remarkable hands and knew how to display them to advantage. He had long decided that Dalgliesh was one of the proudest men he knew. This essential conceit was too carefully guarded to be generally recognized, but it was gratifying to catch him out in one of the lesser vanities. Dalgliesh looked up without smiling.

"I expected you back two hours ago, Sergeant. What were you doing?"

"Extracting information by unorthodox means, sir."

"You look as if the unorthodox means have been used on you."

Masterson bit back the obvious retort. If the old man chose to be mysterious about his injury he wasn't going to give him the gratification of showing curiosity.

"I was dancing until nearly midnight, sir."

"At your age that shouldn't be too exhausting. Tell me about the lady. She seems to have made an impression on you. You had an agreeable evening?"

Masterson could have retorted with reason that he had had one hell of an evening. He contented himself with an account of what he had learned. The exhibition tango was prudently forgotten. Instinct warned him that Dalgliesh might think it neither funny nor clever. But he gave an otherwise accurate account of the evening. He tried to keep it factual and unemotional but became aware that he was enjoying some of the telling. His description of Mrs. Dettinger was concise but caustic. Towards the end he hardly troubled to conceal his contempt and disgust of her. He felt that he was making rather a good job of it.

Dalgliesh listened in silence. His cocooned head was still bent over the file and Masterson got no hint of what he was feeling. At the end of the recital Dalgliesh looked up:

"Do you enjoy your work, Sergeant?"

"Yes sir, for most of the time."

"I thought you might say that."

"Was the question intended as a rebuke, sir?"

Masterson was aware that he was entering on dangerous ground but was unable to resist this first tentative step.

Dalgliesh didn't answer the question. Instead he said:

"I don't think it's possible to be a detective and remain always kind. But if you ever find that cruelty is becoming pleasurable in itself, then it's probably time to stop being a detective."

Masterson flushed and was silent. This from Dalgliesh! Dalgliesh who was so uncaring about his subordinates' private life as to seem unaware that they had any; whose caustic wit could be as devastating as another man's bludgeon. Kindness! And how kind exactly was he himself? How many of his notable successes had been won with kindness? He would never be brutal, of course. He was too proud, too fastidious, too controlled, too bloody inhuman in fact for anything so understandable as a little down-to-earth brutality. His reaction to evil was a wrinkle of the nose not a stamp of the foot. But kindness! Tell that to the boys, thought Masterson.

Dalgliesh went on talking as if he said nothing remarkable.

"We'll have to see Mrs. Dettinger again, of course. And we'll want a statement. Did you think she was telling the truth?"

"It's difficult to tell. I can't think why she should lie. But she's a strange woman and she wasn't feeling too pleased with me at the time. It might give her some kind of perverse satisfaction to mislead us. She might have substituted Grobel's name for one of the other defendants, for example."

"So that the person her son recognized on the ward could have been any one of the Felsenheim defendants, those who are still alive and unaccounted for. What exactly did her son tell her?"

"That's the problem, sir. Apparently he gave her to understand that this German woman, Irmgard Grobel, was employed at the John Carpendar but she can't recall his exact words. She thinks he said something like:

" 'This is a funny kind of hospital, ma, they've got Grobel here, working as one of the Sisters.' "

Dalgliesh said: "Suggesting that it wasn't the Sister who was actually nursing him, otherwise he'd presumably have said so. Except, of course, that he was unconscious most of the time and may not have seen Sister Brumfett previously or appreciated that she was in charge of the ward. He wasn't in any state to recognize the niceties of the hospital hierarchy. According to his medical record he was either delirious or unconscious most of the time, which would make his evidence suspect even if he hadn't inconveniently died. Anyway, his mother at first didn't apparently take the story too seriously. She didn't mention it to anyone at the hospital? Nurse Pearce, for example?"

"She says not. I think at the time Mrs. Dettinger's main concern was to collect her son's belongings and the death certificate and claim on the insurance."

"Bitter, Sergeant?"

"Well, she's paying nearly £2,000 a year for dancing lessons and she's come to the end of her capital. These Delaroux people like payment in advance. I heard all about her finances when I took her home. Mrs. Dettinger wasn't out to make trouble. But then she received Mr. Courtney-Briggs's bill, and it occurred to her that she might use her son's story to get a reduction. And she got one too. Fifty quid."

"Which suggests that Mr. Courtney-Briggs is either more charitable than we had supposed or thought that the information was worth the money. Did he pay it over at once?"

"She says not. She first visited him at his Wimpole Street consulting rooms on the evening of Wednesday, January twenty-first. She didn't get much joy on that occasion so she rang him up last Saturday morning. The receptionist told her that Mr. Courtney-Briggs was out of the country. She intended to ring again on the Monday but the cheque for fifty pounds came by the first post. There was no letter and no explanation, merely his compliment slip. But she got the message all right."

"So he was out of the country last Saturday. Where, I wonder? Germany? That's something to check, anyway."

Masterson said, "It all sounds so unlikely, sir. And it doesn't really fit."

"No. We're pretty certain who killed both those girls. Logically all the facts point to one person. And as you say, this new evidence doesn't really fit in. It's disconcerting when you scramble around in the dirt for a missing piece of the jigsaw and then find it's part of a different puzzle."

"So you don't think it's relevant, sir? I should hate to think that my evening's exertions with Mrs. Dettinger were in vain."

"Oh, it's relevant. It's exceedingly relevant. And we've found some corroboration. We've traced the missing library book. Westminster City Library were very helpful. Miss Pearce went to the Marylebone Branch on the afternoon of Thursday, 8th January, when she was off duty and asked if they had a book dealing with German war trials. She said she was interested in a trial at Felsenheim in November 1945. They couldn't find anything in stock but they said they would make inquiries of other London libraries and suggested that she should come back or telephone them in a day or two. She telephoned on the Saturday morning. They told her that they'd been able to trace a book which dealt with the Felsenheim trial among others, and she called in for it that afternoon. On each visit she gave her name as Josephine Fallon and presented Fallon's ticket and the blue token. Normally, of course, they wouldn't have noticed the name and address. They did so because the book had to be specially obtained from another library."

"Was the book returned, sir?"

"Yes, but anonymously, and they can't say exactly when. It was probably on the Wednesday after Pearce died. Someone left it on the non-fiction trolley. When the assistant went to fill up the trolley with recently returned books she recognized it and took it back to the counter to be registered and put on one side ready for return to its parent library. No one saw who returned it. The library is particularly busy and people come in and out at will. Not everyone has a book to return or calls at the counter. It would be easy enough to bring in a book in a basket or a pocket and slip it among the others on the trolley. The assistant who found it had been on counter duty for most of the morning and afternoon and one of the junior staff had been replenishing the trolley. The girl was getting behind with the work so her senior went to give a hand. She noticed the book at once. That was at four thirty approximately. But it could have been put there at any time."

"Any prints, sir?"

"Nothing helpful. A few smudges. It had been handled by quite a number of the library staff and God knows how many of the public. And why not? They weren't to know that it was part of the evidence in a murder inquiry. But there's something interesting about it. Have a look."

He opened one of the desk drawers and brought out a stout book bound with a dark blue cloth and embossed with a library catalogue number on the spine. Masterson took it and laid it on the table. He seated himself and opened it carefully, taking his time. It was an account of various war trials held in Germany from 1945 onwards, apparently carefully documented, unsensational in treatment and written by a Queen's Counsel who had once been on the staff of the Judge Advocate General. There were only a few plates and of these only two related to the Felsenheim trial. One showed a general view of the Court with an indistinct glimpse of the doctor in the dock, and the other was a photograph of the camp commandant. Dalgliesh said:

"Martin Dettinger is mentioned, but only briefly. During the war he served in the King's Wiltshire Light Infantry and in November 1945 he was appointed as a member of a military Court set up in West Germany to try four men and one woman accused of war crimes. These Courts were established under a Special Army Order of June 1945 and this one consisted of a President who was a Brigadier of the Grenadier Guards, four army officers of whom Dettinger was one, and the Judge Advocate appointed by the Judge Advocate General to the Forces. As I said, they had the job of trying five people who, it was alleged—you'll find the indictment on page 127—'acting jointly and in pursuance of a common intent and acting for and on behalf of the then German Reich did on or about 3rd September 1944 wilfully, deliberately and wrongfully aid, abet and participate in the killing of 31 human beings of Polish and Russian nationality.'"

Masterson was not surprised that Dalgliesh should be able to quote the indictment word for word. This was an administrator's trick, this ability to memorize and present facts with accuracy and precision. Dalgliesh could do it better than most, and if he wanted to exercise his technique it was hardly for his Sergeant to interrupt. He said nothing. He noticed that the Superintendent had taken up a large grey stone, a perfect ovoid, and was rolling it slowly between his fingers. It was something that had caught his eye in the grounds, presumably, and which he had picked up to serve as a paper-weight. It certainly hadn't been on the office desk that morning. The tired, strained voice went on.

"These 31 men, women and children were Jewish slave workers in Germany and were said to have been suffering from tuberculosis. They were sent to an institution in Western Germany which was originally designed to care for the mentally sick but which since the summer of 1944 had been dedicated, not to curing, but to the business of killing. There is no evidence to how many German mentally ill patients were done to death there. The staff had been sworn to secrecy about what went on, but there were plenty of rumours in the neighbouring districts. On the 3rd September 1944, a transport of Polish and Russian nationals were sent to the institution. They were told they were to receive treatment for tuberculosis. That night they were given lethal injections—men, women and children—and by morning they were dead and buried. It was for this crime, not for the murder of the German nationals, that the five accused were on trial. One was the head doctor Max Klein, one a young pharmacist Ernst Gumbmann, one the chief male nurse Adolf Straub, and one a young, untrained female nurse aged 18, Irmgard Grobel. The head doctor and the chief male nurse were found guilty. The doctor was condemned to death and the male nurse to twenty-three years' imprisonment. The pharmacist and the woman were acquitted. You can find what her council said on page 140. You had better read it out."

Surprised, Masterson took up the book in silence and turned to page 140. He began reading. His voice sounded unnaturally loud.

"This court is not trying the defendant Irmgard Grobel for participation in the death of German nationals. We know now what was happening at Steinhoff Institution. We know, too, that it was in accordance with German law as proclaimed by Adolf Hitler alone. In accordance with orders handed down from the highest authority, many thousands of insane German people were put to death with perfect legality from 1940 onward. On moral grounds one can judge this action as one pleases. The question is not whether the staff at Steinhoff thought it wrong or whether they thought it merciful. The question is whether they thought it was lawful. It has been proved by witnesses that there was such a law in existence. Irmgard Grobel, if she were concerned with the deaths of these people, acted in accordance with this law.

"But we are not concerned with the mentally ill. From July 1944 this same law was extended to cover incurably tubercular foreign workers. It might be contended that the accused would be in no doubt of the legality of such killings when she had seen German nationals put out of their misery in the interests of the State. But that is not my contention. We are not in a position to judge what the accused thought. She was not implicated in the only killings which are the concern of this Court. The transport of Russians and Poles arrived at Steinhoff on 3rd September 1944 at half past six in the evening. On that day Irmgard Grobel was returning from her leave. The Court has heard how she entered the nurses' quarters at half past seven and changed into her uniform. She was on duty from nine o'clock. Between the time of entering the Institution and arriving in the nurses' duty room in E Block she spoke only to two other nurses, witnesses Willig and Rohde. Both these women have testified that they did not tell Grobel of the arrival of the transport. So Grobel enters the duty room. She had had a difficult journey and is tired and sick. She is hesitating whether or not to seek permission to go off duty. It is then that the telephone rings and Doctor Klein speaks to her. The Court has heard the evidence of witnesses to this conversation. Klein asks Grobel to look in the drug store and tell him how much evipan and phenol there is in stock. You have heard how the evipan was delivered in cartons, each carton containing 25 injections and each injection consisting of one capsule of evipan in powder form and one container of sterile water. The evipan and phenol, together with other dangerous drugs, were kept in the nurses' duty room. Grobel checks the amounts and reports to Klein that there are two cartons of evipan and about 150 c.c. of liquid phenol in stock. Klein then orders her to have all the available evipan and phenol ready to hand over to male nurse Straub who will fetch it. He also orders her to hand over twelve 10 c.c. syringes and a quantity of strong needles. The accused claimed that at no time did he state for what purpose these drugs were required and you have heard from the accused Straub that he, also, did not enlighten her.

"Irmgard Grobel did not leave the duty room until she

was carried back to her quarters at nine twenty that night. The Court has heard how Nurse Rohde coming late on duty found her in a faint on the floor. For five days she was confined to her bed with acute vomiting and fever. She did not see the Russians and Poles enter E Block, she did not see their bodies carried out in the early hours of 4th September. When she returned to duty the corpses had been buried.

"Mr. President, this Court has heard witnesses who have testified to the kindness of Irmgard Grobel, to her gentleness with the child patients, to her skill as a nurse; I would remind the Court that she is young, hardly more than a child herself. But I do not ask for an acquittal on the grounds of her youth nor her sex but because she, alone of the accused, is manifestly innocent of this charge. She had no hand in the deaths of these 31 Russians and Poles. She did not even know that they existed. The Defence has nothing further to add."

Dalgliesh's bitter voice broke in on the silence.

"The usual Teutonic plea of legality you note, Sergeant. They didn't waste much time with their killings did they? Admitted at seven thirty and injected soon after nine. And why evipan? They couldn't be sure that death would be instantaneous unless they injected a heavy dose. I doubt whether less than 20 c.c. would kill immediately. Not that it would worry them. What saved Grobel was being on leave until late that evening. The Defence claimed that she was never told that the foreign prisoners had arrived, that no one knew until the morning of the fourth. That same plea gave the pharmacist his freedom. Technically they were both innocent, if you can use that word of anyone who worked at Steinhoff."

Masterson was silent. It was all so long ago. Grobel had been a girl. Ten years younger than he was now. The war

was old history. It had no more relevance to his life than
had the Wars of the Roses, less since it did not even evoke
the faintly romantic and chivalrous overtones of the history
learned in his boyhood. He had no particular feelings
about the Germans, or indeed about any race other than
the few he regarded as culturally and intellectually inferior.
The Germans were not among these. Germany to him
meant clean hotels and good roads, *rippchen* eaten with the
local wine at the Apfel Wine Struben Inn, the Rhine curving below him like a silver ribbon, the excellence of the
camping ground at Koblenz.

And if any of the accused from Felsenheim were alive
they would be well into middle age now. Irmgard Grobel
herself would be forty-three. It was all such old history. It
had relevance only because it touched this present case. He
said:

"It happened so long ago. Is a secret like that worth
killing to preserve? Who really cares now? Isn't the official policy to forgive and forget?"

"We English are good at forgiving our enemies; it
releases us from the obligation of liking our friends. Take
a look at this book, Masterson. What do you notice?"

Masterson let the pages fall apart, shook them gently,
lifted the book to eye level and examined the binding.
Then he replaced it on the table and pressed back the
middle pages. There, embedded deep in the folds were a
few grains of sand.

Dalgliesh said: "We've sent a sample to the lab for analy-
sis, but the result isn't much in doubt. It's almost certainly
from one of the fire buckets in Nightingale House."

"So that's where it was hidden until he, or she, could
return it to the library. The same person hid the book and
the tin of rose spray. It all hangs together very neatly, sir."

"A little too neatly, don't you think?" said Dalgliesh.

But Sergeant Masterson had remembered something else.

"That brochure, the one we found in Pearce's room! Wasn't it about the work of a Suffolk Refuge for Fascist War Victims? Suppose Pearce sent for it? Is this another example of making the punishment fit the crime?"

"I think so. We'll get in touch with the place in the morning and find out what, if anything, she promised them. And we'll talk again to Courtney-Briggs. He was in Nightingale House at about the time Fallon died. When we know who he came to see and why, we shall be close to solving this case. But all that must wait for tomorrow."

Masterson stifled a yawn. He said: "It's been tomorrow, sir, for nearly three hours."

II

If the night porter of the Falconer's Arms was surprised at the return of the two guests in the small hours of the morning, one obviously ill and with his head ostentatiously bandaged, he was trained not to show it. His inquiry whether there was anything he could get for the gentlemen was perfunctory; Masterson's reply barely civil. They climbed the three flights of stairs to their floor since the old-fashioned lift was erratic and noisy. Dalgliesh, obstinately determined not to betray his weakness to his Sergeant, made himself take each step without grasping the banister. He knew it to be a foolish vanity and by the time he had gained his room he was paying for it. He was so weak that he had to lean against the closed door for a minute before weaving his unsteady way over to the wash-basin. Grasping the taps for support, he retched painfully and ineffectually, his forehead resting on his forearms. Without lifting his head he twisted on the right-hand tap. There was a gush of ice-cold water. He swilled it over his face and gulped it down from cupped hands. Immediately he felt better.

He slept fitfully. It was difficult to rest his cocooned head comfortably on the pillows, and loss of blood seemed to have left his mind preternaturally active and lucid, militating against sleep. When he did doze it was only to dream. He was walking in the grounds of the hospital with Mavis Gearing. She was skipping girlishly between the trees, brandishing her garden shears and saying kittenishly:

"It's wonderful what you can find to make a show even in this dead time of the year."

It didn't strike him as incongruous that she was snipping full blown red roses from the dead branches, or that neither of them remarked on the body of Mary Taylor, white neck encircled by the hangman's noose, as she swung gently from one of the boughs.

Towards morning he slept more deeply. Even so, the harsh incessant ring of the telephone woke him to instant consciousness. The illuminated dial of his travelling clock showed 5:49 a.m. He shifted his head with difficulty from the hollowed pillow and felt for the receiver. The voice was instantly recognizable. But then he knew that he could have distinguished it from any other woman's voice in the world.

"Mr. Dalgliesh? This is Mary Taylor. I'm sorry to disturb you but I thought you'd prefer me to ring. We have a fire here. Nothing dangerous; it's only in the grounds. It seems to have started in a disused gardener's hut about fifty yards from Nightingale House. The house itself isn't in any danger but the fire spread very quickly among the trees."

He was surprised how clearly he could think. His wound no longer ached. He felt literally light-headed and it was necessary to touch the rough gauze of the bandage to reassure himself that it was still there. He said:

"Morag Smith. Is she all right? She used that hut as a kind of refuge."

"I know. She told me so this evening after she'd brought you in. I gave her a bed here for the night. Morag is safe. That was the first thing I checked."

"And the others in Nightingale House?"

There was a silence. Then she spoke, her voice sharper. "I'll check now. It never occurred to me. . . ."

"Of course not. Why should it? I'll come over."

"Is that necessary? Mr. Courtney-Briggs was insistent that you should rest. The fire brigade have things under control. At first they were afraid that Nightingale House was threatened but they've axed some of the nearer trees. The blaze should be out in half an hour. Couldn't you wait till morning?"

"I'm coming over now," he said.

Masterson was lying flat on his back, drugged with tiredness, his heavy face vacant with sleep, his mouth half-open. It took nearly a minute to rouse him. Dalgliesh would have preferred to leave him there in his stupor, but he knew that, in his present weakened state, it wouldn't be safe for him to drive. Masterson, shaken at last into wakefulness, listened to his Superintendent's instructions without comment, then pulled on his clothes in resentful silence. He was too prudent to question Dalgliesh's decision to return to Nightingale House, but it was obvious by his sullen manner that he thought the excursion unnecessary, and the short drive to the hospital was spent in silence.

The fire was visible as a red glow on the night sky long before they came in sight of the hospital, and as they drove through the open Winchester Road gate they could hear the staccato crackle of burning trees and could smell the rich evocative scent of smouldering wood, strong and sweet on the cold air. It broke Masterson's mood of sullen resentment. He breathed it in with noisy enjoyment and said in happy candour:

"I like that smell, sir. It reminds me of boyhood, I suppose. Summer camps with the Boy Scouts. Huddled in a blanket around the camp fire with the sparks soaring off into the night. Bloody marvellous when you're thirteen and being patrol leader is more power and glory than you're ever likely to feel again. You know, sir."

Dalgliesh didn't know. His solitary and lonely boyhood had been devoid of these tribal delights. But it was an interesting and curiously touching glimpse into Masterson's character. Patrol leader in the Boy Scouts! Well, why not? Given a different heritage, a different twist of fate and he could have easily been a leader in a street gang, his essential ambition and ruthlessness channelled into less conformist paths.

Masterson drove the car under the trees at a safe distance and they walked towards the blaze. As if by unspoken consent, they halted and stood together in the shadow of the trees watching in silence. No one appeared to notice them and no one approached. The firemen were getting on with their job. There was only one appliance and they were apparently running the hose from Nightingale House. The fire was by now well under control but it was still spectacular. The shed had gone completely with nothing but a ring of black earth to show where it had once stood, and the surrounding trees were blackened gibbets, stunted and twisted as if with the agony of their burning. On the periphery a few saplings still burned fiercely, crackling and spluttering in the jets from the fire hose. A single flame, writhing and twisting in the stiff breeze, leapt from tree top to tree top and burned there with the clear incandescent light of a candle before it was scotched by one unerring jet from the hose. As they watched a tall conifer burst into instantaneous fire and exploded in a shower of golden needles. There was a soft gasp of appreciation, and Dalgliesh saw that a little group of black-cloaked students who had been watching at a distance had crept imperceptibly forward into the light of the fire. It shone momentarily on their faces and he thought he recognized Madeleine Goodale and Julia Pardoe. Then he saw the tall unmistakable figure of Matron move across to them. She spoke a few words and the little group turned and reluctantly melted into the trees. It was then that she saw Dalgliesh. For a moment she stood absolutely still. Wrapped in her long black cloak, the hood thrown back, she stood against a single sapling like a victim at the stake, the fire glow dancing behind her and the light flaming her pale skin. Then she walked slowly across to him. He saw then that her face was very white. She said:

"You were right. She wasn't in her room. She's left me a letter."

Dalgliesh didn't reply. His mind was so clear that it seemed to be operating outside his own volition, not so much ranging over all the clues of the crime, but seeing it as if from a great height; a landscape without shadows spread out beneath him, comprehensible, familiar, unambiguous. He knew it all now. Not just how the two girls had been murdered; not just when and why; not just by whom. He knew the essential truth of the whole crime, for it was one crime. He might never be able to prove it; but he knew.

Half an hour later the fire was out. The spent hoses crept and thudded on the blackened earth as they were wound in, sending up little spurts of acrid smoke. The last of the onlookers had melted away and the cacophony of fire and wind was replaced by a gentle background hiss broken only by the orders of the fire officer and the blurred voices of his men. Even the wind had died a little and its touch on Dalgliesh's face was gentle and warm as it passed over the steaming earth. Everywhere there hung the reek of charred wood. The headlights of the fire engine were turned on the smoking circle where the hut had stood. Dalgliesh walked over to it, Masterson on his left, Mary Taylor on his right. The heat struck uncomfortably through the soles of his shoes. There was little to be seen; a grotesquely twisted piece of metal which might once have been part of a stove; the charred shape of a metal teapot—one kick would disintegrate it beyond recognition. And there was something else, a shape, nothing more, which even in death's extreme desecration, was still horribly human. They stood looking down in silence. It took them a few minutes to identify the few details; the pelvic girdle ridiculously small when denuded of its animate wrapping of muscle and flesh; the skull upturned and innocent as a chalice; the stain where the brain had burst away.

Dalgliesh said: "Get a screen around this place and see that it's kept guarded, then ring Sir Miles Honeyman."

Masterson said: "There's a pretty problem of identification for him here, sir."

"Yes," replied Dalgliesh, "if we didn't know already who it was."

III

They went by tacit consent and without exchanging a word through the quiet house to the Matron's flat. No one followed them. As they entered the sitting-room the carriage clock on the mantelpiece struck half past six. It was still very dark and in contrast to the fire-warmed air of the grounds the room was bitterly cold. The curtains had been drawn back and the casement window left open. Matron went quickly across to close it, drew the curtains together with a swift defensive sweep of her arms and turned to look at Dalgliesh steadily and compassionately, as if seeing him for the first time.

"You look desperately tired and cold. Come over to the fire and sit down."

He walked over and leaned against the fireplace, fearing that if he once sat down he might never be able to get up again. But the mantelpiece felt unstable, the marble slippery as ice. He let himself down into the armchair and watched while she knelt on the hearth rug and added the dry sticks of kindling to the still warm ashes of the previous evening's fire. The sticks blazed into life. She added a few nuggets of coal, holding out her hands to the blaze. Then without getting up she reached into the pocket of her cloak and handed him a letter.

A pale blue envelope unsealed and addressed in a round, childish but firm hand "to whom it may concern." He took out the letter. Cheap, blue paper, perfectly ordinary, unruled, but with the lines of writing so straight that she must have used the ruled sheet as a guide.

"I killed Heather Pearce and Josephine Fallon. They had discovered something about my past, something which was no concern of theirs, and were threatening to blackmail me. When Sister Gearing rang to tell me Fallon had been taken ill and was warded I knew that Nurse Pearce would act the patient in her place. I collected the bottle of disinfectant very early that morning and filled one of the empty milk bottles from the Sisters' utility room. I replaced the cap carefully and took the bottle with me to breakfast in my tapestry bag. All I had to do was to slip into the demonstration room after I had finished breakfast and substitute the bottle of poison for the bottle of milk on the trolley. If anyone had been in the room I should have made an excuse and tried another time and in another way. But the room was empty. I took the bottle of milk upstairs to the Sisters' utility room and threw the empty bottle of disinfectant out of one of the bathroom windows.

"I was in the conservatory when Sister Gearing produced her tin of nicotine rose spray and I thought of it when it came to killing Fallon. I knew where the key to the conservatory was kept and I wore surgical gloves so that there would be no finger-prints. It was an easy matter to pour the poison into Fallon's beaker of lemon and whisky while she was in the bathroom and the drink was cooling on her bedside table. Her nightly routine never varied. I intended to keep the tin, then place it on her bedside table later that night so that it would look as if she had killed herself. I knew it would be important to impress her finger-prints on the tin but that wouldn't be difficult. I had to change my plan because Mr. Courtney-Briggs telephoned shortly before twelve to call me back to my ward. I couldn't keep the tin in my possession since it wouldn't be possible to have my bag always with me on the ward and I didn't think it would be safe to leave it in my room. So I hid it in the sand bucket opposite Nurse Fallon's room with the intention of retrieving it and placing it on her bedside table when I returned to Nightingale House. That plan, too, proved impossible. As I got to the top of the stairs the Burt twins came out of their rooms. There was a light shining through Nurse Fallon's keyhole and they said they would take her some cocoa. I expected the body to be discovered that night. There was nothing I could do but to go upstairs to bed. I lay there waiting, expecting every minute to hear the alarm raised. I wondered if the twins had changed their plan and if Fallon had fallen asleep before drinking her whisky and lemon. But I didn't dare to go down and see. If I had been able to place the tin of nicotine by Fallon's bed no one would ever have suspected that she was murdered and I should have committed two perfect crimes.

"There is nothing else to say except that no one knew what I intended to do and no one helped me.

Ethel Brumfett."

Mary Taylor said: "It's her handwriting, of course. I found it on her mantelshelf when I came back after I had telephoned you to check that everyone was safe. But is it true?"

"Oh yes, it's true. She killed both of them. Only the murderess could have known where the tin of nicotine was hidden. It was obvious that the second death was meant to look like suicide. Why then wasn't the tin left on the bedside table? It could only have been because the killer was interrupted in her plan. Sister Brumfett was the one person in Nightingale House who was called out that night and who was prevented on her return from going into Fallon's room. But she was always the first suspect. The bottle of poison must have been prepared at leisure and by someone who had access to milk bottles and to the disinfectant and who could carry the lethal bottle about with her undetected. Sister Brumfett went nowhere without that large tapestry bag. It was bad luck for her that she happened to choose a bottle with the wrong coloured cap. I wonder if she even noticed. Even if she did, there wouldn't be time to change it. The whole plan depended on a substitution which would take merely a second. She would have to hope that no one noticed. And, in fact, no one did. And there is one way in which she was unique among the suspects. She was the only one who wasn't present to witness either of the deaths. She couldn't lift a hand against Fallon while the girl was her patient. That would have been impossible for her.

And she preferred to watch neither murder. It takes a psychopathic killer or a professional willingly to watch their victim die."

She said: "We know that Heather Pearce was a potential blackmailer. I wonder what pathetic incident from poor Brumfett's dreary past she'd raked up for her entertainment?"

"I think you know that, just as I know. Heather Pearce had found out about Felsenheim."

She seemed to freeze into silence. She was curled on the edge of the armchair at his feet, her face turned away from him. After a moment she turned and looked at him.

"She wasn't guilty, you know. Brumfett was conforming, authoritarian, trained to think of unquestioning obedience as a nurse's first duty. But she didn't kill her patients. The verdict of that court at Felsenheim was just. And even if it wasn't, it was the verdict of a properly constituted court of law. She is officially innocent."

Dalgliesh said: "I'm not here to question the verdict at Felsenheim."

As if he had not spoken she went on eagerly, as if willing him to believe.

"She told me about it when we were both students together at Nethercastle General Infirmary. She lived in Germany most of her childhood but her grandmother was English. After the trial she naturally went free and eventually in 1944 married an English sergeant, Ernest Brumfett. She had money and it was a marriage of convenience only, a way of getting out of Germany and into England. Her grandmother was dead by now but she still had some ties with this country. She went to Nethercastle as ward orderly and was so efficient that, after eighteen months, there was no difficulty in getting the Matron to take her on as a student. It was a clever choice of hospital. They weren't likely to delve too carefully into anyone's past, particularly into the past of a woman who had proved her worth. The hospital is a large Victorian building, always busy, chronically understaffed. Brumfett and I finished our training together, went together to the local maternity hospital to train as midwives, came south together to the John Carpendar. I've known Ethel Brumfett for nearly twenty years. I've watched her pay over and over again for anything that happened at the Steinhoff Institution. She was a girl then. We can't know what happened to her during those child-hood years in Germany. We can only know what the grown woman did for this hospital and for her patients. The past has no relevance."

Dalgliesh said: "Until the thing which she must always have subconsciously dreaded happened at last. Until some-one from that past recognized her."

She said: "Then all the years of work and striving would come to nothing. I can understand that she felt it necessary to kill Pearce. But why Fallon?"

"For four reasons. Nurse Pearce wanted some proof of Martin Dettinger's story before she spoke to Sister Brum-fett. The obvious way to get it seemed to be to consult a record of the trial. So she asked Fallon to lend her a library ticket. She went up to the Westminster library on the Thursday and again on the Saturday when the book was produced. She must have shown it to Sister Brumfett when she spoke to her, must have mentioned where she got the ticket. Sooner or later Fallon would want that ticket back. It was essential that no one ever found out why Nurse Pearce had wanted it or the name of the book she had borrowed from the library. That was one of several signif-icant facts which Sister Brumfett chose to omit from her confession. After she had substituted the bottle of poison for the one of milk, she came upstairs, took the library book from Nurse Pearce's room, and hid it in one of the fire buckets until she had an opportunity to return it anonymously to the library. She knew only too well that Pearce would never come out of that demonstration room alive. It was typical of her to choose the same hiding place later for the tin of nicotine. Sister Brumfett wasn't an imaginative woman.

"But the problem of the library book wasn't the main reason for killing Nurse Fallon. There were three others. She wanted to confuse the motives, to make it look as if Fallon were the intended victim. If Fallon died there would always be the probability that Pearce had been killed by mistake. It was Fallon who was listed to act as patient on the morning of the inspection. Fallon was a more likely victim. She was pregnant; that alone might provide a motive. Sister Brumfett had nursed her and could have known or guessed about the pregnancy. I don't think there were many signs or symptoms that Sister Brumfett missed in her patients. Then there was the possibility that Fallon would be held responsible for Pearce's death. After all, she had admitted returning to Nightingale House on the morning of the murder and had refused to give any explanation. She could have put the poison in the drip. Then afterwards, tormented by remorse perhaps, she killed herself. That explanation would dispose very neatly of both mysteries. It's an attractive theory from the hospital's point of view and quite a number of people preferred to believe it."

"And the last reason? You said there were four. She wanted to avoid inquiries about the library ticket; she wanted to suggest that Fallon had been the intended victim; alternatively she wanted to implicate Fallon in Pearce's death. What was the fourth motive?"

"She wanted to protect you. She always wanted that. It wasn't easy with the first murder. You were in Nightingale

House; you had as much opportunity as anyone to interfere with the drip feed. But at least she could ensure that you had an alibi for the time of Fallon's death. You were safely in Amsterdam. You couldn't possibly have killed the second victim. Why, therefore, should you have killed the first? From the beginning of this investigation I decided that the two murders were connected. It was too much of a coincidence to postulate two killers in the same house at the same time. And that automatically excluded you from the list of suspects."

"But why should anyone suspect me of killing either girl?"

"Because the motive we've imputed to Ethel Brumfett doesn't make sense. Think about it. A dying man came momentarily out of unconsciousness and saw a face bending over him. He opened his eyes and through his pain and delirium he recognized a woman. Sister Brumfett? Would you recognize Ethel Brumfett's face after twenty-five years? Plain, ordinary, inconspicuous Brumfett? There's only one woman in a million who has a face so beautiful and so individual that it can be recognized even in a fleeting glance across twenty-five years of memory. Your face. It was you and not Sister Brumfett who was Irmgard Grobel."

She said quietly: "Irmgard Grobel is dead."

He went on as if she had not spoken.

"It's not surprising that Nurse Pearce never suspected for one moment that Grobel could be you. You're the Matron, protected by a quasi-religious awe from the taint of human weakness, let alone human sin. It must have been psychologically impossible for her to think of you as a killer. And then, there were the words used by Martin Dettinger. He said it was one of the Sisters. I think I know how he made that mistake. You visit every ward in the hospital once a day, speak to nearly all the patients. The face he saw

bending over him was not only clearly the face of Irmgard
Grobel. He saw a woman wearing what to him was a Sister's uniform, the short cape and wide triangular cap of the
army nursing service. To his drug-muddled mind that
uniform meant a Sister. It still means a Sister to anyone who
has been nursed in an army hospital, and he had spent
months in them."

She said again quietly: "Irmgard Grobel is dead."

"So he told Nurse Pearce much the same as he told his
own mother. Mrs. Dettinger wasn't particularly interested.
Why should she be? And then she received a hospital
account and thought that there might be a way of saving
herself a few pounds. If Mr. Courtney-Briggs hadn't been
greedy I doubt whether she would have taken it any further.
But she did, and Courtney-Briggs was given an intriguing
piece of information which he thought it worth taking
some time and trouble to verify. We can guess what Heather
Pearce thought. She must have experienced much the
same triumph and sense of power as when she saw Nurse
Dakers stooping to pick up those pound notes fluttering on
the path in front of her. Only this time someone a great deal
more important and interesting than a fellow student
would be in her power. It never occurred to her that the
patient could be referring to a woman other than the Sister
nursing him. But she knew she had to get proof, or at least
assure herself that Dettinger, who after all was a dying
man, wasn't deluded or hallucinated. So she spent her
half-day on Thursday visiting the Westminster library and
asked them for a book about the Felsenheim trial. They had
to borrow it for her from another branch and she returned
for it on Saturday. I think she learned enough from that
book to convince herself that Martin Dettinger knew what
he was talking about. I think that she spoke to Sister Brumfett on the Saturday night and that the Sister didn't deny the

charge. I wonder what price Pearce was asking? Nothing as commonplace or understandable or as reprehensible as direct payment for her silence. Pearce liked to exercise power; but even more she enjoyed indulging in moral rectitude. It must have been on Sunday morning that she wrote to the Secretary of the League for the Assistance of Fascist Victims. Sister Brumfett would be made to pay, but the money would go in regular instalments to the League. Pearce was a great one for making the punishment fit the crime."

This time she was silent, sitting there with her hands folded gently in her lap and looking expressionless into some unfathomable past. He said gently:

"It can all be checked, you know. We haven't much of her body left but we don't need it while we have your face. There will be records of the trial, photographs, the record of your marriage to a Sergeant Taylor."

She spoke so quietly that he had to bend his head to hear:

"He opened his eyes very wide and looked at me. He didn't speak. There was a wildness, a desperation about that look. I thought that he was becoming delirious, or perhaps that he was afraid. I think he knew in that moment that he was going to die. I spoke to him a little and then his eyes closed. I didn't recognize him. Why should I?

"I'm not the same person as that child in Steinhoff. I don't mean I think of Steinhoff as if it happened to someone else. It did happen to someone else. I can't even remember now what exactly happened in that court at Felsenheim; I can't recall a single face."

But she had had to tell someone. That must have been part of becoming another person, of putting Steinhoff out of her thoughts. So she had told Ethel Brumfett. They had both been young student nurses at Nethercastle and Dalgliesh supposed that Brumfett represented something to her: kindness, reliability, devotion. Otherwise, why Brumfett? Why on earth choose her as a confidante? He must have been speaking his words aloud because she said eagerly as if it were important to make him understand:

"I told her because she was so ordinary. There was a security about her ordinariness. I felt that, if Brumfett could listen and believe me and still like me, then nothing that had happened was so very terrible after all. You wouldn't understand that."

But he did understand. There had been a boy in his prep. school like that, so ordinary, so safe, that he was a kind of talisman against death and disaster. Dalgliesh remembered the boy. Funny, but he hadn't thought of him now for over thirty years. Sproat Minor with his round, pleasant, spectacled face, his ordinary conventional family, his unremarkable background, his blessed normality. Sproat Minor, protected my mediocrity and insensitivity from the terrors of the world. Life could not be wholly frightening while it held a Sproat Minor. Dalgliesh wondered briefly where he was now.

He said: "And Brumfett had stuck to you ever since. When you came here she followed. That impulse to confide, the need to have at least one friend who knew all about you, put you in her power. Brumfett, the protector, adviser, confidante. Theatres with Brumfett; morning golf with Brumfett; holidays with Brumfett; country drives with Brumfett; early morning tea and last night drinks with Brumfett. Her devotion must have been real enough. After all, she was willing to kill for you. But it was blackmail all the same. A more orthodox blackmailer, merely demanding a regular tax-free income, would have been infinitely preferable to Brumfett's intolerable devotion."

She said sadly: "It's true. It's true. How can you possibly know?"

"Because she was essentially a stupid and dull woman and you are not."

He could have added: "Because I know myself."

She cried out in vehement protest.

"And who am I to despise stupidity and dullness? What right had I to be so particular? Oh, she wasn't clever! She couldn't even kill for me without making a mess of it. She wasn't clever enough to deceive Adam Dalgliesh, but when is that to be the criteria for intelligence? Have you ever seen her doing her job? Seen her with a dying patient or a sick child? Have you ever watched this stupid and dull woman, whose devotion and company it is apparently proper for me to despise, working all night to save a life?"

"I've seen the body of one of her victims and read the autopsy report on the other. I'll take your word for her kindness to children."

"Those weren't her victims. They were mine."

"Oh no," he said. "There has only been one victim of yours in Nightingale House and she was Ethel Brumfett."

She rose to her feet in one swift movement and stood facing him, those astonishing green eyes, speculative and unwavering, gazed into his. Part of his mind knew that there were words he ought to speak. What were they, those overfamiliar phrases of statutory warning, the professional spiel which came almost unbidden to the lips at the moment of confrontation? They had slipped away, a meaningless irrelevancy, into some limbo of his mind. He knew that he was a sick man, still weak from loss of blood, and that he ought to stop now, to hand over the investigation to Masterson, and get to his bed. He, the most punctilious of detectives, had already spoken as if none of the rules had been formulated, as if he were facing a private adversary. But he had to go on. Even if he could never prove it, he had to hear her admit what he knew to be the truth. As if it were the most natural question in the world he asked quietly:

"Was she dead when you put her into the fire?"

IV

It was at that moment that someone rang the doorbell of the flat. Without a word Mary Taylor swung her cape around her shoulders and went to open it. There was a brief murmur of voices; then Stephen Courtney-Briggs followed her into the sitting-room. Glancing at the clock, Dalgliesh saw that the hands stood at 7:24 a.m. The working day had almost begun.

Courtney-Briggs was already dressed. He showed no surprise at Dalgliesh's presence and no particular concern at his obvious weakness. He spoke to them both impartially:

"I'm told there was a fire in the night. I didn't hear the engines."

Mary Taylor, her face so white that Dalgliesh thought she might faint, said calmly:

"They came in at the Winchester Road entrance and kept the bells silent so as not to wake the patients."

"And what's this rumour that they found a burnt body in the ashes of the garden shed? Whose body?"

Dalgliesh said: "Sister Brumfett's. She left a note confessing to the murders of Nurse Pearce and Nurse Fallon."

"Brumfett killed them! Brumfett!"

Courtney-Briggs looked at Dalgliesh belligerently, his large handsome features seeming to disintegrate into irritated disbelief.

"Did she say why? Was the woman mad?"

Mary Taylor said: "Brumfett wasn't mad and no doubt she believed that she had a motive."

"But what's going to happen to my ward today? I start operating at nine o'clock. You know that, Matron. And I've got a very long list. Both the staff nurses are off with flu. I can't trust dangerously sick patients to first and second-year students."

The Matron said calmly: "I'll see to it at once. Most of the day nurses should be up by now. It isn't going to be easy but, if necessary, we'll have to withdraw someone from the school."

She turned to Dalgliesh: "I prefer to do my telephoning from one of the Sisters' sitting-rooms. But don't worry. I realize the importance of our conversation. I shall be back to complete it."

Both men looked after her as she went out of the door and closed it quietly behind her. For the first time Courtney-Briggs seemed to notice Dalgliesh. He said brusquely:

"Don't forget to go over to the radiography department and get that head X-rayed. You've no right to be out of bed. I'll examine you as soon as I've finished my list this morning." He made it sound like a tedious chore which he might find time to attend to.

Dalgliesh asked: "Who did you come to visit in Nightingale House the night Josephine Fallon was murdered?"

"I told you. No one. I never entered Nightingale House."

"There are at least ten minutes unaccounted for, ten minutes when the back door leading to the Matron's flat was unlocked. Sister Gearing had let her friend out that way and was walking with him in the grounds. So you thought that the Matron must be in despite the absence of lights and made your way up the stairs to her flat. You must have spent some time there. Why, I wonder? Curiosity? Or were you searching for something?"

"Why should I visit the Matron? She wasn't there. Mary Taylor was in Amsterdam that night."

"But you didn't know that at the time, did you? Miss Taylor wasn't accustomed to attending International Conferences. For reasons we can guess she didn't want her face to be too widely known. This reluctance to undertake public duties was thought becomingly modest in a woman so able and so intelligent. She was only asked late on Tuesday to go to Amsterdam to deputise for the Chairman of the Area Nurse Training Committee. Your sessions are on Mondays, Thursdays and Fridays. Then, on Wednesday night, you were called to operate on a private patient. I don't suppose that the operating theatre staff, busy with an emergency, thought to mention that the Matron wasn't in the hospital. Why should they?" He paused.

Courtney-Briggs said: "And why am I supposed to have planned to visit the Matron at midnight? You're not supposing that I would have been a welcome visitor? You're not suggesting that she was expecting me?"

"You came to see Irmgard Grobel."

There was a moment's silence. Then Courtney-Briggs said:

"How do you know about Irmgard Grobel?"

"From the same person who told you, Mrs. Dettinger."

Another silence. Then he said with the obstinate finality of a man who knows he won't be believed:

"Irmgard Grobel is dead."

"Is she?" asked Dalgliesh. "Didn't you expect to find her in the Matron's flat? Wasn't this your first opportunity to confront her with what you knew? And you must have been looking forward to it. The exercise of power is always pleasurable, isn't it?"

Courtney-Briggs said calmly: "You should know that."

They stood looking at each other in silence. Dalgliesh asked:

"What had you in mind?"

"Nothing. I didn't connect Grobel with the deaths of Pearce or Fallon. Even if I had, I doubt whether I should have spoken. This hospital needs Mary Taylor. As far as I'm concerned Irmgard Grobel doesn't exist. She was tried once and found not guilty. That was good enough for me. I'm a surgeon, not a moral theologian. I should have kept her secret."

Of course he would, thought Dalgliesh. Its value would be lost to him once the truth were known. This was very special, very important information, gained at some cost, and he would use it in his own way. It put Mary Taylor for ever in his power. The Matron who so frequently and irritatingly opposed him; whose power was increasing; who was about to be appointed Director of Nursing Services over all the hospitals in the Group; who influenced the Chairman of the Hospital Management Committee against him. Sir Marcus Cohen. How much influence would she retain with that dedicated Jew once he learned about the Steinhoff Institution? It had become fashionable to forget these things. But would Sir Marcus Cohen forgive?

He thought of Mary Taylor's words. There are more ways than one of blackmail. Heather Pearce and Ethel Brumfett both knew that. And perhaps the most subtly pleasurable was the blackmail which made no financial demands but enjoyed its secret knowledge under the cloak of generosity, kindness, complicity or moral superiority. Sister Brumfett hadn't asked much after all, only a room next to her idol; the prestige of being known as the matron's friend; a companion for her off-duty hours. Poor stupid Pearce had asked only a few shillings a week and a verse or two of scripture. But how they must have relished their power. And how infinitely more gratifying would Courtney-Briggs have found his. No wonder that he had been determined to keep the secret to himself, that he hadn't welcomed the thought of the Yard descending on Nightingale House.

Dalgliesh said: "We can prove that you flew to Germany last Friday night. And I think I can guess why. It was a quicker and surer way of getting the information you wanted than pestering the Judge Advocate's Department. You probably consulted the newspaper files and the record of the trial. That's what I would have done. And, no doubt, you have useful contacts. But we can find out where you went and what you did. You can't slip in and out of the country anonymously, you know."

Courtney-Briggs said: "I admit that I knew. I admit, too, that I came to Nightingale House to see Mary Taylor on the night Fallon died. But I've done nothing illegal, nothing which could put me in jeopardy."

"I can believe that."

"Even if I'd spoken earlier I should have been too late to save Pearce. She was dead before Mrs. Dettinger came to see me. I've nothing with which to reproach myself."

He was beginning to defend himself clumsily like a schoolboy. Then they heard the soft footfall and looked round. Mary Taylor had returned. She spoke directly to the surgeon.

"I can let you have the Burt twins. I'm afraid it means the end of this block but there's no choice. They'll have to be recalled to the wards."

Courtney-Briggs said grudgingly: "They'll do. They're sensible girls. But what about a Sister?"

"I thought that Sister Rolfe might take over temporarily. But I'm afraid that's impossible. She's leaving the John Carpendar."

"Leaving! But she can't do that!"

"I don't see how I can prevent her. But I don't think I shall be given the opportunity to try."

"But why is she leaving? What's happened?"

"She won't say. I think something about the police investigation has upset her."

Courtney-Briggs swung round at Dalgliesh.

"You see! Dalgliesh, I realize that you're only doing your job, that you were sent here to clear up these girls' deaths. But, for God's sake, doesn't it ever occur to you that your interference makes things a bloody sight worse?"

"Yes," said Dalgliesh. "And in your job? Does it ever occur to you?"

V

She went with Courtney-Briggs to the front door. They didn't linger. She was back in less than a minute, and walking briskly over to the fire, she slipped her cloak from her shoulders and laid it tidily over the back of the sofa. Then, kneeling, she took up a pair of brass tongs and began to build up the fire, coal carefully disposed on coal, each licking flame fed with its gleaming nugget. Without looking up at Dalgliesh, she said:

"We were interrupted in our conversation, Superintendent. You were accusing me of murder. I have faced that charge once before, but at least the court at Felsenheim produced some evidence. What evidence have you?"

"None."

"Nor will you ever find any."

She spoke without anger or complacency but with an intensity, a quiet finality that had nothing to do with innocence. Looking down at the gleaming head burnished by the firelight Dalgliesh said:

"But you haven't denied it. You haven't lied to me yet and I don't suppose you'll trouble to begin now. Why should she have killed herself in that way? She liked her comfort. Why be uncomfortable in death? Suicides seldom are unless they're too psychotic to care. She had access to plenty of pain-killing drugs. Why not use one of them? Why trouble to creep away to a cold dark garden shed to immolate herself in lonely agony? She wasn't even fortified by the gratifications of a public show."

"There are precedents."

"Not many in this country."

"Perhaps she was too psychotic to care."

"That will be said of course."

"She may have realized that it was important not to leave an identifiable body if she wanted to convince you that she was Grobel. Faced with a written confession and a heap of charred bones, why should you bother any further? There was no point in killing herself to protect me if you could confirm her real identity without trouble."

"A clever and far-sighted woman might argue like that. She was neither. But you are. It must have seemed just worth a try. And even if we never found out about Irmgard Grobel and Felsenheim, it had become important to get rid of Brumfett. As you've said, she couldn't even kill without making a mess of it. She had already panicked once when she tried to murder me. She might easily panic again. She had been an encumbrance for years; now she had become a dangerous liability. You hadn't asked her to kill for you. It wasn't even a reasonable way out of the difficulty. Pearce's threats could have been dealt with if Sister Brumfett had only kept her head and reported the matter to you. But she had to demonstrate her devotion in the most spectacular way she knew. She killed to protect you. And those two deaths bound you and her together indissolubly for life. How could you ever be free or secure while Brumfett lived?"

"Aren't you going to tell me how I did it?"

They might, Dalgliesh thought, be two colleagues talking over a case together. Even through his weakness he knew that this bizarre conversation was dangerously unorthodox, that the woman kneeling at his feet was an enemy, that the intelligence opposed to his was inviolate. She had no hope now of saving her reputation, but she was fighting for freedom, perhaps even for her life. He said:

"I can tell you how I would have done it. It wasn't difficult. Her bedroom was the one nearest the door of your flat. I suppose she asked for that room, and nothing Sister Brumfett wanted could be denied. Because she knew about the Steinhoff Institution? Because she had a hold over you? Or merely because she had lumbered you with the weight of her devotion and you hadn't the ruthlessness to break free? So she slept close to you.

"I don't know how she died. It could have been a tablet, an injection, something you administered on the pretence that it would help her to sleep. She had already, at your request, written the confession. I wonder how you persuaded her to do that? I don't suppose she thought for one moment that it was going to be used. It isn't addressed to me or to any particular person. I imagine you told her that there ought to be something in writing just in case anything happened to her or to you and it was necessary sometime in the future to have a record of what really happened, proof that would protect you. So she wrote that plain note, probably at your dictation. It has a directness and lucidity that has little, I imagine, to do with Sister Brumfett.

"And so she dies. You have only to carry her body two yards to gain the safety of your door. Even so, this is the most risky part of your plan. Suppose Sister Gearing or Sister Rolfe should appear? So you prop open Sister Brumfett's door and the door of your flat and listen carefully to make sure that the corridor is clear. Then you hoist the body over your shoulder and move swiftly into your flat. You lay the body on the bed and go back to shut her bedroom door and to shut and lock your own front door. She was a plump but short woman. You are tall and strong and have been trained to lift helpless patients. That part wasn't so difficult.

"But now you must move her to your car. It's convenient having access to your garage from the downstairs hall and a private stairway. With both the outside and inside doors of the flat locked you can work without fear of interruption. The body is hoisted into the back of your car and covered with a travelling rug. Then you drive out through the grounds and reverse the car under the trees, as close as possible to the garden shed. You keep the engine running. It is important to make a quick getaway, be back in your flat before the fire is seen. This part of the plan is a little risky but the Winchester Road path is seldom used after dark. The ghost of Nancy Gorringe sees to that. It would be inconvenient but not catastrophic if you were seen. After all, you are the Matron, there is nothing to prevent you taking a night drive. If anyone passes, you will have to drive on and choose another place or another time. But no one does pass. The car is deep under the trees; the lights are out. You carry the body to the shed. Then there is a second journey with the can of petrol. And after that there is nothing to do but souse the body and the surrounding furniture and piles of wood and throw in a lighted match from the open doorway.

"It takes only a moment to restart the car and to drive straight back through the garage doors. Once they are closed behind you, you are safe. Certainly you know that the fire will burn with such fierceness that it will be seen almost at once. But by then you are back in your own flat, ready to receive the telephone call which tells you that the fire engine is on its way, ready to ring me. And the suicide note which she left in your charge, perhaps never to be used, is ready to be handed over."

She asked quietly: "And how will you prove it?"

"Probably never. But I know that is how it happened."

She said: "But you will try to prove it, won't you? After all, failure would be intolerable for Adam Dalgliesh. You will try to prove it no matter what the cost to yourself or anyone else. And after all, there is a chance. There isn't much hope of finding tyre marks under the trees of course. The effects of the fire, the wheels of the fire engine, the trampling of the men, will have obliterated any clues on the ground. But then you will examine the inside of the car surely, particularly the rug. Don't neglect the car rug, Superintendent. There may be fibres from the clothes, even a few hairs, perhaps. But that wouldn't be surprising. Miss Brumfett often drove with me; the car rug actually belongs to her; it's probably covered with her hairs. But what about clues in my flat? If I carried her body down the narrow back staircase surely there will be marks on the walls where they were grazed by her shoes? Unless, of course, the woman who killed Brumfett had sufficient sense to remove her victim's shoes and carry them separately, perhaps slung by the laces around her neck. They couldn't be left in the flat. You might check on the number of pairs that Brumfett owned. After all, someone in Nightingale House could tell you. We have so little privacy from each other. And no woman would walk through the woods barefoot to her death.

"And the other clues in the flat? If I killed her, ought there not to be a syringe, a bottle of pills, something to indicate how I did it? But her medicine cupboard and mine both contain a supply of aspirin and sleeping tablets. Suppose I gave her those? Or simply stunned or suffocated

her? Any method would be as good as another provided it
didn't make a mess. How can you possibly prove how she
died when all you have for the autopsy are a few charred
bones? And there's the suicide note, a note in her own
handwriting and containing facts which only the killer of
Pearce and Fallon could have known. Whatever you may
choose to believe, Superintendent, are you going to tell me
that the Coroner won't be satisfied that Ethel Brumfett
intended that note as a confession before burning herself to
death?"

Dalgliesh knew that he could no longer stay upright. He
was fighting sickness now as well as weakness. The hand
which grasped the mantelshelf for support was colder than
the marble and slippery with sweat, and the marble itself
was soft and yielding as putty. His wound was beginning to
throb painfully, and the dull headache which up to now
had been little more than vague discomfort was sharpening
and localizing into needles of pain behind his left eye. To
drop in a faint at her feet would be unforgettably humiliating. He reached out his arm and found the back of the
nearest chair. Then gently he lowered himself into it. Her
voice seemed to be coming from a long way off, but at
least he could hear the words and knew that his own voice
was still steady.

She said: "Suppose I told you that I could manage
Stephen Courtney-Briggs, that no one but the three of us
need ever know about Felsenheim? Would you be willing
to leave my past out of your report so that at least those girls
need not have died entirely in vain? It is important for this
hospital that I stay on as Matron. I'm not asking you for
mercy. I'm not concerned for myself. You will never prove
that I killed Ethel Brumfett. Aren't you going to make
yourself look ridiculous if you try? Isn't the most coura-
geous and sensible course to forget that this conversation

ever took place, to accept Brumfett's confession for the truth which it is, and to close the case?"

He said: "That's not possible. Your past is part of the evidence. I can't suppress evidence or omit relevant facts from my report because I don't choose to like them. If I once did that I should have to give up my job. Not just this particular case, my job. And for always."

"And you couldn't do that, of course. What would a man like you be without his job, this particular job? Vulnerable like the rest of us. You might even have to begin living and feeling like a human being."

"You can't touch me like that. Why humiliate yourself trying? There are regulations, orders, and an oath. Without them no one could safely do police work. Without them Ethel Brumfett wouldn't be safe, you wouldn't be safe, an Irmgard Grobel wouldn't be safe."

"Is that why you won't help me?"

"Not altogether. I don't choose to."

She said sadly: "That's honest, anyway. And you haven't any doubts?"

"Of course I have. I'm not as arrogant as that. There are always doubts." And so there were. But they were intellectual and philosophical doubts, untormenting and uninsistent. It had been many years since they had kept him awake at night.

"But there are the regulations, aren't there? And the orders. An oath even. They're very convenient shields to shelter behind if the doubts become troublesome. I know. I sheltered behind them once myself. You and I are not so very different after all, Adam Dalgliesh."

She took up her cloak from the back of the chair and threw it around her shoulders. She came over and stood in front of him smiling. Then, seeing his weakness, she held out both her hands and grasping his, helped him to his feet.

They stood there facing each other. Suddenly there was the ring of her front door and almost simultaneously the harsh insistent burr of the telephone. For both of them the day had begun.

CHAPTER NINE

Summer Epilogue

I

IT WAS SHORTLY AFTER nine o'clock when the call came through to him, and Dalgliesh walked out of the Yard and across Victoria Street through an early morning haze, a sure harbinger of yet another hot August day. He found the address without difficulty. It was a large red brick building between Victoria Street and Horseferry Road, not particularly sordid but depressingly dull, a functional oblong with the front punctuated with meanly proportioned windows. There was no lift and he walked unchallenged up the three linoleum-covered flights of stairs to the top floor.

The landing smelt of sour sweat. Outside the flat a grossly fat middle-aged woman in a flowered apron was expostulating to the police constable on duty in an adenoidal whine. As Dalgliesh approached she turned on him, spieling forth a flood of protest and recrimination. What was Mr. Goldstein going to say? She wasn't really allowed to sub-let a room. She had only done it to oblige the lady. And now this. People had no consideration.

He passed her without speaking and went into the room. It was a square box, stuffy, and smelling of furniture polish, and over-furnished with the heavy prestige symbols of an earlier decade. The window was open and the lace curtains drawn back but there was little air. The police surgeon and the attendant constable, both large men, seemed to have used all there was.

One corpse more to be viewed; only this one wasn't his responsibility. He need only glance, as if verifying a memory, at the stiffening body on the bed, noting with detached interest that the left arm hung loosely over the side, long fingers curled, and that the hypodermic syringe was still attached to the underarm, a metallic insect with its fang deep embedded in the soft flesh. Death hadn't robbed her of individuality, not yet anyway. That would come soon enough with all the grotesque indignities of decay.

The police surgeon, shirt-sleeved and sweating, was apologetic as if concerned that he might have done the wrong thing. As he turned from the bed Dalgliesh was aware that he was speaking:

"And as New Scotland Yard is so close and the second note was addressed personally to you . . ." he paused uncertainly.

"She injected herself with evipan. The first note is quite explicit. It's a clear case of suicide. That's why the constable didn't want to ring you. He thought it wasn't worth your trouble to come. There's really nothing here of interest."

Dalgliesh said: "I'm glad you did ring. And it isn't any trouble."

There were two white envelopes, one sealed and addressed to himself; the other unsealed and bearing the words, "To anyone whom it may concern." He wondered if she had smiled when she wrote that phrase. Watched by the police surgeon and the constable, Dalgliesh opened the letter. The writing was perfectly firm, black and spiky. He realized with a kind of shock that it was the first time he had seen her handwriting.

"They wouldn't believe you but you were right. I killed Ethel Brumfett. It was the first time I had ever killed; it seems important that you should know that. I injected her with evipan, just as I shall shortly do myself. She thought I was giving her a sedative. Poor trusting Brumfett! She would have easily taken nicotine from my hand and it would have been as appropriate.

"I thought it might be possible for me to make some kind of a useful life. It hasn't been, and I haven't the temperament to live with failure. I don't regret what I did. It was best for the hospital, best for her, best for me. I wasn't likely to be deterred because Adam Dalgliesh sees his job as the embodiment of the moral law."

She was wrong, he thought. They hadn't disbelieved him, they had just demanded, reasonably enough, that he find some proof. He had found none, either at the time or later, although he had pursued the case as if it were a personal vendetta, hating himself and her. And she had admitted nothing; not for one moment had she been in any danger of panicking.

There had been very little left unexplained at the resumed inquest on Heather Pearce and the inquest on Josephine Fallon and Ethel Brumfett. Perhaps the Coroner felt that there had been enough rumours and speculation. He had sat with a jury and had made no attempt to inhibit their questions to witnesses, or even to control the proceedings. The story of Irmgard Grobel and the Steinhoff Institution had come out, and Sir Marcus Cohen had sat with Dalgliesh at the back of the Court and listened with a face rigid with pain. After the inquest Mary Taylor walked across the room to him, handed him her letter of resignation, and turned away without a word. She had left the hospital the same day. And that, for the John Carpendar, had been the end. Nothing else had come out. Mary Taylor had gone free; free to find this room, this death.

Dalgliesh walked over to the fireplace. The small grate,

tiled in bilious green, was filled with a dusty fan and a jam jar of dried leaves. Carefully he moved them out of the way. He was aware of the police surgeon and the uniformed constable watching him expressionlessly. What did they think he was doing? Destroying evidence? Why should they worry? They had their piece of paper ready to be docketed, produced as evidence, filed away for oblivion. This concerned only him.

He shook the note open in the chimney recess and, striking a match, set light to one of the corners. But there was little draught and the paper was tough. He had to hold it, shaking it gently, until the tips of his fingers scorched before the blackened sheet drifted from his grasp, disappeared into the darkness of the chimney recess and was wafted upwards towards the summer sky.

II

Ten minutes later on the same day Miss Beale drove through the front entrance gate of the John Carpendar Hospital and drew up at the porter's lodge. She was greeted by an unfamiliar face, a new youngish porter, shirt-sleeved in his summer uniform.

"The General Nursing Council Inspector? Good morning, miss. I'm afraid this entrance isn't very convenient for the new school of nursing. It's just a temporary building at present, miss, built on a cleared part of the grounds where we had a fire. It's quite close to where the old school was. If you just take this first turn. . . ."

"It's all right, thank you," said Miss Beale. "I know the way."

There was an ambulance standing at the entrance to the Casualty Department. As Miss Beale drove slowly past,

Nurse Dakers, wearing the lace-trimmed cap and blue belt of a staff nurse, came out of the hospital, conferred briefly with the attendants, and stood supervising the transfer of the patient. She seemed to Miss Beale's eyes to have grown in stature and authority. There was no trace of the terrified student nurse about this confident figure. So Nurse Dakers had qualified. Well, that was to be expected. Presumably the Burt twins, equally elevated, were working somewhere in the hospital. But there had been changes. Nurse Goodale had married; Miss Beale had seen the notice in the national Press. And Hilda Rolfe, so Angela reported, was nursing somewhere in Central Africa. There would be a new Principal Tutor to meet this morning. And a new Matron. Miss Beale wondered briefly about Mary Taylor. She would be earning a good living somewhere if not in nursing. The Mary Taylors of the world were natural survivors.

She drove down the familiar path between the parched summer lawns, the flower beds blotched with overblown roses, and turned into the green tunnel of the trees. The air was still and warm, the narrow road chequered with the first bright sunlight of the day. And here was the last remembered corner. Nightingale House, or what was left of it, was before her.

Once again she stopped the car and gazed. The house looked as if it had been clumsily cut in two by a giant's cleaver, a living thing wantonly mutilated, with its shame and its nakedness exposed to every gaze. A staircase, bereft of its banister and brutally hacked, reeled into nothingness; on the second landing a delicate light filament hung by a thread of flex against the cracked panelling; downstairs the front arched windows, empty of glass, were an elegant arcade of carved stone giving a view of faded wallpaper with lighter patches where pictures and mirrors had once hung.

From the remaining ceilings, naked wires sprouted like the bristles of a brush. Propped against a tree at the front of the house was a motley collection of fireplaces, mantelshelves, and sections of carved panelling, obviously selected for preservation. On top of what remained of the rear wall, a figure silhouetted against the sky was picking in a desultory way at the loose bricks. They tumbled one by one into the rubble of the interior of the house, sending up small spurts of dust.

In front of the building another workman, naked to the waist and burnt bronze, was operating a tractor mounted with a crane from which hung an immense iron ball and chain. As Miss Beale watched, hands taut on the steering-wheel as if bracing herself against an instinctive recoil of protest, the ball swung forward and crashed against all that remained of the front wall. For a moment there was nothing but the reverberation of hideous noise. Then the wall buckled gently and collapsed inwards with a roar of cascading bricks and mortar, sending up a monstrous cloud of yellow dust through which the lonely figure on the sky-line could be seen dimly like some supervising demon.

Miss Beale paused for a moment, then gently let in the clutch and steered the car to the right to where the low, functional, clean-looking lines of the new temporary school could be glimpsed between the trees. Here was normality, sanity, a world she recognized and knew. This emotion, suspiciously like regret, at witnessing the violent destruction of Nightingale House was really too ridiculous. She fought against it resolutely. It was a horrible house; an evil house. It should have been pulled down fifty years ago. And it had never been in the least suitable as a nurse training school.

ABOUT THE AUTHOR

P. D. JAMES (1920–2014) was born in Oxford. She married a doctor and had two daughters, the second born in the midst of a German bomb attack during World War II. After her husband returned from the war incapacitated, she went to work in the National Health Service and the British Civil Service. She worked in various departments for thirty years, including the Police and Criminal Law Divisions of the Home Office, and later served as a magistrate and on the Board of Governors of the BBC. Her first novel, *Cover Her Face,* was published in the UK in 1962, and she went on to write twenty-two critically acclaimed crime novels. She began writing an autobiography at the age of seventy-seven, following Dr. Johnson's advice that at seventy-seven it is "time to be in earnest." *Time to Be in Earnest* was published in 2000. In 1991, she was created Baroness James of Holland Park, and she lived in London and Oxford.

An Unsuitable Job for a Woman

1. Are you shocked that Cordelia decides to conceal the facts not only of Mark Callendar's death but also of Ronald Callendar's murder? Why does she do it? Adam Dalgliesh speculates that she is lying for the sake of justice and tells her, "Justice. A very dangerous concept, Miss Gray." Do you agree?

2. Cordelia Gray is an inexperienced young private detective, while James's other frequent hero, Adam Dalgliesh, is a highly experienced professional policeman. Are they alike in some ways? How does their relationship to each other change in the course of the novel?

The Skull Beneath the Skin

1. At the end of the novel, Cordelia Gray says that "it was almost impossible to believe that she had first seen Courcy Castle only three days earlier. In that short span of time she seemed to have lived through long, action-packed years, to have become a different person." In what ways does the murder investigation change Cordelia?

2. James assigns the task of suspect interrogation to Sergeant Robert Buckley and Grogan, yet, ultimately, neither of them helps solve Clarissa's murder. Why is Cordelia so much more successful at getting possible suspects to talk to her and at deciphering clues such as the newspaper clipping and the jewelry boxes?

Innocent Blood

1. When Philippa first learns that her mother was a murderess about to be released from prison, did you expect that her mother would be a threat to Philippa? Were you surprised to find her a gentle, even sympathetic character? Where does the suspense in the novel come from?

2. How does Philippa change in the course of the novel? What does her final encounter with Norman Scase reveal about her growth? Do you accept as true that "it is only through learning to love that we find identity"?

Cover Her Face

1. Chapter Four gives a window into the thoughts of each of the Martingale suspects, including the actual murderer. How does James provide a convincing glimpse of the murderer's state of mind, without revealing the person's guilt?
2. How does the presence of a sleeping drug in Sally Jupp's cocoa function as a red herring? How, too, does the bolted door? Which is more effective in leading Dalgliesh astray?

A Mind to Murder

1. This novel is set in a psychiatric clinic, yet none of the patients is ever seriously considered to be a suspect. Instead, it is the staff who comes under Dalgliesh's scrutiny. Why do you think James chooses to make suspects of ordinary people rather than the mentally ill?
2. In the end, the A.C. concludes, "It was a perfectly straightforward case. The obvious suspect, the obvious motive." Dalgliesh responds bitterly, "Too obvious for me, apparently." Why is Dalgliesh thrown off so long from identifying the killer? Can you blame him as much as he blames himself?

Unnatural Causes

1. Detective Inspector Reckless and Adam Dalgliesh are working to solve the same mystery and have access to the same evidence. Yet Dalgliesh is able to guess the method of Maurice Seton's murder and Reckless is not. How does Dalgliesh do it? What are his particular gifts as a detective?
2. Once the taped confession is played, Jane Dalgliesh goes to the kitchen and fills the kettle. Adam wonders, "Now that it was all over was she even interested in that tumult of hate which had destroyed and disrupted so many lives including her own? . . . Never before had his aunt's uninvolvement struck him so forcibly; never before had it seemed so frightening." Could the same word, *uninvolvement,* be used to describe Adam Dalgliesh? Could his strong negative reaction to Jane's uninvolvement be related to the letter he had just received from Deborah Riscoe?

Shroud for a Nightingale

1. Near the end of the novel, Nurse Taylor begs Dalgliesh to lie for her. To what higher good does she appeal? Why is Dalgliesh so quick to refuse?
2. The nurses depicted in this novel are very different in personality.

Who among them is the best nurse? Is that character also the most appealing human being?

The Black Tower

1. At the beginning of the novel, Dalgliesh makes a decision to quit the police force. Why? How does his disavowal of police work affect the investigation of his suspicions about the deaths at Toynton Grange?
2. During his final confrontation with the killer, Dalgliesh realizes that he has decided to return to the police force. James writes, "The decision to go on, arrived at when and why Dalgliesh didn't know, seemed to him as irrational as the decision to give up. It wasn't a victory. A kind of defeat even. . . ." Do you agree with Dalgliesh that his decision to go on with police work is irrational or a defeat?

Death of an Expert Witness

1. While considering possible murder motives, Dalgliesh tells Massingham that ". . . the most destructive force in the world is . . . love. And if you want to make a detective you'd better learn to recognize it when you meet it." How does the clunch pit murder that opens the novel illustrate this statement?
2. After recalling the loss of his son, Dalgliesh suddenly realizes "that he knew virtually nothing about children. . . . There was a whole territory of human experience on which, once repulsed, he had turned his back, and that this rejection somehow diminished him as a man." How is Dalgliesh's personal loss reflected in his treatment of the teenager Brenda Pridmore and Kerrison's children, William and Nell?